THEY WERE ALL PART OF THE STRUGGLE ...

MAMA FLORA—The matriarch, propelled by a dark secret from her hardscrabble childhood, she vowed to find a better world for her children. Even if she had to make it herself ...

WILLIE—he fled the South for Chicago and nearly drowned in its depths. It took a war and a good woman to bring him back, but he would never be the man his father was. . . .

RUTHANA—she was the daughter of Flora's heart, a superb student who finally understood that the answers lay not in Africa, but within herself, waiting to be realized at home. . . .

DIANA—wild child of Willie, Flora's granddaughter, she was born to revolution, seduced by militant Islam, imprisoned by drugs and despair, until her grandmother showed her how to find freedom. . . .

LUKE—lost but not forgotten, he haunted Flora's nights and days until he suddenly appeared, the stranger she'd waited a lifetime to see. . . .

MAMA FLORA'S FAMILY

"Interesting reading."—*Newport News Press*

"Heartfelt."—*Booklist*

Mama Flora's

Family

A NOVEL

Alex Haley
AND
David Stevens

A Dell Book

Published by
Dell Publishing
a division of
Random House, Inc.
1540 Broadway
New York, New York 10036

ISBN: 0-440-23543-X
Reprinted by arrangement with Scribner, a division of Simon & Schuster, Inc.

Printed in the United States of America

Published simultaneously in Canada

November 1999

10 9 8 7 6 5 4 3 2 1

MAMA FLORA'S
FAMILY

PART ONE

— FLORA —

1

THE SUN WAS SETTING, and young Willie was not yet home.

Flora, his mama, glanced out the window again, and felt an old, familiar knot in her stomach when she could not see him.

She opened the door and called out through the fly screen.

"Willie!"

She counted to ten. The sun disappeared below the horizon.

"Willie!" she called again, and could not keep the fear that disguised itself as anger from her voice. "You hear me callin' you, boy? Willie!"

Still there was no sign of him, but she could see the setting sun, and it was her enemy, the coming of darkness scared her.

Daylight was no friend to her, or to any black she knew, but night was a frightening place. Bad things happened at night. All the woes of Flora's life had happened at night. Her grandparents, who had been slaves, called night the Devil's Time, and told of the many slaves and, later, free blacks who had simply disappeared at night, never to be seen again. In many ways her grandparents thought freedom was worse than slavery, because at least as slaves they had been of value to their massas, if only as livestock.

When freedom came it brought with it the dark riders of the night, who swept down on blacks for slights real or imagined, and carried them away, to burn or hang or drown. Flora's earliest nightmares were of the silent screams of thousands upon thousands of vanished dead crying out from the mighty Mississippi, which had been their watery, unwanted grave. The Delta Lullaby, her gran'ma called it, and it gave Flora a focus for her fear, and it was white.

Raised on this fear, and in the belief that she was safe only among her own kind, she had no armor against Lincoln, who was her own kind, and who had come to her at night. Lincoln had charmed her into giving away her most precious possession, and when the child was born, he had stolen him from her and banished her from home.

The train that took her away from Mississippi left at night. Flora had waited at the depot at midnight, with only her mama and her younger sister, Josie, beside her to wish her farewell. Her pappa was long gone, no one knew where, North, probably, to Chicago or Detroit, and her grandparents were old and infirm.

Flora had grown up in a tiny settlement of less than fifty people, and she could not bear the thought of arriving, alone and friendless, in a big city like Memphis. In the early morning the train pulled into Stockton, in Tennessee, and Flora made her decision. She got off the train and made her way to the church, where the preacher's wife found her a room in a cheap boardinghouse. Flora took what work she could find, cleaning at the hospital, doing laundry and ironing shirts for white folk, or planting and picking cotton in the seasons. The people at the church were friendly, and Flora settled into a semblance of life, but she always locked her door at night.

Because of Lincoln she distrusted men, and for five years she lived without close contact with them, except for Reverend Jackson.

Then she met Booker. A fine, handsome sharecropper, Booker was, if only in golden memory, the man of a young woman's dreams. They married, and for a while Flora was happy.

Night took Booker from her, soon after their son Willie was born. Their tragedy was not of their own making, for no two people could have struggled harder to carve out something from almost nothing, from the wispy, white gold cotton that sustained them at subsistence level.

Their tragedy was that they were poor and black in a world ruled by whites, and they had no way to escape from either condition.

Willie was another mouth to feed with food they did not have. In their despair, they imagined a future bleaker than poverty.

Booker was young and strong, ready to turn his muscle to anything that might earn money, but winter in a Southern country town is a mean provider. Booker drifted to the twilight world, and began "snatching cotton," stealing pitiful quantities of the unharvested crop, in dark of night, to buy food for his wife and son.

He was discovered and shot.

He struggled to the little shack that he called home, to Flora, and died in her loving arms. Not knowing what to do, or to whom to turn for help, Flora had crawled to the apple box that was Willie's crib, took him to her bosom, and held him there all night, safe, she hoped, from darkness, beside the body of his dead father.

Willie was ten now, and it was nearly night and he was not home.

Flora banged open the sagging fly screen and went onto the tiny back porch. She put her hands to her mouth, a megaphone.

"You, Willie T. Palmer!" she yelled. "You don't get in this house, I'm gon' take half a tree to you! Wil-lie! Get in this house!"

Across the street, Flora's friend Pearl chuckled to herself, snug in her own little shack.

"That Willie," she said to no one. "He be the death of Flora."

Flora began tidying the already neat back porch, muttering to herself. She took the old galvanized washtub from its nail and put it back again. She moved the frazzled and nearly worn-out mop to a different place. She rearranged the garden produce she offered for sale, the braided tie strings of red onions and dried hot cayenne pepper.

She did all this by rote, without plan or thought, for she was watching the gathering dusk.

"Every day got to hog-call him in here," she told the bunches of sage dried for sausage. "Runnin' with them young 'uns 'til he come in here tired and hungry."

She looked beyond her kitchen garden again. There was no sign of her son.

"Don' wanna study," she complained to drying ears of rainbow-grained Indian corn. "But he gon' get them lessons if'n I have to skin him!"

She banged back into the kitchen. With luck there might be some Pepto-Bismol left for her now raging stomach, or she would have some milk. It was an ulcer, Pearl said, caused by worry, and there was no cure except the thick pink liquid, or a glass of cold milk, and chewing every mouthful of food forty times. But who could remember to do that with all the other chores, and so much else to worry about?

She heard him before she saw him, the approaching panting breath and the slap of running bare feet on the ground. He burst through the screen door, a ten-year-old bundle of energy, in a ferment of apology.

Flora grabbed him before he could speak, fear for his safety totally supplanted by anger for the worry he had caused her.

"Where you been?" she yelled, cuffing him, but not too hard. "Me out there hollerin' my head off all evenin'! Ain't I told you to be in this house afore sundown?"

She cuffed him again, but not too hard, and Willie yelped again.

"Din't hear you, Mama," he cried. "I 'clare I didn't hear you!"

It became a kind of a game, as both knew it must, as it always did, but a game with serious purpose, for it expressed love in the only way that Flora knew how. Willie escaped from her clutches and sought refuge behind furniture while Flora chased after him, cuffing him when she could, but not too hard.

"Look at you! More I wash, dirtier you git!" She pointed accusingly at his grubby knee-length cotton pants and his open-neck shirt, smudged with dirt. "Think I'm playin' with you, don't cha? You git over there an' wash up an' set down an' eat."

Her anger was subsiding, and she turned her attention to the simmering pot of butter beans on the stove.

"Cook for you, then got to hunt you down." She waved the wooden spoon at him. "You hear me now? Where you been at?"

Willie headed to the sink, hugging the wall to avoid the spoon.

"Yes'm, yes'm, I hears ya," Willie said, moving quickly to wash, to calm his mama and to give her good news.

"We was down by the railroad, huntin' scrap iron. Makin' money, Mama—"

He was rewarded by a smack on the butt with the wooden spoon.

"Stealin'," Flora said, "nothin' but stealin' that rail-road's iron. Done tol' you about that, boy. I'll tear you to pieces!"

Hands wet, Willie danced away, out of range of the spoon. He fished in his pocket and pulled out a quarter and a nickel.

"Wasn't on the track, Mama, was off to the side. We sold it down at the blacksmith shop. I got thirty cents!"

He threw the money on the table, still dodging the wooden spoon. The chink of the coins calmed Flora some-what and, in her mind, they went straight into the money jar she kept buried in her garden.

Lord knew they needed it. Times were as tough as any Flora had known. A year earlier some catastrophe had hap-pened in New York, in a place called Wall Street, and since then jobs had become increasingly scarce. Flora did not read newspapers because she couldn't read very well, and couldn't afford them, but rumor was her messenger. She heard of hundreds, thousands thrown out of work in the big cities. She heard of riots and breadlines and soup kitchens.

She knew the crisis must be enormous because it even affected the white community of Stockton, whom Flora had thought were all well-off and impervious to financial insecurity. An increasing number of hoboes drifted through town on their way somewhere, anywhere, California most often, where there might be work. That most of these hoboes were white was astonishing to Flora, and sometimes she felt a small sense of satisfaction that these proud and cruel people had been reduced to such awful circumstances.

Yet her heart bled for the blacks of Stockton, who were the ones most affected, Flora thought, by the crisis. The price of cotton had fallen to an all-time low, and dozens of men could not find work. Several of the white people for whom Flora did laundry had cut back on the amount or had canceled her services altogether, and she knew that some white women who had employed her were now doing the unthinkable—washing their clothes themselves. Flora still had most of her cleaning jobs, but even at these houses she heard whispers of worries about money, so it was a matter of some pride to her that she was still able to put food on the table for her boy.

She did not tell Willie this. No matter how dire their circumstances, he would be kept honest.

"Don' care what you got," she said, going back to the stove and the bubbling pot. "It's stealin'. You mess around with that railroad again, gon' beat you to death. Now git over there an' wash up an' set down here an' eat. Then you got lessons."

Willie did as he was told, hoping he had won.

"Mama, this Friday," he said smugly. "Ain't no school till Monday."

But it was a war he could not win.

"Hush up," Flora snapped. "You git them lessons tonight. You young 'uns be runnin' loose all day tomorrow, and I ain't gonna be Sunday beggin' you to get no lessons. Not hard as I'm roun' here washin' an' ironin' all these white folks' clothes tryin' to keep us goin'. I know you gon' learn somethin' in yo' head if I have to beat it in!"

To make her point, she gave him a final tap upside the head with the spoon, then turned back to the stove. She dished up a big plate of the butter beans and okra flavored with salt pork for Willie, and a smaller one for herself.

She set the plates on the table, but before she sat down to eat, she went to the back door and locked it.

Neither of them would be leaving the house again that night. She sat down with the washed Willie, who bowed his head.

"For what we about to receive, the Lord make us truly grateful," they prayed in unison.

As Flora spoke the words she watched her son, and saw a young image of his father. She was proud of him and of the learning he had, which neither she nor his father had ever known.

Her determination came from Booker. Looking at Willie, Flora could still hear his father's voice.

"We gonna see this chile get educated, so he can be better than we."

He said it the day she told him she was pregnant, and he said it once a week at least—sometimes, it seemed to Flora, he said it every day—from then until his death.

They ate their meal mostly in silence, for Willie knew that his mama had not quite forgiven him for coming home late. He knew she was scared of nighttime, and although he thought it was silly—he had been with friends, perfectly safe—he respected her fear and moved cautiously to idle chatter about his day.

When they were done eating, Flora saw to the dishes and, even though it was Friday, insisted that Willie read his books. It was his part of their penance. The rest was stories, told before his bedtime, of the dark deeds of night, remembered from her own childhood, told to her by her own mama, and her gran'pa and gran'ma, the things a black child in the South needed to know, and luridly colored, in Flora's telling, as warning to her boy.

Eventually, she drifted into silence. The stories had become something other than she had intended. Memories of her mama and her grandparents flooded her mind, and of growing up in Mississippi, and this had led her to thoughts of the demon Lincoln, who had stolen her first-born. Tears smarted in her eyes.

Willie, without speaking, filled a bowl with water and brought it to his mama. He set the bowl beside her, knelt down on the floor, and with a cloth washed her aching feet.

He did it because he knew that she was tired and knew that her feet hurt. He did it because he appreciated all she did for him. He did it because he loved her, and he wanted to show her something of that love.

And he did it because he hoped that she would let him leave school. He did not say this yet.

Flora stared at him as his gentle hands massaged her feet, as Jesus did, she thought. Her heart blazed with the fire of love.

When he was done, Willie stayed sitting on the floor.

"Billy Nelson leavin' school," he muttered.

Flora stared at him, not wanting to believe that he had been kind only to be cruel. She knew exactly what it was all about. It had been hinted at, like this, several times before, and she knew that gradually the subtle suggestion must become an outright demand.

"No," she said.

"Why, Mama?" Willie whined. "I's ol' enough."

" 'Coz I said so," Flora snapped, wondering why he could not understand the importance of school, and of the dreams for him. He glared back at her with stubborn, pleading eyes and a tiny bolt of lightning burned her heart, for it was his father's look.

"It was yo' pappy's dream," she whispered.

Willie knew this. He had heard it every day of his life. But it flew in the face of a simple fact.

"I ain't no good at school."

She slapped him lightly, eyes locked with his, as if willing him to learn. "You gon' be good at school. You gon' study an' get good grades, an', Lord help me, you gon' go to college."

Willie stared back, and Flora saw in her eyes something that frightened her. Something that one day she might not be able to resist.

She saw laughter. It was his father's way of winning an argument.

The laughter in his eyes became a grin, and then a chuckle, and she laughed with him, because she loved him. It was not time for the argument yet. He had a few more years of boyhood in him.

"You git to bed," she said. "Busy day tomorrow."

Willie stretched and yawned and kissed her and told her that he loved her, and she nodded her head, because in that moment—apart from the matter of his schooling—all was right with her world. It was night, but Willie was home, and the door was locked.

He went off to the closed-in porch that was his room, and Flora sat for a while, thinking of the past, and allowing herself small dreams for Willie's life, which somewhere in her heart she knew were useless.

From the day that she first enrolled Willie, when he was six, at the Stockton Colored Grammar School, Flora had seen to it that he missed no day for any reason, unless he was demonstrably sick, and he was a willing student, at first, if not a very good one. Once in a while, something occurred of which she could boast to friends.

"—dog," she said to Pearl, "if that boy ain't bet me a nickel 'taters' start with a *p* and proved it in a book."

If his achievements were few and she was proud of them, it was not enough, not nearly enough. His grades were only average, but she would not let Willie leave school now, in his tenth year, as most of the other boys did to work in the fields supplementing the family income. That was not why Flora worked all the hours of the live long day, to see her boy pick cotton. She wanted more for him, even though she had begun to realize that he wanted something different for himself. She let herself imagine he would stay at school, and perhaps, in the fullness of time, even do something more. There were colleges for Negro boys, and hard work and good grades—and a scholarship—would get Willie into one of them. He would get his degree, and then a job, a regular job, a well-paying job, one not dependent on the seasons or the white man's whim, and he would be more than his mother and father could possibly have imagined.

But not more than they had dreamed. She was determined, if only for his father's memory, to push Willie toward education as hard as she could, and if later, in a few years, he rebelled against her, he would have to fight her hard.

When Booker died, Flora thought she could not bear to go on living. She had shouted her grief to Jesus, and, perhaps ashamed of what He had wrought, He relented and was kind to her. He couldn't ease her pain—the awful, aching emptiness that swept over her, and like an unpredictable tide returned to her for days, weeks, months, years to come—but He gave her the strength to continue the struggle of life, alone, without Booker, for the sake of the child, Willie.

When Flora looked at her son, she saw only her dead beloved, and she raised him to the remembered image of his father, unaware that no boy can flourish to manhood in such relentless sunlight.

2

THERE WAS ONLY GOD TO ATTEND TO, and then her day would be done.

Flora glanced around the neat and tidy shack and put Willie's books in order, in a small pile on the table, so that he would see them in the morning when he ate his breakfast, and be reminded of the learning that lay in store for him.

She picked up her shoes and carried them through to her tiny bedroom with its one small cot. She put her shoes under the bed and undressed slowly, folding each of her garments carefully before putting them in the small chest of drawers. There was a photograph of Willie on top of the chest, a photograph of all the children at his school. Good Negro boys and girls, scrubbed and cleaned and dressed in the best their poor parents could afford for this momentous day, the taking of the school photograph, the girls so pretty with their hair braided and ribboned, shy and giggly, the boys staring fixedly as if they had never seen a camera before, which many of them had not.

Except for Willie. He was standing in the middle of the three rows of students, and when the camera clicked he was the only one looking somewhere else.

The thin cotton curtain hardly blocked out the night, so she switched off the light, the harsh single, naked bulb that hung in the middle of the room. One day, she promised herself, she would buy a softening shade for it, or even a bedside lamp, but not yet. Willie's education had to be paid for first.

Enough light filtered into the room from the moon and a distant, pallid streetlamp for her to see her way around. She put on her flannel nightgown, thin from too much washing, took off her bloomers, and used the bed pot. She did not like going to the outhouse at night. She sat on the bed for a moment brushing her short hair. The horsehair mattress was lumpy, the single pillow uninviting, old and scratchy, but it was as much physical comfort as she had known in any bed, except when Booker was beside her.

Part of her ached to have him here now, big, taking up most of the bed, flesh warm and embracing, a safe haven for her tiny ship. She missed the smell of him, the touch of him, the feel of him. She had not looked for another man in her life because Willie was her life, and she was thoughtless for herself until that work was done.

But she was lonely, and she wanted Booker, and so she turned to God.

She got up, put the brush in its place, and kneeled beside the cot. A single picture graced the wall before her. This was Jesus, this is what He looked like, and she knew she would recognize Him on that blessed day when she stood beside Him, and He presented her case for admission to heaven.

She prayed to Jesus now, for His was the voice to God. She prayed for Willie, that he might be a better student. She prayed for her sister, Josie, who was not well, and for Josie's husband and her child, Ruthana. She prayed for her friend Pearl, that she might find comfort in the Lord, and for strength for Reverend Jackson. She even had a prayer for Mrs. Hopkins, the white woman for whom she worked two mornings a week, that she might not be so mean with her money, and she prayed for Kevin Hopkins, their son, who had been a well-behaved child but was becoming a ruthless boy. She prayed for herself, that she might be forgiven her sins. She prayed for Booker, for his soul in heaven. And, as always, thoughts of the departed tore at a scab on her heart, opening it up, making the blood run anew. She prayed for her unknown baby.

She did not know where he was, or what had become of him. He was her other life, before she came to Stockton, before she met Booker, before she had Willie, but the pain of not knowing, of never even seeing the child she had borne, never left her.

Lastly she prayed for her own people, all the colored folk of America, that God might be kind to them, and she prayed that they would find the path to Jesus.

For it must happen. The day must come when God would relent and forgive His children for a sin that was not of their making. Her gran'pa had told her the truth of it, when she was a little girl.

Ham, the son of Noah, had mocked his father, and God had banished Ham to Africa. Ham and his children had forsaken God and worshiped false idols, and their children and their children's children and all the generations must atone for that great sin, and pay for it with blood and suffering. It was the reason that God had allowed Ham's descendants to be taken into slavery, her gran'pa said. Forgiveness would come only when all the descendants of Ham had embraced Jesus. He told Flora she must love Jesus and fear God, to help the black people on their great journey to repentance.

It made absolute sense to Flora. How else could God be so cruel? How could God let the white man have such ascendancy over blacks, unless it was the path to redemption? So she loved Jesus with all her heart, and feared God, and was prepared to suffer all that He could smite her with, so that one day, in some distant future, the black people of the world would be restored to favor in His eyes.

She longed to think that it would happen in her lifetime, but doubted it would. There were too many to bring to Jesus. From her gran'pa she had heard of colored folk who did not believe, and of others, not long from slavery, who wanted to return to Africa and its pagan ways. And from Reverend Jackson she heard of the godlessness of the great cities of America—Chicago, New York, and Philadelphia. Even in nearby Memphis lust was publicly paraded, black men flaunted their carnality in lascivious music and dancing, and black women sold their bodies, sinners fallen from grace who had no interest in salvation.

Flora had fallen from grace once, so long ago, and had spent the rest of her life in abject repentance. The baby she had never seen, taken from her and given into someone else's care, was part payment for her sin. Booker, she was sure, had been taken from her for that same sin. She lived in morbid fear that Willie would be taken from her too, that he would go out one afternoon, like today, to hunt scrap iron from the railroad tracks with his friends, and would never come home again.

But she would not bargain with Jesus or with God. She took some pride in the fact that she had survived as well as she had, despite the cruelties which God had strewn in her path. It was a test of her, of her faith and of her strength. Well, she had faith and she was strong. Against desperate odds, she had raised a good God-fearing boy and given him a clean and well-run home. They had enough to eat. Her glass jar of pennies and nickels that she kept buried in the garden was half full. She and Willie went to church every Sunday, and all the feast days, and every church social occasion, and sometimes Flora, rapt in the adoration of the Almighty, would swoon from the sheer wonder of God's work. Perhaps she was forgiven.

Or was He simply biding His time before smiting her again with another furious trial? She prayed not. But she also vowed that if it happened, that if the unthinkable occurred, God would not find her wanting. She would bear whatever God sent her, because the reward was so enormous. She would not, she was sure, see the Promised Land on earth, in America, in her lifetime. Too much would have to change, and she saw no evidence that anything was changing. If anything, it was getting worse. Because of this Depression, many whites, who had never been kind to blacks were becoming increasingly cruel.

But one day, in the fullness of time, she would pass from this vale of tears and stand before the Judgment Throne and have her triumph. Jesus would tell His Father all that she had suffered and all that she had done, and He would know that she, a sinner, had been saved, and welcome her to Paradise.

And then there would be glory.

3

*B*AD THINGS HAPPENED AT NIGHT, but once, out of the night, something good came, something wondrous that filled Flora with awe at the majesty of God's ways.

It was late afternoon, and Flora was tired. She had worked for the relentless Mrs. Hopkins all morning, cleaning house, doing laundry, thankful that young Kevin was at school. Kevin and Willie were the same age, and the boys were the reason that Flora had come to Mrs. Hopkins's attention.

When Booker was killed, Flora had no money, no work, nowhere to live, and a boy to care for.

But she did have milk. Through the good grace of Reverend Jackson she was employed as wet nurse to Kevin Hopkins, whose mother could not feed him.

The creamy skin of the baby Kevin had fascinated Flora. It was in such contrast to Willie, who was dusky like Flora and his father. She would sit in a chair staring at Kevin while he drank, puzzled that this angelic cherub, the image of the baby Jesus, contained within him the seeds of white hatred of blacks. She wondered if her life-giving milk might change his eventual way of thinking. Perhaps, if she stayed with Kevin, she could teach him some charity toward blacks, and avert him from what she was sure was his destiny.

For a while this hope had seemed possible. With Booker gone, Flora could no longer live in the shack that had been their home. It was needed for a new sharecropper. Mrs. Hopkins offered a tiny shed on the back of their property and the grateful Flora moved in there with Willie. The two baby boys became companions, if not friends, and Flora loved to see them play together, squatted on a rug outside the shed, gurgling noises at each other, learning to crawl together, and then to walk.

But once Kevin was weaned, there was no full-time need for Flora, and the Hopkins claimed to have other purposes for the shed. Again, Reverend Jackson had intervened, and persuaded Caleb Brandon to let Flora rent an old shack that he owned behind his filling station. This became Flora's home, and she tended it and cared for it as if it were hers. She planted her vegetable garden and spent what money she could fixing up the shack to some degree of neatness, if not comfort. Later, again with Reverend Jackson as the intermediary, Caleb offered to let Flora buy the property. He had no use for it, and it seemed a Christian thing to do. He asked for no money down, and what she had paid in rent now went toward her ownership.

All that came later. When Flora first moved there, after leaving the Hopkins household, she had needed to find work. Mrs. Hopkins had offered her housecleaning and laundry two days a week, and Flora accepted the miserable pay partly because she needed the money, but also because she wanted to try to maintain some influence over Kevin. She found other work, mostly laundry, and built up a subsistence income by visiting a number of the town's white families, at their back doors, and asking to "take in y'all's washin' an' ironin'."

When he was old enough, Willie helped. She found him a little red wagon at a church rummage sale, and Willie would pull it from house to house, charming the customers as he picked up the bundles of soiled laundry, which later he would pull back, all washed, starched, and ironed, and neatly folded within a wide, plaited cornshucks basket covered with a tucked-in sheet.

"Here y'all's laundry, Miz Vaughan. If it's all right, I bring it on inside yo' kitchen if that's where you want it, yes'm."

So Flora survived, but her hopes for Kevin did not. A big, chunky boy with an engaging smile, as Kevin grew up he became increasingly mean-spirited, learned or inherited,

Flora was sure, from his charmless parents. If he had any residual affection for Flora, he never showed it, and now, at ten, she saw in him all the worst tendencies of his race toward blacks. He became a pugnacious stranger to her, and hardly spoke to her, except to give her orders or demand attention. He called her a jungle bunny or a jigaboo to her face. If she made any mistake, he would laugh and tell her to get back in the trees with the monkeys.

She started to despair of the boy she had suckled, and, as on this day, had been glad that he was at school while she cleaned the Hopkins house.

She had come home to a big pile of laundry, and had spent the afternoon washing and rinsing the three tub-loads of clothes. The first load was already dry and she was sprinkling and rolling the clothes, ready for ironing.

Willie had come home from school and helped her carry the washing inside, but she had no need of him for the ironing, and after he had helped her peel taters with a p to put in the pot for their dinner, she had sent him off to play with his friends.

She was tired and wondering if she had time for a nap, when she glanced out the window and saw Jerry Mitchell driving a pickup truck to her front gate.

It was not night, but she knew it was bad news. Jerry lived near her sister, Josie, and Josie, she knew, was not well.

Josie was never well. As a child in Mississippi, she had caught a fever that had left her debilitated and prone to sickness. Five years ago, Josie had moved to Stockton, to be near Flora, when their mama had died. She met and married a hardwood logger named George, who provided a get-by living and a little house some five miles from Stockton. Two years ago, they had a daughter, Ruthana, but the pregnancy and labor had done nothing for Josie's fragile health.

As if tired of his sickly wife, and not wanting the responsibility of a child, George was seldom home. He spent his long work weeks at the swampy, mosquito-ridden logging camp, and his weekends messing around with a high-yaller woman in Memphis, whose existence was known to everyone but Josie.

Flora had tried to persuade her sister to move back into town, but Josie, out of loyalty to her husband and the home he provided, would not do it. The sharecroppers who lived nearby watched out for her.

So if Jerry had driven into town to find Flora, it could only be bad news. Flora watched as Jerry parked the pickup, came through the gate, and made his way to the kitchen door.

He did not need to knock. Flora had opened the door. Jerry touched his cap.

"I come to git you, Miz Flora," he said.

He fell silent for a moment and looked away, wondering what to say. Flora waited. There was no reason to rush to the inevitable.

"Jes' a while ago, Mr. Johnny Fisher rid on his horse to my place an' he say to git word to you real quick. Yo' sister Josie's real low sick out yonder where she livin'."

Flora guessed the truth, but still her heart fluttered.

"Oh, my Lord," she whispered. "Po' chile sufferin'?"

"Yes'm."

Jerry was reluctant to give too much bad news, but did not know how to avoid it.

"Miss Annie Fisher's sittin' with her now, an' Dr. Pipkin's goin' jes' soon's he come back off'n the call he on. So I ax the Man if'n I could run you out there quick in his truck."

This was almost the worst part of the news. If Jerry's white boss had let him use the pickup, Josie must be very sick. Flora had made her plans while he spoke.

"Jerry, go crost the street, please, an' tell Sister Pearl where I'm goin'. An' ax her to feed an' look out for Willie 'til whenever I git back. Time you do that, I have myself ready."

Jerry touched his cap again and left on his errand. Flora took the irons off the stove and moved the pot of half-cooked stew to the back. She pulled at her straggly hair, put on her hat and shoes, and took her thin coat from the hook. She had no idea how long she would be away, and it might be cold at night.

An armor of disbelief settled on her. Josie's health had always been a problem, but never a real worry. She could not imagine that Josie's life was in danger, but the urgency of Jerry's visit and the loan of the pickup truck belied that hope.

It was dusk when they arrived at Josie's modest, white-washed home. Sister Annie Fisher met Flora at the front porch.

"Sho' glad you made it in time, Sister Flora," she said. "She in yonder, mighty low. She be layin' there so weak, an' been axin' for you every time she able to speak."

Flora heard the words, and the truth of them, but still clung to disbelief. Annie Fisher followed her into the house, whispering. "She so worried 'bout her po' baby, Ruthana, that's over at my house."

When she went into Josie's bedroom, any hope that Flora had for her sister's welfare vanished.

Josie lay on the bed, under a thin blanket, obviously close to death. She, who had been the prettiest child, was now pale and sallow, scarcely able to breathe. The room was filled with a rich, overpowering odor that was familiar to Flora. For a time she had worked at the hospital, and she knew the smell of dying.

A kind of strength surged through Flora, to help her at this time, but the disbelief lingered. She sat on the side of the bed, the thin springs sagging beneath her small weight, and leaned forward to hear Josie's whispered words.

"Flo—you my onliest sister—an' I ax you—"

Josie's voice was only a wisp of a thing, light as air, almost inaudible. Flora clasped Josie's hand.

"I ax you—from my heart—take care my Ruthana—and raise her for me—"

All disbelief was gone from Flora now. This was a living will, a sacred testament. Flora fought back her tears. She leaned forward farther, to kiss Josie's fever-hot forehead, and then moved her mouth close to Josie's ear.

"You know I do it," she promised. "Jes' like she be my own."

Perhaps Josie smiled, it was difficult to know, but she appeared to be satisfied with Flora's vow.

As the day became night, Flora sat in silence, holding her sister's hand, wiping her forehead, and begging God not to let her die. But she knew that, on this occasion, God was not listening, and Jesus would not intercede. She was not exactly aware of the moment of Josie's passing, only that she had gone, and it was night.

Flora felt no anger. She did not rage at heaven as she had when Booker died. Somehow, Josie's death was inevitable. She felt only a fathomless sadness and unbearably lonely.

She felt as if she could not breathe, and, as if gasping for air, cried out, a huge, wordless moan, and cried again, and then once more.

Her sadness was partly assuaged by the kindness of the neighbors. Someone she didn't know had arrived to sit with the body and had lit the lamps. Jerry Mitchell opened the door to the late arrival of Dr. Pipkin. He took command, and someone helped Flora away from the bed, away from her dead sister. Later, she wasn't sure when, only that it was night, Annie Fisher took Flora across the field to her own modest home and gave her Ruthana, who had been in the care of the Fisher daughters. It was Ruthana who filled much of the void of loneliness. The two-year-old child came awkwardly to her aunt, as if aware that something momentous had happened in her life, terrified that it had to do with her mother, and fearful of the future.

The sight of the shy, trembling girl caused Flora's tears of grief for Josie to flood. She held Ruthana to her, and promised her happiness, if only for Josie's sake.

Jerry Mitchell drove them home. Ruthana sat on

Flora's lap, staring out at the passing night, clenching Flora's hand.

Back at the shack, she thanked Jerry, and offered to pay him, but he refused anything except whatever help he could give, and drove away. Flora carried Ruthana across the street to Sister Pearl's house, where Willie was.

"This be Ruthana," she told Willie.

Like Ruthana, Willie knew that something of great importance had just happened in his life, that change had come, but he wasn't sure what it was, or what the change would mean, only that it had something to do with the tiny girl in his mama's arms. Ruthana, who had been asleep, was awake now, clinging to Flora's neck, but staring at him with wide and solemn eyes. Willie had seen Ruthana only once before, shortly after she was born, and although he knew who she was, the only thing he could think to say was the obvious.

"She my cousin?" Willie asked.

"No more, she ain't," Flora told him. "From now on she yo' sister."

Willie looked to the floor and shifted his feet uncertainly. Two-year-old sisters don't usually just appear out of nowhere, and, obviously, if Ruthana was coming into their household it meant that something really bad had happened to his aunt Josie. Willie did not remember the dying of his father and had no other experience of death, and didn't know how he should react because he didn't feel anything but that profound sense of change.

Should he say something to his mother? Should be offer some kind of condolence? Should he hug her or kiss her? He thought he should, but his mama was hugging Ruthana, and that made expressions of affection difficult. Should he cry?

If Willie did not understand the implications of Ruthana's sudden arrival, or what it meant to Flora, Sister Pearl did. She took Ruthana from Flora and hugged her and murmured sweet words of affection. She longed for a child of her own. Pearl, who loved men, had never found a man to love her.

She turned to Willie and was kindly to the boy.

"That mean you bring her to my Sunday school class," Pearl told Willie, "right along with you. You hear?"

It was a lifeline to Willie. At least to this he knew how he must respond.

"Yes'm," Willie said. He hoped it was enough.

4

$\mathcal{J}$OSIE WAS BURIED ON THURSDAY MORNING, with only a handful of family and friends present. Old Tom Lanier pulled the rope of the church bell in a mournful toll, which sent a signal to the people that another one among them was being laid to rest. Reverend Jackson led the simple service, and they sang some of Flora's favorite hymns, "Amazing Grace"—of course, they always sang "Amazing Grace," no matter what the occasion, sad or joyous—and another that Flora loved, "I Must Be True, for There Are Those That Trust Me."

Then the service was done.

As the mourners filed from the church, the newly widowed George, uncomfortably dressed in a blue serge suit, white shirt, and black shoes, spoke quietly with Flora.

"Far as I can 'ford to, Miz Flora, I'm gonna be right with you." He seemed awkward and grateful all at once, embarrassed that his grief was not great, thankful that he did not have to worry about his daughter.

"I wants you to know I sho' do 'preciate you takin' an' raisin' Ruthana."

Flora understood the truth. George, who was only twenty-one, had married foolishly, too young, to a girl he wanted rather than loved, and he had rebelled at the claims of domesticity. Now he was free to live his life without encumbrance, and would be on the next train to Memphis, to his fancy woman. She did not resent his lack of grief for Josie. She was glad he was out of the way and made no claim on Ruthana, who was, in Flora's mind, hers by right of blood and duty. George became in that moment what Flora's own mama had said all black men were, and while Flora knew the generalization was not true, she recognized that George was looking forward to irresponsibility. But she would hold him to his promise of money, and not only for practical, financial reasons.

She held Ruthana's hand tight.

"Long as there's breath in my body," she said, "my li'l sister's baby gonna have my best."

After the graveside service, as the earth was being mounded to receive the few flowers that had come in the hearse, Flora said a small prayer for her sister's soul.

Then she looked at Willie.

"Since we's here, let's go pay our respects to yo' daddy."

Willie nodded, awed by the solemnity of the funeral, and its attendant grief. Flora had made him wear his Sunday clothes, a dark suit that was already too small for him, and his only pair of real shoes, which, because he was growing so fast, were tight and squeezed his toes. He would have blisters on his heels tonight.

They walked slowly between the tombstones and grave markers until they reached a weedy area around a settled grave. Willie knew the words on the modest concrete headstone by heart.

BOOKER T. PALMER
1893–1920

Flora sank to her knees and began pulling at the weeds. Because Booker was so close, because he was so real to her in this place where he was, she could not resist giving Willie a lecture about Booker's dreams that he be well educated.

As always in this place, the pain of Booker's death flooded back to her, and she started to talk again of that night, as she always did here. Of Booker going out at night to snatch cotton, that Flora and Willie might eat.

Of being discovered and shot by the white farmer, the Man. Of stumbling back to the shack, streaming blood, and dying in Flora's arms.

"He did it fo' us," she told Willie. "He did it fo' you. He wanted you to be somebody. That's why you gotta get yo' schoolin', for yo' pappy's sake."

Willie looked at his uncomfortable shoes, and then away, at the sky, or somewhere, wondering when he would find the courage to end this small war.

Then, unaccountably, something happened that made Willie understand the change to his life.

Ruthana started to cry, as if the dam of her grief had burst. The tiny child, who could not understand what had happened, nor the sad tale that Flora told, wept as if she were inconsolable.

Flora was astonished.

Motherhood was Flora's natural condition, and from the moment Ruthana had come to her she had been filled with the potential of love for the girl, but she was still grieving for Josie. Now Flora stared at the tiny, weeping girl, and her heart swelled with new motherhood, and her own tears ran again, but not for Josie. She clutched Ruthana to her, and wept with her, and promised a happy tomorrow, and that all would be well.

Almost as if she had forgotten Willie, and even Booker, she walked Ruthana away, whispering words of love. For a great gift had been given to her.

Willie understood this, without knowing why. As he ambled after his weeping mother and new little sister, he knew that he had found the key he had been looking for. With Ruthana to worry about, his mother would be less interested in plans for Willie's continuing education and more concerned with financial survival. He must become what he wanted to be, a provider of income for his family.

He almost jumped for joy in that solemn graveyard, but did not. He walked behind his mother and Ruthana as if sharing their grief, but his heart sang a glad song of welcome and gratitude to his new sister.

As for Flora, her own secret wish had come true. Much as she had loved Booker, and much as she adored Willie, she had always wanted another child to fill the void in her womb and her heart of her love child, who had been stolen from her. He had been a boy, but she had a boy, Willie, and she had longed for a daughter—to sew for, to dress up, to fuss over and to pamper, to talk to, to "do for," and to warn of the woes of a woman's lot and prepare the girl for the life ahead.

She saw in Ruthana herself when young. Her mind flooded with painful memories, of birthdays without presents, Christmas without cheer, of never having enough to eat, nor decent clothes to wear. She vowed that Ruthana would never know the unhappiness that she had known, nor the privation.

Mostly, she wanted to teach the girl to avoid the mistakes that she had made, that at least one woman in the world would never know the pain of love denied and stolen.

In Flora's mind, and in Willie's, although the reason for it was so sad, Ruthana was just God-sent. Flora walked away with her new daughter, talking to her constantly, not so much of Ruthana's future, but of her own past.

5

O N FLORA'S FIFTH BIRTHDAY, her mama had given her an egg, a big brown egg that had been laid that morning by a Dominick hen.

"Tain't much," Flora's mama said, "but it's all I got to give you."

Flora was not sure what to do with the egg. It was a present and she didn't get many presents, and so she was grateful. But she guessed it was fertile and not meant to be eaten, so she was puzzled, because she was hungry.

"It's yo' egg, yo' own thing," her mama explained. "If'n you mark it with a pencil, then put it under the hen who's just startin' to set, if'n it hatches it will be your own baby chicken."

The egg became a thing of wonder to Flora. She wouldn't let her little sister, Josie, touch it. Josie was only three and careless with her hands, and Flora was sure she would break the egg. She cradled it gently, in awe of the life within, and her mama helped her mark the egg, oh, so gently, with a simple cross. They went together to the hen-house and, oh, so gently, so as not to break it or scare the broody hen, Flora laid the egg under the downy feathers, beside some others.

It was cotton-picking season, and although she was only five, Flora went into the fields to do what she could to help her family. Sometimes this meant just looking after Josie, sitting on a rug at the edge of the fields, so their mama and gran'ma and gran'pa could pick. Sometimes she would help make sun tea, and bring it to the workers, or on really hot days, or when tea was scarce, she would keep the pannikins filled with water from the pump.

Sometimes she would help pick cotton. Five years old was not too young to learn. Gran'ma was her best teacher.

Gran'ma had learned to pick on the plantation, in the slave days. So had Gran'pa, but he was not a lot of help now, he was getting old, and after only an hour or two in the fields his back would hurt so much he would become crotchety and rough spoken. The main money earner was Flora's mama, who picked more than the rest of the family put together, and didn't have time to teach her daughters. Over the years, under Gran'ma's expert guidance, Flora became as good as her mother and, for a time, earned as much money.

That summer, when she was five and learned to pick cotton, Flora longed for the end of each day, not to be done with the work but to be back at the henhouse, watching her egg. At the end of each day, her hands raw and bleeding from the cotton thorns, she would run to the coop when she got home, and sit beside the hen, and whisper sweet private things to her of dreams she had.

Finally, on the twenty-first day, her pencil-marked egg was among others that began to crack, pecked from within. Flora held her breath in the sheer wonder of it, and when the little scrawny thing peeked out from the broken shell, Flora wept.

She picked up the chick, cuddled it in her hands, and stroked it, and told it that she loved it. It was the first thing she had ever had that she could call her own, and it was alive, a living thing, and to her it was miraculous.

She had nothing else.

The family lived in a little tumbledown shack on the edge of the fields that they worked for Massa Yarborough, the tall, gangling white man who owned the land. It was partly an act of charity on his part. Flora's gran'ma had been one of his father's slaves in the old days, and after the war he kept her on, without pay, to look after his aging parents. Gran'ma married, a fine young man who was looking for work, and old Massa Yarborough gave him a job and the use of the shack.

Gran'pa and Gran'ma had two children. The first was a boy, who was known as uppity by the whites, and who simply disappeared one night when he was sixteen, condemned to a watery grave by some slight insolence to a cracker, a young white male scarcely older than himself. Their other child, a daughter, Flora's mama, was shy and withdrawn all her life, scared of her own shadow and, because of what had happened to her brother, terrified of white people.

It was a surprise to everyone when she married a big, brash-talking man who promised much and delivered nothing, other than two daughters. It was no surprise when he took off one day with a suitcase of his own possessions, some cash he had stolen from Gran'ma's purse, and many promises to return, or to send money when he found a job. It was even less of a surprise when the police turned up the next day looking for the man who had robbed the local store.

The family settled into a life of relentless poverty. Gran'pa's health was failing, his back destroyed by too many years of picking too much cotton. Gran'ma and Flora's mama became the breadwinners, but even the best cotton pickers in the land could not earn enough money to last a family through the winter. They cooked and cleaned for others and took in laundry, and raised chickens and sold eggs, and any produce they could grow. They survived, but only because of the kindness of the community and Massa Yarborough's handouts and hand-me-downs.

Both of Flora's dresses came from Massa Yarborough's girls, the simple white dress she wore only on Sunday, for church, and the smock that she wore on weekdays. She did not have any shoes, only a pair of thin sandals that she wore at church. In the winter, she wrapped herself in an old blanket to keep out the cold.

Each spring, a parcel of clothes would arrive from the big house, as the massa's daughters outgrew them. Two would be picked for Flora, and the others patched or altered and sold. Flora's dresses of the previous year would be darned and shortened and handed down to Josie.

They rose before dawn. Flora would draw water from

the well, humping the bucket to the shack on her own at
first, and then later with Josie's help. They had a meager
breakfast and spent the rest of the day doing chores, or
working in the fields, except for school. Even school took
second place in the planting and picking seasons. Flora
didn't mind being called away to the fields. She was never
really comfortable at school, because she never seemed to
learn to read or write well enough not to be embarrassed
when the teacher pointed out her numerous and repeated
mistakes. Whenever she felt she was beginning to learn,
she was needed for work again in the cotton fields.

Yet she was a happy child, with a strong sense of responsibility. She seldom complained about her circumstances because she could see no way to change them, but
she dreamed of something better. Not much, just more
than she had. A nice dress that hadn't belonged to someone else, a full belly, a warm bed, and a release from fear.

Fear was her constant companion. Not of her grandparents or her mother. They might whump her sometimes
but she knew that they loved her and would protect her to
the best of their ability. The fear was of the unknown and
the face of it was white.

Other than the Yarboroughs, she hardly saw anyone
white, but the stories she heard at her mama's knee caused
her to tremble even before her benefactor. Three or four
times a year, or when they were in the fields, Massa Yarborough would come talk them, and Flora was so in awe of
him she would hide behind her mama's skirts, and could
not speak. Occasionally his wife, Miz Yarborough, would
come with her husband, and once she visited them at the
shack to deliver that year's hand-me-downs, but to Flora
she was even more frightening than the massa, because she
tried to be kind. It was too confusing to Flora. She would
prefer that Miz Yarborough be what white folk were supposed to be, stern and cruel.

Once or twice she would see the Yarborough daughters
driving in the gig with their parents, and Flora hated them.
They were so pretty and well dressed, and so self-assured.

She could not forget the stories of the disappearance of her uncle, and the Yarboroughs were of the race that caused it to happen, and Flora did not believe that the men did these things alone, without the connivance of their women.

When Flora had the measles, Massa Yarborough sent the white doctor to see her, but Flora could hardly bear to let him touch her, and, in any case, he seemed unconcerned about her welfare, not really caring if she lived or died.

Sometimes young white men rode down the track in front of their house, sons of the local farmers, and Flora would hide for fear of them. Once she was not quick enough getting away. The white men rode to a halt and shouted at her, demanding water. Flora burst into tears, so terrified of them that she could not move, and they began shouting abuse at her until Gran'pa came out of the shack and saved the day by being servile and overly polite to the arrogant men.

When they went to the few shops that served as their town, if Flora saw a white man there she would cross the street or hide in some corner. She knew, because her mother had told her, what white men did to little black girls.

And more than once, in the dead of night, she heard horsemen riding by, and heard the screams of a man she knew must be black, and saw fire in the form of a cross.

She lived in a black world, a patched-together village of a few shacks, each quite distant from the other. A mile or so from the house was a small, ramshackle wooden church with a tin roof that had once been a plantation building. Two or three miles away was a larger village with a store and, Mama said, a place where liquor was sold, and where good girls did not go alone.

Between the church and the store there was a railway line, and Flora loved to play beside the track, the gleaming lines of steel that went north, as everyone told her, to fortune.

Although the prospect of a journey excited her, Flora
did not believe that she would ever go north. She could
not imagine leaving home; the family would not manage
without her. She could not imagine ever having money, although there was evidence that it was possible for blacks,
the Holy Few, they were called. In their own district there
was one colored family, the Flemings, who were wealthy
enough to own their own land. Mostly, she could not
imagine going north and living among white people. She
was even suspicious of Massa Yarborough's charity, and
hated the annual trying on of the hand-me-down dresses
that had been worn, so recently, by the uppity Yarborough
daughters.

The railway track was as far as Flora ever wandered
from home. For the most part, growing up, she was able to
avoid all contract with whites, and relished her own small
black community, where she understood the rules, and felt
safe, and she basked in the warm shadow of her own
people.

She loved Jesus, and prayed to Him devoutly each
night before bed. That all the pictures and drawings showed
Jesus as a white man was no contradiction to her. White
people were authority, and Jesus was the greatest authority
of all. She believed that there was a small group of white
men, very few in number, who had heard the word of God
and understood the teachings of the Lord. These men
attained great power, were often presidents and, usually,
martyrs, like the saints cut down by their own kind.
Abraham Lincoln was such a man. Years later she would
believe the same of Theodore Roosevelt and, later again,
John Kennedy. Thus the office of the president of the
United States became sacred to her, and some of the men
who held it divinely inspired.

Of ordinary men, she knew very little; she had no experience with them. The family did not socialize much, and
most nights they were too tired to go out, and would be in
bed not long after sunset. Once a week, shopping on Saturday or at church on Sunday, she would meet other men,

but always and only in the company of her family. She was something of a mother hen to the younger boys at school, and shy of the older ones, who were never very old, and no threat to her. By the age of ten, every boy she knew had left school to work in the fields, and so Flora had little to do with them.

When puberty came to her she understood it because her sensible mama had warned her of it, and she accepted it as a fact of life, to be endured, as her mama told her, a woman's burden.

The intensity of her feelings that came with the years after puberty were a surprise to her, and nothing her mama told her made any real sense of them. They were indefinable, as mystical as the moon. They were all connected with young men, but not any of the young men she knew. There were yearnings to be held and caressed, and dreams of someone else's strength to lighten her burden. She did not believe in the fairy tales she heard at school and told to Josie, of handsome princes taking lovely maidens away to peace and perfect happiness, for she had no realistic example of it. She wanted what Gran'ma and Gran'pa had, but could not imagine how they had achieved it, for she could not imagine them young, like her.

Gran'pa must have been some kind of saint, she thought. Despite all his frequent irritability, he was kind and loving, and unlike all the other men her mama warned her about. In her mama's mind, and thus in Flora's, all men, white or black, wanted only one thing from a woman, and would tell any lie to achieve it. They were faithless, cruel, and brutal, and black men were the worst because they had all failed in their one sacred duty. Black men should have risen up years ago against their white oppressors, and made the country safe for their womenfolk, and given them the hope of a future.

It put Flora in an impossible quandary. She had no interest in white men, but, according to her mama, all black men were unmanly. Flora did not have the experience to understand that this condemnation sprang from her mama's bitterness at her own failed marriage, and her determination to protect her daughters from lust.

Flora's mama instilled these beliefs into her daughters with the very best intentions, concerned only for their welfare. She would never understand that this confusion caused, for Flora at least, the thing she feared most.

6

𝓑Y THE TIME SHE WAS SEVENTEEN, Flora could pick cotton as fast and as well as her mama, and better than many of the men. Josie seldom picked. She had caught a fever two years before, and for several days the family feared for her life. The women tended her with cold compresses and forced her to drink copious amounts of boiled water. Josie didn't die, but she never fully recovered from the illness, which left her listless and lacking in energy. She stayed at home most of the time, tending the shack and the livestock, and cooking their simple meals.

Picking season was a curious, miserable time. The late-summer weather was hot and sticky with impending rain, the work was back-breaking, painful as they bent over for hours at a time plucking the wispy cotton, hands cut and calloused from the thorns. Tempers frequently blazed, yet complaints were rare, because the harvest provided the few dollars that would keep them going until planting season, six months hence. It was a torment that had to be endured, for the alternative was starvation. So they sang as they picked, to give them a rhythm, and to help take their minds off their discomfort.

Sometimes visitors came to stay with the Yarboroughs, and those who were not from the South thought the scene a pretty pastoral, lines of apparently happy black field hands earning their keep and raising their voices to heaven in gorgeous harmony. They had no conception that picking could destroy an able-bodied man by the time he was forty.

Massa Yarborough, raised to the land, was no such fool, and was sensible enough to provide a small reward. In celebration of harvest home he would provide beer, food, and a band for a hop, a dance that was held outside one of the barns at the end of the season.

Flora had been allowed to go to the hop as one of the children, not to dance and enjoy herself, but to watch and keep charge of the youngsters. Her mama would have preferred it to stay like this, but Flora had done splendid labor, and this year, Gran'ma insisted, her seventeenth, the girl should be allowed the celebration. Flora's mama put up a halfhearted fight—there would be men and liquor at the hop, a volatile combination—but Gran'ma had a simple, winning argument. How would Flora ever find a husband if she did not meet young men?

She was allowed to wear her Sunday dress, a simple white gown that came down to her ankles, and the black, patent leather shoes that had arrived from one of the Yarborough daughters that spring, but had been kept in a box for fear of their getting soiled. Even her mama caught the spirit, and dug around at a church rummage sale and found some pretty pink ribbons for her hair and to make the dress more festive.

They had no real mirror, only Gran'pa's small and broken shaving glass, but Josie held it up and twisted it in all directions so that Flora could see something of the effect. What Flora saw made her heart shimmer.

She was not particularly pretty, she accepted that, but she was not plain, and the thrill of the ribbons and the dress and the excitement of the coming evening lit her with an inner glow that could be mistaken, by candlelight, for beauty.

Flora turned away from the mirror and whispered a little prayer to Jesus that it would not rain and that she would meet a young man who defied her mama's prejudices.

One of those prayers was answered. It did not rain.

They walked the two miles to the barn. Lightning lowered in the distant clouds and soft thunder rolled, but the track was firm and dry and Flora's dress and shoes did not get muddy. They had to make frequent stops for Gran'pa's sake, his corns and bunions at war with his old boots, and for Josie, who became breathless every few hundred yards, but Gran'ma kept up a steady chatter of reminiscence about her own first dance, years ago, when the war of liberation was still a recent memory, and even Flora's mama expressed a little excitement at the prospect of relief from drudgery, if only for an evening.

When they were halfway there they could hear the music, and then they saw the lights, the hurricane lamps strung about the barn. Other folk on their way to the hop caught up with them, and the track on which they had been the only travelers became a peopled road of good humor and cheerful anticipation.

It had been a good season and other landowning families in the district had joined forces with the Yarboroughs, the Hendersons, and the Mitchells, and even the black Flemings, to make it the party of the year. So there were nearly three hundred people at the hop, the field hands and their families from all the surrounding farms and plantations. Each farm had its own prize fiddlers and musicians, all gathered in informal competition to see who could make the sweetest music. An ox turned on a spit, and the Mitchell cooks were making barbecue.

The party was already in full swing when Flora's family arrived, and Flora's eyes glittered with excitement; she thought it was the most wonderful thing she had ever seen. Too shy to dance, and with no beau to ask her, she hung back with her family as they chatted with others they knew, but her eyes seldom left the dancers. Then some girls she knew from school flittered up and took her away to gossip, and then, wonder of wonders, a young Yarborough field hand asked her to dance.

Charlie was not the man of Flora's dreams. He was short and stocky, his face was flat with very thick lips, and his skin was ebony black. But he was cheerful and he had a good heart, Flora knew. He was the first man who had ever asked her to dance. In that moment, he might have been Adonis.

"I cain't dance," Flora whispered.

"Lordy, Miz Flo'," Charlie laughed, "ev'ry nigger can dance. Jes' move to the music."

He offered his hand, and, with the giggling urging of her friends, Flora allowed herself to be escorted to the open area in front of the barn that was used for the dance floor.

It was a short distance, but a long walk for Flora. Yearning to be part of the crowd and its energy, wanting to give herself to the music, she was sure she would make a fool of herself. And when she saw the finery of the sashaying older women, the brilliant satins and glowing taffetas, the feathers and frills dragged out of old tin trunks for this one night of the year, she was sure her simple dress made her look like a schoolgirl at a church social.

Which is what she had been, until this moment, but when Charlie led her to the dance floor and, without a moment's pause, started moving to the music, a new Flora was born, after a seventeen-year gestation.

The music became everything. The music inhabited her, infected her, entranced her. She heard, somewhere deep inside her, rhythms she did not know she knew, but were suddenly as familiar to her as yesterday. She felt the movement—her mind had no part in this—her body swayed and twisted as naturally as breathing. Charlie was both the impetus and the answer. She had known him, distantly, all her life, from school and from the fields, and felt no threat from him. She had mopped the blood from his knee once, when he was a little boy and had fallen down in the schoolyard. She had seen him grow into an amiable man, had seen him slinging bales of cotton, and had given him water when too much sun made his head ache. She could not imagine Charlie doing anything unwanted or unwarranted.

She was deeply aware that she was surrounded by an

energy that was at least partly sexual, without being able to give it a name, and when she looked into Charlie's eyes she felt senses in her own body that now had a meaning. She knew that Charlie felt it too, but she was certain that it would end with the dance. Even when he held her close, and she felt the heat of his groin hard against her, she did not think it was for want of her. It was the dance. The simple security of Charlie, coupled with the pulsating music, gave her a freedom she had never known before, and one was not possible without the other.

She forgot the crowd around them. She did not notice the small groups of white visitors who came, not to enjoy the dance or the party but to "watch the niggers carrying on," amused by their lack of reserve, and perhaps taking stock of it; there were young white men with guns slung over their arms, in case there was trouble, or to cause it.

Flora saw none of this. There was only the moment.

She had lied to Charlie. She could dance. She had a natural ability and Gran'ma had taught the basic steps as something every woman should know. Twice a year, at church socials, Flora had danced with other girls, and often at home, with Josie or her mama, to music that Gran'pa made with a comb and a piece of paper.

Now, with a real band and Charlie's reassuring energy, in the middle of a crowd of people bent only on enjoying themselves, and having earned that right a hundredfold, Flora became one with the music.

She was not the belle of the ball, but if there had been anything as formal as dance cards, hers would have been full. She was unaware of time, unaware of the changing tunes, and even the different bands; she was almost unaware of her partners. She was simply herself.

She did not lose her reason; part of her recorded the faces of everyone she danced with, that she might remember them in her waking dreams, or to tell Josie, later, of the fun she had had, but they were all different versions of Charlie, young men from the district whom she had known, if only vaguely, all her life.

Then suddenly, one was different.

"My," he said. "Aren't you enjoying yourself?"

His voice was different; obviously he was well educated. His face was different. Flora was used to all the possible gradations of skin color that a so-called "black" might have. Most people she knew were a sort of brown, but there were others, like Charlie, who were dark as midnight, and others whose skin was so light they were called yellow, high yaller, and even one girl, an albino, who had Negro features, but whose skin was pink and whose hair was white.

This man—she could not think of him as a boy—was high yaller and fine-featured, with straight hair that had only a slight wave to it, and he had a bearing, a confidence, which set him apart from the field hands.

His clothes were different, well cut and fashionable. His smile was different, open and apparently cheerful, but very slightly alarming. And his eyes were dark and oddly disturbing. Flora knew, as soon as she looked into his eyes, that this was a man set apart, a man over whom she would have no control. He was a long way from Charlie.

He offered her his arm.

"May I?" It was not a question.

For the first time since she had started dancing, Flora felt unsure of herself, out of her depth.

"I bin dancing too much," she muttered. "I's hot."

He did not put his arm down.

"Then why don't we find you some lemonade," he said, his eyes still smiling, twinkling with—what? Amusement? Danger?

Not knowing what else to do, and because she did want some lemonade, Flora took his arm. He led her away from the dance floor.

"I'm Lincoln Fleming," he said. "I've been watching you dance. You're very good."

Both of his names had enormous meaning for Flora. She knew he must be one of the Flemings, who owned a plantation a few miles away. She thought she had seen this

Lincoln a couple of times in her life, riding with his family to town or to church. The Flemings were high-and-mighty, the object of envy and admiration among the local blacks. No one knew how this family had made its money, but everyone knew they had a lot of it. That she was walking to the lemonade stand with one of these Flemings was both thrilling and daunting to Flora.

His first name, Lincoln, was even more magical to her, because obviously he had been named after the great president, as many blacks were after the war, and while a name is nothing but a name, some names have resonance. But even if he had been called Charlie, she would have been in awe of him.

"And you are—?" he asked.

"Flora," she said.

Lincoln nodded, apparently in approval. "Flora." He said the name as if testing the sound of it. "It means flowers, you know."

Flora did not know, Flora was simply her name, but the fact that it had a meaning and that meaning conveyed beauty was suddenly wonderful to her.

"And you are the prettiest flower here," Lincoln added. He snapped his fingers, and someone gave him two glasses of lemonade. Lincoln offered one to Flora.

She wasn't sure what to do. There was a hint of mockery in his voice, but she didn't think it was of her; he sounded as if he meant what he said. She felt tongue-tied and shy. But she did not want to leave, nor did she want to let go of his arm. His coat was pure wool and Flora had never felt anything so soft. She did not want to look at him, because then she would have to look into those dark, slightly mocking eyes.

"I'll drink them both," Lincoln said.

At last Flora looked at him, and looked into those eyes, despite the peril she knew was there, and, looking, she was lost.

She took the lemonade and sipped it, lowering her eyes again, but Lincoln chattered on, as if oblivious to her silence. He gossiped about the dance and the dancers, and the season, and about picking cotton—it surprised her that he knew so much—and pointed out members of his family, and made silly comments about them.

The lemonade was gone, without Flora being aware of drinking it, or of walking with Lincoln, still holding on to his arm, back to the dance floor.

"Shall we?" Lincoln said, and this time it was a question.

"Yes," Flora nodded.

And when her mama saw her dancing with Lincoln she saw the danger too, and came to her daughter and told her it was time to go home.

7

*D*ESPITE HER VIGILANCE, there was nothing that her mama could do. Flora was lost.

She could forbid Flora to go out, but she could not forbid Lincoln from coming to the shack, for that would have offended his wealthy family.

Flora had walked home from the barn in silence, dreaming of him. She did not sleep that night, she dreamed of Lincoln. And, because her dreams were, she was sure, only dreams, she felt safe with them, and let herself imagine a glorious future as Lincoln's wife. She became irritable with her family, as if they were the barrier to her happiness. She did her chores and all that was asked of her, but she would find ways to sneak away, and sit in trees or by the river, dreaming of Lincoln.

And then, one day, he was there. Flora was cleaning out the henhouse when she heard a horse ride up. She peeped out and saw Lincoln dismounting outside the shack, and speaking amiably to Gran'pa and Gran'ma, who were on the porch. She saw her mama come out of the shack, hands wet from washing, drying them on her pinny, but Flora could not hear what was said.

She ducked back into the henhouse, her heart fluttering. He wanted her, she was sure. He had come to ask her out, and then he would ask her out again and whirl her into courtship, and he would eventually come to ask for her hand in marriage. It was the stuff of dreams.

"He loves me," she told the chickens, and for the first time since she had her own baby chick, she felt there was something in the world that was hers and could not be taken from her. She did not stop to think that the chick, when grown, had made a tasty stew.

She snuck out of the coop and around the back of the shack, hoping to clean herself up before Lincoln saw her. Her smock was soiled from the henhouse, and her feet bare, and there were feathers in her hair.

She was unlucky.

Josie, shelling peas near Gran'ma, saw her and called to her, and then everyone, including Lincoln, looked at her, and Flora wanted the earth to open up and swallow her.

The earth didn't help, and Flora walked shyly to Lincoln, trying to smarten herself. He laughed when he saw her and she blushed, but he made it right by saying something silly, and then came to the point of his visit.

His gran'ma, his nana, was poorly, and he wondered if Miss Flora would mind coming to stay at his house for a time and sit with the woman for a few hours each day. Of course, Flora would be properly chaperoned, would have her own room, and would be paid. He mentioned a weekly sum that was more than any of them made in a month.

It was the tyranny of money.

That night, Flora and her mama hardly spoke to each other. Flora was wrapped up in her own dreams of Lincoln, and her mama was made conspirator in the seduction of her own daughter.

Yet each longed to talk to the other. Flora was foolish, because she thought she was in love, but she was not a fool. She did not understand Lincoln's actual intentions, but she knew if he ever asked her for anything, even that most sacred part of her, she would not know how to say no. And her mama yearned to warn her, to tell her of what must happen, but could not, for fear of compromising the income.

Instead they all embraced the lie. While her mama washed and ironed Flora's Sunday dress, and Gran'pa did what he could to shine her shoes, Gran'ma gave her instructions on how to behave in a great house, all learned from her own slave childhood. In those days it would have been the white massa who summoned the pretty slave girl

to the house, to do what he would with her, and the irony
that now a black man was doing the same thing was not
lost on Gran'ma. But she could not warn the child.

Only Josie dared hint at it, with silly schoolgirl jokes of
unknown, physical love, and she did not understand the
smack it earned her from her mama.

Lincoln came for Flora the next day, in the gig, and behaved like a gentleman, escorting her to the carriage and
complimenting her on her looks. Flora, nervous and made
wary by her family's ambivalent attitude to her new employment, responded to his charm and flattery. Lincoln
guessed she was nervous, and as if to reassure Flora of his
intentions, he made pretty conversation on the journey to
his home.

The Flemings lived in the big house of an old plantation. No one, perhaps not even Lincoln, knew for sure
how his family had made enough money to buy the place,
but there were rumors of shady dealings made with carpet-
baggers during Reconstruction, and hints that old Grandfather Fleming had not behaved honorably to his fellow
blacks, but had ridden to his riches on their backs. All that
was the past and was mostly forgotten, for now the Flemings were the only living example in this neighborhood of
black men succeeding in the white man's world, and they
were respected for it.

The house was not in good repair, there was a sense of
decay about it, of faded riches, but it was grand enough for
Flora. Excitement mingled with awe in her heart as Lincoln brought the gig to a halt outside the main entrance
and servants came to attend them. Lincoln offered his arm
to Flora and led her up the steps through the large front
door. Flora basked in imaginings of this future for herself as
mistress of the mansion, and allowed herself to forget that
she was only here as an employee. Lincoln introduced her
to his mother, a large-hipped, big-boned woman dressed in
florid taffeta, who was scarcely polite and certainly not
friendly to the nervous girl, as if guessing the real reason
for her presence.

A maid was summoned, who took Flora to a tiny bed-room at the back of the house. It was a poor thing, not much bigger than a large closet and furnished with just a cot and a cupboard, but to Flora, who had never had her own room before, it was a bedroom in a palace.

The maid, Bessie, hardly spoke to her, but looked at her appraisingly, and guessed at her dress size. Flora, unsure of herself, nodded, and Bessie left, to return a few moments later with a simple gray dress that might have been a uni-form. She told Flora to change and then come to the kitchen down the hall.

The dress fitted well enough, and Flora made her way to the kitchen. Bessie was there, with the cook and an old manservant, neither of whom spoke to Flora, but stared at her in surly silence, then went on with their duties. Made increasingly nervous by the lack of welcome, or even the most basic conversation, Flora fidgeted and wondered what to do. Then she heard a bell.

Bessie glanced at a board of bells and headed for the door.

"Come wit' me," she muttered to Flora, leading the way to a large sitting room at the front of the house.

The room was musty and filled with the smell of sick-ness and cheap medicines. Paper was peeling from the walls, and the woodwork was cracked. There was a large canopied brass bed in one corner and a bedside table covered with medicines. Lincoln was sitting by the bed talking to an old woman, who lay under a sheet and blan-kets although the day was hot.

Flora guessed this was the grandmother and had a sense that the woman was not as ill as her appearance and sur-roundings suggested.

She playin' possum, Flora thought to herself, and al-most giggled.

Well, why not? She was old and obviously she could af-ford to lie abed all day, demanding sympathy, all her wants and needs attended to. Lincoln did not bother to stand.

"Nana, this is Flora," he said. "She come to sit with you."

Nana, as the grandmother was called by everyone, glanced at Flora, but without welcome.

"Can this one read?" she demanded of her grandson. Lincoln looked at Flora.

"Some," Flora murmured. But her ability was never put to the test.

The day settled into its routine. Cheerful as ever, Lincoln said he had things to do and left after telling Flora to sit with his grandmother. Flora wasn't sure where to sit, or what to do, until Nana snapped at her.

"You in my light," she said. She had a pile of newspapers and periodicals on the bed beside her, and a magnifying glass, and was more interested in these than Flora's welfare.

Flora, feeling a small surge of resentment, went to a chair some distance from the bed and sat, waiting to be told what to do.

An hour passed in silence, then Bessie came in with a tray, a large lunch for the old woman, and a small sandwich for Flora. They ate in silence, then Bessie returned and took the plates away.

They sat in silence for another hour and Flora was drifting to sleep when she heard a sharp voice.

"Need to pee, missy!"

It was Nana, glaring at her. Flora found the pot and helped Nana from the bed. When the business was done, she helped Nana back into the bed and asked if there was anything else she wanted.

"Empty it," Nana said.

For the first time, Flora started to feel a small sense of security. She had something to do. She knew her place, at last.

She covered the pot with a cloth and went back to the kitchen. The cook saw her and nodded at the door.

"Out back," she said. Flora went outside and, following her nose, found her way to the cesspit. She emptied the pot, washed it at the pump, and went back, through the kitchen, to Nana's room. No one she saw spoke to her.

Nana had put down her newspaper and appeared to be dozing. Flora sat on her chair again and, staring out the window, wondered about this unfriendly house. What puzzled her was that Lincoln was so amiable, in the face of the surliness of all the others.

"Idle hands, missy," Nana said curtly.

Flora sprang from her reverie and glared at Nana.

"What you want me to do?" she said with some spirit.

Nana pointed to a small pile of clothes on a chair.

"I guess you can sew," she said, as curtly as before.

Resentment began to breed in Flora as she inspected the clothes. All her dreams of happy days spent in Lincoln's company caring for his sweet grandmother had vanished. She was here as hired help, to wash and sew and empty the pee can, and that was all. She wondered why Lincoln had bothered with her. A small warning bell chimed in the back of her mind, and she wondered what her nights would be like.

She was sure that Lincoln would come to her at night.

She found the sewing basket and began stitching a blouse with a small tear in it. Then, as if from a long way away, she heard Nana's voice. She looked up and saw Nana staring at her, but hardly seeing her.

"Niggers got it easy now," Nana said softly. "You cain't imagine what it was like."

"What was it like?" Flora asked.

Nana snorted and fell to silence for a moment. Then she began to talk again, of her youth and childhood.

It was the same, terrible stories that Flora's own gran'ma and gran'pa had told her of the old days, of slavery, but filled with a bitterness Flora had not heard before. The passage of the years had caused Flora's grandparents to forget the reality of their slave days. After Emancipation and the end of the war, because they were young, they looked to their new life of freedom as a great adventure. Work was easy to come by, at first, because so many of the blacks had fled the South. But as the years passed and they grew older, the work was harder, and freedom did not prove to be the blessing of their dreams, except that they were free. The rules were different in this reconstructed South and life was more precarious, more dangerous. Part of them longed for the security of their youth, and they began to remember their massa with forgiving eyes. At least they had eaten regularly, and had been cared for, if only as livestock, and only seldom beaten.

Nana's stories were more brutal. Her massa, her family's massa, had been ruthless and cruel, treating his slaves as savages. The telling of the tales made Flora tremble at the awfulness of the life they had lived, and brought to her some understanding of the woman. With the ending of slavery, Nana's husband had not believed the promises of a happy future and had vowed that only an abundance of money could ensure his family's welfare.

"It was easy then," Nana chuckled. "Niggers din't have no money but massas din't have no niggers."

The idea of it seemed to make her happy, and she laughed. "Y'could pay a nigger nex' to nothing, and get 'em to do most anything. Din't matter to 'em, except that they was free!"

She painted a picture that horrified Flora, of the furious drive that had brought the family to their present position. Of freed slaves turning their hands to anything that Nana's husband demanded, the most menial jobs, and being poorly paid for it, slaves again in all but name. So this is how the family fortune was made, Flora thought, by cheating their fellows.

Eventually Nana tired of talking and drifted to sleep again, and Flora was left to her own devices.

Thus the pattern of her days was set. She would come to Nana each morning and simply sit with her until some demand was made. Nana, as if irritated by the cost of Flora without some obvious return, would eventually order her to perform some simple task, but then would fall into a reverie of her own awful youth and bring Flora to an understanding of the selfishness and self-reliance of the family and of the surliness and suspicion with which they regarded any outsider, even their own staff. They trusted no one but themselves.

Nor was there any real separation in Nana's mind between whites and blacks. To an extent she seemed to be more sympathetically inclined to whites. They were the cruel enemy, but the Flemings had done battle with them and, at least to a degree, had won, by virtue of the money they had made. Poor blacks, on the other hand, were more dangerous, a constant reminder to Nana of what the Flemings would be without money. She had little but scorn for her own people, whom she saw as lacking drive and ambition.

She gettin' her own back, Flora thought, seething with anger and disappointment at the pattern of her nights with Lincoln. She treatin' us like she was treated.

She had learned the truth about Lincoln on her first night in the Fleming house.

Dismissed by Nana, Flora ate in the kitchen with the silent staff, and then was ordered to help with the washing up. The small conversations she did hear were hardly encouraging to Flora. She got the impression that Lincoln was not the man she thought he was, that his jovial manner masked another side of him more like the others in his family.

Early to bed, the house was hushed and silent an hour after nightfall. Flora lay on her cot in her tiny room, in some despair at the collapse of her dreams, and wondering when—and if—she would see Lincoln again.

When she heard the scratching on her door, she was not surprised. She felt joy for a moment that he had come to her, in the restoration of her dreams, but it was tempered by doubt that his visit was honorable.

$\mathcal{S}$

O N THE FIRST NIGHT he had wooed her with whispered words of love, and she was unable to resist him because those sweet lies allowed her to rekindle her dreams, but when he knew she would not resist him he became careless of her feelings and took her roughly. He finished quickly and left, as if nothing unusual had happened. Flora wept herself to sleep, both from the pain of him and from her enormous disillusion. It was also clear to her that everyone else—the Flemings, their staff, and her own family—knew why she was there and that her presence was temporary.

Flora guessed she was not the first and doubted she would be the last who let herself believe that she was the only woman he had ever loved. It made the pain of the truth easier to bear.

But it could not stop the tears.

He came to Flora's room each night, after that, in the dead of night, and didn't bother to persuade her to his will. He took what he wanted and left, but she had a sense that he was not satisfied. On the fifth night he demanded that she let him do something that was unimaginable to her. She cried out from the pain and he beat her into silence, so she bore him like a dog cowed to submission by a cruel master.

After that he lost interest in her. He came again for two more nights, and on the last of them, after he was done, he gave her money and told her she would be going home tomorrow. It was the kindest thing he had said to her in a week.

No one said good-bye, not even Lincoln, nor did she expect it. She was a whore, brought in for the master's pleasure and dismissed, and she had been paid for her services.

Joseph, an old field hand, took her home in a cart. Her

family was surprised to see her, having not had word of her return, and Flora wondered if perhaps they were disappointed. If she had stayed away longer she would have earned more. She saw that her mother was weeping, and Flora, who needed to be comforted, became the comforter. She embraced her mama and gave her the money she had earned. She took an old tub to the barn, filled it with water, and stripped, and washed herself and washed herself and washed herself, as if she would never be clean again.

Conversation with her came slowly to her family, as if they were embarrassed by their own guilt. The next day her mama went out—shopping, she said—and when she returned she gave Flora a new dress she had bought for the girl, the first new dress that Flora had ever owned.

She wept in her mother's arms—not tears of joy, but just because she was home. She was not safe here, would never feel safe here again, but it was all she had, and she loved her family, and forgave them their omissions. She went to church on Sunday and her heart swelled for love of Jesus, and He became her only comfort.

When she realized she was pregnant, her emotions were in open war. She despised the reasons for it and hated the way it had happened, but the quickening within her brought her to radiant love of the unborn child, greater even than her love of God, and a fierce determination to protect it and bear it and raise it. To flaunt it before the Flemings, the living evidence of Lincoln's foulness, from which pure good had come.

She was not frightened to tell her mama. The shame was shared, but she was puzzled by the silence with which the news was received.

The next day, her mama took Flora to the Fleming house. They walked the five miles to the house, where her mama demanded to see Mrs Fleming. She was taken inside, but Flora was left alone on the veranda. She thought she heard shouting or raised voices from within, and then she thought she saw Nana at the window, peering out at her, but then there was silence again.

After an hour or so, her mama came out and they walked slowly home. Flora longed to know what had been said, but something in her mama's manner caused a small fear to be born in her, and she did not ask. Then she realized that her mama was crying and the fear grew.

When Flora was told what was to happen, it was almost more than she could bear. She screamed her grief, her disbelief, and cried out to Jesus, but He was not listening. She shouted defiance at her mama, but could not hate her. Gran'pa was old, almost unable to work anymore. Gran'ma was old, too, and it would not be long before she could not pick cotton. Josie was sickly, so this left only Mama and Flora as the providers for the family, and Flora had given them an unexpected source of income they could not ignore.

She had a long, hard labor, and Flora was sure the child was a boy, because no tiny girl could have caused such pain.

She never saw him, never held him in her arms. Flora, swooning from exhaustion and disbelief at what was happening, watched as her mama wrapped the baby in a blanket and left the room. She heard voices outside. One, she was sure, was Lincoln's, and then the sound of a gig departing.

Josie, pale with loving apprehension, came into the room.

"They look after him," she whispered.

"A boy chile," Flora whispered, and it was not a question.

Tears flooded Josie's eyes. She ran to the bed and held Flora tight.

"Gwine miss you, Flo'," she sobbed.

"I know" was all Flora said. She had been struck so many awful blows that a devastating loneliness had settled on her, a kind of armor against more urgent, painful emotions.

It was a simple arrangement. The Flemings, desperate for a grandchild, had paid handsomely for Flora's baby. To avoid any possible scandal, or any further claim on the child or the family, Flora was to be given twenty-five dollars to go away, to go north, or anywhere, to start a new life for herself.

On the night after her eighteenth birthday, Flora stood at the railway station with her mama and Josie. She wore the new dress her mama had bought her nine months before, and had a small burlap sack with another dress and her few clothes. From somewhere, a church sale, perhaps, or neighbors, her mama had found a coat—a thin, skimpy thing—for her, to ward off the Northern cold.

The twenty-five dollars was secure in a little purse, tucked in her bloomers.

She had said an almost wordless good-bye to her grandparents an hour earlier, knowing she would never see them again. Gran'ma hugged her, and whispered the blessing of Jesus on her, then went outside to cry in private.

Gran'pa was inconsolable with grief. It fell to Flora to try and comfort him, but he would not let her come near him. He stood in a corner of the shack, making soundless cries, until Flora thought his heart must explode. Born to slavery, he was finishing his days enslaved to money, unable to do anything to protect his family. He could not bring himself to say good-bye.

She walked to the railway with her mama and Josie, each carrying the small sack in turn, as if bearing this small, light load would somehow alleviate the awfulness of Flora's burden. Mama hardly spoke, but the plans were all made, and there was no future to discuss, no past they did not know.

Josie tried hard, fascinated by what the big city of Memphis might be like, but as they waited for the train, the reality of Flora's imminent departure descended on her and shrouded her in quiet.

They heard the coming train and its whistle. They waited in silence, saying nothing. As the train pulled in, Flora's mama held her daughter as if she would never let go, whispered something about God, and then let her go. She moved away, into the night, unable to bear the departure.

Josie, wiping away tears, walked with Flora to the back of the train, to the Jim Crow car. It was filled with the noise of men, and some sounded drunk.

Flora panicked. She did not know what to do, but she was sure she wouldn't be able to cope with this fearful new world. She wanted to run away, anywhere, to some distant place, and hide until this nightmare was over and she awoke to a bright morning in which everything was known and in its place.

She didn't run. There was nowhere to go. The train was all her future. She stayed where she was, clutching her sister and her burlap sack, unable to move.

A cheerful conductor saw her and understood and was kind. He was used to seeing this. At tiny railway depots all over the South he would see country blacks leaving home, for whatever reason, and he recognized their fear. Some men would try to disguise it with boasting and false good humor, but in women it was almost always palpable, as it was now with Flora.

Born and raised in the country, leaving all that was familiar and secure behind, going to an alien place, was a momentous journey.

He took Flora's sack and offered his arm. She took strength from him. Concentrating only on getting on board the train, in itself a daunting process, she did not look at Josie again until she was settled in a space that the conductor found for her by ordering some men to bunch up close.

Cocooned in an island of fear, Flora stared out the window at Josie, who mouthed words of love and waved as the train chugged slowly away. The few lights of the village faded from view, but still Flora stared out at the darkness, trying to be invisible, fearful of looking at any of the men in the carriage.

Burdened with shame and guilt, she felt as if the word

"whore" was branded on her forehead, that any man she met must automatically know that once she had sold her body for money, and thus would do so again, and that she had allowed the child of that lust to be sold away into a new form of slavery. She could not bear to think of her baby and could not keep him from her mind. She could not believe that her darling would have a happy life in the miserable Fleming household. Who would hold him, caress him, and comfort his hurt? Who would love him? How would he survive without his mother's love?

A new sound edged toward her. Flora had kept her eyes lowered when the conductor led her onto the car and to her seat, and she had seen only the male legs and feet, trousers and boots of the other passengers. She thought she was the only woman in the all-black car but then, above the general din, she heard a woman's voice angrily telling the men to be quiet. It was late and her baby was trying to sleep. The men laughed good-naturedly, but fell into a sort of silence, and the woman began to sing softly.

A lullaby. A mother coaxing her tiny child to sleep. It was so sweet, so lovely, and it magnified Flora's misery. In her despair for her lost child, she could not stifle a groan of pain, so intense it startled those who heard it. A man sitting next to her was so shocked, and so moved, that although he could not guess what caused such grief, he did what he could to comfort her.

He put his arm around Flora and whispered words of consolation, but Flora could not accept the kindness. She remembered the honey talk of Lincoln before he had taken her, and thought now that this stranger knew her for what she was, a whore, and that if she allowed this gentleness it would lead to unwanted intimacy.

She tried to push him aside, and, somewhat to her surprise, the man understood.

" 'S all right," he whispered. "I don' mean you no harm. But we all needs someone when we grievin', an', sister, you grievin' bad."

Flora nodded miserably, but the kindness of the man

had done something important for her. Inclined to reject him simply because he was a man, and thus another Lincoln, she recognized the honesty in his voice and in his actions, and it was the first tiny step in her rehabilitation.

The man moved his arm and apparently ignored her, but he stayed close to her, and Flora came to think of him as a guardian angel, watching over her on her journey.

The night wore on. It was late, and most of the passengers were asleep, but a few in the back of the car were having a quiet party, and a couple of men, closer to her, were whispering excitedly of the temptations of Beale Street in Memphis, the big city to which they were traveling.

Flora could not sleep. Distress at what she had left behind mingled with terror at what she was going to, and when she dared to turn and look at her guardian angel, she saw he was awake.

"Where you goin'?" he asked her. "Memphis?"

Flora nodded and turned away again, to the night.

"Got kin there? Anybody?"

Flora shook her head. Her guardian angel whistled softly, increasing Flora's fear of the coming day.

"Don' like to think of it," he said, "pretty thing like you alone in a city like Memphis."

"Got no choice," Flora said.

In fact she did have a choice. When she was first told that she must leave, various cities of the North had been suggested, and Chicago was the dazzling beacon for many blacks. But it sounded so distant and so enormous to Flora that she had settled for the closer, smaller Memphis, of which she knew next to nothing.

Her guardian angel introduced himself as Joe, and painted for her a small portrait of the city, which he seemed to know well, to warn of the dangers awaiting a young girl there. Perhaps he guessed part of Flora's secret; certainly he understood that something awful had caused her to be alone on this train going to a strange city, and it was not difficult to imagine what it might be. He suggested that she not go all the way to Memphis, but get off at a town near to it, a smaller town where she would feel less far from home, a country town.

Like Stockton.

It made sense to Flora. Why had her family thought of a city at all? Why had she? The essential requirement of the Flemings was that she go away, and a place like this Stockton fulfilled that condition. Because she had never heard of it, it sounded less frightening than Memphis. She questioned her guardian angel, who knew very little about the town, having stopped there only once when he first hiked north. It was small and pleasant, he said, with many less dangers than Memphis, and there was work there.

He tried to question Flora about herself, but she gave him only small answers and they drifted into silence.

The train rattled on, and her guardian angel fell asleep. Flora did not. The more she thought about this town she didn't know, the more she liked the idea. If it was a farming community she would at least understand the way it functioned, unlike a city, and she began to be filled with a small sense of adventure.

Toward dawn she closed her eyes and dozed for a while, to be awakened by a nudge from her traveling companion.

"Stockton," he said, nodding out the window.

Flora looked and saw flat, fertile farmland and neat, white-painted wooden houses. The golden light of dawn softened the landscape, and gave it a prettiness that was not true of the country near her home. In the distance she could see the town itself, larger than any she had known, but still of manageable size.

She looked uncertainly at her guardian angel, although she had already made up her mind.

"Give it a day or two, a week." He shrugged. "You don' like it, you c'n move on. Memphis always gonna be there."

It was the push that Flora needed. She would try it, and if she didn't like it, or if it was not kind to her, she would move on. Memphis would always be there.

The train chugged to a halt. Flora's guardian angel

helped her with her bag, escorted her from the train, and wished her luck. He got back on board and, as the train pulled away, waved to her.

Flora waved back, and watched as the train disappeared down the track until it was gone.

She was alone, and a couple of men loitering near the station were looking at her. She picked up her sack and started walking. She knew exactly where to go. She had seen the steeple from the train. If there was a steeple, there would be a church—in fact, there were two, as she later discovered, one for blacks and one for whites—and if there was a church, there would be a preacher, and, in all probability, the preacher would have a wife, who, as a Christian woman, would help.

As always, she had turned to God for His advice, and with Him as her companion she walked through the town that was to be her new home, and found it pleasing.

For the rest of her days, except in the dark moments when Booker died, she would bless her Maker for the stranger on the train, the guardian angel—sent, she was sure, by God—Who had directed her to Stockton.

9

$\mathscr{B}$Y THE TIME she had lived in Stockton for five years, Flora had established a pattern of life for herself, and Saturday was a joyous day. Although her boardinghouse was close to the center of things, she always had the sense, on Saturday, that she was going to town. Rising early, she would dress, not in her Sunday clothes but almost, and dole out a small allowance to herself for purchases. She went across the street to collect her friend Pearl, who sang in the choir at church, and the two young women walked the couple of blocks to the main street, filled with anticipation of what the day might bring.

Saturday was never dull. Saturday in Stockton was always wonderful to Flora, a day of celebration for the working week done, before the calm of Sunday.

The town divided itself, mostly without complaint, mostly from preference, into its two communities, one white, one black, and Flora seldom ventured into the white section of town except to work. She was content to live in the world she knew and understood, with her own people, and everything she needed was available to her, from her own, with her own.

During the week, especially in the dog days of summer, the town was whisper quiet. There was activity near the two cotton gins and at the lumberyard, and a few passersby going about their business, but otherwise the town slumbered.

On Saturday morning, Stockton awoke with energy, for everyone came to town. The folk from the surrounding farms put on clean clothes, loaded their families into their wagons and carts, or walked. Those who had produce to sell loaded up before dawn. When they arrived, they set up stalls, or simply piled their harvest on the roadside, stacked watermelons and cantaloupes, peck-sized baskets of home-grown peaches, pears, and tomatoes for home canning.

Flora and Pearl allowed themselves a treat, a cup of coffee and a doughnut at Clark's Cafe, known to everyone as Pop's Place, although old Pop Clark was long dead, and the cafe was run by his sons. Then they wandered out, aimlessly, among the vendors, inspecting the fruit and vegetables, past a pushcart selling fish—a sign on it proclaiming CAT AND BUFFALO.

Past the Doo Drop Inn. Past the barbershop, packed with young men waiting to get their hair clipped for a dime, in anticipation of Saturday night. Past Sims Pressing. Past Norelle's Beauty Salon, crammed with young women intent on making themselves lovely for Saturday night. Flora and Pearl had never been inside the beauty shop, they could not afford it, and Flora saw no point in it, for she never went to the Saturday-night frolic, but they stood outside for a while, dreaming of one day having a "treatment," giggling about those who went in, ugly ducklings, and admiring those who came out, primped and preened, gaudy with makeup, some even with straightened hair, swans ready for the night.

They ambled on and stopped again to pass the time of day with their friend Bertha, who was selling lemonade from a big galvanized tin bucket, and then moved on to Isaac Dixon's barbecue stand, already planning their midday sandwich.

Isaac's barbecue was the bull's-eye center of the world for the Saturday crowd. The man himself was in his forties, dark and slender, wearing a tall chef's hat, a red cotton neckerchief, and a white duck jacket covered in splotches of red barbecue sauce. His stand was a box-shaped, white-painted, three-wheeled cart, its lower half of wood, its upper half of glass. Long handles supported a meat-cutting shelf, on which were two big bottles of his fabled sauce, the recipe for which was known only to Isaac and his son, Isaac Junior, who worked alongside his father.

The construction of the sandwiches was a show in itself, and Isaac was the star. There was always a crowd to watch, if not to buy. A sandwich being ordered, Isaac would flip open the glass top of his cart, pull out a choice piece of cooked meat, and slap it on the counter. To the crowd's delight, he would sharpen his knife with elaborate and seemingly dangerous swipes and then attack the juicy meat. Thick slices would be laid on open rolls and covered with generous dollops of the sauce. Closing the sandwich, Isaac would move on to the next customer, while Isaac Junior, who had inherited his father's sense of showmanship, wrapped it with smart precision in a sheet of newspaper and, with a flourish, delivered it to its purchaser.

Flora loved to watch them work. They made a flawless, flamboyant team, and standing there on a bright, sunny day, surrounded by the appreciative, vocal crowd, listening to Isaac's endless spiel, made her feel a part of life.

During her five years in Stockton, fear of the night and of men had not left Flora. She eked out an existence by working every daylight hour, washing clothes and cleaning houses, but at night she stayed at home, in her small room, and would not go out, except very occasionally, to visit Pearl.

She did not want to meet men, but she was lonely and missed their company. Part of her longed to dance again as she had at the barn, all those years ago when she met Lincoln, but she would not put herself in a situation where she could meet men, for fear they would do to her what Lincoln had done all those years ago.

Pearl did not understand this side of Flora. Pearl was three years younger and loved to go to the Saturday dance with her family. It was a sadness to her that Flora would never go with her, for in all other things they were best friends, and had an easy communication. Except where men were concerned. Pearl loved men, she loved to be in their company, to flirt with them, to be friends with them, and although she knew why Flora had closed her heart, she did not understand it, and spent endless hours trying to dissuade Flora from her fear.

So it was Pearl who nudged Flora and pointed to a young man waiting at the barbecue stand to receive his sandwich.

"Ain't he gorgeous?" she whispered with a giggle.

Flora looked and knew immediately who Pearl meant. The young man, a stranger to her, *was* gorgeous. He was tall and well built, his chest and muscled arms almost bursting through his cotton shirt and suspenders, giving his body a graceful line. Flecks of cotton in his short, crinkly hair suggested his employment. His skin was brown rather than black and his features were strongly defined, his eyes wide and dark, his lips thick and full.

He was also either careless of his clothes or very poor, and Flora, used to poverty, guessed the latter. Most people on a Saturday morning, were scrubbed and clean, however well darned their clothes, but this young man's shirt was thin and shabby, and his khaki pants were dirty at the knees. He had no jacket and, unlike most men on this day, he wore no hat. His boots, which had been sturdy, were cracked, down-at-the-heel and dull, despite the several shoe-shine boys around who would clean boots for a nickel.

He was also, just as obviously, hungry. Most people brought sandwiches from Isaac for a snack, or for the sheer fun of it, savoring them because it was their Saturday treat. This young man, when he received his sandwich, tore open the paper quickly and wolfed at it, as if he had not eaten for some time. Chewing on a large bite of the meat, he glanced around.

And saw Flora, who was staring at him.

Neither of them looked away, although, after a moment, the young man wiped his greasy lips with the back of his hand. Neither of them smiled, neither was embarrassed; they simply stared at each other.

Pearl, who had started it, broke it.

"I see'd him first," she said, giggling again, and slapped Flora's arm playfully. Flora looked at Pearl and grinned, and when she looked back the young man was moving away, gulping at his sandwich.

Flora did not know what she felt. She had seen a handsome young man who had caused a stirring inside her that she had not known, or had suppressed, for many years, and part of her felt a rare sense of excitement. Yet she could not cast aside all those years of caution, she could not forget the past for the sake of a penetrating gaze from a stranger, even though his look had caused her to flush.

She stared after the young man as he walked away, and then felt secure again. Nothing much had happened. A stranger she would never see again had looked at her, and that was all.

She giggled, with Pearl, in relief, and the two young women walked on.

A medicine man, a middle-aged white man, had set up for business a few yards from Isaac, and the young women stopped to watch. His stage was a large wagon, on which was a table, some glasses, and several cardboard cartons bearing the printed legend BIG CHIEF NATURE CURES.

An American Indian, the "Big Chief," stood beside the wagon in full regalia, a buckskin robe colorfully embroidered with beadwork, thick strands of neck beads, and a high feathered headdress. His arms were folded across his chest, and his face was stern and impassive; he looked neither to left nor right.

He was wonderful to the local boys, who gathered around, asking one another if he was real, fascinated by the tomahawk that hung from his belt, and his bow and quiver of arrows slung across his back.

"Step back, boys, don't crowd Big Chief!" the medicine man called to them, but cheerfully.

Brisk and confident, he pointed to a gallon glass jar filled with pink liquid.

"You see what's the name of this medicine?" he called to the crowd, which was now quite large, and appreciative of the show.

"Big Chief Nature Cure!" the medicine man proclaimed. "It's made from things that grow in the ground. Nature's roots! Nature's own plants! Made of an old Indian formula!"

He moved to the impassive Indian.

"How old do you think Big Chief is? Come on, somebody, just guess!"

The crowd began calling out their guesses as to the chief's age. Fifty. Sixty.

"Forty-five!" Pearl called, giggling beside Flora.

"Wrong!" The medicine man was working himself up to a full head of steam. "Big Chief is eighty-five! Big Chief knows the way to Nature's good, long health! Eighty-five years of age, ladies and gentlemen!"

The crowd gasped in wonder. The medicine man produced a small package from one of the cartons and a glass of clear liquid.

"You can't buy it in no drugstore," he told them. "Can't buy it nowhere but from me. And see how easy it works!"

He tore open the package and poured powder from it into the glass. He stirred the liquid in the glass, which turned pink and fizzed and frothed. The crowd clapped.

The medicine man turned to an old man who was standing near the wagon.

"How old are you, uncle?" he asked.

"Sixty-five."

"Well, uncle, I'm gonna do something good for you." He handed the glass to the old man. "Swallow that and tell us what happens!"

The old man took the glass, looked at the frothy pink liquid and then at the crowd, who roared encouragement. Conscious that he was now part of the show, the old man swallowed the pink liquid in one gulp.

"Cleanses the liver and flushes the kidneys!" the medicine man cried, retrieving the glass from the old man. "Feel better already, don't you, uncle?"

The old man thought for a moment, but only for a moment. He grinned, first at the medicine man, and then at the crowd.

"Yassuh," he said. The grin spread to laughter. "Yassuh! I feels better already. I sure do! Yassuh, I do!"

The crowd clapped and cheered.

"That's the internal medicine, folks, and it's fast-acting, folks," the medicine man told them.

"But now I'm gonna show you the external medicine. Anyone here got any pain? In the neck or the back or the limbs? Don't be bashful, man or woman! No need of hurting when you can get help! Come on up, come on up!"

The crowd looked around for a volunteer. Edna Gildon, a dark, good-looking woman of thirty, moved cautiously forward. The crowd called encouragement and the medicine man helped her onto the wagon.

"That's my cousin Edna," Pearl whispered to Flora and moved forward, into the crowd, as if to watch more closely.

Flora, who was enjoying the show, did not follow. She was aware of the real reason that Pearl had moved away. She knew she was not standing by herself.

The handsome young man was beside her, not close to her, but close enough. Flora stared at the wagon, where Edna was complaining of pain in her shoulder. The medicine man produced another bottle, shook its chalky contents, and poured some onto his hand.

"Snake oil," the young man said. Flora did not look at him. But she edged, casually, very slightly closer to him.

The medicine man put his hand under Edna's blouse and massaged her shoulder vigorously.

"Surface neuralgia," he told the crowd. "Many people suffer needlessly from this and I'm gonna show you how easy it is to cure!"

Edna suffered the massage for a few moments, while the healer kept up his patter and his massage.

"I want you to tell our good friends down there if this medicine is helping you."

Edna's frown cleared. She moved her shoulder a little, and then a big smile lit up her face.

"Yassuh!" she cried. "Pain's gone! Pain's gone a'ready!"

The crowd roared its approval and surged forward to the wagon as the medicine man moved into high selling gear.

Flora did not move; she stayed where she was. The young man did not move forward, but he took a tiny step sideways, closer to Flora.

"That bottle sells for a dollar, folks!" The medicine man came to the point. "But today only it's on special! Fifty cents! Only fifty cents, ladies and gentlemen, for relief from all your aches and pains. And when my supply runs out, won't be no more here today. And it'll be another year before I'm back this way!"

The crowd needed no more encouragement, but there was more.

"And as a very special offer, you get one bottle of my internal medicine and one bottle of my external medicine, and, as a bonus, the new, the brand-new Super X Big Chief Corn Remover. All three bottles for only one dollar!"

By now the crowd was in an uproar, begging to take advantage of the special, dollar bills waving in the air.

Flora and the young man were alone.

"Snake oil," he said again.

"It worked for Edna," Flora said, wanting to believe, and turning to him to show her annoyance with his doubt.

"So would rubbin' alcohol," the young man said, looking directly at her, as he had when they had first seen each other.

Since he wore no hat or cap, he could not take it off, but Flora thought he seemed to bow very slightly as he introduced himself.

"Booker," he said. "Name's Booker."

"Flora," she whispered.

"Pretty name," Booker said.

Flora did not know how to take the compliment, or what to say next, but she wanted to say something.

"I never met anyone called Booker."

"Booker T. Washington," Booker told her. "He started a university for colored folks in Alabama. My pappy named me after him."

"He kin to you?"

"No," Booker said.

There was another small silence between them.

He pointed to a large painted sign that was on the wall behind them, advertising a moving picture show that evening.

"You wanna see a movin' picture show?"

Flora didn't know what to say. She wanted very much to see a moving picture show. Stockton had no movie house, but occasionally a traveling show such as the one advertised came through town, showing newsreels and short features in a large tent.

Did she dare go with a man, a stranger?

In a heartbeat, Flora saw the pattern of her life. Part of it, part of her heart, was empty, and she wanted it to be filled. She looked away and saw Pearl standing a small distance apart, smiling and seeming to nod. Flora threw caution to the winds, and looked back at Booker.

"If'n you like," she said.

"Where you live?"

Flora did not want to tell him; she had already made too great a leap and was not ready for such intimacy.

"Roun' here" was all she would tell him.

Booker shrugged. Perhaps he sensed her fear.

"Meet 'cher at Pop's Place, at six," he suggested.

"Outside," Flora said. Outside was safe. Outside, on the street, there would be other people, as there would be at the park and at the picture show. Outside was as far as she dared to go. What happened after the picture show was another matter, but Flora thought that if she could keep the two of them outside, in the street among people, she doubted that Booker would try anything too forward on their first—

—date?

Had she just agreed to a date with this scruffy, gorgeous man? No, it was not a date. Flora did not date. She was being taken to a moving picture show. And that was all.

Booker smiled. Was he mocking her, Flora wondered, or did he understand?

"Outside," he agreed.

The smile turned into a grin, and the grin into laughter.

"Outside," he said again. "At six."

He looked at her with something like affection, laughter still dancing in his eyes and on his lips, and walked away.

Flora thought he was shaking his head.

"Well?" Pearl demanded. Flora had not noticed that Pearl had returned, to stand beside her. She looked at Pearl and almost blushed.

"I ain't never see'd a moving picture show!" she said, defensively, and Pearl laughed.

"Lord a'mercy," Pearl laughed. "You scared to death a' men, and doggone if you ain't jes' hooked the bes'-lookin' nigger in this town!"

Flora was embarrassed and happy and scared all at once. She looked around for some way to change the conversation. The medicine man was doing a roaring trade at his wagon.

"That stuff any good?" Flora wondered. "Or it jes' snake oil?"

"Don' make no never mind." Pearl laughed. "You don' need it. You got all the medicine you need. Look at you, girl. You jes' glowin'."

And Flora knew it was true.

10

$\mathcal{T}$HEY MET AT POP'S PLACE—outside—as agreed, that evening. Somewhat to Flora's relief, Booker looked almost presentable. He had cleaned himself up and wore a flannel shirt, obviously not new because several buttons had been replaced with others that didn't match, and a pair of dark serge trousers. His Sunday clothes, Flora thought. He carried a jacket and fidgeted with a hat, which he did not wear. He still had on his work boots, but he'd spent a nickel on having them shined, or had done it himself.

It touched Flora that he had taken some trouble with his appearance, just as she had with her own, but when she saw him waiting for her outside the cafe, it wouldn't have mattered to her if he had worn the cheapest, grubbiest clothes in all the world. He was beautiful.

As, in Booker's mind, was she.

Flora and Pearl had spent the afternoon in a small ferment of preparation. She'd washed herself all over from a little basin of water in her room, and Pearl had "fixed" her hair. It hadn't made a great deal of difference to Flora's appearance, her hair was short and tightly curled and resistant to change, but it made Flora feel good.

The long debate was over Flora's dress. She owned three, two work frocks and her Sunday best. For an hour they tried variations of the three, but nothing pleased either of them. Pearl argued that Flora should wear her prettiest frock, but Flora was not inclined to wear her Sunday clothes. They should be saved for Sunday.

In the end, she borrowed a simple blouse and skirt from Pearl's mother, who was one size larger. The clothes were loose, but Pearl found a belt and did some work with a needle, and the result was loveliness. Flora's landlady caught the mood of the moment and loaned her a pretty straw hat, black, with cheap imitation fruit on it, and then Pearl produced a small bottle of scented water that she had been given for her birthday. It was cheap stuff, smelling of vulgar roses, but it added to Flora's sense of occasion.

They walked together to the main street, Pearl giggling and demanding to know everything about the date when the evening was over.

"It ain't a date," Flora snapped, nervous with an unexpected excitement. "We jes' goin' to a show."

"Girl, you goin' out with a man." Pearl laughed. "That's a date!"

Flora didn't reply because she knew it was true, and in any case they were now some fifty yards from the cafe and she could see Booker.

Flora stopped, her heart flittering. She could stop it now, she could turn around and walk home and lock herself in her room and never see Booker again because he didn't know where she lived.

Or she could go on. But could she do it alone?

"Come wit' me," she begged Pearl.

"I ain't no chap'rone!" Pearl, laughing still, was enjoying herself. "Anyways, I'se goin' to the show wit' my ma and pa."

She knew how nervous Flora was and gave her friend a peck of a kiss as encouragement.

"Y'look lovely," she whispered and moved quickly away.

Suddenly alone, Flora still couldn't move, although she knew she would. She stared at Booker, leaning casually against the wall, and sent a small prayer to Jesus that this man would be kind and would not let her down.

Then she walked slowly to meet him.

Jesus must have heard her, because Booker did not let her down. Ever. He did not smile when he saw her walking toward him, but stood up straight, fiddling with his hat, and as Flora came close she saw in his eyes that she was comely and that she pleased him.

Just as he pleased her in everything he did.

"You smell nice," Booker said.

Flora blushed and looked at her feet, at a loss for words.

"Right on time," Booker said, glancing at the clock in the cafe window.

"Don' wanna miss the show," Flora said.

Booker offered her his arm.

"Then we best be goin'," he said.

Because it was a protective comfort, Flora took his arm as if it were the most natural thing in the world, and found that they fitted together beautifully. He was much taller than she, but this was right to her, and he adjusted his stride slightly as he walked so as not to go faster than her smaller steps could manage.

Thus, arm in arm, they strolled through the town, mixing with the throng headed toward the park. At first their conversation was stilted and general.

"Pretty evenin'," Booker said.

"Sho' is." Flora nodded.

By the time they reached the park Booker had already started to talk about himself and his simple, difficult life, and by the time they reached the marquee Flora was starting to talk about herself.

Flora had never felt so content, or so secure.

There were to be two showings of the moving pictures that evening. The first, at this hour, while there was still light in the sky, was strictly for the coloreds. Later, when night had fallen and the picture on the screen would be better, there would be a show for the whites.

They joined a long line of people at the marquee and moved slowly forward, everyone chattering in excited anticipation of what they were about to see. When they came to the little stand that served as the box office, they had their first small argument.

"Two, please," Booker said and fished in his pocket for money.

"I got money," Flora whispered in his ear. She had raided her penny jar and had fifty cents in her pocket.

"I cain't 'ford this, I cain't 'ford nuttin'," Booker replied, firmly enough to end any discussion.

He paid for both of them. Flora was sure it cost him dearly, but she would not embarrass him by arguing.

In the marquee they found good seats, and the rising excitement of the audience swirled into them.

"Damn, when this thin' gwine happen?" a man cried out.

"When you hush yo' mouth!" another on the other side of the tent responded.

There was a big white screen in front of them, and a piano to the side of it. Children played in the aisle. Everyone there had dressed up for the occasion, for it was an important event in their lives, a celebration, something new, something different.

The lights didn't dim because there weren't any, but the closing day made the interior of the tent gloomy. A florid white man in a check suit made a speech of welcome and then a white woman dressed in an evening gown appeared and took her place at the piano, to raucous applause. She played a stirring overture, which was greeted with cheers and whistles, then a man standing by the big machine at the back turned a switch.

Light flooded onto the screen and the big reel of film on the projector started to move. Flora caught her breath, in an ecstasy of anticipation.

The show began with a newsreel, the pianist giving strident accompaniment, and captions on the screen told the audience the subject.

It didn't matter what it was; it could have been a film of anything and the crowd would have loved it. They cheered and applauded and spoke to the screen throughout, calling out their appreciation and their commentary.

Images of New York and Boston came and went, and people of whom they had heard and seen photos of in newspapers, but moving now, like real people. And automobiles such as they had never seen. And great ocean liners.

And of a war in France, and of soldiers going to battle.

Flora was transported to a new world of wonder, at a moving picture show with a handsome man beside her, and when Booker took her hand and squeezed it, she was happy.

There were other films, a short Western full of cowboys chasing Indians, and a comedy with silly policemen driving around the country in cars that always seemed to go the wrong way, and which brought cheers from the audience because there was a black man in it. A man such as themselves, with enormous round eyes, who always seemed to be in a state of nervous wonder at what was happening. As they were.

It was at the end of this film that Booker had put his arm around Flora. She stiffened and did not respond, but Booker did not move his arm. Then the silly policemen on the screen did something silly again, and Flora laughed, and relaxed, and settled into the snugness of him.

The last film was a thriller in which the heroine was always getting into trouble and being saved by the hero. It ended with her tied to a railroad track and a train approaching her at high speed. The audience gasped and called out urgent advice to the hero, who was riding to save her. At the very last moment the hero did, snatching the woman from the track and riding off into the sunset, and every person present in the audience believed that they had contributed to her salvation.

The florid white man came to the front and told them that the show would be back in three months with new films. He thanked them for their patronage and hoped to see them again on his return.

There was no doubt of it. The audience filed out in an orgy of celebration, each telling the other how his particular advice had saved the heroine, and already planning his next visit when the moving picture show man came to town again.

Flora, who had been transported to another world, was elated by what she had seen. Although the distressed heroine was white, Flora had identified with her perils absolutely, and had shed tears at the worst of her tribulations and had cheered her rescue.

They walked away from the tent, from the marquee, arm in arm, to Pop's Place, and Flora did not stop chattering all the way about what she had seen and the excitement of it.

At the cafe they stood outside.

"Fancy a soda?" Booker asked her.

"If'n it's my treat," Flora said, determined to retain some measure of independence, and because she doubted Booker could really afford it.

He hesitated. She guessed that he wanted to accept her offer, and as correctly guessed that his pride would not let him.

"Nex' time," he said, and led her inside.

It was the first time Flora had been in this or any cafe at night, and the first time she had tasted an ice cream soda, the first time she had sat in a booth in such a brightly colored, comforting environment. She and Pearl came to Pop's Place every Saturday, but always sat at the counter and were frugal with their money.

Nighttime was different. Nighttime was all colored lights and laughing, relaxed people, most of whom seemed to have been at the show and were still talking about it. Sitting in a booth with Booker, tasting her first ice cream soda among the cheery crowd, was an alien land, extravagance, and extravagance was new to her. It made a perfect evening.

Booker's reaction to the show was more subdued than her own, and this puzzled Flora. He had enjoyed himself, he told her, he had loved the show, but the newsreel of the soldiers at war had made him angry.

"Din't see one nigger in that army," he said.

Flora was surprised. She didn't know that black men were fighting.

"My cousin Abner, he in that war," Booker told her. "Done got hisself kilt."

It was a small, sobering moment for Flora. She looked at Booker, who wore an air of angry sadness. Despite his care with his appearance, there was one small fleck of cotton in his hair. She leaned across the table and removed the cotton.

He did not smile or thank her. He looked deep into her eyes, grateful for this tiny, caring kindness.

"Walk you home," he said.

Flora wasn't sure if she wanted to go home, because she didn't want the evening to end, but it was late, for farm people, and even though tomorrow was Sunday, they had a necessary habit of early bedtime.

They walked home, arm in arm. All Flora's fear of Booker knowing her address had vanished and she led him there without thinking.

They stood outside the small wooden house. Her landlady's light was on, and Flora suspected that the woman was quite aware of her return, as would be several others in their houses and the street. Especially Pearl.

She didn't care.

"You goin' to church tomorrow?" she asked Booker.

"Don' go to church much." He shrugged. "Too much to do."

Flora nodded, as if she understood, although she could not imagine how anyone could not find time for God.

And when he did, it thrilled her.

"But—maybe this time. Tomorrow."

"I be there," Flora whispered.

They fell to silence. There had to be a resolution to the evening.

When it came, it seemed like the most natural thing in the world, and the most lovely.

He leaned forward to her, bending slightly because she was smaller than he, and touched his beautiful thick lips to hers, so softly, so undemandingly, a strong man gentle, that it removed from her any last vestige of fear that she had of men, or of this man, at least.

He asked no more of her. He kissed her, just the once,

that was all, then he looked into her eyes, whispered good night, and walked away.

Flora had experienced all the great emotions that evening, with Booker and at the moving picture show. Apprehension. Anticipation. Excitement. Laughter. Fear. Happiness. Contentment. The thrill of rescue. The release from the past. The shock of the new. Now came the greatest of them all, and Flora thought her heart would burst.

For now came love.

11

*T*HEY MARRIED THE FOLLOWING SUMMER, because they were in love, and because marriage was the solution to their mutual financial problems.

Booker's few acres were poor soil at the best of times, and the end of the war in Europe and the return of the soldiers caused a disastrous fall in the price of cotton and wool. In that same summer there was an infestation of boll weevil, which damaged much of the crop.

If it had been a good summer, Booker would have proposed to Flora, but since he would not be able to provide for her, he did not. It was Flora's suggestion that they marry, thus pooling their meager resources. They would save the cost of her lodging, and her small income, together with whatever work Booker could pick up and the winter loan, would see them through.

Booker suggested an alternative. He would give up sharecropping and find a job, somewhere, anywhere, but Flora feared this might mean a move to Memphis, or even farther, and argued against it. They had the acres, Booker had invested so much into them already, and a shack in which to live. Why throw all that away?

"Lessen, a' course, you don' want to marry me," she added. She wasn't being sly. Since he had not actually proposed to her, she could not be sure of his intentions, although they had discussed it often enough.

"More'n anythin' in the whole, wide world," Booker said.

So they were married, in a simple service at Flora's church, conducted by the new preacher, Reverend Jackson. Flora's landlady provided the wedding dress, her own, kept safe in a cardboard box. It had been white but the satin had yellowed slightly with age. It didn't matter. Flora looked lovely, if some twenty years out of fashion.

Booker borrowed a suit that was almost new from one of his cousins, who was also his best man, and invested in a new pair of work boots, which he wore for the first time at his wedding. His old ones had rotted to scrap.

Pearl was Flora's bridesmaid, although she had to duck away briefly to join the choir, for she had a top note that was the pride of the choir and the congregation.

Flora's grandparents were dead, but she had written to her mama, hoping she might come to the wedding, and Josie, but her mama had written back that they could not afford it, and that the journey would be too much for Josie. She sent a dollar bill in the letter, their wedding gift.

Pearl's parents gave a simple wedding feast afterward, and almost everyone there made a speech. Some of the men, although not Booker, got merry on too much beer, and it ended as these things do, the women all moving to the kitchen to leave them to their manhood. They had collected a small swag of presents, useful things, mostly, such as a flatiron and a feed bag for a mule, although Booker was too poor to own such an animal. His parents had scrimped and saved, and gave them five dollars toward their future.

Since they didn't own their own wagon, Jerry Mitchell gave them a ride in his to Booker's shack, doffed his hat, wished them well, and then they were alone.

It was a practical wedding for a practical marriage, but the practicality of it did not diminish their happiness. During the twelve months of their engagement they had sorted out their relationship, the things that irritated them about each other and the things that pleased them. Booker was a man of few words, but he had a habit of repeating himself, which sometimes made Flora mad. When that happened they would both be silent, then Booker would look at her with a twinkle in his eye and say the same thing again, and she would laugh and all would be well.

Flora had habits of tidiness that annoyed Booker. She would yell at him if he came into the shack in his muddy boots.

"Din't never matter before," he'd yell back. Flora knew that to be true. When she first visited his shack she was appalled at the jumble of untidiness.

"It matter now," she'd shout. "I got more to do than clean up after you mornin' till night, an' I jes' done washin' that floor!"

Sullenly, he'd go outside and take off his boots and come back in bare feet, and look at her, and she would see laughter in his eyes, and she would melt before him, and shrug, and put his dinner on the table.

The marriage bed was their triumph, and not just the act of love. On their first night Booker was as gentle as it was possible to be and did not try to coax her to more than she could give. He knew that some foul thing had been done to her and he had lived alone too long to be urgent beyond necessity. As Flora fell asleep in his strong arms that night, warm and secure and in love, she thought she slept with angels.

Over the next few nights she relaxed with him, and soon their lovemaking became passionate and the pinnacle of their joy in each other.

It was also their great consolation, for it was a hard winter. Booker had received the usual winter loan from the Man, the white farmer who owned the land he share-cropped, but it was a small sum of money. Even spent frugally, it would last them only until March, and at subsistence level. Booker found a few odd jobs here and there and Flora kept working, but she had to give up her cleaning job at the hospital because the hours were long and because Booker's shack was five miles from town, and a long walk at the end of a full day.

At Christmas, Booker gave her a brooch, a small thing that pretended to be gold. He said he had got it at a rummage sale, but she guessed he had found it, or even filched it, but he had wrapped it nicely, in paper he had painted himself to look festive, and it was enough, it was more than enough.

Flora gave Booker a new clay pipe and a half ounce of tobacco. It was one of the very few pleasures he allowed himself, and then only seldom, but to Flora it was more than his single vice, it was a splendid virtue. Each evening, no matter the weather unless it was raining or bitterly cold, they would sit together outside their shack—they had no porch—on old rocking chairs. It was a time of great union with him for Flora, for it was their time together, work done, sleep not yet on the horizon.

When he could afford it, Booker bought himself a small amount of tobacco, and would puff on his pipe, and the sight gave Flora a great sense of security. If he could not afford tobacco he would simply pull on the empty pipe, but somehow the picture was incomplete to Flora, the lack of smoke from the pipe being a sharp reminder of their poverty.

She had one other present for him that Christmas. There was snow on the ground, so they had brought their rocking chairs inside, and had allowed themselves the luxury of a fire in the potbellied stove. The room was smoky from a leak in the chimney pipe, and from the hurricane lamp, but warm enough and almost cozy. They rocked in comfortable silence, pretending to themselves that their pantry was as amply supplied as their full hearts.

"You gwine be a pappy," Flora said softly.

She was nervous of telling him, not because she doubted that he would be happy, but it would be another mouth to feed. It meant that Flora would eventually have to stop working, if only for a while, and that would be an added burden. She prayed for a good cotton season.

Booker stopped rocking and stared at her.

"In summer," Flora said. "You be a pappy."

He was silent. Flora guessed he must be thinking the same thoughts as herself, of the cost of a child, and partly that was true, but she misinterpreted his silence.

"I sorry," she whispered.

"Oh, my love," Booker said, as softly.

He reached out his hand to her, grasped her hand in his, and held her so tightly she almost gasped at the pain of it. It was then that she understood. He was crying.

She got up and moved to him, and held him in a hard embrace. Perhaps he did not want the child. Perhaps he would want her to get rid of it. Flora did not know how she would be able to do that, but she would do it if Booker asked her.

"Oh, my love," he whispered again. He looked up at her. She saw the wet tears in his eyes.

And then she saw something that thrilled her to the very core of her being.

She saw happiness.

The boy was born the following summer. Old Mammy Perkins was the midwife, and Booker paid her what he could, which was not much, but promised to give her the balance as he earned it. Mammy Perkins complained bitterly, as she complained about everything, but she was used to it. She seldom received her full fee at the time it was due, but the debts she was owed were repaid a hundredfold in gifts of meat and produce and odd jobs done at her house and kindnesses and sometimes even money.

She was a fat woman with a crude tongue, stern with laboring mothers, and rough with newborn babies, slapping them hard to get them breathing, but with a bountiful heart.

After Mammy Perkins had left, Booker came to Flora, who had the tiny baby in her arms. She offered the boy to her husband and he took him and held him in his arms, and walked away a little, and whispered things, private things that are said only by a man to his newborn son.

Flora did not know and did not care what these things were. It was enough that the man had the child and she saw love. The sweetest memory of her life was that image of Booker holding his son.

After a little while Booker brought the baby back to

her and laid him gently in her arms. He sat on the edge of the bed and looked at her with a determination that was fathomless.

"This chile gon' go to school," he said. "This chile gon' get educated. Then he be better than we selves."

They called the boy William, after Booker's father, but everyone knew him, from the moment of his naming, as Willie.

Booker had made a crib for Willie from an old apple box and had begged, or perhaps he had stolen, a warm blanket for the boy. He would sit for hours each evening beside the crib, at first just staring at the boy, or stroking him with a finger, comforting him if he cried, changing him if he was wet or dirty. He would whisper to the baby things that Flora could not hear, but she was not jealous of them. It pleased her that Booker loved Willie, as it had pleased her on the first night of his life.

"This chile gon' get educated," Booker said. He said it almost every day. "Ain't gon' pull no cotton."

Flora nodded every time he said it, tetchy, sometimes, with the repetition of it, but that was what love was. If it was so important to Booker, then it was important to her. If he felt the need to say it, then it must be said. If it annoyed her because it was said so often, well, what else is love but the acceptance of the loved one's failings?

Yet Booker changed, and Flora knew the reason. One of her prayers had not been answered. It was not a good season.

The price of cotton had risen a little from the previous year, but there had not been much rain and it would not be a good crop. It was also true that Willie was a heavy burden, in material terms. Often they did not have enough to eat, and when that happened Booker denied himself food, that there might be milk and crusts of bread for Willie.

Except when he was with his son, or alone in bed with Flora, a kind of despair settled on him. He went out each morning to work, and no man could have worked harder. But it was almost useless. It did not rain. The cotton did not flourish.

They harvested Booker's crop, and it was a miserable reward. By the time the accounting was done, the previous loan and the cost of cotton seed and fertilizer repaid, and all the little intricacies of bookkeeping completed, Booker's share was less than half of what they needed.

Booker's despair deepened.

He went to the Man for the usual winter loan, and, as usual, it was grudgingly doled out. It was not enough for Booker. He asked for more.

The Man glared at him.

"Boy, I ain't no bank," he said. "That ten dollars should see you through."

Booker managed to hold his temper.

"Suh, I thanks you fo' it," he said. "But I needs a li'l mo' than that."

The Man was silent. Booker's temper rose.

"I mean, 'longsides what we needs to eat, our baby need diapers, an' I hates to tell you, but my wife just got to have one pair a' bloomers."

It was the truth. They could not afford to buy bloomers for Flora. It was also humiliating, an intimate admission of Booker's failure as husband and provider.

The Man was not moved.

"Well, y'all make diapers out of rags," the Man said. "And you tell your wife to patch what bloomers she got."

Booker's temper broke. There was a mighty argument, and the Man called Booker a troublemaker, and threatened to turn him off the land.

This ended the argument. Booker was young and strong, and ready to turn his hand to anything that might earn him money, but winter in a country town is a mean provider. Even though he had suggested to Flora before they were married that he give up the land and find a full-time job, that was in spring, when jobs were possible. Now, in fall, there might be a few weeks humping cotton bales, but that was all until spring, and, if it was another bad season, summer would bring little relief but warmth.

To lose his land now would be to lose everything. He was forced to an apology to the Man, and left, ten dollars in his pocket. It was all he would have until spring.

He did not go straight home to Flora. He hitched a ride into Stockton and went to the butcher. He bought a pound of cheap meat. They would eat well that night, and to-morrow. Walking down the street, he passed the Lanier Mercery. He went in and bought a pair of cheap, reject bloomers for Flora and a single diaper for his son. Finally, he stopped at the bakery and bought a loaf of yesterday's bread.

He was the provider. He would provide.

He walked the miles home and gave these things to his wife, and pretended that all was well, that the Man had agreed to a bigger loan.

But Flora knew he lied.

She did not question him, it was not her place, and clearly Booker was in no mood to discuss their finances. She greeted him with kisses and pretended joy. She used a small portion of the meat to make a stew, and as it bubbled in the pot she sat in her chair holding her new bloomers, a sweeter gift to her than jewels, for the price of them, given what they had, was greater than diamonds.

Booker sat beside Willie, in his crib, holding the baby's hand. He did not speak to the boy. He did not speak to Flora. Very occasionally, he murmured something to himself.

The stew was ready. Flora popped the bread on the stove for a moment, to warm it through and make it appear fresher than it was. She served the dinner and Booker snapped out of his reverie, and was almost jolly with her, complimenting her on her cooking and laughing about her new bloomers.

Flora thought that a weight had lifted and that he had come to a decision that pleased him. She was scared, be-cause she didn't know what it was.

The meal done, Flora cleared and washed the dishes.

Booker sat in his rocking chair, puffing on his pipe, and when it was dark he stood up.

"I's goin' out," he said. "Don' wait up for me."

Fear smote Flora like a sharp sword. He never went out at night.

"No," she begged, "don't do it."

Booker looked at her, sternly at first, and then with a twinkle in his eye.

"You don' know what I's gwine do," he replied, and walked out of the shack.

Flora did know. He was going to snatch cotton.

After a field of cotton is harvested, there is a little left on the plants that escaped the pickers. It was generally allowed, in this area if nowhere else, that this was a bonus for the truly poor, that once the harvest was accounted for, what was left was up for grabs. It seldom amounted to more than a dollar for every few acres, but a dollar was a deal of money to some.

But some harvests were not yet home. To snatch cotton from these bountiful fields was illegal and dangerous. Any farmer had a right to protect his property, and would do so with force, with gunfire, if necessary.

Flora doubted that Booker would content himself with the miserable leavings of the picked fields, so what he was going to do was dangerous.

She did not know what to do. She tried to distract herself with housework, but all she could think of was Booker. She kept going to the window, looking for him, longing to see him walk out of the night, safe, home.

Willie began to cry. She picked the boy up, sat in her chair and fed him, then rocked him and sang him lullabies until he was asleep. She put him back in his crib, then went to the window again.

There was only the night.

She knelt and prayed, she begged Jesus to intercede with God to keep her man safe, and then she abandoned even Jesus and spoke directly to God, but did not believe that He heard her.

Then she heard a noise outside, a strange, scrabbling noise and a gasping, like a wounded animal, and she knew she had been right.

She ran to the door and flung it open. Booker fell on top of her, blood streaming from a gunshot wound to his back. Safe, at last, in her arms, he cried out his pain, and clung to her, covering her with his blood, and begging her to forgive him.

Breathless with pain, and telling her with an urgency that she had never heard how very much he loved her.

She tried to pull him into the shack, so that she might shut the door against the world and be safe; she begged him to crawl to safety, but he was already there, where he wanted to be. In her arms. Safe.

She held him to her, rocking him, weeping, his cries of pain mingling with her grief in an agony of despair.

And then there was only her voice, for his cries had silenced. Flora knew at once. He had gone to his Maker, and there would be no more agony for him, no more pain.

Still she rocked his lifeless body. She shouted her grief to Jesus and screamed to God to let him come back to her, knowing He would not. Then she told God, begged Him, to take her too. Without Booker she did not want to live.

It was then that God relented. It was then that He was kind to her. He couldn't ease her pain, the awful, aching emptiness that swept over her, and like an unpredictable tide returned to her for days, weeks, months, years to come, but He gave her the strength to continue the struggle of life alone, without Booker. It was then that He showed her His purpose.

Willie was crying. The sound of it bled into Flora's grief, and filled her with a new fear. He could not be crying because he was hungry; he had recently been fed. Perhaps he was crying because there was something wrong with him. Perhaps he was sick. Perhaps God was going to be unbearably cruel and take Willie from her too.

Still weeping, still covered in Booker's blood, she crawled away from her dead man to her living child. She plucked Willie from his crib and held her to him, pleading that he be all right, with no understanding that Willie was simply frightened. The child had heard dreadful things and, as a faithful dog knows the sound of human distress, was frightened. He needed the comfort of his mother's arms, and safety.

This comfort she gave, although there was none for herself. She walked about the room, holding Willie, hushing the boy to silence, begging God for peace, and was astonished when He answered.

Booker was dead. Willie was alive. But Willie could not survive without her. She was necessary for his existence. She must grieve for the dead, but turn her attention to the living, else she would lose everything.

She did not know how long she rocked the boy. All she knew was that eventually he was silent and that she was filled with fierce determination.

Booker was gone from her, but Booker's son lived, and in Willie, Booker would live again, and all his hopes and dreams and aspirations.

Willie would be his father's triumph. Flora would not allow him to be anything less.

12

F LORA HAD TRIED TO BRING Willie to a love of
God, but he was not deeply religious. God was
simply there, in heaven, but Willie did not think He
played any active role in their lives. He was a kind boy, and
generous, and he said his prayers regularly, was scared of
going to hell, and hoped that one day he would be received
favorably by Saint Peter, but he seldom talked to anyone,
not even his mama, about God or his small faith. Although he loved the Sunday church services, with the
music and the clapping and the hollering and the passionate sermons, and although he loved to see the hysterical women shrieking and swooning, it embarrassed
him when his mother joined in.

Today was different. Today, he was happy to give
thanks to the Lord, because he had been right and because
he had come to a great decision.

The arrival of Ruthana into their household four years
ago had caused a major change in Willie's life. For the first
ten years of his existence he had been the only focus of his
mother's love, and he labored under her fierce determination that he be something other than what he was. Willie
knew why. For ten years he had heard stories of the goodness, the greatness of his father, a martyred saint in his
mother's mind, and of Booker's determination for Willie's
education. It was the burden of his childhood, and it had
not changed, but with the arrival of Ruthana, the energy
of his mama's ambition to fulfill the wish had diminished.
Willie knew that the day would come when she would accept, however unwillingly, his decision to leave school and
get a job.

That day was close at hand, perhaps even this day.

Willie was fourteen. He had done his duty by his father's commandment and had endured school for four years longer than most of his friends. He was the only boy in eighth grade, and it was enough. It was time to leave and get a job. If nothing else, the family finances demanded it.

Such an action was not without its dangers, as Reverend Jackson was telling them now, coming to the end of his Sunday sermon. The church was packed; the congregation, knowing that the climax of the service was at hand, was working itself into a frenzy of rapture.

". . . in this time o' trouble—YAS!"

Reverend Jackson chanted each phrase, and gasped for breath before the next. That pause for breath was filled with shouts of "Yay-man!" and "Blessed Jesus!" or "Jesus Saves!" from the adoring crowd.

"With so many out of work! *[Yay-man!]* With depression and starvation in the land! *[Have mercy, Jesus!]* When we ain't had but a li'l rain an' bo' weevils thick as flies! *[Ain't dat de trut'!]* An' they ain't payin' hardly nuttin' fo' the li'l bit of cotton that's left! *[Yassuh, ain't payin' nuttin!]* Some people sayin' it look like the world is comin' to a end! *[Save us, Jesus!]* That it look like time *will be no more!*"

Willie thought this was extreme. Yes, there was a depression. Yes, work was hard to find, and yes, long lines of unemployed men waited at soup kitchens and begged in the streets, in the cities, if not in Stockton. But he was young and strong and there was some work, and it would go to the young and strong. And the price of cotton had never been satisfactory to anyone during all his life, there was never enough rain for the farmers, and, if you believed them, the world was in danger of being overrun with boll weevils every summer. But somehow they survived.

A group of women were not so sure. They were weeping together, flailing their arms and shrieking their fear of the end of the world. The voice of Reverend Jackson roared above them and he held up his Bible.

"Bit I got *good news*, my brothers an' sisters!" He flung

his arms to heaven. "There's a just God sittin' up there in heaven! A God Who cares about us this mornin'! A God Who knows we *here* this morning! And in His church!"

The prospect of cataclysmic disaster ebbed. Hope flowed anew.

"The greatest book evuh in the livin' world! An' it say in First Kings, the seventeenth chapter, the sixth verse—"

Yes, Lawd! Yay-man! Preach, brother, Preach!

"—that God sent ravens down from heaven wit' bread to feed the prophet Elijah—"

Willie wondered how much longer Reverend Jackson could go on; he was showing signs of exhaustion.

"—because he had *faith!*" Reverend Jackson shouted at them, almost angry with them. "Ain't no such thing as a *li'l* faith, brothers and sisters, ain't no such thing as a *lot* of faith! There's just *faith!*"

The women were close to their climax. One fainted. Mama Flora, caught up in the orgy of belief, cried out, jumped up, and joined the sobbing throng.

Willie wished she wouldn't do that. It always embarrassed him and upset Ruthana. The six-year-old girl was sitting beside Willie, clutching his hand. Although this happened almost every Sunday, it always scared Ruthana. She stared at her mama, eyes open wide, an observer not a participant. Although one day, Willie thought, when she was grown, Ruthana would catch the mood and behave like the other women.

Reverend Jackson's voice had sunk to a husky whisper. The crowd, knowing what was coming, hushed to a kind of silence to hear.

"So, my brothers and sisters, the message this mornin' is this. Without faith you ain't got nuttin'! But if you got *faith*—you got upon you the *grace of God!*"

The congregation roared its approval, stamping its feet, crying "Yay-man!" and "Hallelujah!"

Reverend Jackson pulled out a big white handkerchief, wiped the sweat from his face, and waited until there was comparative silence.

"The choir will sing, and let us sing wit' them."

The choir, in their red robes, rose to their feet. Sister Pearl pedaled the organ and thumped the keys. Reverend Jackson led the hymn.

"Amazin' Grace, how sweet the sound, that saved a wretch like me . . ."

Willie loved the hymn, they all did, and sang along lustily, because it was true. He had been lost in other people's expectations of him, but now he was found. Now he would assert himself. Now he was a man.

He gazed at Ernestine, in the back row of the choir. He loved to look at Ernestine, who was the prettiest girl he knew. A year younger than himself, Ernestine was the focus of most of Willie's growing interest in girls.

As they sang, Deacon Sanford motioned to two younger girls, about twelve. Dressed in white, they picked up small wicker baskets and took them to each row, to be passed along for the offertory.

For as long as Willie could remember, each Sunday morning before they left for church, Flora would dole out small sums of money to them—a dime each for herself and Willie, and a nickel for Ruthana—for the collection. A few months ago this had changed. She gave Willie only a nickel for the offering and a couple of pennies to Ruthana.

Willie knew that even this cost her dearly, because Reverend Jackson was right. Work was scarce, as much for women as for men. Many of Mama Flora's clients could no longer afford to have her do their laundry, and at least two of her cleaning jobs had ended during the last couple of years. Even the Hopkinses, whom many thought well-to-do, had stopped employing Flora, or any help. It was rumored that Mr. Hopkins had lost much of his money in the stock market.

Willie didn't resent giving a nickel, or even a dime, to the church; he knew it was for a good cause. He resented giving his mother's nickels and dimes. He wanted to give his own.

Deacon Sanford was standing, and the choir lowered its volume.

"An' whilst we give as much as we can this mornin'," Deacon Sanford said, "Deacon Dixon will make the announcements."

Deacon Isaac Dixon, the barbecue king changed to sober church man, rose to speak.

"I b'lieve ev'rybody know that our fellow Christian brother Peter Parm is sick, low sick," he said, his subdued manner in sharp contrast to his huckstering at his sandwich stand. "All those wishin' to take part in a special prayer for him are axed to stay on after reg'lar prayer meetin'."

There was a small chink of coins as the baskets passed along the rows.

"Brother Sanford sends us a note that Mr. Johnnie Jacobs's truck will stop on the lane tomorrow at six, for anybody wants to pick cotton in the river bottom lands. Mr. Jacobs is payin' a dollar and a half a hundred."

Willie was triumphant. There was work. He would find work. The pay was lousy, but it would be money in his pocket, not someone else's.

Deacon Dixon could not resist a small commercial.

"An', brothers an' sisters, when you get yo' cotton money, don't forget yo' church."

The basket was headed Willie's way. He took it from the person next to him, dropped in his nickel, and held it for Ruthana, who put in her three pennies. Willie offered the basket to Mama Flora, who took it from him. Willie watched closely. He saw her hand move over the basket, but he did not hear the chink of a coin. He was sure his mother had not given anything.

He looked at Mama Flora, who caught his eye and blushed. She looked away again and passed the basket on. Deacon Dixon was still making announcements.

"An' speakin' of outstandin' members of our community, if there is one that everybody here loves, it's Sister Edna Mae Riley!"

There was appreciative shouts.

"All the Old Sisters we been priv'leged to honor down over the years, ain't none more deserved it than our dear Sister Edna Mae. Fix the date in yo' minds. One month from today."

Willie, still watching his mother, saw her face set and knew why. For church women it was a great honor to be accorded the title "Old Sister," given only to the most devout. Flora was still comparatively young, but she was a loyal and regular churchgoer and she longed for her faith to be recognized.

"We hear that Sister Edna Mae's chillun that gone north," Deacon Dixon said, "even some of her gran'chillun, are gon' make it here to join her an' members of this church for this occasion. Remember—third Sunday next month! We means to fill up ev'ry seat for good Sister Edna Mae."

One day, Flora thought, my children will assemble here to honor me when I am made Old Sister. But it will be different. My children will not need to come back. My children will not have gone north.

"Now, Brother Henderson has a special 'nouncement," Deacon Dixon concluded. He sat, and Brother Henderson stood to speak. The offertory was done. The two girls brought the baskets from the back of the church to Deacon Sanford, who began counting the money.

"I'm gon' lead a workforce next Sat'dee mornin' at eight o'clock to clean up the cemetery. It's a sin and a shame how we neglect our dead restin'." Brother Henderson was angry and there was some applause of agreement.

"An' ev'ry funeral we have, we pass right by the white folks' cemetery, where they've had some of us mowin' an' cleanin' an' rakin', an' our own restin' place look like a briar patch!"

The congregation accepted his lecture; he was right to scold them. Willie sighed. His mama would insist he be part of the cemetery workforce, and Willie regarded Saturday as his own day. He glanced at the choir, at Ernestine, who nodded her head slightly. This cheered Willie up. If Ernestine was going to be part of the workforce, it would make his day brighter.

"An' I want the good sisters of this church to get up food baskets for the workforce! An' our good brother Sweet Owens, who live close by the cemetery, is gon' have a barrel a' ice water fo' us!"

Brother Henderson wanted to go on, to urge them to labor for the dead, but Deacon Sanford coughed slightly, and Brother Henderson got the message.

"An' now our church treasurer, Deacon Todd Sanford, will 'nounce this mornin's free will offerin'."

Deacon Sanford rose from the counting table.

"Now, brothers an' sisters, we've really enjoyed the good sermon an' the good singin' here together this mornin' under God's roof."

He paused. Everyone knew what was coming.

"An' to make the offertory a complete success, we needs ninety-four mo' cents to make it an even five dollars! Only ninety-four cents, brothers an' sisters. Who's gon' give the first dime?"

Everyone looked at everyone else, or at their feet. No one was keen to give more, but a few, sensibly, had kept a little in reserve. To encourage them, Reverend Jackson led the choir in another hymn, with a quicker tempo: "Let Sunshine Come into Your Heart."

Someone's hand went up, holding a dime. One of the girls ran forward with the basket.

"Brother Nash Campbell!" Deacon Sanford proclaimed. "Thank you, brother, fo' the first ten cents. Who's next?"

At intervals, as the singing continued, hands went up holding nickels or pennies, and the little girls would run to each with the baskets. Deacon Sanford would announce the name of the giver, and the sum. After a while, the giving ceased.

"We down to the last few pennies!" Deacon Sanford

urged them. "C'mon, y'all, so Rev'rend Jackson can let us out a' here, to get home to that big dinner."

He looked around expectantly, but no one offered. The congregation held its collective breath.

Willie saw movement out of the corner of his eye. He turned to his mama, who was digging in her pocket. He wanted to tell her not to do it, but it would be wasted words.

Mama Flora gave a nickel to Ruthana and held the girl up, her hand in the air clutching the nickel. The crowd cheered.

"Thank you, Sister Flora!" Deacon Sanford called with relief. "Or should I say thank you to that li'l darlin' daughter o' yours, Ruthana!" Ruthana beamed happily.

"Ruthana Palmer, brothers an' sisters!"

Mama Flora felt completely justified.

"She put us over the top. Five dollars an' three cents, brothers an' sisters, let us give thanks to the Lord!"

The congregation rose for the final prayer.

Willie did not pray. He burned hot with anger. His mama had withheld her offering so that she could have her moment at the end, a nickel's worth of triumph.

Sure, it was only a nickel. But they could not afford it.

13

*W*ILLIE ONLY PICKED AT HIS FOOD. It was a poor dinner, a thin soup of potatoes, turnip greens, and a few small pieces of rabbit, more bone than meat. It was the best his mama could manage, he was sure, but it fueled his anger. It shouldn't have to be like this. It wouldn't be like this anymore.

He glanced about the room. The oilcloth on the table was clean, but it was old, Willie couldn't remember when it wasn't there, and patches of it were worn down to the fabric. The black cast-iron stove had one leg missing and the corner was propped up on a pile of three bricks. The sagging stovepipe was held up by a piece of wire attached to a nail in the ceiling. A rag wrapping had long ago replaced the missing wooden handle of the black kettle on the stove. The pots and pans were dented. One of the half doors was missing from the cabinet where the dishes were stored. There was a galvanized basin on the water stand. It had a hole in it, and although Pearl's father had patched it with a piece of zinc, it still leaked.

All these things Willie knew; he had seen them every day, had become used to them and accepted them as part of their existence. Now it was as if he were seeing them for the first time.

It shouldn't be like this. It wouldn't be like this anymore.

But the inevitable confrontation that must accompany the change weighed heavily on him.

He sighed, and pushed his plate away.

Ruthana, who had already eaten her smaller portion with a healthy appetite, looked at Flora.

"C'n I have Willie's?" she asked.

Flora glared at Willie, but spoke softly to Ruthana.

"Hush now, you go see if there's some beans ready for pickin'."

Ruthana sighed, but she was aware of their poverty, and also knew that, despite his promises, her father seldom sent money for her keep.

"Aw, Mama, you won't fix 'em till tomorrow. I do it then—"

"You just min' yo' business, an' go pick me some beans," Flora said, more sharply, but then softened again for blackmail. "Mebbe there's a cookie left in the jar."

Ruthana cheered, and went out the back door.

Willie sent up a prayer for help. He knew why Ruthana was being sent from the room. It was to be now. His mama had chosen the time and place of it.

He picked at the oilcloth, preferring not to look at his mother.

"What's the matter wit' you, boy?" he heard her say.

He shrugged, intent on the oilcloth.

"You ain't et right all week. You sick?"

Willie shrugged again.

"I got somethin' on my mind," he muttered.

Did she know what was coming? Had she guessed? She got up and started clearing the plates. She put Willie's un-eaten food aside. He would want it later.

"Best say it, then," she said.

So he did.

"Mama, I don't want—"

He drew a breath in the middle of the sentence.

"—I don' want to go to school no more."

He was still staring at the oilcloth on the table. He couldn't see his mother and he was puzzled by the silence.

"I knows you don' want to hear that—"

She hit him, hard, across the back of his head. She had snuck up behind him, and she hit him, hard.

"Then don' say it!"

It was what Willie needed. It brought all his anger and frustration to the surface in an explosion of energy. He jumped up, his head smarting.

"I ain't makin' no money settin' in that school! I'm near about the only boy ain't gone to work!"

Flora glared at him, but she did not hit him again, although she might, yet. She saw how big he was, but that didn't frighten her, he would never hit his mama. She saw Booker, when young.

Years of dreams fell away from her, years of hope. Of illusion.

"Work my fingers to the *bone* to keep you in books an' clothes," she yelled at him. "I don't care if ain't nobody in that school but you!"

But she was only counterpoint to the speech he had practiced for so long. It came flooding out of him, unstoppable.

"That's what I'm tryin' to tell you, Mama! You out scuffin' day in, day out, me settin' up there in school; it break my heart, Mama, watchin' you killin' yo'self. Fo' what? I ain't learnin' nothin', I cain't learn, I ain't no good at school an' I ain't goin' back!"

First passion spent, the statement made, he calmed a little and was gentler with her.

"Y'think I don't know, you think I don' see? Y'only pretend to eat sometimes, an' hides the food away an' gives it to me or Ruthana nex' time we hungry. I see'd it, Mama, I see'd you do it. Y'think I ain't see'd yer cheating the collection basket at church? Y'think I ain't all et up inside when I see's you come home wore out each day, and why, Mama, what for? So I c'n go to school? Y'think I wants to live like this, y'think I wants you to live like this, or Ruthana, all for some ol' school, where I ain't no good? You seen my grades, Mama. Y'know they're bad—"

She did not want gentleness.

"I ain't gonna hear this," she cried, close to crying. "I ain't gwine listen! I don't care what it costs, I promised yo' pappy, on his dyin' day."

It wasn't true, it wasn't a deathbed promise made to Booker, but it might as well have been, because she believed it. Why couldn't Willie see the point?

"You ain't gon' be ignorant, you ain't gon' know nuttin'!" she begged. "Like the rest of us."

It was an awful admission of her own sense of inadequacy, and it did something against which she had no armor. It made him smile.

"But, Mama," he said, "I bin at school eight years, an' I don' know nuttin'."

It caused her tears to flow and she turned away from him.

"But I'm big, big enough to load cotton, an' that's what I's gon' do. I ain't goin' back to that school."

He knew he had won. Part of him wanted to hold her, hug her hard, and tell her he loved her, but some instinct told him he had to take one step more. He had to assert his independence physically as well.

It was nighttime. He did not intend to hurt her, even though what he was going to do would.

"I's goin' out," he said.

She gasped at the shock of it. He never went out at night. Bad things happened at night. Once or twice, perhaps, in the last year or two, she had let him go out to church functions, when she knew where he was and who he was with. But not this.

She heard the door bang and turned to shout at it, the last word.

"You is goin' back to school! You is! You hear me, boy, I mean you is goin' back!"

She spoke to herself.

She fished in her pinny and found the rag that was her hanky and dabbed at her eyes. She went to the stove and banged a pot on it, for no reason other than to release her anger.

She heard the door again, and looked up, hoping it was he, come back to her, to apologize and do some homework and get ready for school.

But it was the other door, the back door. Ruthana came in from the garden with a basin of fresh-picked beans.

She looked at Flora uncertainly, for she had heard the

argument. Although she had lived in this house for four years, she had never heard such anger, and it frightened her. Even though she knew she was loved here, Ruthana was still not secure enough to think of this place as a place of permanence. She did not remember her previous home, but she knew she had not always lived here, and that Flora was not her real mother, and Willie not her real brother.

"Ain't too many ready," she said nervously, offering the beans.

"Put 'em on the table. I see to 'em later," Flora said.

Ruthana put the bowl on the table and stood there, waiting for some expression of favor.

It didn't come. Flora, still angry with Willie, was trying to restore her world to order by tidying her kitchen.

"Y'said I could have a cookie," Ruthana murmured.

Flora turned and stared at her for what might have been eternity to a little girl.

"Look in the tin," Flora said. "I don't know what's left."

Ruthana went to the cookie tin. There was one left. She took it and turned back to Flora, who had sat at the table. She offered the cookie to Flora, who shook her head.

"I bake some mo' sometime," Flora said. She felt suddenly exhausted, too tired to do anything.

"Come sit by me," she said to Ruthana.

It was what the child needed. All was right with her world again. She went to sit on the chair next to her mama, but Flora pulled her to her, onto her lap.

She sat there, hugging Ruthana, while the child ate the cookie.

"You like school, Ruthana?" Flora whispered.

"M'm," Ruthana responded, her mouth full of cookie. School was still a mystery to her, she was only in the first grade, but she liked the company.

"That's good, 'coz you better like school," Flora said. "School's the best thing fo' a girl like you. You got education, you can be anythin' you wants."

Ruthana mumbled an agreement, although she didn't understand what was happening. She was content to sit there, in Flora's lap, being hugged. She hoped that this was love, but she was wise enough, at six, to know that at this moment she was her mother's greatest comfort. If it wasn't love, it was the next best thing, and it was enough.

"Willie comin' home?" she wondered.

Flora didn't reply immediately. She sat with her arms wrapped around Ruthana, rubbing her cheek in the girl's soft hair. So this was what the end of a dream was like. It was curious, because although she felt downcast and cheated, although she felt that all the plans she had made with Booker had been brutally trampled on, deep inside she had known this day would come. She had not been unready. She also felt a sense of relief. It was as if she had been drowning and a small ship of rescue had just appeared on the horizon.

She did something that surprised Ruthana. She giggled.

"What you laughin' at, Mama?" the girl asked.

"I laughin' at you, chile, 'coz you so ugly," Flora said.

It wasn't true. Ruthana wasn't ugly and that wasn't why Flora laughed. But she was determined to save Ruthana from vanity, for that way lay ruthless men. Every small chance she got, she told Ruthana that she was not pretty. It was done with the very best intentions and it never occurred to her that she was doing any harm to the child.

She had giggled for another reason. If Willie did get a job, it would make life easier for all of them. She wouldn't have to work quite so hard. She wouldn't have to cheat herself of food. She wouldn't have to pretend to put money in the collection basket at church.

But she wouldn't let her son know that his decision was, to even the smallest degree, welcome.

"Yeh, Willie comin' home," Flora said. "Later."

14

WHEN WILLIE CAME HOME HE FOUND the door
unlocked and Flora waiting for him. Flora said
nothing, but she glanced at the alarm clock—it was nine—
and then at a clean shirt and a pair of his khaki pants,
neatly folded on the table.

"You gwine get a job, you best look nice" was all Flora
said, without any sign of affection.

It set the pattern for the next two years of Willie's life.

Flora got up and went to her room, closing the door. It
was the end of the argument and its resolution. Willie sat
at the table for a while, wondering what to do, how to celebrate his newfound sense of independence, of manhood.

After he had stormed out of the house he wandered the
streets for an hour, determined not to go home, and found
his way to Pop's Place. He couldn't go in because he didn't
have any money, but a couple of pals that he knew from
church, young men of his own age who had left school and
were working, were hanging around outside, and Willie
fell in with them.

They strolled up and down the street, talking about the
world, and Willie told his friends of his determination to
get a job. He hoped they would have suggestions for him,
but they only confirmed that jobs were scarce and that
humping cotton bales at the gin was his best—perhaps his
only—hope, which Willie already knew.

Beyond that, Willie was a stranger to their conversation because they talked of things of which he knew little.
Of the Saturday frolic and dancing with girls. Of gambling. Of girls again. Willie wondered what had happened.
The subjects were familiar to him by report, but now they
were spoken of in a different way, as if he were a party to

the adventures, as if he were a young man, like them, instead of a schoolboy. He felt as if he had gone through a door that had been closed to him, into a new, exciting landscape.

There was a small, unpleasant moment when three young white men of their own age sauntered along the street, looking for trouble, perhaps, or just to watch the niggers carrying on. White folk seldom came to this part of town, they had no business here, except to cause trouble. One of the young men was Kevin Hopkins; Willie knew him by sight and very small acquaintance. Despite the fact that they had spent the first two years of their lives growing up together, once Flora left the Hopkinses employ, they had little contact with each other. Sometimes, though, when Willie collected laundry from the Hopkins house, or delivered it, Kevin had been there. Mostly, Kevin would ignore Willie, but he always found a way to make some taunting jibe about colored people, and Willie flushed, ready for a fight, but was unable to defend himself. To hit a white, even a boy of his own age, even to defend himself, would have brought the wrath of his mama and the law upon him.

Tonight was different. Willie was with companions of his own kind, and he was not a boy anymore.

The three black youths took up a casual position that blocked the sidewalk. The three white youths kept on walking toward them, and only stopped when they had no choice.

"Git out my way, nigger," one said.

No one moved.

"Screw 'em," Kevin said, glaring at Willie, and began walking again, directly toward the blacks, provoking contact of some kind.

At the very last moment the black boys backed off, but only just. They moved slightly to let the whites pass, but did not attempt to hide their smoldering anger. Kevin and his friends walked on in silence, but their own appetite for some more violent confrontation was blatant. They glared at the blacks, fists clenched, muttering racial taunts.

"Niggers gettin' uppity," Kevin said, his eyes locked on Willie. They were of a similar height and weight, but Willie's friends were bigger and the whites moved on, without physical incident.

Willie guessed that this was not the last of it, that one day he and Kevin would come to blows, if only to eradicate memories of their shared childhood.

It killed the evening. The whites had won, they always did, they always would, and that sense of defeat soured the amiable mood among the blacks. They stood in silence for a while and then one of Willie's friends said a word that Willie had seldom heard before. It began with the letter *f*.

It was a word Willie knew without knowing how or why he knew it, and he also knew that it must not be said in front of adults, especially women, although it was an adult word. To use it as part of everyday speech was to cross an important bridge to manhood, and Willie crossed that bridge now.

"Fuck 'em," he agreed. The moment after he had said it, he was filled with a sense of elation. He was a man among men. The events of that night had been miraculous to him.

His friends ambled away and Willie wandered home for lack of anywhere else to go. He tried the door of his house with some trepidation—he was not sure that his mama would have left it unlocked for him—and was pleased when he found it open.

He went in, ready for more argument, saw his newly pressed work clothes on the table, and knew from the few words his mama said, and her attitude, that the battle was won.

But not the war.

The next morning he presented himself to the foreman, Pete Lanier, at the cotton gin, and was given a job humping bales of cotton. There were many reasons for it. He was Flora's son, and Flora was well liked and the circumstances of her poverty were known. He was Booker's son, and Booker was remembered, and the circumstances of his life and death. Mostly, Willie got the job because he was young and he was cheap.

Many of the single adult males had left town to seek their fortune, or at least employment, in Memphis or the cities of the North. Most of the younger married men who had stayed had jobs on the farms. Despite the massive unemployment that had swept the country, farm jobs were the most secure, if poorly paid, because people still had to eat. It was the older men who found jobs scarce, because humping cotton bales is a young man's game.

It was hard labor, backbreaking work. Even though Pete Lanier kept an eye on him, and ordered several breaks, when Willie came home from his first day he thought he would never stand upright again.

Flora's heart almost melted when she saw him, for he was the living image of his father, young and strong but almost defeated, the familiar cotton tufts in his hair, which Booker had sworn they would never see on their son.

Her manner to him did not change. She was determined on a war of attrition with Willie, that he would some day relent and apologize for breaking her dreams. But he was her son, a working man, and would yet be the provider. She must look after him.

"Y'need a bath," she said.

Willie was slumped in a chair, every bone in his body aching, almost unable to speak.

Flora ordered Ruthana to drag in the battered bathtub while she put wood on the fire so that the water would be warm. She sent Ruthana from the room and told Willie to strip and helped him to the bath. He was careless of his nakedness, only aware of his aching body.

"Be worse tomorrow," Flora said.

She had sent Ruthana from the room because although

the children had grown up familiar with each other's bodies, from their weekly bath, something had changed. Willie was not a child anymore.

She let Willie soak in the bath while she fixed his dinner. She had dipped into her penny jar and bought him a special treat, a nice piece of pork meat. She could afford it. If Willie could keep up the pace, this would be a two-income family by the end of the week, and the new provider must be provided for.

Willie did keep up the pace. The second day, as Flora predicted, was worse than the first, every muscle in his body screamed in pain as he hefted the bales to the truck, but by the third day he was becoming used to this new exercise, and by the end of the week he thought himself a veteran.

When he was paid, all the pain he had borne was amply rewarded. He walked home on clouds of happiness with four dollars in his pocket.

Then he remembered something else. Because it was the picking season, they had worked Saturday, which meant that Willie had not been able to join the work gang cleaning up the cemetery. Being a working man had great rewards. This made him think of Ernestine, whom he had not seen, had hardly thought of in this miraculous week, but he reminded himself that she would be at church tomorrow.

Flora was ironing when he got home. It wasn't how he wanted to see her. He hoped that one day he would come home and find her sitting in a chair, taking things easy. Well, that day would come.

Already he was changed. He stood straight and looked taller, Flora thought, stronger. Tufts of cotton lint bedecked him, his hair and his work clothes, that no amount of washing would completely remove. His shirt was torn at the shoulders as if his muscles had already swelled in this short week. His pants were scruffy. They could be washed but they looked short on him.

There were some ears of fresh corn on the table.

"You been pickin' in the garden," Willie said.

" 'Bout the last of the season," Flora agreed.

Willie dug in his pocket. He took out the dollar bills and put three on the table, for his keep and Flora's money jar.

"I keepin' a dollar," he said. "Needs to buy a balin' hook."

"New clothes too," Flora said. "Good an' tough."

Almost by mutual consent they had refrained from the investment for this, his first week. It was pointless spending money on new work clothes until they were sure that Willie was up to the job.

Willie nodded and sat in his chair at the table, a whole new world of responsibility opening up to him. He needed a baling hook. He had used a spare one at work this week, but every baler should have his own hook. He needed new clothes. These, his school clothes, would hardly last another week, and he felt taller, bigger. These things would eat up the money he had earned this week, and more, but they were necessary. He wondered when spending would stop and saving started, but at least he had his own money for the collection plate. There was something else.

"I gwine out tonight, Mama," he said. Some of his workmates had invited him to join them that evening, the usual celebration of the weekly work done, and Willie, after a moment's hesitation, agreed, as if he had been invited to join yet another new club of men.

Flora didn't want him to go, but said nothing. It was his right; he had earned it. It was the world of men.

"I press you a white shirt," she said, wondering if any of his white shirts would still fit him at the end of this bulging week.

Still, she had to warn him, even though she knew it was useless, that Willie would do what he wanted to do.

"Don' go drinkin' no liquor," she cautioned.

"Ma!" he said, looking at her with reproaching laughter in his eyes.

But he did not say no.

He didn't drink any hard liquor that night, although

someone had a bottle of whisky, but he did have a couple of beers. Although he knew of the usual Saturday frolic and some were going to it, he did not feel ready yet to attend. He met his new friends at Pete Lanier's house and there was a keg, and music, and some women turned up. Willie was awkward, unsure of himself at first and how he should behave, still learning the new language of manhood, but the beer relaxed him, and soon he was laughing at the crude jokes, even if he didn't completely understand them.

There was also some talk of gambling, which fascinated Willie. He'd heard of it some, at school, but never really understood it. The men talked of the bets they had made, on almost anything, it seemed, horses and dogs and prize-fights. They even joked about a man who raffled his pay packet every week and always came out ahead. This was all Willie heard, because no man spoke of the money he had lost, only of money won.

It was amazing to Willie that there was a way of making money without working, and he wondered what more surprises lay in store for him.

He did not want the evening to end, but a few drifted away with their women, to the frolic, and Pete Lanier advised Willie against any more beer. Flora might smell it on his breath. Pete grinned like a conspirator. Willie grinned too, and drank the offered cup of coffee.

He stopped at Pop's Place on his way home for another cup of coffee, not because he needed it, but because he wanted to celebrate the fact that he could. It was the first time he had been there on his own and the first time he had been there at night. It wasn't busy, most people were at the frolic, but a couple of young women were giggling in a booth, and Willie, sitting alone at the counter, could hardly keep his eyes off them. Women had suddenly assumed a new importance in his life, and were part of his new world.

He thought of Ernestine, of seeing her at church the

next day, and because he couldn't think of anything else to do, and because he was tired, he went home.

It wasn't late, perhaps half past nine, but the house was silent. Ruthana was in bed, Willie knew that she would be, but what surprised him was that Flora had also gone to bed. There was a note for him on the table telling of bread and cheese, in case he was hungry.

He wasn't hungry, but he got the bread and cheese and sat at the table to eat.

He didn't want the evening to end because something important had happened. For the first time in his life his mama had gone to bed before he was home.

15

THE MONEY WILLIE BROUGHT HOME each week, and the occasional gifts he gave them, made their lives easier. They had a new stove and a new oilcloth for the kitchen table, and, at Christmas, Willie gave his Mama a bedside lamp.

Although she was grateful, and although she had settled into an acceptance of his working life, the small war between Flora and Willie lasted for two years. Both of them strained at the leash of it, and both mourned something that was lost from their relationship. There was no longer any sense of fun between them, nor any great sense of love.

Wanting this, missing this, both of them turned elsewhere. Ruthana began to assume a place of dominance in Flora's heart, still young but more than a pupil. A careful and caring girl, she had never been exactly sure of her place within the household, but as Willie drifted away, Ruthana came into her own.

By the time she was eight she could cook an evening meal adequately, and she had taken Willie's place on the laundry run. In countless tiny ways, she relieved her mama's burden, but Flora was always careful that the girl had time to study. It had become clear that Ruthana was a gifted student, with a splendid capacity for learning.

Because of this, Flora made remarkable adjustments. The idea of a colored boy—Willie—going to college had always been novel to Flora, but there were examples of it. The concept of a colored girl—Ruthana—going to college was completely alien to Flora. If some had done it, they were unknown to Flora. But as Ruthana's grades got better and better, as her mind seemed to swell before her mama's eyes, Flora started to wonder why not.

She talked about it with Pearl, cautiously at first, and her friend was all in favor of the idea. Pearl, who loved men but had never found one to marry, lived with her aged parents, looking after them. She was devoted to the church and its functions; Sunday school was her domain, and she was organist for the choir, but in the little spare time she had, she read newspapers.

Flora could not imagine what was in those mountains of papers, but Pearl was a treasure trove of garnered information. She began reading to Flora whatever snippets she could find about black girls who had gone to college and earned degrees, and were making headway in the world. The information was scanty, and many of those college girls gave up once they had their degree and settled into matrimony, but that didn't matter to Flora. The degree was, in itself, almost enough.

They began to lay plans for Ruthana's future, and these gave Flora something to dream about again, and reasons for the battle.

Most of all, Flora found that she liked Ruthana, that the child was becoming a friend as well as a companion. She found that she could unburden her heart to Ruthana in ways that she would never have done with Willie. With her son she had always needed to appear strong. To her daughter she could reveal her weakness.

Willie found his friend in Ernestine. He had always thought her pretty and enjoyed her company, but over the two years of his working life Ernestine had become something much more. Willie did not admit it, but his friends at work joked that Ernestine was his girl, and it was accepted by almost everyone that where Willie went, Ernestine went as well. When she was fifteen, her parents even allowed Willie to take her to a dance, an "Ol' Timey Country Frolic," although he was ordered to have her home by eleven.

It was a Saturday evening. Willie wore his new Sunday suit, which was a little too "modern" for his mama's taste, and had put Vaseline in his hair to make it sparkle. Ernestine's mother had made her a new dress for the occasion, her first real party dress, of soft pink organza. When he came to her house and she opened the door, Willie thought her beautiful, although she still wore a schoolgirl's ribbons in her hair. Pete Lanier drove them, and half a dozen others, to the farmhouse in his truck, and even before the short journey began everyone was already in a party mood. Another cotton baler, Clayborn Baker, was a few years older than Willie and always anxious to maintain his superiority.

"Din't know they was lettin' school kids come to the hop," he said without malice to Willie, as he helped Ernestine climb on. "Wha'cher doin' here, boy?"

Leo Barnett, who was twenty, stood up for Willie.

"Ain't no boy helped load hunderd fifty-two bales yesterdee," he told Clayborn, who already knew this. "I was right a'side him."

Already on the truck, he held out his hand for Willie to pull him aboard.

"You all right, Willie," he said.

Willie had the measure of these men, they were his friends and workmates, and Clayborn's constant assertions of his greater age and strength didn't bother him. But it pleased him that Leo had made the compliment and recognized his achievement.

They drove a couple of miles to a run-down country farmhouse, their excitement growing every inch of the journey. The party was already in progress when they got there, in the yard, about fifty people present, with more arriving. Illumination came from the full moon and a score of kerosene-filled Coke bottles, with wicks burning smokily, wired to a clothesline strung between some trees.

They climbed down from the truck and as their eyes adjusted to the hazy light, Ernestine hung back a little. Willie looked at her.

"It's all men," Ernestine said, suddenly nervous among so many adults.

"There's women here too," Willie chuckled. He

pointed to a couple of women dancing in the crowd. "An' mo' comin'."

Another flatbed truck had arrived, with half a dozen raucous party-goers, including, happily for Ernestine, three women. Less happily, they were older, and dressed in violent colors. It was a long way from the sock hops at church, her only experience of dances until now.

"We be all right," Willie said. "You stay by me."

He took her hand and led her to the yard, but Ernestine was still nervous. The music, although she had heard snatches of it before, was still rare to her, a low-down blues sung to a gut-bucket guitar. From somewhere beyond the lighted area she heard other unfamiliar sounds, the cries of crapshooters. Two or three couples were dancing to the blues, the women in their cheap shiny dresses, some of the men in suits, some still in overalls. Their slow-drag, funky dancing was chiefly octopuslike embraces.

Drinks were being sold by Charlie White, a local boot-legger. On the ground beside his crude wooden stand was a large tub containing a fifty-pound block of ice and bottles of colored soda pop. On the stand there were a number of mismatched cups and glasses. Those who wanted soda pop simply took their choice and put a nickel in a plate on the stand. Liquor customers had to pay Charlie first, plunking down their quarters before he filled their shouted orders— "Joe Louis!" or "Gimme a shot!" Bringing a quart Mason jar from under the stand, Charlie poured a shot of the clear, raw moonshine into one of his cups.

Everyone's mood was amiable, but still Ernestine was nervous. She watched a drinker down a shot of moonshine and call out "goddamn" at its burning potency, and she wondered how she would tell her parents about her evening.

It also made her wonder about Willie, and her feelings for him. She had known a tall and gangling boy, but in this place, this company, suddenly he was a man. She didn't doubt the honor of his intentions toward her, she knew she was completely safe with him, but she sensed a potential for violence in the gathering, and she wondered how Willie would respond to that.

She was also intrigued because, despite her nervousness and her feeling that she was completely out of place, part of her was enjoying herself. If Willie was a man, was she becoming a woman?

"Wanna fish sammitch?" she heard Willie ask.

She laughed and nodded. She would worry about the consequences of the evening, and her parents, later. For the present, she was going to enjoy herself.

The sandwich vendor's counter was two wooden planks resting on two bales of hay. On the planks were loaves of sliced white bread, bottles of hot sauce and catsup, and a smaller bottle of hot red peppers in vinegar. The flat top of a large can was heaped high with golden fried chicken, and two other lard can tops were heaped with hand-sized slabs of raw fish rolled in cornmeal.

"Two catfish," Willie said. It was obvious to Ernestine that he knew his way around, that it was not the first time he had been to such a frolic.

The sandwich vendor speared a couple of pieces of fish and dropped them into a kettle of bubbling fat over a charcoal bucket. The fish sizzled and splattered.

Clayborn and Leo wandered up.

"Havin' fun?" Leo asked Ernestine, and she nodded shyly. In a limited way, she *was* having fun.

Leo took a sip from the cup in his hand, grimaced, puffed his cheeks, and handed the cup to Willie.

"Finish this fo' me," he said. "I's goin' win me some a' that gamblin' money."

He left, headed for the crapshoot. Willie looked at the cup in his hand.

"Ain't a man till you drink that." Clayborn grinned.

Willie looked at him, then at the cup, then at Ernestine, who also grinned. Thus encouraged, Willie swallowed what was left in the cup. An instant later he choked, and struggled to contain the burning effect of the raw liquor, punched in the chest. Clayborn laughed and moved away. Ernestine laughed too, astonished at his audacity.

"Hot sauce?" the sandwich vendor demanded, slapping the cooked fish on some bread. Willie, unable to speak, shook his head. The sandwich vendor looked at Ernestine for her choice, and she shrugged.

"Li'l bit," she said.

By the time they had their sandwiches, Willie had recovered, and he looked at Ernestine in surprise.

"Y'like 'em hot?" he asked.

"Some," Ernestine replied. She'd never had a fish—or any—sandwich with hot sauce before, but obviously others had survived it, and she was ready to try. She didn't realize that she was flirting with Willie, but wouldn't have stopped if she had.

She bit on her sandwich, daintily, and chewed the fish for a moment. Then her eyes rolled up in her head, and she spat the food out, choking. Hot sauce, she had discovered, was *hot*.

Willie laughed, and Ernestine slapped him, but not too hard.

"You knew!" she accused him, but Willie only grinned. He took her sandwich and scraped off some of the hot sauce with the newspaper wrapping. He ate this one himself, then gave her his own, sauceless.

"Ever seen a crapshoot?" he asked her as they munched.

They wandered to the back of the yard, where a dozen men were gathered, rolling dice.

'Lonzo, a slender, tan-complexioned young man of about twenty-five, appeared to be in charge. He rattled the dice vigorously in one hand and carried on an aggressive verbal barrage.

"A'right, you chumps," 'Lonzo cried. "Git yo' money down! Six my point! Two bucks say I make it!"

"Put the dice on the ground," Leo Barnett called angrily. He wasn't winning.

"You put some green on the ground!" 'Lonzo called back. Leo saw Willie and Ernestine.

"Let the ol' man have two bucks," he begged Willie. "I got to git my money back."

Willie dug in his pocket and gave Leo money. Leo slapped two quarters on the ground.

"Two bits," Leo urged Willie. "Throw down two bits. Get yo' feet wet!"

Willie laughed, caught up in the mood of it, and put a quarter down.

"The money's down," the shooters cried. "Roll 'em!"

'Lonzo blew on his hand elaborately, then rolled the dice.

The shooters held their breath—then sighed and groaned. 'Lonzo raked in all the money.

"Fo' dollars! Let it ride!" he called in triumph. "Get down, chumps, who bettin'?"

"He too hot for me." Willie laughed.

"Nex' roll cool him down," Leo said, plunking down two more quarters. He looked back at Willie, to encourage him, but Willie was gone, with Ernestine.

They strolled to the dance area and watched for a moment. Then Willie looked a question at Ernestine and she nodded in assent. They moved into each other's arms and danced, happy in each other's arms.

At the end of the number, the guitar player, Allen Shaw, got up from his seat, an upended soda pop crate, and called to Willie.

"Hey, Willie, I bin hearin' 'bout you. C'mon here and knock out a number. Lemme stretch my legs."

Willie glanced at Ernestine, and she thought he blushed.

"Aw, I ain't no good," Willie declined, but Allen wouldn't take no for an answer. He held out the guitar.

"C'mon, boy, take this box!"

Some of the dancers were clapping and urging Willie to play.

Reluctantly, he took the guitar and made himself comfortable on the crate. He began to play the blues, his simple, poignant style in marked contrast to Allen Shaw's reverberating virtuosity.

Ernestine watched him in amazement. Willie was not a great musician, but he was good. What surprised Ernestine was that she didn't know he could play the guitar at all, and she wondered how much else about him she didn't know.

She had some answers later. Willie's set, only a couple of songs, drew applause from the crowd, but it was not dance music, and they were pleased when Allen Shaw returned. So was Willie. He came back to Ernestine, who looked at him lovingly.

"That was good," she said. "How long you bin learnin' the guitar?"

Willie shrugged. "A while" was all he would say. "C'mon, let's get a soda."

As they walked to Charlie White's stand, a big, heavyset man accosted them. As soon as Willie saw him he looked around for some way to escape, but their path was blocked.

"How's about that seven bucks, Willie," he said. His voice was low but threatening.

"Not tonight, Hank," Willie whispered, embarrassed that Ernestine was witness to this.

"Yeh, tonight. Now!" Hank said, his voice less low, more threatening.

Willie did not look at Ernestine. He pulled some notes out of his shabby wallet and gave them to the man, hoping this was the end of it.

It wasn't. The bookie, Hank, moved close to Willie.

"Young blood, lemme tell yer somethin'," he said. "When you man enough to gamble is when you man enough to pay up your debts. You don't, somebody gon' knock your head off."

The point made, he walked away. Willie stood there uncertainly, and Ernestine's heart jumped this way and that. Earlier, Willie had seemed a man, especially when he was entertaining the crowd with his blues. But at odd moments, as when he had drunk the moonshine, the boy kept edging through. As he had now.

"How's 'bout that soda?" Ernestine said, taking command.

Willie looked at her thankfully. She must have had some shocks tonight, the news of his gambling debts not the least of them, but she had taken them all in stride.

He wanted to show his gratitude by taking her in his arms and kissing her. He didn't, because this wasn't the time or place; there were too many people around and he'd never kissed Ernestine before.

But he wanted to, and swore that he would, later.

"Yeh," he said.

He took her by the hand and led her to Charlie White's soda tub.

16

THE FROLIC ENDED IN VIOLENCE, but the evening ended gently, although with more surprises for Ernestine.

Soon after the bookie had accosted Willie, while he and Ernestine drank their soda pops, there were shouts and sounds of a scuffle from the crapshoot game, and then a woman screamed.

"He cut 'im! Lawd, he cut 'im!"

Leo, having lost all his money, lost his temper as well, and picked a fight with 'Lonzo, who defended himself with a knife. By the time Willie had dragged Ernestine through the crowd, men were holding the furious 'Lonzo, and Leo was squealing like a hog, blood pouring from a gash on his arm.

The cut wasn't serious but it needed attention. Willie was sorry for Leo's wound, but fights were not uncommon and part of him was relieved that this one happened when it did. Other than Pete Lanier's truck, Willie had no way of getting Ernestine home by her father's appointed hour.

Leo complained all the way back, vowing vengeance on 'Lonzo, until Clayborn told him to shut it.

"Nex' time you tangle wit' 'Lonzo, we be bringin' you home in a wooden box."

Leo shut it.

Pete dropped them at Ernestine's street. and Willie walked with her to her home.

"You have a good time?" he asked. He was concerned. If she told her parents too much about the evening's events, they might tell his mama. There was nothing she could do but there'd be another row and he might be forbidden to see Ernestine. He didn't want that to happen.

"You do much gamblin'?" Ernestine wanted to know. There was a lot she wanted to know about this new Willie, because there might be answers for herself.

"Some," Willie said. It was slightly less than the truth. He gambled more than he should, horses, mostly, and because he always backed favorites he didn't do too badly, but favorites don't always win.

"Where you learn to play the guitar?"

"Aroun'," Willie replied. He was relieved that Ernestine was taking it all so calmly.

"Wanna go to Memphis, Beale Street," he confided. "Good music there. Or Chicago, mebbe."

Ernestine wasn't shocked that he wanted to go to Memphis, it was so near, and Beale Street was considered by many to be the center of black America. Chicago was something else. She was surprised that Willie was even considering it, it was so far away. And yesterday he had seemed so young. But yesterday, so had she.

"Chicago?" she whispered.

Willie grinned. It was the first time he had ever voiced the ambition, but it had been growing since he started to work. The other men talked of Chicago often enough, those that had been, or those who wanted to go, and their stories fired Willie with a determination to see it for himself. He felt too big for Stockton, or Stockton was too small for him.

"Don' you get bored here?" he asked Ernestine, who looked at him in surprise, as if she had never considered it.

"Some," she agreed. "But what else is there?"

"Plenty," Willie said. "Like tonight, only more so, ev'ry day."

They were standing outside her front door, but far enough away to be out of the light.

"I gotta go in," Ernestine said, and Willie heard the reluctance to part in her voice.

He kissed her. It took her a moment to respond because she had never been kissed before, on the mouth, by a man, but she knew what to do because her older sister had told her.

She pushed her tongue between Willie's lips, into his mouth, and let him savor her for just a moment. Then she backed away.

Willie's eyes were closed. He opened them, staring at her.

"One mo' li'l kiss," he begged. "Jes' one mo'."

He said it with such longing she could not resist him. They kissed again, and this time she let Willie's tongue find its way into her mouth. But not for too long.

She laughed, and said she'd had a wonderful time, and went to the door. Willie walked away but kept looking back at her, smiling, and, once, waving to her. Ernestine waited until he turned the corner and was gone. It had been a momentous evening for her, full of surprises, most of them pleasant, but she would never have guessed it was Willie's ambition to go away, to Memphis, perhaps, and more probably to Chicago.

Flora had guessed. Flora was way ahead of Ernestine. She didn't know how she knew, she didn't know what city it would be, but she was sure that Willie was drifting away—in his mind he'd already gone—like so many other young men. She didn't want to believe it, but she knew the day must come when it would be voiced.

They had fallen into a Friday-night ritual with Willie's pay packet. He would come home, and without making any reference to money, how much he had earned, how much he would give her, he'd take out a few bills and put them on the table.

Flora didn't speak of the money either, not even to say thank you. She'd leave the notes on the table and wait till Willie had left the room and then pick them up and count them and be pleased.

One Friday evening, not long after the frolic, something changed. Flora had a headache, which made her more distant than usual, and she was sick of ironing other people's clothes. Ruthana had urged her to lie down, she'd finish the laundry, but Flora shook her head. Willie would be home soon and she did not want him to think she was sick.

He came in as always, in his work clothes tufted with cotton and with his baling hook hanging in a loop of leather from his belt. He had started wearing an old straw hat to keep the cotton from his hair, and he took it off, hung it on a hook by the door.

" 'Lo, Ruthana," he said.

Ruthana giggled. She loved this small Friday battle between Flora and Willie. She made bets with herself as to which of them would speak to the other first. Usually, like tonight, it was Willie.

"Saw Sister Pearl comin' through town," he said, taking off his work boots. "She axed was you gon' be at the special prayer meetin' tonight."

His mama didn't respond.

"I tol' her I 'magined you would."

"Yeh, I be there," Flora said dully, ironing still. Her head down, she did not see the long glare that Willie gave her. Ruthana did, and Willie saw her watching. He motioned his head. Ruthana understood. She picked up her rag doll, made goo-goo noises to it, and left the room.

Willie stood, took some money from his pocket, and put the notes on the table. Flora did not even glance at them, and Willie snapped.

"Mama, I git tired you actin' like I done kilt somebody since I been working."

He turned away to the basin, to wash. Flora counted to ten before she replied, relieved that it had happened at last, not wanting to lose her temper.

"You bein' your own man. That's what you wanted."

Willie kept calm too.

"Don't b'lieve you ought a hold it against me for wantin' to take care of my mama."

Flora set the iron on the stove.

"You ain't never gon' un'erstan' how I feel, Willie," she said, " 'til one of these days, you gon' have chillun. When you tryin' to get them to see somethin' for they own good, you remember yo' ol' mama then."

"That's somethin' I jes' have to worry 'bout when I gets to it, Mama. Jes' do what I think is right—"

He was trying to be considerate, which infuriated her. She wanted to have a blazing argument, to clear the air. She snatched a shirt from the pile and began shaking it out.

"You do anything you want to do! I ain't tol' you what to do for two years. I ain't tryin' to tell you what to do no more."

She laid the shirt on the table and grabbed the iron. It was hot, and she banged it down on the shirt.

"Mama, if you ain't gon' never feel satisfied 'bout me workin' "—he paused for a moment, wondering if he dare say it—"mebbe you'd ruther I don't stay here."

Was she crying? He didn't know.

" 'Coz I'll go," he said. "Chicago, mebbe."

He looked at her. Flora was ironing the shirt, ironing it to death.

"I knows that's bin on yo' mind," she whispered. She put the iron down. "But I never did think you'd say that to yo' mama."

If she wasn't crying, she was close to it. The money was still on the table.

"Mama, take the money." he sighed. "That's what I's workin' for."

Flora looked down at the money and saw that the shirt was singed, burned, from the too hot iron.

"Damn!" she exploded. She had never sworn in front of Willie, she very seldom used that word, even to herself, and the shock of it made both of them laugh, and the laughter brought Flora to the small tears that had been waiting to be shed.

Willie came to her to hug her, and she let him, folding into his embrace, home again, where, for two long years, she had yearned to be. It was all right again.

"I got one mo' chance, Willie," she whispered. "Ruthana."

She sensed him stiffen. He did not know of the plans that she and Pearl had made for Ruthana's continuing education.

"She a girl!"

"Yeh, she a girl chile," Flora said. "Don't mean she ain't bright. Don' mean she cain't learn. Don' mean she cain't be somebody.

"Yo' supper's on the stove. Ruthana'll fix it, an' help you with yo' bath. I'm gon' get on down to church for the prayer meetin'." She kissed him and left the room.

Willie was lost in thought. Ruthana was only eight and it was foolish to have dreams of college for someone so young. But there was no reason why not, after all, if she was clever at school, that she shouldn't go to college. But could girls go to college? Willie had never heard of it. And what would they do if they went to college, afterward, when they had their degree? What use was a degree to a girl? A black girl.

He became aware that Ruthana was standing in the doorway.

"You hear what she said?" Willie was sure the answer would be yes.

"Uh-huh," Ruthana murmured.

"You like school?"

"Uh-huh."

"You want to go to college?"

"Uh-huh."

"Why?"

Ruthana thought for a long time, and then shrugged.

"What you gon' do, if'n you gets to college? Afterwards?"

Ruthana didn't have a specific answer for this, either, but Willie saw determination in her eyes. He recognized it as similar to his own feelings about leaving school and getting a job, which had first come to him when he was about Ruthana's age.

Ruthana was young, but not too young to have her own dreams, even if they were not yet clearly defined.

"Somethin'," she said.

17

WILLIE HAD NO ACTUAL PLANS to leave Stockton; it was a general intention rather than a defined plan, a dream of a journey, a wider future. For one thing, he didn't have enough money. For another, he was just a little scared; it was a very big jump into the unknown. And for another, Ernestine was becoming increasingly important to him.

But by suggesting to his mother that it would happen, one day, he had cleared the air, and he felt free to talk about it from time to time.

"He jes' like his pappy," Flora complained to Pearl. "He talk a thing to death, that man. If'n he say it one day, he's gotta say it the nex', an' the day after that too."

Pearl was all in favor of the idea. Perhaps because she wasn't a parent herself, but had shepherded scores of children through Sunday school, she took a broader view of life than Flora. Surely, she knew more about boys, and young men.

"They all gotta do it," she said. "Gotta spread their wings, leave the nest. Some make it, some don'. Some come cryin' home to their mamas. Some fall by the wayside. But they all gotta do it."

Flora saw the truth of it. Many of the local men, some young, some not so young, had answered the siren song of the big cities. Most did not come back, except to visit, however well they did or didn't do in those cities. Some came home with their tails between their legs.

She began to think it might be a good thing for Willie. In Chicago there was the possibility, at least, of a decent job. She preferred the idea of Chicago to Memphis, even though it was farther away. Memphis was too close, Memphis was still the South, and, like many of her generation and those before, she believed that in the North, the flame of Emancipation still burned.

She began to wish that he would go, not because she wanted to be rid of him, but because if he had the dream he should realize it. A very small part of her was glad that Booker had not lived to see this day. His passion for Willie's education had been so intense that he would have been so disappointed by the truth. She didn't want the same thing to happen to Willie's dream, because then he would be disappointed in himself.

She also guessed that it would take a push to get Willie going; he had settled into a comfortable rut, talking about his dream but doing nothing toward it. She began suggesting to Jesus that He might like to give her son a little nudge. To her surprise, Jesus heard her prayers, and when He did, she cursed herself, and begged to be able to take them back.

On a warm June evening in 1937, Joe Louis, known as the Brown Bomber, the pride of every black man in America, defeated James Braddock and became the heavyweight boxing champion of the world. Almost every radio and wireless in (black) America was tuned to the broadcast, and the punch that won the fight had the strength behind it of almost every black man and boy and many of their women.

Their elation at his triumph exploded across the country, and so it was in Stockton. Men swaggered down the street that night, drunk, some with liquor, some with sheer exuberance, recounting to each other every detail of the fight they could recall, then told it all again. Boys replayed the fight, in back streets and schoolyards, that night and for days beyond. Reverend Jackson wrote a whole sermon about it.

Even Mama Flora had listened to the fight, with Pearl, and although both women disapproved of boxing, the fight was not the issue that night, the winning was.

Many white men heard the fight too, and most thought the result fair. Because the matter was not so visceral for them, the result was less important. What was important, especially in a small Southern town, was the way the blacks reacted.

"Niggers gettin' uppity," they murmured among themselves.

For the most part, segregation was not a major issue for the whites in Stockton, merely a fact of life and law. The two communities lived in segregated alliance, and the rules were so established that if the line was ever crossed, it was easily restored. Very few whites had any conception of the resentments that burned in their black neighbors on the southern side of town. The victory of Joe Louis brought many of those resentments bubbling to the surface.

It happened in very small ways, at first. Black men, brimming with confidence because the victory could not be denied, made jibes about it to the white men they encountered. A few went further, calling out the news to whites passing by in trucks or cars. Some young men, used to stepping aside for whites on the sidewalk, stopped stepping aside.

Several of the hotheads, for the thrill of it, went looking for trouble, daring to drink at the white water fountain, and sassing those who tried to stop them, until the sheriff came.

A couple of nights later, there was a big fight, almost a pitched battle, in the park, and Willie was there. There, but not part of it, because he was with Ernestine. Willie never knew how the fight began. He and Ernestine were strolling through the park on a pretty evening, and heard shouts and an argument. They saw a group of black youths quarreling with an almost equal number of white lads, and then they saw punches being thrown. Very soon, it was out of control. Other blacks came running to help their friends and other whites to aid their fellows, and at its climax there were twenty on either side. Blood was flowing freely, a couple of noses were broken, and it took some time for the police, and the wiser older men of both races, to restore order.

Willie had longed to be in the commotion, but felt it his duty to protect Ernestine. They watched from a distance, and Willie made a small vow that if the trouble came too close he would lead Ernestine away. The fight never did come that close, but it distressed Ernestine, and so Willie, unwillingly, led her away.

As they walked through the trees, a figure came panting up to them, away from the fight. It was Kevin Hopkins, nursing a bloody nose.

"Out my way, nigger," he yelled.

Willie wasn't sure what to do. He could tell that Kevin was itching for more fight, but there was plenty of pathway and he saw no reason why he should move. He was shepherding a lady. He put his arm around Ernestine and kept on walking.

Kevin stopped in front of them.

"You deaf, nigger? Get out my way."

"We ain't in yo' way," Willie said, more calmly than he felt.

"Don't make no never mind!" Kevin was seething with anger. "You do what I tell you!"

"No," Willie said. "You botherin' the lady."

He was ready for the punch, parried it, and slammed his fist into Kevin's gut.

"Get outta here," he yelled to Ernestine. Ernestine didn't go; she began screaming for help.

Although breathless from the blow to his stomach, Kevin had the advantage of anger and recovered quickly. He was a dirty fighter, but Willie was stronger, from years of humping cotton bales.

It was short and sharp and over very quickly. After a few punches on each side, Willie threw one that landed fair and square on Kevin's already bloody nose, and he heard the crunch of breaking bone. Kevin screamed and sank to his knees, his hands to his face.

Willie was ready for more, on his feet, fists up, yelling at Kevin to get up for more, but Ernestine, crying, ran to him, pulling on his arm, begging him to leave.

"Better do what the whore says, nigger!" Kevin yelled.

Willie could hear people coming toward them, and reason returned to him. He let Ernestine pull him away.

"You're a dead man, nigger!" Kevin shouted after them. "You're dead!"

Always ready for a fight, Kevin wore rings on several fingers, and there was a gash from one of them over Willie's eye. It would not be an easy thing to explain to Ernestine's parents, so they went to Willie's house. Fortunately, Mama Flora wasn't there, she was visiting Sister Pearl.

Ruthana was home, doing schoolwork. She gasped as Willie came in with Ernestine and wanted to know every detail of what had happened. She also did something that surprised Willie. She tended the cut over his eye as if she were a doctor.

Ernestine had slightly gone to pieces, not so much because of the fight, but more because of Kevin's final threat, which Ernestine believed. She worked herself up into a small fit of hysterics, insisting that Willie was never going to be safe here in Stockton, Kevin would keep his vow. He might not actually kill Willie, but he would make mince-meat of him.

Then Mama Flora came home and, when she heard what had happened, added her voice to Ernestine's. She knew Kevin for what he was, and begged Willie never to go out alone at night.

"I ain't gwine be no prisoner," Willie insisted.

"Then where you gon' run, where you gon' hide?" Mama Flora demanded. Memories of the disappearance of her uncle, and so many other black men, in Mississippi came flooding back to her, and mingled with Ernestine's hysterics, until both women were in a frenzy of despair.

Willie shouted that they were being silly, and that he wasn't going to run and he wasn't going to hide, but some of their fear communicated itself to him. He knew there could be consequences from his fight with Kevin, and they would not be pleasant. In the middle of this commotion he heard a sharp voice telling him not to move.

It was Ruthana trying to fix a plaster over his eye. It calmed him. He sat still for Ruthana.

"You a'ways talkin' 'bout goin' to Chicago," she said. "Now be as good a time as any."

"I ain't runnin' away."

" 'T'ain't runnin' away." Ruthana shrugged. "You been talkin' 'bout Chicago fo'ever."

Mama Flora and Ernestine were in each other's arms, comforting each other, although still weeping.

"Who gwine look after them?"

"They don't need lookin' after," Ruthana said. "They doin' jus' fine comforting themselves."

She grinned at the man who was her brother, and he grinned back and they started to laugh, as at some private joke. Their laughter impinged on Mama Flora's distress, and she looked at them angrily.

"What's so funny?" she demanded.

For some reason it made Willie and Ruthana laugh even more.

Still, Willie wasn't sure. He didn't make up his mind until the next evening. There were rumors that there was a Klan meeting outside town, and, later that night, a brick was thrown through one of Mama Flora's windows.

Willie didn't believe it was anything to do with the Klan, he thought it was Kevin, alone or with friends, but the fear it produced in his mother, and even in Ruthana, pushed him to the decision he was on the verge of making.

The following night, the blacks of Stockton watched in despair as their church burned to the ground.

Reverend Jackson organized a line of men with buckets to throw water on the flames, but to no avail. Despite all their urgent pleas for help, the fire engine didn't arrive until the blaze had taken hold.

When he realized it was useless, Reverend Jackson

gathered his congregation to him and, weeping, led them in prayer.

Flora stared at the burning church in horror. She did not pray; she had prayed too much and Jesus had heard her and given Willie the push he needed.

But at what cost?

*T*HE ARSONISTS—FOR ARSON IT SURELY WAS—were never found, no arrests were ever made. After a cursory investigation, the official reason for the fire was given as faulty wiring.

Resentment seethed, even among those who were not religious, but there was nothing they could do, no revenge they could take. Rumors of the Klan were enough to quell any action. No one had seen any white gowns and hoods, there were no burning crosses, no one had proof of the Klan's involvement. It was irrelevant. It wouldn't have mattered if the Klan did not actually exist, if it was a phantom army; it was enough that people believed it existed, such was its power.

Many thanked their Maker that no lives had been lost, and settled back into their lives much as they had been before Joe Louis had given them a hint, if only for a moment, of pride in themselves.

But not quite as they were before. They'd always had a strong sense of community, of themselves against the world, but after the burning of the church, that feeling deepened. Everyone had heard of Willie's fight with Kevin, and Kevin's threats of future vengeance; they determined to give Willie a grand send-off when he left for Chicago, the community standing by its own. And the arrival and departure of a train was always a source of entertainment, as there was little else to do.

Some men, unemployed or retired, sat at the depot all day long, chewing tobacco and the fat of the world, waiting for a train to come and go. The blacks sat on one side of the track, the whites on the other. Sometimes, there was some contact, conversation hurled across the line, for they all knew one another, had grown up in the same town, but the separation remained.

If a train was taking away, or bringing back, one of their own, then all the friends and relations, and many spectators, would gather, and a party atmosphere would prevail. Willie's departure was the biggest party anyone could remember, because there was a sharp reason for it.

Willie had made his decision the night the brick was thrown through their window, but the burning of the church gave him a sense of urgency. He was stunned by the violence Joe Louis's victory had unleashed, and he wanted to be gone, away from here, to the freer, he believed, more liberal air of Chicago.

Flora, who had wanted him to go, now didn't want him to leave, fearful that something dreadful would happen to him if he was away from her protecting arms. But something dreadful had happened to him here, in Stockton, within the scope of her embrace, and she accepted his decision despite the grief it caused her.

Ernestine didn't want him to go because she would miss him, more than she had thought possible a few weeks previously. But she wanted him to have the adventure, because she wanted to have that adventure herself, and because she knew he would be incomplete, and therefore less happy, if he didn't go.

Their last evening together was a ferment of mingled excitement and sadness, and Ernestine had allowed him to do a few things she had not allowed before. When he fondled her breasts she did not stop him. At his request, she put her hand to the most private part of him, hard and urgent, and was fascinated by it, partly because of the need it awakened in her. She would not do more than that, or let him be more intimate with her, however much he begged, but she whispered husky promises for the future.

Ruthana enjoyed Willie's preparations for departure and was practical, making lists of what he should take, and writing down names and addresses that were given to him by friends of folk they knew in Chicago, and especially his uncle George's address, Ruthana's father. She even went with him when he bought his ticket, an adventure in itself.

Willie's biggest concern was money. He had saved a little, but not enough, and he owed twenty-five dollars to Hank, the bookie. He paid some of it and begged for time, and hoped that he could leave town before the debt was demanded of him. Even so, he didn't have enough to last for more than a couple of days in Chicago, or anywhere. Part of this was resolved at work. On his last Friday, his pay packet contained an extra week's wages, holiday money, he was told, and a small bonus for good work done, and all of his friends had contributed to a fund for him, a going-away present, which they gave him, with much ceremony, at a drunken party on that Friday night.

And his mama helped, as he thought she would but did not dare ask. Flora dipped into her money jar and gave her son more than half of it, fifty dollars. It was fair, she thought, for he had contributed that sum, at least, from his wages over the last three years.

He came home late on Friday night, his last night, but Flora waited up for him. She could tell he was slightly drunk, but that was fair, because he was a man and off on a great adventure. She would have forgiven him almost anything that night.

Still, she couldn't let him off the hook.

"You bin drinkin'," she said, making him a cup of coffee.

"Yeh, Ma," Willie said, ready for a fight. "Why not?"

"You be careful a' that stuff in Chicago," was all she said. Willie realized that was the end of his lecture, and was grateful. He slumped in his chair. He'd had a great evening, of laughter and drinking and endless remembrances of his past three years. He'd left his friends somewhat tearfully, with many promises he would never keep to write to them and tell them all his adventures.

Now he was home, with his mama, and for the last time.

"I scared, Ma," he whispered.

Flora's heart almost exploded. He was her little boy

again, getting ready for his first day at school, and even though he was now nearly eighteen, he was not big enough, old enough for such an adventure as Chicago. She had to be brave.

"No need," she said. "Yo' uncle George gon' look after you."

She brought the cup of coffee to him, gave it to him, and smiled.

"You stay away from liquor, is all," she said. Not quite all. She added another caution.

"An' keep away from women. I hear they wild in Chicago."

He looked at her and grinned. "Aw, Ma," he said. But he did not promise to stay away from women.

He put his cup of coffee down and stood, and held his arms open.

"Gimme a hug," he said.

That she did, with all her heart, locked in his arms, feeling the strength of him and the small stubble on his chin, smelling the liquor on his breath, and not caring that it was there, thoughtful only of his welfare, fearful of his future, and filled with love of him.

He was to catch the evening train and Pete Lanier came for them the next afternoon in his truck. Flora and Ruthana rode in the cab with Pete, and Willie slung his small suitcase on the flatbed and climbed aboard. They had to stop to pick up Pearl, and she crammed in with Flora, Ruthana on her lap.

When they arrived at the depot, Willie thought everyone he knew was there, and many he did not. Some cheered as Pete stopped the truck and Willie climbed down.

"Ain't gon' be long now, Willie," Leo called.

"She down roun' Snake Bend," Clayborn, who loved railways, yelled.

Willie was Sunday-dressed, dark-suited, with a white shirt and four-in-hand tie. His cheap, cardboard suitcase was bulging, held together with a leather strap around it.

He moved through the throng, shaking hands, accepting good wishes, and he had never been so excited, even on his first morning of work.

He heard the whistle of the train.

"There she comes!" someone yelled.

Ernestine was there with her parents.

"When you gon' git to Chicago?" Ernestine's mother asked him.

"Tomorrow mornin'," Willie said. "Roun' nine-thirty."

"Lawd," Ernestine's mother gasped. "Ride all night?"

The train whistled again, closer, and they could see the clouds of smoke from the engine.

Flora had stood aside, with Ruthana, to let Willie make his farewells, but women from the church made sure she was not alone. Sister Johnson and Sister Henderson were with her.

"Know you gon' miss him, Sister Palmer," she said.

"Sho' will, sister." Flora nodded.

"He allus worked hard, jes' like his daddy," Sister Henderson said. "Know he gon' do good."

"He say he gon' make money an' make me proud a' him." Flora nodded again. "But I already proud a' him."

Leo Barnett wandered up, and took off his cap.

"I tol' Willie a'ready," he said, "you need help, Miz Palmer, you jes' send fo' me."

"You know I know that, Leo," Flora whispered, close to fresh tears. "Ev'rybody so nice."

It was their kindness that was causing her tears to flow anew, and Ruthana squeezed her hand.

Sister Sanford, used to departure because both her sons had gone, gave Willie a small gift, wrapped in a cloth.

"Here one of my tater pies you allus liked so much, Willie," she said. "It'll help you to Chicago."

Sister Barnett gave him some fried chicken, and Isaac Dixon, the barbecue king, gave him some back ribs, wrapped in greaseproof paper, in an old shoe box.

"Sauce not too hot, Willie," he said. "Know you don't like it too hot."

It was clear to Willie that he was not going to starve on the journey, and already his heart was full.

They could see the train now, chugging toward them. Charlie White was hovering on the edge of the crowd. Willie guessed Charlie's purpose, and moved toward him.

Charlie made sure Mama Flora wasn't watching, and gave Willie a bottle in a brown paper bag.

"My bes', Willie," he whispered. "Four months ol'."

Willie grinned and winked his thanks and hid the bottle of moonshine in Isaac's shoe box as Deacon Sanford plowed toward him.

"Don't forget," Deacon Sanford said, pumping Willie's hand. "You makes money, you remember yo' church."

"Sho' will, Deacon," Willie agreed.

The train was there, coming to a stop, brakes squealing. Steam poured from it, enveloping the crowd.

Willie moved toward his family. Ernestine was with them.

"Don't git up there an' forget me, Willie," she whispered, eyes brimming with the excitement of a loved one's adventure.

"I ain't never gon' forget you, Ernestine," Willie whispered back. He did something that yesterday he might not have dared to do in public. He kissed Ernestine.

The crowd roared its appreciation. The kiss done, Willie glanced at Flora, but she smiled, as if she approved.

Willie was the only passenger to get on the train, and the station agent was already looking at his watch.

A deep, bass voice called from the back of the train.

"Cullud car! This way!" the porter called.

"Time to git on board, Willie!" Clayborn shouted. Willie turned to Ruthana and hugged her.

"Make sho' you gits them lessons good, for me an' Mama, honey," he said, filled with affection for her.

"I do my best," she said.

There was one more good-bye to make, the hardest of them all, but each made it easier for the other.

"Bye, Mama," Willie whispered, hugging Flora.

"Bes' get on board," Flora whispered.

"Boooo'rd!" the porter cried, echoing Flora. Leo grabbed Willie's suitcase and took it to the back of the train.

Flora did not want to let him go and she did want to let go of him. She held his hand tight as they walked together through the crowd to the last car of the train.

Passengers already on board had caught the mood of the moment and were leaning out the windows, calling encouragement to Willie as the crowd shouted its good-byes.

Leo had put the suitcase on the train. He punched Willie's shoulder as he said good-bye, and then put his arm around Flora.

"I look after yo' mama," he said.

Willie nodded, and climbed on board the train. His journey had begun.

The station agent blew his whistle and waved his flag. The train whistled and let out a whoop of steam.

The crowd was close to ecstasy, calling its good-byes. With a mighty sigh, the train began shunting, grinding to movement.

Everybody there, but Flora, waved.

Willie, leaning out the carriage door, waved back.

The train picked up steam, moving faster, chugging away. Willie leaned out the doorway so far he nearly fell out, but the porter grabbed him and dragged him back inside.

They couldn't see him anymore. The train was clattering to the horizon.

Flora was unaware of time. She stayed staring after the train until it had disappeared from view.

"Mama," Ruthana said, touching Flora's arm.

Flora looked around. Half the crowd had gone already, the others leaving.

"Pete Lanier say he take us home whenever you ready," Ruthana said.

Flora nodded.

"Everyone so kind," she said.

She did not want to leave, but there was no point in staying.

"We bes' go home," she said.

PART TWO

19

$\mathcal{W}$ILLIE AWOKE TO THE SMALL PRESSURE of a hand on his knee.

He rubbed his eyes and looked at Taylor, who nodded to the window.

"Windy City," he murmured.

Willie pressed his face to the glass.

There it was in the distance, its tall buildings like beacons, calling Willie's name.

It had been an uncomfortable journey. The colored car had been half empty when Willie got on at Stockton, and he had put his suitcase on the rack and settled in a seat by the window, opposite an older man who introduced himself as Taylor. He had witnessed Willie's farewell, and guessed at the young man's adventure.

"Firs' time in Chicago?" he asked and Willie nodded. Then, because he was nervous and Taylor seemed kind, he added a truth.

"Firs' time leavin' home," he confessed.

Taylor roared with laughter.

"Boy, I done seen that," he said. "An' you got the look of it. Still got cotton in yo' hair!"

Willie was slightly offended, he thought he looked rather sharp and worldly, but as they journeyed on, he recognized the truth of what Taylor had said.

At every stop people got on board, and Willie saw countless replays of his own leaving of home, young men—it was almost always young men—saying good-bye to their families. By the time they crossed the state line the car was full, and Willie thought himself a veteran. Already he had begun to see a difference between those going north for the first time—the hicks, the country boys, dowdy in their simple Sunday suits compared with older men who had, Willie guessed, lived in Chicago and wore a peacock finery. It made him nervous.

More passengers got on, finding space where they could, sitting on their suitcases, spilling into the corridors of the next car, the first white car, only half full. Among some there was a camaraderie of travel. If a woman got on board, some men, those dressed like himself, squeezed together and tried to find space for her. Others, more selfish, were defensive of the small space they had, and a few arguments broke out.

The man already seated almost always won, unless the woman was pretty or aggressively vocal.

Willie, because he didn't know how to behave and was nervous of giving up his seat, his place of refuge, slunk down and pretended to be asleep when others pushed through the car looking for what he had.

Yet there was kindness too. Taylor and the men sitting near Willie shared the food they had, and all had some; there was no dining car for blacks. Once Willie understood the rules, he offered his tater pie and barbecue, which was mostly refused, and, later, in the dark of night, his bottle of Charlie's moonshine, which was not.

"Ain't gon' find this in Chicago," Taylor told him, after taking a healthy swig of the harsh liquor. "This be good."

For a while there was a party atmosphere in some sections of the car, and strangers briefly collided, introducing themselves, the nervous voicing their nervousness, the old hands their bravado. Later, Willie heard the sounds of a poker game and he longed to go and join it, but dared not leave his seat, except once, in the wee hours of the morning, when everyone was settled, to pee.

And to move his small wad of cash from his socks to inside his underpants. From the stories he had heard that night, a young man and his money were soon parted in Chicago.

He slept for a while, but kept waking, his mind filled with the things Taylor and others had told him of life in the big city, and the traps that awaited a young man there, and the wonders. He made a mental list of the places he would visit, the shops on Forty-seventh Street, the Regal Theater, with its movies and live shows, and the Savoy Ballroom. What amazed him, and comforted him most, was that all these places were all-black. He tried to be sophisticated, but the country kept breaking through.

"What about Mr. Charlie?" he asked.

"Lawd A'mighty, boy, honky don' dare come near!" Taylor said, laughing again. "He got his own places."

" 'Cept a few, Sat'dee nights, what likes midnight velvet," he added.

Willie nodded, as if he were a man of the world.

"Ev'n the cops is colored," Taylor added again. "Some of 'em, anyways."

This was a great relief to Willie. He didn't want anything to do with white people; he didn't like them, he didn't understand them, and he resented the obscure, aggressive authority they had over him. He didn't understand why he had to call a mean, potbellied, white-trash no-hoper "suh," obey any order given, and step out of the way. He respected segregation, however unfair it was, because it kept him mostly away from whites. There was a hamburger joint in Stockton, the Star Cafe, and blacks could order only at the back door; they were not allowed inside, at the front. This was fine by Willie.

He had thought that Chicago would be different, that he would have to integrate, and mingle daily with people he disliked. He was relieved to know that this was not necessarily the case.

"Niggers can do anything there," he said to Taylor. It was a question and a hope.

To his surprise, Taylor laughed again, which irritated Willie. "Pull the cotton out yo' head, boy," Taylor said. "South Side, yeh, in the ghetto, they leave us pretty much to we selves. Step outside a' that, cross the line, and it's a honky world."

Willie settled to sleep again, determined never to leave the South Side, the ghetto, and woke to Taylor tapping on his knee.

"Windy City," Taylor said.

The countryside gave way to houses, rows and rows of boxes—Willie had never seen so many—and the tall buildings were lost from view. As they journeyed on, the houses became taller—tenement buildings, warehouses, and department stores. The passengers began gathering up their belongings, and then, at last, they shunted into Union Station.

Willie half hoped that Taylor would stay with him, to guide him through the enormous, unfamiliar station, the strange routines, but as the train stopped, Taylor stood up, shook Willie's hand, wished him luck, and disappeared into the throng.

Willie got off the train holding his suitcase tight and went with the flow. The crowd of passengers, surging with an unfamiliar energy, all headed in the same direction, swept him along the platform into the concourse and then dispersed, leaving Willie alone and uncertain, surrounded by strangers.

Willie stood staring at the passing, bustling mass, which now appeared to be mostly white, and everyone seemed to know where they were going, apart from him. He took a piece of paper from his pocket, with his uncle's address on it, and looked around for help.

He saw what he hoped was salvation, a uniformed redcap, an older black man with gray hair, slowly pushing a cart laden with luggage, following a white couple.

Willie fell in beside him, walking with him, and proffered his piece of paper.

"C'n y' tell me how to get there, mister?"

The redcap knew Willie's generic history in a glance, and saw himself when young. Without stopping, he took the piece of paper.

"First time here, ain't it?" he said, already knowing the answer. Willie nodded.

"You sure git lost on the El train." He chuckled. "Same wit' the bus. I say a taxi yo' best bet."

This scared Willie. He'd never taken a taxi in his life, but was sure it would be expensive.

"I guess be roun' a couple a' bucks from here," the redcap said, answering the unasked question. "Can you stand that?"

"I guess." Willie nodded with relief. Two bucks was two bucks, but less than he had expected, and worth it, if it brought him to refuge.

"You hang on in behind me, 'til I get these folks in a cab," the redcap said. "Then I see can't I get you straight."

Secure in the redcap's company, Willie walked beside him through the vast station, trying not to be overawed by the enormity of it all. They went outside to a line of Yellow Cabs. The white couple got into the first of them and the redcap loaded their luggage.

Willie stood there wishing he had never come to Chicago. The noise was deafening, the jostling throng overwhelming. Yet he was thrilled to be here. He could hear his heart beating above the noise of traffic, from excitement and fear.

"C'mon," the redcap said, startling Willie. "We get you a cab knows South Side, where you goin'."

He hailed a rather scruffy cab with a mulatto driver.

"Homeboy here goin' to five thousand block on Forestville," the redcap told the driver. "How much that from here?"

The cab driver knew Willie's story as well, and upped his price a tad. "Three bucks," he said. The redcap looked at Willie, who nodded and dug in his pocket for a quarter. His mama had trained him well.

"Naw, homeboy, you gon' need all yo' quarters afore you done." The redcap chuckled, waving Willie's offer away. "Looka here, where you from, anyway?"

"Town name a' Stockton," Willie said, as the redcap put his case in the cab. "Fifty mile from Memphis, Tennessee."

The cab driver perked up. "I got a lodge brother say he come from Memphis," he said. "What that place like?"

Willie's only knowledge of Memphis was secondhand, but he knew of Beale Street and the music, and the Peabody Hotel, and it gave him something to talk about as they drove. The cab driver had no real interest in anything other than Chicago, but he listened for a while and then began pointing out the landmarks as they passed.

The faces on the crowded sidewalks denoted their progress. At first mostly white with a sprinkling of black, that changed as they headed south, until every face Willie saw was welcome black.

Finally the cab driver came to a halt outside a five-story tenement in an untidy street of similar buildings. Willie paid, tipped, and thanked him, got out of the cab, and stood on the sidewalk with his suitcase, not sure what to do next.

"Go inside," the driver said, smiling to himself, secure in the familiar. "Number four be on the apartment door. Knock or ring the bell."

Willie thanked him again, went inside, found a door with the number 4 on it, and knocked. There was no reply. He knocked again. Nothing.

He went back outside and sat with his suitcase beside him on the stoop. He was content to watch the life of the street, of the city, until someone came home. He had nowhere else to go and would not have left the area. The address was his lifeline, and he wanted the security of knowing where he would sleep that night.

The street intrigued him at first, the tall brick buildings and iron fire escapes, the wide sidewalks and fire hydrants, the automobiles of every shape, size, and color, some gaudily decorated. The people fascinated him too. No one here had cotton tufts in their hair, and their clothes confused him; some of the women, and a few of the men, were gaudily dressed in colors and combinations he had never imagined. He looked down at his own, best suit, crumpled from the journey and with barbecue sauce on the lapel, and he felt shabby.

It was a world away from Stockton, and Willie felt as if he had the word "country" branded on his forehead.

It was hot, Willie was tired, he hadn't slept much on the train, and the air was different from that of Stockton, close and smelly, not really fresh. He folded his arms on his knees, put his head down, and slept.

He woke at about five. The sidewalk was busy, as if people were coming home from work. Occasionally people came in or out of the building but paid no attention to him, apart from one woman, carrying grocery bags, who stared at him as if she might know him, then went inside.

An hour later, a tall, strongly built man came to the stoop and stopped.

"You Willie?" he asked.

"Yessuh." Willie nodded.

"Come on up," the man said cheerfully, leading the way into the building. "I'm George."

He looked back at Willie and grinned.

"Yo' uncle," he added, unnecessarily, and winked. "You was 'bout hip high last time I seen you."

Willie hardly remembered George from their last meeting, at Josie's funeral, but his cheerful manner put Willie at ease and he followed his uncle inside.

"Hope you ain't had to wait too long," he said, as they climbed the stairs. "Me an' the ol' lady both work."

Ellie, the "ol' lady," wasn't old, but George's age, with a full and ample figure. She was the one who had stopped to look at him on the stoop, and greeted Willie casually.

"I jus' knew it was you," she said, "and I wanted to ax you up, but you don't take no chances here."

"Yes'm, I un'erstan'," Willie murmured.

The apartment was not big, but it was untidily comfortable. There was no spare bedroom for Willie.

"We ain't got no room for nobody," George said, "but you can sleep here two, three nights on the couch."

Ellie served an enormous meal of smothered pork chops, mashed potatoes, and greens, and as they ate, George outlined his plans for Willie's future.

"I already spoke to an ol' lady got a room. Fifteen bucks a week, or twenty wit' yo' dinner meal. You got enough money to cover that 'til you get a job?"

"Couple of weeks, anyway, three mebbe," Willie murmured, doing rapid calculations in his head. Three weeks, four weeks tops, he thought, and that's just for living.

"Cain't git you a job at the stockyards, 'coz they laying off, moving west," George said. "Dunno how long I got a job there myself."

He glanced at Ellie, and Willie sensed financial worry between them. He wasn't surprised. Obviously, Chicago was expensive.

"But a friend a' mine's assistant foreman at a big warehouse," George continued on a happier note. "He say Monday he can start you out temporary, and if'n you cut the mustard he try to keep you full-time."

Willie breathed an enormous sigh of relief, and grinned his thanks.

"But I tell you right now, it's hard work," George cautioned. "Ain't far off from the logging, or throwing cotton bales back home."

"I feels ready, sir," Willie said. Ellie gathered the plates and took them through to the closet that was the kitchen.

Cautions done, George relaxed and lit a cigarette. "Now," he smiled, "tell me all the news from Stockton. How's my li'l girl?"

Willie was surprised. George was Ruthana's father, but he had not mentioned her until now. He guessed it had something to do with Ellie, who was not Ruthana's mother, so he spoke quietly.

"She fine, jes' fine," he said. "She good at school."

He wondered how much he should tell George, and tried to make a bond between them.

"She wants to go to college," he said with a grin,

thinking that George would see the impossibility of the idea.

But George didn't. He looked at Willie in surprise, and then smiled, pleased.

"Well, ain't that somethin'," he said, pride in his voice. He could not resist sharing the news.

"Y'hear that, Ellie?" he called. "My li'l girl wants to go to college."

Ellie was unimpressed. She came back with a pecan pie, a special treat for Willie's arrival.

"What's a nigra girl want to go to college for?" Ellie demanded. "What use it to a nigra girl?"

"Well, it ain't happened yet, an' she be young," George said, ever the peacemaker. He looked at Willie. "How ol' she now?"

"Eight, I think." Willie tried to remember. "No, she nine."

George whistled. "Nine year ol'? My little girl? Time sho' do fly."

He sat in reflective silence, as if wondering where the years had gone, then roused himself.

"An' yo' ma?" he asked. "How is that good lady?"

"She fine, jes' fine," Willie said. He answered all of George's questions about people he remembered from Stockton, but was fascinated by Ellie, who showed no interest in their conversation. She didn't eat pie; she was "watching her figger."

"Lot of it to watch." George grinned, and grinned again when she slapped him, catching her hand and kissing it.

She turned her attention to a pile of magazines, mostly about fashion and beauty, until Willie and George drifted into silence. Then Ellie began chatting to George about her day, and he about his, and Willie was content to sit and listen, as if he were learning a new language, spoken between a couple who had been together for a long time, of which he had no experience.

They listened to the wireless for a while, and then Ellie murmured good night to Willie and went to the next room, the only other room.

"Jes' pull put that couch out, it make a bed," George said, showing Willie how. "And you know where the toilet is. We get up at six. All right?"

"Yessir, thank you," Willie said. George went to the bedroom, and Willie was glad to be alone, at last, and secure.

Although he was tired, he couldn't sleep. Nights in Stockton were silent, but Chicago nights were filled with noise, a continuous rumble of traffic, of cars passing in the street, of distant talking outside and shouts and laughter, dogs barking, and, once, Willie thought he heard a woman scream.

He heard other sounds from the bedroom, things he didn't want to hear, an invasion of privacy. He tried putting the cushion over his head, but George and Ellie were noisy lovemakers.

He envied what they had, not just at this moment, but all of their relationship that he had seen, their ease with each other. They gave the sense that they were a pair united against the world, sharing what they had, defending each other against ill. It made Willie think of Ernestine and he wished that she was with him now to share the triumphs and anxieties of his day. There was still some moonshine left in his bottle, so he had a couple of sips, hoping it would help him sleep.

Then there was a kind of silence, an unfamiliar one that was as close as the city ever came to quiet.

Still, Willie did not sleep. He was pleased with himself. It had been a momentous day, filled with learning, and although he had been nervous, terrified once or twice, he was here, safe, in Chicago, tucked up in bed, ready to face the morrow. He said a small prayer of thanks, and that reminded him of his mama. He vowed that he would write to her the very next day and tell her all was well.

On at least two occasions, standing in the surging,

crowded vastness of Union Station, and sitting on the stoop in the middle of the afternoon, he had thought it was all a huge mistake. He had wanted to get on the first train back to Stockton and never show his face in Chicago again.

He was glad he had resisted that urge. He had survived and he was here, and tomorrow would see him on the road to riches.

20

A WEEK LATER, Willie wanted to go home. A year later Willie still wanted to go home, and the year after that. Four years later he did go back to Stockton, but only briefly. It was only while he was away from the city that he missed it, and realized that it had become his home.

He got the job that George had arranged at the warehouse, and it was hard work, but no worse than humping cotton bales. It was the noise, as much as anything, that disconcerted him, an endless cacophony that made Willie long for silence, and birdsong, and the sweet, clean smell of an open field.

The warehouse was enormous, near the railroad freight depot. The scores of mostly black laborers kept up a din of chatter, shouting, or insults as they pushed two-wheeled handcarts laden with packages and cartons of every size and shape and weight from trucks that brought them from the railroad, to the store, and then again to other trucks for delivery. A dozen foremen shouted orders or abuse. Countless numbers of trucks, massive Macks, or Whites, or Peterbilts, or local delivery vehicles, came and went all day, their engines roaring, their exhaust fouling the air.

Willie, who was strong but careful with his strength, was determined not to let George down, and, simply by following orders and being careful, he did well. For the first two or three days he still thought the word "country" was branded on his forehead, he was the butt of many jokes, but he kept to himself and accepted all the ribbing with good humor. By the end of the week he thought his brand was fading, they no longer made jokes about the hick, but he still did not feel comfortable among these men. They were brasher and more aggressive than his friends in Stockton, they all seemed to know much more about the world than Willie, their mouths were fouler than any he had ever heard, especially where women were concerned, and some of them spoke in a jive talk that Willie simply did not understand.

He took the room that George had found for him, twenty dollars a week with his dinner meal each evening, and because his landlady, Lula, liked him, she made him a brown bag with thin sandwiches each morning to take to work with him.

Lula's apartment was on the fourth floor of a five-floor walk-up. Willie, young and fit, had no trouble with the stairs, but he wondered how Lula, who was frail and old, managed them. Mostly, she did not go out any more than was necessary, but once Willie came home from work and found her on the landing of the third floor, gasping for breath. Willie offered help, but Lula shook him aside.

"You go on up," she wheezed. "I be there direckly." It took her ten minutes to climb the last flight of stairs.

Lula was in her mid-sixties, and tiny, the thinnest, smallest woman that Willie had ever seen; one good puff of wind might blow her over. She was feisty, as little women sometimes are, and she was a widow, but, unlike Flora, she had enjoyed a long and happy marriage, and she missed her husband, who had been a laborer, like Willie, and had died a couple of years ago of a heart attack.

Willie could not imagine how she managed for money, his twenty dollars wouldn't go far, but guessed that her two children, who seldom came to see her, helped her out. She did some mending jobs for others in the building, but her eyes were failing and her stitching poor. Sitting alone in his room in the evenings, Willie would often hear a small cry and a curse as Lula pricked her finger again, or she would come knocking on his door, demanding that he thread the needle.

The apartment was small, seldom clean, and always reeking of overcooked food. There was a tiny sitting area with an uncomfortable, battered couch, a table, and a couple of rickety chairs, and a stove and a sink in one corner. Lula had her own little bedroom, and Willie's room was not much larger than a box with a washstand and a bed. The toilet was on the landing, communally shared by the four apartments on the floor, and often foul.

In summer the apartment was stuffy and unbearably hot, and although it was warm enough in winter—there were radiators that worked in every room—the windows were always closed against the bitter cold, and the air stank.

Despite her circumstances, or because of them, Lula had a devout faith in God. She went to church every Sunday without fail, no matter the weather, wheezing slowly up and down the tenement stairs, and spent her evenings in the little sitting area singing songs of praise and reminding Willie to pray regularly. Especially for the good president.

Lula's faith in Roosevelt was unswerving; he was a saint on earth, sent to deliver the poor from oppression. She speculated that F.D.R. was actually a colored man with a very light skin, God-given, that he might pass as a white man to achieve his present position. He could not actually be white, because how could a white man so utterly understand the plight of the blacks, and strive so steadfastly on their behalf? Similarly, President Abraham Lincoln, she suspected, had a colored ancestor somewhere in his family tree.

It was F.D.R. who had introduced a system of retirement benefits a couple of years ago, and now he was trying to extend those benefits to the dependents, especially the wives and widows, of the retired. Willie guessed, correctly, that Lula's prayers for F.D.R. were as much for the safe passage of this bill as for the president's health.

She did not encourage Willie's company in the evenings, nor did he enjoy her constant hymns, but she did not mind him going out at night, although he was forbidden to bring women or liquor to the apartment. He obeyed the first law, but not the second.

During his first week, Willie spent his evenings in his

room, and ate his dinner there, tired from his work. But he was young and energetic, and disappointed that he had not seen more of the town, the city lights.

Willie slept late on Saturday morning, to Lula's vocal disapproval when he woke.

"Ol' man stop-abed," she sniffed. "Hope you ain't a lazy nigro; too many a' them roun' here."

Willie thought this was unfair, he'd worked hard all week, but he kept his silence, and then George arrived, as promised, to show him the town.

Ellie was waiting for them downstairs, her huge hips and bosom straining at the seams of a thin summer dress, but she looked cool and lovely, and was friendly enough, although she never tried to be friends.

They walked the few blocks to Forty-seventh Street, and it was everything Willie had hoped it would be, and like nothing he could have imagined.

Because it was Saturday morning, the streets were packed, and everyone was in holiday mood. Because it was so hot, nearly naked children danced in fountains of water erupting from fire hydrants on the sidewalk, and ice cream vendors were selling out. The women were dressed in summer finery—pretty cottons, wide-brimmed, frilly hats, and white gloves—and most of the men carried their jackets and wore brightly colored suspenders.

Willie, in his cheap Sunday best, felt out of place.

"Wait 'til tonight." Ellie laughed. "When the zoot suits come out."

Willie asked her what a zoot suit was, but Ellie said he would see.

They walked for several blocks along Forty-seventh Street, and then walked back on the other side, past shops whose windows were crammed with goods and produce— and clothes—such as Willie had never seen before. There was a bank, only for colored folk, George told him, and a very grand hotel. There were cheaper hotels, cafes and restaurants, dance halls and movie theaters, and one, the largest, the Regal, had lines of blazing lights chasing one another like a fantastic sunrise, and brilliantly colored posters.

Despite the shabbiness of some of the streets they had walked through, Willie began to think that everyone in Chicago must be wealthy, but the sight of a few beggars brought him to a kind of reality. A boy tap-danced, spectacularly, for money. Another juggled, badly. A blind man sat patiently with his dog, murmuring thanks when the occasional coin chinked in his mug. Willie began to see the street with new eyes, that many of the old were poorly dressed and not all the stores were wonderland. The veneer of prosperity faded; it was Stockton on a Saturday morning, only a million times larger.

Then they passed a men's clothing shop. Willie stopped in awe, staring at the window.

It was filled with men's suits of a style he had never seen before, on mannequins with black faces, a novelty in itself. Long, flowing jackets and ballooning pants, in all the colors of the rainbow, and hats with enormous brims, some with brilliant feathers in them.

Willie looked at Ellie. "Zoot suits?"

She laughed in agreement. "Boy, I can tell from the look in your eyes, you be in one a' them afore this month is out."

Willie could not imagine himself in such finery, or that he would ever be able to afford such a suit, because the price tags shocked him. George confirmed this.

"You keep yo' money fo' better things," he said.

But when a man came out of the store dressed in a bright yellow suit that seemed to billow all about him, flashing gold teeth in a dazzling smile, cock of the walk, Willie looked at him in envy.

They had lunch in a cafeteria, and Willie had never seen such a display of food: long counters of soups and salads and sandwiches, barbecue and slabs of meat for carving, steaks and chops and stews, half a dozen kinds of potato, greens and beans and vegetables, fruits and puddings and ice creams. Willie walked along the counter with his tray, not knowing what to order because he never knew what would be coming up next, and when he came to the end of the counter and there was nothing on his tray, he had to go back and start over.

He offered to pay his share, but George shook his head. "Least I can do," he said. "You kin, kinda, and yo' mama's been good to my li'l girl."

He always referred to Ruthana as his "li'l girl." Willie began to wonder if George could remember his daughter's name.

After they had eaten, they went outside and Ellie said good-bye because she had shopping to do.

George took Willie for a walk, this time showing him the things that a man might need to know. He assumed that Willie, on Saturday nights, would want to go out, and pointed out several small dance clubs and a couple of bars that were good starting places, where he might not be cheated or robbed. They left Forty-seventh and walked south, George cautioning him never to bring too much money out with him, and always keep some in his socks or underpants.

Some of the buildings they passed now were almost derelict, with windows boarded up, and the sidewalks strewn with trash. They turned a corner onto a street with many bars, loud music coming from them, and the men were poorly dressed, and the women looked vulgar, compared with what they had seen on Forty-seventh Street.

"Whatever you do, you stay away from here, Willie," George said, and it was obviously an important and serious warning. "Lessen you wants to get robbed or cut or kilt," he added. "This is the baaaadlands here."

Willie longed to know why it was so bad, but was afraid George would think the question stupid. He looked around, made a mental note of the street, and promised George he would not come here.

George looked at him as if he didn't quite trust the promise.

"An' keep away from ho's," he said.

Willie looked at the ground. He could not imagine going with a whore, and was embarrassed that George, who had assumed a paternal role, had even mentioned it.

The lecture and the lesson done, they walked back toward Willie's lodgings. They said good-bye and George promised to keep in touch, but they seldom saw each other again. A few months later, when Willie went to visit George, he and Ellie had moved, leaving unpaid rent and bills behind them, and no one knew where they had gone. Willie wasn't surprised; he had a feeling they were nomads, restless riders in the night, perpetually looking for something they had not found.

But on that first, bright Saturday morning, Willie walked back up to Lula's apartment thinking he had found paradise on Forty-seventh Street, and could not imagine why anyone would ever want to live anywhere but Chicago.

That night, because it was Saturday, he went out on the town. He went to the bars George suggested, and drank more than was good for him. He went to a dance club, but he felt out of place in his Sunday suit among the brilliant costumes of the Chicago night, and he found himself wandering toward the area George had prohibited.

He had more to drink in a low bar, which was filled with people who were as cheaply dressed as he. A fat, middle-aged whore tried to pick him up, but no one else was friendly. The whore took his refusal well, but insisted he buy her a drink, and Willie did not know how to say no. She drank to his health, then drifted away and others pressed around him, demanding service from the barkeep.

Then Willie discovered his wallet was gone. He looked for the whore, but she was gone too. Almost weeping with angry frustration at his own stupidity, he stumbled out of the bar.

Other women, whores, accosted him outside, and a man offered him happy dust, but Willie didn't know what that was, and in any case he had no money. He thought he knew his way home, but he was drunk and disoriented.

In a dark street, a couple of young men confronted him, one wielding a knife, demanding money. They didn't believe him when he said he'd been robbed already, and suddenly one moved behind him and got Willie in a half nelson while his pal cut the pockets of Willie's suit, looking for his wallet. Finding nothing made them angry, and they punched Willie in the gut a couple times, then vanished into the night.

Willie stumbled on, lost and hurt. A white policeman, with a black partner, stopped him, and asked him what he was doing. Willie was scared of them, of their authority, but his frustration and pain flooded to the surface. He explained his situation in drunken half sobs, and the policemen laughed and gave him a small lecture, then pointed out the way to his street.

He was only a block away from home.

The cops watched him for a while until they were sure Willie was safe, then turned their attention to the rest of the night.

Willie crept up the stairs, praying that Lula would not be up. His prayers were answered. He snuck into his room, and checked that the money in his socks was still there. Mercifully, it was, and he thanked God for it, and that he had paid Lula that morning.

He lay on the bed, aching all over, but every time he put his head down the bed started to spin. Then he was sick on the floor.

When it was done, he tried to clean things up, but the effort was too much. He lay back on the bed, cursing Chicago. What hurt him most of all was that fellow blacks had done this to him, his brothers and sisters. Only the policemen had been kind, and Willie had always believed that the enemy was white.

It was this, more than anything, that caused his tears to flow, and in his misery he regretted ever coming to Chicago, and vowed to leave this wretched city and go home.

21

*W*ILLIE DIDN'T LEAVE BECAUSE he couldn't bear to admit failure, and things got better after that, if only by degrees.

On Monday morning, the assistant foreman told him that they were pleased with his work and his job was permanent. It was a mixed blessing to Willie, because he still wasn't sure he wanted to stay.

Because of his new status, or because he was becoming familiar to them, the other laborers began treating him differently. They still laughed about his rural background, and still talked to him as if they were ready to pick a fight with anything he said, but occasionally they included him in their jokes or their gossip. A week later another young man, fresh from the country with cotton still in his hair, began working there. They called him Tufty, and made the same jokes about him as they had made about Willie, and treated him as harshly, and Willie realized that it was a general pattern of behavior and not specifically cruel to the individual.

Tufty could not stand the pace, or insults. He picked a fight with the worst of his oppressors, got beaten up, and chucked his job. He was replaced the next week by another country hopeful, and the pattern repeated itself, this time with Willie joining in the jokes.

On a Friday evening after work, a couple of the men asked Willie to join them at their local bar. Willie went and had a good time, and on the following Monday his position altered again. His drinking companions greeted him cheerily, as one of them, and Willie's sense of security deepened.

He passed a series of tests he didn't know he had been given. He kept silent about a scam that was revealed to him. One man was making a sideline profit by "losing" an occasional carton and selling the contents on the street. Willie knew who it was, but when it was discovered and he was questioned, he shrugged and kept his mouth shut. He was surprised that this earned him respect from his fellows.

When another worker, a white man, tried to steal his new watch, Willie confronted him, and there was a fight. Willie won. Again to his surprise, he found that during the fight the other permanents, black and white, were cheering him, and were pleased with his success.

He joined the union because he was pressured to do so, and went to a couple of meetings. He had no great social conscience, and he didn't really understand the speeches or the cause, but one union man, Ab, impressed him. Ab was tall and powerfully built, black as ebony, with a charismatic personality, a deep bass voice, an orator's tongue, and a passionate commitment to the cause of the common man. Willie loved to listen to Ab's speeches. Even if he didn't always understand them, there were things that stayed in his mind long after he had heard them.

"From each according to his ability," Ab declared at the end of one such speech, and the rafters rang with the booming of his voice. "To each according to his needs."

In another speech, Ab talked about the coming war in Europe, for surely war was coming. He spoke of the great evil that had come to power in Germany, the Nazis, the enemies of the working man, and of their leader, Adolf Hitler. He insisted that Americans, whatever their color or creed, should support Joseph Stalin, the leader in Russia, a man who could and would stand up to Hitler.

Willie didn't understand what was happening in Europe, nor did he really care. It was all so far away. He didn't read newspapers much, he glanced at the headlines and scanned the sports pages, and when he heard the news on the radio, his ear only tuned in to things of local interest. But Ab made it seem important. For a few days Willie read the news pages with some interest, but the European politics confused him, and even if there was a war, about which no one agreed, Willie couldn't think that Americans would be involved. Without Ab's passion it was meaningless.

Willie thought that Ab would have made a great preacher, but others told him to steer clear of the union man. He was a communist. Willie wasn't sure what a communist was, except that they had something to do with Russia, which Ab talked about a lot, and were, somehow, enemies to America. Willie was confused. Ab was fighting for the American working man, black and white; how could he be an enemy to America?

Confusion about the politics turned into boredom with the politics, and Willie stopped going to union meetings, except when pressured or, sometimes, to listen to Ab.

Possible friendships flowed and ebbed about him. Willie was lonely, almost unbearably so sometimes, but he was cautious in his choice of company. Although his job was permanent, a sense of permanence came to him only slowly. While he had many acquaintances, he made no real friends, although later, a young man called Josh filled the need for a while.

Willie's loneliness was most acute in the evenings. Because of his misadventures on his first Saturday night, Willie didn't go out very much. During the week he stayed in his room, although occasionally he ate his dinner with Lula and chatted with her about her day for a while, until she turned to thoughts of God and hymns of praise. He occupied most of his spare time by strumming the guitar he had bought for himself, just riffing, or trying to compose songs.

Or writing to Ernestine. The letters began as a simple correspondence, informing Ernestine of his health and welfare and inquiring about hers, but because he had nothing else to do they became a kind of diary, which he sent to her once a week. Each evening he would labor over his pad of paper with a stubby pencil, setting down the things that had happened at work that day, or his thoughts, and because he didn't want her to think his life was dull, he began inventing things that he had done. Writing did not come easily to him, he had to think about each word and labor over its execution, and within an hour his hand ached, but it filled in time.

He was always thrilled to get Ernestine's longer, and neatly written, replies, and, because he was lonely, his feelings toward Ernestine deepened and blossomed into something he began to think of as love.

And, once a week, he wrote, dutifully if briefly, to his mama, with hugs and kisses for Ruthana as well, and, once a week, she sent him simple replies. Willie guessed that Ruthana actually wrote these letters to Flora's dictation, because his mama had never learned to write very well.

He had been in Chicago for about six months when a letter came from Stockton with spidery writing. It was from Flora, written by herself, with a twenty-dollar bill tucked inside. Willie was puzzled until he read the letter.

In her untidy scrawl, Flora explained that the twenty dollars was for him to send to Hank, the bookie in Stockton, to pay the debt that Willie still owed the man, " 'coz you got to keep you good name," Flora wrote.

Shame flooded through Willie. He had forgotten the debt, or put it out of his mind, and he realized that Hank must have visited his mama. He wondered what had been said, and had a vision of his mama digging in the garden to uncover her buried money jar, counting the coins inside, and changing them to a twenty-dollar bill. He determined that he would change his ways, that he would send money to his mama regularly, would repay the twenty dollars, and that he would not gamble again.

It puzzled him that he had so little money. His rent chewed up half his pay packet, but he seldom went out during the week. On Friday nights he went to local bars with his workmates, and had a cheap meal with them, spending at most a few dollars, and it was hard for him to believe that he spent the rest on Saturday nights. Gambling took up some, he knew, but he still backed only favorites, and he still came out mostly ahead.

On Saturdays, in the daytime, he made excursions, to the zoo or the lake while the weather was still warm. There was a small stretch of beach on the edge of the ghetto that was used mostly by blacks, and Willie enjoyed going there, lying on the sand or paddling in the water, and he decided that he would learn to swim. He'd buy an ice cream and wander among the crowds, but all he saw were couples, arm in arm, lovers young and old, and it increased his sense of loneliness, and his feelings of love for Ernestine.

He always went out on Saturday nights, looking for something, but not sure what. A friend, perhaps.

He bought a new suit to replace the one that the robbers had slashed, a simple suit, nothing expensive, although three times what it would have cost in Stockton. Wary of the bars and dark side streets, of George's baaaadlands, he limited his excursions to Forty-seventh Street. He loved movies, and always went to the Regal Theater, no matter what was showing. After the film, the orchestra played and the screen rose, and a live show began, long rows of tap-dancing, high-kicking, prettily dressed chorus girls, and comedians and singers.

The show done, Willie went to the cafeteria for his evening meal, and then to one of the dance clubs. He could never find the courage to ask one of the brightly dressed Chicago girls to dance, so he would sit at the bar, drinking, and wishing Ernestine were with him.

He was bored. He was lonely. And he had no idea how to change either condition.

He was sitting at the bar on one such Saturday night, thinking of Ernestine, when he heard a voice he recognized.

"Hey, bro', what y'doin', man?"

Willie turned and saw Josh, a fellow laborer from work, but it was not a Josh he recognized.

Josh, at work, wore overalls, and was perpetually in a bad mood, cursing the cartons and packages he had to load.

This Josh, in the half light of the dance club, was dapper and dandy and colorfully clad. He wore an electric blue zoot suit, a matching hat with a filmy ribbon around it, several gold chains on his wrists, and as many glittering rings on his fingers. His bad temper had vanished with his work clothes, and this Josh was all cheer and wisecracks.

He offered Josh a drink, which was accepted—Josh never refused a drink—and they chatted for a while, about work at first, and then began exploring each other's opinions.

Relieved that he had someone to talk to at last, Willie lost control of his tongue, and talked about his loneliness, his sense of being displaced in the big city, and of missing home and friends.

Josh sat with his back to the bar, watching the dance floor. He seldom looked at Willie, who began to wonder if Josh was even listening to him. His confession trickled to silence.

Then Josh did look at him, as if appraising him.

"Yo' trouble is," he said, teacher to a small boy, "y'need new clothes. Y'look like shit, man. No bitch gon' come near you."

Willie's temper flared. He was wearing his new suit, and he'd bought other clothes as well, some sweaters and an overcoat, because the weather was cold, and some decent boots for work and for the winter. These things had eaten up much of his money. But he knew he still looked drab compared with Josh.

"Cain't afford it," he admitted.

"Sho' you can, bro'." Josh laughed. "Ain't y'ever heard a' credick?"

Willie had heard of "credick," but wasn't sure what it was.

"Five dollar down, fifty cents a week," Josh explained. "Buys you anything you want."

Willie couldn't believe it was that easy, but Josh was master of his fate.

"Ain't never gon' get nowhere lookin' like that," Josh said.

Willie sat staring glumly at his drink. Josh said nothing for a while, and then seemed to take pity on Willie.

"Come wit' me."

Willie followed Josh to the dance floor. The music was slow and moody. The lights were dim, and spots hitting a revolving mirrored ball cast pretty patterns on the dancers. About fifty couples were dancing, and as many young women were seated on chairs along the wall, giggling or gossiping or swaying to the music, waiting to be asked to dance.

Josh walked along the line of them, Willie in his wake, and finally made his choice.

Two young women, obviously friends, were sitting slightly apart from the others, whispering to each other. They had spotted Josh when he first walked by them, but pretended not to notice when he walked back to them.

" 'Scuse me, sisters," Josh said politely, "but I was wond'rin' if'n you could help me."

They deigned to look at him.

"This be my cousin, Willie," Josh continued. "He a homeboy fresh in town from the country, that's why he dressed so baaaad. He don' know his way roun' an' I wants him to have a good time in Chicago, but he sceered to death a' asking a pretty woman to dance."

Willie could hardly keep a straight face. Surely they couldn't believe such a line?

"Where he from?" the prettier of them wanted to know. Josh looked at Willie.

"Li'l town called Stockton, ma'am," Willie said. "Fifty mile from Memphis, Tennessee."

He heard the Southern drawl in his voice. He knew he was presenting his simplest, hick face. He almost touched his hair to pull out cotton tufts that were not there.

"An' you sho' is pretty," he added.

She tossed her head, as if immune to such compliments, used to them, but then she looked at him.

"I dance wit' you awhile," she said. "To keep you company. But don' you go gettin' no ideas!"

"No, ma'am," Willie said, almost wanting to shuffle his feet. "No ideas at all, not wit' a lady like you. I jus' wants to dance awhile."

The deal done, her honor satisfied, she cast her pretensions aside. She stood. She was attractive in a flashy, fleshy way. Her bosom bulged over the top of her shiny satin dress.

"My name's Minty," she said, her voice dropping to a husky, seductive whisper. She moved close to Willie and ran her tongue over her shiny lips. "Choc'late on the outside, all fresh and tingly unnerneath."

Suddenly, as if she could no longer contain the music and the energy inside her, she let out a whoop and shimmied her body against Willie.

"Be bop da re bop!" she shrieked, grabbed Willie's hand, and dragged him to the dance floor. She exploded into a wild lindy hop, a solo that had no real need of Willie.

Willie could hardly believe his good fortune. He looked at Josh, who shrugged at Minty's friend and offered his arm. She, because she was now alone and because Josh looked very sharp, accepted his hand, and moved with him to the dance floor. Willie turned his attention back to Minty, and for the rest of the evening she was all he saw.

Six months of pent-up energy erupted in him. He grabbed Minty's hand and went with her and the music into frenzy.

They danced until the club closed, and between dances they drank cocktails all at Willie's expense. If Minty and her friend had been pretending to be ladies, that pretense vanished with the liquor; they laughed and joked and swore like warehouse laborers. None of this mattered to Willie. He had forgotten to pretend that he was "fresh in from the country," but Minty didn't seem to mind, all she wanted was a good time, like Willie, and he was having that.

Later, Josh took them to a jazz club, in a smoky, sweaty, crowded basement. They drank some more and listened to great music, and Minty, because space was scarce, sat on Willie's lap. The air was filled with a smell unfamiliar to Willie, and then Josh offered the women a drag from a long cigarette, and Willie realized the smell came from that. When Josh passed the joint to him, Willie accepted. He didn't smoke, but he was having a good time, and anything was possible this night. The cigarette made him choke and cough, but then that passed and Willie felt supremely, lazily happy. He began moving his hips against Minty, gently but in time to the music, and she snuggled back and pushed against him, and time was irrelevant, the pulse of the music was everything.

Later again, when they left the jazz club, they wandered the streets for a while, each couple arm in arm. Josh led them to a dark back alley, where Minty took Willie to the darkest corner and kissed him, thrusting her tongue deep into his mouth. Opening herself to him, she gave him something he had never had before, and guided him to ecstasy.

It was only when Willie was alone in bed, drifting into a sublime sleep, trying to recall each moment of the pleasures of that night, he realized that from the moment Josh had first spoken to him, he had not thought once of Ernestine.

22

*E*RNESTINE PUT WILLIE'S LETTER ASIDE, and tried
to work out how she felt. She had written to him two
weeks previously, telling him of the coming service and
suggesting that Flora would be thrilled if Willie was there.
She did not think he would agree.

She was wrong. Willie was coming home.

He had been in Chicago for four years. For each of
those years Ernestine had thought, had hoped that he
would return, if only for a vacation, if only to see his
mama, but for each of the first two years he wrote saying
that he had hoped, planned to come back, but "somethin's
come up." In his letters of the last two years he had not
mentioned the subject. Indeed, during the last year, he had
hardly written to Ernestine at all.

She was hurt, but she wasn't surprised. When he first
went away, she was too young to worry about their separation. They had grown up together almost, had known each
other since school. Other boys left school to go to work,
but Willie stayed on, and they became friends. They
drifted, slowly, casually to more than that, and the first
time Willie asked her to go out with him, it seemed natural
to Ernestine. They got on well, they had fun together, they
were easy together. She could shout at him, or stomp her
foot, or even hit him, and it didn't affect their relationship
because they were used to seeing each other every day, in
every kind of mood.

The first time Willie kissed her, it was no major jump
for Ernestine; it was a natural extension of what they already had, the display of a new if unfamiliar mood. There
was never a point when they decided to go steady, they had
always been going steady, and dances and movies and

sodas at Pop's Place simply replaced the things they had done as children.

She did not fall in love with Willie. She drifted to love, without any awareness of where she was going; only, when he left, that she was there.

She was the first person to whom Willie had voiced his desire to go to Chicago, and that ambition seemed natural to her as well. She did not think it would change their relationship, because nothing else ever had, and she had no experience of separation from him.

Looking back on it, Ernestine realized she had been naive. The whole basis of their relationship was that they had always been together; being apart was bound to make a difference.

This realization came slowly to her. At first, he wrote regularly. If his early letters were short, they were full of sweet endearments, and heartfelt. As the months went on, his letters became longer, a recitation of the events in his life, and they were filled with a sense of loneliness, and longing. She could see him clearly, in her mind's eye, sitting in his room every night, alone, writing to her, with no friends, nothing to do, nowhere to go, and her heart ached for him. She longed to be with him, and thoughts of a vacation in Chicago filtered into her mind. It wasn't realistic, she couldn't afford it, and she doubted that her parents would let her go, but the dream of the journey, and of being with Willie, was sweet to her. She did not tell Willie of her plans.

Ernestine left school and got a job at the Lanier Drapery, and working life, and functions at the church, brought her into contact with other young men. Several of them asked to take her out, but Ernestine declined all their offers and stayed loyal to the man she loved.

The church had been rebuilt since the fire, and Ernestine saw Flora there every Sunday, and always spent a little time chatting with her and Ruthana. Flora's conversation was mostly a recitation of Willie's welfare in Chicago and from what she said, Ernestine realized that Willie was lying to his mother. His letters to her were short and always cheerful, telling her how well he was doing.

Ernestine also visited Flora at least once a week, making sure to take some little gift—a cake, or some sweet-smelling soap, or a lavender bag she had made. Flora was always pleased to see her, if only to talk about Willie. She missed her son dreadfully, but put a brave face on her pain at his absence.

But one day, when Willie had been away for about six months, Flora was in tears. Ernestine hugged her and asked what was wrong, but at first Flora would not say. Ernestine tried to cheer her up, by telling her some funny thing about work that Willie had mentioned in his letter.

"He workin', he all right fo' money," Flora said suddenly. Ernestine wasn't sure if it was a question.

"Yes, he working at the warehouse," Ernestine said, puzzled. "He doin' good."

Flora sniffed, as if she didn't believe it. "Then why don' he pay what he owe?"

The truth came tumbling out. Hank, the bookie, had visited Flora and told her that Willie owed him twenty dollars, a gambling debt unpaid when Willie left.

"Gamblin'!" Flora almost spat the word out. "My boy gamblin'!"

She glared at Ernestine.

"You know that? You know he gamble?"

Ernestine blushed. She did know that Willie gambled, and she understood why he hadn't told his mother.

"Well, a little bit," Ernestine said. "I'm sure it's not much."

"Twenty dollar ain't a li'l bit," Flora snapped. "Twenty dollar a lot."

She dabbed at her eyes.

"That boy go to the devil, he not careful," she said.

Her prophecy appeared to come true. Willie began writing about a new friend, someone called Josh, who was, Willie said, "sharp." He wrote of the fun he was having on Saturday nights, going to movies and dance clubs with

Josh. He said that he had danced with a few girls, but only to dance, none of them meant anything to him, and that he still loved Ernestine.

The first small pangs of jealousy began to smolder in Ernestine's heart.

His letters became less frequent and less regular. At first, they had come once a week, like clockwork, a constant of her existence. The first time a letter did not come, Ernestine fretted, and worried that Willie was sick. She did not tell Flora.

He did write, a week after that, with a small apology. He said he had been especially busy at work, doing a lot of overtime. He needed the money to pay for the new suit he had bought. A zoot suit, he called it, and he tried to describe it to Ernestine, but she could not imagine it.

The next day, at work, she was gossiping with her friend Clara, who was two years older, and mentioned the zoot suit. Clara's eyes bulged, and she giggled. She found a magazine that had a photograph of a young man wearing such a suit and showed it to Ernestine.

Ernestine stared at the photograph in wonder. She could not imagine Willie so stylishly dressed.

Clara told her she was out of touch with the times. All the sharp dudes, the black dudes in the big city wore zoot suits, and went to dance clubs and jitterbugged.

"Get with it, girl," Clara said. "You wanna keep Willie, you gotta get with it."

Ernestine took the magazine home, and studied the photograph in the security of her room. It had been taken at a dance, and in the background she could see several young women staring at the zoot-suited model. It was those women who worried her, more than the suit. They were wearing dresses that slightly shocked Ernestine—very modern—with skirts almost above the knee and tops that revealed more than they covered. They looked like whores.

Ernestine put the magazine down and stared at

nothing. If Willie was going to dance clubs with such women, there was probably a whole lot more than dancing going on.

Willie didn't write again for a month, and then it was more of a note than a letter, telling her that everything was fine, and he'd write more later. He was busy, he said. He did write again, as promised, but it was only a page, and although he said he missed her, he did not write of love.

That fall, the zoot suit came to Stockton. Dave Lanier, Tom's son, Pete's brother, went to Chicago with his wife, Bess, for a two-week vacation. Dave left in his gray Sunday serge and came back a bright red peacock.

He wore the suit at a frolic on a Saturday night. Ernestine was there with Clara, and Clara's steady, Andy.

When Dave arrived with Bess, the crowd fell into awed silence, and then began chattering about the only thing that mattered in all the world at that moment, Dave's and Bess's clothes.

Dave was in scarlet. His jacket was long and flowing. The trousers ballooned at the knees, then tapered sharply to tightness at the ankles. He wore a huge scarlet hat with a long piece of chiffon draping from it, and several gold chains around his neck and wrists.

Bess wore a short-cut dress of shimmering shot taffeta, a gaudy greeny blue, and enormously high heels.

The piano player began thumping out a fast tune, swing. Dave led Bess to the middle of the floor and spun her into a dance, learned in Chicago.

They jitterbugged.

The crowd went wild, cheering and clapping, and talked of nothing else for a week afterward. Stockton was used to energetic dancing, the lindy hop, the shag, and even variants of the old black bottom, but this was different. This was modern. This was wild. This was funky.

They had seen brief examples of it in newsreels at the movie house, but then the dancers were always white. They had never seen any of their own jitterbugging. They were not slow to learn. After a small, awed silence, a couple of young men led their women to the floor and burst into energy. But Dave and Bess were the stars.

Although Ernestine had cheered the dance, and even admired the clothes, something she heard worried her. Dave, whose family had money, had made no secret of how much his suit had cost, and it was being whispered among those watching the display. Ernestine was shocked. If it was true, and if Willie had bought such a suit, he must be doing very well in Chicago.

But he told her, in his letters, city life was expensive and he was always broke.

And he never sent Flora a dime.

Ernestine wrote to Willie, telling him about Dave's suit and how much it had cost. Obviously, she wrote, Willie was doing well.

Willie didn't reply for three months. When he did write, there was no mention of clothes or dances or even of Josh. What he wrote was a confession, begging Ernestine's forgiveness.

He had been with a white woman, he said. He didn't intend to do it, he was drunk, at a dance, and the devil white woman had seduced him. It was the only time he had not kept faith with Ernestine, he wrote, and it would never happen again. He was telling her because he wanted to be honest with her.

He said he would understand if Ernestine dumped him because of it, but he prayed that she would not. She was the only woman he loved, and he longed to be with her again.

A dozen emotions pounded at Ernestine's heart. Anger hit her first. She wanted to tear the letter up, burn it, and write to Willie telling him to go to hell, but she didn't. She did roll the paper into a ball and fling it across the room, and she did say a few words that she had heard others use but she had not said before. She threw a couple of cushions across the room too, but even as she threw them she made sure they wouldn't break anything.

Disappointment was anger's constant shadow, and because she was disappointed in Willie, she cried. She wasn't foolish enough to imagine that Willie was still a virgin, although she was keeping her virginity safe, as a gift for him, but she didn't want to know about his amorous adventures.

She felt insulted, but only briefly. She was puzzled that she wasn't more hurt. She loved Willie, and the fact that he hadn't kept faith with her should have been painful, but she kept coming back to anger. And then to something else. She wondered why Willie had told her.

He could have kept it secret from her, and she would never have known, so why had he confessed? She didn't believe that the experience had been so shocking to Willie that he had forsworn all women but her. She didn't believe his claim that he had been seduced. Ernestine didn't know much about men, but she knew some. She knew that the word "no" didn't come easily to men, where women were concerned, and the idea of innocent, zoot-suited Willie being set upon by some predatory white woman didn't jell in her mind, however drunk he was. Or claimed to be.

Mostly, she was intrigued by his phrase "I'll unnerstan if'n you dump me."

Was that it? Had Ernestine become an encumbrance to Willie, part of his past that he wanted to be rid of? Was the confession designed to make her break with him?

Was he cutting Stockton, and his past, out of his life? Was he never coming home again? But if that was true, why did he keep writing? It would have been easier simply not to write.

Before Willie went to Chicago, he'd ventured over to the white side of Stockton and had his photograph taken at Dunbar's Portrait Studio. Cheaply framed, he'd given one to this mother and one to Ernestine.

Ernestine looked at his photo now. If Willie was trying to provoke Ernestine into breaking up with him, he was going to be disappointed.

"Uh-uh, sweetheart," she told Willie's photograph. "It don't work like that. Not wit' this girl."

She thought about her reply, and whether she would reply, for some time. On several occasions she began writing to him, but it was never what she wanted to say, and she tore each letter up.

About a month later she was at choir practice, and Pearl introduced a new choir—and church—member to them, Jack Frawley.

Jack was about Willie's age, not as handsome as Willie, and not as tall or strong, but he was good-looking and genial, and he had a shy smile that touched Ernestine. After practice, she introduced herself to Jack. He and his parents were recently moved to Stockton, from Muscle Shoals, a small town in Alabama. Jack's father had offended his white boss, had been sacked, and work was hard to come by there. They'd crossed the river, looking for work and somewhere pleasant to live, and had found both in Stockton.

They talked again, after church on Sunday, and Jack introduced Ernestine to his parents. The following Wednesday, after choir practice, Jack asked Ernestine to join him for a soda at Pop's Place, and she agreed. She found that she enjoyed Jack's company, and certainly he was taken with her. They drifted into an easy, casual friendship, occasionally going to the movies, or to dances, and although Jack kissed her every time he took her home, and suggested more than that, it was never serious between them.

Ernestine didn't tell Willie this. At last, she knew what to write. She did not refer to his confession, or white women, or faithfulness in their relationship. Instead, she wrote cheerily of her life, and of all the fun she was having, and of the several young men, including Jack, with whom she went dancing.

She didn't hear from Willie for three months, and began to wonder if she had done the wrong thing. Perhaps she should have accepted his confession at face value, and written back protesting her love and forgiving him his wrongs, and telling him that she understood the temptations that awaited a young man in the big city, especially from white women.

Or perhaps she should have done as he hinted and broken off with him, ended their relationship. The trouble with that was, she wasn't sure what their relationship was.

His letter, when it came, said exactly those things that, in her heart of hearts, she hoped to hear. His life was full, work was going well, Josh was a good friend, and they went out to dance clubs every Saturday. But only to dance, he insisted. He swore there was no woman in his life. Oh, a few friends at the dance clubs, but no one serious.

He was pleased that Ernestine was having a good time, he wrote, pleased that she was going out and enjoying herself. And he hoped that she wasn't getting too keen on this Jack. Ernestine was young, he said, with no experience of men, and she should be careful.

And he told her how much he loved her.

Ernestine was thrilled, because she still loved Willie. Or the memory of Willie, the idea of him. She wasn't sure how long she would continue to feel this way because if it was ever going to lead to anything, they had to be together, and the one thing Willie didn't say was that he was coming home.

She was also sensible enough to realize that Willie, by admission no longer a virgin, probably did have girlfriends with whom he was doing a great deal more than dancing, but she didn't feel jealous anymore.

They had given each other the freedom to get on with their lives, sure in the knowledge that whatever their relationship was, it was proceeding in the only way it could. What was critical was that they should have a relationship.

Soon after that, war broke out in Europe. Germany attacked some other countries. It caused a small fuss in Stockton, and a few young men talked about joining the army and going away to fight, but that was only the hot blood of bored youth talking. There was no evidence that

America would become involved in that war, or any reason why it should.

Then odd things began to happen in Stockton. Cars arrived with gray-suited white men, who looked at vacant land and surveyed it, then got into their cars and drove away. A week later, another car would come, with more surveyors.

Rumor ran like wildfire. Ernestine first heard the news from Clara, at work.

"Gub'mint's lookin' for land to build a factory," Clara said. "Makin' guns."

A variant of this was confirmed by Clara's boyfriend, Andy, at Pop's Place. The government was to build a factory at nearby Millington, not to make guns, but to manufacture explosives. For bombs.

It was the talk of the town.

"Man, is you gone crazy?" Ernestine's father, Albie, said to Brother Henderson. "You know good as I do there ain't nothing to Millington but a filling station, two stores, an' a few houses."

"I knows that," Brother Henderson replied. "All I'm tellin' is what I heard."

Deacon Sanford had another rumor.

"I done heared somethin' crazier than that," he announced. "I hears they gon' build a place to fly and land airplanes, jes' outside a' Halls. An' Halls sho' ain't nowhere to build nothin'."

The men fell into shocked silence.

Then Jack's father offended his white boss and was sacked. Ernestine thought that obviously he had a habit of doing this. She and Jack said a tearful farewell, amorous but not passionate, and Jack left with his family for somewhere else.

Ernestine drifted into a pleasant life. Old Tom Lanier died, and neither Pete nor Dave, his sons, was interested in the store. It was sold to a man from Memphis, who closed the shop for a few weeks, repainted and reorganized it, and reopened it as Lady Blue. It was a shop for the modern black woman, he proclaimed, Ernestine and Clara both kept their jobs, and enjoyed this challenge of new ideas, pleased that they could consider themselves "modern women."

"Stockton's looking up," Clara said with satisfaction.

A week later, the longest freight train anyone had ever seen moved slowly along the railway line through Stockton. The old men sitting at the depot watching the world go by stared in amazement. The front engine was passing them, but they could not see the end of the train.

They told some boys to tell the world, and the boys ran off, announcing the spectacle to the town.

People stopped what they were doing and walked quickly to the rail depot to watch the train. It seemed to go on forever and had four locomotives at intervals between the freight cars. Each of the flatcars held odd shapes, covered in olive green canvas tarpaulins.

Ernestine was there with Clara, on their lunch break. Andy, who worked at the cotton gin, joined them.

"Them's guns," Andy said of the odd shapes on the flatcars. "Bully White tol' me, an' he done be in the army, so he knows what a gun looks like."

Albie had walked from the service station to watch the train.

"An' what ain't guns is trucks," he said.

"But what's it all for?" Ernestine asked. Deacon Sanford heard her.

"I jes' axed the stationmaster," he confided, as if he had state secrets. "He say he cain't say too much, but that's a gub'mint army train on the way to Louisiana. He cain't say no more'n that."

It didn't answer Ernestine's question, and it worried her. Why was the army making such preparations? America was not at war.

She wrote and told Willie about it, but he did not mention it in his reply.

Ernestine wrote regularly, if not often, to Willie, and he occasionally replied. She went out, sometimes, with young men, as dancing companions mostly, but found no one who filled her heart, because someone else was already there, and in the way.

She still visited Flora once a week, and helped Ruthana with her studies as much as she could. She sang in the church choir, loved Jesus, and helped out at all the church functions and fund-raisers. Her older sister married, and Ernestine was maid of honor, and caught the bouquet when it was thrown, but no man presented himself to her for serious consideration as a husband.

One Sunday morning, in late September, Reverend Jackson made an announcement that pleased her. Sister Flora was to be honored as an Old Sister.

Ernestine hugged Flora afterward, and saw the pleasure in Flora's eyes. And a curious sadness.

Ruthana told her why.

"She want Willie there," Ruthana said. "She wants him to be there when she made Ol' Sister. But she too proud to ask him."

Ernestine hadn't heard from Willie for some time, but that night she wrote to him, telling him of the honor that was to be accorded to his mother, and that it would please Flora is he was there.

She was surprised and pleased when he wrote back promptly, saying that he was coming home.

23

ALBIE, ERNESTINE'S DAD, was a motor mechanic. He had worked for Caleb Brandon all his life and, over the years, had acquired the reputation of being a wizard with automobiles, from the early, rickety Model T's to the modern, enormous, elegant sedans. Albie had acquired his skill by working on the trucks and farm vehicles that were owned by the few blacks who could afford them, keeping them going long beyond their natural life.

As word of Albie's remarkable ability with engines spread through Stockton and the surrounding district, increasing numbers of white men brought their prized possessions to Brandon's Service Station, and entrusted them to Albie's care. Until recently, because whites were the only ones who could afford good cars, they were the majority of Albie's customers, but he always found time to work on a farm truck owned by a brother. Then, when Pete Lanier bought a smart new Chrysler, Albie became the guardian of its mechanics, and now a number of blacks in Stockton owned cars, more than Albie could handle. He persuaded Caleb to take on Andy, Clara's boyfriend and a budding engineer, as his apprentice.

Albie had not owned a car himself until Ernestine was about fifteen. He could not afford it, he said, but then he had the opportunity to buy an Oldsmobile that had been wrecked in a crash. He kept the vehicle in a corner of Caleb's garage, and had spent several years restoring it to perfect working order and lustrous condition.

It was the joy of his life, but he seldom drove it. It was too precious to him, and, work on it never completely finished, he said, there was always something more to do. He often pretended to drive it, though. Alone at night in the garage, working late, Albie would sit in his precious car and drive it over imaginary roads. He rarely turned the engine on, but made vrooom, vrooom noises, and he was happy.

He did use the car when Henrietta, Ernestine's sister, got married, and its appearance in public, in daylight, caused quite a stir because it was beautiful. It glistened and gleamed and hummed with vrooom, vrooom life. The wedding done, it was returned to the garage, and used again only on very special occasions.

This night was one such occasion. Willie was coming home, but Albie did not use the car for Willie's sake. It was a treat for Flora, because of the great honor to be accorded to her.

And for Ernestine.

Albie did not understand the complexity of his daughter's feelings for Willie, and did not approve of Willie's prolonged absence, but he knew that she cared deeply for the man. If Willie was coming home from Chicago in triumph, Ernestine would meet him with as much fanfare as Albie could muster.

Willie was coming in on the night train, arriving about an hour after midnight. Albie and Ernestine drove to Flora's house, causing quite a fuss in the little street, which saw few cars and none as grand as this.

Flora was dressed in her Sunday best, as was Ruthana, who was only thirteen but had been allowed to stay up late. Flora sat in the back with Ruthana as they made their way to the depot, nodding imperiously at the few passersby that stopped to admire the vehicle.

At the depot the women waited in the car, and Albie put the hood up and checked the engine, until they heard the train coming.

Then Flora could not restrain herself. She had been edgy with anticipation since Ernestine told her of Willie's impending return, and this had built to an almost palpable tension.

"He comin'," she said, scrambling out of the car. "My boy comin' home."

Ernestine was oddly moved, and fascinated. She was pleased that Willie was coming back, excited and nervous, but Flora's emotion was so much greater, grander, the love of a mother for a missing son. Ernestine wondered if it was ever thus, if she would feel the same way when she was married and had boys, and some instinct deep inside her told her yes.

But what of girls? Of daughters? Of Ruthana?

Ernestine thought of her relationship with her parents, and her sister's. She knew her parents loved them both, beyond any question were proud of them, doted on them, obsessed with their safety and welfare, but would she and Henrietta have taken second place if there had been a brother?

So how did Ruthana feel? Ernestine knew Ruthana's true history, that she was Flora's niece, not daughter, Willie's cousin, not his sister, and although Ruthana always called Flora her mama, and knew no other family, and although Flora clucked over Ruthana like a mother hen, was there a missing component of love in Ruthana's life?

A great affection for Ruthana swept over Ernestine, sisterly, as someone to nourish and cherish, as Henrietta had cherished her younger sister. She put her arm around Ruthana as they waited for the train, and sensed gratitude.

The train chugged to a halt, steam belching from it, then the steam cleared and Willie was there.

"Oh, my Lawd," Albie murmured, and looked at his daughter, wondering what her reaction would be. Ernestine said nothing, and her expression betrayed nothing of her feelings, but Ruthana giggled.

The Willie that stood before them was not the Willie who went away.

The departing Willie was a simple, pleasant, country youth who melded into a crowd. The arriving Willie was a slick, sophisticated city man, who stood a long way out from the masses and looked, Albie thought, slightly ridiculous.

He wore a tangerine-tan zoot suit. The coat pinched at his waist, but then flared wide over his knees. His shirt was bright canary yellow, with a limp, long collar. He wore a pluming, brilliant orange tie. The trousers were fully thirty inches around at the knees, tapering radically to ankle-hugging cuffs. A long, imitation-gold linked chain looped under the coat. His shoes were yellowish-orange Florsheims, with paper-thin soles and sharply pointed, up-bent banana toes.

His hat was enormous, dark orange, Big Apple felt, with a swooping brim and an enormous feather in the hatband. The several rings on his fingers, and his huge, glass-toned cuff links, glittered, competing with the starry night.

But whatever Flora thought of his appearance, all she saw was Willie.

She moved slowly toward him as he sashayed toward her and then he swept her into his arms, picking her up from the ground, holding her, hugging her, and swinging her around.

As Ernestine watched this reunion, she had a small revelation. The exterior Willie was all big city, but as he hugged his mama the simple Willie broke through, and Ernestine saw that he was relieved to be home.

Flora was crying, and Willie laughed, tears in his own eyes, and put her down, and told her not to be silly, not to cry, that he was home. Then he turned to Ernestine and took his hat off.

"Oh, my Lawd," Albie said again, to no one in particular. "What that boy done done?"

Willie's hair, which had been close-cropped tight curls, was now a shining mane, straight and glossy black, swept back into a ducktail curl.

Ernestine could not keep from laughing as she moved into his arms and kissed him.

"What you done to yo' hair?" she giggled.

"It conked." Willie grinned. "Ain't it sharp?"

Ernestine did not hear pride or happiness in his voice. She heard a need for approval.

"It different," she said, laughing. It was the best she could manage, and she saw, from the look in his eyes, that it was not enough.

Willie turned to Ruthana, who was waiting patiently at the edge of the reunion. Ruthana was always on the edge of things.

"My, Ruthana," Willie said warmly. "Ain't you growed."

He gave her a hug. Then he whispered something to her, something private that pleased her beyond all possible measure.

"I seen yo' pappy in Chicago," Willie said softly. "He sen' you his love."

It wasn't true. George had hardly mentioned Ruthana in Chicago, and Willie had not seen George for over three years, but it was a kindness, kindly done, and it meant the world to Ruthana.

"What he like?" Ruthana whispered. "My pappy?"

Ernestine was shocked. It had never occurred to her that her absent father might mean so much to Ruthana. She hoped that Willie would tell the girl what she needed to hear, and was thrilled when he did.

"Yo' pappy?" Willie said. "He a good man, a hard-working man."

He paused for a moment as if not sure what to say, and then found the right words.

"He golden," he said. "Jus' like sunshine."

Ruthana's lip trembled and she could not prevent a tear welling into the corner of her eye. She looked away.

Willie shook hands with Albie and called him sir, and Albie drove them home to Flora's house. They all went in to see Willie settled.

"You in yo' ol' room," Flora said. "Ruthana sleepin' wit' me."

She turned to Ruthana. "Time you was in bed, chile," she said.

Ruthana longed to stay and talk to Willie, to find out about life in Chicago, to hear all the things this glittering creature had done, and, especially, about her father, but she did not argue. She never argued. Dutifully, she said her good nights and went to Flora's room.

Willie took his suitcase to the closed-in porch that was Ruthana's room now, and Ernestine went with him. The structure of the room had not changed, but there was evidence that it was a girl's domain, with photos cut from magazines and a frilly pillow on the narrow, uncomfortable cot.

"Good to be home," Willie said.

"You bin away a long time, Willie," Ernestine replied.

"Yars," Willie said. He looked around the room. "Too long, mebbe."

He came to Ernestine and put his arms around her. He kissed her, and even his kiss was different, aggressive and experienced. Ernestine submitted to his embrace, even though she wasn't sure she liked being kissed by this man she didn't know.

Willie ended the kiss and looked into her eyes, and Ernestine had another small revelation, although she wasn't sure what caused it.

"Much too long," he whispered.

She didn't think that Willie liked the man he had become.

24

WHEN ERNESTINE AND WILLIE CAME BACK into the sitting room, where Albie was talking to Flora, her dad said it was late, time to go home.

Willie had taken off his jacket and tie and settled in his old chair. If Flora had any negative reactions to his appearance, she did not voice them.

"Does my heart good to see you sittin' there," Flora murmured.

Ernestine longed to know what was said between the mother and the son when they were alone, but over the next few days, whenever she talked to Willie and asked him how he felt about being back, Willie simply shrugged.

" 'Tain't easy" was all he would say. "Wit' Ma. It ain't easy."

Albie took them to church, the regular Sunday morning service, in his car, and Willie's return to the fold was a triumph.

The church had been rebuilt after the fire, a labor of love by all the congregation, with donations of money and timber, some by a few members of the white community who had been appalled by the arson, and even a little ashamed that the destruction of the church might have been caused by whites. Churches were sacred. Churches should not be part of any racial antagonism.

If any of the older members of the congregation were shocked by Willie's appearance, they did not voice displeasure, only pride at his evident success, and among the young he was a hero.

Willie wore another suit that morning, powder blue, and not as spectacular. He was saving his best, the tangerine tan, for the evening. Even so, the appreciation as he

walked up the aisle with Flora, Ruthana, and Ernestine
was vocal.

"Chile, you look like new money!"

"Willie, you sho' look like up Nawth!

"You look so *good*, son. Be sho' come by an' see us."

Any unease that Ernestine had sensed in Willie vanished. He strutted up the aisle, and as they took their
places in the row, he put his arm around Flora, a dutiful
and successful son returned.

Even Reverend Jackson referred to Willie's return, and
took as his text for the sermon the story of the prodigal son.

Ernestine thought this was a little tactless. She had
been taught at Sunday school that the prodigal son had
not done well when he was away from home, and had got
up to all sorts of mischief before returning to the bosom of
his family, but then she began to wonder if Reverend
Jackson had, unwittingly, hit on a truth that she herself
was starting to suspect.

If there was irony in the sermon it was lost on the rest
of the congregation, and the service was joyous, if not as
full-blooded as usual. The congregation was holding itself
in reserve for the evening.

After the service, Pete Lanier killed the fatted calf, or
half an ox, and gave a picnic in the yard behind the church
to celebrate Willie's return. Most of black Stockton, religious or otherwise, was there, all of Willie's old workmates
and school friends, and Isaac Dixon and Isaac Junior organized the barbecue for free.

Dave Lanier, who had not been at church, had heard of
Willie's zoot suit and wore his own. He and Willie greeted
each other like brothers in fashion, but Ernestine thought
that Willie's suit, however spectacular, looked shabby
compared with Dave's, and was obviously cheaper.

She was content to sit with her parents, and Flora and
Ruthana, leaving Willie to catch up on old friendships.

Flora's eyes never left her son. People came to her to
comment on Willie's obvious success, and to them all
Flora gave a similar reply.

"He look good, don' he?"

Or:

"My boy done good up North. I allus knew he had it in him."

It was fall, and the warm day drifted into a pleasant afternoon. Willie came and sat beside Flora for a while. His mama took his hand and held it, kissed it once, and did not seem to need to talk.

Reverend Jackson came by, with Deacon Sanford, and shook Willie's hand.

"It's wonderful, Willie, that you've come back fo' yo' mother's special day."

Willie looked embarrassed.

"I couldn' miss it, Rev'ren',' " he said.

Reverend Jackson looked at the crowd.

"It the goodness in people's hearts that *moves* you, on days like this."

"Hallelujah," someone said.

"The church fo'ever in yo' debt, Reveren'," Deacon Sanford added. "For startin' our Old Sister ceremony."

His heart full of Jesus, he kissed Flora's hand.

Albie offered to drive them home, to get ready for the evening service, but Willie suggested that he and Ernestine walk, and everyone nodded agreement and approval.

Conversation between them was not easy at first.

"Your mama sho' is pleased you back," Ernestine ventured.

"Yars," Willie said.

"I is too," Ernestine tried again.

Willie looked at her, as if needing reassurance.

"Is you?"

Ernestine nodded, and they walked in silence for a while.

"You like Chicago, Willie?"

"It the only place to be," Willie said, but there was no great joy in it.

Ernestine wanted to ask him more, she wanted to know the truth of his life there, because she was sure he was holding something back. But Willie offered nothing of consequence. They went to Pop's Place for a soda and a banana split. Willie had the admiration of everyone there because he looked so sharp.

"Looking forward to this evenin', Willie?" Ernestine asked after another silence between them.

"My mama be proud." Willie shrugged, his mind miles away. He wanted to say something, but hardly spoke. Deciding it was now or never, Ernestine took a stab in the dark.

"How's that friend of yours, Josh?" she asked.

It was exactly the right question, but Ernestine was shocked by the answer.

"Josh inside," he said. "Ten year."

Ernestine didn't exactly understand.

"Jail. Prison. The big house," Willie told her.

"Why?"

"Drugs. Dealin' drugs."

Ernestine knew next to nothing about drugs. She had heard that a few jazz singers were hooked on heroin, and a couple of times at dances she had smelled a sweet smell that Clara told her was grass, Mary Jane, "funny tobacco," but that was the extent of her knowledge. She wanted to know more but was scared to ask.

"I never done nuttin' with drugs," Willie said, his voice low. "Li'l bit Mary Jane, but nothin' heavy. Josh, he done everything."

Slowly, the story came out. Josh and Willie had become friends, a couple of young rams on the town. Willie had aped his hero Josh in everything.

"Got my hair conked." He grinned. "That hot lye nearly cooked my head. But it shine like glass!"

For a couple of years he had lived the high life. He began gambling heavily to pay his debts and had a long losing streak. His landlady, Lula, kicked him out and he moved into a pad with Josh, a filthy basement. He knew Josh was doing drugs, and he had experimented a little, but he didn't like losing control of himself to such a degree.

He hadn't touched his banana split. The ice cream was melting. He seemed to be waiting for another question, so Ernestine asked the obvious one.

"The white woman?"

Willie grinned shyly. "Wasn't her doin'. It was me, all me. Tore her up."

Ernestine looked away, and Willie was embarrassed that he had allowed his tongue to run.

"I don' mean to hurts you, Ernestine," he said. "But I been tellin' lies. To you, To Ma. To me. To everyone. I don' want a' tell any mo' lies."

He pushed the banana split away.

"The cops picked up Josh, he was dealin' heavy shit, I didn't know. He got ten years."

He looked out the window, and then back at Ernestine.

"I got no money, nuttin' to show for it. Ain't nuttin' I own paid for. All credick. That's how come I couldn' send nuttin' to my mama. Time I's paid my room rent and my credicks, and all the stuff I owe—I got nuttin'."

"Then why you goin' back?" Ernestine asked. "There's jobs here. The gov'ment's building a big factory at Millington."

The rumors had been true. The government was building an enormous explosives factory at Millington, and an airfield at Halls.

Willie wasn't convinced. "You think they gon' let colored folk work there?"

Ernestine didn't share his pessimism. In July, President Roosevelt, partly because of pressure by militant black unionists, had signed an executive order banning racial discrimination in defense factories. It had not yet been tested because the factory in Millington wasn't complete and hadn't started hiring, but, like so many others, Ernestine had faith in her president.

"Ain't supposed to make a difference, if'n it's gov'ment work," she said.

"You really b'lieve stuff like that?" Willie shrugged. "Ain't nuttin' fo' me here."

He took Ernestines' hand.

" 'Ceptin' you. I loves you, Ernestine. I cain't ax you to marry me, 'coz I ain't got nuttin' to give you, but I do loves you."

She knew what she was expected to say, but couldn't bring herself to say it.

"You loves me?" he asked her.

"I think I do, Willie," she said. "But what's the use? Me here, you there. An' I ain't goin' to Chicago. Not till you's got somethin'."

She saw hurt in his eyes, but she also saw determination.

"I do it," he said. "I swear I will. Leas'ways, I still got my job."

"Ain't someone there can help?" Ernestine wondered. "A friend—?"

"Ain't got no friends," Willie said bitterly. "Roun' here, you know ev'rybody, know ev'rybody's dog. A cow break loose, we know whose cow. Up there, they got 'point-ments. You cain't tell nobody jes', 'Well, I be by to see you,' you gotta be ev'rywhere at a certain time."

He looked so unhappy, so forlorn that Ernestine's heart quivered with love for him. She took both his hands in hers and squeezed them tight. She was younger than Willie by a year, but she felt years older.

"But I do it, I swear I will. Be easier now Josh not roun'."

Willie looked into her eyes, and now Ernestine saw a flash of hope.

"There be one man at work. Ab. He wit' the union. He got it all worked out. Mebbe I talk to him."

It was time to get ready for the evening service. Willie walked Ernestine home, and now that he had admitted the truth about his life in Chicago, he was easier, unburdened, if still not happy.

They stood outside Ernestine's front door, not wanting to part.

"Don't you tell Mama 'bout Chicago," he said. "She kill me."

Ernestine smiled, and promised she would not tell Flora, or anyone.

"I write," he said. "I promise. Jes' like the old days."

She nodded again.

"I loves you, Ernestine," he said in a sudden rush. He grabbed her to him and kissed her more deeply, more passionately than ever he had done, and she responded to him with love.

Albie took them to church in the car. Willie, oddly nervous, had changed into his tangerine-tan suit, which his mama had pressed for him. At the church, Flora left them to go in the back door, and the others went in the front.

The church was packed, but space was saved for Flora's family and friends in the front row. Again, people called out to Willie, appreciating this more vivid suit, and although Willie strutted to his seat, he whispered to Ernestine as he sat down, "Hope I don' got to say nuttin'."

The rostrum at the back of the church was hidden from view behind two large white sheets, makeshift curtains. Pearl went to the organ and began pedaling furiously, thumping out a hymn. The choir, at the side of the rostrum and in view, sang their praises of the Lord lustily, and then Reverend Jackson went to the lectern.

"Let us pray," he thundered. The congregation hushed and bowed their heads.

"Heavenly Father, we gather here today to render special honor to one of Your servants among us. She has served her God faithfully—"

"Amen," a voice concurred.

"—she has served her church faithfully—"

"Hallelujah! Ain't that the truth!"

"—she has served her community faithfully—"

"Praise the Lawd!"

"—an' she has served her family faithfully—"

"Yay-man!"

"In Thy son Jesus' name, we ask Thy blessings upon our presence and upon our purpose here this evenin'—"

"Bless us, Jesus, bless us, Lawd!"

"—and we beseech Thy continued blessings upon our dear sister *Flora Palmer!*"

"Amen! Amen! *Amen!*"

Two girls in white, offertory girls, each carrying a bou-quet of long-stemmed lilies, made their way up the aisle. They climbed the steps to the rostrum and put the lilies in vases on either side of the white sheet curtains.

Obviously nervous, and anxious to perform correctly something that had been carefully rehearsed, they went to the center of the sheet curtain and pulled on cords there, dragging the two sheets, suspended by hooks on a wire, apart.

Mama Flora was revealed behind the sheets, wearing only white, dress, stockings, and shoes. A corsage of tiny white roses was pinned to her dress. Her hair had been groomed by Pearl, and she wore a white headband.

She was sitting in the carved-wood, high-backed min-ister's chair, staring gravely, solemnly ahead.

The two flower girls sat on cane chairs beside her, flanking her in white.

"Sister Flora Palmer was not born in Stockton," Rev-erend Jackson began, "but since she came to us as a young woman, she has devoted herself to others."

He proclaimed the simple facts of Flora's life in Stockton, with especial reference to Booker, and then to Willie. If Willie took pride in this, he didn't show it; he looked at his feet, praying, Ernestine thought, that he would not be called upon to say anything.

"An' when her dear sister died, leaving behind a tiny child, Sister Flora Palmer took that child to her bosom and raised her as her own," Reverend Jackson continued. "An' I am happy to say that the girl chile, Ruthana, is with us here today as a young pillar of this, our new church."

There were shouts of approval. Ruthana looked around, her face solemn but interested. It was impossible to know what she was thinking. Ernestine never knew what Ruthana was thinking.

"All her life, Sister Palmer has served here among us, known throughout this town," Reverend Jackson was sweating, "an' *respected* throughout this town, as a good Christian woman."

"Praise the Lord!"

He beamed at his flock.

"An' it is our privilege here this evening to pay to Sister Palmer our church's highest honor of *Old Sister!*"

"Hallelujah!"

The preacher had done his part. It was the congregation's turn. Willie slunk even deeper into his seat.

"May we now have the testimonies?"

Deacon Sanford was on his feet at once.

"The *brethren* of this church have witness for *years* that when*ever* the help of church *sisters* was needed, that among the first always to come forward to put her shoulder to the *wheel*, has been *that sister*—"

He pointed dramatically at Flora, who sat impassive as a graven image, gracious as any sovereign accepting allegiance from her subjects.

"—Sister Flora *Palmer!* Settin' right up there!"

There were shouts of agreement and approval, and Pearl rose from her place at the organ. A chorus of parishioners urged her to testify.

"*Sister Pearl!* Yes! She know de truth!"

"Flora Palmer," Pearl cried, "every woman in this church, in her heart, cling to you like one of her own family!"

Flora's composure broke. She dabbed at her eyes with a small white handkerchief. Sister Pearl was deeply moved by the evident emotion, and by her own words.

"You visit anybody in this town that's sick, day or night, with a helping hand—"

Sister Pearl broke down, weeping.

"It too well known for me to need to say mo'," she

choked, and fell into the arms of Sister Jessie, who comforted her.

"It's hard to say what's in our hearts!" Sister Jessie shouted, weeping too.

All the sisters were united in joyous tears, sobbing audibly. The brothers provided a counterpoint of "Yaymans!" and "Hallelujahs!"

Everyone was having a great time, except for Willie.

Reverend Jackson took command, his voice hoarse with love.

"We have in our midst this evenin' a young brother of this church—"

"Oh, shit," Willie muttered. Only Ernestine and Ruthana heard him, and both of them grinned.

"—young Brother Willie Palmer, who is with us, to help us honor his mama, all the way from *Chicago*!"

The congregation was close to ecstasy, but Willie was on the edge of despair.

"*We ask him for his testimony!*" Reverend Jackson shouted, and it would have been impossible for Willie to decline.

Reluctantly, he stood up, still looking at the floor. Ruthana bent close to Ernestine and whispered in her ear.

"Bet he wishes he wasn't wearin' that suit," she giggled. Ernestine slapped her hand lightly, and shushed her, but deep inside agreed with Ruthana. In his tangerine finery, Willie was the focus of all attention.

"I ain't never knowed no daddy," Willie began, and stopped. And started again. "But my mama always tol' me the right things to do."

He stopped again. Words did not come easily to him.

"An' I ain't always done them!" Willie announced.

The crowd cheered in agreement. Confession of sin, especially in public, was good for the soul.

"Far back as I remember," Willie went on, "Mama was bringin' me to this church."

"Praise the Lord."

"She tried hard to keep me in school. She didn't want me to quit!"

"Ain't that the truth!"

Willie had a little head of steam going now. Ernestine watched him carefully, guessing he was going to justify himself.

"But I wanted to help her out! Mama needed help!"

"He heard the Lord!"

"An' I lef' home, lef' Mama by herself! But she been wit' me, whatever I done!"

"Hallelujah!"

Willie's steam ran out. He couldn't think of anything else to say. He looked around at the congregation, at the people he had known all of his life, and found inspiration there.

"I got a good mama! I know it! An' y'all know it!"

They knew it, and loved to hear it from a son, and their enthusiasm gave Willie the push he needed. He looked at his mama, who was still dabbing her eyes.

"God knows, I *love* you, Mama," he shouted at her, and abruptly sat down.

Ernestine was surprised to see tears in Willie's eyes, and reached over to him. Willie squeezed her hand gratefully, but kept his eyes to the floor.

He had done his best, but it was not quite enough. Reverend Jackson saved the day. Sensing an anticlimax, he leapt to feet.

"*Love*," he cried. "Ain't that the word? The *love* of a son for his mama. Ain't that the most beautiful thing in all the world? Look at him, brothers and sisters, his heart choked up so full he can only find one word to say what he's feelin'. An' that word is *love*."

He picked up his Bible and held it high in the air.

" 'An' now abideth faith, hope, and love, these three, but the greatest of these is *love*!' "

The congregation had what they wanted. Mama Flora wept. Pearl wept. The sisters wept. The choir wept. Some of the brethren choked up.

Even Reverend Jackson was moved.

"We'll all stand and join in song!"

It was an order not a request, and everyone, apart from Willie and, of course, Mama Flora, rose, and lifted their voices in song, led by the booming baritone of Reverend Jackson.

It was "Amazing Grace." At critical moments, at times of high emotion such as this had been, it was always "Amazing Grace."

Although Ernestine sang with the rest, her mind was going in other directions. "Faith, hope, and love," the Bible said, but that was not the original translation. Ernestine had studied the King James version because she loved the language of it, and in that book the three that abided were faith, hope, and charity.

It was charity that concerned her, because to her it meant kindness. It occurred to Ernestine that none of the white women who employed Mama Flora had bothered to come to pay tribute, or even just to be there, on Flora's day of days. She hadn't expected it, but it did happen, sometimes, at the Old Sister ceremony. And it would have been kind.

Albie drove them all to the railroad the next day, and Willie was in a good mood. It pleased Flora, although she wept when she said good-bye, and clung to him, not wanting him to go.

He kissed Ernestine and Ruthana and shook hands with Albie, then got on the train.

"I reckon he had a good time," Flora said, after waving a frantic good-bye as the train pulled away. "I reckon it done him good to be home."

"Yes," Ernestine said, taking Flora's arm and leading her to the car. "It done him good."

It was true. In some way, talking about his problems with Ernestine had helped Willie to resolve something, and she believed that he would change his life when he was back in Chicago.

She determined that she would write regularly, supportively, being honest with him, and urging him to success. But she would also be kind, she would be the lover that he wanted, needed, even if only at a distance. She would buy him a good Christmas present, and spent happy hours deciding what it would be.

Three months later, she and Clara decided to spent a day in Memphis to do their Christmas shopping. It was different, an outing, and they would be able to buy nicer gifts than were available to them in Stockton. It was also an adventure for Ernestine. She had never been to Memphis, but Clara knew the city well.

They did not go, because something happened that changed both their immediate plans and the future direction of all their lives.

*F*LORA WAS IN DESPAIR. The train on which Willie left was taking him straight back to hell.

She wept as she hugged him good-bye and clung to him, because she believed she would not see him again for many years, and never as himself. She tried to lie, to pretend to herself and others that his holiday had done him good, but it was no use. Willie had been happy that last day and never more so than when he got on the train and waved good-bye. He was returning to the damned City of the Plain, and glad to do so.

She was silent on the short car ride home, numb with grief, and scarce able to thank Albie and Ernestine for their kindness. In the house, she hardly heard Ruthana's small attempts at kindness, and said she was tired and was going to bed.

She went to her room, but not to bed. Alone, she took an old shoe box from the bottom drawer, where she kept it, and examined the contents, every letter Willie had ever written to her from Chicago. The record of his journey to damnation.

Lies, all lies.

The first time he went away, Flora had been miserable, and lonely when he was gone, but she had wanted him to go, for his own sake. He was a good boy and a hard worker, and despite the many temptations that awaited him in the city, she believed she had given him, through his faith in God, the strength to survive.

His early letters had been short and simple, but filled with positive news. George had been kind and he had a job and was lodging with Lula, a good Christian woman. The first indication that something was wrong came to her not from Chicago but from Stockton, when one of Lucifer's messengers arrived at her door, disguised as Hank, the bookie.

He wanted the money that Willie had gambled and lost.

It was shocking to Flora. She knew that Willie drank hard liquor with the men from work, and drinking was the first step on the road to evil, but all men did it, even some Christian men. Willie had gone farther down the path. If he was gambling in Stockton he was gambling in Chicago, and all her attempts to keep Willie from sin had failed.

She voiced her fear to Ernestine. She knew that the two wrote to each other regularly, and Ernestine's voice, added to her own, might bring Willie to reason.

"That boy go to the debbil, he not careful," she said.

She sent him the twenty dollars to pay Hank so that Willie would know she knew, and that it might shock him back to grace, but he did not mention the money, or the gambling, when he wrote to her again.

She thought of going to Chicago and beating sense into the boy, but she didn't think it would do any good; she did not have the strength to defeat Satan on her own and she would not tell anyone else of her son's shame, because it was her own as well.

She had failed as a mother.

This belief in her own failure nagged at her and festered and grew, because Willie was not the only example of her inadequacy. There was her firstborn son, whom she had allowed to be stolen away and delivered to a loveless life. The more she worried about Willie, the more she thought about that other son, and a dormant seed that had lain in her heart for years began to swell and burst into life, watered by her tears.

She wanted to see her other son, or know what had become of him.

The first tangible evidence that Willie was damned came to her a year later. Hank might have been all talk, the gambling debt a lie, but the photograph that Willie sent her of himself in his first zoot suit was the proof that demolished any small hope she harbored for her son.

No good Christian man would wear such a suit; it was the devil's armor, the uniform of the drinker, the gambler, and, she hardly dared admit it to herself, the fornicator. Willie had asked her to show the photo to Ernestine, but she did not, she could not show it to anyone. She wanted to burn the photograph, tear it to pieces, get rid of it, but she did not. She kept it hidden in a drawer, and each evening when she knelt to pray she took out out to show God, to alert Him that a soul was lost, and she begged Him to recover the boy.

In her letters to Willie, she hinted at what she knew. She suggested that she understood the temptations of the city, and hoped he was avoiding them. Perhaps this would bring him to reason, to confession, to a promise, if only for his mother's sake, that he would abandon his wicked ways. But in his letters to her he talked only of hard work and no money, and did not mention sin or redemption. It was clear to her that he was lying. If he was working so hard and leading a blameless life, why did he not have money?

Lies, all lies.

The worst of the Depression was over, but times were still hard for Flora because she was getting older. She had arthritis in her left hand, and winter caused her back to ache with lumbago. Her ulcer, which had been quiet until Willie went away, flared again. She was going through the change of life, and menopause brought its own complications of unwanted depression and anxiety. Her reproductive life was over, and all she had to show for it were two lost sons and a girl child who wasn't her own.

It was only that girl child, Ruthana, who gave her reason to go on. She was hard on the girl, harder than she had ever been with Willie, but she persuaded herself it was for Ruthana's own good. If Flora's life had any meaning it would be in Ruthana. Happily, she had no need to force Ruthana to schoolwork; the girl was a natural study and loved learning, her head always stuck in a book. The idea of Ruthana going to college, which had begun as a silly, impossible dream, now took hold with a vengeance, and Flora mentioned it at least once a week, and sometimes every day.

But a college degree was not, in itself, enough. A woman's mind was not her problem in life, it was her body. Flora did not allow Ruthana a single vanity. She did not have a pretty frock, not even for Sunday, her dresses were all drab, she wore no ribbons in her hair. As Ruthana came to her own change of life, to puberty, Flora, as her own mama had done, told her the blunt truth of it and where it would lead. It was a woman's curse, for with it came lust, and lust was the devil's business.

She did not allow Ruthana to go out, except on the laundry run or in Flora's company, or that of some other woman whom she trusted such as Pearl. She insisted that Ruthana, who did not sing very well, join the church choir, but on practice nights, Wednesday evening, she walked Ruthana to the church, or Pearl took her, and brought her home. She did not allow Ruthana to talk to boys, and her girlfriends were monitored with great care. She fed Ruthana well, perhaps to encourage the girl to unattractive plumpness, but would not allow her to finish any meal. Some small portion of the food always had to be left on the plate, no matter how hungry Ruthana was, to learn control.

And on every occasion that she could, she found some way to denigrate Ruthana's natural prettiness.

"You sho' is ugly, chile," she'd murmur. "Thank the Lord."

Yet Flora loved Ruthana, and through the difficult years of Willie's absence in Chicago, the girl gave her strength and purpose.

She loved Ernestine too, who was always kind. Ernestine came to visit at least once a week, and always brought some small gift with her, to make Flora's life easier. She trusted Ernestine and harbored the hope that Willie might yet come to his senses, return to Stockton and marry his childhood sweetheart. Because she trusted Ernestine, she allowed her to develop a friendship with Ruthana, and even, on occasion, to take her out, but only to places that Flora knew to be safe, such as social functions at the church.

The changing times, the snail-slow return of prosperity, hardly changed Flora's financial situation. Because of her arthritis, the laundry took her longer these days. Ruthana helped with the ironing and folding, but Flora never allowed her to do the actual washing. That was not to be Ruthana's future.

She had to give up some of her laundry customers. Cleaning houses was easier because she could set her own pace and take occasional breaks. Mrs. Hopkins, whose husband had recovered financially from the slump, asked Flora to work for her again, and Flora, against her better judgment and because she had few options, agreed. This brought her into contact with Kevin Hopkins, who was now a young man, Willie's age. The years had not mellowed him. Charming with his own kind, white folk, he was casually cruel to any black person he encountered, and Flora was no exception. He expected her to wait on him hand and foot, and never gave her thanks, only tiny, hurtful insults of her race. He called her the porch monkey.

In their dealings with blacks, the milk of human kindness ran sour in all the family, and Mrs. Hopkins was a mean employer. No matter how careful Flora was, Mrs. Hopkins always managed to find some corner that had not been dusted. If, because of her arthritis, Flora dropped and broke a cup or glass, it was paid for out of her miserable wages. And Kevin, if he was there, cussed and laughed and called her "stupid nigra."

Flora bore this like a cross, a penance she must pay for her own increasing sense of failure as a mother. Since God's hand was everywhere, there had to be a reason why Kevin was so cruel, and Flora thought it was to illustrate

the contrast with Willie, because, to his parents and to all
outward appearances, Kevin was everything a good son
should be. Handsome, hardworking, and successful, and
engaged to be married to a local beauty.

As always, Flora turned to God, and one day He was
kind. She was sitting in church one Sunday morning in late
summer hardly paying attention, scarcely involved. Her
mind was filled with worry, about herself and Willie and for
Ruthana. She sang the hymns without fervor. When other
women went into their customary hysterics of worship,
Flora did not join them, she was too tired. Only her faith in
God was not diminished, and she prayed with all her heart
that He might give her some relief, some small indication
of His purpose, and, once again, He answered.

Reverend Jackson announced that she was to be honored as Old Sister.

The honor itself was not what filled Flora's heart. She
took pride in it, but she felt it was well earned and long
overdue. It pleased her that her years of faithful service
were being recognized, but she saw in it a great opportunity. This would be a way to bring Willie home, and to lead
him to salvation.

She did not know how to go about it. His letters had
become fewer and less frequent, and never much more
than a grudging recitation of the hardness of his life. Her
letters to him had become prayers for his welfare and reminders of his Savior's love. There was no intimacy between them anymore, and she thought that if she asked
him to come home, even for this special occasion, he
would decline. So she mentioned it to Ruthana, who suggested it to Ernestine, who wrote and told Willie that he
should come home, and he did.

The news of Willie's impending return fell on Flora like
a benediction. Here was her chance to restore them both
to favor, he from his wicked ways, and she to prove, to
God, to herself, and to the world, that she was a good
mother.

But the moment she saw him at the depot, in his

tangerine-tan finery, doubt beset her, because what she saw was a sinner condemned to hell. She took him in her arms and wept for him.

She prayed, that night, for strength, but Satan was too strong for her. She told Willie, repeatedly, that it did her heart good to see him home, sitting in his old chair, hoping he would take the hint, but it only made him irritable.

She thought Reverend Jackson's choice of the story of the prodigal son for the Sunday morning sermon was brilliant. Willie was lost but could yet be found if he opened his heart, to the Lord and to Flora, but already the devil had revealed to her the depths of Willie's depravity. She had pressed his suit that morning, hating the gaudy thing and the evil it represented. She loathed his conk, she missed his tight curls; this straight hair seemed to her to be an attempt to deny his colored blood, to pretend that he was, however darkly, white. Then she found in the jacket pocket a small end of something that looked like a half-smoked, stubbed-out cigarette. Flora, who had no experience of these things, guessed it was not tobacco.

She did not confront Willie but took it to Pearl, that her fears might be confirmed. Pearl sniffed the roach and pulled it open with her fingernails, revealing a green substance.

"Drugs," Pearl said sadly. "Reefer madness."

Flora, who was already angry with Willie, became irritated with Pearl. Despite the many newspapers that Pearl read every week, how could she know?

"I seen a movie," Pearl said smugly. A few years previously there was a movie *Reefer Madness*, a cautionary tale of marijuana and the madness to which it led. Pearl had not seen it, but had read about it in her newspapers, and the debate surrounding it, and now considered herself an expert on the matter.

"Ain't nuthin' y'can do for him now," Pearl warned. " 'Ceptin' pray."

Flora did pray, but to no avail. At her Old Sister ceremony, Flora prayed so hard she almost went into a trance, but when Willie made his woefully inadequate testimony she wept, not tears of joy, but of grief.

The devil had given him impregnable armor against her. He resisted all her attempts, all her pointers to righteousness, but what puzzled her was that she knew, as mothers know these things, that he was bitterly unhappy in Chicago.

Finally, she had to confront him. On the Sunday night, his last night, she waited up for him. He came home late; he'd been out with Ernestine. She didn't smell liquor on his breath, but she did smell the cheap scent that Ernestine always wore. For a brief moment she hated Ernestine and wondered if she had seduced Willie, but then she saw a tiny light at the end of a long, dark tunnel, and it was Ernestine.

"You gon' marry that girl?" she asked. "She sho'ly loves you."

Willie shrugged. He had asked Ernestine to marry him that very evening, and she had declined.

"Be a good life," Flora said, trying to paint a happy picture of married life in Stockton. "Good jobs here now."

Willie didn't reply. He took his guitar from its case and began strumming it.

"Them Du Pon' chem'cals building a big fac'try in Millington," Flora continued. "Work for any man as wants it."

"Wouldn't want a' be the first nigro that goes for a job there," Willie said. "An' gits kicked out the door."

Flora sat in angry silence while Willie made sad music on his guitar.

"Then what you gon' do?" she exploded, unable to contain herself. "Go back to Chicago, an' drink yo'self to the debbil, wit' harlots an' gamblin'?"

Willie stopped strumming the guitar, but did not look at her.

"An' drugs," Flora added, the nail, she hoped, in Chicago's coffin.

But all she had done was to make him angry.

"Ain't nobody's business what I do," he muttered.

"Yes, 'tis," FLora cried. "It my business, you my boy, my baby—"

"I ain't yo' baby, not no more," he shouted. "I be a man, an' I be makin' my way in the world bes' way I knows how!"

"Makin' yo' way to hell," Flora shouted back. "On a 'spress train straight to hell!"

"You don' unnerstan', Ma," Willie said more quietly. "I done some wrong things, like I 'fessed up in church, but that be behind me now."

"Wish I could b'lieve that!" Flora was still angry.

"What you want from me, Ma? You wants I come back here an' work at the cotton gin all my days, an' end up wit' a busted back an' a broken heart? 'Tain't the way of things, not no more. 'Tain't what I wants to be."

"Better'n a wasted life a' sin," his mother snapped.

"I cain't come back, Mama," he said. "Mebbe I ain't done too good in Chi-town, but I gotta try. I ain't comin' home wit' my tail atween my legs, I ain't gon' go to Pete Lanier an' say, 'Well, I didn't make it in the big city, c'n I have my ol' job back?' That what you want me to do?"

"I wants you to go to heaven when you die!" she shouted.

He stared at her in astonishment and then did something that almost destroyed her. He became, before her eyes, his father. She saw the old, familiar twinkle of laughter in his eye.

"If'n the Lord made me, He know I ain't so bad," Willie said.

Even though she believed in God's infinite mercy, she wasn't convinced, but the argument frittered to trivia. She had laid herself open to him, told him she knew the worst of him and had shown him the way home, all to no avail. Pearl had been right. All she could do was pray for him.

Still, he was her son. Lost, he might yet be found, but it would need a force greater than she could muster.

Her ulcer flared, she lost her energy. There was only the pain in her stomach and her wayward son. She kissed him

and told him that she loved him and that no matter how
far he strayed from the Lord it was only a very short way
back, one tiny step to Calvary.

He told her that he loved her too, and not to worry
about him.

But how could she not worry? When she went to her
room Ruthana was asleep on the thin mattress on the floor,
but Flora could not sleep. She could hear him in the next
room, strumming on his guitar, and then he started to sing,
a soft, sad lament.

> *Bo'n in a cotton fiel',*
> *Raised on corn an' greens.*
> *My mama she a fiel' hand,*
> *My daddy I never seen.*
> *God know, I couldn't help it.*

The pain of it, to Flora, was that Willie was right. The circumstances of his life were not his fault, but her own.

She had been a bad mother, unable to save her sons.
She had sinned in the eyes of the Lord and she had to
make the sin right. Only then would Willie have a chance
of salvation.

26

*S*HE COULD NOT AFFORD TO TAKE TIME OFF WORK, so she had to leave on Friday night and come back at the latest on Sunday night. She did not take Ruthana with her, but sent her to stay with Pearl. She told Ruthana that she was going to visit a distant relation who was ill, someone who had been kind to Josie, Ruthana's mother.

She told Ernestine the same story. Ernestine volunteered to go with her, but Flora said no. Ernestine said she'd ask her father to drive Flora to the station, but Flora said no. She didn't want to make any fuss or bother about her going, and she lied to Ernestine, and told her she was leaving on Saturday morning, not Friday night.

Other than buying her ticket, she made no plans. Perhaps she hoped she would be greeted with hospitality, if not warmth, and offered accommodation on the Saturday night, or perhaps she dared not consider the alternative.

On Friday night she settled Ruthana with Pearl, then went home and packed a change of clothes in a small bag. She made some thin sandwiches, which she put in a brown paper bag. She wore her overcoat because the weather was turning cold. She walked the mile to the railroad and got there much too early. She sat on the bench marked COL-ORED ONLY and kept her head down, hoping no one she knew would see her.

At last the train came. She clambered into what she still thought of as the Jim Crow car. There weren't many passengers and she found a seat next to a window, although it was night and there was nothing to see.

Her mind was blank. She had no idea of what she would find when she got there, and the past was too painful to remember. She was tired, it had been a busy day, and Kevin Hopkins had been more than usually unpleasant. The repetitive sounds of the wheels and the gentle rocking of the car lulled her. She asked the conductor to make sure she was awake for her stop, and went to sleep. Blessedly, she did not dream.

She woke up before dawn. She sat staring out the window, watching the black night turn to indigo, then darkest blue, and then a strip of gray showed on the distant horizon, and nothing but flat land, cotton land, Delta land, before it.

With the light came memory. The fields were empty, harvested, and a familiar morning mist lingered. Outside the few shacks she saw field hands getting ready for the day. A man chopped wood, as she had done when young, when Gran'pa was too sick. A girl let chickens out of a coop, and threw dried corn for them, as she had done when young. She saw a young woman, poorly dressed, perhaps fifteen, standing near the rail tracks, staring at the train. She saw herself when young.

She was ready well before the train stopped, clutching her bag, and nervous, wishing she had made some plans, but not knowing what they could be. The conductor helped her from the train, and she stood in wonder and confusion, staring at the place she had left so many years ago, and never thought to see again.

The rickety wooden depot building had weathered some, but otherwise it had not changed, and she could not remember it, ever, freshly painted. She heard the train leave, but she could not move. She was fixed in a different time and did not know where to go, or what to do, for fear of what she might find.

She became aware that the station agent, a white man, was staring at her.

"What'cher doin', girl?" he said without kindness.

"Nuttin'," she said.

"Best do it, then." He shrugged and walked away, to close up the depot. There would not be another train for several hours. He was going home for breakfast, but he did not offer Flora a lift in his car.

She started walking down a road that had once been familiar to her, that would take her to a place that had once been home.

The station agent passed her in his car, but did not stop. Otherwise there was no sign of life, only a few crows in a field.

After about three miles she began to see things she remembered. A wooden shack, smoke rising from its stone chimney, was where it had always been. If Flora thought very hard she might be able to remember the name of the family that lived there, but then it seemed unimportant. She came to a turning and knew which way to go. There were more shacks, and a few people, but no one she thought she knew. Her pace quickened slightly. She was almost there.

It was deserted, falling down; no one lived there. She saw the old chicken run, but the wire was gone and the coop had been plundered for firewood. The floor of the porch was rotted and there was a broken rocking chair lying in the yard. For an instant, she saw her gran'pa rocking in that chair and tears sprang to her eyes, but she brushed them aside. It was the past, it was gone, and she would not waste tears on this, for they would have been a river and she still had much to do.

She turned away from the old shack and saw a man of about fifty on a buggy, staring at her. The horse was munching contentedly on grass at the side of the dirt track. Flora had the strangest feeling that she was, even against her will, being dragged back to a place where she did not want to be. There were no cars, no telephone lines, no streetlamps, nothing to suggest she was in her present day. Only a man on a horse-drawn buggy, and it was timeless.

"Y'ain't from these parts," the man said. He did not sound interested, but in the relentless boredom of his life, Flora was a distraction.

"Use to live here," Flora said.

"Lawdy, Lawd," the old man said. "Ain't anybody lived there since . . ."

He scratched his head and tried to remember.

"Ol' Maz' Yarborough war' gon' give it a' me," he said. "But it too big for me. I on my ownsome. I lives in that shack yonder."

Did she know him? She thought she did.

"You work for Maz' Yarborough?"

"Lawdy, Lawd, he dead now, pas' five year."

He looked at the sky, content to pass the time of day. He had nothing else to do.

"I work'd fo' him twenty year, 'til I did my back, humpin' cotton bales. Ol' Maz' was kind, he give me that shack yonder. I still do errans fo' the family."

"Who got it now, the Yarborough place?"

"Miz Ellen's man. She done marry well."

Ellen was one of the two Yarborough daughters, Flora couldn't remember which, if she ever knew.

"He brung in machines t' pick cotton, don' got much use for nigros," the man said.

She did know him, she was sure of it. She wasn't sure she wanted it to be him.

"Yo' name Charlie?"

He chuckled and wheezed.

"That be me," he said. "Who you?"

She stared at him, so old, so poor, so broken. Did she look so old?

"My name be Flora," she said.

He stared at her for the longest time, but he could not remember. He nodded at the shack.

"You lived there?"

"Wit' my gran'ma an' my gran'pa an' my mama."

"I 'members 'em," he said, with some relief. "Yo' mama, she sho' could pick cotton."

He remembered something else, but not Flora.

"There was a girl chile," he said. "But she warn' called Flora."

"Josie?"

A big smile spread across his face.

"Yars, Josie," he said, and then he chuckled. "We was goin' steady fo' a while."

"She my sister," Flora said. "She dead."

His smile faded.

"Right sorry to hear that." He looked at her, squinting his eyes.

"I don' 'member you," he said.

Why should he? Why should he remember that she used to bring him water in the fields? Why should he remember that once when he was young and strong he danced with a girl called Flora?

"It don' matter," Flora said.

"Why you come back?" he asked. He seemed relieved that the burden of remembrance had been taken from him.

"I's goin' to the Fleming place," she said. "I got business there."

"The Flemings?" Charlie chuckled. "Ain't too many got bizness there, not no more. Ain't nuttin' there."

Flora's heart sank.

"Nuttin'? No one?"

"Big house still there," Charlie said. He chuckled again. "Fallin' down, like yo' place yonder. An' ol' Miz Fleming still live there, on her ownsome since her man done leave her. Don' see too many folk."

He must mean Lincoln's mother, not his nana, Flora thought. But where was Lincoln?

"You wants a ride? Long ways to walk."

It was kind and Flora said so, but she didn't want to take him out of his way.

"Lawdy, Lawd." Charlie grinned. "I ain't got nuttin' else to do."

He helped her up onto the buggy and flicked the reins. The horse ambled away.

"Young Maz' Lincoln live wit' his mama?" Flora asked, as casually as she could.

Charlie looked at her, as if he wasn't sure what effect his reply would have.

"Maz' Lincoln dead," he said. He scratched his head. "N'Orleens, far as I 'member. Some trouble wit' 'nother man's wife. Never did hear the trut' of it, but Maz' Lincoln done got hisself kilt."

Flora's heart sang a small song. There was a God and He was just. But what of Lincoln's son?

"I hear'd there was a boy chile," she began, but Charlie was not listening.

"Jes' 'bout drove his mama plum crazy," Charlie remembered. "At the fun'ral she was screamin' and yellin', 'nuff to wake the dead."

He chuckled again.

"But the dead is dead; it don' wake Lincoln."

Flora let him ramble. It was coming together, piece by piece.

"Shut hersel' up in her room, won' see to no one, won't talk to no one, 'ceptin' li'l Maz' Luke."

Was that his name, Luke?

"Maz' Ol' Fleming done got sick of her. Sol' all the land to Maz' Yarborough an' took off fo' the high life. New York, they do say."

He was silent, as if that were the end of the story. Flora saw her chance.

"An' li'l Maz' Luke?"

"Stay'd wit' his gran'ma. Maz' Ol' Fleming din't want him."

Flora's heart skipped a beat.

"He there now?"

Charlie shook his head.

"Nuttin' here fo' him. He done go to college in Atlanta. Come home sometime, see his gran'ma."

They were passing the fields that once belonged to the Flemings. She could see the big house on the hill. She could get to the truth at last. Now she could know.

"Where his mama?"

Charlie stopped the buggy in front of the gate. He looked at Flora and grinned and winked.

"Li'l Maz' Luke ain't got no mama." He chuckled as he got off the buggy to open the gate. "Dey done find him in the cabbage patch."

He did have a mama, Flora wanted to scream at him, and his mama was me! But she didn't. She sat on the buggy staring at the house where her baby, Luke, had grown up in such unhappy circumstances. But she felt no grief, only joy that she had found him. Or, at least, could give him a name.

"Turn up one day, out a' the blue," Charlie said. "An' from the day he come, his gran'ma love him like he was her nat'ral-born son. Loved him mo' than she ever loved Maz' Lincoln. Ain't too many loved that fella."

He flicked the horse. They began moving slowly up the long drive to the house that Flora hated.

"She done call him Luke, from the Bible."

It was a good name. It was not a name Flora might have chosen, had she been given the chance, but it was a good name. But was Luke hers?

"He musta had a mama somewhere," Flora said.

"Yep, ev'ry boy got a mama somewhere," Charlie agreed, but he did not seem to know any more.

They stopped outside the big house. It was in terrible repair, unpainted, boards hanging loose, windows boarded up.

"I waits fo' you here," Charlie said. He chuckled again as Flora climbed down from the buggy. "You won' be long."

Old habits die hard. Flora did not go to the front door, she walked around to the back. She could hear her heart beating. She knocked on the kitchen door, and knocked again when no one answered.

She heard movement inside, and then a lock being turned. The door opened, but only a crack. A woman with white hair was there. She glared at Flora.

"Come to see Miz Lincoln," Flora said.

"She sick," the woman said. Suddenly, Flora knew who she was.

"Bessie?" she said. It was the maid, Bessie, who had not been kind to her.

Bessie stared at her.

"I be Flora," Flora said, and added the explanation, "Maz' Luke's mama."

She had hit some kind of a target. Bessie stared at her, without recognition, but with knowledge of a truth.

"Bes' wait here," she said. She nodded at a bench on the back porch and waited until Flora sat. She closed the door.

Flora waited patiently, not knowing what she felt. Luke could be her son, but it occurred to her, for the first time in her life, that she had no way of knowing what other girls Lincoln had seduced, what other babies there might have been.

She heard the back door open, and Bessie came out to her.

"She won' see you," Bessie said.

Flora was disappointed, but not surprised. Then she felt a small sense of relief, because she did not know what she would have said. Then she felt anger.

"She gotta see me!" she cried. "I be Luke's mama! You were here! You know!"

Bessie sat down on the bench beside her and took her hand.

"It the past, chile," she said, not unkindly. "Let it be."

"I gotta know!" Flora said. "I gotta know fo' sure that he be mine!"

Bessie squeezed Flora's hand.

"Y'know a'ready, you got yo' answer," she said. "Why you think she won' see you?"

So it was true.

"I gotta see him," Flora said, letting the tears fall freely, the tears she had held back. "Where he live?"

Bessie put her arm around her, and held her while she cried.

"Let it be, let it be," she whispered.

"I cain't," Flora cried. "You don't know what it's like. You don't know the pain of it."

"There, there," Bessie said, "let it be, let it be."

She sat holding Flora until the tears were spent.

"She kill me if'n I tells you where he is," Bessie said. "Mebbe he kill me too."

"But I his mama," Flora said, wiping her eyes.

"An' look what you done to him, girl," Bessie whispered. "Mebbe he don' want a' see you. Mebbe he don' want to meet the mama who give him away."

"Tell him," Flora demanded. "You tell him what they done to me. You tell him that I never stopped thinkin' a' him, not one day or one night I din' think a' him. You tell him I was here!"

"He don' come home too often," Bessie said, and then smiled. "He don' like it here. An' who can blame him?"

"He got a right to know his mama," Flora insisted. "An' if'n he hates me, that's all right too. But he got a right to know."

Bessie considered this for a moment.

"Where you live?"

"Stockton, Tennessee," Flora whispered, a small hope flaring.

"Y'can write to him here," Bessie said. "When he come home, he get his mail."

Flora gasped in relief and shock. It was such a simple solution.

"Yes," she said. "I write."

She heard the sound of a bell in the kitchen. She knew it was a call for Bessie, probably so that Mrs. Fleming could find out what had been said.

"She let him read the letter?"

"I gets the post," Bessie said. "Letters come to me."

She got up and went into the kitchen to answer the summoning bell. She did not say good-bye.

Charlie looked at Flora in surprise when she walked back to the buggy.

"You see her? You be gone awhile."

"I got what I wanted," Flora said, climbing into the buggy.

"Where you wan' go now?"

"Home," Flora said.

There was no train until the evening, so Charlie took her back to his shack and warmed up some beans and gossiped about the things that had happened over the years. It had no meaning for Flora, none of this was part of her life anymore. Her life was elsewhere. In Stockton. And Atlanta.

In the afternoon they sat on the porch, Charlie in a rocking chair, Flora on a stool. He suggested that she should stay the night, but Flora said no. She didn't entirely trust Charlie, he had a small gleam in his eye when he made the invitation, and in any case, she wanted to be home. She had a letter to write.

Charlie dozed for a while, and Flora cleaned up his shack; he was an untidy housekeeper. When she came back to the porch, Charlie woke and stared at her.

"I 'member you," he said. "You danced wit' me."

His hair was gray, his face was wrinkled, his body bowed, his skin dull. But once he had been shining ebony.

"Yes." Flora smiled. "I danced wit' you."

She kissed him on his forehead and pulled her stool to him and sat beside him, holding his hand. He was alone, his wife dead, his two sons gone north. They seldom came to visit.

"Lawdy, Lawd, girl," Charlie said. "The things we seen."

Flora stared at the setting sun.

"The things we seen."

He took her to the depot in his buggy, and wished her well. She kissed him again and thanked him for all he had done.

She slept for most of the journey home, her heart filled with other people's tiny kindness. Already she was preparing in her mind the letter she would write to Luke, but the letter was only possible because strangers had been kind.

She got home on Sunday morning, but did not go to church. Ruthana would be there with Pearl, and although it was the first Sunday of her life when she did not go to church, she worshiped God in her heart and believed He would understand.

She spent the morning writing to Luke. It was not easy for her. Glancing out the window she saw Ruthana with Pearl going into Pearl's house, but she did not call out to tell them she was home. She was not expected back until that night.

She tore up the letter she had written to Luke, and wrote it again, and this time she thought she had it right. She took a little nap, and when she woke she went across the road to Pearl's house.

Pearl opened the door, obviously in great distress.

"Flora, you heard the news?" she cried and clung to her friend, weeping.

"The Japanese bombed Pearl Harbor," she blurted between sobs. "It on the radio."

At that moment, a boy of about ten came running down the road.

"The Japs is comin', the Japs is comin'!" he shouted to alert the town. "My pappy done seen 'em comin' up the creek!"

27

THE FOLLOWING SUNDAY, Reverend Jackson gave what he considered to be the most important sermon of his ministry. When he was old and looking back on his life, he thought of other sermons that were more passionate or joyous or aggressive, but when he spoke on that Sunday morning in December, it was a turning point in his life.

"Brothers and sisters, young and old, *whatever* your heritage, black, colored—or white," he began, "we stand united before our Maker today, the children of *America*, and our country is at *war*."

Someone muttered "Hallelujah!" but the congregation was unusually subdued. They were in uncharted waters.

"We did not *ask* for this war, we did not invade another country, but it has come to us, a test of our *strength* and our *resolve*. An' it is our duty, as Christians and Americans, to pray, to struggle, and to fight for our country's *victory!*"

The response to this was more enthusiastic, because the shepherd had revealed the way to his flock. Almost everyone in the church agreed with him, if not everyone in the town. A few thought it to be a white man's war, and wanted no part of it, and a couple of the young hotbloods were suggesting that life might be better, easier, at least, for black people if the Japanese conquered America.

"Now, America has not always been *kind* to us," Reverend Jackson continued. "Sometimes America has been *cruel* to us. We were brought against our will from Africa and were *enslaved*. But the children of Israel, God's chosen people, were slaves in Egypt. An' the Lord took pity on them, and sent Moses to deliver them, as He sent the blessed *Abraham Lincoln*—"

"Amen, amen, amen," the congregation cried.

"—to deliver us from bondage. An' he *did!*"

"Hallelujah! Praise the *Lord!*"

"But Pharaoh regretted letting the children go, and went to bring them *back*. Moses raised his staff and parted the waters and the children went on. But they had *sin* in their hearts and wandered in the wilderness for *forty years* before they found the *Promised Land!*"

He paused for a moment, and his mood changed.

"As we wander in the wilderness," he said sadly, "and cannot find the *Promised Land*."

"It be true, it be true!"

"No one struck Pharaoh down, and we are enslaved again, to the *evil* of segregation."

Some women were weeping. Reverend Jackson paused again. He had never criticized America before; his sermons were seldom political. This one had to be.

"An' we have labored under the yoke of oppression these many years. They tell us we are *free*, but there are places we cannot go. The law says we are *equal*, the laws makes us *separate*.

"Separate, we are not equal. We cannot *vote* lessen we got college degrees; we cannot choose our leaders. There are jobs we cannot do. An' in the jobs we can do, we are paid *half* what a white man earns.

"We cannot *drink* from the same cup, we cannot *eat* at the same table, we cannot *sleep* in the same bed.

"Is this *freedom?*"

"*No,*" the congregation roared.

"*Yes!*" Reverend Jackson thundered back. "This is *freedom!*"

This shocked everyone into silence.

"This is freedom!" he said. "But this is not *equality!* And it is not *right*, and it is not *just*, and it is not *fair!* But it is what we *are*."

He gave them a moment to consider this.

"So why should we pray and struggle and fight for this America, why should we ask our mothers to give their sons and ask those sons to spill their blood for this country that *oppresses* us?"

No one had an answer, because he had made his case too well.

"Because we are *Americans*!" he told them. "Whatever our grievances, this is our *country*!"

He had them in the palm of his hand, because they were Americans, and, however illogically, irrationally, they loved their country.

"Some say we should go back to *Africa*," he said. "But I say *why*! We were *born* here, and our fathers were born here, and our fathers' fathers, and all the generations that we know! Yet a white man who arrived here yesterday is better regarded than us."

He came to what was, for him, the crucial point.

"But we are *Christians*, and we must show our *love*. We must turn the other cheek! We must forgive our oppressors, and stand shoulder to shoulder with them and fight to prove our love.

"We wander in the wilderness of segregation, of inequality, but we are Daniel in the lion's den, and when we are found blameless, we will have shown our worth.

"This is the time of our *testing*! This is the time when we must prove to America that we are equal to the task of full *citizenship*. This is the time of our great *sacrifice*. It will be hard, and there will be many burdens to bear, and lives will be lost. But I believe, with all my *heart*, that the *love* of God will guide us, and deliver us from evil!

"It is up to us, to each and every one of us, whether we pass the test or *fail*."

There was pin-drop silence in the church.

"So I ask you to pray, for our country and for our leader, President Roosevelt, who has shown himself to be a friend to us. Pray to the Lord to give our president courage and strength and wisdom to lead us through the Valley of Death to *victory*!"

He bowed his head.

"Our Father," he prayed, "Who art in Heaven, hallowed be Thy name."

The congregation rose and spoke the prayer with him, many women and some men weeping, in fear, but also in joy. At the end, the rafters rang with the shouts of "Amen!" The floorboards shook with stomping feet, the windows trembled from the hands clapping.

Reverend Jackson turned to the choir. He had chosen the song after great thought and deliberation. It was not the national anthem, it was "The Battle Hymn of the Republic."

"Mine eyes have seen the glory of the coming of the Lord," they sang, and every voice in the church joined in.

28

*F*LORA WAS INSPIRED BY Reverend Jackson's sermon, but, like every mother in America, fear stalked her heart. Already a score of the town's young white men had enlisted, and several blacks.

They discussed it at a special meeting of the sisters on a Tuesday night.

"Our boys is safe," Sister Lake said. "Ain't no colored combat units."

"Won't let 'em fight," Sister Sanford agreed. "They jes' use 'em for supply and mess halls."

"Not fo' long, you mark my words," Sister Pearl contradicted them. Pearl, the voracious reader, knew her history. "Our boys fought las' time, in the Great War, had got theirselves kilt."

Pearl, who had no children, did not understand the fear that plagued the mothers.

" 'Tain't fair," Flora complained, forgetting the point of Reverend Jackson's sermon.

"No, it isn't fair, but that's the point," Vera Jackson, the preacher's wife, reminded her very gently. "We must share the burden of war equally before we can be equal in peace."

"But what can we do?" Sister Henderson wanted to know, speaking for all of them. They were an enormous resource of energy, all anxious to help. They needed direction.

"Many things," Vera said.

They must be ready. There were rumors of enemy bombers flying over California. If the Japanese invaded the West Coast, there would be millions of refugees, and they would need to be fed and sheltered. The women must plant victory gardens in the spring; every available inch of land must be productive. They must organize collections of clothes for the destitute and scrap metal for salvage. They must have war fund sales, of donated goods and produce, the proceeds to help buy military supplies. They must help to sell war bonds. They must learn simple nursing skills.

Sister Henderson, who was fully trained, offered to give lessons in basic first aid every Tuesday night. These lessons became the core of the Tuesday meetings, which expanded over the next couple of years into a simple, well-run organization with many skills.

Within the town, things began to happen that were shocking at first to many, and a cause of celebration for some.

Andy, Clara's boyfriend, enlisted. This left Albie, Ernestine's dad, without an apprentice and overwhelmed with work. He advertised, he spread the word, but could not find help. Young men with mechanical aptitude were in high demand and short supply. So Albie persuaded Caleb Brandon to employ Henrietta, Ernestine's sister, at the service station as an apprentice auto mechanic.

Henrietta loved her father and his cars, and from her early teens spent hours with Albie in the evenings, in the garage, when he worked on his own car. Sometimes, if he worked on a Saturday, she'd be with him then, and sometimes, if Caleb was shorthanded, he let Henrietta pump gas. To have her work with her father on a full-time basis was only an extension of this to Albie and Caleb, and Ruthana, but to the town it was momentous.

"Ain't nat'ral," Flora gasped when she heard.

"Why not?" Ruthana asked. "She like it, she good at it, and ain't no man to do it."

Flora had no real argument against this, but still it didn't seem proper.

" 'Tain't a woman's work," she said, but mildly.

"Oh, Ma." Ruthana laughed. "What are women s'posed to do? Cookin' an' washin' and cleanin'? Is that why you wants me to go to college, to get a degree in ironing shirts?"

"No, chile." Flora laughed as well. "You ain't never gon' to do that, not so long as I got a say in it."

"Women gon' be doin' a lot a' things they ain't done before," Ruthana predicted. "You wait an' see."

She was right. More men went away, and the factory at Millington replaced them with women, many of them black. A munitions plant in Brownsville took more, and the airfield at Halls.

The women at the Tuesday night meeting, practicing bandaging pretended broken arms, were agog with rumors. It was said that some of the women in factory jobs were earning as much as ten dollars a day.

"Hush yo' mouf!" Flora said with more than a trace of envy. "That much pretty soon break even the gub'mint."

As usual, Sister Pearl had the best gossip.

"Y'all heard 'bout ol' Sister Toog done quit cookin' for Mr. and Mrs. Anthony?" she said, knowing they had not because she had only just heard it herself, and old Sister Toog wasn't at the meeting.

"This very day, she jes' cooked an served 'em a big, pretty meal, an' whilst they was eatin' she walked in pullin' off her apron, an' tol' 'em she was leavin'. Tol' 'em her sister had drove down in her car from Brownsville to git her for one a' them gov'ment war jobs. An' I knows that for a fact, 'coz Sister Toog tol' me today on my new telephone party line."

She added the last detail with no small sense of triumph, and was well satisfied with the awed, and envious, reaction.

"You done got a tel'phone a'ready?" Sister Sanford inquired tartly. "We expectin' ours any day."

Everyone correctly guessed that Sister Sanford would go directly to her husband after the meeting and demand they have a telephone installed, and that she would give him no rest until he agreed.

"Tel'phone company say they doin' their best, but they swamped 'coz a' the war," Sister Sanford told them, to explain the delay.

Vera Jackson tried to restore a little charity to the meeting.

"If this all keeps going," she said, "before long there be more jobs than there are colored folk."

This prediction came true too, at least in Stockton. As cooks and maids left their employers for the well-paying factory jobs, Flora was swamped with offers of work. The best of these came from Mrs. Vaughan, who lived in a big house with a couple of acres of well-tended garden. Flora had done her laundry for years, but now Mrs. Vaughan wanted more.

"Ya'll colored folks rushing off to the wartime jobs payin' more'n ya'll know what to do with, until it's no more maids and cooks left to hire," she complained to Flora.

But she had invited Flora into her sitting room and had served her iced lemonade. That was a first.

"And, Flora, you know I can't sweep and mop and dust this big house all by myself."

"No'm," Flora said, content to wait for the offer she knew was coming. It was worth it when it did. Mrs. Vaughan offered her fifty cents an hour for three full days a week.

"I don' rightly see how I can, Miz Vaughan," Flora said. "I does Miz Hopkins three days a week, an' all my other cust'mers."

"But, Flora, I need you," Mrs. Vaughan wailed. And upped the offer to sixty cents an hour. Flora hesitated. At sixty-five cents an hour, plus fifty cents a day traveling expenses, more than the bus fare, Flora agreed.

"Dunno what I's gon' tell Miz Hopkins," she said.

"Edna Hopkins will manage just fine," Mrs. Vaughan said tartly. "After all, she had to clean her own house for years, when Mr. Hopkins was bankrupt."

She looked out the window.

"And what am I going to do about the garden? Tommy upped and left me Saturday without a word of warning."

Flora agreed to make inquiries about a new gardener, but without hope of success.

Before she gave notice to Mrs. Hopkins the next day, she sent up a small prayer of thanks that Kevin Hopkins had enlisted in the air force, and was not there.

"Flora, I am shocked," Mrs. Hopkins said. "And hurt. And bitterly disappointed."

"Yes'm," Flora said.

"After all I've done for you, how can you be so ungrateful?"

"Yes'm, " Flora said again, not bothering to argue.

"How shall I manage?"

"I's gettin' sixty-five cents a' hour from Miz Vaughan." Flora shrugged. If Mrs. Hopkins made her a better offer, she'd consider it. It was a seller's market.

"I couldn't possibly match that!" Mrs. Hopkins seemed genuinely shocked. "And, you know, Flora, when this war is over, you'll all be running right back to those of us who stood by you in the lean years."

"Yes'm," Flora said.

"But don't you have a daughter?" Mrs. Hopkins wondered, uncertain because she had never shown much interest in Flora's life.

"Yes'm, Ruthana," Flora said.

"Well, couldn't she come and work for me? Even two days a week would help, and I'll pay her the best I can."

Flora savored her moment of triumph. Even if Ruthana didn't go to college, or didn't get her degree, cleaning for Mrs. Hopkins, even on a part-time basis, was not to be in her future.

"Miz Hopkins, I sho' hates to tell you, my Ruthana ain't doin' too well at school," she lied. "An' how much her pappy send us, to help us git along, depend on how well her report card say she doin'. An' I jes' know sho' as she starts to workin' it'll git her mind off'n them books an' she'll fall even further back than she is already."

236 * ALEX HALEY and DAVID STEVENS

It was a sweet, if tiny, vengeance, and only white lies.
You done it to me, you old heifer, Flora thought, but over
my dead body, you ain't gon' do it to Ruthana.

"Y'unnerstan' me, Miz Hopkins?"

Mrs. Hopkins looked at her steadily.

"Yes, Flora," she said with scarcely controlled anger. "I
understand you perfectly."

She swept out of the room. To celebrate her victory,
Flora picked up a glass and dropped it on the floor.

She was as ruthless with her laundry customers, abandoning the meanest of them to the mercies of the Memphis Steam Laundry, and only keeping those who had been
kind to her and had good hearts. New customers came to
her almost daily, and Flora put them through a short but
thorough questioning before accepting or, more often, de-
clining them.

Her days were filled with work, her evenings were devoted to keeping her own house and looking after
Ruthana, but her small private time was filled with worry.
She'd only had a couple of letters from Willie since he
went back to Chicago, and they were only dutiful.

A few months later a letter came. It was the one she
had been dreading. He had enlisted in the army, with his
friend Ab.

Flora put the letter down and sat at the table staring at
nothing. All the rumors she had heard rang in her ears,
that there were no colored units, that blacks in the military were given only menial or labor jobs, that there was
no chance he would actually have to fight.

They were meaningless to her. Ports and cities can be
bombed; shipboard sailors were not the only ones who had
lost their lives at Pearl Harbor. Even if he did not go overseas, he could still be in danger. The Japanese bombers had
not reached the West Coast, but there was the chance that
they would, and military bases would be their first targets.

To be a soldier in a war was to be in harm's way, and
Willie was to be a soldier in the war.

Ruthana came home from school and saw her mama sitting at the table, a pile of ironing still undone.

"What's up, Ma?" she asked.

Flora said nothing. She held up the letter and Ruthana read it. She was thrilled that Willie had enlisted; to her it was an adventure, and, if nothing else, it would get rid of Willie's silly conked hair. But she loved her brother, and the prospect of his fighting in the war frightened her.

"He be fine, Ma," she said, hugging Flora.

"Yeh, he gon' be fine," Flora whispered, and wiped the tears from her eyes.

He began writing regularly, once a week. He was at boot camp, in Georgia, he told Flora, and the character of his letters changed. Previously they had been short and simple. Now they became long and full of the details of his life and the woes of a training soldier, but cheerfully recounted and filled with love.

He sent her a snapshot of himself with another man, tall and handsome, well built, and black as coal. "Ab," Willie had written on the photo, an arrow pointing to his friend. And "Me," with another arrow pointing to himself.

She did not know why he had thought it necessary to point himself out, she would have known him anywhere, in any disguise, but this was not the son she had last seen in Stockton, in his conked, zoot-suited, tawdry splendor. Nor was this the eager boy who had first gone to Chicago.

This was a new Willie, with shorn head and a man's confidence. This was Willie the soldier, in uniform, too young, by far, for such a perilous adventure, and far too old to stay at home.

This was the sinner saved, and Flora thanked her Maker for it. Her journey to her past, her journey to find Luke, even if it had not been fulfilled, had been the start of it, and the war its culmination. She prayed that the end would not be more painful than she could bear.

Thoughts of Willie never left her mind, and nor did thoughts of Luke. She had written to him but had not received a reply. She tried to imagine him sometimes, and what he might look like, but no image of him came to her, and only Willie's face appeared. It grieved her that she had no picture of her firstborn son, but at least she knew his name, and could include him, by name, in her prayers. He was a living being to her, unseeable, unknowable, untouchable, like God, but nonetheless real because of that.

Then Willie came home, a soldier. Albie took Flora and Ruthana with Ernestine in the Oldsmobile to the railroad, and it thrilled Flora's heart that several of Willie's friends were there, cheering and waving tiny flags.

He jumped from the train in triumph, more handsome in his uniform that Flora could ever have imagined. He swept his mama into his arms and off her feet and swirled her around, laughing at her tears of joy and hugging her. After another hug for Ruthana, he walked slowly to Ernestine, put his hands on her hips, and stared at her, and she at him. Whatever each saw was obviously pleasing to both of them, and to the cheering crowd when, without embarrassment, he put his lips to hers in a kiss that lasted forever.

He did not stay long, only four days, but they were among the sweetest of Flora's life. This was the man she had always hoped her son would be, and if he lacked his father's dream of a formal education, it was irrelevant. Life had taught him more than any schoolbook, and he faced the future confidently, without fear.

"Is you scared?" she said to him one evening.

"Lawd, Ma." Willie laughed. "Course I is. I scared they ain't gon' let me fight."

"What you wan' do that fo'?" Flora snapped. "It's enuff yo' in the army."

"No, it ain't." Willie laughed again. "I's a soldier. Soldiers fight. An' until they lets us fight, I ain't a real soldier."

"Get yo'self kilt," Flora grumbled.

"I scared a' that," Willie admitted. "I scared to death a' dyin'. But I joined the army to defend my country, and until they lets me fight, I ain't a real American."

Suddenly, urgently, he was a different Willie, a political Willie that she had never seen before.

"Don't you see, Ma?" he said. "Until we is equal wit' the whites, we is only ever half men, not complete. An' until they lets us fight alongside wit' the whites, we ain't equal."

But he laughed again.

"What you want us to be, cooks an' stevedores an' messmen, jus' 'coz we black, part of the army but not soldiers? When we are ev'rywhere, officers an' sergeants an' grunts, an' when we fight—an' when we die—then we is men. When we can make our mamas proud, then we is men. An' if'n we have to die to do it, then it be worth the price. An' lessen we do that, then all we ever gon' do is hump cotton and clean latrines."

"I proud of you," Flora whispered stubbornly. "I don' needs you to die to be proud a' you."

"I ain't gon' die, Mama, not in this war, anyways. But I ain't gon' be a hero, either. An' I deserves the chance at that. Black blood is as good as white."

It did not ease her pain, but it had deep meaning for her. For the rest of the time she was happy enough to have him home, and pretended she was happy about his future. He had been posted to Fort Huachuca in Arizona, and that pleased her. There appeared to be less and less chance that the Japanese would invade California, but if they did, he would still be a long way from the front.

She did not begrudge the time he spent with Ernestine, for it was clear to everyone, including Flora, that they should be together, and everyone guessed that they would be together, permanently, when Willie came home from the war.

Obsessed with the welfare of her own son, Flora had not really been aware of the sacrifice that the mothers of America were making, but it was brought home to her with some force at the railroad depot, when Willie left.

A dozen sons of Stockton were waiting to catch the

train, two other boys she knew, and nine whites, including
Kevin Hopkins, who had been home on furlough. Much of
the town, black and white, was gathered to see them off,
for it was an event of moment in their lives, and all had
flags to wave and the depot building was decorated with
bunting.

As they waited for the train, Flora stood aside with
Ruthana to let Willie say his farewell to Ernestine. She saw
Kevin Hopkins with his young, already pregnant bride,
and with his mother and father, and she recognized in Mrs.
Hopkins an emotion exactly similar to her own.

The train arrived and every mother at the depot, with
eyes only for her own son, saw something else. The train
was packed with military, mostly soldiers, a few sailors and
airmen; there was hardly a civilian to be seen. From every
station and siding and halt for a thousand miles, the train
had picked up young men in uniform, on their way to war,
and each, each mother knew, had said a farewell to his own
mother as painful as that which she must make now.

The men already on the train were cheerful enough,
white men in the first six cars, black in the last three, and
leaned out the windows to call encouragement to their
joining fellows, and, perhaps, to watch the sad good-byes
and be reminded of their own.

It was almost more than Flora could bear; she felt she
was drowning in a sea of the war's making. Some of those
men would never come home.

She tried to be brave for Willie's sake, but at the end
her resolve faltered, and she grabbed him to her. He was
tender with her, and hugged her and kissed her hair.

The whistle was sounding.

"I gotta go," he whispered thickly, and looked at Ernestine and Ruthana. They came to Flora and took her away
from him. He got on the train, and looked back, and
waved and grinned, and it was the grin that caused her to
cry out his name.

The crowd cheered and waved their flags, the station

agent blew his whistle, the engine blasted steam and chugged and shunted, and the train moved away.

She wanted it to be over. She thought the train would never be gone; it seemed to inch away, as if unwilling to deliver its burden, but she would not leave, for the train was the last of him that she might see. She watched it, and the soldiers, white and black, leaning out windows to wave good-bye, and one of them, she was sure, was Willie.

She was not aware of anything else except the noise of the train, which dimmed to silence, and the cheering of the crowd, which slowly faded. She was not aware of anyone leaving the station, but then Ruthana squeezed her arm.

"He's gone, Ma," Ruthana said softly. "We go home now."

Flora nodded and turned to walk away. The crowd had gone, there were a few small knots of people left, the families of the departed, not wanting to go home.

She saw Mrs. Hopkins weeping, and Mr. Hopkins trying to comfort her, and again she recognized the depth of the emotion because it was her own.

White tears were the same as black. They sprang from an identical source, the fathomless reservoir of a mother's love.

29

SHORTLY BEFORE CHRISTMAS, Flora was traveling to work on the bus. As they passed the town hall, she saw that a temporary Red Cross station had been set up in a marquee, a blood drive.

She thought about it all day long, and hardly heard Mrs. Vaughan's complaints about her new, temporary gardener, and the terrible job he had done pruning her roses, and the difficulty of finding anything decent in the stores for Christmas gifts, and the burden of the new food rationing cards; it was so silly, America was a land of plenty. The war was a huge inconvenience to Mrs. Vaughan, but she did not have sons in the military. One of her boys was at college and the other, exempt because of chronic asthma, was still at his job in Memphis.

Something Willie had said to her kept sounding in Flora's ears. "Black blood is as good as white."

She decided to give a small, anonymous Christmas gift to a soldier she didn't know. It would cost her nothing, and yet it might be priceless to him.

On her way home, she got off the bus at the town hall and stood uncertainly for a moment. Although she journeyed through it almost every day on the bus, she seldom came to this part of town. It was not barred to her, any black could come here, and several did, just as some whites walked freely through the black section, but Flora always felt like a stranger here. The law was the same but the rules were different, except in this regard: as everywhere, blacks took second place.

There had been a small line outside the marquee that morning, but now no one was waiting. Flora concentrated on the big red cross on its white background, and walked to the tent. She hoped it wouldn't hurt; she'd never had an injection of any kind. Then she thought it could be no worse than when she pricked her finger with a needle, sewing, and that was a small pain to bear.

There was no one outside and Flora wondered if she should go around the back, if there was a separate entrance for colored, as at the Star Cafe, across the road. She walked around the marquee but she could see no other gap in the canvas, nor any sign. She went back to the front and went inside.

A white-uniformed white nurse was sitting at a desk inside the entrance. Beyond her, in the body of the tent, there were several cots, a few screens, and another, older nurse. A couple of men were lying on cots, tubes attached to their arms filling pint-sized bottles suspended on stands with blood.

The nurse looked at Flora, a small unease in her eyes. She did not speak.

"What I do?" Flora asked.

"What do you mean?" The nurse was puzzled.

"To give blood," Flora said.

"You want to give blood?"

Already, Flora knew that she had done something wrong, she had crossed some invisible line of segregation, but she could not imagine what it was.

"That's why I be here," Flora said. "I looked for the colored entrance."

At least this made sense to the nurse.

"There isn't one," she said. She looked around the tent. She looked at her papers, and then at the tent again. She did not look at Flora. She was obviously uncomfortable.

"Wait here," she said. She went away and whispered to the older nurse. They both looked at Flora. The young nurse came back.

"You have to leave," she said, speaking softly.

"But I wants to give blood," Flora insisted.

"You can't," the nurse said.

The truth did not hit Flora like a sledgehammer. It

flooded to her more slowly, because she did not want to believe it, but still with speed. But if it was true, she was going to hear it said.

"Why?" she wanted to know.

"We don't want your blood," the nurse said. She was getting irritable.

"Why?" Flora demanded.

The nurse's reserve broke.

"We don't take nigger blood," she snapped.

It was inconceivable to Flora. Her milk had suckled a white boy, Kevin. Her blood might save another. A deep anger rose inside her.

"Black blood the same as white," she said, remembering Willie's words.

"Just go away," the nurse whispered fiercely. She was only young, not fully trained, it was her first day doing this, and she had not had to deal with this situation before.

"My boy a soldier," Flora said. "An' if'n he wounded, what blood you gon' give him?"

"We have enough," the nurse said, begging God to make this woman leave.

"Then why these folk givin' mo'?" Flora said, pointing to the two donors, who could hear the argument.

"Get out a' here, nigra," one of the two donors said. "Stop makin' trouble."

"I tryin' to do my Christian duty!" Flora raised her voice so that he would hear and lost her temper. She turned on the nurse.

"Well, I don' wants you givin' white blood to my boy," she said. "I don' wants no drop a' white blood in his body! So what you gon' do 'bout that?"

She knew she would not get any adequate reply, but had to have the last word.

"Huh?" she demanded. "What you gon' do 'bout that, missy?"

She turned and walked out of the tent. She did not go to the bus stop; she did not want to have to sit at the back of a bus full of white folk. She was angry with white people, and their wretched, unwarranted superiority, and she was angry with herself for being such a fool.

She should have known or she should have guessed. When she had passed by the Red Cross marquee on the bus that morning, not one black person had stood in the line to give blood.

She stomped along the street, shouting at herself inside to release her anger. She wanted to be among her own kind.

It was not very far to go, but the distance was enormous, a whole other world away.

30

FLORA TOLD THE OTHER WOMEN at the Tuesday night meeting that the Red Cross was not accepting black blood, not even to save black lives. Most of the women were shocked, but Pearl, as usual, took a loftier view. Pearl was starting to irritate Flora.

"How can they?" Pearl said, slightly smugly. "Make a mock'ry a' all their laws."

"How come?" Sister Sanford demanded.

"One li'l drop a' black blood make you colored, they say," Pearl answered. "They give black blood to white boys, those boys all come back colored."

Pearl chuckled.

"An' then where would they be, 'coz the blood bank is 'nonymous, an' they wouldn't know who was white an' who was black! An' fo' some reason, they jus' gotta know."

Because it was so ridiculous, and so true, it broke the tension, but did not ease the puzzlement or indignation.

"But if it saves their lives . . ." Vera Jackson said, voicing their confusion.

"Sister Pearl right, they don' care about that," Sister Lake confirmed. "Some a' them cracker boys rather kill theirselves if'n they had one li'l drop a' black blood in 'em."

"Kevin Hopkins," Flora murmured. Kevin's mother, Mrs. Hopkins, might pay any price, however high, to save her son from dying. But not Kevin.

They talked about it for a while, and when the women went home they told their husbands or their families, and the matter was discussed among the men and other women, and it joined with other discussions of similar injustices that were being talked about by blacks all over the country, and it swelled to a roar and it exploded, one day, in Detroit, in a riot that left several dead.

It wasn't just the blood, nor, however indirectly, was it Flora's humiliating experience at the blood drive. It was the culmination of thousands, millions of similar tiny incidents all over the country, North and South, grievous injustices that the irony of the war magnified to explosive force. What were they fighting for?

The answer came to Reverend Jackson like a revelation, and he was compelled to share it with his congregation. He was also sure that a similar revelation had been given to other black preachers across the country, and that God was speaking to them in a powerful voice that they dare not ignore.

"We fighting in two wars," he proclaimed during his next sermon. "An' one will be longer and harder than the other, an' we are the army, an' only we can win the *victory!*"

There was the war overseas, the war against the Japanese, he explained, which would be won.

"Hallelujah!" they cried, for it appeared to be true. The enemy had been stopped from advancing, and some small islands in the Pacific had been reclaimed, though with tremendous loss of life.

And there was the war at home, which would be tougher, longer, more directly painful to them, because they were all in the army; every man, woman, and child had been conscripted by God for the fight.

"Praise the Lord!" they cried, for there were the first small glimmers that it might be true.

The radio was the messenger that brought them the hope. The riots in Detroit and other cities were widely reported, and not always favorably because the country was obsessed with its other, overseas war. But much of that war could not be broadcast; it was classified, too secret, or too stagnant. The first small forays by blacks into the white world were not classified, not secret, not stagnant, and filled the news broadcasts and the newspapers.

There was also evidence, however minute, that the enemy was not united. In Chicago, white diners had

cheered when some black men had demanded, and had received, service in a white restaurant.

"But I hears your question," Reverend Jackson said. "I
hear you askin', what can we *do*?"

He was right; it was the question in all their minds. The
shock of the overseas war had fired them all to activity, but
they did not know how to fight on the home front, because
they did not want to be disloyal to their country, and because the enemy, segregation, seemed invincible.

"Not much," Reverend Jackson said blithely. "Not in
the South, in the country. There ain't enough of us to win."

He was in a very good mood. Those few, tiny victories
up North had inspired him. He doubted there would be
many more, he knew this home-front war would be very
long indeed, but he was filled with a sense of change, and it
could only be for the better.

"But we can do somethin'!" he said. "Raise yo' hands if
you know what the N double A C P is?"

Half a dozen hands went up. Pearl was the first.

"It is the National Association for the Advancement
of Colored People!" Reverend Jackson thundered at them.
"It has existed fo' many *years*, and it is for the betterment
of *all* colored folk in America!"

They accepted the lecture in silence.

"An' how many of you is members?" he asked them
again.

Pearl put her hand down.

"Then that the *first* thing that you *do*!" Reverend
Jackson told them, a clarion call. "You *join* that 'ssocia-
tion! You be *good* members! You support what they *do* an'
what they *done*! You show our black brothers and sisters up
North that you *care*!"

They cheered lustily, and Reverend Jackson was satisfied. Not all of them would join the association, perhaps,
but some would, and even a few were, for the moment,
enough. He would remind them again, and more would
join, and they would make an army.

Flora did not join. She intended to, and she discussed it with Pearl, but something always got in the way.

Ruthana was one of those things. Ruthana was starting to show the first small, dangerous signs of independence. Flora still dressed her drably, but Ernestine gave her ribbons for her birthday, and Flora did not have the heart to forbid the girl to wear them.

She started to worry about Ernestine's increasing influence over Ruthana. Ernestine came by several times a week, bringing news of Willie from the letters he wrote to her, or asking for news that Flora might have. In many ways, Ernestine eased Flora's burden; often she made an evening meal for them, while Flora rested, and taught Ruthana to cook things that were beyond Flora's simple kitchen skills.

She allowed Ernestine to take Ruthana to the black movie house once a week, and did not get too angry when they came home late, having stopped at Pop's Place for a soda. It was what they talked about when they were alone that worried Flora.

Not that she questioned Ernestine's morals. Ernestine was, undoubtedly, a "good girl," who was probably going to marry her son, and she was sure that Ernestine was keeping her virginity for Willie. But Ernestine was more than several years older than Ruthana and worked in a shop that sold very modern clothes, and had ideas that worried Flora.

Ernestine had known of Willie's gambling problem. How much else did she know about him?

In many ways, Flora wanted Ruthana to be like Ernestine, avoiding the temptations of the world and saving herself for a good man.

It was simply that Flora didn't trust anyone else with Ruthana's upbringing, not even Ernestine. She was determined that Ruthana would not make too many mistakes too soon, and the only way she could do this was to limit Ruthana's choices.

Fifteen, for example, was much too young to go to dances.

"Mama," Ruthana cried as she rushed into the house. "Up at that big air force base at Halls, the colored soldiers is gon' be givin' a big dance two Saturdays from now. They've sent invitations to all the colored high schools wanting all the girls to come, Mama!"

Flora had never seen her so excited.

"They're even gon' have their own band, a sixteen-piece band, an' it's got some real famous musicians in it! You got to let me go!"

Flora had not gone to her first dance until she was seventeen. Nor would Ruthana.

"Naw, baby, you ain't goin' to no dance, soldiers an' nobody else," Flora said, trying to be gentle.

She saw the hurt on Ruthana's face, the boundless disappointment.

"Aw, Mama, why?" the girl demanded.

Flora didn't have a reason that Ruthana would accept, not even the rumors that dozens, scores of girls, some younger than Ruthana, had gone to dances with soldiers and found themselves pregnant.

"I wouldn't do that!" Ruthana cried, close to weeping.

"You don' know what you'd do if'n some smart soldier made sweet talk," Flora insisted. "It's like I allus tol' you, girl, they only wants one thing."

"It isn't fair," Ruthana shouted. "You never let me do anythin'!"

She went to her room and slammed the door.

Flora was shocked. It was something she remembered shouting at her own mama more than once, but Ruthana was a placid girl, who seldom complained. Obviously, the dance was an important event for her, if only because all her friends from school would be going, and Flora wondered if her decision had been too harsh. She had no intention of relenting, but she thought she must loosen Ruthana's leash a little, and tried to think of some nice outing for her, or some little fancy gift to brighten her life.

She went to Ruthana's door and scratched on it.

"Hon', I's sorry, let me talk to you," she said.

There was silence. Flora opened the door and went in. Ruthana was lying on the bed, staring at the wall.

"I cain't let you go to that dance," Flora began. "It for yo' own good, you's only fifteen."

"All the others is gon' go," Ruthana mumbled.

"Maybe their mamas think diff'ren'," Flora allowed.

Ruthana turned and glared at her accusingly.

"Don't you trust me?" she challenged.

"I trusts you, hon," Flora promised. "It's men I don' trust."

It was not true, she realized, she did not trust Ruthana. She remembered her own first dance, and Lincoln, and would have done anything the man asked of her.

"Tell y' what," she bargained, relenting a little. "First dance there be after you is sixteen, I lets you go."

"That's only three months away," Ruthana said sulkily. "What diff'rence is there 'tween now an' then?"

"I cain't explain it," Flora admitted. "I jes' know."

It was silly, Flora knew that; what difference did three months make? But it did. She tried to make amends.

"An' mebbe I bin too hard on you," Flora said. "Mebbe you don' have too much fun in yo' life."

She grinned wryly.

"Mebbe both a' us don'. Why don' you an' me go out together Sat'dee night to the movies, and a soda at Pop's. Ernestine too, if'n you like. Have a li'l fun together."

She made one more concession.

"An 'mebbe we start lookin' for a nice dress fo' you, a party dress to wear at dances, when you is sixteen. Somethin' pretty, somethin' special."

Ruthana didn't smile, as Flora hoped, but she gave up the fight, for the moment, anyway. She reverted to her usual self, reliable, withdrawn, and, Flora thought for the first time, slightly sad.

"All right, Mama," she said.

They did go out, the following Saturday, to the movies,

the small flea pit that served the colored community, which was in considerable contrast to the grander cinema for the whites. Ruthana enjoyed herself, but Flora did not. The newsreel was all about the war and, in particular, the fierce fighting on an island in the Pacific Ocean, in which many American lives were lost. It distressed Flora, and all she could think about for the rest of the show was Willie.

Willie's last letter had been full of excitement, because, after several boring months at Fort Huachuca, he was then posted to San Francisco. He enjoyed the city in his off-base hours, but work was tedious, an extension of his warehouse work in Chicago, loading and unloading supplies. Now, at last, he wrote, he had the possibility of seeing some action. He and Ab were being sent to Australia.

Flora didn't know where Australia was, so she looked it up in Ruthana's atlas and found it on the other side of the Pacific Ocean.

She was so scared. All the great battles of the war, so far, had been fought in the Pacific, and countless thousands of lives had been lost. Even though Willie was not in a combat battalion, he still had to cross that violent ocean to get to Australia. When the newsreel showed Japanese planes attacking an American aircraft carrier, Flora was in despair. She thought that to die in a battleship at sea, trapped between fire and drowning, must be a cruel death.

Two features followed the newsreel. The first was a jaunty, cheerful film about ice skating, with Sonja Henie wearing, to Flora, outrageously short skirts, but then there was a more somber film, about an English family's experiences of war. It was harrowing to Flora, but she could not take her eyes from the screen, hypnotized by black-and-white images of other people's lives that were piercingly real to her, and by some curious process of osmosis she identified absolutely with the white, well-spoken English star. Color and country became irrelevant; the mother's pain was all.

Flora had not invited Ernestine to join them; she had decided she and Ruthana should have a night on their own, to talk and, hopefully, to laugh and make up for the argument over the dance. They went for the promised soda at Pop's Place, which, to Flora's surprise, had changed in the years since she had last been there. It was brighter, better lit, the furniture was new and modern, the booths were all bright red imitation leather, and cheerful, unfamiliar music blasted from a brilliant jukebox. Flora tried to be jolly, for Ruthana's sake, and part of her was enjoying herself, but she could not rid her mind of the newsreel she had seen, and thoughts of Willie's welfare.

She was relieved when Ernestine came in with Clara, and somewhat surprised with herself when she suggested Ruthana stay with them for a while, but not to be home too late.

She walked home alone, glad to be by herself, and, at home, she sat in the new rocking chair she had bought herself. It wasn't exactly new; she had found it at the back of Pete's Emporium, slightly battered but comfortable and cheap. Rocking in it eased the winter pain in her back, and she sat for an hour trying not to think of the films she had seen, trying to remember only Ruthana's smiling face, but the images of Willie, and of burning ships and drowning men, would not go away.

And another face, that had no shape or form, but which she knew to be that of her other son.

She ceased to worry about Ruthana, she was in good company, and went to her room and knelt at her bed to pray for Willie and Luke. While she was praying she heard Ruthana come in, and heard the girl singing softly.

Her relationship with Ruthana was on the verge of change, because she couldn't remember Ruthana as a little girl, only as the young woman she now was. She almost relented, she almost changed her mind, she almost went out to Ruthana to tell her she could go to the dance.

Then another face drifted into her mind, that of Charlie when young. She remembered her own first dance, outside a barn all those years ago, and she remembered the dazzling joy she had seen in Charlie's eyes as she danced with him, and knew it was in her own. She remembered the soft desire that had flooded through her then. Ruthana must be feeling some of those same emotions, and there was nothing Flora could do to prevent them, but she would not let go, not yet. There was too much temptation out there.

She got into bed and drifted to sleep, but then she had a nightmare of burning ships and drowning men, and she woke again. She lay awake for an hour trying to think of anything but the war. Eventually she fell asleep again, but restlessly, as all her sleeping was.

She was alone in the house the next Tuesday, ironing shirts. She was tired and irritable; she seemed always to be ironing other people's shirts, or on her knees cleaning other people's floors and toilets. She began to wonder what the point of it all was. Her money jar was almost full these days, she had even taken the extraordinary step of putting some money in a savings bank, but what was it all for? Surely simple survival was not enough. Willie had left home and would never come back to live. Ruthana would leave home within a few years. Would she end up like Charlie, old, alone, and forgotten?

There was a knock at the door. Flora was puzzled; very few people ever came to visit at this time of day, unless it was Pearl, wanting a cup of sugar as an excuse to gossip. She put her iron aside and went to the window.

She saw a car and a man in uniform, a soldier, an officer, standing outside her door, and her heart almost stopped. Something must have happened to Willie.

Even as she thought this, she knew it was irrational; bad news came by telegram. But this was the war, the rules could have changed, and why else would an officer come to her?

She dared not open the door, and he knocked again, more sharply. She edged to the door, slowly, and opened it a tiny crack. She had to know.

The officer was older than Willie, by some five or six years, but still young and quite handsome. His skin was coffee-colored, his eyes were gentle brown. He was trim and crisp and neat. He had a serious manner, and was slightly nervous, which reinforced her belief that he was the bearer of awful tidings.

"Mrs. Palmer?" he asked. His voice was soft and well spoken.

Flora nodded.

"I'm Luke," he said. "Luke Fleming."

31

*S*HE MADE HIM A CUP OF COFFEE and sat staring at
him as he sipped it. He looked out of place in his
smart lieutenant's uniform and Flora was acutely aware
that her little house, however clean and well kept, was also
slightly shabby.

She thought he did not belong here, and she could not
imagine what to say to him, although for years she had
planned what she would say if this day ever came. She felt
as if there was a gulf between them that she did not know
how to bridge. Then the unthinkable happened. Part
of her wanted to take him in her arms and hold him, just
hold him.

But, because she did not know what he thought of
her, and was scared to find out, part of her wanted him to
go away.

"Why you come?" she asked him.

He looked at her as if he was looking at a stranger,
which she was to him. She did not understand that it was a
stranger he wanted to know.

"Because I could," he said with a small smile. "And because I wanted to."

The smile faded.

"Because I had to," he said. "Is it true, are you my
mammy?"

She didn't like the word. It was a Southern word, an
old slave days word, it was what white children called their
black nurses, and she was more, so much more, than that.

"Yes," she said. "I's yo' mammy."

He nodded, but not as if she had told him anything
new.

"I got your letters," he said. She had written to him

three times over the past three years, once a year, on his birthday.

"I didn't know what to do, what to think at first," he said. He smiled that small, shy smile again.

"I wanted you to know why," Flora murmured.

"I think I always knew," he said. "Or I guessed. My pappy was not"—he searched for the word—"a kindly man."

He took a sip of coffee.

"At first they told me you were dead," he said. "But they wouldn't talk about you, they wouldn't tell me what you were like, how you and Pappy met, or how you died. It was like you had never really existed for them."

She knew he spoke true.

"Gran'ma told me I should think of her as my mammy, but I was a li'l bit darker than her and a whole lot darker than my pappy, and it didn't make sense to me."

What could she say?

"Was he kind to you, my pappy?"

She stared at him. Should she lie?

"No," she said. "He waren't kind."

He nodded again.

"Din't think so."

He sat in silence for a moment, and Flora understood this was as difficult for him as it was for her, but he was building the bridge.

"He never did marry. He was always away, in Atlanta or New Orleans, and ol' Nana was locked up in her room sick all the time, and Gran'ma, well, she was tough. And Gran'pa. They kep' telling me I was special, and that I had to do well at school 'coz I was better'n the other boys, because I was a Fleming, and I had to carry on the family name, and I didn't feel special, I felt—I don't know—lonely."

He looked at her again, and she saw his eyes were glistening.

"And I missed you, Mammy."

In that moment, he became her little boy.

"Ol' Nana died and Pappy got killed and I thought the end of the world had come, alone in that big, empty house with Gran'ma, who didn't love me. She loved her son, my pappy. Gran'pa sold the land and cleared out and she locked herself up in her room, and I think somehow she blamed me for Pappy's death. She blamed everyone else, why not me?"

Flora could not bear to think of him alone in that loveless house.

"Bessie looked after me. You know Bessie?"

Flora nodded.

"And ol' Joseph, and they were kind. And I asked them one day where my mammy was, if she was in heaven. I think I was, oh, mebbe fifteen. They didn't answer directly, and I shouted at Bessie, said I wanted to know, and she told me. But she didn't know where you were. She couldn't even remember your name."

He was silent again, and then looked straight at her, almost accusingly.

"And I hated you. 'Coz of what you done."

She could not meet his eyes. She looked down. Why shouldn't he hate her? She hated herself.

"I went to college in Atlanta, and I was glad to be away from that place. I was almost happy, on my own."

He did not tell her how miserable he had been, even at college. He was the only black in a law school full of whites because his family had money. He did not tell her how he tried to be white and how he had failed.

"And then I got your letter."

Now it would be all right, now he would understand she thought.

"And I was so angry with you. I couldn't understand how you could give me away."

"I din't want to!" she cried. "They took you! I didn't have a choice!"

"I know that now," he said softly.

He did not tell her that it was Bessie who made him understand, and old Joseph, and even Charlie. Brought up to money, in privileged if lonely circumstances, he had never understood that the poor had few options.

After he had received Flora's first letter he had been angry, but when he went home he showed the letter to Bessie and asked her for the truth. She had told him the truth of her life, of all their lives, and it had opened his eyes. He went to Joseph, who was sick and dying, and after years of labor for the Fleming family had nothing, no money, no family, and few friends. He went to visit Charlie, and saw what he had never seen, because before it had not been important.

He went back to college, determined to succeed, but not in the white man's world. When he got his degree, he found a job with a not very good black lawyer, one of the few of his kind, and had devoted himself to improving the lot of colored people, the poor and the dispossessed, fighting their battles on their behalf. He had become everything his family—but not his mother—had not wanted him to be.

"Why you in the army?" Flora asked him, intensely proud of him.

Luke shrugged.

"Things to do," he said. "Battles to fight. Army just as unfair to colored men as the rest of the world."

He corrected himself.

"As the rest of America," he said.

He told her a funny story. In Britain there were bars where white American servicemen were not allowed. Only English people—and black Americans—were served.

She smiled at the story, pleased by it, but it was trivia compared with the matter at hand.

"Why you come?" she wanted to know.

Luke shrugged.

"I don't know. I've thought about it a lot, and don't

know. You weren't real, and I wasn't sure I wanted you to be real, in case I didn't like you. Then I got posted to Europe, I'm leaving tomorrow, and I had to see you, I had to know— anything happens to me—"

Again she thought his eyes were glistening wet. If what he had said seemed formal, almost rehearsed, that fell away from him.

"I wanted to know what you look like, at least, in case anything happens to me."

He paused again.

"No, that's only part of it," he said. "I wanted you to know what I look like. If anything happens to me, I wanted to think that somebody might care."

This smart, handsome officer became, at that moment, the loneliest boy in all the world. He had no one who loved him. Except Flora, and that had not been established yet.

He looked around the little shack.

"You doing all right?" he asked.

Flora nodded, her own tears welling up.

"Oh, yes," she said. "I doin' jes' fine. Now."

His voice sunk to a whisper; she could hardly hear him.

"Then give me a hug," he said.

She didn't know if it was what he needed, or if he was doing it to be kind. But it was what she needed.

She went to him and thirty years of love flooded from her, and as he held her he whispered the words that she had longed, for thirty years, to hear him say.

"I've missed you, Mammy," he whispered.

They were sitting together at the table when Ruthana came home. She was puzzled to see the handsome stranger, and shocked when Flora said who he was. She wanted to feel more emotion than she did, but her overriding concern was for her mama. She knew how much this must mean to Flora, and wondered how she was coping with it.

Luke was pleasant to her and asked her about her day and her schoolwork, but Ruthana felt she was intruding on something that was beyond her emotional grasp.

"You needs to talk, I'll go see Auntie Pearl," she said, but Luke looked at his watch and rose.

"No," he said. "I gotta go. You stay and look after my mammy."

Flora begged him to stay the night, but he had to be back in Memphis to catch the train for New York. He promised he would write.

Flora walked with him to his car. She remembered that she didn't know his job in the army.

"You gon' have to fight?"

"No." He smiled. "I speak and write English pretty good so they've made me a journalist."

This hardly settled Flora's fears for him. She remembered the newsreel of the battle in the Pacific. Somebody had to take those pictures. Someone had to write the stories of the battles for the newspapers.

"You stay 'way from them Germans," she blurted out.

He nodded, then he moved to her and held her in his arms again, hugging her. Neither of them spoke. Words were useless, meaningless.

He broke away from her.

"I'll write," he said, getting quickly into his car. Flora nodded and watched as he turned on the engine. He waved, and tried to smile, and drove away down the street. He didn't look back, and she didn't want him to. She wanted to remember him trying to smile, and she knew she would never forget.

She stood in the empty street, staring at nothing except a dream fulfilled.

Ruthana came out of the house and put her arm around her mama.

"You all right?" she asked softly.

Flora heard her, but didn't respond for a little while.

"Yeh, I all right," she said eventually. "Bes' get somethin' to eat, you be hungry."

"I cook," Ruthana said.

While she busied herself at the stove, Flora sat at the table twisting her handkerchief in her hands.

Her firstborn son, Luke, was lost to her for many, many years, but now he had been found. Her second son, Willie, was lost for a while but then he was found again.

Now both had gone away, and she did not know if she would ever see either of them again.

She could not contain the enormous complexity of emotion that she felt. All she could see were the faces of her sons, and all she could hear was a sound she had heard so many years ago.

On the train that took her away from home, from Luke, a mother had sung a lullaby to calm her infant child. She heard that lullaby again, and she felt the pain that the lullaby had provoked in her, and she remembered that she had cried out, on the train, just once.

That sound came from her again, magnified a thousandfold, from the deepest recesses of her soul, an animal sound, something between a scream and a moan, and she fell to the floor in a faint.

32

*W*ILLIE GOT HIS WISH, his chance to be a hero. Ab had always said it was inevitable, that the United States didn't have the manpower to wage war on two fronts without using black troops in combat, but even so, it was a long time coming.

After two years in the army, they were on active duty. They were stationed on the island of New Georgia, in the Solomons group, north of Guadalcanal, guarding an airfield by a pretty, tropical beach. They were four hundred miles from the Japanese stronghold of Rabaul, on the island of New Britain. It was as close as they came to the war, but it proved to be close enough.

The port and airfield at Rabaul were the main base for all Japanese operations in the southwestern Pacific, heavily fortified and as heavily defended. Rather than risk an all-out assault on the fortress, General MacArthur had concentrated on Papua New Guinea and the islands surrounding New Britain to cut off the Japanese supply lines. After two years, he was close to reaching his objective, and was now turning his attention to the recapture of the Philippines.

The Japanese still had a capacity to strike, and strike hard. Once a week at least, their planes came flying low over New Georgia, some bombers but mostly fighter planes, strafing the airfield that Willie and Ab were helping to defend.

Although New Georgia was technically under American control, on many of the surrounding islands large numbers of Japanese soldiers still roamed free, in the hills and jungles, and they still held a large section of the nearby island of Bougainville.

Some of these Japanese had abandoned the war. With

no information or supplies reaching them from headquarters, they had made themselves comfortable in the hills, in well-fortified huts or dugouts, and had planted gardens for produce. They defended these ferociously.

Others were less complaisant, and small groups of stragglers formed attack units to try and retake some ground. Such as the airfield.

The U.S. troops were constantly on the alert. Apart from the weekly small bombing runs or attacks by fighter planes, days would go by with only sniper fire to distract them, but sometimes these snipers found a target. And sometimes, mostly at night, a small group of stragglers would rush the perimeter, cause what havoc they could, and disappear again into the night.

Despite this, the men fashioned a pleasant existence at other times, swimming in the lovely lagoon, although they were always guarded, and planting their own gardens for fresh vegetables. The speed with which plants grew in this sultry, humid climate astonished Willie, who was used to the more sedate seasons of Tennessee. There was no summer here, or spring or winter or fall, only the wet and the dry, and the dry was wet enough. They would fish, trying to match the astonishing accuracy of the native island spearmen, and almost always failing, and a few of them went night fishing with some islanders. It was said that one young New Georgian fisherman could hold his breath underwater for seven minutes. When snipers shot two nighttime fishermen, the expeditions ended.

Willie and Ab had fallen into a pattern. They had their own well-constructed gun emplacement halfway along the runway, sandbagged and with a good view of the strip, and not too far from shelter or assistance. They spent their days on guard against attack, cleaning their rifles, watching the sky and the nearby jungle, and talking about everything in the world.

"Them powdered eggs was good this morning," Ab said, yawning one day.

It wasn't true, they hated powdered eggs, but it was a change from complaining.

"Sure was," Willie agreed, yawning himself. "I ain't ever gon' eat real eggs again."

They had become more than friends. Ab was the father that Willie had never known. Three months before the war began, when Willie went back to Chicago after his mother's Old Sister ceremony, he was in despair. He was conked, zoot suited, and broke. Josh was in jail and because Willie had allowed Josh to dominate his life, he had no other real friends.

Without Josh, the dark underbelly of Chi-town night-life became meaningless and slightly frightening to Willie. Josh knew his way around, and although Willie liked to think himself a man of the world, all he had really wanted from Josh was to have a good time and not be lonely. Without Josh he felt out of place in the dark bars and scrungy dance halls, filled with brazen women and aggressive men.

He wanted to do something with his life, and he didn't want to end up like Josh, behind bars.

He was also flat broke and he didn't know why. He worked hard, and even though he knew he was paid only slightly more than half what the white men at the warehouse earned, this didn't explain the financial disaster of his life. There was his rent, but the cheap basement wasn't expensive, hardly more than he had paid Lula, and there was his food, but he ate cheaply, poorly. There were his "credicks," but that was only about three bucks a week. The rest, he realized, went to pleasure. He gambled more than he should, and he'd had a losing streak, and he always seemed to pay for the drinks when he went out with Josh, for Josh and whatever women they picked up, and some of those women had wanted more than drink money.

He was determined to turn his life around, for himself and for Ernestine. He had changed from loving Ernestine to being in love with Ernestine, and he wanted to marry her. But she would not have him until he got himself on his feet and had something to offer her. Then there was his mama. It embarrassed Willie that he had seldom sent his mother more than a dollar or two, and he knew she was disappointed in him, not because of the money so much as the chance he had wasted.

He wanted to be the man he had promised his mother he would be, but he didn't know how to achieve it.

So he went to Ab.

"What's up?" Ab asked him.

Willie had gone to a union meeting, not because of the union but because of Ab, and he hung around afterward until all the other men had left. Ab gathered up the notes of his speech, did some bookwork, and tidied the room. He was aware that Willie was hovering by the door, but did not think it was because of a union problem. He knew Willie slightly and knew him to be a good worker, but he also thought Willie was on a fast train to becoming the kind of black man that Ab despised, caring only for drink and sex and, possibly drugs. He knew that Josh, Willie's friend, had been imprisoned for dealing drugs, and because the two were friends, Ab did not think Willie could be innocent.

"What's up?" he said to Willie when he was ready to go home.

"Got a li'l problem." Willie shrugged.

Ab waited.

"I ain't got no money," Willie said.

"I ain't lendin' you none," Ab told him.

Willie's temper flared; he wasn't looking for a handout, only for help.

"I don' want a loan," he snapped. "I earns good money, I c'n pay my way, nearly. I jus' . . ."

He didn't know how to explain it, so he simply presented the problem.

"What am I doin' wrong?" he asked.

Ab walked slowly to him and stared at him without sympathy.

"Jus' 'bout everything, man," he said. "Look at you."

"What's wrong wit' the way I look?" Willie demanded defensively. He was wearing his work overalls, but his conked hair was sheened with brilliantine, he had imitation gold chains on his wrists, and he wore a couple of cheap glass rings.

"Your hair, for a start," Ab said. "What you want hair like that for? You ashamed of your black blood, you tryin' to look white?"

"I jus'—" Willie flared, but he had no real reason. He had his hair conked because it was the sharp thing to do. "Ev'ryone do it!"

"Not everyone," Ab said. His own hair was short and tightly curled. "Only fool nigros doin' it."

Willie wanted to hit him, but Ab was a big man. He almost walked out of the room, but Ab was his lifeline. So he didn't say anything.

"You dealin' drugs?" Ab asked him accusingly.

"If I was dealin', I wouldn't be broke!" Willie said, still edgy with Ab.

He sighed. He might as well be honest.

"Josh, he done 'em," Willie explained. "I din't know."

He realized he'd been a fool, and that he had known, but had not wanted to know. He had ignored it, and gone out whenever Josh had secret visitors.

"I gotta fin' somewhere to live," he muttered.

"That's a start," Ab said more cheerfully.

He stared at Willie as if he was making up his mind about him, as if he was deciding whether Willie was worth the bother.

"Come along a' me," he said, walking out of the room. Willie followed.

Ab lived in a boardinghouse a few streets away. It was sparsely furnished but clean and tidy, run by a big, heavyset, aggressive woman called Martha, who glared at Willie.

"I cook, but I don' clean," she told him. "You keeps yo' own room neat an' tidy."

"Yes'm," Willie murmured, wondering if he wanted to live here.

"And if'n you wants to cook for us all one night, I ain't gon' stop you," Martha announced.

Willie was shocked. Men didn't cook.

"Men do here," Martha snapped. "Men do ev'rything women do here, an' women do ev'rything men does."

There was a large communal sitting room, again sparsely furnished, a long table, and hard wooden chairs. A man, as serious as Ab, was sitting at a desk in a corner, writing. Ab and Willie sat at the table.

"Trus' me?" Ab asked Willie.

Willie nodded, and Ab asked him questions about himself and about his family in Stockton. He wrote several things in a small notebook and then explained his plan. Each week, Willie would give his pay packet, unopened, to Ab. Ab would pay Willie's rent and his bills.

A dollar a week would be put into a special account, to be sent to his mama once a year. He would give Willie five dollars for spending money. The rest would go to paying off his debts, fast, and when that was done, into a bank account.

"Five dollar?" Willie said. Five dollars a week was not a lot of spending money.

"That too much?" Ab asked, poker-faced.

"No!" Willie cried. "That ain't enough!"

"Gon' have to be," Ab declared. "An' first thing to-morrow, you get a haircut."

He looked at his watch.

"We go get your things."

They walked the few blocks to Willie's basement and collected his belongings. Willie was grateful that Ab dealt with the landlord.

As they walked back, Ab voiced his opinion of the man.

"Men like that," he said, "traitors to their race. Makin' money off the backs a' kids that don't know better, or fallen on hard times. Or bums, like you."

"I ain't a bum," Willie muttered.

"You headed in that direction," Ab told him.

They walked in silence for a moment. Willie tried to think of ways to be friendly, and remembered what others said about Ab.

"You a communist?" he asked Ab.

"What you think a communist is?" Ab asked in reply.

Willie didn't know, and had the grace to admit it.

"Do I think the system is unfair? Yes," Ab explained. "Do I think the capitalist bosses abuse the workers for their own benefit? Yes. Do I think there's a better way, with workers governing theirselves? Yes. If that make me a communist, that's what I am."

It didn't seem so terrible to Willie and he didn't understand, from that first small lesson in politics, why communists were so detested by so many. He guessed there was a whole lot more than Ab was telling him, but he liked the man, if only because he was so straightforward.

"Do I want to go an' live in Russia?" Ab finished. "No. I want to make a better America."

Willie wasn't quite sure where, and how, Russia fit into the picture, but it was late and he was tired.

"Why you called Ab?" he asked, to make the talk more personal. "I never heard a' Ab fo' a name."

"Short for Absalom, from the Bible," Ab grinned. "My mama was religious, an' my pa. I ain't."

Willie was confused.

"Y' b'lieve in God, though?"

"No," Ab said. "God's an invention and the church is just part of the system to keep the workers where the bosses want 'em."

Willie couldn't think of anything to say because he thought that everyone believed in God, however loosely. He was to meet several people over the coming weeks who didn't.

It did not stop him from kneeling down to say a prayer that night, in his small, less than comfortable room. There was a narrow bed, a chest of drawers, a small mirror, and a washstand. A single, naked lightbulb hung from the ceiling, and the curtains at the window were thin. The walls were bare, apart from a picture of a man called Lenin, and another of a man called Stalin. There was no rug on the floor.

Yet Willie thanked God for his surroundings, and for Ab, who had taken the burden of money from his shoulders, and even for the curt and testy Martha.

So began a period of great learning for Willie. All the eight men and two women who boarded at the house were socialists, and some, including Martha and Ab, were card-carrying members of the Communist Party. All were deeply dedicated to the cause of equality of all people, regardless of sex, nationality, or race. They spent hours planning how to bring about their utopia, and as many hours in helping others less fortunate than themselves.

They kept their own rooms clean and there was a roster for sweeping and tidying the communal rooms, and doing the dishes. Martha cooked most of the meals, often with the help of Sarah, the other female boarder, but a few of the men took turns in the kitchen.

During the evening meal, and for an hour or so afterward, they would sit at the tale discussing the politics of the day. At first, Willie listened with some attention, but the talk was of things he didn't understand, or the implications of them, and he would go to his room and strum his guitar, or write to Ernestine and his mama. No one minded. Although they all accepted his presence in the house and were kind to him and contributed to his education, they did not seem to regard him as a potential convert to their cause.

Willie had the sense that they were under siege, because of the war in Europe, and because the Russian leader, Stalin, had signed a pact with the despised German leader, Hitler. When the Nazis attacked Russia that summer, it was a day of rejoicing in the boardinghouse. Even though they doubted that Russia could withstand the German onslaught, and wept openly at the blood that would be shed, it brought Joseph Stalin back to favor in American eyes.

Saturday nights were Willie's biggest problem. It was not easy for him to abandon his old life of dancing and nightclubs, but five dollars wasn't going to get him very far, and Martha made it clear that if he ever came back to the house drunk there'd be hell to pay.

He became an avid moviegoer, and sometimes Ab went with him. Willie wasn't too keen on this. He was content to sit and watch the film roll by, laughing at comedies, thrilling at cowboy films, and entranced by musicals. But Ab almost always found some political fault with the films they saw together.

Cowboy films were wrong because the Indians were always the villains. Comedies were usually wrong because if there were any black characters they were usually of the Stepin Fetchit kind, wide-eyed and fearful, and if there were no black characters, why? Musicals were fine as far as they went, but mindless.

"Don' you ever have any fun?" Willie exploded after a lecture about a film he had enjoyed. "Y' know, when you jus' laugh an' enjoy you'self, an' don' worry 'bout the politics?"

"Sure!" Ab laughed. "But ev'rything's political, an' there's diff'rent kinds of fun."

A couple of weeks later, to prove his point, he took Willie to a concert in a theater outside the ghetto.

It was a novelty for Willie. He seldom left the black district because he was always uncertain in the company of whites. Nor did Ab have much to do with whites, except on union business. He preferred to spend his time with fellow blacks, and his money in black shops.

"The black dollar is black power," he told Willie. "We have to use the system until we can change it."

For this occasion, because the singer was a black man, Paul Robeson, a larger than usual section of the back of the auditorium was reserved for colored only, and it was full.

The rest of the packed house was white, and wildly appreciative of the singer.

Willie thought he had never heard anything so beautiful. There was a full orchestra and a large black choir, and the tall, powerfully built Robeson had a voice like gorgeous thunder, deep and resonant.

His last song was "Ol' Man River," which everyone but Willie seemed to know. When it was done there was absolute silence in the theater, and then a sudden avalanche of applause and cheering, and the entire audience stood to show their appreciation of the beauty they had heard.

They walked home because it seemed the right thing to do; each wanted the silence of the night to consider the evening.

"Don't know if it was your idea of fun, exactly," Ab said eventually. He wanted to know how the concert had affected Willie.

And Willie did not have the words to tell him.

"I 'spect there's diff'rent kinds of fun, like you said," he murmured, and then added a truth he had felt.

"He make me cry."

Willie had been moved to tears several times during the concert, but especially during the last song. It said exactly, more perfectly, more beautifully everything he had tried to say in the simple songs he had written.

He was shocked when Ab told him that a white man had written the song.

"You got a lot to learn." Ab chuckled. "There's white folk feel the pain. It ain't a war between black an' white, it's a war between good an' evil. That song written by a great artist, an' great art is color-blind, like all the world should be."

Willie didn't reply, because the leaning curve was too steep, and then Ab made it sharper still.

"That man Jesus that you pray to, if'n he existed, he was colored," Ab said casually.

Willie stopped, stunned by this heresy. Jesus wasn't colored, Jesus was white, with fair hair and blue eyes.

"They's white man's pictures," Ab said. "You think they gon' bend their knee and pray to a nigro? They don't even like to think he's Jewish."

That made some kind of sense to Willie. He'd never thought about it, but, yes, Jesus might have had Jewish blood.

"Man called Rembrandt," Ab said, "painted portraits of Jesus. But he went to the Jewish quarter of Amsterdam and used Orthodox Jews for his models, with ringlets an' those funny hats."

He laughed.

"Those pictures under lock and key, don' ever see the light of day."

Willie didn't care about a Jewish Jesus, he was still trying to imagine a colored Jesus.

"But Jesus waren't from Africa," he said.

"Right next door," Ab told him blithely. "An' a'for the Crusaders went to Palestine with all their white blood, the Jews was pretty dark."

Willie never really came to terms with this. He saw the logic of it, but his heart refused to accept Ab's conclusion. He wondered if Ab was pulling his leg, to shock him and confuse him and make him think. Ab did that sometimes.

Besides, another problem was occupying his mind. Christmas was coming. Willie loved Christmas, but the people at his boardinghouse did not celebrate the festival.

"Nuttin' to do with us," Martha said. "That's a Christian thing."

Willie didn't care because he accounted himself Christian. He remembered Christmas at home as being a special day of celebration. Even though his family was poor, there were always tiny presents, however cheap, and a special dinner. Even in his days with Josh they had celebrated Christmas by going to a bar and getting drunk. Willie wasn't looking forward to a bleak and somber holiday, alone in his room or sitting at the table with the others discussing Karl Marx and the workers' revolution.

He thought about going home. He was sure Ab would

let him have a little extra from his pay packet for the trip, on such a special occasion.

He started rehearsing his speech to Ab, asking for the money, telling him how much it would mean to his mama and sister, but he never made the speech because he didn't go home.

At the beginning of December the Japanese bombed Pearl Harbor, and the next day President Roosevelt declared war on Japan and then Germany declared war on America.

This was enough excitement for any young man, and Christmas, and going home, took second place in all his thinking.

33

THEY ENLISTED THE FOLLOWING SUMMER. Willie had wanted to join up from the moment war was declared, but Ab counseled caution.

"Every man an' his dog enlisting," Ab said. "An' there's going to be some trouble while they sort it all out."

"But what if it all over afore I gets there?" Willie moaned.

"This war gon' be around for quite a while, boy," Ab said. "You jes' hold your horses."

What Willie didn't know, because Ab didn't tell him, was that if they tried to enlist immediately there was a fair chance that they'd be turned down. There were only a limited number of black regiments, and the army had the pick of those who applied.

What he also didn't know, because he wasn't told, was that Ab was hoping for a major shift in government policy. Ab believed that eventually the country must see the light and form black combat divisions, of which Ab intended to be a part.

"First thing they gon' do is put black soldiers as far away from the war as possible," Ab said. "Messmen, stevedores, laboring, construction, anything but give 'em a gun."

"Why?" Willie demanded.

"'Coz they don't trust us not to cut an' run," Ab said. "If'n we come under fire."

Willie laughed.

"Don't laugh, it's true. It happened in the last war, an' it's the way they still think today."

"How you know all this?" Willie asked. He was always amazed at the breadth of Ab's knowledge.

"'Coz I read books, an' I talk to folk about the things

that matter," Ab said. "When was the last time you read a book?"

Willie shrugged, and Ab explained. During the last days of the Great War, a black unit serving in France lost its way during a nighttime action and drifted to the rear of their own army. Rumors about this supposed cowardice grew to such an extent that eventually the conduct of all black troops was questioned.

"Got so bad they had to have an investigation," Ab said. "It wasn't true, the men had not run. Their officers, who were white, had led them the wrong way."

He stopped and turned away, and when he turned back there was an expression on his face that combined pain and anger.

"Truth was that three black soldiers in that battalion won medals for extraordinary heroism. My pappy was one, but it was too late for him to know it. He was dead."

Ab seldom talked about his family; Willie had only gleaned bits and pieces from the few things Ab had said.

Ab's father had gone to war to serve his country when Ab was only seven. A year later, Ab's father was dead, killed in an advance on German lines. Ab's mother had raised seven children on her own, in grinding poverty. Two of his brothers were dead. One, a coal miner in West Virginia, from lung disease, the other, Ab's youngest brother, shot by policemen during a riot in the Depression.

It was this that brought Ab to political awareness.

"He wasn't doing nothing bad," Ab said. "Just trying to get himself a job. But they was only hiring whites."

Willie knew that Ab's mother was still alive, because he went to see her once a week, every Sunday. He wouldn't talk about her, but Martha knew the truth and told Willie.

"She crazy," she explained. "She married again 'coz she needed a man to support her, or thought she did. He used to beat her up, but she didn't complain. They had a li'l girl, and when the girl was ten her daddy raped her. Ab's ma, she gone crazy. She took a knife and kilt him, and they locked her up."

She looked at Willie with withering scorn.

"You men. If'n you get married an' you lay a finger on your wife, an' I hear about it, I cut your balls off."

Willie did not doubt that she would do it.

"We ain't all like that," he said.

"No, mebbe you ain't," Martha conceded. "But too many are."

This led her to a speech about the brave new world of her communist dreams, in which all men and women were exactly equal, and women and children were not regarded as property but as individuals, with individual rights.

Willie had heard similar speeches from Martha many times before. He agreed with the principle behind it, but was bored by hearing it again. Soon as he could he excused himself and Martha let him go. He was not revolutionary material.

Spring came, and the Japanese had conquered most of the western Pacific and seemed invincible.

"I gotta do my bit!" Willie cried to Ab.

"You been watching too many war movies." Ab chuckled.

Willie didn't know what he was waiting for, but he did know that a number of the black men from work had tried to enlist and had been rejected. Willie didn't want this to happen to him, so, however unwillingly, he waited.

Three things happened that spring, and Willie was never sure which one provoked Ab to action, or if it was some combination of all three.

In the middle of April an American lieutenant colonel, James Doolittle, led sixteen B-25 bombers on a raid on Japan itself. It was an audacious, stupidly dangerous attack, but it succeeded, and America loved Doolittle for it. It was the first proof to the public that there were chinks in the Japanese armor. Men swarmed to enlist.

Three weeks later, in the Battle of the Coral Sea, the American navy was victorious and twenty-five Japanese ships were sunk or disabled. More men rushed to enlist, including three of the men from work who had previously been turned down. This time they were accepted.

Then some young black men in Chicago formed the Congress of Racial Equality and immediately began a campaign of nonviolent sit-ins at theaters and restaurants that did not serve blacks. They were surprisingly successful and, even more surprisingly, struck a chord of sympathy among many whites.

"That's all right." Ab smiled at Willie. "We can go now."

It was as if he felt he was leaving the political war on the home front in good hands.

They enlisted in the army the next day, and a week later they were on their way to boot camp in Georgia.

The night before they left, Ab gave Willie an accounting of his money. All his credit accounts and gambling debts had been paid off, and Willie now had about a hundred and fifty dollars in a savings bank. There was a further forty dollars in another account for Flora.

"You want to send it to her now?" Ab asked.

Willie nodded, astonished at his riches. He mumbled his thanks to Ab, who shrugged.

"You lookin' after your own money now," he said. "You man enough to be a soldier, you man enough to do that."

Willie nodded again, something else on his mind.

"Ab . . ." he began, but didn't know how to finish.

Ab waited.

". . . should I—case anythin' happen to me—what I do wit' that money?"

"You want to make a will?" Ab asked him, and Willie nodded again, grateful that his friend always had the answer.

Ab got a pad and a pen.

"Who you want to leave it to?"

"To my mama, I guess," Willie said. "An' some for Ernestine. An' Ruthana."

He wondered if he should offer Ab money for looking after him.

"An' a li'l bit fo' you," he said, but Ab shook his head.

"I ain't done this for money, boy," he said softly.

Willie mumbled his thanks again, and sat patiently while Ab wrote the will.

"Y'ever been married, Ab?" he wondered. "Got a girl-friend?"

He had never seen Ab with a woman, or heard him mention one, apart from his mother and his two sisters. And Martha, who meant a very great deal to Ab.

"No," Ab said. "I ain't the marryin' kind."

"Ah," Willie said as if he understood, although he could not imagine that a man wouldn't want to get married.

Let Willie think what he would, the truth was that Ab was so appalled by the violence of his mother's second marriage, by the appalling poverty of his early life, and by the inequities and inequalities that existed everywhere, he had sworn that he would not bring a child into the world until the world was different, and he would not inflict his own battles and battle scars on a wife. He found release for his physical needs with Martha, and it was enough for both of them, for she had sworn a similar vow. Martha had been gang-raped when she was young, and again five years after that. A child of that second rape, who might have had any one of a d———————, had died in infancy.

Ab called Martha in, and they witnessed Willie sign the piece of paper. Ab folded the will and put it in an envelope.

"Martha, keep it safe," he said.

Willie was suddenly flooded with love for this remark-able, unsentimental couple who had been so kind to him without ever being gentle. They had helped him when he needed help and taught him important lessons he had needed to learn, and they had done so without any prospect of return, or want or need of it.

Tomorrow he was going away to learn how to be a sol-dier, and even though Ab would be there, watching out for him, watching over him, his life was changing. He was excited, but he was also scared of his brave new adventure, and he wanted to say something that showed them both how much he appreciated what they had done.

"I wants to say . . ." he began formally. "I wants to say . . ."

He tried to control the choke in his voice.

"I dunno what I wants to say, 'ceptin' thank you fo' all you done for me, and that I loves you."

"Don't you start blubbin' on me, boy," Martha said warningly. " 'Coz if'n you do, I'll start blubbin' myself."

But it was no use, she was already crying. She moved to Willie and held him hard. He put his arms around her and hugged her as hard and let his own tears flow, because in front of these people he could be anything and not be ashamed of who he was.

34

WITHIN A WEEK, WILLIE HAD DECIDED that the top army brass didn't know what it was doing. Georgia was the stupidest place to send black men to learn to be soldiers, or Alabama, or either of the Carolinas, or any of the old Confederate states.

"It's part of the training," Ab said. "You in the army, but you still a nigro an' they don't want you to forget that."

An officer had told them that on the first day.

"You may be soldiers in the army of the United States," he told them, "but you are still Negroes, and you will be treated as Negroes by the police in this town."

"An' by the army," a man sitting near Willie muttered.

Both had spoken the truth. As recruits, Willie and Ab could not leave the base, but others could and did, and there were repeated stories of encounters with the citizens and, especially, with the local police, who had a reputation for violence toward any black accused of almost anything, no matter how small or how unwarranted.

Within the confines of the base, segregation ruled. The black men had their own barracks, showers, and latrines, their own mess, their own canteen, their own shop. Their officers were white but other than that they had no contact with other white men during their hours on duty.

Their day began at dawn, with reveille, and was a sweaty, arduous, often painful haze of drill, physical exercise, more drill, fatigues, drill again, obstacle courses, and even more drill.

Willie was lucky, he was good at drill, and he had Ab to guide him. Others were not so fortunate.

"You lazy, shiftless, no-good nigger!" a sergeant screamed at someone. Sergeants were always screaming at someone. "This ain't a tap dance; don't you know your left foot from your right?"

Willie thought that was stupid too, because drill was just like tap dancing, a series of steps learned by rote and executed to a certain rhythm.

Ab was also good at drill and Willie began to think that it wasn't new to him, that somehow Ab had done this before, in some other war. But what other war? Ab was eight when the last war had ended.

At the end of the day, he was exhausted. He collapsed on his bed and maybe dozed for a while, but then a corporal or a sergeant would come in and scream at them all over again, and have inspections of bodies and uniforms and beds that were already scrupulously clean and tidy, and find fault with most of them.

He learned how to polish his boots to a mirror shine and press his uniform into razor-sharp pleats. He learned how to look after his possessions, for several men in his barracks were expert cat thieves, and clothes hanging out to dry would go mysteriously astray or, more seriously, money or any small thing of value.

He had no idea how Ab, who was a natural soldier, found time to spend with other men, informing them of their rights, or helping them write letters home, or defending them against the worst abuses of the sergeants. Within a short space of time, Ab had a reputation as a sort of saint to the other men, and a troublemaker to any officer.

The one comfort of their lives was the food. There was plenty of it. It all tasted much the same—it was hard to know chipped beef from creamed chicken, or chocolate pudding from apple pie, except by the color of it—but they went to bed with full bellies, at least. And for some men there, that in itself was a thing of wonder.

Their real problems came in their few off-duty hours, and it was here that Willie decided the army brass was at its most stupid. It was one thing to put several hundred young black men in a base near a Southern town, but all the white recruits and soldiers seemed to be bigoted Southern redneck crackers with the most extreme racial attitudes. If there were men from the Northern states or even a few liberal whites on the base, and there must have been many, their voices were seldom heard.

"Outa my way, nigger" was the constant chorus they heard as they walked through the base and white soldiers approached them, and that was the least of the insults. The Southern blacks were used to it, even if they didn't like it, but because it was so relentless, even they rebelled. The Northern blacks, used to less formal segregation and unfairness, but not to such continuing and ruthless insults, responded with their fists. Fights broke out every day, stopping, by common consent, if an officer came by and continuing when he had gone.

"There gon' be trouble," Willie said to Ab.

"There's going to be trouble," Ab said to Willie.

The swimming pool was the first focus of the discord. The weather was still hot and there was only one pool, although another was planned. The army simply had not been ready for the mass of black recruits that Washington had ordered. They were supposed to share the pool, but a number of whites objected, and a compromise was reached. The blacks could use the pool for two hours, and then the whites had it. This was not good enough for some whites, who objected to swimming in water that blacks had recently used. Then a few blacks didn't get out of the pool at the appointed changeover time, and there was a fight, and blood was spilled. Blacks were banned from the pool until a new, temporary one could be built.

The biggest riot happened because of the movie theater. There was only one, although again, another was planned. The side sections of the movie house were reserved for blacks, but some Southern whites objected even to that. They wanted separate screenings of the films for separate audiences. They wanted what they had at home.

It came to a head because of Betty Grable. A new film of hers was to be shown on a Saturday night, and the trailers and the posters showed her in a revealing swimsuit. A number of white soldiers spread the word that they did not intend to sit in a theater with a bunch of niggers ogling the swimsuited star.

This was not acceptable to many, and especially to Ab, whose influence now extended well beyond his own hut. On the Saturday night, he and a couple of others, with a somewhat reluctant Willie at Ab's side, led a hundred black men to the cinema. The whites were waiting for them and refused to let them in. Someone called the MPs but they didn't hurry to get there, and by the time they did two hundred men were locked in battle. Noses were bloodied and several arms broken. Ab and the other ring-leaders from both sides were arrested and put on a charge, but in the end, Ab and the blacks were let off with only a caution. As Ab said, arguing his own case, the blacks were only following the camp commander's orders.

Within a week, there was a second movie house, for blacks, in a converted drill hall. Ab was disgusted. Segregation had won.

Willie wrote to his mama and told her of the riot, but he tried to make it seem less serious than it was; he didn't want her to worry. He wrote to her regularly, every week, and was pleased to do so because he had news to tell.

To Ernestine he wrote once a day, if not a complete letter then scraps of a letter that, by the end of the week, filled several pages. He was doing, he told Ernestine proudly, what he had said he would do; he had changed himself. His life was full, and he was happy. He was surviving the rigors of basic training, and he knew he would be a good soldier.

Yet despite the many surprises the army had in store for him, the most surprising thing in Willie's life remained Ab. He was constantly learning more about the man, and constantly grateful for his friendship.

Weapons training provided the biggest surprise of all, because it was clear from the word go that Ab knew as much about a rifle as any sergeant.

"Where you learn that?" Willie asked him one night.

"In Spain," Ab said.

"When was you in Spain?" Willie demanded. He'd never heard Ab talk of Spain, or even of having left America.

"In the war," Ab said.

"What war?" Willie exploded, although he knew which war Ab meant. Martha had given him the details of the Spanish Civil War in one of her evening lectures.

"The only war that mattered then," Ab said. The civil war in Spain had been the political world in microcosm, a battle between the left and the right. The right had the support of the Italian and German Fascists, while the Russians and many socialists from many countries fought for the left-wing legitimate government. The Fascists had won.

"You kill a man in that war?" Willie asked.

"I reckon I did," Ab said softly. He was lost in memory for a moment.

"But the thing I remember most is that no one cared about the color of my skin. I went to Paris to enlist, an' I went to a bar. I ordered a coffee and a drink an' thought maybe they wouldn't serve me, they'd send me to some other bar, for blacks. Not that I'd seen any others."

He smiled as at a pleasant memory.

"But no one gave a damn. I drank my coffee an' my brandy an' no one cared about the color of my skin. I sat there for hours thinkin' how nice it was, just to be like anyone else."

Willie turned away with a grin. Ab was many things, but he was not just like everyone else.

Basic training, which Willie thought would never end, did, and then he was a soldier. Later, looking back on those weeks that had been such hell, he remembered them fondly. He and Ab were both posted to Fort Huachuca, in Arizona, but were given four days of home leave first. Ab went to Chicago, to see Martha, his mother, and his friends, and Willie went to Stockton.

It was in Stockton that Willie realized how much he had changed. The army, for all its faults and inequities, had given him a sense of pride in himself. He felt he had earned the uniform he wore so proudly, and he also knew that he wanted to be more. He wanted to be able to fulfill the full potential of that uniform. He was a soldier. He wanted to fight. He wanted his chance to be a hero. If that meant he might die, it went with the uniform. He tried to explain it to his mama, that he didn't want to die, that he was scared to death of dying, but that until that possibility was available to him he would not be complete. All his life he had been a second-rate citizen just because of the color of his skin, and he wanted to be just like everyone else. It didn't seem a lot to ask. He wasn't sure his mama understood.

He realized how very much he loved Ernestine, but he did not want to ask her to marry him, although he thought she would say yes if he did.

" 'Tain't fair on you," he told her. "Not while there's a war on."

"Other men doing it," Ernestine protested. "Other soldiers gettin' married. Or at leas' "—she hinted—"engaged."

Willie laughed, and she laughed, and they agreed they were "going steady."

Willie stared at her, wanting her more than he had ever wanted any woman. She was more to him than beautiful, she was his friend. She knew the best of him and the worst of him, she had stuck with him through the good times and the bad. He could not bear the thought of dying without ever knowing the completeness of her, but even if he was careful there was a chance she would become pregnant, and, if he was later killed, he would not leave her with the unfair burden of a fatherless child.

He asked for a new photograph of her; the old one he kept in his wallet was scrappy and torn around the edges, and it was a picture of the girl she had been, not the woman she had become. She gave him a new photo on the last night they were together, and he laughed because he had a photograph of himself for her. They had both snuck into the photo studio at different times.

At the last moment, he could not stop himself. The train was about to leave, packed with soldiers. The station was crammed with friends all waving flags. Flora was crying. The station agent was blowing his whistle and the conductor was calling "All aboard!"

Willie had kissed Ernestine good-bye and hugged his mama and Ruthana. He picked up his bag and began moving to the train. Then he stopped and looked back at Ernestine. She was about six feet away from him and the shouting and cheering and noise of the station was all around him. He did not say the words aloud because he didn't think she would hear them. He mouthed them, silently.

"Marry me."

He saw a bolt of happiness illuminate her eyes and he knew she had heard him, and he saw her lips move although the answer was as silent as the question.

"Yes."

35

*A*RIZONA WAS PLEASANT, the winter desert air fresh and clean. Fort Huachuca was a large base, efficiently run, and Willie thought the blacks outnumbered the whites. Because they were soldiers and not raw recruits, the officers were more relaxed, and the sergeants did not always shout. The laws of segregation still applied and were enforced, but with more tact than in Georgia.

But they still hurt.

A large number of German prisoners of war were interned nearby, and it was a matter of continuing bitterness among the black troops that the Germans could be served in restaurants and bars where black American troops were not allowed. This bitterness was only slightly alleviated when rumor spread that the army was to form the first colored combat division, and it would be here, at Fort Huachuca.

"At last!" Ab shouted in triumph. He had to prove to himself and to the world that black men were not cowards, for his dead father's sake.

"At long last," Willie echoed, hoping he would be allowed to join.

It was not to be. Although the 93rd Infantry Division was formed at Fort Huachuca, Willie and Ab were assigned to a different unit in San Francisco, initially to work as stevedores.

"Chocolate soldiers," Ab grumbled.

At least they felt closer to the war, and at least they had some junior officers who were black, and they did not stay in San Francisco long. They were posted again, overseas, to Australia.

Willie was thrilled. He'd never been overseas before,

and could not imagine what a foreign country was like. More important, it was one more step closer to the war.

The journey was less than romantic. They traveled on an old freighter that had been converted into a troop ship, packed together like sardines. Willie was seasick for the first three days, and so, to his surprise, was Ab.

"Gimme dry land!" Ab moaned. "I can't stand all this ocean!"

There was nothing but water, day after day, with not a single island or even a seagull to break the monotony, only, sometimes, flying fish that landed on the deck, or dolphins that raced beside them.

After two weeks they crossed the equator and had a ceremony that broke the monotony. Those who had never crossed the line before had to be introduced to King Neptune and his court and get their heads dunked in a barrel of seawater. Everyone entered into the fun of it, although many of the men from the heartland, the Plains states, had never heard of Neptune, and, never having seen the sea, were astonished at the extent of his domain.

They bunked down happily that night, they were halfway to their destination, but at about two in the morning the ship's alarm sounded. Men fell from their bunks and hammocks and hit the deck, grabbing their life preservers.

It shocked Willie into a new reality. Until then they had been sailing alone across a vast, empty ocean, and he had never considered the possibility that they would be attacked, or, if they were, that it would be in daylight, by aircraft.

He had not thought about submarines.

They mustered on deck and assembled in formal ranks. No one spoke except the officers, who moved among them checking that their life preservers were properly tied, and they spoke in whispers.

The ship rolled and changed direction, and then again. Willie stood beside Ab and every man was united in fear, and each was asking himself the same question. What if a torpedo hit them? What would it be like to die on a burning ship, or drown at sea?

He began to hate the submarine he couldn't see and wasn't even sure was there, and he hated even more the enemy below. Up until then, even in boot camp during bayonet training, that enemy had been a faceless mass, lacking individuality or personality, simply the distant aggressor. Now the enemy was only a torpedo's range away, and Willie acquired the critical sense a soldier needs in war, of survival, of readiness to kill.

They stood for an hour, silently, and then someone broke wind and the tension lessened.

"Shit, man!" a voice whispered. "How long this gon' go on?"

It lasted for another hour, and then they were stood down. They went back to their bunks, but no one slept easily that night.

In the morning they were all changed men, soldiers ready to fight, and with the morning came information they had not had before.

They were not going to Australia as stevedores or janitors or messmen, potato peelers or latrine cleaners. After a brief period of weapons and jungle training, they were going on active duty.

At last they were going to fight.

Three months later they found themselves on a picture-perfect Pacific island guarding an airstrip by a palm-fringed beach, surrounded by friendly islanders and hostile Japanese.

The first time they were attacked by Japanese aircraft, Willie panicked inside, but his training, his determination to be a good soldier, and his fury at the enemy made him stand his ground. He grabbed the AA gun and started firing long before he had any real target, and kept firing until long after the planes were gone.

"Damn!" he swore, because he hadn't shot one down.

Ab, who had stood beside him all the way and, guessing

Willie's nervousness, had shouted encouragement as he fired his own gun, grinned.

"Yeh, hot damn!" Ab said.

Willie looked at him and saw the enormous smile on Ab's face and realized that Ab had enjoyed himself.

"That's why we here," Ab said. "An' it's better'n being bored to death!"

He was exultant, and Willie began to catch his mood. He was alive. He had had a very close encounter with the enemy, and he had survived.

He let out a whoop of joy and put his arm around Ab's shoulder, and the two of them almost danced in glee.

Their excitement faded when they found out that the strafing planes had killed two men, and now Willie had to face another fact of war: it might as easily have been he and Ab. He mourned the dead, as he hoped others might grieve for him if he died, and he felt the loss of two men he didn't know all that well very sharply, and his hatred of the Japanese increased. But not even this loss could completely eradicate the absolute exhilaration he had felt that day, the surging of the life force.

The pattern of the next few months was set, and they became used to it, veterans of attack. Willie never lost the fear he felt whenever the planes came, but he became a fine gunner, and the day he scored a hit there was not a prouder man in all the world.

He didn't have any proof that it was his gun that brought the plane down—it might have been Ab's, or that of any one of the dozen gunners ranged around the strip— but Willie was sure of it. He saw a piece of the wing tear off, and smoke began pouring from the fighter. Then the plane lurched and started falling. The pilot must have regained control because he veered the aircraft upward and limped away to the sea, to safety. When it was a mile from land, the plane lurched again and fell into the ocean.

Every man watching, and all them were, cheered and clapped, and they had a drunken party that night.

At dawn they heard distant pops of sniper fire. Every

man grabbed his rifle, ready for action, but there was only silence. Then they were told that two of the perimeter guards had been attacked; one was dead, one was injured.

Willie hated the snipers most of all. At least he could see attacking aircraft; he had a target for his gun and a focus for his rage. But snipers were invisible and gave no warning. There was only the dense green wall of the jungle and then a tiny belch of smoke, and, a millionth of a second later, the sound of the gun. It didn't matter how much gunfire they poured into the jungle, the sniper was long gone.

Almost the pleasantest part of the months they spent on the island was the easy camaraderie among the men: mostly blacks, some whites, as there was no segregation of this tropical island far from home. They didn't have room for separate mess halls, and they were united in complaint.

Always, and as usual in the army, most of the complaints were about the food.

"Damn, I hate these powdered eggs," Ab said one morning, staring at the bright yellow scrambled mass on his plate. Someone said it every morning, usually more than once.

"I c'n put up wit' the eggs better'n them dried potatoes," Willie said.

" 'Fore you come here, we had a cook made them things taste fresh," Tate Kilmer, a veteran of island war, told them. He said it every morning. "Where the hell did he go?" Willie demanded, although he knew the answer.

"Officers got him!" Tate grinned. "An' he ain't cookin' no more powder!"

It was at breakfast that they heard that the marines had landed on New Britain and were attacking Rabaul, and shortly after that the air raids ceased. There was talk of victory and even of leave in Australia. Willie had liked Australia, or the little he had seen, and he wanted to go back to the Barrier Reef. After their jungle training, they had been given a few days leave. Willie and a few others had gone out to the reef on a charter boat. He had stood on the reef, twenty miles from land, waist deep in water, and for three hundred and sixty degrees he could not see land.

Ab had a different view of Australia. They sat in their gun emplacements day after day, waiting for air raids that didn't come anymore, and keeping their eyes open for snipers, or even islanders chasing a runaway pig, anything to alleviate the boredom, and Ab made plans to go somewhere else when they got their leave. Fiji, perhaps, or one of the other safer islands. He didn't like the Australian attitude to their own native population, the Aborigines. They were a dispossessed and disadvantaged people who had been hunted almost to extinction in some parts of the country and had no standing as citizens in the land that had once been their own. What concerned him most was that there didn't seem to be any desire for change in Australia, and he talked fondly of America.

It made Willie look at America with fresh eyes of hope. In the last three or four years there had been considerable change, and Willie, all of them, were part of it. Just this year, some of the voting laws in the Southern states had been changed to black advantage, and Willie began to believe, as Ab did, that there was a possibility of a more equitable future society, however distant it might be.

Orders came, but no mention of leave. Rabaul had fallen. MacArthur had returned to the Philippines. The men on New Georgia were given a new mission. They had to clear the island of Japanese.

They operated in small units of a dozen men. They had rifles and machine guns, grenades and flamethrowers.

At first it was easy. There were a few isolated Japanese dugouts about a mile from the airstrip, the snipers', Willie guessed. Although they tried to defend themselves, they were demoralized, out of contact with their comrades, and often hungry, their supplies long gone, their ammunition depleted.

As Willie and Ab moved farther from the airstrip, higher into the hills, the resistance became fiercer. The dugouts were larger, holding up to six men, and well camouflaged, although broken supply boxes or small, well-tended gardens of vegetables often betrayed their whereabouts or proximity. These men had more ammunition because they had expended less, and many had a determination to fight to the death rather than be taken prisoner. Nor did any of them know that, to all intents and purposes, their war was over.

Willie didn't mind killing them, as long as it was in a small battle and he never saw their faces. He hated it when they surrendered, because then he found that he could not hate them, they seemed so pitiable.

He was sick to his stomach one day, when they came to a foxhole. There had been no gunfire, but they were wary. Then Willie saw Ab staring at something. perhaps because he heard the Americans coming, and perhaps because he had run out of ammunition, the Jap had committed suicide by disemboweling himself. Willie turned away and vomited.

He was sick again the first time he used a flamethrower and smelled burning human flesh. He couldn't understand why they, outnumbered, fighting impossible odds in a war they had already lost, wouldn't surrender.

But sometimes the Japanese were more successful and several Americans were injured, and a couple killed. Because of this, medics were attached to each unit, or at least someone trained in first aid.

They got word that they were to have leave, in a week's time, when they had finished mopping up their area. The numbers of Japanese they found had diminished markedly, and sometimes Willie almost enjoyed the days, walking on tropical green hills with a view of the lazy, rolling Pacific. He thought how pleasant it would be to go on leave, duty done, and he began to think of a peacetime future. Or Ernestine. And marriage. And children.

He was so lost in his own thoughts that when the gunfire came it shocked him. He felt someone pull him down, Ab, and he fell to the ground, rifle ready.

The pillbox was a hundred feet farther up the hill, a small cement bunker dug into the hill and well hidden by camouflage. Obviously they had a machine gun because it blazed occasionally in continuous fire, and the men of Willie's unit were pinned down.

They returned fire, but to no effect. They couldn't use the flamethrowers, they were too far away for them to be effective, and it had rained that morning, the jungle was wet. Willie thought about a grenade, but it was a long throw, and probably useless. He fired a few shots at the pillbox, to release his frustration, and whispered a call to other men near him to see if anyone had any ideas.

Then he became aware that Ab wasn't firing. He looked at his friend, slumped on the ground.

"You all right, Ab?" he cried.

There was no answer.

Willie felt as if he'd been punched in the stomach, hard.

He turned Ab to him and saw the terrible wound in his chest, gushing blood.

"Willie," Ab whispered piteously. "It hurt . . ."

He was still alive, if barely, and in that awful moment their roles reversed. Willie became the father and Ab his darling, dying son.

"Medic!" Willie screamed. "Needs a medic here!"

He saw the medic get up, and then drop down again as there was another burst of gunfire from the pillbox.

A great rage churned in Willie and seethed and boiled and exploded.

"Cover me!" he screamed again to anyone who could hear him.

He crawled away from Ab, and, when he thought he was safe, hidden among the dense foliage, he got up and ran, keeping his head well down, up the hill, farther and farther up the hill, well to the side of the pillbox, and up again and up.

Gasping for breath, he arrived at a point some forty feet

above the pillbox. The other men were keeping the Japanese busy with gunfire, and Willie thought he hadn't been seen.

He didn't care either way, for he was an avenging angel now, furious with wrath, and mighty with righteousness. He didn't care what happened to him, he only wanted vengeance for his friend. He wanted the Japs to hear him, to know that he was coming, and know that he was death.

He grabbed the grenade from his belt and began running downhill toward the pillbox. He pulled the pin out with his teeth and then began screaming at the top of his lungs.

He waited until the last possible moment, until he was at the pillbox. The grenade must explode at any time, but he was not going to give them a chance. He saw their astonished faces and saw them frantically trying to turn the machine gun from its fixed position toward him. He saw them grabbing at their rifles.

He almost fell into the pillbox as he hurled the grenade, slipping on the mud and dank undergrowth, and, as he threw it, he jumped to the ground away from them and rolled down the hill toward his own men.

The explosion deafened him, but he heard their dying screams. He landed against a tree and it winded him, and stopped his fall. He was aware of pain in his leg, from a bullet or a piece of shrapnel, and he lay there crouched as small as could be, his hands over his head as the tiny battle raged about him, his troops firing machine guns at the two survivors who had half clambered out of the dugout.

Even before the firing ceased he was on his feet again, limping down the hill. He stopped some fifteen feet from Ab.

He saw the medic kneeling beside his friend. He saw him put his hand to Ab's face and close his eyes. He saw him sit back on his haunches and murmur a tiny prayer for the departed.

"No!" Willie roared. "No!"

Tears streaming down his face, he ran to Ab and

clutched him, grabbed him, pulled the body to him as if to drag him back from death.

"Don't die!" he commanded Ab.

He knew it was too late, that Ab could not hear him and would not obey the order, but that didn't matter. He felt he was drowning in an ocean of grief, and the only thing that mattered was to strike out for some distant shore where everything might be what it was.

He laid Ab's body to the ground and stayed kneeling beside it, and slowly the understanding came to him that he would never find Ab again, on any shore, no matter how distant, and that nothing would ever be what it had been.

Even though he would not have wanted prayers, Willie prayed for Ab, that he had found, at last, the golden country of his dreams, where everyone was equal, and that he had labored so long to achieve.

Ordinarily, his friends would have surrounded him, cheering and clapping him on the back, but they did not, for they understood what had happened. Some cleaned up the mess at the pillbox, and others stood together, talking quietly.

It began to rain, a drenching tropical rain. Willie lifted his face to the sky and thought it proper that the heavens wept for Ab, but no amount of rain would ever wash Ab's blood from him.

Tate Kilmer came to him and offered his hand to Willie, to help him to his feet, but Willie shook him away.

"I c'n do it," Willie snapped angrily.

He struggled to his feet and let the medic tend his wound, and then he could not imagine why he had bothered, for then, and for a long time afterward, he could not see any point in going on.

PART THREE

— WILLIE —

36

*T*HE BOARDINGHOUSE LOOKED THE SAME but not
the same, shabbier than Willie remembered, in
need of a coat of paint. The downstairs windows were
boarded up, but not against the snow. One of the gutters
had come loose and was hanging away from the roof. It was
as if no one lived there anymore.

Martha looked the same but not the same, older by
more than the years since Willie had last seen her. Her
hair was gray and she'd put on some weight, and her eyes
lacked any spark or luster.

Willie guessed that he too looked the same but not the
same. He limped slightly, from the wound to his leg, the
reason for his discharge, and he was older, yes, by time and
a weight of war.

The other boarders were out, those that still lived
there. Martha was polite, and almost kind, but not much
more than that. She made him a cup of coffee and asked
how he was, but did not ask how he had been. She did not
want to know what he had done. She did not want to hear
about the war. She did not want to talk about Ab. She
didn't care about the manner of his going; it was too much
that he was gone.

When she turned away to refill his coffee, Willie put a
little packet on the table, some of Ab's personal things
that he had kept and thought that she would want.

She saw the packet but she did not mention it, she did
not thank him. While he drank his coffee, she picked up
the packet, casually, as if it were a thing of no value, and
took it to a drawer. But it was something of value to her,
because when she put it in the drawer and closed it, she
locked it with a key, and put the key back in her purse.

"Y'need a room?" she asked him eventually.

Willie shook his head, and she gave no indication that she was sorry or glad.

"What you gon' do?" Willie asked.

Martha looked away, to the window, and did not speak for a while.

"Go on fighting the battle," she said wearily. "The war ain't over yet."

She meant her war, her political war, her war against inequality, but Willie did not think Martha looked forward to the future with any zeal.

Nor did Willie. He was sick of segregation. He had fought hard and well for his country, had courted death, and many black servicemen had given their lives. Yet in Honolulu, on his way back from the South Pacific, there were beaches and bars and restaurants that were barred to him because he was black. So it was in San Francisco, and so it was in Chicago. So it would be in Memphis and in Stockton, and if he went farther south it would be worse.

He knew that some small advances had been made. After Ab died, several white men, and some officers, came to him and told him how sorry they were, and how much they admired what he had done. When he was presented with his medal for valor, several white men, and some officers, shook his hand. A few places in the big cities had been integrated, but many more had not. His prospects of a job were much as they had always been, a laborer, and even then he would be paid less than a less experienced white.

And all around him he found anger, and a determination that, somehow, there had to be change. Many black men who had served overseas knew what they would be returning to, and only the thought of seeing loved ones again, family and friends, gave them cause for celebration, for no one knew how to bring the change about or had any real belief that it could happen.

"I'm leaving here," Martha said. "Closing this place up, selling it."

She had not moved, she was still staring out the window.

"Going to Detroit. Things is bad here, but they's worse there."

She wanted to be away from here, Willie understood, away from all memory of Ab.

"Work to do," Martha said softly. She meant the future, but she could have meant she had work to do now, so Willie used it as his opportunity to leave.

She went with him to the door, and suddenly she did not seem to want him to go.

Willie waited.

"Was you with him?" she asked softly. "When it— when he—?"

"I was there," Willie said, as softly.

"That's all right, then," she said. She closed the door. Willie never saw her again.

His return to Stockton was joyous, for several reasons. During all of the long journey home, Willie had made certain decisions about his future, but it wasn't until he had closed the door on the past, when he said good-bye to Martha, that he felt free to put those decisions into effect. After leaving Martha he went to the warehouse and was told that there was a job for him whenever he wanted.

On the train to Stockton he practiced his speech to Ernestine. They would marry, in Stockton because their families were there. They would move to Chicago and live there. They would have babies, lots and lots of babies. And they would be happy.

He had no need to make the speech; Ernestine did it all for him.

"When we gon' get married?" Ernestine whispered.

They were comfortable in her sitting room, in each other's arms. Albie and Ernestine's mother had, tactfully, gone visiting to leave them alone.

"Whenever you want, if'n you still wants to," Willie said. "Next week. Next month."

"Tomorrow!" Ernestine laughed, and kissed him.

"Where we gon' live?" she asked a little later.

"Chicago," he said.

She kissed him again.

"How many babies we gon' have?"

"As many as we can," he told her.

Ernestine looked at him with a twinkle in her eyes.

"Better get busy, then," she said.

He did not take her, she gave herself to him. Even though they weren't married they would be soon, and they had waited long enough. And it was everything he had ever imagined it would be.

"You still wants to?" she whispered to him afterward. "Marry me?"

"More than ever," he said, kissing her again.

They planned a summer wedding and Flora wept when he told her of it, just as she had wept when she first saw him at the station, the soldier coming home from the war. When he sat in his old chair, she brushed tears from her eyes again.

"Does my heart good to see you sittin' there," she said.

"You always say that, Ma," he laughed.

"Well, it true," Flora muttered.

They had a small argument about where he should sleep. Flora had made arrangements for Ruthana to stay with Pearl, so that Willie could have his old room.

" 'Tain't my room anymore," Willie said. "I stay wit' Pearl."

Flora insisted that whenever her son came home there would be room for him in her house, but Willie laughed again and said she'd have to get a bigger house because she had two sons now, and what if they both turned up at the same time?

Luke had spent the war in Europe, first in Sicily and Italy, and now in France. With victory against the Nazis imminent, he was already planning to work in New York after his discharge from the army.

Willie had not met Luke, and was not sure how he

would react when he did. He had been his mama's only son for most of his life, and for most of those years Flora had never mentioned the existence of his brother, or half brother. After Luke had visited her, her letters to Willie had been full of him, and Willie was angry that this stranger occupied so great a place in her heart. Then he calmed down, and was pleased for his mama, because she was so pleased. He hoped they could be friends, but he hoped that Luke would not try to exert any fraternal authority over him, and a small part of him was jealous of Luke because he had been born to money.

He won the argument and stayed with Pearl, and it was easier for him and, very obviously, better for Ruthana.

"That girl, she never have no fun," Pearl said to him one day. "Yo' mama keep a leash on her like a naughty dog, an' one day she gon' snap."

She didn't say much more, and she didn't need to, because immediately Willie knew she was right. Ruthana had always taken second place in everything, and although Flora had always been kind to her, more than kind, had loved her, it was not the love she had showered on Willie.

"Ain't got but one pretty dress," Pearl murmured, "an' don' get to wear it too much."

It was true, Willie thought. Ruthana was always neatly dressed, but he'd never seen her in anything that wasn't serviceable.

He decided he would spend some time with Ruthana, and do silly, frivolous things with her, and take her to a dance. When he suggested to Ernestine that Ruthana should be her bridesmaid, Ernestine immediately agreed.

"Of course!" she said. "Why didn't I think of that?"

Then she said something that startled Willie, more so than anything Pearl had said.

"We never think of Ruthana first. An' she's so kind an' good with yo' ma, an' everyone. She know she's class valedictorian?"

Willie didn't know, and was shocked that no one had told him.

So it pleased him to be able to go to Ruthana's high school graduation ceremony, and, sitting in the garden on a warm victorious day, he took stock of his sister.

She was seventeen years old and she was lovely. Her eyes were bright and shining on this, her day of days, and she looked confident, but also still slightly shy. The long black gown and the brightly tasseled hat suited her, the uniform of the successful student, as if she took her authority not from herself, but from what she had achieved.

Ever since she was a little girl, ever since Willie's decision to leave home and go to Chicago, his mama and Pearl had discussed the possibility of Ruthana going to college. Willie had discounted the idea as simply a transference of Flora's ambition for him to Ruthana, but now he was briefly angry with himself. He thought of Martha and her many lectures about the role of women in society. Other black women went to college, and to dismiss the idea for Ruthana was to discount, discredit her potential. If she could do it, why not?

Ruthana made a short speech that was full of hope for the future. If not in any way memorable, it caused Flora to dab at her eyes with her handkerchief and grasp Willie's hand. Then, speeches done, Ruthana came running to them, clutching her diploma.

"Was I any good?" she asked Willie, filled with happiness, knowing she had done well.

"You done great," Willie assured her. "I was very proud."

He *was* proud of her. During her speech he had tried to remember the little, dutiful girl, always anxious to please, that she had been, but he could not find her. He could only see this confident young woman.

But she was still anxious to please. She turned to Flora. She needed to hear it from her.

"Mama—?"

Willie guessed that Flora would be kind, but she was more than that. She hugged Ruthana to her, then held her away, at arm's length.

"Chile, you don' know how good you make me feel this day," she said. "You jes' makin' all my dreams come true."

She hugged Ruthana again, and Willie understood something else about them. If Flora had been hard on the girl, it was not from any malice. Nor was it so that his father's dream of having an educated child be realized. It was so that Ruthana would be able to be the best she could be, and in that sense there was a covenant between the two women. Flora had made this day possible, and Ruthana had accepted the possibility of it. They had worked for her success together.

That evening, Ernestine was with them, but they did not talk about the coming wedding very much, except to get some details out of the way.

This was Ruthana's day.

"Mama, things been flyin' so fast, what wit' the weddin' an' all, I ain't had a good chance to tell you," Ruthana said quietly. "But Fisk College, in Nashville, they offers a partial scholarship."

"That right?" Flora said, knowing there was more.

"But Nashville's a long way away."

Willie saw an opportunity he had been waiting for. No matter what Luke's position was in his mother's love, Luke wasn't here. Willie was the head of the family, and he wanted to do something for Ruthana.

"Ain't so far these days," he said. "You think you c'n get that scholarship?"

"I c'n get it, yes, I think." Ruthana nodded. "I dunno if'n I c'n keep it. You gotta average C minus every year."

"That shouldn't be hard fo' you." Ernestine laughed. "You always got yo' head in a book."

That wasn't what was worrying Ruthana. She looked at Flora.

"But I can't hardly bring myself to be thinkin' about goin' off an' leavin' you alone by yo'self," she said.

Flora had been fiddling with some darning. She wore glasses these days. She put the needlework aside and looked at Ruthana.

"Honey, I wants you to listen close to yo' ol' mama, 'coz I don' never want a' have to say it again," she said.

Willie held his breath.

"I'd be mad as I could be if'n you even think about stayin' here in Stockton, when you got all the world afore you."

Willie almost cheered, not only for Ruthana, but for himself, going to Chicago. He clutched Ernestine's hand.

"Ain't nuttin' fo' you here, nor nobody like you. So git yo'self busy to git to that there Fisk College," she ordered.

She picked up her needlework again, as if there was nothing more to discuss.

"Oh, Mama!" Ruthana cried, and hugged Flora and kissed her.

Willie was pleased, and Ernestine laughed.

"How's your dress coming along?" she asked. Ruthana was making her own bridesmaid's dress.

"It nearly ready, you wants to see it?" Ruthana grabbed her by the hand and led Ernestine to her room.

"You cain't come," she called back to Willie.

Willie stayed sitting with Flora.

"Why didn't you tell me she was valedictorian?"

Flora concentrated on her sewing, but pricked her finger. She muttered a tiny curse and dropped the needle. She looked at Willie.

"'Coz I cain't even say that word," she said. "An' I din't want you thinkin' I was igner-ant."

Of the several small shocks Willie had had that day, this was the most acute. It had never occurred to him that his mama was embarrassed about any aspect of herself.

"You be all right on your own, Ma?" he asked her gently, when she had started sewing again. Flora looked at him over the rim of her glasses.

"I be jes' fine," she said. "And if'n I said no, what you gon' do 'bout it? You gon' come back here to live when you's married? I hopes not, boy, fo' yo' sake, 'coz I kick you right out the door."

She put down the darning.

"You was right an' I was wrong, all those years ago," she said softly. "I dunno what there is fo' you in that Chicago, but I do knows this. Ain't nuttin' fo' you here in Stockton."

It was one of the sweetest things she had ever said to him, and Willie was moved. He went to her, hugged her, and kissed her hair.

"We get you a telephone," he said. "In case anythin' happen, you on your own."

"I don' want one. Y'know what them things cost?" she insisted. "Pearl's got one, an' she take messages. That's good enuff fo' me."

The next few weeks were mostly about the wedding, a little bit about Ruthana, and a lot about money.

Ruthana was accepted by Fisk College and offered the scholarship. She and Flora got on the bus and went to Nashville, so that Flora could see where her daughter would be, and could find out about the finances.

When they came back, they spent a lot of time whispering together, and, again, Willie felt slightly excluded. He came home one day to find them sitting at the table, making a lot of notes.

"What's goin' on?" he asked.

"Nuttin'," Flora said, tidying up the notes.

"Think you should tell me," he said, head of the family.

Flora glanced at Ruthana, who nodded.

"She gon' have to get a job," Flora explained. "It all worked out."

It was arranged with the dean that Ruthana should work in the college dining room to help meet her expenses for books and living.

"And?" Willie asked.

They had to pay twenty-eight dollars every month, but that was no problem, Flora insisted, she had that money.

"And?" Willie asked again.

It was only a partial scholarship. They had to pay three hundred dollars in advance for her tuition.

Willie whistled.

"It's all right, it ain't nuttin' to do wit' you," Flora said airily, as if three hundred dollars was nothing to her.

"Where you gon' get money like that?" Willie demanded.

"I got nearly that," Flora said. "The money you give me afore you went away, an' the money you sent while you was in the army, I bin puttin' all that aside."

"But that money's for you," Willie said, and wished he hadn't because he didn't want to appear mean to Ruthana.

"Reckon if'n you give it a' me, it's mine to do what I like wit'," Flora said tartly.

"Oh, Ma." Willie sighed. "I got money, I c'n help."

"No," Flora said sharply. "You gettin' married, you gon' need every dime you c'n lay yo' hands on."

"We only needs a hundred dollars," Ruthana said. "We gon' ask my pappy."

Willie was astonished.

"George? Ain't no one knows where he is!"

"I know," Ruthana said smugly.

"How you know?" Willie asked. "He done up an' leave Chicago, an' din't tell no one where he was goin'."

"He got a mama an' a papa too," Ruthana said. "So I writes to them, an' they tell me. He in Denver, workin' in the meat works there."

Willie looked at them in amazement, this pair of devious, scheming, plotting women, and he laughed. They would take on the world to get Ruthana to college.

To Willie's considerable relief, and to Flora's, and to Ruthana's, George was more than generous. He wrote to them apologizing for not having sent money for Ruthana's keep for so long, and he enclosed a check for two hundred dollars. He promised to send more in six months, and every six months after that, for Ruthana's education. It was a simple letter, badly written in a scrawling hand, but it meant the world to Ruthana. It was the first direct contact that she had ever had with her father.

There was a frightening new bomb that brought victory, and peace added to the joy of the wedding. Even though everyone guessed she was pregnant, Ernestine was all in flowing white satin and pretty lace and carried white gardenias. Ruthana was in pale apple green, a color that suited her exactly. Flora wore the Sunday-best dress she had bought only a year before, but she allowed herself the extravagance of a new hat. Pearl bought a new dress, of crushed purple velvet, which was too heavy to wear on such a hot day, and she sweated as she banged away at the organ.

Willie was in a new suit, and Pete Lanier was his best man, and the only moment of sadness for Willie was when he turned to Pete at one point, and saw Ab.

Reverend Jackson conducted the service, and the choir sang to raise the rafters, and everyone had a good time, the women weeping, the men shouting "Yay-man" throughout.

Albie did his daughter proud, and they had the reception in the new church hall, which had been built while Willie was away. Isaac Dixon supervised the barbecue, although Isaac Junior did the work; his father was mostly retired. When Ernestine threw her bouquet Clara caught it. This pleased everyone who knew her, because Andy, Clara's boyfriend, was killed on the last day of the war, and no one thought that Clara had smiled since then, until that moment.

They caught the train to Chicago that night. They weren't going to have a proper honeymoon because they had decided it was an extravagance they couldn't afford, but Willie had booked them into the bridal suite of a good hotel for their first night in Chicago.

It wasn't the best hotel in town—they couldn't stay there, because they were black—but that didn't stop them from loving each other.

Willie started work the following day at his old warehouse job, and Ernestine found them lodgings, one small room, nothing special, but it would do until they were more secure financially.

In November, the twins were born.

They called them Don and Diana, and when Willie held them in his arms for the first time, he choked up, for the wonder of them, these two, tiny, vulnerable creatures that he and Ernestine had made. He was their defender and provider, and he vowed to defend and provide. He would do his best to equip them for the future, but they were coming into a complex and frightening new world.

Battle lines were being drawn in Eastern Europe, and although America had the atomic edge, Willie did not believe that the Soviets would easily surrender. War, in some form, was an inevitable part of their future.

Tears glistened in his eyes. They were beautiful, those tiny babies, but he wept because of the indignities and injustices the color of their skin would bring to them, and from which he could not protect them.

They were the first tears he had shed since Ab had died.

37

*F*LORA'S HEART WAS FULL. It had been a mighty battle, it had taken five years instead of four, but it had all been worth it. Ruthana was graduating from college.

It was a hot, sunny day. Flora was sitting with three hundred other parents, people like herself, who had come to see their children's triumph. She was grateful that George was with her, because she had been nervous. She had been to Fisk once before, when Ruthana was first accepted, but this was different, this was a public ceremony, and Flora didn't know how to behave at public ceremonies such as this, because she had never been to anything so formal before.

She had been worried that her clothes, although neat and clean, would be dowdy compared with others', that they would see that the heels of her shoes were worn, or that she would say something to someone important that would somehow endanger Ruthana's achievement.

She had approached the campus almost unwillingly, but then she saw that most of the other parents were like herself and George, hardworking people with little money to spare. They had put on their Sunday finery but this did not disguise the sacrifices they had made for their children's sake, and most of them spoke as Flora did, simply, with bad grammar.

Flora was very conscious of grammar these days, because grammar was the rock on which her dreams, and Ruthana's, had almost foundered.

They took their places in the audience, and when Flora looked at the stage she thought she had never seen anything so grand or so important, the teachers and graduates all in their gold-tasseled caps and brightly hooded gowns, and the sense of occasion that everything imparted.

The dean began his speech, and Flora, who knew exactly where Ruthana was sitting although she could only see her back, grabbed George's hand.

"Ain't this wonderful," she whispered.

"Jes' wunnerful," he whispered back. "You don' know what this mean to me."

But Flora did, because she knew what it meant to her.

George's promises of financial help had proved to be as elusive as his whereabouts. He had sent some money sometimes, but never very much, and always, it seemed, from a different address. Flora had borne the brunt of the cost of Ruthana's education, and to do it she had to take on yet more work.

She tried to keep this secret from Ruthana. Five years ago she had put her on the bus to Nashville with two new pressed-cardboard suitcases crammed full of sensible clothes, nothing fancy, and had given her a shoe box stuffed with food for the journey.

"Here some fried chicken an' deviled eggs an' sweet tater pie," she said. "'Coz I don' want you startin' out hungry leavin' home."

Ruthana, close to tears, embraced her, and Flora took the opportunity to deliver, for the last time, the lecture she had given so many times before.

"Now you 'member what I tol' you, 'bout all them boys you gon' be meetin'."

Ruthana brushed her eyes and laughed.

"Yes, Mama, I know. I keep myself to myself."

"Well, make sho' you do, honey chile," Flora commanded. "Now git on board an' let the man close his door. I loves you."

Ruthana got on the bus. The driver closed the door and pulled away.

Ruthana's face was pressed to the window, and she was waving.

"G'bye, sweetcake," Flora cried, waving back.

She watched the bus until it had turned the corner, filled with love and concern, and the greatest of these concerns was men. She was sure that Ruthana was a good girl, but she wasn't so sure about all those young men she would be meeting at college. She had done her best, and she had to let Ruthana fly the nest one day, but she was still worried.

It was because she didn't trust men that she didn't trust George's promises of financial help. Once she was sure Ruthana was gone, she got on a bus herself to travel the short distance to the town hall. Nervous among all the white people there, she found the office she was looking for, and was glad that the man she had to see was black.

She wasn't as surprised as she would have been once. The wartime employment situation had radically altered the old hiring customs of staff, and blacks popped up in the most unexpected jobs these days.

"I come to see if'n I can get that job y'all got advertised," she said, "fo' a janitor."

He looked at her in surprise.

"Well, we had a man in mind—" he began.

Flora was ready for that.

"Well, I knows fo' sho' I c'n clean up good as any man," she said. "An' I 'spect better."

After some discussion she got the job, three hours every evening, five nights a week. On top of her regular work it would make a long day, but it was worth it if it ensured Ruthana's place at college.

Flora went home feeling pleased. Ruthana's immediate future was settled. Willie and Ernestine were in Chicago, and Willie had written to say that Ernestine was expecting a child. Flora counted the weeks in her head and guessed that they had not waited till their wedding night to consummate their marriage, but they were married, so she forgave them.

She was suddenly, unexpectedly lonely. The tiny house

was empty, and no one would be coming home that night, and she had never been alone in the house for any extended period of time. There had always been Willie and then Ruthana. She gave herself a little lecture and went across the road to visit Pearl.

She was pleased that Ruthana's early letters were cheerful, but then they changed, and Flora guessed something was wrong. When Ruthana came home at Christmas, she found out what it was.

Ruthana's first-semester average of C minus had thrust her into the strict university's probationary status. In view of her D's in English, Composition and Diction, unless her second-semester grade levels improved, her scholarship would end.

Ruthana was weeping.

"Mama, I swear I ain't knowed I wasn't passin'," she cried. "I c'n do better, I know I can. I jes' got to learn to talk more the way them teachers an' others do."

Flora thought her world was collapsing. She prayed to God that night, and God gave her an answer.

During the lean years of the Depression, Mrs. Hopkins had supplemented the family income by returning to her old profession as teacher at the white high school.

Swallowing all of her pride, Flora got on the bus and went to visit Mrs. Hopkins and begged for her help.

"Well, I don't know, Flora," Mrs. Hopkins said. "You did let me down very badly when I needed a maid."

"Yes'm, I know, an' I's sorry, but you did fin' Gloria."

Gloria was the present Hopkins maid and a hard worker.

"Well, yes, that's true," Mrs. Hopkins admitted. "But even so—"

"An' I pay you whatever you wants," Flora cajoled.

"It isn't a question of money," Mrs. Hopkins said. She didn't need money, and resented the suggestion that she might.

But she was bored. Mr. Hopkins spent the working week in Memphis, and she didn't see very much of Kevin, who was married, with two sons of his own, and living on his farm a few miles out of town. Teaching a nigra girl to speak properly might be amusing, although she doubted she would achieve much in the short time available.

She agreed to give Ruthana a crash course in English during the two weeks of the Christmas break, and if she was the most ruthless of teachers, she was good.

What surprised Mrs. Hopkins was Ruthana's capacity to learn and her dedication to hard work. What surprised her even more was that she found she was enjoying herself. It was thrilling to her, a good teacher, to find a willing and capable student, even if she was colored. A tiny, inflammatory, slightly unwelcome idea began nagging in the back of her mind. If Ruthana could do this, what else might she achieve? And if Ruthana could do this, were there other nigra girls who, given the opportunity, could do as well or even better?

At the end of the break, she gave Ruthana a farewell gift, several books to study, and thereafter, she took an interest in Ruthana's progress, and whenever she came home on vacation Mrs. Hopkins insisted she come visit two or three times a week for more lessons, and for these she would not take Flora's money.

Flora did her part. Each evening, she insisted that she and Ruthana listen to the radio, not music or quiz shows or comedies, but the news and current affairs, where the announcers were well spoken. When Ruthana went back to Fisk, Flora could hear the beginnings of change in the way she spoke, and felt rewarded. She gave Ruthana a little extra spending money, as a show of confidence.

She decided to get a telephone, to call Ruthana at least once a week and nag her to improvement. When the telephone was installed she was glad of it, because one day Willie rang her to tell her she was a grandmother, Ernestine had given birth to twins, and the cost of the telephone became utterly irrelevant.

But, oh, she was tired. She no longer went to the Tuesday night women's meeting, which had continued after the war, and she missed the counsel and company. She told herself it was all worth it because Ruthana's next semester grades, especially in English, were better, and better again the semester after that, and her place at Fisk was secure. She came home for the summer brimming with pride in her achievement, but sounding, to Flora, like someone else. She did not rest on her small laurels. She got a part-time job at the old Lady Blue women's shop, which was now Modern Modes, and was a great success because she was so courteous and well spoken. She enjoyed her sessions with Mrs. Hopkins, and almost came to like the woman, although she would never go if she knew Kevin was visiting his mother.

The summer break did Flora good, because she could see a return on the investment she was making, but it didn't lessen her tiredness. One Sunday morning in fall she got down on her knees to pray with the rest of the congregation and fell asleep. Albie, who was sitting next to her, prodded her, and she jerked awake, and wondered, for a moment, where she was.

After the service, Reverend Jackson and his wife, Vera, cornered her.

"We all know why you making this sacrifice," Vera said. "We jus' don't want you taking on a cross that's too heavy to bear."

"I'm doin' fine. I can handle whatever I'm doin'," Flora said testily.

Reverend Jackson was ever the peacemaker.

"Sister, let me say what's on my mind," he said, his voice soft and coaxing. "We've all been talkin' and prayin' for you, and maybe there's another way to take less of your time and energy, and make more money besides."

Flora was embarrassed and opened her mouth to speak.

"Let me finish, Sister Flora," Reverend Jackson rolled on. "Ev'ry person in Stockton know you this town's best baker of just about any kind of pie. If you'd sell them downtown on Saturdays, we think you could make more in that one day than some of those laundry jobs you doin'."

Flora, still testy, saw a glimmer of sense in this. She experimented with the idea the following week and sold the six pies she had made within half an hour. The following Saturday she made a dozen pies and sold them all. It became a regular and additional source of income for her, but she did not give up any of her laundry jobs for another year.

One Friday night, six months later, she had put a batch of pies in the oven and fell asleep at the table. The telephone woke her. It was Willie.

She was a grandmother again, of a fine and chubby baby boy. He was to be called Booker, in honor of his grandfather.

Joy battled with fatigue in Flora, and tears won because when she put down the phone she realized that the pies in the oven were burning. But she laughed through her tears as she threw that batch of pies away, and she did not bother to bake any more.

She was almost unaware of the passing years, because she was so busy and so constantly tired. The government announcement that the armed forces were to be integrated had little meaning for her, other than as something that was right and proper and long overdue, but she understood it was important. In celebration of it she gave up a couple of her laundry jobs, although she had been planning this for a while. She was able to stay in bed for an hour or two longer on those mornings, if not to sleep, because she was, by habit, an early riser; it was a luxury not to have to get up.

Suddenly it was all over, and she wondered where the years had gone. Ruthana was to graduate with a B-minus average, an English major with a Spanish minor.

She rang Willie, who was thrilled and promised to send Ruthana a gift. He couldn't come to the ceremony because he was so busy, and Ernestine wasn't quite well, but he sent his love.

Flora hadn't expected Willie to come, but she was worried that Ernestine wasn't well. Ernestine had been poorly for some time, since little Booker was born. The doctors said there was nothing wrong with her, but a small warning bell was ringing in the back of Flora's head.

She tracked down George in Kansas, and he was thrilled too. He would certainly come to his daughter's graduation, he said, and would stop in Stockton on the way, to take Flora to Nashville. He was on his own these days, Ellie had left him years ago, and he was glad to be involved in Ruthana's life, the only family he had left to him.

On the spur of the moment, she rang Mrs. Hopkins to tell her the glad news.

"Well, Flora, I am very, very pleased," Mrs. Hopkins said.

"Yes'm," Flora agreed.

"And when she comes home, be sure to tell her to come and see me," Mrs. Hopkins added. "I shall give her a little gift for all her hard work."

The gift turned out to be fifty dollars, which thrilled Ruthana and touched Flora so deeply she didn't quite trust her own reaction.

She made one more phone call, to Luke, in New York. He sent his congratulations to Ruthana, and apologized that he had not been back to Stockton. He was working as a lawyer in Harlem, badly paid and with little tree time. Flora understood this. Luke had written to her regularly since he went to Europe, and he always ended his letters by saying that he missed her.

Flora wished that once, just once, he would say that he loved her, but he did not say that until he came to visit her a year later, bringing his young wife, Jessica, with him. He waited until the last moment, until they were just getting on the train, then he hugged Flora and said those little words she had waited for so long to hear, and because they had not come easily they were priceless to her.

She and George arrived in Nashville the evening before the graduation ceremony. Ruthana was at the bus stop to meet them, and Flora embraced her, but then stood aside. Awkward and shy, George didn't know how to greet the daughter he hadn't seen since she was two years old, but Ruthana did all the work. She moved slowly to him.

"Hello, Pa," she whispered. She was crying. George put his arms around her and held her while she cried.

"Oh, my baby," he said.

The next day, nothing mattered but the ceremony itself and the work and sacrifice it represented. There were speeches in Latin and Greek, during which Flora dozed, then the president of the college announced that the diplomas would be issued.

"In the interests of efficiency," he ended, "we would appreciate it if all applause is withheld until we have finished."

He should have saved his breath. When the first student received his diploma, his parents could not contain themselves and clapped. Six students later, everyone was cheering and clapping for every student, and when Ruthana's name was called, Flora's pride burst every barrier of reserve.

She jumped to her feet.

"Thank You, Jesus!" she cried, and again, "Thank You, Jesus!"

"Hallelujah," someone called, and then everyone did, and laughed and applauded Mama Flora, for her joy was their own, her pride was theirs, her years of self-denial were shared by all of them.

And the rest of the commencement was like a Baptist revival meeting.

38

THE EVENING, LIKE THE DAY, was unbearably hot. Flora and Ruthana sat on the tiny back porch sipping lemonade, fanning themselves, praying for a breeze.

Flora was content to be silent, because she knew that soon it would be over, and Ruthana would tell her what she was going to do. Since Ruthana had come back from Nashville, she had been preoccupied, as if deciding her future, or how to tell her mama of a future already decided.

At first, Flora had urged her to relax and enjoy her hard-earned vacation, and Ruthana had gone through the motions of having fun, but there wasn't a lot for her to do in Stockton. Ernestine, who had been her best friend, was in Chicago with Willie, and while Ruthana was at Fisk all the other girls she knew from school had grown and changed, or moved, or married, or settled down to a rural existence.

"She be leavin' soon," Flora said to Pearl. "An' the bes' thing fo' her."

Then she began to worry that Ruthana wasn't going to leave. She didn't seem to be very interested in finding a job, although she had written a couple of letters to someone, and in the evenings she began gossiping with Flora about the things that had happened in the town that day. Then she went back to her old summer job part-time at Modern Modes. After six weeks of this, Flora was alarmed. To get a college degree and then settle down in Stockton was a waste of everything they had worked so hard to achieve.

Then that morning, Saturday morning, a letter had come, postmarked New York, but it wasn't from Luke.

Ruthana had read the letter twice, then put it away in her room and was preoccupied for the rest of the day. Flora didn't ask any questions, she waited patiently to be told, but now it was evening, the sun was setting, and Ruthana still hadn't said what was on her mind.

She decided to give her daughter a little push.

"What you gon' do, chile?" she asked as casually as she could. "A li'l teaching or somethin', mebbe?"

Ruthana stared at the red sky, and then looked at her mother and smiled.

"How do you always know?" she wondered.

"'Coz I yo' mama, honey, an' mamas always know," Flora said. "You find that out when you got young 'uns a' yo' own."

"I don't want to leave you alone," Ruthana said.

Flora looked at her over the rim of her glasses.

"I thought all that was finished an' done wit' a long time ago," she said, slightly sternly. "Afore you went to college."

It still pleased her to say it, and she said it as often as she could, that her daughter had been to college.

"Yes, but Nashville wasn't so far away," Ruthana agreed.

She waited for a moment and then took the plunge.

"New York is different," she said softly.

Flora felt smug because she had been right, it was to be New York. Still, it scared her slightly because New York was a very long way away, and the idea of Ruthana being in any big city worried her. But the idea of her staying in Stockton worried her even more.

"You think I don' know that?" she said. "But now I gots me a tel'phone; it ain't so far these days."

She was relieved that it was to be New York. Luke was in New York and would look after Ruthana.

There was the possibility of a job, Ruthana told her, as a project worker at the Henry Street Settlement.

"What they do there?" Flora wanted to know.

"I'd be a social worker," Ruthana explained. "Looking after people, sorting out their problems, helping them with their lives."

It made complete sense to Flora. Ruthana had always helped people with their problems, tactfully and generously. Then it occurred to her that, apart from some quarrels in adolescence, Ruthana never talked about any problems of her own.

"One of the men who runs it came to Fisk in my second year and told us all about it. That's why I started taking Spanish. A lot of the people they deal with are Spanish, from Honduras and places."

"Is it a good job, chile?"

"No, Mama, I should think it's a terrible job!" Ruthana laughed. "It's the bottom of the ladder, and the pay's not very good, but I have to start somewhere."

She mistook her mother's silence for concern.

"And I haven't actually got the job yet. I have to have an interview. And it's a long way, just for an interview."

Flora's only concern was that Ruthana would talk herself out of it, and not go.

"You never get the job if'n you don' go, an' I 'spect there's other jobs in New York too. An' you got to start somewhere."

She added a little more sugar.

"An' yo' brother Luke's in New York, he keep an eye out for you."

One more spoonful couldn't hurt.

"An' if the pay's not enuff an' you need a li'l extra, I can manage a few dollars, now we ain't got to pay fo' college."

She saw relief and determination come into Ruthana's eyes, and knew that it was going to be all right.

"You really think—?"

"Girl, what's wrong wit' you?" Flora snapped. "You be talkin' this thing to death afore you're done!"

Ruthana laughed and looked at the sky. It was dark now, the stars were out, and, thankfully, there was a small breeze.

When she talked to God that night, Flora prayed that the interview would go well and that Ruthana would get the job. She asked God to look after her little girl, and not let anything bad happen to her. And, if she hadn't asked for too much already, she wondered if a decent, honest, reliable man, if there was such a thing in New York, could come along to keep Ruthana from harm.

She prayed for her other children, and for her grandchildren, and that Ernestine, who was poorly, would get better.

She got up slowly and eased herself into bed and lay listening to the quiet of a country town at night, and she knew she was going to be lonely when Ruthana was gone, because she doubted that Ruthana would ever come back here to live.

Well, she would get used to it. She would find things to do. And she would never be completely alone, because, always, there would be God.

She rang Luke the next day and told him. He was very pleased, and quite impressed. The Henry Street Settlement was old and well established and did splendid work. He promised to look after Ruthana, but said he would not try to stifle her.

Ruthana would be all right for money, for a while anyway. She saved a little from her summer pay packet, George had given her a hundred dollars as a graduation present, and there was the fifty from Mrs. Hopkins. Flora gave her a hundred dollars as well.

They had decided that the Greyhound bus was more sensible than the train—slightly cheaper—and Albie, as a kindness, drove them to Memphis to catch the bus.

As soon as they drove into the big city Flora knew that she had been right, all those years ago, not to venture there but get off the train at Stockton. Just the look of Memphis frightened her. They drove through dirty streets, with cheap bars, and flashily dressed women, who all looked like whores, and then they drove through the smarter downtown, where the buildings were impressive but most of the faces were white, and the traffic and energy were alarming.

Flora decided that the idea of Ruthana going to a

bigger city, alone, was madness. How could she possibly avoid temptation and misfortune in such a place? She remembered Willie's first expedition to Chicago, and the disaster that had been.

Then she remembered that Willie had survived the disaster and had become a fine man, the father of her grandchildren. And a long time ago she had left her own family, and had made a bigger journey from a smaller place than Stockton.

She would not stop Ruthana, could not, but in the crowded, echoing Greyhound bus depot, she panicked. She clutched Ruthana.

"Ruthana—" she began. But Ruthana was way ahead of her, and laughed.

"I know, Mama," she said. "I'll keep myself to myself, and I won't trust men."

The reminder of the lesson learned, and the laughter, made Flora relax. If she wasn't happy about Ruthana going, she was going to send her off on the right note. She put her mouth close to Ruthana's ear.

"That's jes' till you fin' the man that's right fo' you," she said. "An' soon as you do, you give him ev'rythin' you got!"

Ruthana gasped in shock, and looked at her mama, who almost winked.

It all happened very quickly after that. Ruthana got on the bus, and waved, and Flora waved, and Albie waved, and then the bus was gone, and the depot seemed suddenly quiet, and rather empty.

Albie drove her home and made small talk all the way so that Flora wouldn't have to speak. Mostly he talked about the insides of cars, and how well Henrietta was doing. He didn't mention his daughter, Ernestine, until the car was stopped outside Flora's house.

"What be wrong wit' Ernestine?" he wondered. "Women's trouble?"

Flora didn't know what was wrong with Ernestine, and she was worried. She was more worried that the doctors kept saying that there was nothing wrong with her.

"Mebbe," she said.

She thanked Albie and went into her house, alone. She took off her hat and sat in her chair and eased her shoes from her feet. She sat for a while, not sure quite what to do, then she made a sandwich because she couldn't be bothered cooking for one. She thought about going to visit Pearl, but then remembered that Pearl was at choir practice.

She turned on the radio and listened to a quiz show, trying to answer the questions before the contestants did, and was surprised that she did so well.

Pearl called later, when she was home, to check that she was all right, and suggested they go to a movie Saturday night.

"Mebbe," Flora said.

She didn't want this to be the pattern of the rest of her life, growing old with Pearl because there was no one else to grow old with. She would do things. She'd go out and about more. She wasn't sure where she'd go, but she'd think of things. She'd given up her part-time janitor's job, but she still had her cleaning work, and she still sold her pies on Saturday morning, and that would keep her busy in the daytime. The evenings would look after themselves, and Sundays were filled up with God.

Ruthana rang four days later to say she'd arrived safely in New York. Luke had met her and was kind and helpful, and she was settled in a room at the YWCA. Her job interview was the next day.

She rang again the next evening to say that she had the job, and would start work the following week. She hadn't been out much because she didn't know where to go, and because New York was a very big city indeed. She was going to spend Saturday with Luke and his family. She asked Flora to call Mrs. Hopkins to give her the good news.

Flora called Mrs. Hopkins the next day, and, to her surprise, Mrs. Hopkins sounded pleased and asked Flora to keep her informed of Ruthana's progress.

So Flora settled into a life of growing old alone, but she

kept the promise she had made to herself. She found things to do. She always went to the movies on Saturday night, usually with Pearl, because, realistically, she and Pearl *were* going to grow old together. On Monday she stayed at home, to tidy or darn or clean, or listen to the radio. Tuesday nights she went to the women's meeting at the church, Wednesday nights she made social calls to Old Sisters who were too old to go out very much, widows, or mothers whose children had all left home. Thursday nights she gave herself a treat; she had her evening meal at Pop's Place, sometimes with Pearl, and she enjoyed being in company. Friday night she baked her pies and Saturdays she sold them. And Sundays there was God.

With her children gone, Flora found that money became less and less of a problem. She was sending Ruthana twenty dollars a week to help out, but she was still working four and a half days a week, and selling her pies, and was still careful about her spending. She had abandoned her buried money jar after the war, and now put all her money into a savings account. It was constantly surprising to her that the account was, by her terms, healthy.

All her children called once a week to give her their news, and all seemed to be doing well. Luke, married, had two children, a boy and a girl, and Ruthana was happy in New York, or said she was. Willie was doing fine in Chicago, although Ernestine's health was still a problem. She had good days and bad days, good weeks and bad weeks, good months and bad months, and no one knew what was wrong. Their children were all doing fine, and the twins, Don and Diana, had started school.

They sent their gran'ma hand-painted cards on her birthday, silly, childish things, but potent to Flora, and her heart ached to see them.

The days drifted by, and then one day, unexpectedly, Mrs. Hopkins called. Her maid, Gloria, had fallen from a ladder when she was hanging drapes and had cracked a bone in her arm. She knew Flora was busy, but if there was any way that Flora could help, even one day a week, perhaps.

Flora rearranged her schedule and went there the following Thursday. Mrs. Hopkins seemed pleased to see her, made her welcome, and asked about Ruthana. In the middle of the day, she suggested they share sandwiches at the kitchen table.

Flora was intrigued; this certainly would not have happened twenty years ago. They sat eating the sandwiches and drinking iced tea, and as Mrs. Hopkins talked Flora started to feel slightly sorry for the white woman who was trying so hard not to reveal her feelings, and was desperate to share them with someone.

Her husband was spending more and more time in Memphis, staying overnight sometimes, for several days in a row. Flora began to get the drift. Mrs. Hopkins believed that her husband was seeing another woman.

Mrs. Hopkins didn't see much of Kevin and his wife, they were so busy at the farm, but thankfully, Kevin's oldest boy, Gavin, was at school in town and came to visit his grandmother.

"He a good boy?" Flora asked.

"Oh, he's a darling," Mrs. Hopkins said. "He's—well— he's very like his father. It's like having Kevin young all over again."

This wasn't a concept that appealed to Flora, but she didn't argue.

"Yes'm," she said.

When she finished work that afternoon, Mrs. Hopkins paid her and showed her to the door. She asked to be remembered to Ruthana, and then a boy of about eleven came scooting up the path on his bike.

Flora knew at once that it was Gavin. He was his father's son, the spitting image of him.

"Hi, Grandma," he called. "What's the nigger want?"

He was his father's son. Flora felt exactly as she had felt all those years ago, when Kevin had been as casually cruel to her. She felt as if he had slapped her in the face, but for nothing, for no reason, just because she was black.

She saw Mrs. Hopkins flush with anger.

"Nice boys don't use that word, Gavin," she said sharply. "We say Negroes."

"What's the difference?" Gavin said blithely. "Niggers, jigaboos, Neeeeegroes, it's all the same."

He pushed past them into the kitchen, calling back as he went, "Any lemonade?"

Mrs. Hopkins looked at Flora.

"I'm so sorry, Flora," she said. "It won't happen again."

"No'm," Flora said.

Still, the embarrassed Mrs. Hopkins thought she had not apologized enough.

"He's so like his father," she said.

"Yes'm," Flora said.

Traveling home on the bus, Flora realized she had been living in a fool's paradise. All the white folk she dealt with were longtime customers and employers, and had long ago defined their relationships with her, in courteous, if sometimes patronizing terms. She'd had very little to do with other white people, and she had obeyed all their silly laws and kept out of their way. Thus she had arrived at a pleasant life and her children were doing well.

Gavin's silly, casual comment had shaken her back to reality. Despite the few things that had happened in the bigger world, such as the integration of the armed forces, or the small change in voting rights, more than half of her hometown was barred to her, and, in the real South, in Alabama, less than a hundred miles from here, black men were still being lynched. She was a second-class citizen in a white man's world, and whites still had the power to hurt.

39

*D*EPENDABLE AS DAYLIGHT, Albie drove her to the railroad depot. Pearl went with them, her handkerchief screwed up in her hand, ready for the tears that Flora knew would come. Pearl had been crying, on and off, for a week, ever since Flora told her the news.

"Gon' miss you, Flo'," she wept.

Flora had wept with her on that first occasion, but Pearl's tears continued throughout the days of Flora's preparations, and she was getting irritable with Pearl. Not, she thought, for the first time in her life.

"How long you gon' be gone?" Pearl wept as she watched Flora pack.

"Long as it takes," Flora said.

Willie had called, in need of help. Ernestine was low sick, and still the doctors didn't know what was wrong. She had no appetite, was losing weight, and, always listless, she was spending most of her days in bed. Willie, who was working two jobs, couldn't manage the house and the children on his own, so would Flora consider coming to Chicago for a while?

Although she was concerned about Ernestine, Flora was also thrilled. She had a purpose in life again, someone needed her, and she would see her grandchildren.

"If'n you needs me, baby, I be on the nex' train," she said.

The next train wasn't practical, she had things to do, her life in Stockton to put in storage, because Flora had the feeling she would be gone for a while.

She gave up all her jobs, was irritated by the displeasure this caused some of her customers and touched by the generous bonuses several of those same employers gave her on her last day.

She thought about trying to find a tenant for her house but decided against it. She didn't know exactly how long she would be away, but she wanted the freedom to return, and she didn't like the idea of a stranger, or even an acquaintance, messing around in her kitchen. Pearl, tears flowing again, promised to look after the house and forward any mail.

Flora made arrangements with the savings and loan to pay her monthly mortgage and took out sufficient money to last her for a little while in Chicago. If necessary she would get a part-time job there; people always needed cleaners.

Albie was at her side throughout all her preparations, concerned for his daughter Ernestine, and told Flora not to worry about money. He was doing well these days. He'd gone into partnership with Caleb Brandon, and now that Caleb was dead, Albie owned the service station. If Flora needed any help, financial or otherwise, she should contact him at once. He drove them to the railroad station. Flora sat in the front passenger seat beside him, and they shared a small smile every time Pearl, in the backseat, wailed again, and dabbed her eyes with her handkerchief.

"What'm I gon' do without you, Flo'?" Pearl continued to weep as they hugged good-bye, and now Flora cried as well. Pearl had been a constant of her life for over forty years, and that part of her life was ending.

Filled with apprehension about life in the big city, Flora was also extraordinarily excited. She was off on a brave new adventure, because someone needed her again.

She was astonished by the comfortable changes that had been made since her journey back to Mississippi, even in the colored cars. Despite her apprehension, she was able to sleep.

She was overwhelmed by the vastness of the station, and the sense of bustle and purpose of the people, the strident noise, but then she saw Willie in the crowd, waving and calling to her. He looked older than she had expected, and she guessed this was because of worry.

They took a cab to the apartment, and although Willie gave her something of a guided tour, Flora was hardly conscious of her surroundings. Willie was all she cared about, because he was at his wits' end.

"Them doctors say there's nuttin' wrong wit' her," he said, explaining Ernestine's condition. "But summat's wrong."

The moment Flora saw Ernestine she knew that Willie was right. Ernestine was thin and pallid, and obviously weary. But she smiled, for Flora's sake.

"Look, Booker," she said. "This here's your gran'ma."

The boy was six years old and shy, standing behind his mother, staring at Flora.

Care for Ernestine would come later. At that moment all Flora saw was the darling boy who bore her husband's name.

"Hello, baby," she whispered. "You gon' give yo' gran'-ma a hug?"

He didn't seem too happy, but he looked at his mother, who smiled encouragement. He came slowly to Flora, who sank to her knees to be at his level.

"An' I got a li'l present fo' you," Flora said, knowing that bribery worked well with children you didn't know.

She took a small packet of brightly colored candy out of her bag and held it out for him. Shy still, little Booker looked at his father, who nodded.

"You say 'thank you' now," Willie said. "An' give yo' gran'ma a kiss."

"Thank you, Gran'ma," he said, and dutifully brushed his lips against Flora's cheek.

She couldn't help herself. She put her arms around the child and hugged him. Booker allowed himself to be hugged, but the candy was his greatest concern. Flora didn't care. Love would come later, with familiarity. For now it was enough that she was holding him, at last.

"Thank you," she whispered to Willie and Ernestine. "Thank you."

The apartment was pleasant and, to Flora, spacious.

334 * ALEX HALEY and DAVID STEVENS
334 * ALEX HALEY and DAVID STEVENS

There were two bedrooms, one for Willie and Ernestine, one for the children, and Flora assumed she would sleep on the couch. There was a portrait of Franklin D. Roosevelt on one wall, and Flora was pleased to see a poker work sign on another, the words JESUS SAVES burned into the wood. To one side of the room there was a large, obviously new overstuffed chair covered in imitation leather, which Willie said was Flora's chair.

She sat in it, and Willie laughed.

"Does my heart good to see you sittin' there." He chuckled.

Flora smiled too, as at an old family joke, but it had meaning for her.

"Does my heart good to be sittin' here," she said.

They chatted for a while, and then Ernestine excused herself to rest. Flora inspected the small kitchen, and every time she turned around she saw Booker standing in the doorway. She began asking him where things were, and he would point. He didn't say very much, but stared at her continually, as if fascinated by her.

The twins, Don and Diana, were less shy with her when they came home from school, but she was still a stranger to them. Like Booker, they allowed themselves to be kissed and hugged, and accepted her gifts of candy, but then they turned their attention to their parents, to tell them of their day.

"What do you think, Ma?" Willie asked her.

They were alone in the kitchen, Flora preparing the evening meal. Ernestine was sitting on the sofa, talking with Diana, and Don was outside, playing with some friends.

"They jes' li'l darlings," Flora said of the children. "I'm gon' eat them all up, they so sweet."

Booker was still standing in the doorway, staring at her.

"I meant Ernestine," Willie said softly.

"She sick," Flora said, as softly. "An' we gon' find out what it is."

She looked around, pleased with what her son had achieved.

"You done so well," she said. "Ain't gon' let no sickness spoil it."

He had done well, but he had worked hard for it. He was now the assistant foreman at the warehouse, and had a part-time job three evenings a week as a watchman.

At the dinner table Booker insisted on sitting beside Flora, which pleased her, and she helped him with his food. Willie said the blessing, and Flora was surprised to see Don and Diana cross themselves when they said the amen.

"They go to Catholic school, Ma," Willie explained. "They gon' have the best education they can get. It gon' be different for them."

Flora wasn't sure how she felt about that, she didn't know any Catholics, but that was for another day. They seemed to like her food, which made Ernestine smile.

"Willie been telling them all week," she said, "jes' wait till they taste Gran'ma's cooking! Like I ain't been feeding them!"

"Still thinkin' about his belly." Flora smiled. She was watching Ernestine, who only picked at her meal.

Diana helped her with the dishes. She was a quiet, re-served girl, much as Ruthana had been, Flora thought. Af-terward they sat together talking, and Booker climbed up on the big new chair to sit on Flora's lap, and he fell asleep in her arms. Don and Diana said they liked school and were doing well; they were in third grade. Willie took Booker from Flora and carried him to the bedroom, and Ernestine shooed the twins off to get ready for bed.

"An' what's wrong wit' you?" Flora asked Ernestine.

"I don't know, Ma," Ernestine said. There were tears in her eyes. "Some of them doctors say it's all in my head, that I ain't sick at all, but I knows I is sick. An' I don' know how to get better."

She tried to stem the tears.

"It ain't fair. It ain't fair on Willie and it ain't fair on the kids."

"Ain't fair on you, neither," Flora whispered.

She asked why the twins were going to a Catholic school.

"It's a better education," Ernestine said. "There's a lot of problems in the public schools fo' colored children."

That was why Willie was working two jobs, and why Ernestine had worked for as long as she could, so they could afford a private school for their children. Now she was sick and couldn't work, and the cost of school was a financial burden.

The twins came bounding back in their pajamas. Willie followed.

"Lawd, pajamas!" Flora laughed. "I'm jes' gon' eat you up, you so sweet."

They stood in front of her, formally, and Willie had his guitar with him. He started to strum.

"Ain't played much since I been workin' two jobs," he said, "but they wants to sing you a song."

The guitar was slightly off-key but it didn't matter.

"My country 'tis of thee," the twins warbled. "Sweet land of liberty, of thee I sing."

"You jes' li'l angels," Flora said at the end. They kissed her good night and went to bed. Willie went with them, to tuck them in.

"He raisin' them so good," Ernestine said.

"He ain't doin' it on his ownsome," Flora told her.

Ernestine looked at her gratefully, but Flora saw a tiny glint of something else, and probed at it a little.

"That's what I'm gon' tell your mama back in Stockton, Ernestine, and Albie, yo' pa. Willie ain't raising these children by hisself."

Ernestine looked at her hands.

"My mama reared me to help my man," she murmured.

Willie came back and they talked of Stockton and Ernestine's parents until it was late, and Flora yawned.

"'Scuse me, yawnin' in y'all's faces," she murmured. "Jes' git me a pillow an' a blanket, an' I make myself right at home on that couch."

Willie glanced at Ernestine and smiled.

"Get up, Ma," he said.

Flora got up, and Willie pulled a lever on the back of the chair. He pressed down on the back, and the chair turned into a bed, already made up with sheets, blankets, and pillows.

"Have mercy, Lawd!" Flora cried. "That's a magic bed!"

"Special for yo' comin'." Willie laughed with her.

He put the radio on a table beside the magic bed and turned it on low.

"There's a gospel program, Ma," he said. "You'll like that."

They made their good nights and Willie and Ernestine went to bed. Flora opened her suitcase, took out her nightgown, and went to the bathroom to change, then she came back and kneeled beside her magic bed, well pleased with her day.

"Lord, You've brought me what I needed," she said. "An' where I's needed."

On the radio, a choir was singing a joyous hymn, which Flora thought was heaven-sent. She climbed into bed.

"This is Radio Ministry," the preacher purred. "Your servant in Christ, Reverend G. Wilson Daniels, speaking. Once again it has been the privilege of South Side Baptist Church to bring you this one hour of the true gospel of our Savior, in song, seven days a week."

The program ended, but Flora, although she was tired, could not sleep. She twiddled the dial on the radio, and found another station.

"It's the witchin' hour, kitties!" a deep, energetic voice boomed. "Anybody ain't coppin' z's can jump till the early gray with this wailin' whomper, Br'er Bo Diddly!"

A frenetic blues shouter, backed by a searing blues combo, screamed out of the radio.

"Big leg woman, keep yo' dress tail down!"

Flora snapped off the radio. She would have to be vigilant. She had allowed her joy of family reunion to beguile her, and had forgotten that she once called Chicago a damned City of the Plain, like Sodom and Gomorrah. There were bad things out there in the night, things that were dangerous to growing children.

She realized that she was not alone. She turned and saw Booker standing beside the bed, in his pale blue pajamas, sucking his thumb.

"You wants to come in wit' yo' gran'ma?" Flora whispered.

He nodded, and Flora helped him climb up into the bed beside her. It was a tight squeeze, but both of them were comfortable.

Within moments, Booker was asleep, his head on Flora's shoulder. She stared at the ceiling listening to the unfamiliar sounds of the city at night, stroking the boy's hair.

She was glad she had come; there were things to attend to, and not just Ernestine.

But already, something important had been accomplished. Her grandson was starting to love her.

40

*F*LORA TOOK CHARGE OF THE HOUSEHOLD and insisted that Ernestine rest as much as possible. At
first Ernestine resisted her, there was so much to do, and
Flora couldn't manage it all on her own.

"Lawd, girl, what you think I am?" Flora said quite
sharply. "You think I cain't manage a li'l shoppin' an'
cookin' an' cleanin'? That's what I been doing all my life,
it jes' like Stockton."

She softened.

"You rest up good," she said, "so when those twins
come home you c'n spend some love time wit' 'em."

Ernestine saw the sense of this and rested most of the
day. Fortunately, Booker attached himself almost permanently to Flora, which thrilled her. At the same time, she
had a nagging feeling that she knew what part of Ernestine's problem was, and she made sure that Booker spent
time with his mother too.

On the first Saturday, Willie took them out to see the
sights of town. He had wanted Ernestine to come, but
Flora said no.

"I 'spect this be about the first day since you was married she had a li'l time to herself," she told Willie. "You jes'
leave her be."

Willie took them to Forty-seventh Street, as George
had taken him there when he first came to Chicago, and
he enjoyed watching Flora's reaction to the busy street.

"I ain't never seen such things," Flora said almost every
five minutes.

They had lunch at a cafeteria and ate ice cream afterward. They did a little shopping, and then Flora said she
wasn't tired but her feet were, so they went home.

She had been fascinated by all she had seen, the display

of city life, but she had kept a careful eye on Willie and the children all the time. Booker had held Flora's hand almost every step of the way, and chatted to her almost as if he knew her. The twins were less extroverted, but laughed at Flora's reactions. She played this up, she became the complete country hick to make them laugh some more, and by the end of the day she thought they liked her.

Willie had been good with all his children, and had carried Booker when he got tired, but he was firm with the twins. Although they behaved well, he was always demanding that they behave slightly better. In the cafeteria, he chided Don for his table manners.

"You don' put yo' knife in yo' mouth, boy," he said sharply. "You know better than that."

Don said nothing, but kept his eyes on his plate.

When they got home, Ernestine was pleased to see them and looked more rested, and Flora was sure that her intuition was right.

They took her to church the next day, and Flora was impressed, although not with the preacher. The Calvary Baptist Church was an enormous building and was packed; Flora guessed there must have been six hundred or seven hundred in the congregation. The big choir, impeccably robed, sang beautifully, with great energy, and a female soloist had a voice that would rival an angel's. Flora had heard great gospel music before, on the radio, and she'd heard some marvelous improvisations by the choir in Stockton, but never anything to rival this.

She was ready to enter into the full spirit of the service, and weep, or even faint, perhaps, although Willie was praying that she wouldn't, and then the preacher made his sermon and deflated Flora's emotions.

"Oh, he shout good and loud," she said on the way home. "But it ain't got meanin', it ain't got soul. Reveren' Jackson make hamburger out a' him."

They introduced her to some churchwomen after the service, who invited Flora to a women's meeting on

Wednesday. Flora agreed to go because she was determined to find out all about Chicago, and what she was up against.

She wouldn't let Ernestine cook but insisted she spend time with her children, and packed her off to bed at the same time as the children, so that she could be alone with Willie.

"You like it here, Ma?"

"It int'restin'," Flora said.

They chatted about the city and the things she had seen, and then Willie got his guitar and strummed for a while.

"How often you tell Ernestine you loves her?" Flora asked casually.

"Jes' about every day, I reckon," Willie said, concentrating on his guitar.

Then he stopped strumming and looked at Flora.

"Mebbe not as often as I should," he admitted. "But she knows I loves her. I's married to her."

"Never hurt to tell a body you loves 'em," Flora said.

The next day when Willie was at work and the twins at school, Flora made Ernestine take a nap in the afternoon, and gave Booker some candy to keep him occupied for a while. His mouth good and full, she phoned Ruthana in New York.

Ruthana was doing well, and wanted to know what was happening in Chicago. Flora said Ernestine was simply overworked, and changed the subject by talking about the children.

When she thought she had covered her tracks, she tried to sound very casual, and asked Ruthana about her work. Ruthana began a recital of what she did, but as soon as she said that her work was mostly with women, Flora asked her a question.

"You ever meet women, married women, who gets sick for no reason?"

There was a small silence at the other end.

"You mean Ernestine?" Ruthana guessed.

Flora cussed silently.

"No," she said. "I jes' askin'."

Ruthana didn't argue, although she knew what Flora needed.

"Yes," she said, "there are women like that."

Almost formally, she told Flora the little she knew of such cases, and said she would find out more.

The information that Ruthana gave her convinced Flora she was on the right track. She continued to run the household firmly, but now she encouraged Ernestine and Diana to help her sometimes, with little things, and she always thanked them for what they had done.

The next week, Ruthana called and had a long talk with Flora. That night, when everyone else had gone to bed, she sat with Willie. He was strumming his guitar.

"How often you tell Ernestine 'thank you'?" she asked casually.

Willie looked at her in surprise.

"What you mean, Ma?"

"I think she done real good," Flora said. "Keepin' this house nice, an' raisin' them kids when she sick an' all. An' so far away from her ma an' pa. I was jes' wonderin' how often you tell her what a good job she done."

"How often anyone tell me that?" he asked.

"You a man, you don' need to be tol'," Flora said.

Willie looked at her steadily.

"Yes, I do, Ma," he said.

She didn't know if he understood what she was saying, but over the next few days, he was especially considerate to Ernestine, and somewhat more relaxed with Don.

One night in May, he came home late. He was not sober. Ernestine was upset, and Flora was grateful that the children were in bed. But Willie had reason for celebration. That day, the Supreme Court had ruled that separate schools for blacks and whites was unconstitutional.

The case had been brewing for some time, although Flora was hardly aware of it. Willie had the newspaper, and read to them.

"Separate education facilities are inherently unequal," he read. "Racial segregation violates the equal protection clause of the Fourteenth Amendment.'

"You hear that?" he said, beaming. "You hear that?"

"'Separating children in schools on racial grounds generates a feeling of inferiority as to their status in the community that may affect their hearts and minds in a way unlikely ever to be undone.'

"At last!" Willie cried. "At last. Dear God Almighty, thank You!"

He went to Ernestine and hugged her, and kissed her.

"I sorry I's late, hon," he said. "I should a' rang."

Ernestine forgave him, because of the news.

"How they gon' do that?" she asked.

"I don' know." Willie laughed. "But it's gon' be all right, you see."

Flora didn't understand how it was going to work either. Whites, at least in the South, were never going to let their children go to the same schools as blacks.

"It gon' make a diff'rence?"

"I don't know, Ma," Willie said again. "But it's something. After all this time, it's something!"

It didn't make much of a difference, at first. Preachers thundered sermons from pulpits, and editorials argued the rights and wrongs of the Court's decision. Schools in some of the larger Northern cities began to integrate, while some of the Southern states attempted to form a new confederation against the ruling, but otherwise their lives were unaffected.

Except that it had an extraordinary effect on Ernestine. She still didn't eat very much, but she regained some energy and something of her old vitality returned. She wasn't always so tired, and she began taking more of an interest in the running of her house and the raising of her children.

Flora discussed it with Ruthana, who took a very broad view. She thought that the Chief Justice had been exactly right. A lot of black children carried the stigma of inferiority all their lives, especially women. They were never good enough, no matter how good they were. They had no self-esteem. It was possible that this applied to Ernestine.

Flora didn't argue because perhaps it could be true, and because she had learned a lot in Chicago.

The women's meetings at the church were her starting point. Again, she played the country hick at first and almost scratched her head and shuffled her feet, but then she began to ask questions. In particular, she wanted to know about the schools, and she wanted to know about the drug problem, and she wanted to know about employment prospects for young people.

The answers to all her questions were totally depressing, especially about drugs. Five years ago, the *Chicago Defender*, a black newspaper, had published an alarming report by a writer who had spent a month undercover observing the sale of various drugs to and among the pupils in the black schools. It caused a public outcry, but in a recent follow-up article, the newspaper suggested that nothing much had changed.

This was why Willie and Ernestine had decided to send Don and Diana to private school, and this was why Ernestine had taken a job. Working and running a house and raising children exhausted her, and this was when she first became ill.

So Flora didn't entirely agree with Ruthana's assessment of Ernestine's problem. In her mind, Ernestine had worked too hard and needed the rest that Flora had provided, and now she was on the road to recovery.

Flora even began to think about going home, but not quite yet. She was still worried about the twins.

Diana was a curious one, so like Ruthana when she was young, but with a hard and brittle edge to her. She was a good student and did well, but she always claimed she could have done better. Flora went out of her way to praise the girl, but the girl resisted her praise.

Don was even more difficult. As reserved as his sister, but not as clever, he seemed to be constantly trying to please his father, but nothing he did pleased Willie enough.

"You awful hard on that boy," Flora said to Willie one night. "He ain't in the army yet."

Don's shoes had been dirty, and Willie had shouted at him.

"You was hard on me, Ma," Willie said.

"Times was diff'rent then," Flora said.

Willie looked at her in surprise.

"Was they? It's a tough world out there. Only way a boy c'n get ahead here is if'n he got a college degree."

"An' if'n he don' want to go to college?"

"He goin' anyway," Willie said. "Jes' like you pushed Ruthana there."

Flora was surprised. Yes, she had pushed Ruthana into college, but Ruthana had wanted to go. She had tried to push Willie into college, and he didn't want to go. She had let him go to Chicago instead, and she was puzzled that Willie didn't remember this.

Having sweltered through a Chicago summer and enjoyed the fall because Ernestine was getting better, Flora experienced the biting cold of her first Chicago winter, and, because she thought her work was done, she began to talk about going home. Almost immediately, Ernestine had a small relapse, and Flora didn't talk about going home anymore. She endured the winter, and told herself she would leave in the spring.

On a pretty April Sunday they were leaving church and Flora drifted apart from her family to talk to some women she knew. Two young men were moving among the crowd, giving out small cards. They had close-cropped hair and were as neat and clean as pins, wearing dark suits, bow ties, and white shirts. They were extremely courteous.

They came to Flora and her friends.

"'Scuse us, sisters," they said. "Please join us at three this afternoon to hear our preaching of our love for each other."

They gave out small white address cards, which were embossed with a green crescent.

They impressed Flora. They were the sort of young men she hoped Don would become, and she thought of going to their meeting.

Ernestine laughed when Flora showed her the card. Willie was having a nap, and Don was out.

"I don' think you'll enjoy it, Ma," she said.

"She might," Diana said, to everyone's surprise.

"They preachin' love," Flora said.

"If you want to go, I'll go with you," Diana murmured.

That settled it for Flora. If Diana wanted to go somewhere with her grandmother, the grandmother was going to go.

"Don' say I din't warn you." Ernestine laughed again.

"They tell it like it is," Diana whispered, so quietly that no one heard her.

Diane knew exactly where to go. Outside the small building, a couple of young men, as neatly dressed and impeccably mannered as those who had first approached Flora, smiled and bowed slightly as they greeted the trickle of people arriving. A few women going in were dressed in flowing white robes and turbans, and wore no makeup. Flora remembered she had seen women similarly dressed occasionally on the streets of Chicago, but had never thought to ask who they were.

Inside, incense burned, sweet and heady. Folding wooden chairs had been set up in rows, an aisle between them. White robed, turbaned black women politely directed Flora and Diana to one side with other women, while more of the smartly suited young men directed men to the other side.

On the small stage there was an easel and a color portrait of Jesus, and in front of it, facing the seats, eight dark-suited young black men stood like statues.

"They're the Fruit of Islam," Diana whispered, and Flora wondered if this was the first time Diana had been here.

Most of those present were in ordinary clothes, like Flora and Diana, and when the room was full another young man, also impeccably dressed, came in. He was carrying a book that looked like the Bible, and Flora guessed he was the minister. He stood on the stage and looked at the audience.

"A-salaam-alaikum," he intoned, and bowed his head.

"Salaikum-a-salaam," a number of voices responded.

"Praise be to Allah," the minister said. He raised his head.

"To those who have not been here before, we want to thank you for coming," he said.

"We want you to know that you may see and hear things from us that may be unlike your previous religious experience. We want you to know that we are not necessarily seeking to convert you. We ask only that you listen to what we say, and that when you go home you will do us the honor of thinking about the things we have told you and shown you about our beliefs."

Flora was feeling uncomfortable; she didn't want to think about changing her religion, or really want to hear about other religions, because she already had her faith. She looked at Diana, who was concentrating on the speaker intently.

"We want to ask each and all of you a question," the minister continued. "It is possibly a question you have never been asked before."

He pointed at the portrait of Jesus.

"Would you tell me, please, who is this man?"

At last, Flora was on familiar ground.

"That's my Jesus!" she cried out.

"Sho' is!" a man shouted.

"Yay-man!" another man called.

Flora thought she heard Diana giggle.

The minister waited until there was silence, and smiled at them politely.

"Is it true that all of you who worship this man consider yourselves to be equals in his sight?"

"Yassuh!" some voices called, and "That's right."

"And this is the man you pray to every night?"

Again, there was a small chorus of agreement.

"Brothers and sisters, do not be angry with me," the minister said, as gently as before. "But why do you pray to a man with long blond hair and white skin, who doesn't even look like you?"

There were audible gasps of shock. Flora sat bolt upright, stiff with tension.

"Do not be angry with me," the minister said again. "We love you as our own. We just ask you to think about what we say. Why does a black man or a black woman or a black child go down on their knees, praying and begging to a blond-haired white man who doesn't even faintly resemble you or me, but looks exactly like those who oppress us?"

Flora was furiously angry. She wanted to get up and hit the man, she wanted to shout out her faith, she wanted to leave, dragging Diana with her. But she didn't, because of Diana.

Fortunately, there was a lot more, about the way the white man had oppressed the black, denying him individuality, personality, and a sense of his own history. Flora didn't hear most of it because she didn't want to listen, and it allowed her to control her temper.

Finally, it ended.

"Brothers and sisters," the minister was saying, "we are so brainwashed that even the very word 'black,' if applied to us, upsets many so-called 'colored' people, offends so many of we so-called 'knee-groes.' We have become so brainwashed that we despise what we are, we despise ourselves."

He smiled at them as gently as before.

"Do not be angry with me," he said. "Go home, and think about what we have said."

Flora did not remember leaving, but only feeling that she had to get away. Then another problem presented itself.

"What did you think?" Diana asked her, when they were about halfway home.

Flora knew she had to be careful. What she had heard was a kind of blasphemy to her, but she knew she dare not say this to Diana. By now she was calmer, and she also knew that she had heard a very good preacher, and that some of the things he had said, although not those about Jesus, had elements of truth to them.

"It was very—int'restin' " was the best she could do.

"You hated it!" Diana laughed.

"Yes," Flora admitted. "What he say about Jesus. But some of it—"

"I think they're wonderful," Diana said. "They tell the truth, what it's like to be black."

Flora wondered how this child could know what it was like to be black, and then remembered herself at the same age. She had known, and she had grown up in a tiny village. Diana was growing up in Chicago.

She asked Diana how she knew about these people.

"They come and talk to us sometimes, after school," Diana explained. "They do wonderful work, feeding and helping the poor, and teaching people to be proud of themselves."

Flora didn't say anything. She still thought the teachings were blasphemous, but anyone who did charity work, especially in this city, must have a good heart.

"Are you going home?" Diana asked her. "To Stockton?"

"Soon, mebbe," Flora said. "Yo' ma's gettin' better, an'—"

"Don't go," Diana said, interrupting her. "If you go, Mama will get sick again."

41

DIANA WAS RIGHT. Ernestine did get sick again, although Flora did not say she was leaving, and, when Ernestine got sick, she could not go.

She got sick because she was not well enough to work and so they could no longer afford to keep the twins in private school, and Ernestine thought it was all her fault.

Flora rang Albie and explained the schooling situation to him. He was angry that no one had told him, and immediately arranged to pay for the twins' education, and his daughter's medical costs.

This made Willie furious; he had a blazing argument with his mother. He was the father of his family and it was up to him to provide.

"Why you thinks we do this?" Flora shouted at him. "Why you thinks we work an' scrimp an' save? It fo' our children, an' our gran'children, so they can be better than we was!"

"Tain't the point, Ma!" Willie shouted back. "I's the man!"

"Oh, you's the man, is you?" Flora cried. "An' you gon' let yo' wife die afore you asks fo' help?"

Eventually he calmed down, and accepted Albie's generosity, and apologized to his mama. But none of this helped Ernestine.

If she ate, she vomited, and so she did not eat.

The doctors said there was nothing wrong with her, but she was wasting away before their eyes.

"It happens in some women," a doctor said. "They believe they're sick, and so they are."

"If she doesn't eat, she will die," another doctor said.

But she could not, would not eat.

Flora could not leave. Ernestine was spending more

and more time in bed, and someone had to run the house and cook and clean and raise the children, and the more Ernestine was unable to fulfill these wifely, motherly duties, the sicker she became.

Because she needed money for herself, Flora found a job three mornings a week cleaning for a Jewish couple, who had a pleasant apartment with a view of the lake, and problems of their own that were beyond Flora's understanding.

Mrs. Brooks, her employer, seemed to have an enormous weight of worry on her, and quite often she asked Flora to sit with her rather than clean. Then she would pour out her troubles. Her husband, a good and decent man, had a socialist past. Even though the communist-baiting Senator Joseph McCarthy was dead, the House Un-American Activities Committee was still investigating those suspected of extreme left-wing views, and Mr. Brooks had been called to testify. It was possible he would lose his job. It was remotely possible that he would go to jail.

Flora was sorry for the woman, and murmured sympathy, but there was nothing she could do, and, in any case, her concern for her own family obliterated her concern for others.

Don was hardly ever home, and was moody and surly all the time. Just before Christmas, when Flora was going to buy presents, she found that five dollars was missing from her purse, and she was sure Don had taken it. She started to hide her purse in different places.

Diana, worried about her mother, was withdrawing further into herself, or into a world of which they were not a part.

The light of Flora's life was Booker. Always kind and considerate to his mother, always happy with his father, he adored his grandmother and spent much of his spare time with her. He was Willie reborn to her, and Luke, and she gave to Booker the love that she had longed to be able to give to Luke.

Earlier that year he had begun strumming on his father's

guitar, and had a natural talent for it. This thrilled Willie, and he loved to sit with his son, giving him pointers about the guitar and teaching him about music.

When Willie and Flora went to a PTA meeting— Ernestine was too sick to go—Booker's teacher said they must be very proud of his musical talent and told them how well he played the piano.

This was a surprise to both of them; Booker had never mentioned it. Flora made a point of picking him up from school the next day, and she found him in an empty room where there was an old upright piano, which Booker was playing well for one so young.

They couldn't afford to buy him a piano, and there wasn't room for one in the crowded apartment, but Flora made an arrangement with the music teacher to give Booker extra lessons.

Luke wrote every two weeks. His letters were not long, but gave her simple news about himself and his family. Once or twice Flora had the feeling that he was holding something back from her, but couldn't imagine what it was, and because she doubted that there was any real problem she devoted her energy to Willie's family.

Ruthana called once a week, and they talked about Ernestine at length. Not long before Christmas, Ruthana had suggested that since they were getting nowhere with traditional medicine, they might try other things.

"Faith healers?" Flora asked.

"Well, no, but why not?" Ruthana laughed. "I meant chiropractors or osteopaths, but if faith healing works, why not?"

Flora put down the phone.

"Witch doctors," she said to Booker, who was sitting at the table drawing a picture of her and did not hear her.

They were hardly aware of the rest of the world. If they listened to the news on the radio, it was only noise. They read newspapers but only scanned the headlines. Their world revolved around Ernestine.

So when a black woman in Alabama refused to give up

her seat on the bus to a white man, it had no meaning for them, although everyone they knew talked of it. It was a small thing that might have gone unnoticed, but it was an idea shared by millions of people, and it was an idea whose time had come. In terms of the eventual effect on all their lives, it was the match which lit a fuse which exploded a bomb greater than the entire nuclear arsenal.

Christmas was a miserable time. Ernestine's weight was down to about a hundred pounds, and she looked dreadful. She spent most of Christmas Day in tears, apologizing to her family. Don got surly and went out. Diana snapped that her mother should stop apologizing, she had nothing to be sorry about, and Willie was sharp with Diana, and Booker burst into tears because everyone was arguing.

In January, Ernestine was so sick they took her to the hospital, and again the doctors said there was nothing they could do.

"There's nothing wrong with her," they said, and told Willie the blunt truth: unless Ernestine ate proper food in decent amounts, she would die. She tried to eat, but every time she did she vomited, defeating the purpose of the prescription.

In his despair for his wife's life, Willie abandoned traditional medicine, because it had abandoned Ernestine.

He took her to a faith healer, but that didn't help, because Ernestine didn't believe it would help. She weighed hardly more than ninety pounds; her face was gaunt, her body skeletal.

The distraught Flora phoned Ruthana, who said that she would come to Chicago.

Ruthana was full of news when she arrived. Flora met her at the station and went with her to the YWCA, where Ruthana was staying.

Small fires of protest were burning all over the South. In Alabama, the first black students had been enrolled at the state university, and the home of the young minister Dr. King was bombed. He had organized a protest against the bus line that had arrested the woman who had refused to give up her seat. There were protest marches by blacks and their friends everywhere, and counterprotests, often violent, by whites.

Flora heard these things, but they were unimportant to her because Ernestine was dying.

"Let me take her to a naturopath," Ruthana said, and explained what a naturopath was.

Flora was inclined to dismiss them as witch doctors, but nothing else had worked.

"Cain't make her any worse," she said to Willie.

Ruthana made an appointment and she and Flora took Ernestine to the naturopath. The walls of his office were decorated with charts of the human body, the shelves were lined with boxes of pills that had the names of plants and flowers, and there was a smell of burning incense.

The man himself was inconsiderable, small and gaunt, with wrinkled, nut-brown skin. But when he held Ernestine's hands and looked deep into her eyes, Flora felt a force of personality emanate from him that surprised her.

"My Lawd, girl," he said unsentimentally. "You low sick. You gon' die if'n you ain't careful."

Flora looked away, and then at Ernestine, and saw something that astonished her.

She saw trust.

"Yes," Ernestine whispered.

"I ain't never seen no one as sick as you," the naturopath said.

"Yes," Ernestine whispered again.

To Flora's amazement, Ernestine put her arms around the man and wept. They were not tears of grief, but of relief. For the first time, someone with medical authority, no matter how obscure, had told Ernestine what she knew to be true.

"Yes," she said again as she wept.

"There, there, girl," he said gently. "It ain't your fault. Ain't none of it your fault."

He didn't give her sickness a name because it was unnecessary, or perhaps it didn't have a name, or he didn't know it.

He told her that unless she did exactly as he said, she would be dead within a month. She was to eat a cup of yogurt with half an apple grated into it every day, three times a day. Exactly nothing more. And exactly nothing less.

Flora didn't know what yogurt was, but if it was going to help Ernestine she would find out. When Ruthana told her, she had no real faith in the cure, but that didn't matter if it persuaded Ernestine to eat.

Three times a day for a week, Ernestine ate her apple and yogurt, and then the healer increased it to two cups three times a day. Then he added a slice of whole-meal bread to her diet, and then a tomato.

And Ernestine began to get better.

"It's a miracle," Flora said to Ernestine.

Ruthana laughed. It wasn't a miracle, it was that someone had believed Ernestine. Her work with women in New York had shown her that people in authority, many men, including doctors, simply did not believe that women with problems had problems, because the causes of them were so obscure. And too many women didn't complain because they believed they shouldn't complain. It was their lot in life to support their men, to be perfect wives and mothers, even though they were fighting insurmountable odds to do this. There were even women who didn't complain when their husbands beat them up, because they believed the husbands had a right to do so.

Ruthana couldn't stay. She had taken three months off work and was going South, where the battles were being fought, but she promised she would come back to Chicago when she could.

"What about you, girl?" Flora asked her. "You foun' a good man fo' yo'self yet?"

Ruthana looked away before replying, and Flora guessed that there had been a man, and that the experience had not been happy.

"No, Ma!" Ruthana said with a laugh. "I'm too busy for all that."

Under the watchful eye of the naturopath, Ernestine continued to get better. By the end of the fourth week, she would eat a large salad for her dinner, and then one day, encouraged by her recovery, she ate a piece of cheese, but could not keep it down.

Flora took her back to the naturopath, who was ruthless with her.

"What you doin' eatin' cheese? I din't tell you to eat no cheese!" he shouted. "Be a year afore you c'n look at a piece of cheese!"

But he was pleased with her, and increased her diet with other good things, fruits and vegetables and more bread, and she stuck rigidly to her regimen and began to put on weight. Within three months he allowed her to have a small piece of boiled fish or chicken for her evening meal, and within six months he told her what they already knew. She would always have to be careful with her diet, but she was not in danger of dying anymore.

"Happen to a lot a' folk," he said. "Women 'specially."

Ruthana had come back from the South in an odd mood. She had boycotted bus lines and taken part in protest marches. She had been knocked to the ground by police with fire hoses. Whites had beaten up some of the marchers. She had been arrested twice and imprisoned once, overnight. When she spoke of the young minister Dr. King, who was leading the movement, she likened him to a saint, or to a man called Gandhi, of whom Flora had never heard.

But she still had time for Ernestine and, more particularly, for Willie. She spent time with her brother, and because he trusted her, because she was the key to Ernestine's cure, Willie took what she said to heart. Flora saw a change in his attitude toward his wife. He praised her often, and thanked her, and offered to help with housework, although he was working two jobs and was frequently tired.

Ernestine usually declined his help; it was enough that he had offered. She gained weight slowly, and regained energy quite quickly, and when Flora suggested she was thinking about going back to Stockton, Ernestine did not get sick.

It was time to go home, Flora decided. She had done all she could. Ernestine and Willie still had a long way to go, but they had started down the road and it was a journey they had to make for themselves.

She was pleased that Ruthana and Diana had become good friends, always whispering together, mostly about revolutions, Flora thought, and being black women, and about Africa.

Don was still a problem, but Flora didn't know what to do about him, and because so many problems had been solved, or had been addressed, at least, this one could wait for a little while.

She missed her friends, she missed her house, she missed her home. She was fascinated by Chicago, but she didn't like it, and she thanked her Maker one night for being so kind to her all those years ago, for sending a guardian angel to her on a train to direct her away from Memphis, from a big city to a small country town, and to a life with which she was well content.

The one small hole in her heart would be leaving Booker, who loved her as she loved him, and, for the rest of her life, would be her darling.

42

T HAD BEEN A TIME OF CHANGE FOR FLORA, but the change that shocked her most was revealed to her at the Chicago station.

"You wants to sit at the front, Ma?" Willie asked her.

"That where the colored car is?" she asked.

"Ain't no colored cars anymo', Ma," Willie told her with a grin. "You c'n sit anywhere on that ol' train you wants."

Flora stared at him in disbelief.

"Honest, Ma," Willie said. "Where you want 'a sit?"

Flora stood for a moment to make sure the earth wasn't moving under her, and then, shocked, she whispered to Willie.

"Y'mean I got to sit wit' white folks?"

"I fin' you a nice seat," he said. He searched the cars and saw one that was mostly black. The interstate train lines had only recently been desegregated, and while a lot of black people were embracing the new freedom and sitting everywhere on the train, old habits die hard, and some, especially older people, preferred to be with their own.

"Wonders never cease," Flora said, and felt slightly guilty for the whole journey, because although she was surrounded by blacks, there were white people in the car as well.

It was with some relief that she got off the train at Stockton, and hoped there wouldn't be any more surprises for her there.

Then she wondered why she had thought anything would have changed. Nothing much had changed in Stockton in the forty years she had lived there. The streets were the same, broad and lazy, and the shops were the same, except that Pop's Place had a big banner outside saying UNDER NEW MANAGEMENT and the Star Cafe still only served blacks at the back door, and would not allow them inside.

The people hadn't changed, except that they were all a little older. Pearl certainly hadn't changed. When Flora had first announced she was going to Chicago, Pearl behaved as if the heavens had fallen. When Flora came back, Pearl acted as if she had been gone for a couple of days. But Flora would never forget Pearl's look of shock and jealousy when she first got off the train.

As a going-away present, Ernestine had taken Flora on a shopping expedition. They went to a beauty parlor. Flora had a manicure and a pedicure. She had a facial. She had a shampoo. Then, at Ernestine's urging, she had her hair tinted bluish gray. They went to a shop and bought a new outfit, and Flora was wearing those clothes now, a tulle hair net over her newly colored hair, a smart new dress, brightly colored and shiny, a new purse harmonizing with the dress, and Enna Jettick matron's shoes.

The green of jealousy in Pearl's eyes disappeared in a zillionth of a second, and then there was only love.

"Well, Flora," Pearl said, dabbing her eyes. "It's so good to see you."

It was true for both of them, and Flora hugged her and was glad to be in her company again. Pearl did not mention Flora's appearance.

Albie did. He was alone, his wife was sick, and he told Flora she looked beautiful, and kept saying it, and every time he did Flora grinned inwardly, because she saw Pearl wince inwardly.

On Sunday when Flora went to church, she laughed. She hadn't seen Pearl since Friday night, and when Pearl walked to the organ her hair was coiffed and rinsed mauve pink.

Flora went back to cleaning for Mrs. Vaughan twice a week, and Mrs. Vaughan had friends who needed a maid, and soon Flora's working week was full.

As the months went by, Flora realized that if nothing much had changed, things *were* changing, and not only the color of Pearl's hair.

Reverend Jackson was a little grayer at the temples, and his waist was thicker, but the tone of his sermons was different. He preached change. He praised the government, which was introducing, slowly, all sorts of legislation that protected the rights of blacks. He hailed the leaders of the movement, this Dr. Martin Luther King who had suddenly become so famous, and Ralph Abernathy and Medgar Evers and Asa Philip Randolph and a dozen others of whom Flora had never heard. He said they stood on the verge of extraordinary times, when black people were rising up, at last, and were demanding their place at the table.

It was the first time he had ever called them "black" instead of "colored," and Flora was shocked, not because he said it, but because she remembered a Muslim minister in a small bare room in a back street in Chicago suggesting that they call themselves black and not colored. And she had been shocked then and wasn't anymore, and it was happening.

There were changes in the congregation too. Many of the faces were the same, her oldest friends, or people she had known all their lives, but many of the young men and women had a new energy about them and, again, a fiery anger. Often, during the sermons, while the older men called "Yay-man!" and "Hallelujah!" some of the younger men would be silent, but raise their right arms in the air, their fists clenched.

Other things changed too. Flora found a pamphlet in her mailbox, a printed handbill. It was the Memphis Steam Laundry and gave the telephone number of their Stockton office.

Flora took it straight to Pearl, who also had one of the handbills.

"Soon as I read that thing, I felt like the ground fallin' out from under me," Pearl announced.

"I sho' knows what you mean, girl," Flora agreed. "Sho' is a new day when white folks is axin' to do washin' and ironin' fo' us!"

Willie called once a week, or Ernestine, to say that all was going well, and when they rang she talked to Booker and even, sometimes, Diana. But Don was never home.

"He never home," Flora said.

"He got a lot of frens, Ma," Willie said, but she heard the edge of worry in his voice.

Ruthana rang once a week, to make sure Flora was all right. She seemed happy, but she never mentioned men.

Luke also phoned regularly, or wrote, and one Sunday when he called he said that he wanted to bring his wife and children to visit the next summer. Flora was thrilled.

When they came, all of Stockton looked twice. They looked like all big-city people, but not quite the same; there was something more to them, that hinted of Africa.

Luke had taken off his suit jacket, it was a warm day, and was wearing a brightly colored loose-fitting vest and a small round cap on his head. His wife, Jessica, who was beautiful, wore a dress that flowed, in red and green, and an oddly carved wooden necklace. Their children were gorgeous. Janine, the eldest, was eight, and wore a simple dress that, like her mother's, flowed gently, without a restricting belt, and the boy, Bobby, who was seven, wore an airy, loose-fitting shirt that was not tucked into his pants.

It was decided that the children should stay with Flora, while Luke and Jessica slept at Pearl's, but in the daytime they were all together, all the time, and it was a week of unalloyed happiness for Flora.

Luke was in his early forties, and had matured into a very handsome man. He was working as a lawyer, in Harlem, an advocate for black people, and seemed to be doing well. Jessica was quiet and gentle and softly spoken, and obviously shared her husband's commitment to her people's cause. The children were beautifully mannered, and quite ready to give affection to their grandmother.

Luke hired a car, and every day they drove around the

countryside, and every day Jessica made sandwiches for their lunch, so they could picnic in the open.

One day, Janine asked why they didn't stop at a diner, and Luke hushed her gently and said they were on vacation, that this was their grandmother's time, and this wasn't New York. It occurred to Flora that he was trying to avoid something, but she wasn't sure what.

It didn't matter to her. Nor did it matter that when they ate and Luke blessed the food, he never mentioned the Savior. It didn't matter that they didn't go to church with her on Sunday, because they couldn't. They had arived on the previous Sunday evening, too late for church, and they left the following Saturday night, before church was a possibility. It was only afterward, when she knew them better, that Flora found out that Luke had arranged their schedule with great care, so that church didn't become an issue.

One evening, she asked him about Mississippi, and the Flemings.

"I never go back there," Luke said. "No reason to now. No reason to wake up those ghosts."

Both his grandparents were dead, like his father, and the house had been sold, like the land, to the Yarboroughs' daughter and her husband. His grandmother had left him just a small amount of money; his grandfather had lost the family fortune, investing in grand schemes that came to nothing and living the high life.

"You are the only part of my past I care about," he said to Flora. "You are the only part of my past I want to know."

"I waren't there," Flora said.

"No," he said softly. "But you are now."

Thus Flora had her vengeance on the family that had been so cruel to her, but she felt no sense of triumph. She felt only joy that out of the dreadful past good had come, for when she looked at Luke and his family all she saw was goodness.

At the railroad depot everyone hugged her, and Luke promised that he would bring the children to see her again, next year he hoped. He embraced his mother in his powerful arms, and although Flora was deeply moved, she did not cry. She had wept an ocean for him in all those years she had lived without him, but now he was part of her life, no matter how tiny, and there was no reason to cry.

The following fall, Reverend Jackson shocked his congregation. He was planning to retire the following year, he told them. He didn't want to leave them in such stirring times, but he was old and he felt they needed the guidance of a younger, stronger man. He was raising the issue now so that they would have plenty of time to decide on his successor.

It was a small earthquake in their lives. Tears were shed. Many people could not remember when he had not been their pastor, and even the older members of the congregation had trouble remembering his predecessor's name.

Special meetings of the deacons and Old Sisters were called, and under the guidance of Reverend Jackson it was decided that they would cull the applicants down to three. These three would be invited to give a sermon, one each at various, differing times, and the best of the three would be selected.

The choice of the three caused endless discussion.

Reverend Jackson insisted that they needed someone young. The deacons were not so sure.

"Young fellas these days, cain't trust 'em," Deacon Sanford mumbled, having trouble with his false teeth, which didn't fit.

"Don' want one a' them young firebrands," Deacon Henderson announced fierily, forgetting that he had been something of a firebrand when he was young.

"Don' want someone gon' stir up trouble," Old Sister Pearl insisted.

"Mebbe we do." Flora giggled quietly to Vera Jackson. But then Flora was considered something of a radical these days. She had lived in Chicago, and had a daughter who lived in New York and was involved in the protest marches, and a son, Luke whose family had African leanings.

Eventually the three were decided, and the first, an older man, was invited to give a sermon just before Christmas.

It was not a disaster, it was actually very moving, but he was from another time and place. Halfway during the sermon, which was about the meaning of Christmas and the great gift from God of the boy child Jesus, he fell into an old-time, singsong chanting, which was very beautiful but seemed very old-fashioned, and the younger members of the congregation announced they would not accept him.

The deacons and Old Sisters got huffy, because it was their decision, the young people had no real voice in this, but the young people spoke loudly enough to make their elders listen.

The second, in February, Reverend Hawkins, almost caused Deacon Sanford to have a heart attack, and Deacon Henderson told anyone and everyone who would listen that if Reverend Hawkins were chosen, it would be over his dead body.

Everyone else loved him.

He was young, only thirty, and very handsome, with a deep voice like dark honey that made the rafters ring.

He took his text from the book of Romans. He was a New Testament man.

"Now it is high time to awake out of *sleep*!" he thundered. And Deacon Sims, who was old and had been dozing because he was sure this would not be the man, woke with a start.

"For now is our salvation *nearer* than when we *believed*!"

"Yay-man!"

"The night is far spent, *the day is at hand!*"

"Hallelujah!"

"Let us therefore cast off the works of *darkness*! And let us put on the armor of *light*!

Young men raised clenched fists in the air.

Reverend Hawkins looked up from his Bible.

"*We* have been sleeping, brothers and sisters," he said, "but now it is time to *awaken*!"

Reverend Jackson was beaming. This was his kind of man.

Throughout the South, throughout his great country, black men and women are casting off the works of *darkness*! They are putting on the armor of *light*!

His intention was simple. Because he was young he doubted that he would get the job, and so he had nothing to lose. But the spirit moved in him that was moving through black people throughout America.

He had perpared his sermon sensibly and thoroughly, and had given it several times at other churches that were considering him. Wisely, he had talked to Reverend Jackson to get the measure of the town and the congregation.

He talked about the many protests that were happening in the South, but only briefly. He mentioned the integration of the high school at Little Rock. The pictures of young black children going to the school protected by soldiers with guns from a violent and aggressive mob had shocked the nation, and had caused many a black mother to grieve and moved many a black father to anger.

But he did not dwell on this recent past. He concerned himself with Stockton, and urged them to the future.

"And what will you do?" he asked them. "Will you *awaken*? Will you cast off the works of *darkness*, will you put on the *armor* of light?"

Time finds the man, and the town had found their man.

"Will you be part of the great *battles* before us? Or will you *sleep*?"

He did not suggest a specific course of action, he only

demanded that there *be* action, and that if they did not grasp the moment, they would sleep, undisturbed, for another hundred years.

"Will you let others do your work for you? Will you leave it to the government? But the government is the people, the government is you! *Shout* and ye shall be *heard*! *Fight* and ye *win*!"

Everyone was calling out approval. He glared at them and willed them to silence.

"For if you do not, what will you say to your children, and your grandchildren, and all the generations? Will you say to them, I was there, it was the time, and it was the hour, and I was there, but all I did was *sleep*?"

Even if he hadn't got the job—which he did—he had done enough, he had made his mark. Because his sermon caught the mood of the time so exactly, within a week Stockton was irrevocably changed.

The next Wednesday afternoon, three days after the sermon, two young men, Washington and Billy, went to the white section of the town to the Star Cafe, which would not serve them, and demanded that they be served.

All of black Stockton knew they were going to do it, because it was premeditated. It was discussed at length at a meeting on Tuesday night.

Most of white Stockton knew they were going to do it too; the word of it spread like wildfire.

The town held its breath.

Flora and Pearl and half of the congregation held a prayer meeting at the church. If Washington and Billy were successful, they would be cheered and applauded at the church on their return. If they were not successful they would be cheered anyway, for trying, and two other young men had already volunteered to be the next to try.

Washington and Billy were not successful. Young Jerry James ran into the church, shouting out the news.

"They been beat up!" he cried. "They bleedin' bad."

Others were hard on Jerry's heels. A group of young white men had been waiting outside the Star Cafe. They had let Washington and Billy go in, and the young black men had asked for service and were refused. Washington and Billy sat at the counter and the young white men began pushing them out. Although Washington and Billy had sworn to nonviolence, tempers flared, and when Gavin Hopkins punched Billy in the nose, Billy fought back. They were seriously outnumbered and overwhelmed. Washington had a bloody nose and a broken arm, Billy had two cracked ribs and a gash on his face that needed stitches.

The congregation sat in stunned silence. No one had expected this level of violence.

Reverend Jackson stood.

"Let us pray for our brothers," he said. He led them in prayer, but the moment it was done, Freeman Lanier, who was seventeen, and his brother Abe stood up.

"We gon' be next," he shouted. "We goin' in Saturdee!"

His mother, Bess Lanier, wept, and although some of the congregation cheered, it was only halfheartedly.

Perhaps they had awoken too soon.

Flora did not sleep well that night. She'd always heard that if you were dying, your whole life flashed in front of you, so perhaps she was going to die, for her whole life flashed before her.

She thought of Washington and Billy, battered and bloody, and she heard again the Delta Lullaby, the screams of all those black men who had mysteriously disappeared at night, never to be seen again. She remembered cradling her dead husband in her arms, shot by a white man because he could not afford to live. She remembered that only five years ago a teenage black boy was murdered, because, they said, he had whistled at a white woman. She thought of Luke's son, Bobby, who might be that boy, or Don, or Booker.

She remembered, oddly, Ernestine, thin and gaunt and dying, and doctors saying there was nothing wrong with her.

There was something wrong with Ernestine. Willie had told her what it was when he read to her the Supreme Court ruling on segregated schools. She couldn't remember the actual words, but she remembered their meaning. She remembered that all her life she had been told by white people that she was inferior to them, a porch monkey, a jungle bunny, a chimpanzee jumped down from the trees. That she was inferior. Ernestine had been told this too, and Ernestine had believed it.

She remembered thousands upon countless thousands of insults and slights she had endured and had believed, because a lie repeated often enough becomes the truth, and her children had suffered the same.

This made her think of Ruthana, and suddenly she was filled with remorse and guilt. Ruthana was over thirty and had never once spoken of love in her life. Had Flora done this to her? In order to protect Ruthana from men, by telling her she was ugly, had she protected her too well, had Ruthana believed her too much? Had the lie, so often repeated, become the truth?

She sat up, turned on her light, and picked up her Bible from the table beside her bed. She knew exactly where to look.

"Ask, and it shall be given you; seek, and ye shall find; knock, and it shall be opened unto you."

She had found Luke only after she had gone looking for him. If she atoned for her sin, would God smile kindly on Ruthana?

She knew what she had to do and she was fearful of it, yet she had no choice. Only she could do what must be done, for Ruthana and for Ernestine, for Willie and Luke, for her grandchildren, and for all the generations.

She got out of bed and knelt and begged God for guidance. Then she remembered what Willie had said to her before he went away to war, that black blood is the same as white.

She remembered how Mrs. Hopkins had cried when

her son went to that war, and white tears were the same as black.

She wept now, in awe and gratitude, because God had displayed His infinite mercy.

He had shown her the enemy's weakness.

43

*T*HE NEXT MORNING, at about ten, she put on her coat and hat, for it was cold. She walked to the end of her street and got on the bus.

At the stop outside Pop's Place, Freeman Lanier got on.

"Where you goin', Miz Palmer?" he asked politely.

"Well, now, Freeman," Flora said, "I's goin' into town. I's gon' have me a cup of coffee."

"That's nice," he said. But he was puzzled.

They were driving away from Pop's Place.

"I's goin' to the Star Cafe," Flora said casually. "I hears they make a nice cup of coffee."

Freeman stared at her as if he didn't believe what he had said. Flora hoped he wouldn't say anything else. She hardly knew him, and she had to do this on her own.

"I don' think that's a good idea, Miz Palmer," he said.

"Well, now, Freeman," Flora said, "I don't really care what you think, 'coz that's where I's goin'."

Freeman didn't know what to say. He stared out the window, and then back at Flora.

"They don' serve colored folk there, Miz Palmer," he said.

"Freeman, I ain't colored," Flora said. "I's black. How's yo' pappy doin'?"

He mumbled a sort of reply, and then stared out the window again.

Flora got off at the town hall. So did Freeman. He wandered a few paces away, as if he had something to do, but then stopped and watched Flora.

She looked around. It was really quite a pleasant place, she thought, but it was so silly to have two of everything. Two drinking fountains, two park benches—it was such a waste of money. She knew that Freeman was following her, at a respectable distance, her guardian and protector, and she wished he wouldn't. She didn't want a guardian and protector, because she already had one.

She had God.

She walked through the little park in front of the town hall, and remembered that this was where she had once tried to give blood and was refused because she was black.

This reminded her of her present purpose and she went across the street to the Star Cafe.

"Don't do it, Miz Palmer," Freeman called. He was a few feet away.

"You jes' mind yo' business, Freeman," Flora said sharply. "An' don' come wit' me. I gotta do this on my own."

She went in, looked around.

It was plesant enough, but no nicer than Pop's Place, and it was busy but not full. She decided she'd like to sit at the counter. She took her seat, and waited patiently. She was aware that everyone was looking at her.

A waitress came up to her, a young blond woman in a pretty pink uniform. She seemed nice.

"We don't want no trouble here," she said.

"No, we surely don't," Flora agreed. "All I wants is a nice hot cup a' coffee, wit' a li'l cream an' sugar."

"We don't serve colored," the waitress whispered.

"Oh, I 'spect you will," Flora said. " 'Ventu'lly."

The waitress went away to talk to someone. A couple of white men got up from a table and went out, whispering to themselves, doubtless about her. Flora looked around and saw that Freeman was standing outside, watching her through the window.

A man she guessed was the manager came up to her.

"You'd best get out of here," he said. "Go on home."

"I don' feel like goin' home," Flora said. "Not till I's had my coffee. It cruel cold out there today."

"We ain't going to serve you," the manager said.

"Oh, I 'spect you will," Flora said sweetly. " 'Ventu'lly."

The manager didn't know what to do. The violence of the previous day had shocked him, and he didn't want anything to happen to this little old lady.

"Y'know we don't serve nigras," he whispered fiercely.

" 'Spect you will," Flora said. " 'Ventu'lly."

The manager decided on discretion. If they ignored her, she would go away. Eventually.

She didn't go away. She sat there, waiting patiently, smiling at people sometimes. She glanced out the window and saw Freeman, his face pressed to the glass.

Then she saw the person she had been waiting for. She had now seen him for several years, but she would have known him anywhere. He was his father's son.

Gavin Hopkins came in with three or four of his friends, and sauntered over to Flora.

"Wha'cher doin' in here, nigger?" he demanded.

She didn't care what he called her anymore.

"Waitin' fo' my coffee," Flora said, without looking at him.

"You best get out of here," Gavin said.

Flora turned and looked at him.

"An' what you gon' do if'n I don't?" she asked him calmly.

"Ain't you niggers ever gonna learn?" Gavin said. "Don't you know what happened here yesterday?"

"Yes, I do," Flora said. "An' are you gon' do that to me too? You gon' beat me up too?"

Before he had a chance to reply, Flora made the speech she had been preparing for the last several hours.

"Let me tell you somethin'," she said, not quietly. "When yo' pappy was a li'l baby boy he drank my milk, so he got nigger milk inside a' him, an' milk's the same as blood. So what you gon' do now to the woman what nursed yo' pappy? You gon' beat me up, an' break my arms, an' then go runnin' home to yo' pappy an' yo' gran'ma, an' tell 'em what you done? Tell 'em what a big man you are, beatin' up on a li'l old lady was sittin' at a counter waitin' for a cup a' coffee? That gon' make you feel good? That gon' prove what a big, strong man you are?"

She stopped because she couldn't remember all the things she had planned to say.

"An' what you think yo' gran'ma gon' say when you tell her what you done?"

Gavin was furious. She knew he wanted to hit her and she knew he did not dare.

The standoff lasted for several moments, because she wore impregnable armor and Gavin didn't know how to back down. He'd never had to back down before.

Then the sheriff came in, a newspaper under his arm, and sat at the counter.

"What's going on?" he asked calmly.

He looked at Gavin, waiting for a reply.

"Ah, the hell with this," Gavin said, and went out. His friends followed. They would have their revenge. They would beat up some black guys in some dark alley at night. They had lost this battle, but the war went on.

There was pin-drop silence in the cafe.

The sheriff nodded at Flora.

"Morning, ma'am," he said. "Cold out there today."

"Sho'ly is," Flora agreed. "A nice hot cup a' coffee's gon' warm me up."

He glanced at the menu and then at the waitress, as if ready to order, opened up his newspaper, and started to read.

The waitress came to him, the coffeepot in her hand.

"She was here first," the sheriff said, nodding at Flora.

Again, for a moment, time stood still.

Then the waitress shrugged and came to Flora and poured her a cup of coffee.

"Thank you kindly," Flora said. "An' p'raps a nice piece a' apple pie?"

The waitress went away to get her a piece of pie.

Freeman came in. He sat a few seats away from Flora.

"Mornin', Miz Palmer," Freeman said, as if it was the first time he had seen her that day.

"Mornin', Freeman," Flora said, pouring cream into her coffee, and otherwise ignoring him.

44

*Y*OU HAVE TO TELL HER," Ruthana said to Luke.
Luke was very uncertain.

"She won't like it," he said. "She's so—Christian."

Ruthana laughed.

"She loves you, and she'll get used to the idea," she said. "She's not senile, she knows what's going on. When she was in Chicago she went to a Nation of Islam meeting with Diana."

Luke was intrigued. Flora had never told him this.

"She hate it?"

"Of course," Ruthana said. "But she listened. And she does call herself black and not colored."

Something puzzled her.

"What happens when you go Stockton?"

"I'm careful." Luke grinned. "I fix it so we never have to go to church, and the first time we took the kids we never went anywhere that was segregated. I didn't want trouble, for her sake."

"It isn't fair not to tell her," Ruthana insisted. "She'll know anyway, the next time you take the kids there. And you have to go. It would be cruel not to let her see her grandchildren."

Luke and his family had converted to Islam. The parents had not yet taken Muslim names, but Bobby, Luke's son, liked it when his father called him Daoud, which means "beloved," and Janine called herself Jasmine.

"Yeh, you're right," Luke agreed. "It's just . . ."

Ruthana waited.

"For the first twenty-seven years of my life, I didn't have a mammy"—he corrected himself—"a mother. Then I found her and I don't want to lose her again. Or hurt her."

"You couldn't lose her." Ruthana laughed. "You could

become a Buddhist monk and go and live in a monastery in Tibet on top of the highest mountain, and she'd still track you down."

Now Luke waited.

"And the only way you could hurt her is to stop loving her."

Luke nodded. It was true. But he didn't give up without one last barb.

"You tell her everything about you?"

Ruthana shrugged and looked away, and then looked back at Luke.

"Of course not."

Daoud and Jasmine came in to say good night to her. Ruthana kissed and cuddled them, oh, she loved them, and said good-bye to Luke and Jessica because she had a big day coming up.

She walked home through the balmy night. Her small apartment was only three blocks from Luke's and she loved walking through Harlem at night. It was not late and the streets were thronged with people enjoying the evening. Some called greetings to her as she passed by; she was well known and admired for her work. She stopped to talk to a woman she knew, Shona, who was sitting on her stoop selling trinkets on a small rug beside her, a thin baby asleep on her lap.

"Hi, Shona," Ruthana said.

"Miz Palmer." Shona nodded in greeting. One of her eyes was bruised and swollen.

"He do that to you?"

Shona shrugged.

Ruthana thought about making a speech, but decided against it. Shona had heard the speeches too many times, and although she always nodded and agreed, she would not leave her abusive husband.

The sound of the Marvelettes' "Please, Mr. Postman" drifted to her from an open apartment window, but then was lost to Chubby Checker twisting and shouting as two boys went by with a transistor radio.

"'Lo, Miz Palmer," one of them said. Ruthana nodded and tried to remember his name and his offense or his problem, but could not, because there had been too many like him, too many offenses, too many problems.

"How are the kids?" she asked Shona.

They chatted for a few moments, then Ruthana moved on. Shona was not one of her success stories, although she was one of the reasons for Ruthana's present success. It was because of women like Shona that Ruthana and some others had opened their own shelter, in Harlem, for women five years previously.

When she first came to New York to work and live, Ruthana had been frightened of Harlem, and depressed by the scale of its problems. Now, after ten years of social work and hardly making a dent in those problems, she wouldn't live anywhere else.

Except Africa.

Ben had shown her the reality of Harlem, and told her the truth about Africa. But if Ben had told her Antarctica was a great place to live she would have gone there with him. She would have gone anywhere with Ben, except to where he was now, lost to her.

She let herself into her tiny apartment. It was one room, with a small cupboard that served as a kitchen. She shared a bathroom with the people next door. It was clean and comfortable and it was her nest, her home, and crammed with photographs of her enormous family, real and surrogate. She was mother, big sister and aunt to dozens of people whom she had helped over the years, and while she did not love them all equally, she liked to keep photographs of them because when she looked at the photos she remembered their stories, and their pain, and the reason they had come to her.

In pride of place was a photograph of Ben, framed in brass, and next to it a photo of Zora, gaudily dressed, who had been her best friend, and had taught her how to survive in New York.

Ruthana had arrived in Manhattan with not much more than a pocketful of dreams and the possibility of a job. Although many of her dreams were dashed, she got the job and was plunged into a teeming world of which she had no experience and almost drowned. The Henry Street Settlement was based in the Lower East Side, and a massive influx of Dominicans and Hondurans was swamping the area. This had caused problems with the traditional residents, the Italians and Jews, and there were small riots. The old-time residents conceded the war and moved to other areas, and now Spanish was almost the first language of the district.

All the immigrants were poor, come to seek their fortunes, and many were illegal. Within a week, Ruthana's enormous heart was full to capacity and overflowing with the problems she had seen. Within another week she was sure she'd never make a good social worker and by the end of the following week she was ready to go home.

Luke, who was keeping an eye on her, tried to help, but warned her that the only way she would survive was by being tough, or else she was no use to anyone.

"It's sink or swim," he said.

Zora taught her how to swim. Zora was a year older than Ruthana, from Detroit and streetwise. She had just moved to New York because of a bruised heart from a busted love affair, was staying at the YWCA, and she was bold, brassy, and confident.

Zora strode into the elevator at the Y one evening just as the doors were about to close, in a low-cut dress of gold lamé and high dudgeon.

"Can you b'lieve the men in this city?" she said to the elevator, and Ruthana, who happened to be there. "He axes me out on a date and I thinks we be goin' to the movies, and he thinks he gonna get what he want without so much as a cup of coffee or a by yo' leave!"

She snapped her gum.

"I sez to him, 'Shug, if you be thinkin' I'm that kinda

girl, you get yo' sorry ass outa my sight!' He needs to be
takin' me out and buyin' me cocktails afore he lays down
the blanket for *this* picnic. You know what I'm sayin'?"

She glared at Ruthana.

"What's the matter wit' you, girl? Look like you gonna
bust into tears."

Which was all Ruthana needed, because she'd had a
lousy day of wayward husbands, abandoned mothers, and
undernourished kids, all speaking a low Spanish that she
hardly understood because her Spanish was more formal.

She burst into tears. Zora was shocked.

"Chile! Hope it wasn't nuttin' I said," she murmured
loudly. "Some man let you down?"

In Zora's world, men were the root of all and every evil,
and she adored them for it.

"No." Ruthana wept. "It wasn't a man, at least, not
what you mean. It's just—I can't cope with it all! I want to
go home."

"Hush, now, shug, it cain't be as bad as all that,"
Zora said. "You come along and tell yo' auntie Zora all
about it."

An instant mother figure in the face of another
woman's distress, she lowered her voice a decibel or
twenty.

"I gotta bottle of bourbon in my room," she almost
whispered. "I knows it ain't allowed, but what the heck, a
girl needs a li'l company on a rainy day."

She shepherded Ruthana to her room, and would not
accept protests against alcohol.

"What you mean, you ain't never drunk liquor? Where
you *bin* all yo' life, girl?"

It wasn't true, Ruthana had drunk liquor occassionally,
at college, but had never really liked the taste, and she
tended to avoid it.

There was no avoiding it now. She sipped at the proffered bourbon, diluted with a splash of water, coughed, and
took another swallow.

The alcohol loosened her tongue and she poured out

her problems to Zora, who listened attentively and had a simple solution for those problems.

"That's men fo' you," Zora said, like a litany. "Don't you take no shit from none of them."

It didn't matter what the problem was, men were the key to it, in Zora's world.

After a while, Ruthana began to giggle, and although she had almost no experience with men she started to agree with Zora's estimation of them. The giggles turned into laughter, and then, because she had drunk too much, into tears again, and then Ruthana was sick. Zora helped her to her room and tucked her in bed, and sat with her for a few moments until Ruthana passed out.

The next day, Ruthana felt lousy. She was short-tempered with everyone and lost her temper with one Dominican because he couldn't understand her, although she was speaking good Spanish. In the face of her fury, he apologized profusely and thereafter had no trouble understanding her.

When she had calmed down, Ruthana felt very much better. She had just learned the most important lesson for her future life as a social worker. She took her heart off her sleeve and tucked it away where it belonged. She listened attentively and she helped where she could, but she didn't take any crap from anyone.

She turned to Zora like a lotus to the sun, and the unlikely pair reveled in each other's company and explored the city together. They decided to share an apartment and it almost ended their friendship, but they liked each other too much to let this happen. Zora agreed not to bring men back to the apartment and Ruthana agreed not to be so prudish about Zora's many men friends.

"Time you got yo'self a man, shug," Zora said to her. "You ain't never gonna be Miss I-da-ho, but you ain't bad-lookin'."

The trouble was, Ruthana didn't believe her, she believed what she had been told all her life, and it had become the truth. She believed that she was ugly.

She didn't date because she believed that men could only want one thing, and so she had almost no experience of men. What she knew about men, and about relationships, was from her work, but because she saw only troubled marriages and families, she had no great hope for a domestic future. Although she longed to find a kind man who would love her, she didn't really believe that he existed.

Above all, she wanted children, and she almost contemplated bedding the first man who asked her in order to achieve her dream, but there were enough fatherless children in the world already, her work had shown her that. And she was impossibly romantic. She wanted what she thought Willie had with Ernestine, and what Luke certainly had with Jessica. Their two children became her darlings, and she their adoring aunt.

Zora tried taking her out on Saturday nights, and lined up several men whom she thought would treat Ruthana well, or not badly, but nothing came of it because Ruthana didn't know how to proceed.

"What's the matter wit' you, girl?" Zora asked her after every failed encounter.

"He wasn't right for me," Ruthana said.

"Won't know till you sample the merchandise," Zora trilled.

After a while, Zora gave up on her search for a man for Ruthana, and they lived their different lives, each needing what the other gave.

Zora, because she loved men so much and so indiscriminately, was often hurt by them, and then Ruthana was her comforter and her counselor and provided a strong shoulder on which to cry.

Ruthana, who loved her work and did well, would not have done so well without Zora, who kept her on an even keel and restored a sense of proportion, and a lot of much needed laughter, to her life.

"Shug, I been workin' like a black woman all week so's I

can act like a white woman on the weekend!" Zora said on Friday nights. She said it every Friday night.

It was because of Zora that Ruthana got arrested for the first time. Reverend Adam Clayton Powell was organizing a picket of a Harlem department store, and Zora roped Ruthana in. Zora, who was a waitress in a diner, longed to work in a department store, selling makeup and perfume, but this store didn't hire blacks.

"Makes me puke," Zora said. "Black people's buyin' keeps 'em rich, but they won't employ us."

Ruthana was reluctant because she saw it as a political activity that might endanger her neutral status as a social worker, but she agreed the cause was just, and so she went along.

A hundred of them picketed the store, to a cheering crowd of many hundreds more, and then Ruthana heard the wailing sirens and saw the police cars arrive, and her heart sank. As press cameras flashed and the police bundled her into a paddy wagon, Ruthana was grateful that Mama Flora could not see her now.

In the paddy wagon, once she had recovered from the shock, Ruthana realized that Zora was not with her, and her heart sank. She had no idea how to handle the next hour of her life.

A man sitting opposite to her grinned.

"It won't be so bad," he said.

Ruthana look at him gratefully.

He was tall and thin and not very attractive until he smiled. His face was slightly lopsided, but somehow his smile restored balance to his features, and he had an embracing personality that made Ruthana feel safe.

He said his name was Ben.

They were charged with disturbing the peace and released on their own recognizance. Ruthana's boss blasted her, as he had to do, but then, because she was a good worker, made some phone calls. The charges against Ruthana were dropped, and most of the other cases fizzled away to nothing. A few of the picketers were fined, and a fund was started for those that could not afford the fine, and somehow everyone thought that the picketers had won, although the store didn't change its hiring policy for some little while.

Now, years later, things were very different, Ruthana thought, staring at the photos on the wall of her little apartment. Zora was back in Detroit the last time Ruthana had heard. Schools were desegregating all over the country, even in the South. Jobs that had been barred to black people were opening up to them. The Supreme Court had been an astonishing ally to the civil rights movement, a new, young president who offered hope for the future was in the White House, and tomorrow Ruthana was to start a new job, working as an adviser on social problems for the mayor's office.

She was pleased with her life, but desperately lonely. She missed Zora. And she missed Ben.

She had known almost from the beginning that it was pointless loving him, but she could not stop herself from falling in love.

45

A FTER BEN HAD INTRODUCED HIMSELF in the paddy wagon he had stayed beside Ruthana as much as he could, whispering what to do, or smiling encouragement. When they were released, Ruthana stood outside, not sure what to do next, and looking for Zora, and then Ben was there beside her.

"Look like you could use a drink," he said. "First time you been arrested?"

Ruthana nodded.

"There's a first time for everything." He shrugged. "Second time ain't so bad."

He was quite tall and very gangly, and his arms had a life of their own, madcap windmills underscoring everything he said.

"What about that drink?" he prompted.

"I'm waiting for someone," Ruthana answered.

His face fell and she thought he looked hurt, or disappointed. Just then Zora came rushing out of the precinct in a fury.

"The things that cop said!" she fumed, having loved every minute of it. "I says to him, Listen up, li'l white boy. You put that chicken back in yo' basket 'coz I ain't yo' picnic. You dealing with a lady here, you know what I'm saying?"

She looked at Ben.

"Who he?" she demanded.

Without waiting to be told, she gathered both Ruthana and Ben in her embrace and herded them to a nearby diner. She kept up her tirade about the way the police had behaved for half an hour, while admitting that the cop who had made a pass at her had been cute, but one of those skinny-ass white-boy fellas who didn't know how to keep a woman happy, and in any case she had a date with a man who had been on the picket line.

As suddenly, she was gone, and Ruthana was alone with Ben.

"Ain't she somethin'?" Ben said.

"Yes, she's surely something," Ruthana agreed. She felt perfectly safe because Ben seemed so harmless, and because any man, given a choice between them, would inevitably choose Zora over Ruthana, she thought.

She was wrong.

"Too much woman for me," he said. "She'd bust my ass."

Ruthana giggled, and he looked at her and smiled, but then he let the smile fade.

"Who are you?" he asked, staring at her.

She told him who she was and what she did, and that she was nervous she would lose her job because of the arrest.

"Won't happen," he said. "Ain't enough people to do the work you do already. They'll just yell at you some."

"Who are you?" she asked him.

He was a writer, he told her, or a poet, and he made his living working in a menswear store nearby.

"Which is it, a writer or a poet?" Ruthana asked him.

"Depends what I write," he said with a grin. "On the days I write my novels I'm a writer, and on the days I write poems, I'm a poet."

Already she was fascinated by him. She had never met a writer or a poet.

He was born and raised in Cincinnati, but had come to Harlem to find what it had been. He longed for the glory days of the tens and twenties, the great years of the Harlem Renaissance, when the most talented black people in America had flocked there. He made it sound as if poets and painters, writers and artists and jazz singers and musicians were a dime a dozen, littering the streets.

Ruthana had heard of the Harlem Renaissance, but she had never understood what it was, and he opened her eyes to it, a world where a black man could be anything he wanted, in a black society.

There was a Harlem for everyone then, he told her. There were concerts and speakeasies and jazz clubs for those that wanted them, although the most famous, the Cotton Club, was mostly for whites. There were elaborate and unusual churches for those that wanted them, filled with fantastic choirs and exotic rituals. The street funerals would be watched by hundreds, with bands following the spectacular carved wooden hearses, drawn by black horses. Although such funerals still happened occasionally, they were a thing of the past. There was the life lived on the edge of the law, if you wanted that, with bootleg liquor and street gangs who kept a kind of peace, except among themselves.

There were books written and published by blacks, and magazines, and art galleries, and salons, an astonishing confluence of talent and blazing energy.

"It's still there, some of it," he said. "But not like it was. Hungry?"

Ruthana was surprised that it was dark already, and she nodded. He led her to a little restaurant around the corner where he ordered things that she had never eaten before, gumbo and jambalaya and étouffé. It was spicy but she loved it, and she was hungry for more than food.

"New Orleans," he explained. "Creole food. It's okay, but it ain't the best. Low-country cooking's the best, she-crab soup, but it ain't the season."

"Tell me more about Harlem."

Ben grinned.

He told her more, lots more that evening, and on the evenings that followed. They became inseparable, more than friends but not lovers. Undoubtedly Ben wanted her company but didn't seem interested in her body, and she understood that, because she was ugly. It surprised her when he kissed her good night one evening, and surprised her again when he held her hand all the next evening, but she didn't complain, because it felt so natural. They drifted into a pattern of cuddles in movie houses, and hands held, and ardent good nights, but he didn't ask for more, and Ruthana was confused.

Zora wasn't much help.

"Dunno what you see in him, shug," she said. "He ain't my idea of a man's man, you know what I'm saying, but if'n he makes you happy, I's jones."

"He's fun," Ruthana said. "He's intelligent, and he's good company, and, well, he's—harmless."

"That's my point," Zora said. "I likes a little boom-da-boom in my men."

She giggled.

"That ain't true," she said. "I likes a whole lotta boom-da-boom in my men!"

Ruthana giggled too, but she didn't agree with Zora about Ben. He had a lot of boom-da-boom, although not the boom-da-boom that Zora meant. He could be oddly aggressive, although never with her, and he had a short, blazing temper, which was always directed at others, not at her. She thought he was trying to prove something about himself to himself.

He seldom talked about his own past, although she gleaned bits and pieces. His mother had brought him up, he was her middle son and not overly loved. His father showed up from time to time, usually drunk, and was abusive to Ben. He didn't want any son of his to become a writer or a poet or any kind of artist. When Ben was fifteen, his father had found some of his poems, which were mostly fantasies about sex. He had beaten Ben up and kicked him out of the house. Ben had survived because he was a survivor. He'd made his way to Harlem and had fallen in love with Harlem's recent past.

She knew so little of that past, or any black history. For most of her life, Ruthana had been told that black people were, with a few spectacular exceptions, illiterate peasants, incapable of learning, only a few generations from the jungle. Her sense of pride in her people and their achievements had begun only at college, where she learned of some extraordinary black achievements against impossible odds. This was a paradox to her. If exceptions proved the rule, why wasn't this true of blacks?

If Madame C. J. Walker could become a multimillionaire in the twenties, for example, in Memphhis of all unlikely places, why were most black women relegated to menial jobs?

"It was differernt then," Ben said.

"No, it wasn't," Ruthanan argued. "For most people it was worse."

"For most people, yes, it was much worse," Ben agreed. "But there were the exceptions. There were people who had hope."

He meant Marcus Garvey, who was his hero. Garvey had been one of the most magnetic personalities of the Harlem Renaissance. He organized a black nationalist movement that, at its peak, had more than a million followers. He advocated a return to Africa as the only hope for American blacks, and he even founded a steamship company to take people there.

"Of course, they got rid of him," Ben said bitterly. "They put him in jail, then deported him to Jamaica."

He stared at the ceiling.

"They get rid of anyone who stands up for the black man."

They were lying on the bed together. They often lay together like this. They kissed and cuddled, but had not done much more than that.

"Who got rid of him?" Ruthana wondered.

"You can't give them a name. Just to say whites is too easy. The government? They're part of it. Mostly, it's the capitalists and bankers who really run the system and don't want it to change. They don't want to have to pay blacks proper wages; they think it would ruin the economy. They say that's what killed the South, anyways."

He stroked her hair.

"I love you," she whispered.

"I know," he said.

But he didn't say that he loved her.

She had tried to stop herself from falling in love, because it was stupid to fall in love with a man who wasn't in love with her, but she had failed. She adored him.

Her happiness with him was tempered only by her concern for Ernestine, who was sick. Flora was in Chicago to help, and had, by instinct, hit upon a clue to Ernestine's problem, which she shared with Ruthana. Ruthana agreed with the diagnosis, but couldn't imagine a cure.

Ernestine had grown up in a small country town and then one day Willie whisked her away to a big city, where they set up home. Ernestine had to run that home and care for her man and bear children and raise those children, and work as well, with her husband hardly there because he was working two jobs, so that they could give their children a better life. Of course Ernestine was sick. She had no close family to turn to for help, only strangers. She had Willie, but Ruthana knew Willie well. He was a kind and loving man, but his own life had been hard, and she knew from her work at the shelter that men changed when they married. They believed they had been cast into a particular role that they must fulfill, of breadwinner and provider, and that their family's welfare depended on their ability to put bread on the table. It was an overwhelming responsibility for some, and Willie had never been good at sharing his feelings.

Ruthana tried to help, with advice to Flora, but since none of them knew the extent of the problem, there was little she could do. And then Ernestine seemed to get better.

On the night of the day the Supreme Court ruled that segregated schools were unconstitutional, Ruthana and Ben made love. Although they achieved their basic purpose, it wasn't very successful for either of them. Ruthana knew he was disappointed, and assumed it was with her. She never understood that his disappointment was with himself.

But she knew how to reach him.

"Tell me about Africa," she whispered. He loved to talk about Africa.

They lay on his single bed in his shabby room, and he conjured up ancient and magnificent kingdoms and took her on fabulous journeys.

From the glories of Egypt, astronomy and mathematics and architecture, to the spectacular riches of Ethiopia, and Sheba and the mines of Solomon. Down through the Mountains of the Moon to the source of the Nile, and to the coast again, the spice-laden coast, sailing in dhows past fabulous beaches to the southern land of jewels and gold that was so despoiled by white colonialist adventurers, who had accumulated untold fortunes on the backs and blood of black men.

Past the Cape of Good Hope, the ship of his imagination sailed north again, past deserts crisscrossed with rivers of diamonds, to the jungle coasts of the west, and inland again, to the ancient city of Timbuktu.

Patterns of Africa interlocked in her mind. The capital of the country of Nigeria was called Lagos, and Cleopatra, two thousand miles away, was of the House of Lagos. Aesop meant Ethiop, and the fables that white folk taught their children were first told by an Ethiop in Athens. The people of the north were different from the people of the east and west and south, but they were all united by the color of their skin.

Except for the south, where a cruel and vicious system of segregation had been instituted, Africa gave Ben hope. In several of the central African countries, blacks were rising up against their colonial masters, the British and the French and the Belgians, and one day would achieve their independence, as India had.

Ben longed to be part of that revolution. He yearned to be a freedom fighter in Africa, and was tolerant of the violence against whites that was happening in Kenya. Ruthana couldn't see this writer and poet as revolutionary. He was stick thin, scarecrow tall, and urban flamboyant.

"Pen's as mighty as the sword," he said.

390 * ALEX HALEY and DAVID STEVENS

Ruthana believed that. She was sure the advances being made by the legislation in America would eventually bring about the elusive dream of equality. The Supreme Court was demanding the integration of schools, and even the state of Georgia seemed likely to comply.

"You think them crackers down South are going to lie down and accept it?" he asked in wonder. "They getting ready for war down there, and one day it's gonna blow up in all our faces."

He was right, as he was right about so many things. The match was struck when a woman in Alabama refused to give up her seat on the bus to a white man, and a young minister organized a bus boycott.

"I'm going," Ben said. It was one of his Christmas gifts to her.

"No," she begged, fearful for him, or because she was fearful of life without him.

"I gotta do it," he said. "We gotta stand up and be counted."

She agreed, but she didn't want him to go. Just as she could not imagine him waging war in Africa, she couldn't imagine Ben in the South, could not think he would be safe there; just the look of him, and his extrovert personality, was enough to drive Southern whites to action.

She knew she could not stop him. He had to go, as much for himself as the cause, as if to prove something about himself to himself. They made love that night, and it was intense and satisfactory for both of them, as if the prospect of imminent and possibly dangerous action had made him the man he had always wanted to be.

She wept for him, but did not let him see her tears. She talked to Luke, who was all in favor of it, but was not going himself. The South was an important battleground, but it was not the whole war. The cities of the North were where the true victories would be achieved. He was impressed with the teachings of a young black Muslim preacher, Malcolm X, who was warning of dire urban violence to come.

Ben left, a soldier off to war, and Ruthana wasn't sure if

her tears and fears were those of a mother or a lover, and then she knew that she could not let him be alone. She arranged to take a leave of absence from the shelter, and was planning to join Ben in Alabama, when Flora phoned to say that Ernestine was dying.

It was when she saw her family again that Ruthana realized how much she had changed in the six years she had been in New York. She had a confidence and sophistication that made them turn to her almost as head of the family, and they listened to what she said, and, when the naturopath she had suggested cured Ernestine, they believed her.

Ruthana had not believed that the naturopath would be able to do very much, but her years in a cosmopolitan community had taught her that there was more to healing than traditional Western medicine. Ernestine's condition was so desperate that anything was worth a try, and even though he had some success, she knew that the cure would need more than grated apple and yogurt.

She went to Alabama with her family very much on her mind. She had helped Ernestine and thought she could help Willie. Booker was darling, and Diana had blossomed in Ruthana's company, seeing her as a black woman who was doing something of value. Don was the real problem. Ruthana was sure that he was running with some wild friends, and guessed he was not a stranger to marijuana.

Then there was Alabama and Ben, and an odd kind of loving, and her family took second place to her adventures.

At first Ben had attached himself to the group following Dr. Martin Luther King, but they were committed to nonviolence, and Ben was all for action, even if it was violent. He fell in with a splinter group of young radicals, hotheads like himself, and they traveled the South to wherever they thought action might be, or to provoke it.

Ruthana was alarmed that Ben had become such a radical, but she had become almost peripheral to him. He was pleased to see her, and they pretended they were lovers, but his heart was with the battle.

They went to Florida, to Tallahassee, to join the bus boycott there, and when small fights broke out with protesting whites, Ben was always in the thick of them. When the NAACP forced the University of Alabama to enroll its first black student, Ben and Ruthana and his friends were there. They appointed themselves guardians of any black child going to a white school for the first time, and even if there was no likelihood of violence, somehow Ben found fights with angry whites, in the back streets. They organized protest rallies, often simply to provoke reaction from extremist whites, including fire hoses and arrest.

After two months, Ruthana had had enough. Her leave was over, and that gave her the excuse she needed.

"I'm not coming back," Ben said.

"I know," she said.

They parted as friends, not as lovers, although she loved him.

"I love you," she said.

"I know," he said.

He kissed her and wished her luck, and she hugged him and made him promise to be careful, although she knew it was a waste of time.

She went back to Chicago because there was work to do with her family. She became their counselor, and spent hours talking to Willie. She told him he was not alone in his feelings, that many men felt swamped by the responsibility of family. But she pointed out that Ernestine felt swamped too, and had few friends in the city to turn to for help. He had chosen Chicago of his own accord, but she had come to Chicago because Willie had demanded it, and had cut herself off from the support of her family. He had to be the anchor that held her in place, not the rock on which she foundered.

She began to understand more about Diana, who knew what her mother's problem was, and was determined not to go the same way.

"I'm proud to be black," Diana said. "I'm not going to let them make me think I'm inferior just because of the color of my skin."

Diana admired the Black Muslims, but she adored the young and aggressive Black Power radicals, who were becoming increasingly strident. Ruthana suggested caution, but then wondered why. Why shouldn't they stand up and demand what they were only slowly being given? She smiled, because she thought that Ben and Diana would have made a splendid couple, soul mates.

She tried talking to Don. She thought he was pleased that she was ready to listen to him, but she doubted they would make any headway in the short time they had. She suggested, gently, to Willie that he ease up on the boy, for this was the root of his problem, but she already believed that too much damage had been done.

She loved Booker, everyone loved Booker, but the main joy to Ruthana was the pleasure she found in Flora's company.

Flora had not changed, but she had grown. Ruthana was amazed that a woman of Flora's years and limited education, and so set in her ways, could accommodate extraordinary, new ideas. She knew that Flora, deep down inside, had been strongly offended by the idea of taking Ernestine to a naturopath, but then she realized how little she knew about her mother and how little she knew about love.

Flora would have done anything to help Ernestine; it was a primal need to protect her family and it transcended the literal.

"Wish we'd had one a' them in Stockton when yo' ma was dying," Flora said.

Ruthana asked her about the Black Muslims. Diana had told her that they had been to the meeting.

"Blasph'my," Flora said. "But it makes you think."

It was then Ruthana noticed that her mother had stopped referring to herself as colored and called herself black.

She did not tell Flora about Ben, because she saw no point. She hadn't told any of her family about Ben, not even Luke, because she saw no point. He had been a friend, her closest friend, an intimate friend, but she was not sure that they were lovers, and she was too insecure in her relationship with him to try and define it.

She didn't talk to anyone about Ben very much, except Zora, whom she saw only occasionally, because they had drifted apart. Zora had fallen in love with a man who lived in Pittsburgh and had gone to live with him there.

Ruthana preferred to let her family think there was no man in her life, because now it was true. There was no man in her life.

She left Chicago and went back to New York, and she did not hear from Ben again for a year. He called to say that he was in Washington for the Prayer Pilgrimage, and even though it was essentially a religious occasion, it was inspiring. It was to be held at the Lincoln Memorial and thirty thousand people were expected to attend. He had never been so happy, he said; things were exploding in the South.

"I love you," she said.

"I know," he said.

Talking to him again had opened up the wound on her heart that she thought was healed, and she prayed for his safety.

Her relationship with God was ambivalent. She believed, but she wasn't sure what she believed. She still went to the Abyssinian Baptist Church every Sunday, because it was a habit, and because she loved and needed the expressions of devotion, but she stood outside it, as she stood outside of life, concerned, deeply, deeply concerned, but not involved.

Ben was right, things were exploding in the South, but not just in the South. The Little Rock High School in Arkansas was integrated, but the National Guard had to protect the nine black students. In New York, Luke's hero, Malcolm X, led a protest outside a police station

because the police had beaten up a man from the Nation of Islam.

Ghana became the first African country to gain its independence, and an ambassador was appointed to the United Nations. Ruthana laughed, because this simple thing showed segregation for the farce that it was. On the one hand, the United States was welcoming the winds of change in Africa, but the arrival of African diplomats in Manhattan was almost too windy. It caused some small chaos and considerable rethinking, because a lot of the best hotels and restaurants in the city were, effectively, still segregated. That soon changed, but Ruthana wondered what would happen if one of those diplomats went to, say, Atlanta.

The winds of change were not only blowing in Africa, but sweeping across America as well. Ruthana took no overt part in the revolution, but she was a tiny cog in the engine that made it turn, for she was dealing with ground zero, the streets where it was being fomented.

She was sitting at her desk one day, trying to find accommodations for a woman with nine children and no money whose husband had abandoned her, when a neatly dressed young man approached her. She thought she knew him, but could not place him.

"Miss Palmer?" he asked her.

She knew him as soon as he spoke; his voice reminded her. He was a friend of Ben's whom she had met in the South. Her heart sank. His manner was too grave for him to be bringing good news.

"It's Ben, isn't it?" she whispered.

"I'm sorry," he said.

Ben was dead. No one knew what had happened. They were in Mississippi, and there was an argument because a white woman complained that Ben made a pass at her. This led to a fight, but that resolved itself, and Ben went to get cigarettes and didn't come back.

The police found his body the next morning, half submerged in a muddy river, beaten to death.

She went to church because she couldn't think of anywhere else to go. It was empty, like her heart, and she found no solace there.

She called Zora, who said she would come back to New York, but Ruthana said no, and wasn't sure why she had made the phone call.

She went home and tried to cry but could not. She went out on the streets, looking for human company and comfort, but although many people knew her, no one knew what she needed or thought to offer it.

She felt utterly alone, and had never been so lonely. She went to the only person who might understand. She went to Luke.

He did not know what was wrong, only that something was. He left his office and walked her to his home, to Jessica, who was laughing with her children.

It was the children that made her cry. They didn't mean to, it was only that they were so happy and so innocent and so uncaring of the world, and loving, and loved.

Above everything, they were loved.

46

*I*T TOOK HER A LONG TIME to get over Ben's death, longer than she realized, and things he had said continued to affect her life, for a long time to come.

Work became her life because she had no other, and again, she almost drowned because she could not see hope. All around her, at least in the North, the civil rights movement was making impressive progress, but at the same time there was a rising edge of violence. Many young blacks were demanding a faster, more aggressive revolution and Black Power began to hold more sway for some than the nonviolence of Martin Luther King.

In the South, the war was accelerating, and for every small advance there was a violent setback. After a march by blacks on the old Confederate capitol building, the Alabama university expelled nine students who had participated. Diners and luncheonettes were integrating in major cities, but then bombs were thrown at the houses of movement leaders in Nashville, and collateral damage injured many medical students at a nearby college.

Martin Luther King led a sit-in at a lunch counter in Atlanta. He was arrested, imprisoned, and sentenced to four years' hard labor, and was only released after Senator Kennedy, the presidential candidate, interceded.

Aware of these things, Ruthana developed tunnel vision and saw only the dark side. She had hoped that the women's shelter in Harlem would make a difference in people's lives, and even, unrealistically, that one day the shelter might not be necessary anymore, but instead the numbers who came seeking assistance swelled, and Ruthana did not think she was making any difference at all. She went on because she had no choice, working sixteen and seventeen hours a day, fueled by a deep rage because of what had happened to Ben.

She forgot to be attentive to her family, apart from Luke and Jessica, and she began to think that she might follow their example. She knew they were thinking of converting to Islam, but she couldn't see the point for herself, because she didn't believe. She didn't believe in anything much, anymore.

Her only comfort was Africa.

Many nights, as she drifted to sleep, she heard Ben's voice again, taking her on remarkable journeys to the Mountains of the Moon, and there she was almost happy.

"Shug, you needs a hairdo and a facial baaaaaad," she heard a familiar voice say one day. She knew who it was at once. She looked up from her desk and there was Zora, resplendent in crimson satin and four-inch high heels.

Ruthana started to laugh and couldn't stop, it was such a relief to see her.

"Don't be laughing at me, Harriet Tubman!" Zora said, pretending to be aggrieved. "I look good, and someone needs to class up this joint!"

They went out to lunch. Zora was only in town for a day, on her way to Boston to set up house with another man who was going to be Mr. Right for a year or two.

"I dunno about New England, shug," she said. "They's all icy ass up there."

"It's pretty in the fall," Ruthana said, trying to see the bright side.

"Gonna take a lot more'n leaves to keep this girl entertained." Zora grinned.

The smile faded, and with it went her brassiness.

"I'm sorry about Ben," she said.

"Well, you know—" Ruthana said, and couldn't say any more because the kindness hurt.

"Yeh, I know," Zora said softly.

They were only together for an hour or two, but it was enough. Zora's blazing personality and unexpected gentleness warmed Ruthana's heart, and, slowly, with the spring, things began to get better.

They had a new, young president, who offered hope. Ruthana was interviewed for a job with the mayor's office, and then a week later was told that she had the job, and was to start in a couple of months. It was advisory and supervisory, and it would take her out of direct contact with the streets, and Ruthana agreed with Luke when he said that was no bad thing.

Luke and Jessica joined the Nation of Islam, and Luke took his family to Stockton to tell Flora in person, so she might see for herself that they were still themselves.

"How did she take it?" Ruthana asked him when they came back.

"You were right, of course." Luke grinned. "She was so wrapped up in the kids I didn't think she'd heard me. Then she asked if she could still mention Jesus in front of them. I said, sure, they know who Jesus is. I didn't realize how crafty she can be."

"What happened?" Ruthana demanded, loving her mother's guile.

"She said that since she'd been to a Nation of Islam meeting, it was only fair that I let her take her grandchildren to a service at her church. How could I say no?"

Already, Ruthana was laughing.

"Well, it was wonderful." Luke grinned. "I told the kids beforehand, and made them promise to behave, but of course, we all went."

Flora hadn't been able to keep quite, Luke explained, and told Pearl, who got on the phone and told everyone, including young Reverend Hawkins, that a Muslim family was coming to church. Luke was sure it wasn't planned, but the congregation gave them a service to remember. The choir sang as it had never sung before, the congregation thundered "Yay-man" and "Praise the Lord" and "Hallelujah," as if to prove to these Muslims that old-time gospel was the real answer, and Reverend Hawkins welcomed them and gave a sermon to wake the dead. His theme was simple. No matter what their religion, they were all united in the color of their skin.

"Was she pleased?" Ruthana asked.

"She was thrilled," Luke said. "She was queen for a day."

After the service, Isaac Dixon Junior gave a barbecue, and everyone had wanted to talk to Luke and his family, perhaps to prove their inclusiveness, or perhaps to convert them back, by good example.

"What did Daoud and Jasmine make of it?"

"They were very good," Luke explained. "They said nice things to their gran'ma, but they were very quiet. On the train home, I asked them what they thought."

"They all carry on like that?" Daoud had asked his father.

"Yes," Luke told him.

Daoud grinned at Jasmine and they both gave a sign of relief. They were glad to be Muslim. The service had been too noisy.

Ruthana laughed about it several times on the way home, but she was pleased that Flora had taken it so well, and that Stockton had given such a clamorous reception.

She wanted her family to be in order, because an idea was forming in her mind that would take her away from them.

She wanted to go to Africa.

It had no shape or structure yet, she had so specific destination in mind, only a continent, and no leaving date, but the seed was there.

She rang Willie. The news of his family was mixed. Ernestine was well, as was Booker. He was an accomplished piano player now, and doing well at school.

Don and Diana were in their freshman year at Roosevelt College. Diana was becoming something of a radical and had joined the Black Student Union.

Don was not doing so well. He had little interest in college; he had very little interest in anything, except music and his friends, and the hopelessness of the human, that is, the black, condition. Willie admitted something he had not told Ruthana before. A year previously, he found some marijuana in his son's pocket.

He'd tried to be reasonable, because he'd smoked it when he was first in Chicago, but he thought Don was too young, and told him so. Of course there had been an argument, and when the dust cleared, father and son came to an agreement. Don would go to college, to please his father, but he really wasn't interested in a formal education. He recognized everything his parents had done for him, and he was grateful, but he didn't think they understood young people.

Willie had not argued with him, it was enough that Don agreed to go to college, but Willie thought he wouldn't make it past his first year.

"It wouldn't be the end of the world," Ruthana said. "You didn't go to college either."

There was a small silence at the other end of the line.

"No, I didn't," Willie agreed. "An' that gets thrown in my face often enough. But I wants him to be better'n me."

There was nothing Ruthana could say. Willie had carved out a good life for himself and his family, against overwhelming odds, but by nature of his time and place and the few opportunities that had been available to him, it was a life of limited expectations. It was not surprising that he should want so much more for his children.

But his children wanted something different for themselves, as children do, and the gulf might be unbridgeable.

Ruthana loved her new job, and was good at it, but by the end of the first year she found she was missing the hurly-burly of the shelter. Although her life was full to capacity with paperwork and politics, she had very little contact with people, other than her fellow workers, and she longed to be able to sit down with someone in distress and bring a little comfort to his or her life. She visited the shelter from time to time, but she wasn't much use on a practical basis because she wasn't there to follow through.

Zora came back from Boston and stayed for a few days. Falling leaves had not been enough to save her relationship, and Zora was headed back to Detroit to see her family for the first time in years. She still had all her zest for life, and her furious optimism, and they had fun while she was there.

"Ain't you ever gon' get married, shug?" Zora asked her more than once, and Ruthana didn't mind, because it was Zora.

"One day," she said.

"Well, chile, you better get a move on," Zora said. "The clock's tickin' an' as far as I know you ain't ever even been laid!"

She went off to Detroit promising to return the following summer, but it was years before Ruthana saw her again.

She was right, Ruthana decided. The clock was ticking. She thought about taking a vacation. Perhaps in some romantic situation, she might meet a man, if only for the vacation, but she decided against it. She was saving for Africa.

She was worried about Flora, who had been ill, and Ruthana decided to go to Stockton for a few days. She had not seen her mother for several years. And because she knew there was to be a big civil rights march in Washington, she stopped there for a couple of days on her way to Stockton, and was glad she did.

The city was packed, but someone at the mayor's office called a colleague in Washington who found her a room. On the morning of the rally, Ruthana decided to walk, and found that slowly she was being engulfed by black people, all in a joyous and determined mood, and she became part of a crowd that eventually numbered more than three hundred thousand.

Years later, it pleased her to be able to say that she had been there that day, although she had not seen very much except the press of people around her. But she heard, through loudspeakers, what Martin Luther King said that day.

"Go back to Mississipi, go back to Alabama," he said, "go back to Georgia, go back to Louisiana, go back to the slums and ghettos of our Northern cities, knowing that somehow, this situation can and will be changed. Let us not wallow in the valley of despair."

He shared his dreams.

"I have a dream today. I have a dream that one day every valley shall be exalted, every hill and mountain shall be made low, the rough places will be made plain, and the crooked places will be made straight, and the glory of the Lord shall be revealed, and all flesh shall see it together."

It was a powerful speech filled with dreams, and it did something profoundly important for Ruthana, as it did for so many who heard it.

It gave her hope.

It was what Ben had told her was necessary as a condition of a full life.

"Free at last!" he cried at the end. "Thank God Almighty, we are free at last!"

She went on to Stockton, filled with what she had heard and seen, and filled, for the first time in years, with some optimism for the future.

The only thing that was unclear to her was what her own future would be. Flora had recovered from her ailments, and was pleased to see her daughter. She wanted to know about Luke and his family, and was full of the story of their going to church in Stockton, and Stockton's enthusiastic response to these Muslims. It was clear to Ruthana that Luke's change of religion had made not one jot of difference in Flora's feelings for her son and his family. She loved them. It was simple, pure and unalloyed.

She loved Willie, too, but was concerned for his family, and told Ruthana things she didn't know. Albie and his wife had gone to see their daughter and son-in-law and their grandchildren, and had come back with worrying news. Don had dropped out of college. He had a job as a barman in a jazz club. He moved into a room with some friends, and saw his parents only once a week at most.

Diana was radical in her politics. She and some other female students had successfully ousted the leader of the Black Student Union, for talking black, sleeping white, Diana said, and now Diana had been elected to head it.

Willie and Ernestine could hardly talk to her anymore without a violent argument. Willie tried hard to be reasonable. Many of the things Diana said were things he had heard in his youth, from the communists he knew: the dreadful conditions in the ghettos, created by slum landlords, and starving children, not just in the Third World, but here in America. Each day, it seemed, Diana became more extreme, inclined to violence as an answer.

Only Booker brought happiness to all his relations. He had come to Stockton for a vacation the previous summer, and everyone had adored him. He gave a concert in the church hall one evening, playing piano, and everyone agreed that here was a boy with a great musical future.

The few days passed pleasantly, in renewing old friendships, and one afternoon, Ruthana went to visit Mrs. Hopkins. She was glad she did so.

"Why, Ruthana," Mrs. Hopkins said. "I never thought to see you again."

Ruthana was puzzled. Mrs. Hopkins seemed oddly disturbed, even alarmed.

"Well, I guess I just came to say thank you," Ruthana said. "For all you did for me. You were so kind."

She thought she saw tears in Mrs. Hopkins's eyes.

"Yes," Mrs. Hopkins said. "Please, come in."

Yet still she seemed slightly unwilling, or nervous. She led Ruthana to the living room and ordered coffee from her new maid, Connie.

"I don't get many visitors these days," she said.

"How's Mr. Hopkins?" Ruthana asked.

Mrs. Hopkins was surprised.

"Haven't you heard?" she said. "He left me years ago. He's living with some fancy woman in Memphis."

Ruthana was shocked.

"I'm sorry, I didn't know—"

Mrs. Hopkins gave a bitter description of a young floozy who was only interested in Mr. Hopkins's money and would ditch him one day.

"I was sure your mother would have told you."

"No," Ruthana said. "We talk about local gossip, but she never mentioned that."

There was a small silence.

"Has she told you about the Star Cafe?"

"What about it?" Ruthana said, puzzled.

"And my grandson?"

"I really don't know what you're talking about, Mrs. Hopkins. I'm sorry," Ruthana said.

She saw relief on Mrs. Hopkins's face, and a need to unburden herself. Quietly, edgily, she told Ruthana the story of the day that Flora had, single-handedly, desegregated the Star Cafe.

"I am not proud of how my grandson behaved," she said. "Except that he walked away."

She was staring at the handkerchief in her hands, fiddling with it. She looked up at Ruthana.

"That's why I was so surprised to see you here. I thought you must hate me."

Ruthana was stunned. She managed to find nice things to say to Mrs. Hopkins, but could not imagine what she would say to her mother.

Ruthana went straight to Pearl and demanded to know if her story was true, although she could not imagine that Mrs. Hopkins had invented it.

Pearl confirmed the story, but said Flora had sworn her to secrecy. She didn't want any of her children to know because they'd worry about her.

So Ruthana kept the confidence until the morning she was leaving, then she had to let Flora know how much she admired her.

"I heard a story about you," she said casually. "At the Star Cafe."

Flora sniffed and turned away, but whens she looked back at Ruthana her eyes were filled with pride.

"Folk roun' here got busy tongues," she muttered. "It waren't nuttin'."

"Yes, it was, Ma!" Ruthana said, as proud as her mother. "It was something. Something wonderful."

"Well, I done it," Flora agreed. "Things is diff'ren' here now."

They parted at the station, and Ruthana tried to choke back her tears, for Flora's sake. She looked old, and her health was a concern, and Ruthana wasn't sure when she would see her again.

That was the year the long-simmering war in the South exploded. Civil rights demonstrators in Birmingham, Alabama, led by Dr. King, were attacked by police with water cannons and dogs. The images of violence brought strident calls for action from the North, and Ruthana wondered what was different now. Smaller versions of the same thing had been happening in the South for several years, and there had not been such an outcry.

It was agreed at work that television had crept up on them all. Before there had been simple reportage, or some still photos, or short film pieces of specific events, such as the Little Rock Nine. Now there was full and spectacular coverage, because of newer and more mobile film cameras.

It was not the only answer. Some things were not seen by the television cameras, only their aftermath, but perhaps because of television, the level of violence grew to shocking heights.

Also in Alabama, four young girls were killed during Sunday school when their church was bombed by a group of white men.

Medgar Evers, a leading civil rights worker, was shot outside his home in Mississippi.

And in November, in Texas, the young president was killed.

The world stood still for Ruthana when she heard the dreadful news that the president had been assassinated. All she could hear was Ben's voice, ringing in her ears.

"They get rid of anyone who stands up for the black man."

Could it be true? Were "they" so powerful, so determined against change that they would even kill a president? The grief and the shock that assailed her that day took from her something important. If "they" could kill presidents, as Lincoln had been killed, and Kennedy, if "they" got rid of anyone who stood up for black people, what hope was there for the future?

She knew she was being irrational. Others had stood up for blacks, such as Roosevelt and Truman, and had not been killed or got rid of, but rationality deserted her for a while, because there was more bad news.

Willie phoned, begging her to come to Chicago for Christmas. Diana had been expelled from college. Willie was at his wits' end, and needed help.

It was an ugly story. Diana and half a dozen others had burst into a college board of directors meeting flinging jars of roaches onto the table and shouting that these roaches came from local ghetto homes. Someone, it was said Diana, had alerted the local news, and a television crew was there to cover the event.

The college had been inclined to let her off with a warning, but she had made a speech outside the dean's office saluting her revolutionary brothers and sisters, and denouncing the college as a bastion of elitism, an eggshell within a pigsty.

She had been expelled.

Ruthana went to Chicago for Christmas. She did not think she would be able to do very much, but she could try. And she needed to be with her family that Christmas.

Diana was surly and truculent, still living at home because she couldn't afford to live anywhere else. She resisted all of Ruthana's attempts to reach her, and accused Ruthana of being part of the black bourgeoisie. She adored Malcolm X, but Martin Luther King was an Uncle Tom. She stayed in her room most of the time, listening to loud and aggressive rock music.

Willie and Ernestine were in despair; even Booker, usually so blithe, was affected by Diana's rage and his parents' inability to understand what had gone so dreadfully wrong.

Don turned up one day, greeting everyone casually, including Ruthana, whom he had not seen for many years. He was flip and passionate by turns, making jokes about things that were sacred to his parents, and defending all of Diana's convictions and actions.

While he was there, Albie rang from Stockton. Ernestine's mother had died. Ruthana thought that Ernestine would break. She stood stock-still, bolt upright, her arms stiff at her sides, when Willie told her. Then her eyes rolled and she put her head back, her body shaking.

"Lord Jesus!" she screamed. "Oh, Lord Jesus!"

She began crying violently. Willie and Booker grabbed her and took her to the bedroom, and then Willie came back to Ruthana.

"She need a doctor," he said.

"Yes, of course," Ruthana said. She went to the phone. Diana came out of her room to see what the fuss was, and Don was lolling in a chair.

"I guess that's killed Christmas," Don said to Diana.

It was then that his father hit him.

Ruthana went with them to the station, and wished she hadn't. Don and Diana were both going back to Stockton under protest, Don still seething about his father's blow, and Booker was furious with both of them.

They were standing in a group near the ticket booth, while Willie bought the tickets. The ticket seller, who was white, was passing the time of day.

"You folks goin' home for Christmas?" she asked.

"No, ma'am," Willie said. "There's bin a death in the family."

"Tell her to mind her own goddamned business," Diana muttered. Fortunately there was thick glass at the booth, and the ticket seller did not hear.

But Willie and Ernestine did. Ruthana, who was standing close to Diana, tried to stop it there.

"Don't do it, Diana," she urged.

But Diana wouldn't be stopped.

"Her fucking job is to sell tickets, not interrogate black people," she said.

Ernestine turned on her daughter.

"She jus' doin' her job," she said, her own temper rising. "Don't you respect nothin'? Nobody?"

Don didn't help.

"Cringing to these crackers," he egged Diana on. "'Yes'm, no'm, we don' want no trouble.'"

"Oh, for God's sake," Booker muttered. He walked away and sat down on a bench. He wanted no part of this.

Willie had collected the tickets and came to them, his eyes filled with anger.

"What is this?" he asked them, trying to keep his voice calm.

"You actin' like a nigger," Don said.

It was then Ruthana knew that his problem was more than marijuana. His eyes were sparkling. He was enjoying himself.

"What you want me to be?" Willie demanded.

"Be what you want," Don said, turning away. "I'm making my own life."

"We done ev'rything fo' you," Ernestine shouted.

"Oh, let's sing that song again!" Don said, turning back to them. He mimicked their country voices. "Givin' y'all all we din't have! Savin' fo' yo' college when we couldn' 'ford it!"

Diana giggled. Ruthana was sure that whatever Don

was on, he'd given some to his sister too. She also thought that Willie was going to hit his son again. His fists were clenched.

"An' what you gon' do fo' yo' kids?" he demanded of his son.

"Make damn sure they ain't like you," Don said. He stuck his chin out, as if inviting the punch he guessed was coming.

Willie didn't hit him. He looked as though Don had punched him instead.

"Son, don't," he begged. "This ain't the time. We got to go—think of yo' mama—"

Ernestine was crying in Ruthana's arms.

Don glanced at Diana and she nodded. They picked up their bags.

"Let's split," Diana said.

They turned and walked away.

"You gone crazy?" Booker shouted.

Ernestine saw what was happening and pulled away from Ruthana.

She moved a few paces and shouted after the twins.

"You *listen*!" she screamed at them. "I'm yo' mama! That's yo' pa! Where you going?"

They did not turn back, they kept on walking.

"You *hear* me?" Ernestine screamed again. "You *see* me? Talk to *me*!"

Diana stopped, and turned back. Don looked at her.

"Let the dead bury their dead," Diana said, and walked away. Don giggled and followed her.

Booker got up and came to his mother, put his arms around her.

"Come on, Ma," he said. "We'll miss the train."

He picked up her bag and led his weeping mother away.

Willie stood still. Ruthana tried to think of words of comfort.

"They'll come back," she said.

Willie was staring after his children, and hardly seemed to hear her.

Then he shook his head slightly, and looked at his sister.

He had heard her, but he did not believe her.

He did not speak. He picked up his bags and went to the train.

Ruthana stayed where she was, shivering because it was a cold day.

Too cold. Hopelessly cold.

She did not want to be here anymore. She wanted to be somewhere else, somewhere far, far away.

Somewhere warm.

47

$\int$HE THOUGHT SHE COULD SEE FOREVER and felt she was suspended in time.

The land stretched away to the horizon in almost every direction; only if she looked to the west could she see any evidence that the world was not completely flat, a cliff that rose up two thousand feet to the plateau that became the rest of the world.

She was in Karamoja country. She was in the land of Ben's dreams.

To the south, two hundred miles away, was a great lake bordered by mountains that nurtured other lakes. To the east was Pokot country, and then another great cliff that rose up to a plateau that became Kenya. To the west was Uganda, and to the north was Nubia and then Sudan and then Egypt.

The vegetation was sparse and angular, thorn trees and bushes, that seemed able to survive for years without rain. When it rained, the water ran down the dry courses and became streams that ran into a distant lake that fed other rivers, which became the Nile.

The Karamoja tribe lived on the western side of an arm of the Great Rift Valley, which extended north and east to the Dead Sea. Their customs and culture had been established in the time of the pharaohs, and they had found no reason to change them in four thousand years. The eastern half of the arm was Pokot country, an exactly similar group of people with whom the Karamoja were deadly enemies. For most of the recorded history of mankind the two tribes had occupied this valley, almost unnoticed and unvisited by the rest of the world, raising their few crops and tending their cattle and occasionally going to war with each other, and they had never found any good reason to invent the wheel.

The men were stocky and well built, when young, and fearless warriors, with beautiful, finely honed spears. They were able to fire a bow and arrow on the run with deadly accuracy. The wore a square of cloth hitched at one shoulder, and sometimes a feather or two in their hair. A few men still had a small disc of silver embedded in their lower lip, a form of disfigurement to discourage Arab slave traders from taking them.

The women were more elaborately dressed, in complex skirts made of dried grass and wooden beads, and, sometimes, a strip of cloth around their upper body. Some of them liked to smear themselves with a mixture of cow dung and rancid butter that made them more attractive to their men, who were oblivious to the odor, or found it desirable.

Ruthana was living in a birthplace of mankind, and if sometimes she thought she had found a kind of paradise, most of the time, especially recently, she could not imagine what she was doing there. She was in the middle of a small tribal war that was being fought with bows and arrows, and a few guns, and in Uganda proper a greater civil war was being fought with more efficient weapons.

These days she told herself that she had not intended to come here, but of course she had. Ghana, although wonderful to her, was not enough, the edge of a continent, not its epicenter.

After the dreadful scene in Chicago station between Willie and Ernestine and their two eldest children, Ruthana had returned to New York determined to realize her dream. Because of her position with the mayor's office she was easily able to arrange to meet with Reverend James Robinson, whose organization, Operation Crossroads Africa, had been a major source of information and experience for the founding of the Peace Corps, of which he was an adviser.

It was an essential problem of the Peace Corps that most of its volunteers were white, and they were regularly castigated in some of the African press as wealthy white kids enjoying a year or so slumming among the natives. Reverend Robinson was delighted that a black woman with Ruthana's experience and credentials, and, more important, a rural background, was now offering her services.

She was offered transport and a small stipend to spend a year or two in Ghana, which resisted white volunteers. She took an extended leave of absence from the mayor's office, packed up her apartment, and two months later landed in Africa.

It dazzled her. It shocked her. It delighted her. It appalled her.

Although used to the packed streets of Manhattan, she was unready for the surging mass of people she found in the African capital, the sense of barely controlled chaos, and the raw vitality of an alien culture, at once enchanting and embracing and disturbing. She loved the vibrancy of it, the bright colors and extravagant clothes, the welcoming friendliness and the exotic food. She was horrified by how much work there was to do.

The departing British had left behind a functioning infrastructure, but, perhaps because of the speed of their departure, had only halfheartedly prepared the local people for government. The educated ruling class was comfortable, the middle class was struggling, and the great mass of people still lived in poverty, and even though all were united in the euphoria of independence, and a determination to prove that they could be what they had promised, there were evident strains in the fabric of society.

What was shocking to her was that she had found what she had been looking for. She was unnoticed and unnoticeable in the crowd. She was not a minority in a white culture, she was anonymous in blackness. No one cared what she looked like; they were only concerned with who she was, and what she could do.

What was even more shocking to her was that she discovered that here she was not ugly. Because there were no comparisons with white ideals, no constant reminders of how much she differed from white concepts of beauty, in face or hair or figure, she began to appreciate the woman she had always been.

She began to like herself.

She was pleased when she was sent to a small coastal village about a hundred miles from Accra, and slightly overwhelmed by what was expected of her. She was to be schoolteacher, district nurse, and village counselor, and she was, to a large extent, on her own. For the first few days she was filled with self-doubt, but then she accepted the challenge, rolled up her sleeves, and went to work.

Thus Ruthana passed the two happiest years of her life, and when romance came to her in that little African village, she was ready for it, and relished it, although she did not fall in love.

Joseph was a medical technician, and, to Ruthana, very handsome, black as midnight, with small, neat scars of manhood initiation on his cheeks.

He came to the village for two days as part of a government program of vaccination for the children. He was neat and efficient, and relied heavily on Ruthana's help, because many of the children were terrified of the needle he wielded.

At the end of the day they walked together on the lovely beach at sunset and watched fishermen casting nets into the surf. They bought a fresh fish and Joseph grilled it over an open fire. They lay on the beach, side by side, basking in the tropical warmth, and Ruthana stared up at a sky vaster than any she had ever seen, and filled with more stars than she knew existed.

"There's a satellite," Joseph said.

He pointed to the sky and Ruthana saw a small, flashing light moving steadily through the heavens. She was filled with a sense of awe and of being, at last, in a place where she belonged, and when Joseph kissed her she did not resist, although it was a fiercer kiss than any she had known.

He wanted to make love to her and she did not resist because she was so happy, and when he loved her she felt filled with Africa.

They had a steady, intermittent relationship, rather like the flashing of the satellite, she thought. His work took him all over the country, but he would come back to her every few months, and they would walk on the beach at twilight and eat grilled fish and make love. She knew he had a wife and children in Accra because he told her, and so she did not fall in love with him, but loved him, and the times they were together. She was too busy to fall in love.

She did not fall in love with Ghana, although she loved it, and loved her village and its people. She felt she was nibbling at the edges of something greater, something even more fulfilling. If she had come so far in such a short space of time, how much farther could she go, because even here she had the sense she was a visitor to their lives and not a participant.

Much as the villagers respected her, and much as Joseph said he loved her, she had no sense of permanence. She was a foreigner, and she would leave, eventually, as all foreigners did.

When she did leave the village, two years later, they gave her a wondrous farewell. Children hugged her and wept and begged her not to go, although they knew she would. Women embraced her and shed tears and told her they would miss her, and she knew it was true, because she would miss them, but still she went. Men came to her formally, and some shook her hand, and others gave her tiny, useless gifts that she would treasure always, and as the Land Rover pulled out of the village, they all gathered in lines and sang a song of farewell, and danced their fascinating line dance, consisting mostly of swaying and jumping, and when they couldn't see her anymore they stopped dancing and went on with the rest of their lives.

Ruthana had written to Reverend Robinson explaining what she wanted to do. After counseling caution he had contacted a mission group in England who also counseled caution and welcomed her services.

After a tender farewell to Joseph in Accra, she flew to Cairo, which she didn't like, a crowded dusty city, and then to Entebbe, which she didn't like, a falling-down town on the edge of bloody civil war that had once been the pearl of Africa. After a cautious welcome and more cautions by the church group, Solomon, a placid middle-aged man from the mission drove her two hundred miles northeast of Entebbe to a faded, crumbling town that had once been a colonial jewel.

Ruthana had the sense that she was on the edge of a remarkable adventure. She had seen giraffe and zebra and wildebeest. They had stopped at a water hole and she had seen dazzling flocks of pink flamingos.

She and Solomon spent the night at an old hotel that had once been grand, and had eaten alone in a huge dining room where the menu promised much but offered little, and the next morning, after loading up the vehicle with supplies, Solomon drove her to where she was going.

"Why you going there?" Solomon asked her.

They were driving through lush, fertile farm country.

"To work." Ruthana laughed in response.

"Bad place," Solomon said, but would not elaborate.

Ruthana, who was loving the journey, could not imagine anything bad. She was going to the Mountains of the Moon.

But Solomon was right. The decent road became a dirt track that suddenly veered down a perilous slope of sharp, winding turns, and although Ruthana trusted his driving, she sent up small prayers for their safety.

They turned a tortuous corner, and a wonderful vista appeared, a vast land, flat to the horizon, except for a few small, distant peaks that might have been the mountains she was seeking.

At the bottom of the precipice, two thousand feet

down, they drove through the arid land, and heat assailed her, and a sense that it hadn't rained for months, and dust filtered in through the closed windows and filled her eyes and mouth and nose with sand.

After several miles she saw small herds of cattle such as she had never seen, but which Ben had described to her, African cattle, paintings of which had been found in ancient tombs. Karamoja warriors guarded the herds, gaunt, unmoving, and nearly naked.

An hour later they arrived at the tiny mission settlement, a few scattered shacks at the edge of a village of mud and branch huts. The missionaries, an older British couple, Peter and Sarah Mills, greeted her cheerily, and Ruthana's life changed forever.

She thought she had come home, at last, but instead she had arrived at a place that taught her where home really was.

48

RUTHANA WAS SHOCKED. Nothing made sense to her anymore.

"Why do they do that?" she asked Sarah.

Sarah was a sparrow of a woman, crisp and neat and efficient, full of energy and authority. She and her husband, Peter, had come to Uganda forty years previously, dedicated missionaries, and had spent most of their lives in villages near Entebbe. Five years previously they had discovered the Karamoja and their vocation. They had established their mission, living in a tent at first while Peter built their shack, and in five years they had converted six people to their Anglican cause, of whom two were backsliders.

If they were discouraged, they did not show it or admit it. They lived a life of example, built wells for the village, and were confident that the word of God would prevail.

Ruthana could not imagine the faith that sustained them in the face of such indifference.

The Karamoja accepted what they gave, the wells they dug, the food they offered, and the medical assistance they provided and otherwise almost completely ignored them, except when they needed help with a problem.

"They've lived like this for thousands of years, dear," Sarah told Ruthana. "One can't expect them to change overnight."

So they labored on. They built another shack, for their very few visitors, and a tiny church that was nothing more than a cement floor and half a dozen thin tree-trunk pillars supporting a roof of branches. Peter and Sarah held regular services in the church, which Ruthana attended, although she felt foolish.

The congregation inside the church never numbered

more than half a dozen, but scores of other villagers would stand outside, staring in at the obscure ritual. Sarah banged out hymns on a little pedal organ and Peter preached the Word, but to an uncaring audience.

At first, Ruthana had seen it as an enormous challenge, and had believed that change was possible. Three months later she discovered a truth that eventually demolished her ideals. The Karamoja circumcised their women.

It was shocking to Ruthana.

"Why do they do that?" she asked Sarah.

"Because they're men, dear," Sarah said, "and you know what men are like."

The angry Ruthana knew what Karamoja men were like. To her they were vain, shiftless, and lazy, almost constantly stoned. They spent most of their days guarding their cattle, but then they would burst into action and go hunting, and for a while they were storybook warriors. They were as brave as it was possible to be, their spears and bows and arrows were lethal weapons, and they could run for ten hours without stopping. These spurts of activity over, they would return to their idleness.

The women did all the real work. They cooked and kept house and humped water from the wells. They built the huts under the stern direction of the watching men. They raised the children but were not involved in any decision making. They obeyed their husbands' orders and accepted the laws of the elders, who were all men. At thirteen, every young woman was circumcised, to make sex undesirable to her. Their vaginas were cut out with sharp stones, or, these days, knives, a twig was inserted in the wound to make a hole for urination, and the tissue was bound in place with leaves and mud until it healed. On their wedding nights, some husbands had to cut their wives open to enter them. It was a barbaric ritual that had existed since the time of the pharaohs.

What disturbed Ruthana most was that no one seemed to want change.

"Well, of course we don't like it," Sarah said. "But it's what they believe. What would you have us do?"

"Stop it," Ruthana said.

"Don't you think that would be impertinent?" Peter said. "It is a custom of their tribe. Who are we to tell them that they're wrong?"

"We do try," Sarah added. "But we have never found a reason that makes sense to them."

Impertinent or not, Ruthana had found her cause. She taught English every day, and several young girls were proficient in the language. Ruthana used them as her interpreters, to spread her message of women's rights over their own bodies to the others. She wasn't ready for what happened next.

"You have to stop," Sarah told her sternly. "The elders are complaining, and many of the women."

"It's wrong!" Ruthana insisted.

"It is not your place to decide that for them," Sarah said, as firmly. "These are decisions they must arrive at for themselves. This is not America."

Peter was more gentle, if just as firm.

"What is the point of giving all these African countries their independence," he asked her, "if we then tell them what to do? We have given them the right to decide their own future, and who is to say that the Western model is right for them? If they decide they want socialism, that is their right. If they decide that democracy as we know it is not for them, that is their right. If they decide they want to return to the tribal boundaries and stick with the tribal customs, that is their right."

Ruthana had no answer for this, but seethed inside.

"Otherwise, everything that has happened in the last fifteen years, everything they have fought for and shed blood for is a waste of time," Peter concluded.

Ruthana conceded the point, but on this issue did not agree with him. She decided on a small war of attrition. She made friends with a couple who were Christians, Peter and Sarah's first and most successful converts. They had a daughter of twelve. Ruthana spent long hours persuading the couple that their daughter should be the first of the tribe not to be circumcised, and they eventually, if reluctantly, agreed.

When the time of the ceremony came, they imprisoned their daughter in a hut. The next morning, Ruthana was shocked to see the girl at the ceremony. Happy to accept the mutilation, she had broken out of the hut and hidden with other girls.

"Peer pressure," Sarah said, somewhat smugly. "Why should she want to be different?"

"Perhaps you should consider," Peter said, less smugly, "that this is not the right place for you."

Ruthana had already come to that conclusion, although she was reluctant to accept it; she found it hard to let go of Ben's dream.

Here, where she should have felt at home, she was an outsider, different, with different ideals, different aspirations. She thought of going back to Ghana, where she had been happy, but she was an outsider there too. She might be African-American, but she was more American than African. She longed for the certainties, the verities of the American ideal, however great the battle to achieve them. Africa might change, would change, but not necessarily to what she wanted it to be, and the change would take longer than she had life.

She was lonely. At the simplest level, she missed the visits of Joseph in Ghana, but there was no future in that relationship, and she was not going to find a Joseph among these Karamoja warriors.

At a deeper level, she missed her family and friends desperately. News from home came only sporadically, as the mail was unreliable, and the few newspapers that came to them were British and not filled with American news.

She knew Malcolm X was dead, gunned down by assassins. She knew Martin Luther King was dead, gunned down by an assassin. She heard Ben's voice again.

"They get rid of anyone who stands up for the black man."

It was a truth, but it wasn't always true, and in any case, was that any reason to abandon the fight, to give up? She knew that there had been massive changes in America; she had heard of Lyndon Johnson's Great Society, and the many advances that had been made.

And she was homesick.

She knew her country was at war with Vietnam, and Booker was fighting in that war. She bitterly regretted that she had not been there to say good-bye to him, and wish him well, and pray for his safe return.

Flora was seventy-four, and Ruthana longed to see her again, for who knew how long she had to live? She missed Luke and Jessica, and yearned for Daoud's and Jasmine's loving embraces. She wanted to see Willie and Ernestine and find out what had happened with Don and Diana, because no letters told her.

She missed her friends from work in New York, and she missed Zora and everything that Zora represented.

She missed Stockton. She even missed Mrs. Hopkins. She missed hamburgers and hot dogs and smothered pork chops. She missed gumbo and jambalaya and ice cream with hot fudge sauce. She misssed winter, she missed snow, and she missed the cherry blossoms in spring. She missed the world she understood.

She made up her mind to go home, and then war broke out and she couldn't leave.

There was a small gold mine in Pokot country, and a young Pokot warrior had sold his cattle for a matchbox full of gold in order to buy guns to raid the Karamoja herds and get more cattle.

After a short battle in which several Karamoja warriors were killed and two hundred head of cattle stolen, the Karamoja warriors sold some of their cattle and bought guns and raided the Pokot.

There were more battles, and the wounded flooded the mission with their injuries, overwhelming Peter and Sarah's small resources. Ruthana bound gunshot wounds and tended the dying, and tried to persuade herself that she was doing some good.

Nor was Uganda safe. The two presidents, Milton Obote and Idi Amin Dada, ruled in uneasy alliance, and small civil wars broke out constantly between their factions. Although her citizenship and honorary missionary status gave Ruthana immunity and freedom to travel, there was the problem of getting safely to Entebbe.

Peter and Sarah talked of sending Ruthana out through Kenya but that meant a journey through Pokot country, which could be dangerous. So, for the moment at least, Ruthana stayed where she was and longed to be somewhere else.

She was in the cement shed that served as the clinic one day, binding a gunshot wound on a warrior who intended to go straight back to battle the moment the wound was bandaged. She was in despair. She could achieve nothing here. Nothing she said or did made any difference to anything.

She heard shouting and the toot of a car horn. She looked out the open square that was the window, and saw village women sweeping the open ground with brooms, raising clouds of dust that immediately settled again. Obviously an important visitor was coming.

She saw the Land Rover driving in, but from the east, from Pokot, and she wondered who was foolhardy enough to have made the journey.

She went outside and watched as the vehicle pulled up near the mission. An armed bodyguard got out.

She saw a man who looked oddly familiar. He was wearing long white flowing robes, sandals, and a small white skullcap.

He looked around and saw her and waved.

Her heart jumped into her mouth and she let out a whoop of joy and ran to him and hugged him and wept on his shoulder, laughing through her tears.

It was Luke, come to take her home.

49

$\mathcal{F}$INDING RUTHANA WAS NOT Luke's primary reason for being in Africa. He had come to make the hajj, the Muslim pilgrimage to Mecca. Malcolm X had made the pilgrimage four years previously and had experienced a revelation. He returned to America with a broadened compassion, and founded his own Organization for Afro-American Unity.

After Malcolm X was assassinated, Luke had struggled with his feelings, and had eventually decided that perhaps the pilgrimage might answer some of the complex questions in his mind. He flew to Cairo and then to Mecca, and like Malcolm X before him, he was astonished to be in a place where the color of his skin was irrelevant, but there was more, much more than that. The faith of myriad pilgrims was deeply moving to him, and strengthened his own beliefs, and changed and broadened them beyond the horizons of where he had been. He did not want to live in Arabia or Africa, he did not want to follow their rule of law, however much it was based on faith.

Like Ruthana, Luke wanted to go back to America to bring about changes there.

Since he was in Cairo and so close to Ruthana, he wanted to see her to share his experiences and question her as to her own. He flew to Nairobi and at the mosque he heard of the troubles in the Rift Valley. He hired a Land Rover and a driver, and an acquaintance from the mosque offered his services as bodyguard and translator, and he went to find Ruthana.

They traveled safely back to Nairobi, which Ruthana thought was a clean efficient city after Entebbe. She had her first hot bath in years, and was not sorry to wash the dust of Karamoja from her, although she already knew that she would look back on her time there with enormous affection.

Luke gave her family news. Daoud and Jasmine were at college. Flora was frailer than before, but well, as were Willie and Ernestine. Booker had been wounded in Vietnam but was home again, safe. He was to be married next spring. The one tragedy was that his right hand had been injured in Vietnam and had not properly healed. His piano-playing days were over.

"Any news of Don?" Ruthana asked, because he had not mentioned the twins and was talking of other things.

"Don's in prison," Luke said.

His parents had not seen him again since he walked away from them at the Chicago train station, and it was only now that he was in jail that they knew what had happened to him. After drifting for a while, he had gone to Cuba, to help the revolution and the establishment of a Marxist society. He stayed there three years and came back as disillusioned with Cuba as he was with American society. Like his hero, Che Guevara, he had joined a small, radical militant group who believed that revolution was everything. They robbed a small bank in Detroit to finance their cause but were caught and imprisoned.

"I think I need a drink," Ruthana said, appalled but not surprised by Don's fate.

"I don't drink," Luke said.

"Well, you can have a Coke while I have a good stiff cocktail." Ruthana grinned. And for some reason she thought of Zora and giggled.

They went into the bar of the Hilton Hotel, and both remarked how pleasant it was to be the majority. There were a few white tourists, but it was not safari season, and most of the customers were black.

Ruthana didn't know what to order because she hadn't drunk liquor for a long time, and settled for the barman's suggestion of the house cocktail, a bright, highly colored concoction that she didn't like but drank anyway.

"And Diana?" she asked. She knew it could only be bad news, because Luke had not mentioned her.

"No one knows." He shrugged. "Don was the last to see her, when he first came back from Cuba. She'd joined the Black Panthers, but since then . . ."

He sipped his Coke, then looked at her.

"And you?"

"Oh, I'm fine," she said. "Now."

It was true, she was fine now, and she did not regret one moment of her experiences. She regarded herself as an old Africa hand, and she was pleased when a waiter who was having trouble understanding a German tourist who spoke bad English looked to her for help.

She had one last moment of Africa to take with her. At the airport she had too many Kenyan shillings, and was not allowed to take so many out of the country.

"What do I do with them?" she asked the policeman.

"Give them to someone," he suggested. He glanced at a porter who was standing beside him. The porter was grinning from ear to ear and Ruthana immediately understood. She gave her excess shillings to the porter, who thanked her cheerfully and put them in a pocket already bulging with other people's excess shillings. It was a very neat scam, Ruthana thought, and wondered how many people shared the shillings.

They flew to London and then to New York, and Ruthana understood why people kissed the ground when they came home.

She stayed with Luke and Jessica for a few days, and reveled in the company of Daoud and Jasmine, who had grown into young adults as pleasant and as studious as the children they had been.

She called Flora, who asked, demanded that she come to Stockton for a few days.

"You know, I's ol' and I might not be aroun' too much longer," she blackmailed. "An' if you ain't got no money after that Africa bizness, I can pay yo' train fare."

Ruthana laughed and said that she did have money and would come, but when she put down the phone she shed a few tears, because hearing Flora's voice again was a constancy in an inconstant world.

She was all right for money. She had been thrifty all her life, and even though she had been paid very little while she was in Africa, she had arranged that a small part of that small sum be put into her account in New York.

She saw old friends and fellow workers, and was offered several jobs, which she said she'd think about, because she wasn't sure what she wanted to do yet. It was enough, for the moment, to be home, and to try to comprehend the enormous changes that had happened. The first time she walked through Harlem, she almost thought she was back in Africa, because many people had grown their hair into an Afro style and wore African gowns, or brilliantly colored flower power clothes. She also saw militancy everywhere, and the insistence that blacks still had an enormous journey to make to equality.

But Ruthana saw the country with the eyes of someone who had been away, and, returning, saw how very far they had come.

She went to Stockton and there was Flora at the station, Albie beside her. Flora held out her arms, and Ruthana moved into them and was embraced, and loved.

"Oh, my baby," Flora whispered. "I din' think I was ever gon' see you again."

It was only then that Ruthana understood that the things their children do, the journeys they make, can be terrifying to parents. Once or twice, in Africa, Ruthana had been scared for her physical safety, but only once or twice, and only in Karamoja.

Flora, who had no concept of Africa, had thought Ruthana had lived in grass huts surrounded by lions, and swum in waters infested by crocodiles. Ruthana had sent her postcards from Accra, showing the tall buildings, the bustling city, but these were irrelevant to Flora. When she heard that Ruthana was going to live and work in a village, she had imagined the worst.

She seemed almost disappointed when Ruthana admitted that she'd never seen a lion, except at a zoo, and so she told her a few stories of Karamoja that were more alarming than the actuality, to keep her mother happy and give her something to tell her friends at church.

Flora looked old but was as spry as ever. Later in the evening, before she went to bed, she also seemed embarrassed.

"Albie be roun' here a bit," she said. "Me an' him's seein' each other."

Ruthana stared at her in astonishment.

"He lonely since his po' wife, Ernestine's ma, died, so he stay here some nights," Flora said, coy as a virgin. "An' I stay there some nights. He wants fo' us to live together, but I ain't leavin' here an' he ain't leavin' there. Leastways, not till I sho' a' his intentions."

Ruthana started to giggle.

"You don't mean—?"

"Don' you go gettin' no ideas like that!" Flora said huffily. "We both too ol' for that kind a' thing. But sometimes it nice to go sleep wit' a man beside you."

She glared at Ruthana.

"An' it's high time you foun' yo'self a man to sleep wit'," she said. "You more'n forty year ol', girl an' yo' clock is tickin'!"

"There was a man in Africa, Ma," Ruthana said. She didn't know why she told her mother that, except that she didn't want Flora to be disappointed in her.

"Well, I's sho'ly pleased to hear that," Flora said. "But what you doin' with some African? You fin' yo'self a nice American boy."

"Easier said than done." Ruthana grinned.

"No, it ain't," Flora said. "You jus' too picky fo' yo' own good. Pretty thing like you."

To hear her mother say she was pretty, a thing she had never said before, was breathtaking to Ruthana.

"Night, Ma," she said, kissing Flora. "Mind the lions don't bite."

Flora giggled and kissed her and went to bed.

Albie called for them on Sunday to take them to church in his new car. They made a splendid couple, fitting together like a pair of old gloves. Flora nagged him gently, constantly, and Albie loved it. They picked up Pearl, who looked much older than Flora and frailer. Arthritis had caused her to give up playing the organ at church, and she hardly stopped complaining about it.

"That girl they got now," Pearl complained, "she ain't got no rhythm, no feeling, she don't let the spirit of the Lord move inside her to make the music!"

The new organist was a woman of forty, hardly a girl, and Ruthana thought she played wonderfully.

She spent pleasant days in Stockton, deciding her future. She went to see Mrs. Hopkins, who was old and still waiting for her wayward husband to come home to her. She was pleased to see Ruthana, but her world revolved around her great-grandchildren, Gavin's children. Although she talked about them all the time, she never once mentioned their father's name in Ruthana's company.

She sat with Flora on the back porch one evening. It was fall, and the weather was lovely.

"What you gon' do wit' yo'self now you back?" Flora asked her.

Ruthana looked at the evening sky.

"First of all," she said quietly, "I'm going to find Diana."

She was not looking at Flora, but she heard her gasp. When she turned to her, she saw that Flora's hand was clutched to her mouth, and she was crying.

"Yes!" she said. "Yes!"

She recovered from her tears and dried her eyes. Then she glared at Ruthana.

"An' when you fin' her," she said, "you bring her right here to Stockton. That girl gon' need some attention."

"I might not be able to find her, Ma," Ruthana said cautiously.

"You better," Flora snapped. "You better!"

Again, it was something easier said than done. Ruthana went to Chicago and had a joyful reunion with Willie and Ernestine. They looked older than their years, carrying an enormous, unspoken weight of sadness about their two older children.

Then Booker came to visit, bringing his fiancée with him, a lovely, cheerful young woman, and for a little while there was only happiness in the tiny apartment. Booker was as blithe as ever, and if he had any bitterness about the injury that prevented him from playing the piano, he did not show it. He had a whole new future. He was at college, studying psychology, because he believed his experience in Vietnam had equipped him to help other veterans coming home from that war, men not as lucky as he.

They had a conference about Diana, but no one had heard anything of her. Don had given them the only clue. The last time he saw her she was in Baltimore, in a house where she'd crashed with some other Panthers. Ruthana went to Detroit, to see Don in jail, and he was able to provide her with a few names of Diana's friends.

Don had been wary of her at first. He did not know her well, and could not guess what her reaction to his circumstances would be. All Ruthana's years of social work, of tactful interviews with suspicious people, helped to bridge the gap between them.

"You need anything?" she asked him toward the end.

He shook his head.

"Would you like me to visit again?" she asked him.

He looked down at his hands, and then at her, and she thought she saw his eyes glisten with tears. He nodded.

"Yes," he whispered.

She did not dare think what his life in prison was like. When he was young, despite the troubles with his father, or perhaps because of them, Ruthana had seen a sensitive and caring young man who wanted only to be shown that he was loved. He had given the abundance in his heart to the socialist revolution, and he had ended up here. He would leave prison hardened and embittered, and she swore to herself that she would be there to help when he came out.

She telephoned some old friends at the shelter in New York, who tracked down someone who might be able to help her, and she went to Baltimore.

Johnny Metz was a probation officer. He was a year or two older than Ruthana, slightly overweight and very overworked. His desk was laden with case files and he did not seem pleased to see her, but she came recommended by people he knew, and so he found time for her.

Ruthana explained her problem and gave him the small information that she had.

He stared at the ceiling and then at Ruthana.

"You know what you asking?" he said.

"Yes," Ruthana said. "I know it's a needle in a haystack, but it's important to me."

He looked at his watch and glanced out the window. Already it was getting dark.

"Fancy a drink?"

Ruthana shrugged.

They went to a small bar around the corner, and it seemed as if everyone on the street and in the bar knew Johnny.

"Wish I could remember all their names," he said. "Their faces, yeh, that's easy, but there's too many names."

Ruthana didn't think that was true. To everyone who had greeted them, he had replied with their name. She thought he must have a photographic memory. But she understood the problem, from her own years in New York. Being known by name was important to those who have little else.

Johnny was gruff and brusque and a little cynical, but gradually a sharp sense of humor began to reveal itself, and Ruthana understood that the gruffness was armor against a bulging heart.

"Got a photo of her?" he asked.

Ruthana nodded and gave him a photo of Diana. He stared at it, as if memorizing her face, but she saw no recognition in his eyes.

"Could be anyone," he said.

He put the photo in his pocket. That, in itself, gave her hope. He wasn't dismissing her.

"Why's it so important to find her?" he asked, although the reply was obvious.

"She's family," Ruthana said, stating the obvious. She tried to explain, and in doing so she began to talk about Ernestine and Willie, and Don and Diana, and Flora, and then she found she was talking about herself, and before she knew where she was, she had revealed more of herself than she had intended.

"You're clever," she said to Johnny, laughing.

He grinned at the compliment and looked at his watch again. There were never enough hours in his day.

"Where you staying?"

"At the Y," she said. She always stayed at the YWCA, in any city. It was easy and comfortable and cheap.

"Hungry?"

Ruthana nodded.

He took her to an inexpensive seafood restaurant a couple of blocks away, near the port. It wasn't glamorous, but the food was great and the atmosphere cheerful.

Over dinner he told her a few things about himself. He'd been a probation officer most of his working life, and it was more than a job— it was a consuming passion to him. He'd been married, but his wife had left him after five years, taking their two children with her. She claimed that he thought more about the deadbeats he dealt with than his own family.

"They ain't deadbeats," he said. "Most of 'em's just looking for a little love."

It wasn't sentimental, it was exactly similar to her own reaction to Don, only less specific. Children were not born bad.

He and his wife were divorced, and although he was supposed to have visiting rights with his children, she had taken them to California. He saw them maybe once a year.

He drove Ruthana back to the YWCA.

"How long you planning to stay?" he asked.

"I hadn't thought about that," she said. "A few days."

She thanked him for dinner and got out of the car.

"Is there any chance we'll find her?"

"Don't get your hopes up," he said.

He glanced at his watch again, and drove away.

Ruthana stood outside the Y feeling foolish. There was no real reason to suppose that Diana was still in Baltimore, or that she could be found. Although Johnny had been kind, she wasn't sure he'd be able to help.

Ruthana had no idea where to start. She hadn't seen Diana for years, and so she was searching for someone she didn't know all that well in a city she didn't know at all.

But no power on earth would keep her from looking.

50

$\mathcal{J}$OHNNY CALLED THE NEXT DAY.

"No news," he said. "I was wondering what you were doing for dinner tonight."

"I don't have any plans," she said.

"Pick you up at eight, then."

It was only when Ruthana put down the phone that she wondered if he had asked her out for a date.

She spent the day at *The Baltimore Herald* going through old newspapers. Don had given her the names of a couple of Diana's Black Panther friends and had suggested that some of them had been involved in criminal activity. She found references to the Panthers and photos of some of them, but she saw no mention of Diana, nor anyone who might have been Diana.

She changed into her nicest dress that evening and stood in the lobby waiting for Johnny. He was late.

"Sorry," he said. "You know how it is."

She didn't mind because she knew how it was.

"There's a place serves African food," he said. "Thought you'd like that."

The restaurant was small and the food wasn't very good, a mishmash of several types of African cooking, mostly mild curries with too many peanuts, but the atmosphere was fun. The couple who ran it came from Ghana, and she was able to say a few words to them in their own language, which pleased them.

Johnny didn't talk about Diana. He spoke about a case that was bothering him, a young man who was going back to jail for constantly breaking his parole. It was frustrating because the kid was intelligent, and Johnny doubted he would survive jail.

"Tell me about Africa," he said.

She talked about Africa. She saw it now as a golden time of her life, even in Karamoja, and she made him laugh. He dropped her at the Y.

"Same time tomorrow," he said, glancing at his watch.

"Yes," she said.

She spent the next day at the newspaper office, but again she had no luck. Then she had an idea.

She had two other photographs of Diana apart from the one she had given Johnny. She got a market pen, and on one of them she drew Afro hair.

"Makes a difference," Johnny said, looking at the photo. He did not give it back to her, he slipped it in his pocket.

They ate Chinese that night, and he dropped her at the Y, as usual.

"Same time tomorrow," he said, as usual.

Ruthana agreed, wished him good night, and he drove away. She stood on the sidewalk puzzling about something.

Was he ever going to kiss her?

She gave herself a day off from old newspapers and explored Balitmore and liked what she saw. She bought herself a new dress and wore it that night to dinner.

"Pretty," he said.

They were back at the fish restaurant, eating a huge, shared bowl of boiled shrimp. Johnny had big hands and a bigger appetite, but he peeled the shrimp delicately, neatly.

"Same time tomorrow," he said, when he stopped outside the Y.

"Yes," she said. She leaned across and kissed him, gently, on the lips.

"What was that for?" he asked her.

"No reason," she said. "Because I wanted to."

"Do I get another one tomorrow?" he asked with a grin.

"If you want," she said.

"Yes," he said. "I do."

The next day was Saturday, and she wandered the city

some more and went to a movie. Johnny was working, because Saturday was the day he caught up on his paperwork.

They had pizza that night, in a rowdy, cheap Italian
place, and a bottle of rough red wine.

He stopped the car outside the Y.

"Thought we'd go for a drive tomorrow," he said.
"Around the bay. Unless you got plans.

"No," she said. "I don't have any plans."

She waited for him to kiss her, but he didn't. She was
disappointed, and started to get out of the car.

He grabbed her arm.

"You gotta understand," he said. "I can't ask anyone to
share what I've got, and I'm never going to change, the
work will always come first. I'm not making any moves."

She looked back at him.

"Do I have to do all the work in this relationship?" she
asked him.

"Yes," he said. "You do."

She got back into the car.

"At least I know what the ground rules are," she said.

She kissed him on the mouth, and he responded. His
lips were full and soft and yielding, and then she felt his
thick, hot tongue probe her mouth and she was glad, oh, so
glad, because it was what she wanted.

It was raining the next day, Sunday, but that didn't
dampen their spirits. They drove around the misty bay and
stopped at a cheap fish house for lunch. The rain eased and
they walked on the beach that wintry afternoon, wrapped
up in each other, against the cold.

"I don't have a lot of experience with men," she said.

"Well, I'm pleased to hear that." Johnny grinned.
"Neither do I."

She punched him and he laughed.

"I don't know why you told me that," he said, more seriously. "You think I didn't know?"

"How?" she wondered, not sure if she should be insulted.

"It's my job," he said. "To evaluate people. Listen to

what they say, and work out what they're really saying. You know that. You do that. They tell me you're good at what you do."

"Who've you been talking to?" she demanded, laughing.

"Does it matter?"

"No," she said. "It doesn't matter at all."

Now he did all the work. He pulled her to him and wrapped his arms around her and kissed her, long and languorously.

She felt him hard against her, and pressed to him, to let him know it was all right.

"What are we going to do?" she whispered.

"I don't know," he said. "It'll work out."

She went back to the newspaper office the next day, but by midmorning, she gave up. It was useless, a needle in a haystack. She didn't know what to do anymore. She had no idea how to find Diana, and staying in Baltimore was costing her money. But then there was Johnny, and she didn't want to leave. She decided to try and work something out with him that evening.

When she got back to the Y there was a message from him. She called his office and he said he'd pick her up in half an hour.

"I guessed she'd be on welfare," he said. "So I put the photo out, the one with the Afro. We don't know if it's her."

They stopped outside a slum tenement in the worst part of town. The street was filthy, the building half falling down, half boarded up. Flashy, jaded young men did illegal business on the corners. Flashier, jaded young women were touting for illegal business, although it was only the middle of the day.

"Don't get your hopes up," he said. "I don't know if it's her."

He led the way into the building. The hallway stank. The walls were peeling, the woodwork rotted. Somewhere, distantly, Ruthana could hear a child crying.

Ruthana wanted to turn around, go away. She had seen

as bad, or worse, in New York, but she couldn't bear the thought of Diana living in such circumstances. But Johnny led the way, and she followed. The crying of the child was louder now, and upstairs a woman was shouting at someone, and then the same woman screamed and cried.

They came to a door that had no number on it, and Johnny shrugged.

"Must be it," he said, knocking on the door.

There was no answer, except that the crying child was certainly in that room.

Johnny tried the door. It opened, and he went in. Ruthana followed.

It was dirty as the hallway, and almost bare of furniture. There were a couple of rickety chairs and an old table. There was a double mattress on the floor, with a couple of filthy blankets and a man passed out. There was a small stove in the opposite corner and a woman was standing there, a two-year-old child on her hip. The child was crying. The woman was fiddling uselessly at the stove with an empty pan, and was obviously stoned. Ruthana thought it was something more than marijuana.

Her hair was matted and dirty, an Afro that hadn't been tended in some time. Her clothes were ragged.

"Diana?" Ruthana asked cautiously.

The woman turned to look at her, to focus on her.

"Diana?" Ruthana said again, sharply.

For the smallest moment, Ruthana was not sure, and then she was sure, although she never knew why, and moved to her.

"Diana," she said. "I've come to take you home."

The woman gave no sign that she had heard or understood, but tears started rolling down her face and she held out the child to Ruthana.

"He hungry," she said. "Mickey hungry."

They took her away because she seemed to want to go; she would go anywhere if she could get food for the boy. They went to Johnny's office, where someone found some food for Mickey and a sandwich for Diana. She sat in a corner of the office clutching her son to her, and would not let anyone else touch him or feed him.

Only when the boy was fed and quiet again did she allow Ruthana to try to take him from her, and then there was recognition in her eyes. But Mickey screamed and would not leave his mother. Johnny came to him, and the boy quieted and allowed Johnny to pick him up.

They went to a house that Johnny knew of where Angie, a kindly, motherly woman, took charge and looked at Diana with an appraising eye.

"Needs to sleep it off," the woman said.

They put Diana to bed in a small clean, sparse room. She fell asleep, or passed out, almost at once.

Johnny was still holding Mickey. Ruthana tried to take him, but he would not go to her.

Angie showed them a bathroom, where Johnny bathed Mickey, washed the filth from him, and changed his diaper.

"Haven't you got calls to make?" he said.

Ruthana went to the phone and called Ernestine in Chicago. Willie was at work, and Ruthana hoped there was someone in the house with her, because the weeping Ernestine would need someone.

She called Flora, who thanked the Lord.

"Bring them here," she said.

Ruthana wasn't sure.

"That's for Willie and Ernestine to say."

"You leave them to me," Flora said.

"It's early days, Ma," Ruthana said. "She's not well; we've got to take her to a doctor—"

"You do what you's got to do," Flora said. "Then you bring 'em to me."

The phone was in the hall, and as Ruthana made her calls, a young man had come in with a slightly hunted, haunted look about him. He went into a room, and then a young woman came in with that same, nervous look. She nodded at Ruthana and went upstairs.

Johnny was in the main room, sitting on a chair with Mickey, talking with him. The boy was wearing clothes that Angie had found, too big for him but clean. The walls were covered with posters against drugs.

"You talk to your auntie," Johnny said to Mickey. Mickey looked very uncertain.

Ruthana went to them and kneeled down so as not to be frightening to him.

After some coaxing by Johnny, Mickey allowed Ruthana to take him. Johnny looked at his watch.

"I gotta get back," Johnny said.

"Thank you," Ruthana said. "Thank you with all my heart."

"I'll come by later," he said, and left.

Ruthana sat in the chair with Mickey on her knee, whispering softly in his ear. Eventually he fell asleep.

Angie came to her.

"Best put him with his ma," she said. "She need him when she wake up."

Ruthana carried Mickey to Diana's room and laid the sleeping boy in his mother's arms. Still asleep, Diana curled around him, as if protecting him, and slept on.

Ruthana went to Angie, who said that Diana and Mickey could stay there. A doctor she knew was coming by later to check them out. Ruthana had already guessed that this was a rehabilitation house for kids with drug or alcohol problems, or just problems. Ruthana, who wasn't sure if she believed in God, thanked Him that there were women like Angie in the world.

Angie made her a cup of coffee and Ruthana went back to Diana's room and sat with her.

When she woke, Diana looked at her slightly suspiciously. Mickey woke up too, and Ruthana gave him an old, worn-out stuffed toy that she had found. Mickey loved the eyeless teddy bear; he grabbed it and nursed it.

"You want some coffee?" Ruthana asked Diana.

Diana nodded.

"It's all right," Ruthana said as they sipped coffee

together. "It doesn't matter. Whatever's happened, whatever you've done, it doesn't matter."

Diana sat in silence for a moment. Then a violent sob broke from her, and she spilled her coffee.

Now she wept, and Ruthana held her as she cried.

"I want to go home," Diana said.

Johnny came by later.

"She be all right," Angie said. "She safe here."

They went out to eat at the fish restaurant. Johnny had been able to piece together a little of Diana's history. She had a small police record for some violence when she was with the Panthers, but nothing that would affect her future. After that she seemed to have drifted from city to city, from man to man. He did not know who Mickey's father was, and doubted that Diana knew.

"How can I ever thank you?" Ruthana said.

He shelled a shrimp.

"That's a tough one," he said, not looking at her, concentrating on his shrimp.

"You could move to Baltimore," he said, popping the shrimp in his mouth. "Find a job here and marry me."

Ruthana didn't answer immediately. She picked up a shrimp, peeled it, and ate it.

"Yes," she said. "I could do that."

Willie and Ernestine flew in from Chicago on Saturday. It was a difficult reunion with their daughter at first, for Diana was suffering from drug withdrawal and was suspicious of her parents.

Mickey broke the ice. Mickey, who was suspicious of all women except his mother, was perfectly content to be taken into his grandmother's arms and to be hugged by her.

Diana was different. She accepted their hugs but without enthusiasm.

They wanted to take her back to Chicago, but Ruthana was against it. Diana's rehabilitation would take some time, and Ruthana didn't think that Chicago, with its many temptations, was the best place for that to happen.

She knew she had to be cruel, but she and Johnny had

discussed it, as professionals, and she and Diana had discussed it, as relatives.

"She doesn't want to go to Chicago," Ruthana said.

She saw the hurt in their eyes.

"She wants to go to Stockton," Ruthana said. "Mama
will look after her and you can visit her there and get to
know her again.

"Flora cain't manage, not on her own," Ernestine said.

"Yes, she can," Willie said with a small grin.

"Then I's goin' there too," Ernestine said. "I stay with
Pa fo' a while."

"Yes," Ruthana said. "That's a good idea. But not yet;
give it a few weeks, see how it goes."

She still wasn't sure that Flora would be able to
manage, but she could think of no better place for Diana
and Mickey to be. She decided she would stay in Stockton
herself for a couple of weeks, to make sure that Flora
understood the enormity of Diana's problems.

She found a job in Baltimore, and then a small apartment. She suggested that she and Johnny live together for
a while, when she came back from Stockton, but Johnny
would not hear of it.

"You afraid of commitment?" he asked her.

"I love you," she said. "That's a commitment."

"Marry me," he said.

"Yes," she said.

Three weeks later, Angie thought that Diana was well
enough to travel, but she doubted the wisdom of her going
to Stockton. Diana had been deeply hurt and would have
many scars, and she wasn't sure that a little old lady living
in the country would have the resources to deal with those
things.

"You don't know the little old lady." Ruthana smiled.

The moment they got off the train, Ruthana knew it
was going to be all right.

Flora was there with Albie. She paid no attention
to Ruthana or, even, initially, to Mickey, although she
yearned to take him in her arms.

She cared only, in that moment, about Diana. She walked to her granddaughter and looked at her appraisingly.

"You need feedin' up," she said.

"Oh, Gran'," Diana said.

She gave Mickey to Ruthana and folded into her grandmother's arms, and let herself be loved.

REUNION

51

O N THE OCCASION of her eightieth birthday, Mama Flora's family gathered in Stockton for a celebration and a reunion.

There was no room at Flora's little house for anyone, because Diana and Mickey were there, so the family had to be billeted throughout the town.

Willie and Ernestine stayed with Albie, as did Booker with his wife and four-year-old son, Albie Junior, who was, of course, the apple of his grandfather's eye.

Ruthana and Johnny stayed with Pearl, who was now very frail. Ruthana thought she could not live much longer, but Pearl was determined not to go before Flora. Ruthana worried that having a two-year-old girl in the house would be too much for Pearl, but Pearl, who had no children of her own, adored Floretta, and wept when they left.

Reverend Hawkins had specifically asked that Luke and Jessica stay with him and his wife, Tesa. He was intrigued by the idea of having full-blown Muslims stay in his Christian house, and the two men spent happy hours in religious debate. Jasmine stayed with them, with her husband, Jamal, and their son, Yahyah.

It was a sadness to Flora that Daoud could not be there. He was doing a postgraduate course at a Muslim university in Cairo, and his wife and sons were with him, but he sent photos of the family at the pyramids, and Flora was proud.

It was a greater sadness that Don was not there. He was elegible for a parole in a year's time, and Flora had hoped the authorities would be kind and let him come to her for her birthday, but knew it was not realistic.

There was to be another big celebration in Stockton

the next year, for the American bicentennial, and Don promised her that he would come for that.

Diana, already in Stockton, would attend the celebration with Mickey and with her boyfriend, Rusty Simpson, called Rusty because his hair had a reddish tinge to it.

Things had not been easy between Flora and Diana for the first two years that Diana was in Stockton. She was moody and pensive, suffering from withdrawal for some time, but Flora had persevered with her, simply by being herself and by loving Mickey.

At first, this had caused some tension between them. Mickey was all Diana had in the world and she resented Flora's intrusion on Mickey's love. There had been several arguments about small things, but Flora had recognized the true cause of the problem and adjusted her behavior to Mickey.

There had been other arguments, about church. Flora believed, devoutly believed, that God could help Diana, but she, as forcibly, denied the deity.

As usual, Flora prayed for guidance, and perhaps God answered, because Flora did something that helped the relationship.

Despite her restoration to her family, Diana still had many of her youthful radical ideas. She strained at the leash of Stockton, and was inclined to dismiss the simplicity of the lifestyle there as evidence that the local blacks were complaisant.

Pearl fixed some of that. Although Flora had never told any of her family of the events at the Star Cafe, she was pleased when Ruthana found out, and thought it might help Diana. Since she couldn't tell Diana herself, she asked Pearl to do it.

Diana did not talk about what she had heard, but one evening she remembered their visit to the Nation of Islam meeting, and asked Flora how she felt about Luke and his family being Muslim.

"Long as they b'lieve," Flora said, "I don' care what they call Him."

The following Sunday she did not insist that Diana and Mickey come with her to church, but in the afternoon she told Diana she needed help.

They walked to the cemetery, to Booker's grave. Flora still went there once a week and tended the grave. She weeded it and tried to keep fresh flowers in a little jar by the headstone. Lately, it had become too much for her, and she bought a potted plant that she transplanted to the grave site. It grew every spring and flowered every summer and rested in the winter, and that seemed right and proper to Flora.

Diana helped her kneel beside the grave, and then Flora sat on the ground and pulled up weeds. She did not ask Mickey to help, but he did anyway.

"How did he die?" Diana asked her.

Flora told her the story of Booker's death. She told it simply, trying very hard not to make it greater than it was, although it was very great.

Diana said nothing, but as they walked away, she asked about Luke.

So Flora told her the story of Luke's conception and birth, its awful aftermath, and its joyous resolution.

"God done it," Flora said. "God showed me how to find Luke, an' I done what He said, an' I found him."

She wondered how far she should push it.

"Jes' like He did with Ruthana."

They were back at the house and Flora pretended to be busy with something.

"What happened with Ruthana?" Diana asked.

"I made some mistakes," Flora said. "Like parents do."

She would not discuss it any more that night, but over the days, she talked about Ruthana's life and Josie's death. Small piece by small piece, she led Diana to the point that she wanted to make.

"I din't want anything bad to happen to her," she said.

"I din't want her life to be like mine. So I tried too hard to protect her."

"But Ruthana's had a wonderful life," Diana said in amazement.

"Now she has," Flora agreed. "But you talk to yo' aunt, girl. You ask her how happy she been afore she went to Africa."

Diana said nothing, but a few days later she sat down and wrote to Ruthana, a simple letter asking no great questions—a contact, a return to her family and an involvement with it.

Ruthana replied, a simple letter with no great answers in it, but a week later, Diana phoned Ernestine in Chicago.

Ernestine had moved back to Stockton for a few months after Diana's return there, partly to be with Albie, mostly to renew her relationship with her daughter.

It had not been a success. Albie loved having his daughter with him, and was pleased to see Ernestine making friends with his sister, Henrietta, and her family again, but then he suggested that Ernestine return to her husband.

"You go there or he come here," he said. "He's yo' man, an' you ain't got long wit' him. No matter how long you live, it ain't long enough."

Diana had completely resisted her mother. She was polite to her and allowed her to make friends with Mickey, but the scars were deep and had not yet healed.

Ernestine went back to Chicago to the man she loved, to the man with whom she had endured so much, and was happy there with him and Booker, but she missed her firstborn children.

So when Diana called that day from Stockton, not to say anything important, simply to say hello, it was a treasure beyond the dreams of avarice to Ernestine.

Shortly thereafter, Diana decided she would like to get a job, if only part time. Flora walked into town with her to look after Mickey during the interview.

They stood outside the shop, Narelle's Beauty Salon many years ago.

"Use' to be called Modern Modes," Flora said. "An' afore that it was—Lady Something—but ol' Tom Lanier started this shop afore I come here."

She was lost in memory for a moment.

"They done well, the Laniers."

Diana got the job and it made a great difference to all their lives, because Diana had a purpose and Flora had to look after Mickey while she was at work, and smothered the boy with love.

"You're spoiling him." Diana laughed.

"Yeh, I is," Flora agreed. "That's what gran'mas do."

So the family of Mama Flora gathered in Stockton for her eightieth birthday, and whatever problems any of them had with one another, or within their own families, were put aside, for this was someone else's time.

Everyone went to the Sunday service, even the Muslim members of the family, because it was in honor of a woman who believed in God in a very particular way, and those of a different faith and those without faith recognized that her faith had sustained her through many trials.

The choir sang lustily, and when young Betty Jackson went for the top C that sometimes eluded her and got there, everyone cheered and stomped.

"Yay-man!"

Although Pearl complained bitterly about the quality of the organ playing.

Reverend Hawkins gave a short but very moving sermon, and took his text from Matthew. He was a New Testament man.

"Behold my mother, and my brethren."

"For *whosoever* shall do the will of God," he proclaimed, "my Father which is in heaven, the same is my *brother*, and *sister*, and *mother*."

He glared at them. They loved it when he glared at them, because they knew that something good was coming.

"Behold my *mother*," he thundered, pointing at Flora. "Who hath done the will of God!"

They didn't have a barbecue afterward because the birthday party was to be in the early evening so that the old folk and the children might get home to bed at a reasonable hour. Isaac Dixon Junior was providing the food at no charge, and was cooking a side of beef because he knew that some of Flora's family did not eat pork.

They all went to their various houses and rested and then changed. Albie came to Flora's house in his car at about four. She was wearing a new dress bought specially for the occasion, and Albie gave her a small corsage of gardenias, her favorite flower.

He drove her to the church with Diana and Mickey. Almost everyone was already there, half the town, it seemed, and Ruthana was especially pleased to see that Gavin Hopkins delivererd his grandmother, Mrs. Hopkins, to the party, although he did not stay himself.

It was a perfect evening, warm, and it did not rain. There was a band, led by Freeman Lanier's son. It wasn't very good, but no one cared, and Betty Jackson got up and sang a spiritual.

Diana was inclined to protest that spirituals were not spiritual but evidence of the white man's authority over blacks, but Booker told her to be quiet and enjoy the music.

At about six, the family moved into the church hall, where the photograph was to be taken.

The photographer was already set up, with a line of chairs in place. Booker led Flora to the middle chair, the place of honor, and she insisted that Albie Junior kneel on the floor beside her, in front of her, with her other great-grandchildren beside him.

The rest of the family sorted themselves out as to where they would sit or stand, under Flora's direction, and the photographs were taken.

A year later, Diana moved out. She married Rusty, whose first wife had left him after only a short marriage for the bright lights of the big city, leaving their baby daughter with him. Thus Mickey had a sister and Diana had a husband, and it was a good marriage.

Pearl, who had grown old with Flora, died, and so Flora was on her own, apart from Albie.

Albie tried to pressure Flora into moving in with him, but she could not bear to leave her little house. So he visited three or four times a week, and sometimes he stayed the night, and they were happy.

On the nights when Albie was not there and Flora was alone, she liked to sit on the back porch on warm evenings, promising herself that she would do something about her vegetable garden, which was overgrown.

On cool evenings and in the winter, she sat inside watching television or writing letters to her family, which were always short, because writing had never come easily to her and arthritis had worsened her hand.

When Don was paroled the following year, he kept his promise and came to Stockton for a month to see Flora and, especially, Diana. Flora did not ask him about his time in prison, he would tell if he wanted to, but she did ask him for a photo of himself. This he gave to her before he went to Chicago to spend some time with his family.

Every night before she went to bed, Flora would look at the photograph taken on her eightieth birthday. She'd had it framed and had tucked into the frame the photos of Daoud and his family taken at the pyramids, and the photo of Don.

She also had a small, very old photograph of Booker, taken before she met him, when he was part of a work gang. She cut his face out of the group photo and put that into the frame too.

Thus they were together at last, reunited, all of Mama Flora's family, all the generations, and it gave her a great sense of satisfaction to look at them, everyone smiling happily for the camera.

And if she felt proud of what she had wrought and

achieved with her life, then surely not even the good Lord could account that vanity.

Don' care who they is an' where they been or what they doin', Mama Flora told herself, if it hadn't been for me an' what I always believed in an' done, then none of it wouldn't never have happened.

Praise for the novels of New York Times bestselling author
CARLY PHILLIPS

"Fast-paced and fabulously fun, Carly Phillips entertains
with witty dialogue and delightful characters."
—*New York Times* bestselling author Rachel Gibson

"Popular Phillips' first attempt at romantic suspense should
be eagerly received by her loyal readership, and the
denouement hints at a future romance for Hunter, as well."
—*Booklist* on *Cross My Heart*

"Who doesn't love a reunion of long-lost loves?
Add a diabolical villain as Carly Phillips does and
you have everything you need for a beach read."
—*Columbus Dispatch* on *Cross My Heart*

"Contemporary pizzazz with a good
old-fashioned happily ever after."
—Michelle Buonfiglio, *Romance: B(u)y the Book*,
WNBC.com/romance

"*Cross My Heart* engages readers with a light
and perky story that will absorb you from
start to finish.... You'll be smiling while you read
the book, and grinning when you finish."
—Lezlie Patterson, MCT News Service

"Phillips has penned a charming, fast-paced
contemporary romp."
—*Booklist* on *Hot Item*

"A great summer read that should not be missed."
—*BookReporter.com* on *Hot Item*

"A sassy treat full of titillating twists
sure to ring your (wedding) bell."
—*Playgirl* on *The Bachelor*

"A titillating read...on a scale of one to five: a high five
for fun, ease of reading and sex—actually I would've
given it a six for sex if I could have."
—Kelly Ripa on *The Bachelor*

Also by

carly
phillips

Ty and Hunter's stories
Cross My Heart
Sealed with a Kiss

The Hot Zone series
Hot Item
Hot Number
Hot Stuff
Hot Property

The Simply series
Simply Sinful
Simply Scandalous
Simply Sensual
Simply Sexy

The Chandler Brothers series
The Bachelor
The Playboy
The Heartbreaker

Also...
Body Heat
Brazen
Seduce Me

carly
phillips

Hot
PROPERTY

HQN™

ISBN-13: 978-0-373-77333-6
ISBN-10:   0-373-77333-1

HOT PROPERTY

Printed in U.S.A.

Dear Reader,

I love writing, but no series has given me more joy than the Hot Zone, maybe because of the many personal connections for me in these books. Uncle Yank is based on my grandpa Jack, may he rest in peace, and macular degeneration runs in my family. Giving Uncle Yank a love of life despite his limitations has truly been a labor of love. From your many wonderful letters, I sense you have the same warm, fuzzy feeling for the Jordan sisters and the Hot Zone characters as I do. Thank you so much for letting me know!

Thank you, too, for being diligent, intelligent, smart readers. You picked up on inconsistencies in this series that are—frankly—embarrassing for me. As I explained to those of you who wrote me about the errors, I wasn't trying to see if you were paying attention (although you definitely were!). All I can say is that I'm human. I have tried to address the inconsistencies in this story and have clarified that both Annabelle and Micki have daughters.

Hot Property is the last in the Hot Zone series of books. John Roper (Micki's best friend and high-maintenance client) and Amy Stone (Riley's cousin from Florida) are about to meet—and when they do, sparks fly!

So enjoy the heat and the fun, and the next time you write to me, I hope it's because you miss these characters as much as I will!

Best wishes always and happy reading!

Carly
www.carlyphillips.com
e-mail: carly@carlyphillips.com

8/08

I write best when I'm on vacation. Maybe it's the sand, the surf or maybe it's the company. This book is dedicated to The Smith Family— Gary, Tracey, Matthew and Robbie, the greatest (and funniest) family friends ever. Thanks for giving a Table for Four new meaning.

As always, to Phil, Jackie, Jen, Buddy and Bailey— for making me crazy and keeping me sane... all at the same time.

To the editor who knows me best and always makes me better, Brenda Chin; and to Janelle Denison, for all you do, they're all for you!

And to the Plotmonkeys: Janelle, Julie Leto and Leslie Kelly—www.plotmonkeys.com —for having a brain when mine is fried. Love you guys!

Hot
PROPERTY

PROLOGUE

AMY STONE WAS SURROUNDED by testosterone. Not everyday, average testosterone but the heavy-duty testosterone that could only belong to athletes. She couldn't stop staring at the quarterbacks, the baseball stars and other large, muscular guests attending her cousin Riley's wedding reception. The bride, Sophie Jordan, her sisters and their friends appeared unfazed by so many hot men in one place. As publicists for the Hot Zone, a PR firm specializing in athletes, they were probably used to the sight. As a single woman more accustomed to living and working as a social director at a Fort Lauderdale retirement community owned by her relatives, Amy was out of her element.

But that was about to change. Starting in January, Amy would be working at the Hot Zone, too, and she'd have to learn how to handle herself around these big-shot athletes without melting at their feet. She'd already made a few trips to the city and had begun settling into the apartment Micki Jordan Fuller had leased to her. After spending the holidays with her family, Amy would be leaving her easy life behind.

She'd turned twenty-five on Halloween—there was some irony there, she was sure—and she'd woken up, looked at her life and realized a change was long overdue. She belonged in a crowd of young people, not refereeing irreverent retirees who preferred skinny-dipping to swimming with bathing suits and Long Island iced teas to the nonalcoholic variety. But she was worried about the trouble her mother and her friends could get into left on their own.

Which reminded her... She scanned the area looking for her family. The acreage was huge, the view beautiful. Amy couldn't find her mother or her aunt Darla, but she consoled herself with the notion that if she couldn't see or hear them, they couldn't be causing a ruckus. That had to be a good sign. Especially since the reception was being held at the Brandon, Mississippi, estate of *Senator* Harlan Nash, the man who'd raised Riley as his own son.

She prayed her mother and aunt would behave for a change. As she'd instructed them this morning, no nude bathing in the fountain, no playing tag in the yard. Her relatives lived to enjoy life. And they did— a little too much sometimes, which often got them into trouble, making them all the object of public ridicule. It had often been a point of contention between her parents when her father was alive. When Amy had made the decision to move back home and had taken the job as director, aka babysitter, she'd known her father, who'd died when she was twelve, would approve.

The sun beat down on her head and she envied the senator's guests who had parasols to shade themselves from the heated rays. The humidity was really getting to her. Her skin was sticky beneath her dress as she strode to the bar.

"Can I get you a drink?" a deep male voice asked.

Amy turned, shading her eyes against the glare of the sun, and stared into the most gorgeous face she'd ever seen on a man. His eyes were a deep shade of green, his features more chiseled than rugged, and when he smiled, dimples embraced his white teeth and oh-so-sexy smile.

"I was just about to order a cola," she said.

"I think I can manage that for you." His easygoing smile grew wider. "Do not go anywhere."

Amy wouldn't dream of it. It was one thing to be surrounded by testosterone, another to have one of these men turn his attention her way. Heat suffused her and her pulse rate kicked up so she found it hard to breathe. Amy wasn't a nun and she'd been with her share of men, but she'd never dated a guy as rugged and…well, hot as this man.

He eased his way between the people at the bar and quickly returned with her drink in one hand, one for himself in the other. "Here you go."

She accepted the glass. "Thank you."

"My pleasure." He nodded and tipped his glass, clinking it against hers. "So, pretty lady, are you a guest of the bride or the groom?"

She tried not to preen under the compliment, but

he'd gotten under her skin already. "I'm a guest of the groom. Riley is my cousin," she explained, before taking a cool, welcome sip of her soda.

"Are you related to the senator?" he asked.

"No, actually, Spencer Atkins is my uncle." Riley had a complicated family situation, but Amy figured this man, probably an athlete, knew of renowned sports agent, Spencer Atkins, who was Riley's biological father. "What about you? Which side of the family do you know?"

"I'm a guest of both, actually."

"Which would make you a client of the Hot Zone PR and Athletes Only?" she said, referring to her uncle's sports agency.

"Not only beautiful but perceptive, as well."

She was certain she blushed. "What sport do you play?"

"You don't know who I am?" His eyes widened. "I'm wounded," he said in an affected tone with a little boy's hurt in his expression. But immediate laughter let her know he was just teasing.

Amy smiled, enjoying his sense of humor and easygoing personality. The attraction went without saying. The man was definitely irresistible.

"John Roper, New York Renegades center fielder at your service." He tipped his head toward her, then extended his hand.

"Amy Stone." She placed her palm inside his. Searing heat branded her, sizzling up her arm and into her chest, knocking the wind out of her completely.

Wow.

She'd *never* had such an intense reaction to a man before. She caught a whiff of his sensual cologne, which caused an erotic spike in her body temperature. "It's nice to meet you, John."

A cute smile pulled at his lips. "It's nice to meet you, too, Amy Stone." His voice dropped a husky octave.

She ran her tongue over her dry lips. "So what table are you seated at?" she asked him.

He'd been holding her gaze with a look hot enough to melt the ice sculptures she'd seen earlier, but suddenly he twisted his body, looking around before turning back to her again. "Listen, the seating is…um…complicated."

"Tell me about it. It's a wedding. Seating is always complicated. I'm just hoping I'm not at the same table as my mom and her sister." Amy had picked up her place card earlier, but she hadn't seen her relatives since they'd left the ceremony to ask where they were seated. Amy rolled her eyes at her predicament and laughed.

John didn't join her. "It's not that kind of complicated." He mulled something over in his mind for a while before finally speaking. "I just didn't expect to meet someone like you here," he said, warmth and something inherently more in his tone.

"Tell me about it." She hadn't come here with a date or intending to meet a man, either, but she was definitely glad she had met one. Now she didn't have to survive those awkward moments during slow songs. If John didn't ask her to dance, maybe she'd just ask him instead. Though that sounded more like something her mother would do than Amy, this man was worth stepping out of her comfort zone for. A tingle of anticipation rippled through her at the thought of a slow dance, his arms wrapped around her waist....

He bent his head close to hers. She inhaled and his aftershave filled her with deep yearning. He leaned closer. For a whisper? Not a kiss, it was way too soon.

But her heart pounded in anticipation.

"Roper! Roper!" A shrill female voice called out his name.

The chance for her to discover his intentions disappeared as Amy and John jerked back and turned toward the sound. A beautiful woman walked, teetering on high heels, across the lawn, making a beeline his way. Her long dress kept catching beneath her shoes, and although she held up the hem with both hands, the trip was obviously a difficult one.

"There you are," she said. "Didn't I ask you to stay on the patio? I told you I didn't want to ruin my dress on the lawn." She whined through heavily glossed lips that turned downward in what was obviously meant to be a pretty pout.

It *was* pretty, though Amy hated to concede the point. The other woman was model-thin and attractive in a waiflike sort of way, elegant despite her awkward trek across the lawn. And judging from the possessive way she aligned herself against John, she was his date.

His date. Disappointment rushed through her. All the while he'd been initiating conversation and coming on to her—at least that's how she'd read his words and his body language—he'd had another woman waiting for him.

How naive could she be, thinking a hot baseball player would be interested in a country bumpkin? And that's what she felt like compared to the chic woman standing next to him. She resented the emotion, hating that she allowed herself to feel inferior.

"I leave you alone for five minutes and I find you racking up another conquest in my absence," the other woman said.

"I—" He paused. Obviously he couldn't find an acceptable excuse because there was none.

Amy's heart beat hard and fast while nausea overwhelmed her. She turned and started for the house, trying to get as far away as she could get from John Roper.

"Amy, wait!" He called after her. "I know this looks bad, but—"

She refused to turn around. It looked like what it was. He'd brought a date to the party, but he'd definitely come on to *her.*

He caught her arm, forcing her to face him.

His date followed, coming up beside them. "You're worried about her and not me? You *jerk!* I flew out to this godforsaken place to be with you and this is how you repay me? By trying to hook up with a local bimbo?"

Before anyone could blink, the woman grabbed his drink from his hand and deliberately poured it down his shirt.

"Come on, Carrie. This is a Hugo Boss shirt!" He pulled at the stained material and glared at his date. "Was that really necessary?"

She forced a smile. "I think it was."

Amy couldn't believe this. The crowd around them grew silent and began to edge closer for a better look. Amy cringed. She hated being the center of attention and she resented that this man had done it to her now.

"You two obviously need privacy." This time she ran from the circus act that was John and his date.

She slowed as she approached the patio, disappointment in John Roper and the way this day had turned out as strong as the sun overhead. She'd really been attracted to him, but she didn't need a man like that in her life. She would begin her new job as a publicist for the Hot Zone, operating behind the scenes. But she definitely had to grow a thicker skin if she was going to deal with this kind of high-maintenance client on a daily basis.

A commotion broke out on the other side of the patio and Amy glanced over. Apparently the bride had decided to toss the bouquet early. She squinted for a better view and groaned aloud.

Amy's mother, Rose, and Aunt Darla both jumped

for the prize and were now rolling on the lawn, both determined to claim the flowers. Neither wanted the tradition that went along with the bouquet, since they'd sworn off remarriage. And they weren't interested in the flowers, either. They just wanted the attention due them from catching it.

On one side of the house was John and his date. On the other side wrestled the crazy redheaded sisters who needed someone to separate them and give each a time-out.

This day couldn't possibly get any worse.

But when the New Year arrived and with it, her new life, Amy swore to make it her mission not only to succeed, but to thrive.

CHAPTER ONE

One month later

SPORTS AGENT YANK MORGAN sat in the backseat of his Lincoln and rubbed a hand over his scruffy beard. Scruffier now since his wife, Lola, had thrown out his razor to prevent him from accidentally slitting his throat. Dang woman had also somehow discovered where he'd hidden his spares. Apparently an almost-blind man had no privacy in his own bathroom.

Normally he'd be angry, but considering his eyesight had gotten worse, he was forced to admit Lola had a point. Macular degeneration was messing with the balance of power in his marriage. Telling a woman she was right about anything, though, especially his woman, would be the equivalent of relinquishing his throne. And that wasn't happening at home or at work.

"We're here, Mr. Morgan," J.D., the ex-football player he'd hired as his driver, said. "Want me to walk you inside?"

Yank shook his head. "No, thanks. It's bad enough

you had to drive me here. I don't need you as my guide. I got Noodle for that." His Labradoodle sat beside him and Yank patted her furry head. He'd got the dog when she was a pup, but now she was the size of her standard poodle mother.

"Be careful. I don't want to end up at the emergency room again because you tripped over something you and the mutt didn't see."

"She's not a mutt, she's a mix of two pure breeds," Yank said proudly as he opened his car door.

"I still say you should have bought a real guide dog and not a pet." J.D. came around and met him.

Yank frowned. "Keep sounding like my wife and you'll have to find yourself a new job."

J.D. merely laughed. "You say that every day," he said as he helped Yank out of the car.

Yank did his best to ignore the indignity of needing aid at basic tasks. A man accepted what a man had to accept. "You remind your father we're playing poker tonight," Yank said.

Nobody asked how Yank played without being able to see the cards, and Yank refused to discuss it. He'd rather lose money every month than give up the things he loved. And J.D.'s father, Curly, had been in Yank's poker game for years, even before Yank had become his nieces' guardian when they were little girls.

J.D. scratched Noodle's fluffy fur and helped Yank pull the dog out of the car. "You think I need to remind Dad of something he's been doing every

month for most of his life? At least now with Lola
around I know he won't be smoking. You and my
father. Neither one of you listen to your doctors," J.D.
muttered.

"Wait till you get older before passing judgment.
I'll only be about fifteen minutes." Yank pulled his
heavy jacket tighter around him and let the dog lead
him toward the door of the gym.

Part Labrador retriever, part poodle, completely
dense when it came to being in charge, Noodle
wasn't the guide dog Yank should have gotten, but
he enjoyed the pretense. It was fun making people
think he was a little bit crazy. There were worse
ways to spend his life, he thought, laughing.

He made his way to the weight room in the back
of the gym. The trainers and employees were used
to him visiting clients and bringing Noodle along. He
headed for where he knew he'd find John Roper, letting years of experience lead the way. The main part
of the gym was noisy and crowded, but as he approached the private rooms in the back, Yank could
hear that there weren't as many people there.

Which Yank figured was the reason his not-so-star
baseball player client John Roper chose to work out
here and now. Unfortunately, the televisions were on
and the sound coming from the speakers told Yank
that morning sports talk-show host, Frank Buckley,
was spouting off at the mouth as usual.

"Spring training is around the corner and this New
York Renegade fan still hasn't gotten over John

Roper's disastrous last season or his role in the Renegades Game 5 World Series loss. Call in and let me know if your lack of expectations match mine for the highly overpaid hero. The Buck Stops Here, folks."

The television station went to commercial at the same time Roper yelled aloud, "Somebody shut that damn thing off before I rip the speakers off the wall."

When nobody moved, Yank added his two cents. "Can't you hear the man? Shut off the noise or we'll sue you for intentional infliction of emotional distress."

The weights clanged hard as Roper dropped them to the floor. "Morgan, what are you doing here?" he asked.

"Visiting the dumbbells." Yank laughed at his own joke.

Roper didn't.

"You still upset over Buckley the Bastard's tirade? Grow up and get over it," Yank said. He'd already tried coddling Roper through his rough patch and it hadn't worked. He was moving on to tough love.

"Someone dropped off a Roper bobblehead doll with my doorman. Damn thing had a knife stuck in the shoulder."

Yank groaned. The fans wouldn't let Roper forget his nightmarish last season. He hadn't been able to hit or throw, and to make things worse, he'd sprained his shoulder in a failed attempt to stop a game-winning home run by slamming it into the center field wall.

This in addition to striking out earlier when the bases were loaded and the Renegades had a chance at the go-ahead run. Their team had lost, the fans needed a scapegoat, and they'd chosen the highest-priced center fielder in the game to sacrifice. Not that the man wasn't in a slump, but losing had been a team effort.

Now Buckley insisted on continuing the torture in the off-season. Roper had every right to be pissed. He didn't need Buckley riling up the fans against him in his daily tirades.

"Are you sure Buckley doesn't have a personal grudge?" Yank asked.

Roper rose to his feet, looming large over Yank. "I screwed his ex-girlfriend. She just didn't see fit to mention she was no longer his ex on the night in question."

Yank chuckled. "He oughta let it go."

"She's his wife now," Roper said.

"Shit."

"Yeah," Roper agreed. "You do realize that if this was a lesser market, nobody would pay attention to anything Buckley said?"

Yank shook his head. "But it isn't a lesser market. It's New York." And that said it all.

Athletes were like movie stars here, back- and front-page news and fodder for gossip. "You used to love the attention," Yank reminded him.

Prior to his funk, Roper had been known for being a high-maintenance outfielder. ESports TV, Magazine and Radio named Roper among the top metrosexual athletes of the year. Yank didn't get why grown men like Roper spent good money on the best clubs, gyms and hairdressers. What normal man had his back waxed? Yank had no idea. But Roper's good-looking mug had made them both a boatload of money, so Yank wasn't about to complain.

"I did love the attention," Roper said. "Until my talent went south." Roper leaned forward on the bench, elbows on his knees, and stared ahead at nothing in particular. "So what are you really doing here?" Roper asked.

"I came to cheer you up. I don't want the media to see you down and I sure as hell don't need you taking a swing at one of them, no matter how much they provoke you."

"That sounds like a message from Micki."

Yank's niece, Michelle, was Roper's close friend, as well as his publicist. She was the resident expert at the Hot Zone for keeping her high-maintenance client out of trouble and out of the press.

Then again, maybe some good press was exactly what Roper needed. "I have a present for you. Here's a gift certificate." Yank pulled a piece of paper from his back pocket. "Go get yourself a massage and a manicure."

"Not in the mood."

Yank didn't know what else to do in order to help his dejected client. "Don't you want to look your best for the annual Hot Zone New Year's party?"

"I'm not going."

Yank smacked him upside the head. "You sure as hell are. You're going to hold yourself up and make like life's grand. Attitude is everything and right now yours sucks."

Yank couldn't see well but he figured Roper was scowling at him about now. "I'm sure you're having a rough time after the series, but obviously something more has you bent out of shape. The happy-go-lucky guy I know wouldn't be sulking like a pansy."

Roper rose and Yank felt the other man's height close beside him.

"You want to know what's bothering me? Where should I start? I could live with last year's disaster if I thought I was definitely coming back, but we both know the shoulder's not healing the way it should. That means my career may be shorter than we'd anticipated. Not a financial problem given my huge contract, right?"

"Unless you pissed it away…" Yank said, not at all serious.

"You know me better than that. But my family's working hard at doing it for me."

Yank blinked. "Ever hear *just say no?*"

"You try telling them that."

Yank wasn't worried about Roper's future. The younger man had come to him for investment advice and Yank knew he'd diversified wisely. But if his career was shortened due to injury and his family was going through his money like water, Yank could understand the man's distress. "Slow 'em down, then," Yank suggested.

"Yeah, I'm trying," Roper muttered. "Do me a favor? Tell Micki I need time to myself. If she doesn't quit worrying and sending you around to check on me, I'm going to let the Hot Zone go. Who knows? If I can't play this season, I may not need a PR firm at all."

Yank frowned. "Micki's not worried about you as a client, you ass. She's worried about you as a friend."

"I know that," Roper said, sounding more subdued and apologetic. "I appreciate her concern, but there's nothing she can do unless she's got a magic cure for the shoulder."

Even Yank knew when to give a man space, and John Roper needed it more than Yank had realized. "I'll make you a deal," he said to the man he both liked and admired.

"What's that?"

"Come to the party and I promise nobody will be talking business. You could use some time to relax. No media invited. What do you say?"

Roper remained silent for too long.

Obviously the man was tense and strung tight if he couldn't bring himself to say he'd come to a party. "When was the last time you got laid?" Yank asked, voicing the first question that came to mind.

"None of your damn business."

Yank chuckled at the quick answer. "Then it's been too damn long."

Yank had seen the symptoms in other good men, as well. Men who spent too much time alone and needed a woman in their lives. Not that he'd know… No sir, but he knew Roper needed a distraction from focusing on his World Series screwup or the start of spring training in February.

Too bad Yank had already hooked up his three nieces with solid men. But just because his girls were taken didn't mean Yank couldn't work his magic with Roper and another woman.

But who could he find to put up with a man who liked things orderly and neat, designer and upscale? He went through the women in his office, then smacked himself for being so dense. He should have thought of the female solution to Roper's problems sooner.

Amy Stone, the niece of his partner, Spencer Atkins. She was feisty, pretty and single, and only an idiot could have missed the sparks between Amy and Roper at Sophie's wedding. Roper's date had been a bimbo but not an idiot, Yank thought, recalling the drink she'd spilled down Roper's shirt and their immediate exit right afterward. And since Amy had just moved to the city and taken a position at the Hot Zone, she didn't know many people in town. Yes, sir, Amy was his answer.

He didn't intend to tell Roper, though. Yank loved surprises. "Come to the party," Yank insisted.

"You'll leave me alone if I do?"

Yank nodded. "Scout's honor," he said, raising his hand.

Roper shrugged. "Okay, then. Why the hell not?"

Yank tugged on Noodle's leash, and as they walked out the door, Yank whistled, pleased with his handiwork.

J.D. met him by the car. "Why are you in such a good mood?"

"Because I'm not a Boy Scout and I never have been," Yank said, laughing. John Roper was about to benefit from Yank being a lying, meddling son of a bitch.

AMY LOVED FLORIDA. SHE enjoyed the warm weather all year, the ease of never having to wear a winter jacket. It was one of the reasons she'd stayed down South instead of going away to college. She also was a person who appreciated comfortable surroundings, and her home and family in Florida represented the familiar.

Her father had died of a heart attack when she was young. But thanks to her mother and aunt, and her uncle's frequent visits, she'd never felt alone or neglected. Still, she'd been old enough to remember her father and she'd always felt his absence in her life. While her mother was wild, spirited and free, her father had been more reserved, the epitome of good manners.

When she was a kid, she'd had some wild antics of her own, like when her father had insisted they give the puppy she'd found to the pound. Granted it was a no-kill shelter, but she'd wanted that dog, and

to prove her point, she'd picketed—with signs—
from the garage roof below her bedroom window. He
had insisted she come down before she fell off,
making his disapproval with her technique clear
along with his fear for her safety. He preferred she
use traditional, safe methods to make her point instead of alerting the neighbors and causing them to
panic and call both him and 9-1-1.

She laughed at the memory, because it had been
one of the few times she'd made use of her mother's
genes—the ones she usually kept hidden inside her.
From that point on, she'd tried to please her father
and rein in any wildness. Even after he was gone,
Amy had never stopped trying to please him.

Being a social worker, helping out others in need,
was something she knew her father would have been
proud of. When she'd lost that job, thanks to one of
her mother's more outrageous stunts, she'd been devastated and she'd retreated home to lick her wounds.
While there, she fell into the habit of looking out for
her mother and her friends, again something her
father would have approved of. She'd ended up as the
social director of the seniors' community and she had
to admit the job had been a good fit for her.

But she'd spent enough time watching over her
mother and she missed being with people her own
age. Amy had woken up on her birthday and realized
not only hadn't she accomplished her old dreams,
she'd forgotten to make new ones. Uprooting herself
from the familiar was the first step in forging a new

life. One that included a new career—with the Hot
Zone thanks to her uncle Spencer and the generosity
of the Jordan sisters in giving her a chance.

Now, on New Year's Eve, she stepped off the
elevator at the Park Avenue offices of the Hot Zone
and glanced at the guests, the male ones in particular, and an immediate feeling of déjà vu swept over
her. Just like at Sophie and Riley's wedding, she felt
out of her element. Would she ever get used to being
surrounded by buff, hot men? She hoped not, she
thought, as she glanced around at her new normal.

The coat-check woman greeted her and took her
jacket. A server offered her a glass of champagne,
which Amy declined. She wanted a clear head for all
the new faces and names she'd encounter, as well as
access to her memories of those she'd already met
at the wedding. Those memories were vivid. Especially the ones of John Roper and how disappointed
she'd been by his deception. Of course, maybe he'd
have told her about his date given more time.

And maybe he hadn't leaned close enough to kiss
her cheek, she thought, still disappointed by the outcome. No matter how much she wanted to believe
he'd been as blindsided by their attraction as she'd
been, that he couldn't help but act on it, date or no
date, she knew she was deceiving herself. In all likelihood, the man was exactly what he seemed to be—
a guy trying to juggle more than one woman at a
time.

The man was a superstar athlete, a celebrity who

was probably used to women falling at his feet. Amy had grown up listening to her uncle's stories of his famous clients. And Amy had inadvertently played the role of doting admirer. But that wasn't who she was. Amy wasn't into the glitz, glamour and fame celebrity brought.

She exhaled a stream of air, annoyed at herself for giving Roper any thought at all. She forced herself to focus to the holiday decorations that lingered from Christmas and the pretty silver balls hanging from the ceiling. A professionally decorated tree sat in the corner twinkling with lights that were sure to be taken down soon after the first of the year. The decor outdid anything she, her mother and aunt back in Florida had managed to set up in the clubhouse each year.

"Amy?"

She turned at the sound of her name above the noise of the happy crowd. Sophie Jordan approached quickly, a warm smile on her face. No matter how many times Amy saw Sophie, she was always shocked by her beauty and perfection. Tonight her honey-blond hair was pulled back in a neat knot, her face beautifully made up.

Amy hugged Sophie, the sister who was the organizer behind the Hot Zone. She had met Sophie for the first time in Florida last year. Though Sophie wasn't as touchy-feely as Amy, she hugged right back.

"You look happy. Marriage to my cousin must

agree with you," Amy said, taking in Sophie's glow-ing face.

Sophie grinned. "Well, marriage to Riley *is* pretty darn good."

"I just bet it is. Where is my cousin, anyway?"

"He'll be here soon."

"And your sisters?" Amy glanced over Sophie's shoulder. "Are they around here somewhere?"

"Unfortunately Micki's still on the island—her husband, Damian, owns a slice of paradise. Her daughter had a respiratory infection and Damian insisted on taking the family to a warmer climate for a little while. From what they say, it seems to be helping. But Annabelle is here working the crowd. I'm sure you'll see her soon."

Amy nodded. "Well, please send Micki my love."

"I will. And you can do it yourself at the first staff meeting in a few days."

Amy already knew she was stepping into a high-profile, high-pressure place with loyalty and dedica-tion in spades, and she wanted to play a successful part. Nepotism might have gotten her the job, but only proving herself would keep her here. She was definitely ready for the challenge.

"Well, look who's here!" a booming male voice said. Her uncle's partner, Yank, pulled her into a big hug at the same time Amy caught sight of his wife, Lola, standing behind him.

Amy waved to the other woman, who smiled right back.

"Just tell me your crazy mother and aunt are still at home in Florida," Yank said as he stepped back.

Lola groaned. "Ignore him. He's had a drink or two and doesn't know what he's saying." She smacked her husband on the shoulder.

"I'm stone-cold sober. You've been watering down my drinks all night." He leaned closer to Amy. "She thinks just because I can't see, my taste buds have gone, too."

And he thought Amy's relatives were crazy? She shook her head and laughed. "No problem, Lola. I've heard from Uncle Spencer that Yank says whatever's on his mind." She shot the older man a grateful look. "Thank you for giving me a chance here," she told him.

Yank grinned, obviously pleased. "You see? The only one who's got a problem with me is you," Yank said to his wife.

Sophie rolled her eyes. "Okay, you said your hellos, Uncle Yank. How about giving me a chance to introduce Amy to some other people at the party?"

"I'd like that." Amy rubbed her hands together.

"Why not start with someone she knows and ease her in. John Roper's over there in the corner," Yank said without much tact.

Amy's stomach flipped. "Oh, I think we can skip over him," Amy said, only partially meaning it. A traitorous part of her wanted to get a glimpse of him again.

"Nonsense. Amy wouldn't want him to think he

was avoiding her, considering he's been eyeing *her* since she walked into the room," Yank said.

"He has?" Amy asked, then wished she could bite her tongue and take it back. Still, she had to admit it stroked her ego to know Roper's eyes had been on her since she'd arrived. She had to force herself not to glance at the corner and look over at *him*.

Lola scowled at her husband. "Leave Amy alone," she instructed.

"Lola's right," Sophie said. "But tell me something. Just how would you know where Roper is, considering you can't see well enough to identify anyone?" Sophie perched her hands on her hips and eyed her uncle warily.

"She's got your number, old man," Lola said, laughing.

"Who are you calling old?" he grumbled.

Lola ignored him, meeting Sophie's gaze instead. "Actually, Yank's been checking up on Roper ever since he arrived. I feel like the man's personal GPS system."

"Speaking of guides, where is Noodle?" Sophie asked.

"One of the staff took the dog out for a walk." Lola gestured toward the windows overlooking the city. "They'll be back soon."

Sophie nodded. "Gotcha. Well, I can understand your concern for Roper. We've all been worried about him lately. The papers have been brutal."

Despite her better judgment, Amy's curiosity got the better of her. "Why? What's going on?"

The other three stared at one another, wide-eyed and surprised.

"I guess New Yorkers forget that not everyone else's world revolves around sports," Sophie said, realization dawning. "You know that the Renegades made it to the World Series?"

Amy nodded. She just hadn't kept up with the details since the opposing team hadn't been from Florida.

"Roper went into the post season in a serious slump," Sophie said in a low whisper. "He didn't play well at all in the series, struck out in the clutch and injured his shoulder in an attempt to stop a home run. The team lost the series and Roper became the media scapegoat."

"Ouch." Poor man, she thought, then caught herself. The *poor man* didn't need her pity, that much she knew for sure.

Despite herself, Amy's gaze came to rest on the sexy guy who had made her pulse kick up a notch and her mouth go dry.

And he still had a female cozying up to him just like the last time.

"He doesn't look happy," Sophie murmured.

She was right. Despite the attention of a woman who appeared to be hanging on his every word, Roper appeared dazed and bored.

"How odd," Lola said. "Normally Roper loves every bit of attention he can get, female or otherwise."

Amy pursed her lips and kept silent. She'd once

been all too happy to shower him with that attention. Thanks to the scene made by his date at the wedding, everyone here knew it.

"Must be today's paper that's getting to him," Yank said. "Lola read it to me earlier. The *News* ran a list of New Year's resolutions. Said if Roper didn't get a renewed dose of talent from Santa, he should resolve to take a one-way ticket to Siberia as his contribution to the team."

"That's awful," Amy said, shocked by the brutal treatment despite her feelings about Roper at the moment.

"That's New York," Sophie replied. "Something you'll be getting used to, I promise."

Amy nodded. "Still, I can't imagine being the center of such negative press day in and day out."

Yank shrugged. "In this city, it comes with the territory. The bigger the contracts, the worse the scrutiny and the higher the expectations. Let's go save him," Yank said. He practically gave Amy a shove forward, calling Roper's name at the same time.

So much for steering clear of him, Amy thought. And one glance his way had her wondering why she wanted to.

"I'm sorry," Sophie whispered, catching up with her.

"Not a problem," Amy said with a forced smile as they walked forward.

Yank Morgan trailed right along with them until Lola deliberately pulled him away for a scolding.

Amy chuckled at the family dynamic, one to which she could relate. But she had something more important to focus on now than Yank and Lola.

Roper's gaze locked on Amy's and her insides twisted with the familiar sense of awareness he'd invoked in her once before.

"Ladies, please come rescue me from wedding talk," Roper said, reaching out and putting an arm around Sophie's shoulder.

But he never broke eye contact with Amy.

"Wedding?" Sophie asked, her voice rising. "I didn't know you were even seeing someone special."

Wedding? A voice inside Amy's head echoed and her stomach cramped.

"As in, you and a member of the opposite sex making a permanent commitment? Someone give me a fan. I think I'm going to faint." Sophie waved a hand in front of her face, mocking him and chuckling at the same time.

"Did you hear that, John? They think *you're* getting married." The woman by his side, a different woman from the last one Amy had seen him with, laughed in real amusement.

When she turned around, Amy realized the other woman was much younger than she'd originally thought. Certainly younger than Amy and definitely younger than John Roper.

"John's not my fiancé, he's my brother," the other woman explained.

Amy let out a breath she hadn't realized she'd

been holding. She wanted to dismiss the wave of relief washing over her, but she couldn't. Roper wasn't getting married and she could breathe again. Obviously, despite her frustration with him over their first meeting, the attraction was still there, strong as ever.

"Ah, now that makes more sense." Sophie nodded in understanding. "I couldn't see you taking yourself off the market, and I definitely couldn't see the papers missing out on the courtship."

"Ha, ha," Roper muttered.

While they were sparring, Amy took a moment to look at the younger woman with fresh eyes. With the family connection made, Amy saw the resemblance now—the sandy-blond hair, the shape and color of their green eyes and the matching dimples.

"Sabrina, meet everyone here." Roper inclined his head towards his sibling. "Everyone, meet my sister, Sabrina." He finished the introductions with a quick wave of his hand.

"Nice to meet you all." Sabrina smiled, once again reinforcing the family resemblance. "I wish I could stay and hang out, but I've got to go find my fiancé."

"Nice to meet you," Amy murmured, but Roper's sister had taken off before she could hear the reply.

Sophie glanced at her watch. "I should follow her lead. Riley should have been here by now."

"Go on. I'll take good care of Amy while you're gone."

Sophie shot Amy a look of concern, but Amy didn't want the other woman worrying about her or thinking she couldn't handle herself with one of Hot Zone's clients.

Amy put on her brightest smile. "Say hi to Riley and tell him I'll catch up with him in a few minutes," Amy said.

"Are you sure?" Sophie's gaze bounced between Amy and Roper.

Roper pushed off from where he was leaning against the wall and rose to his full, overwhelming height.

"Don't worry about me," Roper said, treating Amy to a wink and a grin that caused a tingling straight down to her toes.

"I wasn't. Amy?" Sophie asked.

"Go find my cousin and give him a kiss for me." She dismissed the other woman's worry with an encouraging smile.

Sophie turned to Roper. "You know that Riley will kick your ass if you misbehave, so be good to Amy. She's new in town."

He cocked an eyebrow, throwing a sexy look her way. "When am I ever not good?"

Which was exactly what had Amy on edge. But she was a big girl. She could handle herself, as well as John Roper.

Sophie frowned, but after a lingering glance at Amy, took off to find her husband, leaving them alone.

Roper stepped closer. And Amy knew she was in deep trouble.

CHAPTER TWO

WHEN YANK INSISTED ROPER show up at this gig, he'd agreed under duress. Now Roper realized fate wanted him here so it could present him with the one thing he needed—a distraction from his career problems, his sister's wedding and his brother's constant whining about a loan. Amy Stone provided that distraction. Apparently life had given him a second chance, and he decided to take this as the first positive sign in ages. Maybe things were looking up after all.

He vividly recalled the instant attraction he'd felt for Amy the first time he'd laid eyes on her. And the stirring in his body told him *that* much hadn't changed. He'd gone to the wedding out of obligation, still in a funk over the blown World Series. But one look at the pretty brunette and all thoughts of his problems had fled. She'd been a breath of fresh air in his down-and-out life. He'd actually forgotten all about his date, mostly because she was simply arm candy and hadn't meant anything to him at all. Not that that was an excuse. Although Roper liked women, all women—blond, brunette or redhead, natural or from a bottle—when he looked at Amy, the punch in the gut had been harder and more defined.

He hadn't lost sight of the fact that he'd made an ass of himself the last time they were together and he owed her an apology for what had transpired. Now, with everyone gone, he and Amy were alone in their own corner of the party and she met his gaze head-on, not blinking or backing down.

He admired the fact that he couldn't rattle her and refused to rush his perusal. She had tanned skin only someone from a southern state could manage, a fresh, unjaded look in her eyes, and curly hair that didn't appear overly set with sprays or products. He could definitely get into tangling his hands in the soft brown curls.

But most of all he wanted to be with a woman who in all likelihood didn't keep up with New York sports news and Roper's humiliations. One who wouldn't pity him, judge him or want something from him in any way. Of course, he was getting ahead of himself. Chances were good she hadn't forgiven him for the scene at the wedding, and he couldn't blame her.

"So how have you been?" he asked once they were alone, or as alone as they could be in a room full of people.

"Just fine, and you?" She folded her arms across her chest, causing her cleavage to swell above the glittery gold tank she wore beneath a white silk blouse.

He knew Amy's movement was unintentional, and he had to admit her lack of pretense was one of the things he found most appealing about her. "I've been better," he admitted, opting for honesty.

But he didn't want to get into his recent problems. He cleared his throat and asked, "Been in town long?" Not his best line, but he wanted to change the subject.

She shook her head. "Not very."

She wasn't making this easy. For the first time, he was uptight around a woman and unsure of how to reach her. "So, um, when do you leave?" he asked.

She raised an eyebrow. "Anxious to get rid of me already?"

He shook his head, exhaling hard. "I'm blowing this big-time. Let's backtrack, okay? It's good to see you again."

"Same here." She immediately pursed her lips.

He'd bet she wished she could take that comment back, but he liked her refreshing honesty.

She turned, obviously scanning the crowd.

He followed her gaze but couldn't pinpoint any-one or anything that would have distracted her. "Looking for someone?"

"As a matter of fact, I am," she said as she pivoted back to face him. "I was trying to locate your date."

A grin tugged at his mouth. "What makes you think I brought one?" he asked.

"Experience."

"Touché."

She shrugged. "I can't imagine you spending New Year's Eve alone." She reached her hand out, tapping a finger against his pink Ralph Lauren dress shirt.

She was bolder than he thought she'd be, but the slight trembling of her fingers told him the movement was forced. He'd bet she didn't want him to think he could get to her again.

Well, hell. *She* got to him. "You wound me," Roper said.

"You'll live."

He laughed hard, something he hadn't done in way too long. "I suppose I deserved that."

She grinned. "You supposed right." Her hand lingered. Her pink fingernails were short and blended with the color of his shirt.

His flesh burned hot underneath the material. He couldn't tear his gaze from her delicate fingertips lingering so close to the buttons that would let his skin touch hers.

She followed his stare, glanced down, realized she hadn't removed her hand and snatched it away, leaving him to wonder if she'd felt the same searing heat.

She cleared her throat. "Well, your shirt's clean so I assume you've been a good boy. You haven't ticked off your date, at least not yet. So where is she? Ladies' room? Buffet table?"

They were bantering easily and he was glad. But he'd like for her to get to know him better so he could erase the bad first impression he'd made. "If I admit that was tacky and I apologize, can we start over?" he asked.

"That depends." She narrowed her gaze, assessing him in silence, but assessing him nonetheless.

Roper decided the fact that she couldn't take her eyes off him was a good thing. At least it was mutual. He couldn't stop staring at her, either. The more he thought about it, the more he realized she'd be good for him. A welcome break from physical therapy for his sprained shoulder and from wondering whether or not he'd return in time for spring training.

"I didn't come with a date," he admitted, refocusing on Amy. "Lesson learned the hard way." Thank God.

She inclined her head. "That's a start," she murmured.

"What if I told you I was so taken by you at the wedding that I couldn't help myself, date or no date?"

She swiped her tongue over her lightly glossed lips. "I'd say you were pushing it and would be better off with just the apology."

"Even if I was telling the truth?"

"Especially then," she said, her voice huskier than before.

He stepped closer, so close he could examine each freckle on her nose and cheeks. "Come on, give me another chance. Let's start fresh." On impulse, he reached out and ran his finger down the tip of her nose. Skin touched skin and his hand sizzled on contact.

Her eyes widened with awareness, but she didn't back away.

Pleased, he tipped his head even closer. "So what do you say?"

She bit down on her lower lip, pausing in thought.

The seconds that he waited were the longest of his life.

"For the sake of peace, why not?" she finally said.

He had the second chance he'd sought, he thought with relief. "Can I get you some punch?"

She wrinkled her nose. "I think I'm going to stay away from alcohol. Besides, I should really get—"

A loud bell-like sound clanged, drowning out her voice.

"What's that?" Amy yelled over the noise.

"Sounds like a fire alarm."

And he must have been right because the guests, talking loudly among themselves, headed for the front of the offices leading to the hallway.

"Let's get moving," he said.

"Are you serious? We're twenty floors up!" Panicked, she grabbed for her heels.

"What are you doing?"

"I was going to take off my shoes so I could run downstairs easier!"

He swallowed a laugh, knowing her fear was real. "In my experience, more often than not it's a false alarm."

She narrowed her gaze. "Haven't you ever seen *The Towering Inferno*?"

He chuckled aloud this time. "It's a bad seventies movie, not reality. But you have a point. Let's get going. If the shoes don't hurt, you can keep them on. We're not going to be running. Just moving quickly."

She nodded.

"Shoes on or off?" he asked, talking loudly to compensate for the clanging bell.

"On. The heels aren't that high. I'll be fine."

Before she could make a run for the stairs or push through the crowds, Roper slipped his hand into hers and took control. He led her to the fire exit along with the rest of the guests and they maneuvered the long walk down in silence, punctuated by the alarm but with no hint of smoke or fire. Finally they stepped into the front lobby and were greeted by firemen in uniform directing people to the sidewalk across the street.

From what Roper could gather, the fire chief thought it was a false alarm, but until they checked out the building, they couldn't be sure. Everyone needed to evacuate.

Outside, he caught up with one of his teammates.

Jorge Calderone lifted a hand in greeting. "Someone say Yank Morgan trip on his Noodle and accidentally pull on the fire alarm," he said in his heavy accent.

Roper shook his head and laughed. "You're kidding. Was the old man hurt?"

"He's fine. But Sophia *mucho* angry that he ruined the party."

Roper thought of perfectionist Sophie and said, "I just bet she is."

"I'm not staying to freeze my ass off out here. See ya, *mi amigo*." Jorge strode away without looking back.

Roper turned to Amy. "I'd have introduced you to my friend but he took off too fast."

"Not a problem." Her voice shook as she spoke and she had wrapped her arms around her upper body as she shivered in the below-freezing temperatures.

He slipped his sport jacket off and wrapped it around her shoulders.

She smiled appreciatively. "Thanks. I left my jacket at the coat check when I arrived, and my body is used to much warmer temperatures."

"I should have figured as much. Can I take you somewhere for dinner? I know a nice place with good food." The party might be over, but he wasn't ready to part ways with Amy just yet.

"No thanks. I really should just go home, change and get warm. Oh, no." She swung around and glanced back at the building.

"What's wrong?"

She shut her eyes, frustration clear in her expression. "I left my key in my coat pocket."

He shoved his hands into his front trouser pockets for warmth. "I'm sure the hotel would issue you another one, unless your ID is in your pocket, too?"

"No. But I'm not talking about a hotel key card. I'm talking about the actual key to my apartment."

"Wait, you live here? In New York?" Suddenly he was wary. Earlier when he'd pursued her, somewhere in the back of his mind was the knowledge that Amy was in town for a short time. No hopes, no expectations to add to his burdens. Except, apparently, he was wrong.

"I just moved here. I'm subletting Micki's apartment since it's too small for her whole family and they stay at Damian's when they're in the city, anyway." Amy hopped from foot to foot in order to keep warm. "I take it Micki didn't mention it?"

Roper shook his head. He was going to strangle his best friend for the omission. If he'd known Amy was a permanent resident, he wouldn't have restarted his flirtation. He was looking for a quick fix and a good time. Not a relationship with a woman nearby who, though she kept her distance now, would undoubtedly begin to expect something more eventually. He'd had enough of that already.

"I could talk to Sophie or Yank and see if they have an extra key, but they look tied up with the firemen," she said, glancing over his shoulder. "I guess I'll just wait."

Her eyes were wide, her cheeks flushed red from the cold and her curls were tousled around her pretty face. Oh, hell, who was he kidding? Even if he had known she'd moved to town, he'd have had a hard time staying away. Besides, he wasn't going to overthink this, just make the most of it.

She shivered and he stepped toward the curb, hailing the first yellow cab that appeared and opening the door so she could get in first.

"Where are we going?" she asked.

"My place." Where she could warm up before he took her back to her building to see if the doorman or super had a spare key.

It was New Year's Eve and he wanted to keep her with him for a while longer.

AMY HADN'T AGREED TO go to his apartment. She just wanted to get warm. She settled into the taxicab seat, then Roper sat down beside her. His body heat rippled through her, warming her when just seconds before she was chilled inside and out.

He rattled off an address to the driver.

"Wait."

"You need warm clothes and maybe some hot food before dealing with Micki's grouchy doorman," he said, before leaning forward and telling the driver to go.

She knew better than to sound like an ungrateful brat, considering she was freezing, hungry and she had nowhere else to go. "Good point. Thanks." Teeth chattering, she leaned back in her seat for the duration of the ride to his high-rise farther uptown.

When she finally walked into his apartment twenty minutes later, she was immediately reminded that she still wasn't used to city living. In her old world, one-floor ranch homes were the norm. Her house in Florida hadn't been huge, but because everything was spread out on one level, the square footage seemed larger. Her father had left her mother with enough insurance money to let them live comfortably, and once her uncle had bought the real estate he'd turned into a retirement community along with his fellow investors, he'd insisted his sisters move there, as well. Amy had lived in one of the smaller units, paying token rent. Here in New York, her new apartment was small and quaint.

Roper's place was enormous. She sensed how large it was just by looking across, past the sliding doors to the terrace off the living room. Then there was the decor. In a masculine cocoa-and-cream color scheme, the living room held a plush suede sofa and ottoman, two club chairs and a rectangular marble cocktail table in the center. A massive large-screen TV hung on the wall across from the sitting area, while behind the couch, framed artwork made the room come alive.

"Like it?" Roper asked as he tossed his keys into a bowl in a practiced movement.

"It's gorgeous."

He grinned. "Thanks. I decorated it myself." The pride in his voice was unmistakable.

"I'm impressed." What other hidden talents did he have? Amy wondered.

He shrugged. "Why pay a professional if I can just as easily do it myself? That's my motto. Anyway, let me get you something to change into. My sister leaves comfortable clothes here in case she's too lazy to go home, which used to happen pretty often before she met her fiancé. She won't mind if you borrow them."

Amy rubbed her hands up and down her arms, covered only by her thin blouse. "Thanks."

"After you warm up, we'll talk about what to eat. I'll be right back."

She turned to study her surroundings once more, her gaze coming to rest on the trophies in a dark wood cabinet with glass doors. MVP, Golden Glove and other notable mentions were inscribed on plaques with John Roper's name.

He walked back into the room with a stack of clothes in his hand. "Take your pick."

"Nice set of awards. Once again, you've impressed me," she said as she accepted a sweat outfit.

"I hope the awards aren't the only things you like about me, because you know what they say, all good things come to an end." He studied her through narrowed eyes.

"I don't know you well enough to know what I like about you." She knew better than to mention the career problems she'd just learned about tonight.

"Good answer." He smiled and his eyes softened, warming her a bit more.

She supposed it couldn't be easy to meet women and not know whether they were interested in him or in his status and money. Amy had no use for either. She'd grown up comfortable and didn't need excessive luxury, although what her mother couldn't afford, her uncle had always provided. But Amy never took having material things for granted. Love and family were much more important than money. But he didn't know enough about her to understand she was a genuine person and she knew better than to try to convince him with mere words.

She had already seen there was more to Roper than the player she'd assumed him to be. Like his ability to apologize for mistakes and his chivalry in bringing her back here to warm up with seemingly no ulterior motive.

"Let's get to know each other better over a good meal. While you change, I'll fix us up something to eat," he said.

"There's no need for you to go to any trouble. We can order in. It's easier. And I ought to know—I've been living on takeout."

Although she had essentially been the caretaker in the family, keeping everyone busy and out of trouble, she'd also been spoiled by living near her mother and aunt. They'd served her home-cooked meals and delivered them to her doorstep if she wanted to be alone. She hadn't had to worry about fixing things for herself, which was a good thing, because she was a hazard in the kitchen. Here in New York, she'd been too busy making Micki's apartment her own and learning her way around the city to attempt making meals, too.

"That settles it, then. I'm definitely cooking. It relaxes me, and besides, it's healthier than eating the fried food and heavy sauces you'll find in takeout."

She couldn't help but laugh. "A man who cooks? Now, *there's* something to like about you. I knew that list wouldn't be all that hard. I'll change and then maybe you can give me some pointers in the kitchen."

"I'd be happy to." His eyes sparkled with pleasure. "Bathroom's down the hall on your right." He pointed toward the back of the apartment.

She headed to change in his spare bathroom, something her apartment didn't have, and a few minutes later she returned to the kitchen dressed in sweats that were a little snug but much warmer and more comfortable than the outfit she'd worn to the party.

She stood in the doorway and took in the gorgeous state-of-the-art kitchen. "Wow. My mother would be impressed."

"I'm impressed, too." His gaze traveled leisurely over her, his eyes darkening with distinct approval. "You dress down as well as you dress up. The rumpled, fresh-out-of-bed look suits you," he said with a sexy grin.

Her face warmed at the compliment and her body followed suit.

"I didn't realize you were that much taller than my sister," he said, taking in the sweats that she'd rolled around her calves.

She glanced down at her bare ankles. "Well, at least capris are in style."

"They are and they look great on you."

"Thanks." A flush rose to her cheeks. She could say the same about how good he looked, too.

He'd opened the first few buttons on his shirt and

rolled up his sleeves, giving him an edgy, sexy look. "So let's get started. You said you wanted lessons. I take it cooking's not your thing?"

She sighed and lifted her hands uselessly in the air. "Nope. They say children learn by watching, but I'm afraid I never picked up Mom's talent. Not even the basics."

"Well, then, sit and I'll teach you."

She realized he'd already taken out presliced chicken strips and now he was slicing fresh vegetables on a cutting board. A wok sat ready and waiting for him to use.

"Starting with precut and sliced food helps," she said, laughing.

He raised an eyebrow. "So you're that much of a novice, hmm?"

"And you're that much of an expert?"

He nodded.

Everything about the man took her by surprise. A really pleasant surprise.

She settled herself onto a barstool near the island, where he was working.

"I buy presliced chicken because my schedule's so hectic I never know how much time I'll have. On a night like tonight, it comes in handy. You can buy precut vegetables, as well, but it takes me no time and I'd rather eat fresh. Now I'm nearly ready to toss the vegetables into the wok."

She blinked at how fast he'd prepared a meal that would have taken her an hour minimum.

"Maybe I should be taking notes," she mused as she reached over and plucked a carrot from the cutting board.

"Hey, quit nibbling or you won't be hungry enough to enjoy my masterpiece." He playfully smacked at her hand, but she was faster.

She nabbed another carrot before he could stop her.

In two steps he stood by her side, his presence big and overwhelming, the heat in his eyes matching the desire pulsing through her veins. From the moment she'd laid eyes on this man, she'd been seduced by his looks. What sane woman wouldn't be?

But in the short time she was with him tonight, she'd seen glimpses of the everyday guy he really was. She really liked what she saw.

He reached for the carrot and she tucked it tighter into her hand.

"Give it up," he ordered, clearly amused by her game.

She bit the inside of her cheek. "Make me."

He tickled her but she held on fast, eagerly anticipating his next method of extraction.

Their eyes met and held. Her pulse pounded hard in her throat and the anticipation of his lips hot and hard on hers sent tremors quaking through her body.

She slid her tongue over her mouth, moistening her lips, waiting, hoping...

The jarring ring of the telephone broke the thick silence surrounding them. His head jerked toward the sound.

Needing space, Amy jumped up from her chair. "You should answer it," she said, her voice unusually shaky.

He shot her a glance filled with equal parts heat and regret before grabbing the portable phone behind him. "Yeah," he barked into the phone, then listened to whoever was on the other end.

"Sorry. Happy New Year to you, too, Mom. Why aren't you out at one of those Hollywood parties you love so much?"

Hollywood? That was an interesting tidbit of information, Amy thought. And far better to focus on that than how close they'd come to kissing.

"Oh, right. Time difference. I forgot. I'm distracted, that's all." His gaze settled on Amy, his stare deep and consuming, letting her know he hadn't forgotten what had almost happened between them. What could still happen if she let it.

He cleared his throat. "That's okay. What's going on?" he asked. His expression darkened the longer his mother spoke. "No, Mom, I'm not giving Ben money to invest in a gym."

He listened, then said, "Because giving money to my brother is like throwing it away, that's why." Roper pinched the bridge of his nose. "Have you forgotten about all the failed businesses that I did subsidize for him? Never mind. I can't talk about this now. I have company."

He winked at Amy, but she didn't miss the fact that his previously playful side had disappeared.

"Yes, Mom, *female company*. Just how long am I supposed to compensate Ben because I made it in the majors and he didn't?"

Obviously his mother wasn't listening to what Roper said, and Amy winced. As an only child, she wasn't used to dealing with siblings. But she *was* used to coping with stubborn adults who acted like kids and who wouldn't take no for an answer. She was being given an inkling into Roper's family dynamics, and they seemed to be in as much turmoil as his career.

"I didn't say family wasn't important, Mom. Go to your party and we'll talk about this tomorrow," he said, his voice softening.

He obviously loved his mother. He also had a complex family situation, but really, who didn't? She'd had to leave home to get a life, but that didn't mean she wasn't worried about every move Rose and Darla made. She loved them, but there were times they grated on her nerves, pushing every emotional button she possessed.

Roper obviously felt the same way about his family. His life wasn't easy, she thought. She quietly slipped the carrot they'd fought over into her mouth and waited for him to finish his call.

"Yes," he said, raising a finger toward Amy to indicate he'd be off soon. "Yes, I know. Go enjoy and forget about it for now. Oh, and Mom? Happy New Year," Roper said.

He hung up the phone and turned her way. A flush

highlighted his cheekbones and a muscle ticked on one side of his face. "Nothing like a call from Mom to kill the mood," he said too lightly.

Amy figured he needed a minute or two to calm down, so she let him turn away and place the food into the heated wok.

She tried to use the minutes wisely, reminding herself she wasn't going to be taken in by his charm, something he possessed and no doubt knew how to use in spades. After all, he was not just an athlete but a showman. Yet already she was coming to know him better and to like him despite all common sense. She tried to calm her still-racing heart, but Roper's effect on her was very strong. And the whole night lay ahead....

CHAPTER THREE

ROPER COULD NOT BELIEVE his mother was bugging him about helping Ben yet again. On New Year's Eve. Just as he was finally going to kiss Amy.

Still wound tight, he tossed the last handful of vegetables into the wok with too much force and oil splattered up at him. He stepped back to avoid being hit.

"Families can be a bitch," Amy said at last, breaking the tension.

He turned toward her. "Especially mine."

"Um…" She bit down on the bottom lip he'd been on the verge of devouring minutes before. "If you missed my mother and aunt in action, then I'm sure you heard the wedding stories. I hardly think I'm in a position to judge other people's relatives." She laughed, lightening his mood in an instant.

He didn't know another woman capable of getting into his head that way. He ought to be wary, but right now, he was just grateful. "You've got a point. My mother likes to lay on the guilt when I don't give Ben what he wants."

"Your brother played baseball, too?" Amy leaned forward and perched her chin in her hands.

He stared into her curious gaze. Discussing his personal life with anyone, especially women, had always been a big no-no. Inevitably something private made it into the papers after the relationship ended. He'd learned it early in the minors and had never violated the rule since.

Yet here he was, ready to talk to Amy. He drew a deep breath and forged ahead before he could stop himself. "Ben never made it past the minors. He blames me for inheriting talent from my father. His father, his and Sabrina's, wasn't good for much of anything. He walked out on my mother and us kids, which frankly wasn't much of a loss. But after baseball, Ben just ventured from job to job. You know the expression *jack of all trades, master of none?*"

She nodded in understanding, listening without judging, which only made him want to tell her more. "Over the years Ben's come to me for money for one investment after another, promising me a huge return. At first I thought he'd find something that gave him financial security. Eventually I realized that would never happen, but I helped him out, anyway, just because I could."

While he spoke, he took plates from the cabinet and she helped him set the table.

"You're a good brother," she said. "Uncle Spencer's taken care of his sisters the same way. He bought the retirement complex that my mother and her sister live in. It keeps them out of trouble. Or should I say, it confines their trouble. Anyway, it seems to work."

"Real estate is a smart investment. Ben's last idea was a franchise that would put condom machines in restrooms around the country. My brother was calling himself the future Condom King of America."

Amy pursed her lips to keep from laughing.

Roper grinned. "You can let it out. It's ridiculous, I know. But at my mother's insistence, I gave him the franchise money and he promptly passed it on to a guy who ran away with the cash. Last my detective heard, he was sunning himself in Mexico, avoiding extradition for embezzlement. Meanwhile there were a lot of disappointed, broke future Condom Kings he'd bilked out of large amounts of cash."

"So you'd like to help him but can't because he's stubborn and invests in pipe dreams. Meanwhile you feel guilty that you won't help him anymore because he's still your family."

He gave her a quick nod. She'd nailed his dilemma perfectly, he thought, not all that surprised at her insight. But he was uncomfortable with how well she understood him. He stirred the vegetables and poured them into a bowl, covering it with foil to keep warm while he cooked the chicken.

Eventually the silence got to him. "So there you have the story of my life. How about you? Any brothers or sisters to tell tales about?"

She shook her head. "I'm an only child."

"Lucky you." A few more preparatory steps and he served the food, dividing up the meal and putting it on their plates.

She sat down at the table to eat. "I wouldn't say I was lucky. It was pretty lonely growing up by myself."

He tipped his head to one side. "I never looked at it that way." He'd had Ben to fight with and toss a ball to. And he'd had Sabrina trailing after him with doting eyes.

"That's because right now you have issues with your brother."

"Here's the thing." He set two full glasses of water on the table. "I love my family, but everyone needs something from me. They pull at me from every direction and like you said, I feel guilty not responding on the minute."

"Because you always have before."

"Exactly." He placed his hand on the top of his chair. "Now, how about some champagne? It *is* New Year's Eve."

She crinkled her nose in that cute way she had whenever she wasn't sure she wanted to do something. "Maybe just one glass."

He obliged, pulling a bottle from the fridge, popping the cork, pouring and finally sitting down beside her at the table. "A toast," he said, raising his glass.

She raised hers, as well.

"To…new friends," he said. He hadn't known

how much he needed someone like Amy in his life until tonight. She was special.

A warm smile tilted her lips. "To new friends," she said, a gleam in her eyes as she touched her glass against his and took a sip.

"Good?"

She nodded. "Excellent. Now, you were saying that everyone in your family needs something from you. Care to elaborate beyond Ben?"

He lifted his fork and tasted his meal. "Mmm. Care to compliment the cook first?"

Laughing, she took a bite and paused.

And paused. And paused so long he nearly fell off the edge of his chair waiting for her opinion.

"This is unbelievably good!" she said at last with a smile on her face that bordered on orgasmic.

All he could imagine was putting that same expression on her face in a more intimate setting. But somehow, he managed to clear his throat and continue their discussion. "Thank you," he said, ridiculously thrilled that he'd pleased her palate.

He loved to cook and often did so to relieve tension when he had home games or just to help himself relax during the off-season. And he'd needed one helluva a lot of relaxing lately.

"Well? You were saying about your family?" Amy prodded without shame.

"Anyone ever tell you you're like a pit bull when you get your teeth into something?" he asked. She didn't reply, merely continued eating and waiting, knowing he'd have to answer eventually. "Oh, all right. I'll tell you, but I'll probably put you to sleep with my family saga."

She shook her head. "Try me."

He shrugged. "Mom's an actress, or at least she was until she aged beyond the point where cosmetic surgery enabled her to take youthful roles."

"Would I know of her?" Amy asked.

"Her stage name is Cassandra Lee."

Amy's eyes lit up. "From the movies *Maiden Lane* and *On Sandy Shores!* My mother is a huge fan and took me to her movies all the time when I was growing up!"

"That's her," Roper said. "These days she's too vain to accept the more mature roles, so she's settled into living her life with me supporting her. Not that I mind, since she worked hard to take care of us while I was a kid."

"It must be hard aging in Hollywood."

"There are plenty of better-known actresses who've handled it. Sharon Stone, Meryl Streep, Annette Bening. Mom has truly made *Poor Me* into an art form. But I'm used to it by now."

Amy finished her meal, leaving nothing on her plate. She wasn't one of those women who pushed the food around instead of eating, and that pleased him.

She raised her glass and sipped her champagne. "What about your father? Is he still alive? Mine isn't. He passed away a few months after I started junior high," she said, her tone wistful.

"I'm sorry." He wanted to squeeze her hand, but she didn't seem to want or need sympathy.

She finished her champagne and smiled.

He poured them both another glass. "My father is still alive. He just wasn't ever much of an influence in my life, except for the fact that I inherited my baseball talent from him. Eduardo Montoya. He was a big-time player in his day. And before you ask, Roper was my mother's name before she had it changed."

Amy inclined her head. "I've never heard of him, but that isn't saying much."

He nodded. "It's kind of nice that you don't know the professional me."

She nodded in understanding. He couldn't get over how much he'd revealed to her tonight. Other than with Micki, he never discussed his famous parents with anyone. He didn't need another reason for people to be impressed with something about him that had nothing to do with who he was inside. Amy was different. She was easy to talk to and genuinely interested in him, unlike the usual women he dated, ones who were more interested in his career, status and what he could buy them. Before now, all he'd wanted from his companions was a good time, in bed and out. Yet here was a woman he could talk to....

Unwilling to think about that, he rose and started to clean up. Amy helped and in the process, they managed to finish the bottle of champagne. Once the plates were in the dishwasher, and the kitchen was sparkling, he finally led Amy into the family room and turned on the big-screen TV to watch the ball drop in Times Square. He'd have offered to take her home, but he was enjoying her company too much and he didn't want to ring in the New Year alone.

She snuggled into the corner of the couch and didn't object when he eased in close beside her. From the way she'd tripped once on her way into the den and giggled a few times over a joke he hadn't made, Roper knew the champagne had gone to her head.

She was adorable to watch, and he liked having her in his home. Another first.

She narrowed her gaze at the TV screen depicting Times Square. "I can't believe all those people are standing outside in that freezing-cold weather. It was awful when we were there and it wasn't by choice!" She shivered at the memory, giving him just the excuse he needed.

"Spoken like a true Florida girl." Roper pulled her close at the same time the countdown to the New Year began.

"Know what I was doing last year at this time?" Amy asked him, her eyes wide, her face close to his.

"What?"

"Breaking up a fight between two men who wanted to kiss Aunt Darla first once the ball dropped," she murmured. "It's been ages since I spent New Year's with someone my own age."

"Oh, yeah? And when was the last time you were kissed?" he asked, staring at her moist lips.

"Way too long," she said as her eyes fluttered closed.

He knew she had to be slightly tipsy, because he couldn't imagine her letting her guard down this easily otherwise. Still, she'd seemed willing enough earlier in the evening before they were interrupted by the telephone.

He had every intention of taking that next step with her now.

AMY'S STOMACH FLUTTERED as she waited, delicious ripples of anticipation licking at her from deep inside. Roper's eyes darkened and he lowered his head, slowly dragging out the anticipation until finally his mouth came down on hers.

The initial touch set off more sparks. Spiraling whirlpools of desire started slowly and built larger, filling her from inside out. His kiss was silky smooth, the stuff of sensual dreams as he drew his mouth back and forth over hers and lulled her into a hazy stupor of wanting. She lifted her hands and wrapped her arms around his neck, pulling him closer, something he seemed to appreciate because he slid his tongue over the seam of her lips, teasing her back and forth until she opened her mouth and let him inside.

Her tongue tangled with his, matching every fantasy she'd ever had of him and providing even more. He ran his thumbs over her cheek, gently caressing her face while he ravished her mouth. She didn't need food, not when she had this. Wanting to taste more of him, she curled her hands into the hair at the nape of his neck, then tilted her head back, giving him better access. He swept his tongue one last time around her mouth, then began a warm, wet trail of kisses down the side of her face, her neck, her throat, until his head came to rest on her chest just above her cleavage.

Her heart pounded and her breasts felt full, her nipples tightening into hardened peaks at the thought of his wicked mouth suckling her hard. Moisture pooled between her legs, dampening her panties as desire pulsed through her body.

"You taste sweet," he said against her skin.

She moaned. The sound tore from deep inside her at the same time the crowds cheered at the dropping of the ball.

"Happy New Year," she said, drunk with happiness.

"Happy New Year." He pulled back, and she tilted her head, smiling at him, expecting him to kiss her again. After all, the first time had been spectacular and he obviously wanted her, too.

Instead, he pushed himself up and rose to his feet.

"Where are you going?" she asked.

"To get you a blanket so I can tuck you in. Much as it kills me, I'm going to be a gentleman."

She started to rise, then decided it was too much effort. She hadn't had alcohol in a long time and the champagne had gone straight to her head. Of course, it could also be his kisses that made her feel light-headed and dizzy.

"Sit tight," he said, a sexy smile lifting his lips. "I'll be right back."

Amy lay her head back against the couch and shut her eyes, waiting for him to return. Maybe she'd be able to pull him down so they could finish what they'd started. Her mind might be hazy, but she was clear on what she wanted.

Amy wanted John Roper.

AFTER HANGING UP WITH JOHN, Cassandra Lee opened the screen door to her patio and walked outside into the warm air. Although she had to leave in half an hour for the New Year's party she was attending, she had some things to work out in her mind first. Family things. Personal things. Scary things.

She paced the length of her outdoor pool. Normally the rhythm made by her small heels clicking against the stone provided a soothing sound that helped her think more clearly. But her life was truly overwhelming right now and she found it hard to concentrate.

On the one hand, she had director Harrison Smith pressuring her not just to take the role he'd created for her but to let him back into her life. Her daughter was getting married, and instead of enjoying the planning, Cassandra felt more distant from Sabrina than ever. Her youngest son couldn't find himself and her oldest wouldn't cut the youngest any slack. On top of it all, John was undergoing the worst career crisis of his life and Cassandra didn't know how to help him.

At least he wasn't alone on New Year's. He'd said he had company, which in John's world could mean a one-night stand, but something in his voice told her otherwise. The annoyance in his tone indicated he hadn't appreciated the interruption. Normally John took her calls without question. Cassandra hoped there was something special about this woman, because her son needed happiness in his life. She just hoped whoever she was, she liked a close-knit family, because that's what they were.

She picked up the phone and dialed her youngest son's cell phone. "Hello, Ben," she said when he answered on the first ring.

"Did you speak to John about the money for the gym?" he asked.

Cassandra sighed. She loved all her children, but truly Ben was the most selfish.

"Happy New Year, darling." Lowering herself onto a cushioned lounge chair, she eased back against the pillow. "Yes, I tried to talk to him, but the timing was wrong. John was busy. He said he had company and I think it was a woman. You know we have to approach your brother at the right time. He's got so much on his mind right now."

"And I don't? I could lose this opportunity," Ben said.

"Not on New Year's Eve, Benjamin." Cassandra didn't want to outright scold him. After all, he'd never had things quite fall his way, not the way John had. "What if you try talking to your brother yourself?" she asked.

"He hates me, Mom. He never wants to help, and when he does, he blames me when things go wrong. But he can't say no to you. He never could. This is the big thing. I can feel it," Ben said, his tone pleading.

Her heart squeezed tighter in her chest. "I'll talk to him as soon as I can," she promised.

"Thanks. I have to go."

"I love you. Happy New—"

The phone line disconnected before she could finish.

Cassandra sighed. That was Ben. Well, at least she'd reached Sabrina and then Roper, wishing them both Happy New Years and receiving one in return.

She rose and headed inside to change and get ready for the party she was attending. The most mellow one of the year. A ladies-only affair among her closest friends, where she could end the old year the way she planned to start the new.

Avoiding her ex-lover Harrison Smith.

AMY AWOKE WITH A SLIGHT headache and fuzzy memories of an incredible night with a sweet man she'd once thought was anything but. She was glad she'd been wrong about him. As she stretched, she rolled over, and when she nearly fell face-first off the couch, she suddenly remembered where she'd spent the night.

On Roper's couch.

In Roper's apartment.

After that kiss.

"Oh, my God," she groaned, tossing her arm over her face.

"Good morning," he said in a gruff voice.

She peeked out and saw Roper standing over her with a glass of orange juice in hand. "Hi," she managed to say through the fuzzy cotton taste in her mouth.

Knowing she'd have to face him sometime, she scooted upright, bending her knees in front of her. "Is that for me?" she asked, eyeing the cold juice hopefully.

He nodded. "I figured you'd be up soon." He handed her the glass.

"Fresh squeezed?"

He rolled his eyes. "Now, that's pushing your luck."

She laughed. "I was curious just how far your culinary talent went." She took a sip and then downed the glass in two big gulps. "Mmm. That is so good. I'm sorry I fell asleep." The last thing she remembered was planning his seduction while waiting for him to bring her a blanket.

"Me, too." His intense gaze burned into hers.

She swallowed hard. "I hope it wasn't inconvenient having me stay over."

"Only if you consider me lying awake in my bed knowing you were right in the next room inconvenient." He spoke like a man who'd been a gentleman but who'd definitely had second thoughts.

Thank goodness she couldn't hold her champagne. "You're a good guy, John," she said, calling him by his given name.

"I like when you call me that." His face actually flushed. "As for being a good guy, I'm pretty sure it was a first."

She untangled herself from the blanket he'd covered her with. "I really should be getting home. The daytime doorman will let me in without a problem." She hoped. She got up and folded the covers, leaving them in a neat pile on the couch. "I'll just change and give you back your sister's clothes."

"There's no rush. Why don't you wear them home and I'll get them from you the next time I see you."

Meaning he wanted there to be a next time. So did she. But she had a plan for her life, and while last night she'd gotten carried away in the moment, helped by the alcohol, she had to put the brakes on here and now. Even if he was the guy she'd gotten to know last night and not the showman from the wedding, she needed time and space to get a foothold in her new life before getting involved in a relationship.

But she wasn't going to make an issue out of a magnanimous gesture. "Are you sure your sister won't mind?"

"She hasn't stayed over since getting engaged, and even if she wanted to, there are more clothes in the closet. Trust me, she won't care if you borrow some things." He grinned then, a sexy gesture meant to sway her, and it worked.

"Okay, but I'm going to look pretty ridiculous wearing these sweats and my high heels from last night."

"You'll look cute, not ridiculous." He ran his finger down the bridge of her nose, over the freckles she'd always found embarrassing because they made her look so young. It wasn't the first time he'd done it, and the gesture felt incredibly intimate and sensual.

"Excuse me for a minute, okay?" she said, slipping by him so she could head for the bathroom before she got caught up in how delicious he looked wearing low-slung, unbuttoned jeans and no shirt.

His hair had been messed either from sleep or from running a hand through it in place of a comb or brush. First thing in the morning he looked endearingly sexy, and she'd have to convince herself not to notice if she wanted to get out of here quickly, with a minimum of fuss. She was determined to make her morning-after-nothing-happened escape, thank you very much.

"Amy, are you okay in there?" Roper knocked on the bathroom door, startling her back to reality.

"Fine! I'll be out in a sec." She brushed her teeth with minty toothpaste and one finger before drawing a deep breath and heading out to face him again.

He'd slipped on a royal-blue Renegades sweatshirt and a pair of Nike sneakers.

No less handsome, she thought, holding back a frustrated frown.

He grabbed his keys from the bowl by the door.

"Where are you going?" she asked.

He narrowed his gaze. "Where do you think? I'm taking you home."

She shook her head. "I'll be fine. It's broad daylight now."

"And I'll feel better knowing that your doorman is willing to let you inside the apartment without your key." His tone left no room for argument. Neither did the fact that he picked up a garment bag in which he'd obviously hung her outfit. He handed her shoes to her and waited while she slipped them on.

"I feel silly," she muttered as she followed him into the hall.

"Adorable," he corrected her. Placing one hand on her back, he led her to the elevator. A moment later, the door opened and they stepped inside.

People joined them at various floors, leaving no time for conversation, and Amy was relieved. She tried not to feel as if she was sneaking out of a man's apartment in last night's clothes, but she wasn't a pro at this. It didn't matter that she hadn't slept with him, she was embarrassed, anyway. She couldn't help but feel people were looking at her—and him—and staring.

Because John was famous in this city and was certainly well known in his own apartment building, Amy figured it wasn't her imagination, nor was she being paranoid. By the time the elevator came to a halt on the ground level, she practically ran toward the revolving doors.

Roper watched Amy teeter on those silly heels, which made her look both sexy and cute at the same time. He wanted to yell out and tell her they could take his car instead of a cab, but he figured that would call even more attention to her, something she obviously didn't want.

He could understand her need to escape. She wasn't used to strangers gawking at her the way he was. Since most women—heck, *all* the women he'd dated up until now—*liked* the fact that being with him put them in the spotlight, this was but another facet of her personality that made Amy unique. And special.

Ironically he was more convinced than ever that he'd done the right thing by not having sex with her last night. Now she would appreciate his sense of decency. No matter how hard it had been and how much sleep it had cost him.

Instead of following her through the revolving doors, he hit the handicapped automatic door and caught up with her outside on the sidewalk.

Just in time for the paparazzi to greet them with flashing lightbulbs and microphones shoved into their faces.

ROPER FENDED OFF THE vultures by answering their questions about who had spent the night in his apartment with deliberately chatty nonanswers, giving Amy time to escape.

From the corner of his eye, he saw her flag and get into a yellow cab before the press could stop her. He still held on to her clothes but decided not to worry about that now. No matter how hard he prodded, nobody in the group of reporters was willing to divulge their source or tell him why they'd chosen this morning to stake him out. It made no sense. Despite his recent notoriety, he was small-time news for a New Year's Day morning.

Eventually he returned to his apartment, which felt emptier somehow without Amy in it, and he spent the day watching Bowl games with some teammates who showed up uninvited. He was grateful for the company and even ordered pizza as a show of goodwill. He might have cooked to impress Amy, but the guys could damn well eat takeout.

He called her to apologize and to make sure she'd gotten home okay, but her voice recording picked up. He didn't know whether she was deliberately not answering the phone or if she had plans for the day. He left a message along with his number.

She never returned his call, which left him feeling surprisingly bummed out.

He awoke the next day, a Tuesday, feeling as if he'd never slept at all. Not a good sign. He'd hoped the coming year would be kinder than the last.

He had a meeting with Micki scheduled at the Hot Zone offices that morning—at her request. He figured he could pump her for information about Amy then. Roper hadn't wanted to bother her yesterday, because he knew how rare her time with her husband and daughter actually was. After his New Year's Day incident with the press, Roper could understand the appeal of solitude.

"Maybe I ought to buy myself an island," he muttered. "Oh, that's right, I can't. I'm frigging cash poor and tapped out." Okay, he knew that was an exaggeration.

He'd made damn good investments with his money and had prepared for the future from day one of his first big contract. He never wanted to be one of those athletes who pissed away their money and were left with nothing to show for it after their successful career was over. But his family was spending cash like water and he was the spout. He had no choice but to keep an eye on things—in case his career ended sooner than planned. He rubbed his shoulder and hoped the rehab and physical therapy would do the trick.

He finished his cappuccino, brewed in a state-of-the-art machine he'd bought last year, and decided he couldn't wait to meet with Micki later this morning. He picked up his cell phone, needing to talk to his best friend now.

Roper wanted nothing more than some basic information on how to win Amy over. Who better than Micki, who'd rented Amy her apartment, to fill him in?

Roper already figured a girl like Amy might be intimidated by his status and celebrity. Last night he'd questioned the wisdom of getting involved with her once he'd discovered she was living and working in New York. One evening in her company had shown him how different she was from the other women he'd dated. He could no longer just walk away. He was determined to show her he was worth the hassle that came along with him, because he realized they could have a good time together.

And Roper believed in good times. Man, he could use some....

THE WOMAN LOOKED SPOOKED, he thought, watching as she ducked into the nearest cab, running from the paparazzi he'd notified. She wore sweats, a sweatshirt and high heels. A ridiculous combination, he thought. Just as ridiculous as the fact that her outfit from last night still dangled from Roper's hands. He snickered. It's about time Roper looked ridiculous.

He intended to make sure the media continued to know where Roper was and when, keeping him in the news, maintaining the negative press.

Shoving his hands into his jacket pockets, he turned and walked down the street, away from the luxury building. He had no doubt the swarm of paparazzi would continue to circle and create trouble for John Roper.

CHAPTER FOUR

NEW YEAR'S DAY in a new town was a bummer, Amy thought, staring at the walls of her small apartment. She could pass the day alone, cooped up inside, or she could brave the cold and hit the department stores. She'd already gone shopping with Sophie and Annabelle for a new work wardrobe, but she still needed heavy sweaters and clothes for the change in climate. Even if shopping hadn't been a necessity, keeping busy was. Anything to stop her from thinking about John Roper and the media circus that was a part of his life.

She could fall hard for the man, that much she knew. Never mind that he had one hot body and he'd singed her with kisses that left her wanting more. He was sensitive and he cared for his family, he cooked, for goodness' sake, and he'd decorated his own apartment. Yet what should be a perfect start to a possible relationship wasn't. Everything about John Roper and his life was detrimental to her goals and needs.

She'd grown up with a father who instilled in her the need to make a difference in the world, and her short career as a social worker had been a sure way of doing just that. She understood she was idealizing her dad, but even her mother always spoke of what a good man he'd been. Make your father proud, Amy. She'd tried.

She'd failed.

She'd been let go from her job as a social worker for the state because her mother's antics, captured in the paper with Amy by her side, contradicted the necessary level of decorum her boss insisted went with her job. Instead of looking for other employment, she'd moved back home and taken the position of social director at her mom and aunt's retirement community to watch over them. Surely her father had been nodding in approval over that move.

Her dad had been a stabilizing influence in Rose Stone's life, but after he died, she'd gotten more wild. Uncle Spencer had never tried to control his sisters. They were extremely close to him, as was Amy, but he believed in letting people make their own mistakes. Besides, considering he lived in New York, Amy knew there wasn't much he could do even if he'd tried. So Amy had stepped in, taking over where her father had left off. She could be stern when she needed to be, and she'd had things in Fort Lauderdale well in hand.

She'd bailed her mother and aunt out of the local jail more times than she could count for being a public nuisance. From raucous parties to turning the water in the fountain in the local mall pink in honor of Breast Cancer Awareness Month, Amy's mother and aunt had indulged in an array of bad behavior.

The only reason none of the arrests had resulted in anything more serious than a warning, a fine or community service was because their local judge had a crush on Aunt Darla and Rose baked for the police officers, allowing them to avoid the greasy doughnut shops during their downtime. Amy wasn't a complete stick-in-the-mud and she did find her relatives amusing at times, but she'd always had to be the rational one, the savior. Like Roper, she was the responsible caretaker of the group.

But she had the chance now to make a career for herself even if it wasn't a world-changing job. She needed to make herself, her mother and, by extension, her late father, proud.

Amy sighed and shook her head. She hated being the center of attention, which was why she was so thrilled to be working at the Hot Zone. She'd be the person behind the celebrity. Even if she wanted to give a relationship or even an affair with Roper a chance, his lifestyle demanded anyone in his personal sphere succumb to the media attention. And that was something she wasn't willing to be a part of, especially in the big way his life demanded.

She'd just have to push her intense feelings for the man aside in favor of focusing on work and creating a life for herself here in New York.

With one last glance at the answering machine holding his phone number and the recording of his husky voice asking her to call him, she grabbed her purse and headed for the stores instead.

THE DAY AFTER NEW YEAR'S, Amy sat in the conference room of the Hot Zone offices. All seats around the table were filled and she fidgeted in her seat, ready to begin.

Yank cleared his throat. "The weekly meeting of the Hot Zone and Athletes Only will now come to order." He slammed his gavel down on the table, missing the rubber padding made to cushion the blow. The wooden hammer hit the conference table and Amy felt the vibrations rippling throughout her body. She jumped up from her seat, then discovered she was the only one who had. Micki, Annabelle, Sophie, Lola and even her uncle Spencer had already slid their chairs back, away from the table in anticipation of Yank's move.

Amy's cheeks burned as she lowered herself slowly back into her chair.

"Sorry. We should have warned you he has no aim." Micki, tanned from her time on the island, resettled herself in her chair and the rest of the group did the same.

"And he doesn't care that he's scarring an expensive table," Sophie added.

"Stop talkin' about me like I'm not in the room," Yank muttered. "I'm the one in charge. The meeting's been called to order. As you all can see even if I can't, we have a new member of the team. Amy, we're happy to have you."

"Thank you," Amy said, touched.

"No thanks necessary," Annabelle said.

"Besides, change is good." Lola patted Yank's hand.

"Even if it means I'm getting older and blinder?" he asked.

"Even then," Lola said softly.

"Amen," Uncle Spencer said, probably because he was aging along with his friend, something Amy preferred not to think about too long or too hard.

She remained silent instead, sensing it was the wrong time to interrupt. Even the three sisters remained quiet, letting Yank be comforted by his wife.

Of course the silence didn't last long. "Well, what are you waiting for?" Yank asked, all bluster once more. "First order of business. Michelle?" he asked, calling Micki by her given name.

The first half hour of the meeting consisted of a run-through of current clients, assignments and status updates, along with banter most often begun or finished off by Yank. Amy found the dynamic interesting, considering the family-run business operated smoothly despite it all.

"Now, on to the new assignments," Yank said.

"Amy, we have your first client all lined up," Micki said. "After Spencer came to us with the idea of hiring you, one of the things that impressed us most was your organizational ability. After all, you've spent the past few years single-handedly running the activities at a retirement community where the older residents are cantankerous at worst and difficult at best."

Amy couldn't hold back a laugh. "That's a better description than any I could have come up with."

"Hey, are you picking on us old folks?" Yank asked.

Uncle Spencer rolled his eyes. "It takes one to know one."

"Look who's talking," Yank said to his best friend.

Annabelle rose from her seat. "Grow up, both of you! Micki, go on."

Sophie and Lola applauded while Annabelle re-seated herself.

"Okay, as I was saying, when this assignment came in, we immediately chose you because of your ability to micromanage."

"I'm grateful for your faith in me." Amy rubbed her hands together, the idea of digging into her new job exciting her. "So tell me more."

Micki nodded. "We have a client, a baseball player, who is having serious career issues and who needs to focus completely on both the game and on *his* life. Unfortunately he has family complications that are distracting him."

Amy shook her head. "If I didn't know better, I'd think you were talking about John Roper," she said, without really meaning it.

But every last person at the table turned their gaze her way.

Oh, no, Amy thought. Not Roper. Somehow she

managed not to say the words aloud. She couldn't. Whoever the client was, Amy had no choice but to accept him with a smile. It was her first day, her first assignment, and she could not afford to act like a prima donna.

"So it *is* John Roper?" Amy asked.

All heads at the table nodded.

"Okay, then." She pasted on her brightest smile. "At least it's someone I already know." Thank goodness nobody at the table knew just how well she'd almost come to know Roper.

"That's what we thought," Micki said, obviously pleased with the business pairing.

"Although, if you aren't comfortable…" Sophie's voice trailed off, her offer clear. The other woman obviously sensed now, as she'd indicated at the party the other night, that Amy's history with Roper might make it uncomfortable for her to work with him.

Amy shook her head. "It's fine. I'm fine." Nobody at the table knew she'd spent the night at Roper's place New Year's Eve.

A knock sounded on the conference-room door and her uncle Spencer's secretary, Frannie, walked in. "I'm sorry for interrupting but I have news that can't wait."

"Come on in and let's hear it," Annabelle said, gesturing with her hands. "Something juicy, I hope?"

Micki leaned over and whispered to Amy. "Frannie gets the morning papers and fills us in with anything we need to know about our clients that the press got their teeth into first."

"Got it," Amy said, nodding.

"You, my dear, have *arrived*." Frannie strode over to Amy, taking her by complete surprise. "Photograph and articles."

"Excuse me?" Amy asked, confused.

"Page Six in the *New York Post!*" Frannie exclaimed.

"Get out! What are you holding back?" Annabelle asked Amy. At the same time, Micki snatched the paper from Frannie's hands and began riffling through it.

The other woman, Amy noticed, had a second copy beneath her arm.

"What is on Page Six?" Amy finally managed to ask.

"Only the premier source of celebrity gossip in New York City," Lola pointed out, her voice calm in the midst of the sisters' excitement.

Amy thought she might throw up. "Celebrity?" A sick feeling settled in the pit of her stomach as the memory of the flashing cameras outside Roper's apartment came back to her, more vivid than ever.

"Liz Smith and Cindy Addams's columns are featured there," Sophie said. "What does it say about Amy?"

"Quit keepin' it to yourself," Yank ordered.

Their curiosity piqued, everyone seemed oblivious to Amy's anxiety. Everyone except her uncle Spencer, who glanced at her through worried eyes.

Micki began to read aloud. "What troubled Renegades player needs a distraction from his problematic moves on the field? On New Year's Eve, hottie John Roper forgot his troubles with a lady friend who is surprisingly not of the garden-variety sexpots he normally dates. Who is she and is it serious? Considering this photo was taken outside Roper's apartment building on New Year's Day and the woman was wearing very comfortable clothes, *anything* is possible. Stay tuned."

At least they hadn't mentioned her by name, Amy thought.

"Anything else?" Annabelle asked.

She wanted more?

"The *Daily News* picked up the piece and ran with it." Frannie pushed her glasses farther up on her nose and began to read. "'John Roper is numbing his pain in the arms of a woman. Amy Stone, a Florida transplant and the newest member of the Hot Zone team, was caught sneaking out of his apartment building New Year's Day wearing nothing more than sweats and high heels from their aborted soiree at the Hot Zone the night before. A new year, a new relationship and maybe a *renewed* career. I say, "Go for it, Johnny!"'"

Yank snickered.

Amy winced. She'd been trying to forget the incident, going so far as to give up on the outfit she'd left with him. Thanks to the New York press, she was big-time news. She might even have outdone her mother and aunt, and that was saying something.

"What's the original source?" Sophie asked.

"Gawkerstalker.com." Frannie offered her copy of the paper to Amy.

She shook her head.

"Even though we didn't invite the press to the party, I'm guessing someone saw Roper outside the office after the fire alarm went off and called it in. Either they were followed back to Roper's apartment or they found the information on the Web site and staked out his building hoping for a story."

"Well, they got one," Amy muttered. "What is gawkerstalker.com?" she asked.

"A celebrity-sighting Web site. People e-mail, text message or call in celebrity sightings," Micki explained.

"You're kidding. I didn't know there was such a thing."

"Celebs are big news, and in New York, athletes are prime targets, too. In fact, there's one more mention," Frannie said.

"Let's get it over with, please," Amy said, resigned.

The older woman cleared her throat and silence settled over the room. "We're not the only ones who keep up with Page Six. Frank Buckley picked up the story, too."

"Buckley is Roper's number-one nemesis," her uncle explained.

Frannie nodded. "I downloaded his comments from his Web site. He says, 'Premier sports agents Spencer Atkins and Yank Morgan may have one helluva time unloading Roper to any team this off-season, and not just because of his poor playing skills. But if his New Year's Eve activities are any indication, Roper's only interested in one kind of game.'"

"Poor playing skills, my ass," Spencer said, jumping up from the table. "The man still had a batting average of 290, thirty-five home runs and 121 RBIs, even with his problems. He's got a no-trade clause and he's not going anywhere," he said, then lowered himself back into his seat.

That was her uncle, Amy thought. Yank might bluster but Spencer spoke when he had something deliberate and calculated to say. She wondered what he'd have to say to her. Then again, considering his hands-off approach to her mother, maybe he'd forgo the lecture.

Sophie spoke, calming the room. "I suggest we all settle down and discuss things calmly and rationally."

Lola grabbed the gavel before Yank could second the motion with a smashing blow.

"Does anyone else have anything to add?" Sophie asked.

Yank rose to his feet again, and for the first time Amy realized his brightly patterned shirt clashed with his brown pants. He must have fought Lola on helping him, she thought. Pride was a valued commodity and Amy could understand holding on to it at any cost.

Right now hers was in shreds.

"Uncle Yank, it's your turn," Sophie said, obviously having taken control of the meeting.

Amy wondered if she did the firing. The memory of losing her social-worker job was still clear in her mind.

"I don't like none of this," he said, shaking his head.

Here it comes, Amy thought, nausea rolling through her.

"There's no reason for the reporter who wrote that article to give me second billing to that yahoo," Yank grumbled, pointing at Spencer. "Athletes Only's a Morgan Atkins production. Not vice versa."

"Sit down and shut up," Lola said, grabbing his arm and pulling him back into his seat. "This isn't about you and your mammoth ego."

"No, it's about me and I want to apologize to all of you," Amy said. "I know I've humiliated this firm by getting involved with a client. If you want to let me go, I completely understand."

Without warning, Yank burst out laughing. "What's to apologize for? You didn't do anything different from any of my other girls."

All three sisters nodded in agreement.

"Amy," Micki said, walking over and placing an arm around Amy's shoulder. "You didn't cause trouble for the firm. In fact, you single-handedly changed public opinion about John Roper."

"How so?" she asked, now thoroughly confused by their reaction.

"I've been trying to get Roper to act up again and

take the spotlight off the World Series disaster. You did it without even trying! And the paper is right. You're nothing like the bimbos he usually hangs out with, which lets people see him in a new light. A more respected light, even." Micki's grin said more than her words ever could about how she felt about the situation.

There were murmurs of agreement from around the table.

Amy narrowed her gaze, confounded by the entire morning. She didn't understand New York celebrity at all, but she'd better get a handle on it and fast because her job depended on just that.

"Amy, your client is waiting for you in your office."

She blinked, the pronouncement taking her off guard. "You still want me to work with Roper?"

"Of course! You're still perfect for the job," Micki assured her.

"Uncle Spencer?" Amy glanced at her uncle, needing his affirmation more than ever.

He nodded. "You're our girl," he said with confidence.

Her heart filled, thanks to their support, but pounded hard in her chest with the knowledge that she'd been firmly placed in Roper's universe. Still, no matter how difficult she'd find keeping her distance from the man on a personal level, compartmentalizing was what she did best.

She had no doubt she could handle the job of organizing his life. She only hoped she could handle John Roper.

AFTER THE MEETING ADJOURNED, Micki followed her uncle to the break room. Refusing help, he'd had his assistant bring Noodle to him and let the dog bark and woof her way to where the food was located before Micki took charge and led them both to his office. They sat side by side on the comfortable couch he'd had since she was a little girl who'd come to live with him when her parents died. Unlike her sisters, she'd follow him around, and even insisted he bring her to work. This place had always been in her heart.

"Well, well, well," Uncle Yank said. "Exciting morning."

Micki nodded. "Poor Amy. She doesn't understand New York and what it means to be an athlete here."

Micki herself had been baptized by fire into the New York PR world. Micki felt awful about the unplanned coverage, but if Amy was going to survive here, she'd have to weather storms like this. Especially if she was going to get involved with Roper. The man was a media magnet.

Not that Micki knew the extent of their relationship. Roper hadn't mentioned that Amy had spent the night at his place New Year's Eve, but Micki understood why. Roper was nothing if not a gentleman.

She turned to her uncle. "Roper never mentioned the papers when he stopped by early this morning, so I'm sure he hasn't seen the articles yet." Because he'd been solely focused on Amy, Micki thought.

"He probably figured a bigger story would hit and make him old news before the photos were ever published," Yank said.

"Probably." Micki stood and paced the office, taking in the awards on the walls and photographs of her uncle and famous athletes he'd represented over the years—including one of Roper the day he'd signed his multimillion-dollar contract with the Renegades. "I feel bad that Amy's upset, but you have to admit that the media talking about Roper's love life and not his career is exactly what he needs right now."

Yank snickered. "The boy needs more than that. But you're right. It's a good start. I knew you'd come around to my way of thinkin'."

Her uncle was referring to his notion of setting up Roper and Amy. After he'd decided on that course, he'd gone to Micki for help. But having been on the receiving end of her uncle's matchmaking schemes, Micki had refused, despite the fact that she believed the two would make a great couple. Micki wanted nothing more than to see her best friend settled and happy just as she was with Damian.

But she wouldn't meddle. "I didn't come around to your way of thinking. I just happen to think assigning Amy to Roper works for the business." That it would work for them personally, as well, was a bonus. Or so Micki told herself when she'd paired them as a business team—the idea occurring to her just this morning while Roper was questioning her about Amy Stone, his interest clear.

Her uncle laughed. "Either way, the result's the same. They're together. Nature can do the rest."

AMY WALKED INTO HER OFFICE only to find it empty. She returned to check back with Kelly, the receptionist she shared with one of the other publicists. "Good morning again," Amy said.

Before she could ask, the woman handed her a stack of pink message notes. "These are for you," Kelly said with a smile.

Amy narrowed her gaze. "I don't know many people in town and this is my first day. What gives?"

"You're experiencing your fifteen minutes of fame. The papers want to interview you. Mind if I give you a suggestion?" the other woman asked.

"I'm all ears," Amy said, wanting any help she could get.

Kelly leaned closer, her bangs falling over her eyes as she leaned in, and whispered, "Ignore them."

Amy blinked. "That's it? That's the magic formula?"

"That and praying for some other athlete to make a scene or screw up so he replaces you and Roper in the headlines." Kelly nodded sagely.

"Got it. Speaking of Roper, did he—"

"Leave a message? Yes, he did. Here." She handed

Amy a white envelope with her name written on the front. "He was waiting patiently until he got an urgent phone call. Then he asked for paper to leave you a note and rushed out." Apparently her new secretary was the epitome of efficiency.

Amy was grateful something was going right today. "Thank you, Kelly."

"That's my job. Oh, you have a lunch date at 1:00 p.m. today at Sparks. It's a steak house on Forty-Sixth between Second and Third. Since that's prime lunch hour and we're farther uptown, you might want to give yourself some time to get there. Would you prefer cab, car or subway?" Kelly asked, pen in hand, ready to tackle anything.

Florida girl that she was, Amy wasn't ready to take on the NYC subway system just yet. "I'll just go down and grab a cab."

Kelly rolled her pen between her palms. "No, never mind, that won't work. You might not get one at that hour. I'll make sure a car is waiting." She placed her hand on the phone, obviously ready to do just that.

"It seems like an extravagance to take a car for lunch," Amy said.

"We bill it to the client. It's fine, really. SOP," Kelly said.

"SOP?"

"Standard operating procedure."

Amy smiled. "Got it. It looks as if you have everything covered except for one thing."

"What's that?" Kelly glanced up at her, surprised. "Who am I meeting for lunch?"

Kelly tapped her head with her hands. "I didn't mention that? Roper. It's all in the note he left. Since he couldn't have his business meeting with you due to a family emergency, he said he wanted to take you for lunch and do it there."

"Aah." Family emergency. Amy glanced at her watch. At 11:00 a.m. in the morning. Apparently Roper needed her even more than she realized.

"Take a paper and pen to lunch," Kelly said. "Make notes so you don't forget anything. Not that I'm suggesting you're forgetful, but if it were *me* having a business lunch with that perfect specimen, I'm sure I wouldn't remember anything he said. And I'm pretty on-the-ball," Kelly said, laughing.

Amy grinned. "That you are, and something tells me I'm going to need your expertise during this transition period."

"Did anyone tell you that Rachel, the other publicist I work for, is out on maternity leave? I'm all yours for the next three months."

And Kelly seemed eager to help, for which Amy was grateful. "That's even more good news."

"Do you need me to join you at lunch?" Kelly asked hopefully. "I could hold Roper's hand. I mean, I could hold *your* hand." Her eyes twinkled with mischief and Amy chuckled.

"I think I can handle it," Amy said.

Those words were becoming her mantra.

"You're definitely lucky. The man is one hot property," Kelly said, returning her focus to her ringing phone.

Amy remembered his lips on hers and merely nodded in agreement. Hot property. Yep, Roper was definitely that and more. Keeping her mind on *business* during lunch was going to be *very* difficult.

ROPER ARRIVED AT SPARKS a few minutes early and the maître d' led him to his favorite table, a private one in the corner where he and Amy wouldn't be disturbed by prying eyes. It was bad enough his sister had called crying, begging him to meet her at her apartment. She'd been beyond upset. He couldn't understand the reason for her hysteria, but he'd scrawled an apology note for Amy all the same and headed to the SoHo loft she shared with her fiancé, Kevin. There he discovered the breakdown had been caused by a distraught message from their mother, threatening to come to New York and take over the wedding plans if Sabrina didn't start returning her calls.

Roper could understand his sister not wanting their mother in control of her life. Even more, he could relate to Sabrina's fear of having Her Highness show up on their doorstep. Roper adored his mother, but he loved the fact that she lived in L.A. even more. She still managed to do her share of driving him crazy, but at least it was from a distance. Still, as much as he understood Sabrina's feelings, he wished she'd called Kevin home from work for sympathy instead of him.

She'd pulled him away from Amy. Roper hadn't known Amy was working at the Hot Zone. In fact, the more he thought about his night with her, the more he realized he'd been the one to reveal things about his family and his life while she'd listened, not giving away much about herself at all.

He was glad. For one thing, she remained a mystery he could unravel at his leisure. For another, if he'd known she would end up in his life in such a big way, he'd probably have had second thoughts about getting involved. This way, he was already hooked and he wanted her too much to back out now.

He owed his best friend for assigning Amy as his handler, although he hadn't thought he really needed one. Then again, he did need someone to organize his life, lightening his load so he could concentrate on recovering enough to make it to spring training in February. Micki had made the right call by assigning him Amy. A win-win situation, just the way he liked it.

Not knowing whether she liked red wine or white, he decided on champagne. He thought twice about splurging on Dom Pérignon, then decided his bank account could take the hit. Amy was worth it. The champagne on ice was waiting for her when she joined him at the table.

He wasn't surprised, when his cell phone rang, to find his mother was on the other end. "Good morning," he said, refusing to let his good mood dissipate.

"Hi, darling, how are you?"

"Not bad, considering I spent the morning calming Sabrina down. Do you think you could let her plan her own wedding?" He didn't hold out much hope he'd get through to her, but it couldn't hurt to try.

"What daughter doesn't really want her mother involved in the most important day of her life?" his mother asked.

He leaned back in his seat. "She wants you involved, not taking over."

"I'm just making helpful suggestions." She sniffed. "It's my only daughter's wedding. Can't you just talk to her and explain I love her and want what's best?"

"What's best is what makes Sabrina and Kevin happy." He looked up and saw Amy at the front of the restaurant, handing her coat to the check girl. "I have to go, my lunch date's here."

"Not that crazy agent of yours?" his mother asked.

She'd met Yank on one of her trips to the city. There'd never been two different people placed on this planet, he thought, laughing. "No, with Amy Stone."

"Your Page Six girl!"

He winced. "I didn't know you read the *New York Post* in L.A."

Her light laugh traveled through the phone line. "Darling, you rushed me off the phone New Year's Eve and Ben sent me the *Post*. I put two and two together. You should have told me you were in a new relationship. Where are you taking her?" she asked.

He rolled his eyes and raised a hand, waving at Amy as she approached. "I'm at Sparks. On business. Bye, Mom. Love you." He snapped his phone shut and rose to greet Amy.

"Hi, there," he said, taking in her business attire and trying not to drool at the sight.

She wore a cream-colored pantsuit that accentuated her tanned skin, and though she'd clipped her hair back, soft curls framed her face, giving her a tailored yet sexy look. Micki had mentioned that Annabelle had taken Amy shopping for a New York work wardrobe and he applauded both women's taste. On Amy, the pantsuit looked feminine, especially when paired with pointy-toed shoes peeking out beneath the hem of the slacks. Beneath the tailored suit jacket, instead of a blouse she wore a V-necked three-button vest cut low enough to tempt and dazzle, but covered enough to be appropriate for work. Business casual and chic—Amy had made the transition from Florida native to New Yorker in no time.

And even dressed for the office, she managed to turn him on.

CHAPTER FIVE

AMY WALKED THROUGH SPARKS, the steak house chosen by Roper for their lunch, and found herself taken in by the old-boy charm of the establishment. She appreciated the decor and she tried to focus on that—on anything except the man watching her intently as she approached.

Roper rose as she came closer and waited until she was seated and they were alone before settling back in. "I'm glad you could join me," he said, his voice warm and welcoming.

"I'm glad, too." She placed her napkin on her lap and took a second to cover her stomach with her hand, hoping to ease the butterflies inside, made worse because the car ride had taken longer than it should have. The vice president was in town, roads were closed and *gridlock* was the word of the day. "I'm sorry I'm late. The traffic was horrendous."

"Not a problem. It gave me time to relax a little first." He glanced down and pulled his phone from a holder at his waist. "Excuse me. Phone call." He answered, had a quick conversation that sounded much like the one she'd heard New Year's Eve with his mother, before meeting her gaze once more. "Sorry, that was my sister," he said, placing his phone on the table.

"No problem." She clasped her hands together, thinking that his family most definitely *was* his problem.

"Where was I? Oh, yes. I'm glad you're here and I ordered us champagne." He inclined his head to the side of the table, and for the first time she noticed the ice bucket and the bottle chilling inside.

Memories of New Year's Eve rose quickly and vividly in her mind before she could shut them out. But she couldn't concentrate on business if she was busy remembering how soft and moist his lips had felt on hers or how the intoxicating scent of his cologne had wrapped around her, enveloping her in heat.

She cleared her throat. "It's a working lunch," she reminded him, hating that she sounded stiff, but knowing it was necessary.

"And we will work. But first—" he treated her to a sexy smile "—I'd like to toast our new relationship."

"Relationship?" The word came out more like a squeak.

"Working relationship." A teasing sparkle lit his gaze. "Isn't that why we're here?"

She exhaled hard. "I'd love to toast. I just can't promise to drink."

"Still recovering from New Year's?" he asked.

She shook her head. "I'm over it. I mean—"

"I understand what you meant." He laughed and leaned forward in his seat. "And if you'd just relax around me, I won't even ask why you haven't returned any of my calls."

Her cheeks grew uncomfortably hot. "I needed to distance my work and my personal relationships."

"Which I might have understood if you'd called me back and explained. Or if you'd told me you were working at the Hot Zone to begin with." He gestured to the waiter, who began to unwrap, uncork and pour the champagne.

"The subject of where I was working never came up. But I admit not returning your phone calls was a little cowardly of me. I'm sorry."

"And I'm sorry about the reporters and the articles in today's paper." His normally easygoing smile disappeared, replaced by obvious regret. "I have no idea how they zeroed in on us after New Year's and I certainly never thought they'd make us newsworthy. I took a private booth back here, so hopefully we're safe from prying eyes."

His cell phone buzzed suddenly, shaking on the table and breaking the connection subtly flowing between them. Although he'd set the phone to vibrate, the intrusion was just as noticeable.

Shooting her an apologetic glance, he picked up the phone. This time, however, his tone was different, brittle even. "Bad time. I'm busy. I'll call you later." He disconnected the call and placed the phone back on the table.

She met his gaze. "Your brother."

He nodded. "You're astute."

"I just remembered what you told me the other night. Where does he live?"

"Nowhere permanent. Right now he's staying with a friend not too far from here."

"So all three of you are in the city."

He nodded. "We love our mother, but distance seems to work best for all of us," he said, laughing.

"Speaking of your mother, I suppose she's going to call next?" she asked.

He groaned. "Probably, but I'd rather not think about her right now. So back to New Year's... I'm sorry for the press showing up like that. If I'd known, I'd have taken you out the back or used my car so they never would have gotten a shot of you in the first place."

"Apparently I need to get used to the New York media. According to the rest of the office, the articles about us did you a favor by directing everybody's attention to your personal life instead of your career." She raised an eyebrow, curious about his view on their joint minutes of fame.

He burst out laughing, a response she didn't expect.

"That's rich," he said. "Eight months ago, those same Hot Zone people wanted my personal life out of the papers. Now they're applauding the coverage." Without warning, he reached over and placed his hand over hers.

The heat was immediate and intense.

"But you don't deserve the publicity." His voice grew low and husky. "So I am sorry."

"I thought, as a publicist, I'd be remaining behind the scenes. But it's fine. Really." She waved away his apology, trying to act in control and, oh, so nonchalant over the incident, which at the moment affected her less than the man himself.

Ever since their first meeting, it didn't take more than a touch to remind her of how easily he could seduce her with a look, a glance or a simple gesture. She'd never had such an immediate connection with a man before and she didn't know how to ignore the sparks that sizzled between them now.

"Okay, then, it looks as if once again we're starting over," he said, pleased. He lifted his hand off of hers and raised his glass.

Relieved he wasn't touching her anymore and disappointed at the same time, she lifted her glass.

"To us," he said simply.

Unable and unwilling to argue, she repeated his words. "To us."

She took a polite sip and placed the champagne back on the table. They looked through the menu, then listened to the daily specials. She ordered a mixed green salad and rainbow trout, he chose oysters on the half shell and prime sirloin steak.

She studied him as he spoke to the waiter. Roper was a man comfortable in his own skin and too handsome in his tan-and-white-striped dress shirt,

opened at the throat. He might be suffering personally and professionally, but he hid it well. She
guessed his years of dealing with the press had given
him a thick skin. Personally, she'd never had one
herself. She wasn't surprised he'd ordered steak and
opted not to read too much into his choice of appe-
tizer, assuring herself it was only *her* mind that was
on aphrodisiacs and sex, not his.

After the waiter walked away, she folded her
hands and decided to hit on the reason for their lunch.
"I understand you need my services to clear out the
clutter in your life so that you can better focus on
your career."

He tipped his head and nodded. "That's one way
of putting it."

Micki had told her she'd be his handler, but somehow she didn't think he'd appreciate the term, which
implied he needed babying. "Well, you'll be happy to
know I've given your situation some thought already."

It helped that she'd spent New Year's with him
and seen his family dynamics firsthand. The phone
calls today had merely cemented her earlier impression. Taking her secretary's advice, she pulled a notepad and pen from her large handbag. "Let's start by
listing the things or people in your life causing you
to get sidetracked. If we tackle and eliminate them one
by one, that will leave your mind clear for baseball."

Roper raised an eyebrow, amused by her suggestion. "You think you can take on my family and
eliminate their issues?"

"If they're the sole source of your distraction, I know I can." Her eyes were on fire with determination.

He pictured Amy, petite in stature but not personality, dealing with his larger-than-life, never-take-no-for-an-answer mother, and he glanced heavenward for strength.

"You start talking. Tell me more about each family member and their main problem, why they need your attention constantly each day. I'll take notes and put together a plan." She raised her pen, ready to write.

No sooner had he chuckled than his cell phone vibrated once more. He glanced at the number, shot Amy a you-were-right look, and felt more certain than ever that not only was Amy outnumbered, but she'd be outmaneuvered in a matter of days.

He spoke quickly, then disconnected the call.

"Third call in…" She looked at her watch. "Ten minutes. No wonder you can't find time to get healthy. You're mentally and physically drained by the forces around you."

"*Force* is a good word to describe my mother," he mused.

She held out her hand. "Give it over."

"What?" He hadn't a clue what she was talking about.

"Hand the cell phone over. And the BlackBerry."

"It's a Treo and you may not have either one," he said, shocked by her gall.

She withdrew her hand. "Fine. Then shut them off.

Vibrate's not cutting it. You're at a business lunch and common courtesy dictates you keep your mind on business."

He grinned, finally getting it. "Aah, it's my attention you want," he said in a cocky tone. "I can assure you that even if I answer the phone, my thoughts are solely on you, babe."

She rolled her eyes. "Did you forget why we're here? To organize your life. To make sure you learn how to compartmentalize and make baseball your priority again. So it's your choice. Shut them off or hand them over," she insisted, not backing down.

Roper glanced at Amy's fiery brown eyes and determined expression and realized she was deadly serious. Who knew the woman was a ballbuster?

Who knew he'd like that in a woman?

The last female who'd demanded that he put her first had been pushing for a ring. And since he'd been as interested in a commitment with her as he'd been in the blond highlights his hairdresser had been trying to talk him into, he'd bought her a diamond bracelet goodbye gift and broken things off.

"Well? Choose one or I'm walking away from this assignment." And in case he wasn't sure she meant business, she turned and reached for her purse hanging from the back of her chair.

Damn, she was cute when she was being bossy.

He shocked himself by turning both his phone and Treo off, pushing them to the side of the table and focusing completely, solely on her. "I'm all yours."

"Good. That's how it should be." She swallowed hard, obviously not as at ease around him as she wanted him to believe.

Their attraction was something neither could ignore. He could let her have the upper hand when it came to their professional relationship, but he had no doubt that sexually, he was in control.

And he intended to make use of the upper hand. When the time was right.

"Let's hear your game plan."

The waitress served their appetizers, and while they ate, she outlined her goals. "You have three family members pulling you at all hours of the day. You need to set limits. But first, let's tackle each one of them. Your mother. What is the main reason she's been calling you?" Amy asked. She put a forkful of salad into her mouth, then licked a crumble of blue cheese off her bottom lip with her tongue, wreaking havoc with his attention.

He stared at her moist lips, moving as she delicately chewed her food.

She met his gaze. Obviously embarrassed, she cleared her throat. "Your mother?" she reminded him.

"Right." He paused to suck an oyster from its shell. The food might be considered an aphrodisiac, but Amy supplied all the arousal power he needed. "Other than asking me to lend Ben money?" Which he was sure she would have done again on the phone today if he'd given her more time. "My mother needs a job of her own. Her lifestyle is killing my bank account. And she's bored. She misses acting, not that she's willing to admit as much."

"Hollywood won't hire her because of all the roles she already turned down over the years?" Amy guessed.

He laughed. "Hell, no. Harrison Smith—he's a big-time director—sent her a script for a television pilot over three months ago that was tailor-made for her. He even offered her more money than she deserves at this point in her career."

He shook his head in disbelief. "She said no, but apparently he's waiting for her to change her mind. For some reason, the man only wants Cassandra Lee for the role and has been pursuing her relentlessly."

Amy nodded in understanding. "That's because she's good," Amy said. "What will it take to convince her?"

He shrugged. "She won't change her mind. First, she thinks television is beneath her. But more important, my mother refuses to play the role of a grandmother, no matter how elegant, dignified or perfect the role may be. She thinks spending thousands in plastic surgery and Botox justify her desire to be cast as an ingenue." He shook his head in disgust and frustration. "Sad thing is, she's been saying it to herself for so long, she believes it."

He glanced at Amy, looking for a glimmer of understanding. Heaven only knew why he needed it from her when he'd never wanted it from anyone else. At least she was too busy jotting down notes to realize.

"So tell me more about your brother."

The busboy had cleared their plates, and the waitress set their lunches in front of them. Talking about his family had killed his appetite. "Ben needs a job and a life."

"I've been there," she said with more compassion than he'd afforded his brother lately. "I lived at home for so long it became too comfortable. Maybe that's what's going on with Ben. He just needs the right incentive to get him moving again."

Roper had thought the same thing.

"Does he have any job options? I don't mean investments, but legitimate employment opportunities that you know of?"

Roper took a long sip of water. "His head is so far in the clouds, he wouldn't know an opportunity if it was handed to him. I've offered to make some calls and see if there are any openings as a high school baseball coach in a decent community. He's good enough to teach, he just wasn't solid enough to play pro. Ben won't even consider it."

"When he runs out of money, he'll have no choice. Why don't you give me some leads and I'll see what I can come up with for him."

Roper raised an eyebrow.

"It's my job, remember. Come on."

He rattled off some old ball players he knew were into coaching who might be able to use a guy like Ben. Although he loved his brother, it rankled to have to call in favors knowing Ben wouldn't appreciate the effort and would probably turn down any opportunity Roper uncovered because *he* felt he deserved better.

"Just be prepared. Ben won't make it easy. He'll play the guilt card because I had the father with the talent, while his dad had none. He likes living on pipe dreams of what life owes him, instead of what he could actually do to make it on his own."

Amy jotted down a few more notes. "Delusions of grandeur," she said without glancing up. Her brows were furrowed in concentration and her lips puckered as she wrote. Lips he still wanted to kiss more than he wanted to breathe. But she was working with him now. There would be time.

Neither one of them had eaten much, but he sensed until she finished dissecting his family, she wouldn't be interested in food.

"Are you ready to talk about Sabrina?" she asked.

He leaned back in his chair and stretched. "Sure am. She's the easiest one. My little sister is marrying a great guy. A normal accountant. The wedding is planned for next fall, after my season ends. I'm paying for the big day, but that isn't a problem. I want to pay. She deserves the best. Problem is, she isn't in charge of her own wedding, our mother is. Or at least she wants to be."

"Long distance?"

He nodded.

"Sabrina calls me several times a day with another

of Mom's outlandish ideas, things Sabrina doesn't want but Mom thinks are best. Sabrina wants me to mediate, but frankly, I don't want to do any more than write the damn check."

Amy chuckled. "Typical man."

He grinned. "I tune them out when possible, but if I don't answer the phone right away, they hunt me down. Don't get me wrong. I love them but—"

"They need to live their own lives," Amy finished for him. "But they haven't had to since you've always done everything for them." A few more notes and Amy finally put her pen down and met his gaze. "Got it all," she said, then picked up her knife and fork. "God, I'm starving." She dug into her meal with a gusto he'd never seen in a female.

Just watching her renewed his appetite and they finished their meal in comfortable silence. As soon as their waiter placed the check on the table, he placed his hand on the leather folder.

"I've got it," she said, reaching for the billfold at the same time so their fingers met.

He'd always let Micki pay when they went out for business and he should allow Amy to do the same, especially this first business lunch when he figured she needed to feel in control.

But he let his hand deliberately linger so he could touch her a little longer. "You already talked me into turning off my phone and Treo. Don't add insult to injury by paying the check. My fragile male ego can't handle it."

She laughed. "I don't think your ego has been fragile a day in your life."

"You'd be surprised," he said, sobering. She probably thought the insults from Buckley and the fans rolled off his back. Maybe at one time they would have, but not any longer. He was afraid they were right and he was a washed-up has-been.

Without warning, she slipped her hand from his. "I'll get it next time," she said, leaving him with the distinct impression she did understand the fragile ego thing.

Just as he understood hers. "No, this is business. I don't mind letting the Hot Zone pick up the tab." Before she could get too cocky, he added, "I'll get it on our next date."

She opened her mouth to speak, but he glanced down at the check, ignoring her so she couldn't argue. Because there would be a real date.

She could count on it.

Once the check was paid, he walked her out of the restaurant and onto the street. To his surprise, they'd made it through the meal with only a few stares. No one asked for an autograph or bothered him with stupid questions, like how did it feel to single-handedly blow the series?

He waited as she glanced up the street to locate her driver, then held the car door for her as she climbed inside. He had a physical-therapy appointment downtown so he declined a ride and sent her back uptown alone.

But not before she promised she'd be in touch with a plan to help him reclaim his life. She believed she could fix things for him, and for the first time, he admitted to himself that he needed her to be right.

He'd always been the one taking care of others. No one had ever given much thought to what *he* needed, not because they didn't care, but because they knew he could take care of himself. Even though Amy was only doing what the Hot Zone paid her to do, he appreciated her efforts. He believed she'd do her best, although he had less faith in her ability to get his family under control. It wasn't personal, nor was it a lack of belief in her abilities. He just knew his family, and short of doing their bidding, there was no denying them.

But he was looking forward to seeing Amy try.

HE CALLED IN THE TIP ABOUT Roper's lunch at Sparks Steak House with the niece of Spencer Atkins. He supposed he ought to feel guilty about causing the guy trouble, but Roper's life was already imploding. There was no reason not to help the process along by placing him squarely in the public eye.

He wouldn't want people to forget about Roper or his part in destroying the Renegades' chances of winning the World Series. Not when the man was paid more than anyone else on the team to come up with the ultimate post-season win.

Besides, wasn't it time that the high-and-mighty realized how fragile fame and fortune were? Some people worked hard for their talent. Others thought it was their birthright. Roper was one of the entitled. He took what belonged to others without thought or care. Roper would soon learn otherwise.

He hung up his disposable cell phone and tossed it in the trash. Nobody could trace this call. Celebrities and athletes showed up in papers and columns all the time, but he felt better covering his tracks. He wouldn't want anyone to discover his grudge.

Better to just help Roper's fall from grace anonymously and enjoy the spectacle from a distance.

AMY LEFT THE RESTAURANT on a euphoric high. She knew what she needed to do to help Roper and she had some ideas already to research and implement. On the way back to her office, she stopped by Micki's and ran the plan by her, receiving a thumbs-up in return. She had her secretary following up on some of the coaching possibilities Roper had mentioned for his brother. She felt certain once each of his needy relatives was squared away, they'd leave Roper in peace, allowing him to get back to what he did best.

All he needed was some organization, some direction and a firm, guiding hand. *Her* firm, guiding hand.

She wished she could share her excitement with someone other than her boss, but she hadn't made any real friends in the city yet. So she fell back on the familiar. She called her mother.

Rose answered on the first ring. "Hi, Mom."

"Amy!" her mother said, clearly excited. "Darla, it's Amy!"

Amy could envision her yelling across the small kitchen even though her aunt was always within whispering distance.

"Your aunt Darla sends her love," her mother said.

"Send mine back," Amy said.

"Darla, Amy sends her love right back," Rose yelled.

Amy smiled, a pang of homesickness hitting her despite the fact that she was exactly where she wanted to be. "How are things down South?"

"Bo-o-o-r-ing. It's been raining nonstop. We've seen all the movies playing in theaters. Twice." Her mother let out a long-suffering sigh. "How are things with you?"

"Pretty great." Amy knew better than to tell her mother anything specific about John Roper or she'd be on the next flight out to matchmake. "I have my first client and things are really working out for me here."

"No need to thank me. I knew I was doing the right thing throwing you out of here," her mother said smugly.

"Need I remind you I left on my own?"

"And I must tell you, your replacement is fantastic," her mother said, ignoring her. "Better than fantastic. She's organized daily bingo—for *money*."

Amy winced. Clearly the new director didn't know what she was up against. "There's too much cheating going on to use real prizes." Amy had kept the prizes small and manageable, so nobody would win a jackpot at someone else's expense.

"You're telling me. Marilyn Hornsby stole my card right out from under me and won a jackpot of one hundred and one dollars, the weasel," Rose said.

Her mother went on about the new director and the goings-on in the community. Amy missed them, but she definitely had more of a challenge here. And she couldn't help feeling a sense of peace that came from not being in the center of her mother's world. "I've really got to get back to work now," she explained.

Rose cleared her throat. "I understand. Just make sure your uncle Spencer isn't working you to death or I'll have to have a talk with him."

"Stay out of it," Amy ordered.

"Are you sure?" her mother asked.

"Quite sure. I came here to get a life, not to have you meddle—I mean—interfere in mine. I know you mean well, but no thank you."

"Fine." Her mother sniffed.

Amy grinned. "Stay out of trouble and don't give the new director a reason to quit," Amy warned.

"As if I can possibly cause any trouble. It's boring here, I tell you. She's running the place like a military base," Rose whined.

Amy laughed. "I thought she was wonderful."

"Wonderfully uptight," her mother muttered, the truth coming out.

Amy wasn't surprised her mother had fibbed at first so Amy didn't feel bad for leaving. Or maybe so she would. Knowing her mother, Rose figured if

Amy thought the new director was so perfect, she'd get jealous and run home. She wouldn't put anything past her mother.

"Have you met any nice men?" Rose asked.

"No one in particular." She crossed her fingers as she lied.

Another drawn-out sigh sounded over the phone line. "Leave it to my daughter not to meet men when she works for a sports agency loaded with hotties. Rich hotties."

Amy pinched the bridge of her nose. Definitely time to hang up. "My secretary's calling me. I have to go. I love you, Mom. And I miss you."

"I love you, too. And we miss you. Don't we miss Amy, Darla?"

"We both miss you," Rose said, blowing a loud, smacking kiss through the phone.

Grinning, Amy hung up, and with her mood light, she went back to figuring out how to change John Roper's life.

AFTER ROPER LEFT AMY, he headed straight for the physical therapist's. Taking her cue, he kept his cell phone and his Treo off, and sure enough, got through his physical-therapy appointment uninterrupted. He even fit a short gym session into the day. Amy's solution worked well for him so far.

But by the time he arrived back home, there were no less than half a dozen messages on his answering machine, most of them from his mother. Roper thanked God she lived long-distance or else his life would be more of a hell than it was now. In her messages, his mother managed to hit all of his buttons and he called her back immediately, feeling guilty for taking an entire afternoon to himself.

That's what he got for jumping into the role of man of the family too early in life. His parents' affair had been hot, heavy and had petered out just as fast as it had started, leaving his mother pregnant in an era when women didn't have kids out of wedlock. The beautiful starlet had turned to a man she'd thought would save her. Another impulsive decision, leading to the birth of his siblings. Ben and Sabrina's father soon tired of living with his famous wife and took off, leaving Cassandra with three kids. Though Roper had been young, he'd taken charge. The family had come to rely on him, and he had been the decision-maker and fixer of everyone's problems ever since.

He called his mother back and left a message both at her home and on her phone, hoping that would buy him some peace until morning.

Then he headed for a hot shower. As he stripped and flipped the water on hot, his thoughts turned to Amy, and he changed the temperature to icy cold instead. He wished that the effect she had on his body was all he liked about Amy, but in the short time he'd known her, he'd learned there was so much more. The take-charge attitude he hadn't expected, the understanding of his relationship with his family, her pure determination to succeed in her new job that he could see in her eyes.

Eyes that made him crazy with desire.

He finished showering, dried himself and fell into bed, exhausted.

What seemed like moments later, he woke to the sound of his doorbell ringing. His doorman had a list of approved people to let up, so his uninvited guest had to be someone he knew. A glance at the clock told him he'd crashed all night. It was morning.

He reached for the nearest pair of jeans lying on a chair and made his way to the door. Without coffee, he wasn't ready to see anyone.

He glanced through the peephole and let out a groan. He especially wasn't ready to deal with the woman standing impatiently on the other side. Cassandra Lee had arrived.

CHAPTER SIX

NO SOONER HAD ROPER OPENED his door than his mother barged right in. "Darling!" She presented her cheek for a kiss, which he dutifully gave.

Then he stepped back and looked at her linen pants and blouse, obviously wrinkled from travel. "Did you tell me you were coming and I forgot?" he asked, knowing he'd done no such thing.

She narrowed her gaze. "Don't play games with me, John. You didn't answer your phone, you didn't return my e-mail or text messages, so I'm here." She waved her hands around expressively, ending by cupping his cheek in her hand. "I was worried about you."

He narrowed his gaze, which didn't take much since he was still half-asleep. But mentally, he was now wide-awake. That his mother loved him was fact. That she might have been concerned about his silence also might be true. But no way would she fly across the country just because he hadn't picked up his cell phone.

"What's really going on?" he asked.

"I don't know what you mean. But I do need coffee." She headed for the kitchen, leaving him no choice but to follow after her. "I took the red-eye and I'm exhausted," she said, speaking with dramatic effect as she always did.

She blamed her original drama coach. Roper blamed her love of drama.

She made herself at home in his kitchen, looking through cabinets in her search for caffeine. Finally he took pity on her and opened the correct canister, removed the beans and ground them. Maybe once she had her coffee she'd tell him why she was really here.

Out of habit, he switched on the radio and Buckley the Bastard's voice sounded around him. Though he cringed, he believed in dealing with life as it came. He needed to know what was being said about him if he was to deal with it.

He handed his mother a steaming mug. "So how was your flight?"

"Long." She wrapped her hand around the cup and sighed. "Then to add insult to injury, the airport lost my bags. Of course they promised they'll deliver them as soon as they find them, but who knows when that will be." His mother paused to take a sip of coffee. "Mmm. You always did have the touch." She lowered herself into the nearest chair, obviously exhausted.

But only one word rang in his ears. "Your *bags?* Plural?"

"Well, yes, bags." She tucked her set blond hair

behind one ear, the shoulder-length strands somehow managing to look sophisticated on her and not at all too young despite her best attempt. "How else can I stay indefinitely unless I brought enough clothes? Although New York does have the best stores. Better than L.A., even, and that's saying a lot. I think I'll call my favorite personal shoppers and have them start putting things away for me," she mused.

"What do you mean, you're staying indefinitely?" Roper felt a blinding headache coming on.

She placed her cup down and stared at him as if he were the crazy one. "Darling, your sister is getting married and she needs her mother to help her. And of course, you're going through a career crisis of your own."

"Thanks for reminding me," he muttered.

"Not to worry. Mother's here." She treated him to her brightest smile.

That's what he was afraid of.

"This just in." Frank Buckley's voice spoke into the silence. "Guess who had lunch at Sparks Steak House yesterday? Nice that our friend John Roper has time for wining and dining his new lady when he should be getting ready for the season." The man waited a deliberate beat. "But that's a high-paid athlete for you. No sense of responsibility. The Buck Stops Here, folks."

"Son of a bitch." Roper bristled at the report and accusation. "Who the hell called it in?" he asked.

"It could have been anyone from a waiter to a

patron," his mother said, rising and putting her arm around him. "You know what it's like to be a celebrity. You grew up under a microscope. Let it go."

He twisted his neck from side to side, releasing tension. He wished it was as easy as his mother said. "I just don't like feeling as if my every move is being tracked and scrutinized," he muttered.

"It's part of the life," his mother said.

"The difference between us is that you enjoy it. I just want to play baseball."

His doorbell rang, cutting off whatever his mother might have replied.

He pinched the bridge of his nose. "Who knows you're here?" Roper asked her, resigned to more company. "Ben? Sabrina? One of your actress friends you charmed the doorman into letting up without my okay?" He saw his privacy going down the drain.

His mother shrugged, her gaze wide-eyed and innocent. "Actually, no one. When I couldn't reach you, I packed and headed straight for the airport."

He headed back to the front door and peered through the viewer, needing advanced warning of the person he'd be dealing with next. One look and his mood lifted. This was someone he didn't want to disappear.

Roper opened the door, welcoming Amy, an addition Roper himself had made to his doorman's list. "Thank God," he said, pulling her inside.

He needed someone on his side when dealing with the steamroller he called his mother.

"Strange welcoming but I'll take it." Her smile broadened, easing his strain.

"Not so strange. You aren't a member of my family, so I'm glad you're here." He shut the door behind her and drank in the sight of her.

Dark denim jeans covered her legs like a second skin, while a deep indigo top with bell sleeves floated around her, belted at the waist. Only a hint of a lace tank peeked out from beneath the flowing top. Once again she looked work appropriate and yet so damn sexy, he didn't care that his mother was in the other room.

"So what brings you by?" he asked.

"Well, first the doorman asked me to give you this," she said, handing him an oversize envelope with a handwritten scrawl he recognized as belonging to his most persistent fan. And not a fan in love with him, either.

Ever since the end of the series in October, Roper had been receiving letters and packages from a fan who called himself Season Ticket Holder, a not-so-veiled reference to the fact that he expected more results for his money than Roper had provided.

"Thanks for bringing up my mail," he said, not wanting to make a big deal of the letter and draw attention to the fact that he had someone determined to remind him of his failures. He accepted the envelope from Amy and tossed it aside.

"You're welcome. Now, I'm here because I have a plan." Amy's eyes glittered with excitement. "I was up late working on a way to organize your life and give you the time you need. I really think you're going to be impressed."

"Who's at the door?" his mother called, her voice coming closer with every word she spoke.

"Your sister?" Amy whispered.

He shook his head. "Worse."

At that moment, Cassandra Lee joined them in all her dramatic glory. "John, aren't you going to introduce me to your—"

"Mom, this is Amy Stone, Amy this is my mother, Cassandra Lee," he said, cutting her off before she could draw any conclusions about who Amy was. No way was he playing "fill in the blanks" with his mother.

Amy's eyes opened wide. Clearly she hadn't been expecting to find the movie star in the flesh. To Amy's credit, she recovered quickly and stepped forward, her hand extended. "I'm a huge fan," she admitted. "It's wonderful to meet you. John's told me so much about you!"

"All of it good, of course?" his mother said, lightly clasping Amy's hand.

"Is there anything else?" Amy asked, working his mother like a pro. "I had no idea you were coming to town."

"That's because John didn't know, either. I just love surprises and I missed my children." Her gaze darted away from Amy's just enough for Roper to know his mother was lying.

Just enough. Because Cassandra Lee was an accomplished actress, only her son would have caught the slip.

"I'm sure you know John's sister is planning a wedding and she needs my help," his mother continued.

Unfortunately for him, it didn't matter why his mother was here. Only that she'd arrived and planned on staying. Which meant what little peace and quiet he had, which admittedly wasn't much, was now over.

He had one source of salvation and she just happened to have arrived at the right moment. He wondered if Amy could save him from his family or if she just believed she could. He supposed he'd know soon enough.

Amy met John's gaze over his mother's head. He winked at her, but in his eyes, she saw the plea for help. She had to admit being needed by him was seductive, even if it was her job to keep his mother out of his way.

She'd planned on talking to him about his brother, but she could adapt to the unexpected. Surely even a famous actress had to be easier to deal with than the perpetually naked residents she dealt with back in Florida.

"I'm exhausted after traveling all night. Would you mind if we got to know each other later? I need to lie down." Without waiting for a reply, Cassandra started for the guest room down the hall.

"Wait!" Amy strode up to her. "You don't want to stay here, do you? John gets up early in the morning. Wouldn't a hotel suite be more comfortable? You'd have room service day or night, turn-down service in the evening and a full staff to make you more comfortable," Amy said, finishing on a winded breath.

Cassandra's eyes lit up at her suggestion. "That's a wonderful idea. John, wherever did you find her?" his mother asked.

Amy glanced at Roper, whose tight smile had turned into a full-fledged grin. A sexy grin, not that she wanted to admit as much.

"I work for the Hot Zone," Amy said.

He walked over and slung a casually draped arm over her shoulder. "Isn't she the best?" Roper asked.

"I must admit she's got more on the ball than the usual women you associate with." Cassandra looked Amy over with practiced ease.

She tried not to fidget under the scrutiny or imagine how she came up short compared to the other women in Roper's life. A New York makeover could only go so far....

As if sensing her discomfort, Roper pulled her closer. His body aligned with hers, bare chest and all. Heat shot upward as his masculine morning scent wrapped around her, making her tingle.

She swallowed hard, then cleared her throat. "Well, why don't I go make that hotel reservation?"

"Good idea, but not the Ritz Carlton or the

Waldorf. I prefer the London NYC. Their staff is my favorite. Book me one of their specialty suites."

"Mother, you do not need twenty-two-hundred square feet of space for a short stay. Book her a Vista Suite."

"A two-bedroom," Cassandra countered.

"Fine," Roper said through clenched teeth.

Obviously this was a vintage performance by his mother.

"Please ask if Chef Gordon Ramsay is in town. If so, invite him to dinner. We're old friends," she said, as if Amy were her assistant.

Amy accepted the direction with a nod, and his mother continued to instruct Amy on her likes and preferences. She wished she had her pen and paper ready.

"When you call, you may tell them who I am, but put the reservation under John's name and ask them not to let *anyone* know I'm there."

Amy nodded. Another celebrity quirk she assumed. One that would get Cassandra Lee the perks due her by virtue of her name but assure her some privacy at the same time.

Desiring anonymity with the media was something Amy could understand. "No problem. Anything else?"

Cassandra shook her head. "No, I'll talk to them when I arrive and make sure I have what I need, but thank you. You're a doll."

Roper squeezed Amy's forearm lightly, which she took as a show of appreciation.

A few phone calls and no less than three interruptions later, Amy had arranged for a Vista Suite that overlooked Central Park with extra-special service to compensate for the fact that the two-bedroom rooms were booked, lucky for Roper. She hired a limousine to pick Cassandra up and drive her over, with a stop at Saks on the way so she could pick up some clothes to tide her over until her suitcases were found.

And thirty minutes after that, Roper's mother was gone in a flurry of air kisses and promises to call after she'd napped and taken a refreshing bath. It was only 10:00 a.m.

Roper collapsed on the couch in the living room, patting the space beside him.

"Your mother is a living, breathing tornado," Amy said, flopping down next to him.

"Welcome to my world. Yet you handled her like a pro." Awe tinged his voice as he tipped his head to one side.

She met his gaze and tried not to read more into the molten stare than gratitude, but it was hard. The problem for Amy was more than attraction. She liked doing things for him. She enjoyed helping him and being successful at it. And she definitely liked it when he looked at her with those bedroom eyes that held promises she just knew he was capable of keeping.

"It's what I'm paid to do," she reminded herself, and him. Too bad she wasn't listening.

"And you did it well."

She didn't miss the sudden drop in his tone. The husky sound had her heart skipping a beat.

"Now, about that date…"

The one she'd refused to think about since he'd mentioned it at lunch the day before.

He stretched his arm over the couch, not so subtly reaching her shoulders with his fingertips. She recognized the practiced move for what it was and shot him a knowing look he ignored.

She wished she could do the same with his suggestion they go on a date. "It isn't a good idea to mix business with pleasure," she told him.

"I couldn't agree more."

She grew immediately wary. "You agree with me?"

He nodded. "Of course I do. Business is business. That's what you did for me this morning and that's what we'll discuss in a few minutes. Our date will be personal. We won't mix the two at all."

She rolled her eyes, unable to hold back a laugh. "That's ass-backwards logic." But a damn good attempt at manipulating her into saying yes, she silently admitted.

He chuckled. "I'll pick you up tomorrow night at eight?"

"I don't remember saying yes."

"I don't remember you saying no, either. So tell me, what brings you by?" he said as if that settled that.

But switching subjects gave her time to compose herself. She started filling him in on her plan to manage his life, starting with his brother. She informed him of the progress she'd made in getting Ben interviews at various schools in the northeast, leaving Roper to figure out how he'd approach Ben.

Amy then suggested he win Cassandra over to the idea first. Getting his mother on his side would all but ensure Ben's agreement. But she knew convincing his mother that coaching wasn't beneath her son was the equivalent of convincing Cassandra that television wasn't a step down from the big screen. It was a daunting task and they both knew it.

And all the while they talked business, Roper's invitation lay between them. Knowing she should say no to dinner was one thing. Actually doing it was something else. She had few friends in town, and like it or not, Roper was one of them.

Deep in her heart she knew she'd made her decision. Besides, dinner was harmless. Wasn't it?

CASSANDRA GENEROUSLY TIPPED the doorman, who had brought up her many purchases and deposited the bags in the foyer. Shopping usually brought her inner peace, but not today. She was running as fast as she could from L.A. and she wondered how long she could hide the reason from her son.

John always saw through her, more so than any of her other children. She couldn't let him know she was running not just from a role he'd demand she take, but from a man she'd once loved. She'd lived on her own for so long, she was afraid of the pull this man had over her.

All the drama she lived for in acting was suddenly part of her life, and she wasn't ready to face it. Instead she'd decided to go to New York to help her children.

And they needed her, Sabrina and her wedding, Ben and his inability to find himself and John and his career problems. The fact that a big city like New York was the perfect place to hide from Harrison Smith was merely a bonus.

AFTER AMY LEFT, ROPER picked up the envelope she'd delivered. Just as he'd thought, his Season Ticket Holder fan had written yet again. This time he went beyond expressing his displeasure with Roper's performance last season. Thanks to the recent spate of news coverage, his fan had another gripe. He said in his computer-generated note, "Instead of spending your money on women and entertainment, I suggest you work harder at digging yourself out of the hole you're in. Otherwise instead of the Hall of Fame, you'll be looking at the Hall of Shame."

Roper groaned and tossed the paper into the garbage. The guy wasn't even original. He was just a pain in the ass.

Roper spent the next two days taking care of his daily workout regimen, then either refereeing his mother and sister or spiriting his mother around Manhattan, during which time she refused to discuss her life in L.A., the role she was avoiding or job possibilities for Ben.

She dismissed a future for her younger son in coaching as squarely as she did the role Harrison Smith wanted her to take. She felt it wasn't fair to make Ben feel any more belittled than he already did with all the failed enterprises behind him. Roper knew better than to argue with a woman who had made avoiding conversations she didn't like an art form.

Instead he tried to call his brother to set up a meeting. He figured a face-to-face discussion might help Ben understand why Roper didn't want to invest more cash in any more get-rich-quick schemes. Then he could pump up his brother's ego by explaining all the good he could do by coaching kids. It wasn't that Ben didn't have baseball talent. He did. He just didn't have major league talent.

Roper had thought Ben would appreciate the chance to plead his case for the gym money, if nothing else. But Roper couldn't reach his brother. Ben had no phone other than his cell, where Roper's number would show up. And since Ben refused to return Roper's calls, it was obvious Ben was avoiding him—which led Roper to believe that his mother had tipped Ben off.

Which left Roper more frustrated than ever.

AMY SPENT THE NEXT TWO DAYS familiarizing herself with the New York press and media, their names, as well as those of other Hot Zone clients. Roper was her first assignment, but she wanted to show she was on top of things and ready to go at a moment's notice.

She also was learning to check the papers and relevant Web sites each morning, and for the second day in a row, she clicked on Frank Buckley's blog for eSports. Without a doubt, the man had it in for Roper. As she looked back at his daily rantings, each day started off with a line drive aimed directly at the Renegades' center fielder.

Unfortunately yesterday's was the worst, at least as far as Amy was concerned. She read aloud, "'Guess who had lunch at Sparks Steak House yesterday?'"

Amy was outraged, and not just because she'd once again been linked romantically with Roper. "The man calls himself a reporter? He ought to check his facts. It was a *business* lunch," she said aloud. And she'd rather any attention she received be for acting as his publicist rather than as his girlfriend.

A knock startled her, and she glanced up from the papers on her desk to see Annabelle standing in the doorway, an amused smile on her face.

"You heard me talking to myself?"

The other woman nodded. "Want some advice?"

"Gladly."

"You can ignore the rantings or you can send a professional letter correcting him. My vote would be to ignore it. I wish I could say that it would make it go away, but at least it'll keep you calm. Mind if I come in and say hi?" she asked.

Amy waved her in. "Of course not. I could use the break." Amy put her pen down and pushed her chair back so she could relax. "You're right. I'm going to ignore it. I wonder how Roper does."

Annabelle seated herself in a chair across from the desk and smoothed her short skirt over her legs. "Frankly, I doubt he does ignore it, which is another reason why he's so stressed."

Amy nodded, knowing the other woman was right. "So how's your daughter?" Amy asked.

"Delicious. She is the sweetest thing." Annabelle's expression softened at the thought of her little girl. "I don't have pictures on me, but they're in my purse and on my desk. Stop by later and I'll show them to you," she said like a proud mother.

Amy smiled. "I can't wait to see them."

"What about you? How have your first few days been?" Annabelle asked.

"Oh, a little like trial by fire," Amy said, only partially joking. "Between the newspaper incident the first day and Roper's mother showing up unexpectedly yesterday, I have my hands full. Short of getting him out of town—" No sooner had she said the words than she realized she had the solution. "That's it!"

"What's it?" Annabelle leaned forward in her seat.

Amy bit down on her bottom lip, wondering if her idea was pushing it. "Well, I realize Roper's family issues can't be solved overnight, but spring training is around the corner. He's got to do something—and

I just realized taking him out of town is the key. Getting him away from his family to a place where he can work out, where he can do his physical therapy and focus solely on getting his game back is exactly what he needs." She glanced at the woman across from her. "What do you think?"

"I think it's brilliant. Of course, who knows how Roper will feel, but he's dedicated enough to his career to like the notion." Annabelle nodded. "Yep, the more I think about it, the better I like it. And I have the perfect place for him to escape to."

Amy grabbed her pen and a fresh piece of paper. "Where?"

"Vaughn's place in Greenlawn," she said of her husband's lodge.

Amy had heard about the Upstate New York retreat from her uncle Spencer. Next to his wife and daughter, the place was Vaughn's pride and joy. "Tell me some more."

"Well, during the summer it's a camp for underprivileged kids, but during the winter it serves as a retreat. The price tag is high, but that's because he wants to attract a clientele who will help him fund the summer camp for the kids."

"That's such a wonderful thing," Amy said.

"That's Vaughn. He just gets what these kids need." Annabelle's pride in her husband was unmistakable as her blue eyes softened. "But for guests like Roper, there are rooms and suites. Each has a fireplace. There are a variety of restaurants for meals, room service for privacy and a state-of-the-art gym. And it's about an hour and a half from the city, which can be a hassle if you need a physical therapist to travel there, but since Vaughn's football buddies make use of the place, we've managed to locate a really good P.T. nearby. I'm telling you, it has everything you need."

Amy's mind was reeling with the possibilities. "It sounds as if it does."

"The best part is the people who can afford it understand the idea of privacy. Nobody will bother Roper at all." Annabelle spoke with animation in her voice, her hands waving in the air as her excitement grew.

"Will it be booked now? It *is* a winter resort…."

Annabelle shook her head. "Yes and no. Yes, it's booked, but that doesn't mean there isn't room for Roper. The Hot Zone reserves a suite each year for clients or family members who need the break. No one's using it now that I know of."

Wow. Roper could escape, and while he was preparing mentally and physically for the season, Amy could help him with anything his family needed here in the city. She liked the idea. A lot.

After jotting down the name of the lodge and its location, Amy glanced up. "Sounds perfect. The only question is whether I can convince Roper to leave without telling his family exactly where he's going." And seeing how Cassandra had reacted when he'd ignored a phone call, Amy knew she could be court-

ing disaster. "There's another issue, too." A big one,
Amy thought.

"What is it? I'm sure we can figure out a solution."

"Money. Although Roper doesn't discuss it
much, Yank told me to keep his expenses low because his family isn't only soaking up his time,
they're a drain on his cash flow, as well. He's hardly
broke, but what's liquid goes fast. And if his rehab
doesn't go as planned, he'll take a big hit. I don't
know if he'll agree to spend money on the lodge
when he has a gorgeous Manhattan apartment sitting empty."

"Hmm." Annabelle's forehead wrinkled in
thought. "Well, the Hot Zone has already paid for the
season. And he is our client..." she said. "Don't
worry. I'll clear it with Uncle Yank."

Annabelle rose and Amy stood to walk her out.
"Thanks for stopping by. Talking to you helped me
flesh some things out," Amy said.

Annabelle grinned. "My pleasure. That's what
we do around here, help one another any way we
can. Remember that and feel free to knock on my
door anytime."

"I'll do that," Amy said.

Annabelle paused. "You work on Roper and let
me know when he wants to go."

Amy nodded. She couldn't possibly commit to a
time frame yet. Coming up with the idea had been
the easy part. Convincing Roper to take her up on

spending the rest of his off-season at Vaughn's lodge in Greenlawn would be her greatest challenge.

CHAPTER SEVEN

THE REST OF THE DAY PASSED quickly and too soon, and Amy had to head home and get ready for her dinner with Roper. He picked her up as planned and drove her in his Porsche to a small restaurant called Leto's in Little Italy.

He'd taken over an entire restaurant where his friend was the owner and chef, ensuring their privacy. When she'd questioned the expense, he'd assured her his friend owed him a favor. Then he'd gone on to regale her with amusing tales of his baseball exploits and time on the road. She'd engaged him with her crazier stories about the residents at her mother's retirement community and the fun she'd had trying to keep them out of jail.

Roper at his most charming left Amy without any defenses to resist. Nobody had ever gone to such lengths to impress her before. It wasn't the fact that he'd arranged to shut down an entire restaurant that struck a chord with her, but the fact that he cared enough about her desire for privacy to bother. She forgot her resolve to keep her distance. During dinner, he covered her hand with his and she let him, enjoying the contact. She promised herself she'd turn the discussion to business and her idea for him to go into seclusion, but instead, she let herself be swept away by his charm, and not once did the subject of work come up.

In short, she allowed the impulsive part of her nature, the part she'd inherited from her mother and her aunt, to overrule her common sense. Amy didn't like denying herself the things she enjoyed, and though she'd spent years in Florida smothering those yearnings, it had been easy when she was away from people her own age, away from temptation.

And John Roper was a temptation she couldn't ignore.

Once dinner and desert ended and they were settled back in his car, he lay an arm over the back of her seat. "So, my place or yours?" he asked, staring at her with those sexy, mesmerizing eyes.

She knew what she ought to say, just as she knew she couldn't. She wasn't ready to end their time together. She'd been alone for too many nights, and he made her feel too good to cut the evening short now.

"My place," she answered before she could change her mind.

ROPER DIDN'T EXPECT anything to happen between himself and Amy. He didn't. She'd made her feelings perfectly clear, yet he couldn't help wanting her, desiring her, needing her.

He'd never clicked with a woman the way he connected with Amy. From the food they had in common to her understanding of his family and the on-the-road lifestyle he lived as a ballplayer, there had never been a lull in their conversation. Normally women's eyes glazed over when he talked about his time on the field. Locker-room stories only interested them if he mentioned famous names. Not Amy. She tried to get a grip on who his friends were and who he merely tolerated. She talked about her time in Florida with a self-deprecating humor he appreciated.

He already knew he had a good friend in Amy, something he valued. She'd seamlessly stepped into his life and had taken over where Micki had left off. As much as he loved his longtime friend, she now had a husband, a daughter and a life that kept her busy. Roper understood the changes, but he was grateful to have Amy to fill the void. Grateful enough that he didn't want to screw things up and lose her before their friendship had time to take hold. Yet by the time she let them into her apartment, his desire was becoming hard to control.

He'd talked her into dinner by respecting the fine line she drew between work and pleasure. As much as he desired to kiss her, hold her, feel her body around his, he'd have to let things progress without pushing too hard too fast. Somehow.

"Coffee?" Her soft voice broke into his thoughts.

He nodded. "That would be great."

"Make yourself at home while I go make us

some." She gestured to the small couch with a sweep of her hand. "I should warn you, though, it won't be freshly ground," she said as she disappeared into her kitchen.

"I'll manage," he said, laughing.

She peeked out from behind the dividing wall. "Good, because otherwise I wouldn't be able to invite you back."

He was just glad she wanted him here.

She disappeared back into the small kitchen area.

While waiting for her to finish making their coffee, he glanced around, seeing the personal touches and changes Amy had put on the apartment. Over the plain white wooden slatted blinds, Amy had put up new ruffled curtains that gave the place a womanly feel. She'd added plants on the windowsills and photographs of palm trees, of pink and yellow homes and southern landscapes on the walls. So feminine. So Amy.

"Coffee is served," she said, returning with two white mugs. "I remembered you ordered yours with a little milk, no sugar at the restaurant, so that's the way I made it. But if you want to add anything, just let me know." She placed both mugs on coasters on a glass table in front of the couch.

"Thanks. I'm sure its perfect."

He sat beside her on the sofa, keenly aware of her sweet scent. "I love the changes you made to the apartment," he said, reminding himself to take things slow. "Especially the curtains."

She smiled in appreciation. "They're homemade."

"That makes it even nicer." He took a sip of the too-strong, practically burnt coffee and somehow managed not to wince.

"Well?" She rocked back and forth in her seat, eager for his approval.

"Delicious." He even managed to keep a straight face. Insulting her coffee wouldn't exactly endear him to her. "So how do you like living in New York?" he asked.

"It's different. The pace is faster, the expectations higher, but somehow I'm loving it." Her eyes glittered with an excitement he found arousing.

She'd kicked off her black pumps. Her simple black dress was casual and not intentionally seductive. She wore just enough makeup to accent her pretty features, but not enough to disguise her freckles or tan.

At a glance she was so Floridian—laid-back and at ease—but inside, he knew she had definite strength of character. He admired the adventurous spirit it took to pick up her life and move to a new city. This strong woman drew him to her and he found it difficult not to put his coffee cup down and pull her into his arms, showing her just how much he desired her.

"I'm glad you're happy here. It's better than being homesick." He leaned back and lay one arm over the couch cushion, feigning relaxing though his body was strung tight.

She nodded. "True. I miss my family and the warm weather, but this change was way overdue."

"So how did you end up working at the retirement community in the first place?" he asked, taking advantage of the opening to learn more about her.

She placed her coffee mug on the table and he followed her lead.

"Let's see. I didn't start that way. I graduated college with a degree in social work. I took a job working for the state. It was heartbreaking and difficult, but I was making a difference in the world."

"So what happened?"

"My mother happened. My boss was extremely conservative. All he cared about was propriety and how our behavior reflected the office and the work we did."

"Which shouldn't be an issue for you. You're the epitome of propriety." But obviously her mother wasn't.

Amy curled her legs beneath her and the hem of her dress slipped higher, creeping up her thighs.

His mouth grew dry. His fingers itched to slip his hand beneath the short dress and touch her bare skin in an intimate caress.

"Propriety isn't easy to come by in a family like mine," she said, obviously unaware of the direction of his thoughts.

Amy was exactly what he saw. She was real and she appealed to him on a gut level. One that forced his imagination to go into overdrive. He wondered what she wore beneath the dress and drew a long, steadying breath.

"My mother and my aunt have this tendency to get themselves arrested for things like indecent exposure and being a public nuisance."

He couldn't suppress a grin. "I'm sorry. I know I shouldn't laugh, but it's funny."

She shook her head. "Not to the man who hired me. Or to his very proper boss."

"Go on." He squeezed her hand, encouraging her to tell him the rest. "I promise I won't laugh."

"Don't make a promise you can't keep." She smiled, surprising him. "Mom got a part-time job at a wig store in town. Not just any wig store but one specializing in wigs for cancer patients. She took it on herself to advertise during the annual Halloween Parade." Amy paused, picked up her mug and took a sip of her vile coffee, keeping him in suspense.

Not wanting her to question him about his drink, he took a sip from his mug, too.

"Anyway, Mom dressed up as Lady Godiva wearing nothing but a long wig and a sign with the shop's name around her neck."

He nearly spit out his coffee in shock. "Oh, God."

Her own mouth twitched with humor over the situation. "The police called me to come get her. I bailed her out, but she'd already gotten the press she wanted, including a photograph of her wearing the sign on the front page of the paper with me walking beside her on her way home from jail."

"Let me guess. Your boss lacked a sense of humor?"

She nodded. "I was damned immediately. Guilt by association. That's when I decided somebody needed to keep an eye on my mother and keep her in check. Since my father died, she'd become even more outrageous. So I moved back home. Uncle Spencer had just bought land with some real-estate partners and they were developing a seniors' community. I stepped right in and took over."

He shook his head. "You have some very interesting relatives."

"Coming from you, that's quite a statement," she said, laughing.

"Good point." He glanced down at their hands. He still held hers and she hadn't pulled away. "I take it this is why you hate being on the receiving end of publicity?"

Amy nodded. "It's part of the reason." She didn't know how to further explain, but she tried. "My dad was nothing like my mom. From the time I was little, he taught me the importance of making a difference. He was a lawyer who specialized in family law and he did his part to make the world a better place."

He squeezed her hand lightly and she appreciated the gesture. She smiled, and one look into his eyes told her his understanding wasn't an act. He got what she was saying.

What she couldn't explain to him, what she didn't want to even admit to herself, was that her fear of the press went deeper. Being fired from her first job just for being photographed beside her naked mother reinforced her belief that her mother's wildness was a trait she had to suppress—in her parent and in herself. Because a secret part of Amy admired her mother's brazenness. That same part sometimes yearned to be set free so she could jump in pools on a whim and openly enjoy life without fear.

She had more of her mother in her than she cared to admit. Amy had gotten drunk at college and joined her best friend in streaking outside the boys' dorm. When she'd woken up the next morning, she had a fuzzy recollection of a wild night, but nothing more—until the football players whistled at her the next day. "Nice ass, Amy!" they'd called, and the memory of what she'd done came flooding back. It wasn't the first time she'd done something crazy. But she always tried to make it the last. And by attempting to temper her mother's antics, she managed to control her own.

During her years at the retirement community, she hadn't exactly excelled at keeping her mother in check—but short of enforced confinement, not even her father had been able to do that. What Amy had accomplished, however, was to turn her uncle's retirement home into a successful establishment, and she'd proved to herself that working behind the scenes was her forte.

"Hey." Roper reached out and brushed a strand of hair off her face.

She trembled at his touch, her body immediately responding.

"Not everybody's cut out for my kind of life. Hell, sometimes I'm not cut out for my kind of life," he said, chuckling.

"Poor baby." She spoke lightly, but she was feeling anything but casual toward him at the moment.

He understood her feelings. He cared. And from the moment she'd met him, she'd wanted this. Wanted to be alone with him and see where things went.

Maybe it was that damned wild side and maybe this yearning for Roper was real. She didn't know, but when she looked into his intense eyes filled with desire for her alone, everything inside her told her to go for it.

Her heart pounded hard, echoing in her ears. The tension had been building between them all night, and sharing her past, her fears, herself, only intensified the connection.

She wondered if he'd make the first move or if she'd just throw caution to the wind and kiss him first. It was a tie. They met in the middle, lips lightly touching at the same time he wrapped his hand around the back of her neck, locking her in place.

She wasn't going anywhere but liked the pressure of his palm pressing her ever closer, deepening the kiss. Fireworks went off inside her brain while sizzling heat seared her body inside out. She was lost in the moment while he seemed to grow frenzied. His hands threaded upward through her hair, while she grasped his shoulders and dug her nails into him, needing more with each passing second.

With shaking hands, she moved to his shirt, working on the buttons, opening one at a time, making sure her fingers grazed his chest. "Did I ever mention that I like how you're always so nicely dressed?" she managed to ask him.

He lifted his head and smiled. "No, but I'm glad you noticed."

She laughed softly. "I noticed everything about you. Of course, it's hard for a woman who's used to running around in shorts and flip-flops to compete with you. I changed at least fifteen times tonight," she said, embarrassed at the admission.

His eyes grew darker, hotter, if possible. "I've never seen you looking anything but perfect," he said as he brought his hands around to the back of her dress.

Her nipples tightened even more than they already were, puckering hard as he slowly undid her zipper, lowering it until he reached the small of her back.

"I'd like to see Florida through your eyes," he said in a husky voice. "And I'd love to be with you when you're running around in those skimpy little shorts and tank tops."

She licked her damp lips. "I don't recall mentioning that my shorts were skimpy or that I wore tank tops."

"It's my imagination. Let it get carried away, will you?" He splayed his hands across her back and sucked in a shallow breath. "No bra." He closed his eyes and counted to ten, all the while skimming his hand up and down her bare back. "I'm glad I didn't know about this before now."

"Honestly, this dress didn't call for one."

"Honestly, I'm glad." He pulled the dress down over her shoulders, releasing her breasts.

She tried not to squirm or show her embarrassment as he stared at her full breasts, tight nipples and overall bare top half.

He leaned his head back against the couch and groaned. "Amy, you are so gorgeous."

She shook her head. "I've seen the women you've been with, so let's not go there, okay? If I wasn't so far gone with wanting you, I'd be more self-conscious. Let's not give me time to get there." She glanced away as she spoke.

It wasn't that she didn't think she measured up as much as she knew how hard the women in his circles must work to keep up appearances, cosmetic and otherwise. She was just an everyday woman with an everyday body. It was a reality she understood. How could she not mention the obvious?

He shook his head. "Listen," he said in a serious voice. "Considering I'm here with you, and you can feel how much I want you, I think we're clear on what looking at you does for me." He covered her breasts with his palms and she forgot all sense of embarrassment.

Heck, she nearly passed out from the glorious

sensation of his warm palms and hot touch. And when he slowly, gently, cupped their weight, palming her flesh, she writhed, squeezing her thighs together, letting small waves of pleasure build higher.

A soft moan escaped her throat and he reacted immediately, lowering his head and pulling her nipple into his mouth. She whimpered. He merely suckled her harder, using his tongue to lick and his teeth to lightly graze her flesh. Nerve endings on fire, unable to control herself, she rocked her hips from side to side, desire and longing building inside her. And when she couldn't take the sensations he evoked any more, he seemed to know and transferred his attention to her other breast, giving it equal loving attention.

Bells went off in her head and it took some time before she realized it was a cell phone and not ecstasy causing the sound.

Hers? His? She wasn't sure, but reality, which had been far away, dawned slowly. It wasn't her phone.

"John?" she asked, calling for his attention.

He didn't respond.

"John?" She curled her fingers into his shoulders. "What?"

"Your cell phone," she said, pushing him away.

He blinked and raised his head, his eyes glazed. "Ignore it," he said, leaning closer, obviously intending to kiss her again.

But she wasn't lost in the moment anymore. Nor

was she so far gone she wasn't aware of what she was doing. She shook her head and scrambled to her feet. "No, it might be important."

He raised an eyebrow. "The woman who insisted I shut my cell phone off when I'm with you now wants me to answer it?" he asked in disbelief.

She rose and began to work her dress back up over her shoulders. They'd moved too fast and she needed space. "Get the phone, okay?" she asked, hoping he'd take the hint and give her a minute.

He ran a hand over his eyes and groaned. "It's stopped ringing."

"Then listen to your voice mail."

Obviously she'd made her point, because he stood. His shirt hung open, a reminder of how close she'd been to heaven.

He walked up behind her and reached for her dress. She flinched, but when he ignored her reaction and merely did up the zipper, she felt badly. "I'm sorry. This was just… I got carried away." She hoped he understood, because she didn't want an argument.

Roper stared at Amy. They'd been hot and heavy until his damned phone ruined the moment. He had no choice but to be a gentleman and respect her wishes. Talking could come later.

He grabbed for his phone and dialed his voice mail.

For once it wasn't his family interrupting. One of his teammates wanted to meet for drinks. Roper had no desire to leave Amy or to hang with the guys, but the damage here had been done.

"Anything important?" Amy asked, as she turned to face him.

He shook his head. "Nothing that can't wait."

"Well, at least it isn't an emergency." She ran a hand through her hair, trying to fix the strands he'd messed with his fingers.

"Amy—"

"It's getting late," she said.

Obviously she wasn't going to let him talk about *them,* which was quite a contradiction to her planner personality. She liked things discussed and analyzed as long as *she* wasn't the one under the microscope.

He flexed and unflexed his fingers, grasping for calm. He was frustrated. But getting angry at her withdrawal wasn't going to get him anywhere. He forced himself to remember she'd given him insight into her past, and maybe he could work with that, given time.

"You're right. I should get going." Maybe he would meet his teammate for a drink. He was definitely too wired to sleep.

She walked him to the door. He met her gaze, and in her eyes he saw vulnerability. He lost his anger in an instant.

"Listen, I'm supposed to meet my mother at my sister's apartment tomorrow. Some sort of wedding-planning talk that is bound to turn into World War III. Join me and you'll get a firsthand view of the situation we're dealing with. Maybe you can offer some ideas about how to keep me out of it." And this way he could keep Amy with him while he figured out how to best handle her fear.

"I'll come tomorrow and see what advice I can offer."

"Good. See you at nine?" he asked as he opened the door.

She nodded. "And, John?"

He turned, placing an arm on the door frame. "Yes?"

"Thanks for dinner. I had a really nice time."

He smiled. "Me, too." On impulse, he leaned in and placed a kiss on her cheek. He lingered for a moment, inhaling her scent to remember in his dreams later that night. "See you in the morning." At which point he hoped to have figured out how to breach her defenses again.

Because now that he'd had a taste of her, there was no way in hell he was going to let her walk away.

AMY'S HAND SHOOK AS SHE locked the door behind Roper and headed for her bedroom, the events of the night fresh and vivid in her mind. How in the world had she let things go so far?

She knew the answer to that.

Roper. He was the reason she'd gotten so carried away. One minute they'd been talking and getting to know each other better and the next he'd looked at her with those golden-green eyes and she'd melted into him like a snowflake in July. Pathetic, that's what she was. She couldn't even keep the resolution she'd made to herself the day before.

She pulled an old T-shirt from her drawer and awkwardly unzipped her dress, remembering how sensual it had felt when Roper had undressed her, his strong fingers skimming her back. She shivered at the memory, her nipples puckering into hard knots.

She let out a frustrated sigh. She'd told herself going into the date that she needed a friend, but she'd lied to herself. She'd agreed to go to dinner because she didn't want to turn him down. She liked him too much and wanted him too badly.

They hadn't discussed business and she hadn't wanted to ruin their time together by bringing up the lodge. Instead she'd put herself and her needs before the job.

Her mistake had been in thinking she could resist his charm. That she could deny her desire for him just because it was the smart thing to do. It was time for her to put her priorities back in order.

He was a client. Her relationship with him was professional. And her first order of business tomorrow would be to convince him to head upstate for some R and R—Rehab and Running away from his family.

In other words, she needed to be hands-on when it came to her job, not when it came to John Roper.

ROPER PICKED AMY UP THE next morning with a game plan. It wasn't solid and it had more than a few holes, but it was a start. Every plan had a goal and his was to sway Amy into thinking there was nothing wrong with them picking up where they left off. She didn't like the fact that he attracted the media and he didn't blame her. But there was nothing wrong with a discreet affair between two people who were extremely interested in each other.

The first step in convincing her was to keep them together. He picked her up with lattes from Starbucks for both of them, a grin on his face and an attitude that let her know he wasn't holding a grudge over her turning cold on him the night before.

Once they were settled in the car, she turned to him. "Before we get going, I need to talk to you about a few things."

He raised an eyebrow. "What is it?" She sounded serious but not panicked, which he took to mean she was about to hit him with a professional, not personal, matter.

"I should have brought these things up sooner but I was distracted." Her cheeks flushed and her gaze darted from his, leaving no doubt just what that distraction had been. She drew a deep breath. "Anyway, the first thing I want to talk about is the media. I read Buckley's blog."

He leaned his head back against the seat. "That's a surefire way to ruin my morning. What about it?"

"Well, we were spotted at lunch. You didn't mention it to me but I'm sure you know."

Yeah, he knew. He gripped the top of the steering wheel with both hands. "I didn't think you needed another reason to avoid me."

"That's personal. Professionally, I'm the person

you're supposed to go to on things like this. So if our friendship or relationship or whatever you want to call it is going to hinder our professional relationship, then we have a problem. I can turn you over to another publicist—"

"No."

Losing daily access to her was the last thing he wanted. "You're right. I should have told you right away about the blog. But you have to realize that I'm his target right now. Buckley's going to keep hitting on me until he finds someone else."

She pursed her pink-glossed lips and nodded slowly. "Which begs the question. *Why* are you his target? There are other things going on at the moment. Basketball brawls. Hockey suspensions. Why you? Why now?"

He swallowed hard and decided to whitewash the truth. "I, um, *dated* his ex-girlfriend. She's now his wife."

She narrowed her gaze. "So it's jealousy."

"Insanity is more like it," he muttered.

"Well, whatever the reason, that's twice in one week you were spotted out and about without any promotion ahead of time." She leaned forward, giving him a view into her soft blouse and the cleavage he'd tasted last night. "Is that kind of coverage normal?" she asked.

He cleared his throat and tried to focus. "No, it's not."

"So how does the press just happen to know

where you are?" she asked, persistent in her curiosity.

"Don't know. Don't care." Actually, he did care. A lot.

He just couldn't change it.

"Well, you need to start to pay attention. Who knows your schedule and routine? Who do you speak to and mention your comings and goings?"

"As in you think someone close to me is reporting to Buckley?" he asked in disbelief.

"Not just Buckley. Gawkerstalker.com knows where you are, too, way too often to ignore them. Someone is phoning in information."

He frowned. She was new to this business and to his life. She didn't know his inner circle as well as he did. Nobody would deliberately sabotage him. "Maybe it's just a coincidence. Someone might have recognized me and decided to leak the information. It happens all the time."

She drew a deep breath. "Fine. Just pay attention in the future. That's all I ask."

He conceded with a jerk of his head, then glanced at the dashboard clock. "We need to get going." He turned and reached for the handle, but her hand on his shoulder stopped him.

"There's something else I need to run by you," she said.

He turned back her way. From her serious expression, he wasn't going to like this subject, either. "What is it?" he asked, resigned.

"What's your biggest priority at the moment?"

He let out a laugh. "Come on, you know the answer to that. My career. The upcoming season."

"Then why not act like it? Why aren't you at the gym this morning instead of playing mediator between your mother and your sister?"

He sat up straighter in his seat, his shoulders stiffening. "Not that I need to answer to you, but I'm going to the gym later today." He resented being put on the defensive just because he cared for his family. "Right now they need me. They're my responsibility and I won't turn my back on them."

She ran a hand through her hair, her frustration obvious. "They're adults, despite how they act. They should be able to look after themselves." She paused, then reached out and placed her hand on his arm. "You have a good heart, John, but if you don't start putting yourself first and get your shoulder healed and strong, they won't have you to turn to financially, now will they? Not with a lot of your future money tied to playing time and performance?" she asked softly.

If it was anyone else asking the question, he'd turn on them in a heartbeat. But he knew Amy had his best interest in mind by pushing him to face things he'd deliberately been ignoring.

"How do you know this?" He spoke through clenched teeth.

"Yank thought I should be filled in. So I'd know how important this assignment was," she admitted.

He hated that Amy was privy to his secrets. "So it was just business."

"Exactly." She inclined her head. "And in that vein, so is my suggestion. Are you aware of the fact that Annabelle's husband owns a lodge in Upstate New York? A town called Greenlawn?"

He folded his arms across his chest. "What about it?"

"The Hot Zone has a suite available and I think it would be a good idea if you went into seclusion there until spring training."

Nothing could have surprised him more. He was speechless.

"They have a full-scale gym and trainers and there's a physical therapist in town who caters to the athletes who stay there. You'd have no distractions, no family complications. You could focus totally on rehab and getting yourself in shape for the season," she said, her hands waving rapidly as she described her vision.

He shook his head. "Won't work."

"Why not?"

"Because my family will have no problem calling me upstate with their problems. Hell, they'd drive up in a heartbeat."

Her brown eyes glittered with anticipation. "Not if they don't know where you are. All you need to do is tell them that you're on a business trip of sorts. We'll sneak you out of town and I'll put out any fires here."

Her enthusiasm for the idea would have been infectious if not for the fact that there was no way in hell it would ever work. "I appreciate the thought. But I have a responsibility to my family. I've been the one they turned to from the day my stepfather took off. They need me. I can get strong and juggle them at the same time. It'll be fine," he assured her.

She shook her head and shot him an I-don't-believe-you look. "Just promise me we'll revisit the subject when things get too intense?"

He shrugged. A promise to revisit wasn't the same as a promise to leave town, but it would keep Amy satisfied. "If things get out of hand, I'll rethink things. Feel better?"

"I would if I believed you," she said, laughing. "But that's okay. I'm not finished trying."

CHAPTER EIGHT

AMY FOLLOWED ROPER DOWN the hallway to his sister's apartment. "I'm not sure I'll ever get used to the musty smell in these places," she said. The odor assaulted her every time she stepped off an elevator in Manhattan. Considering she'd practically grown up outdoors, she wondered if she ever would.

"I hear you. When I'm on the road, the thing I appreciate most is the fresh air and the wide-open spaces."

She blinked, surprised he noticed it, too. "Really? I'd think you were a city man, Mr. Metro," she said, laughing.

He turned toward her. "I see you've been reading my old press."

She shrugged. "It's my job to keep up on where you've been so I can help you with where you're going." In truth, she'd enjoyed digging through the old interviews and articles on Roper, learning more about his public persona and how different his personal, private one was.

"You could ask me," he said, stepping closer. "Where you're concerned, I'm an open book."

She inhaled and his scent immediately replaced everything else around her. Her heart rate accelerated as she finally let herself take notice of *him*. His pressed khakis, the sprinkling of hair peeking out of the unbuttoned space on his shirt. The desire to back him against the wall and feel his hard body against her was almost overwhelming.

Without warning, the door behind them opened and Sabrina stepped into the hall. "John, thank God you're here. You have to do something about Mom," she whispered.

Amy breathed out, releasing the tension but not the desire pulsing inside her.

He closed his eyes for a brief moment, obviously composing himself before turning to face his sister. "Can anyone stop a tornado?" he asked. "How did you know I was here? I didn't even get a chance to knock," he said, shooting Amy a look of regret.

Why? Had he been about to act on the chemistry that drew them to each other, even when minutes before they'd been at odds on how to handle his career and family? If so, what would she have done?

Before Amy could formulate an answer that satisfied herself, Sabrina grabbed her brother's hand and yanked him into the apartment.

With the quick instincts of a ballplayer, he encircled his arm around Amy's wrist, so she ended up dragged along with him.

Once inside, Sabrina glanced over Roper's shoulder at Amy. "Hi, again." She obviously remembered Amy from the New Year's party.

"Hi." Amy lifted her hand in a partial wave. "I hope you don't mind that I'm here."

"The more backup the better," the other woman said, sounding pained.

Having met Cassandra, Amy understood.

Apparently so did Roper, because he walked over to his sister and wrapped an arm around her shoulder. "Breathe in and out," he instructed.

Sabrina shut her eyes and complied.

"Better?" he asked a few seconds later.

She nodded.

"Good. Now, let's deal with her together. Come," he said, in a reassuring tone.

Sabrina visibly relaxed.

Amy marveled at the calming effect Roper had on his sister, but then, when she let him, he had his own unique effect on her, as well.

They walked a few steps into the next room, where Cassandra sat beside Kevin, a pen and pad in hand. "So let's go over your guest list," Cassandra said.

"Hi, Mom, Kevin. How's it going?" Roper asked, making his presence known.

"It's going," the other man said. With his dark hair and dark eyes, Kevin was good-looking in a studious way. His rimless, fashionable glasses added to his attractiveness.

Of course, in Amy's eyes, he didn't compare with

her jock Roper, but she could definitely see his appeal. *Her jock?* She caught herself and blinked.

"Kevin, I'd like you to meet Amy Stone. Amy, my soon-to-be brother-in-law, Kevin Reynolds," Roper said, interrupting her thoughts.

Kevin stood and shook Amy's hand. "A pleasure to meet you. And now that you're here to handle your mother," he said to Roper, "I'm going to take the dog for a walk." He paused to kiss Sabrina's cheek before heading for the door.

Cassandra merely laughed. "You know I'll be here to finish up later," she said to Kevin.

"Wait," Sabrina said, running after him but not before giving their mother a frustrated glare. "We don't have a dog!"

Amy turned her unexpected laugh into a cough. "Hello, Miss Lee, it's nice to see you again."

Cassandra looked up, appearing more rested than she had earlier. "Please call me Cassandra. It's lovely to see you again," the other woman said, but her voice sounded uncertain. She was obviously confused by Amy's presence. She settled her glance on her son. "John, we were discussing wedding plans."

"It looked as if you were torturing Kevin," Roper said.

He was too far away for Amy to nudge him in the ribs, so she settled for a warning look instead.

His mother ignored his comment. "Did you know they haven't chosen a reception hall yet? They can't pick a place unless we know the number of guests on the list and what the venue can hold. I already have one hundred of my own—"

Roper nearly choked. Even Amy's head started to pound. She couldn't believe how the actress bulldozed her way into everyone else's life. No wonder Roper was concerned about finances.

"Didn't you hear us say we wanted a small wedding?" Sabrina asked as she rejoined them in the living room.

"Is Kevin okay?" Roper asked.

Sabrina nodded. "He's fine. He just needed some fresh air. Mother, did you hear me? We want a small, intimate affair."

Cassandra waved her hand back and forth in the air. "No, that's what you think now. But when you look back, you'll realize you wanted a big wedding, so that's what we're going to make sure you have."

Sabrina looked at Roper with big, pleading eyes.

For the first time, Amy realized exactly why he felt so strongly about not abandoning them to go to Vaughn's lodge. Each member of his family needed him for their own reasons. But they would take and take until there was nothing left—and that included cash. And it wasn't as if anybody was actually in the wrong. They were just needy. Roper had fallen into the caretaker role and now they all expected it of him, at his own expense.

Roper stepped between his mother and sister. "Mom, look, it's their wedding. I think they can make their own decisions."

Cassandra tipped her head in her elegant way. "And you know this because you've been married before?" she asked him with sweet sarcasm. "*I* know best."

"Because your big wedding and subsequent divorce make you an expert?" Roper asked.

"Argh!" Sabrina stormed out, heading to what Amy assumed was her bedroom.

Cassandra placed her pad and pen on the table, rose and strode to the window, all without meeting Roper's gaze.

Amy couldn't imagine the stress these kinds of confrontations put on him. Watching the commotion today, Amy was even more certain now. All the reasons he didn't want to go to the lodge were the exact same reasons he needed to go so badly. So he could take care of himself for once and let his family learn to stand on their own.

Amy walked over and put her hand on Roper's shoulder for support. He surprised her by covering it with his own.

"Weddings are stressful," Amy said. "Perhaps there's a way you all can sit down and talk and really hear one another," she suggested.

Cassandra swirled around. "I never did find out what exactly you are to my son. You mentioned working for the Hot Zone, his public relations firm?"

"Officially Amy's my go-to person at the Hot Zone." Roper jumped in and spoke for her, something Amy didn't want or need him to do.

"You see, Cassandra, the Hot Zone felt that given Roper's current situation, he could use someone to help keep him on track with his physical therapy before the start of the season," Amy said, eager to speak for herself.

"Sort of like a handler," Cassandra said.

Amy nodded. "Exactly."

His mother studied Amy for a long while, enough to make her uncomfortable. But she held her ground and refused to fidget even though Cassandra didn't hide her blatant attempt to take stock. "So you're here with him today because he needs help handling his family?" Hurt suffused Cassandra's tone.

Amy's heart constricted. She didn't want wounded feelings. "I'm just here for support," she said, deliberately backing off.

She saw Roper's dilemma so clearly now. His aging mother was unsure of her place in Hollywood and in her children's lives. It wasn't Amy's place to butt in. She could guide Roper, but she couldn't tell his family what to do. She realized that now.

Amy turned to Roper. "Don't you have an appointment with the doctor and then with the physical therapist today?"

He glanced at his watch. Surprise at how fast the morning had gone registered on his face. "I do, but my family needs me right now. I'll call Aaron and reschedule."

She might as well start *handling* him now. "No,

you won't. Your shoulder might heal on its own, but you won't get your strength back without hard work."

"Amy's right, John," his mother said, shocking Amy.

If the stunned look on Roper's face was any indication, he agreed.

"I'm tired. I've upset your sister and obviously overstayed my welcome. I'm going to go back to the hotel. First I'll go talk to Sabrina and make peace. We can pick up the wedding talk another time. I still say they'll regret a small wedding later." With a wave, his mother headed in the direction Sabrina had gone, leaving Roper and Amy alone.

Roper leaned against the wall and let out a low groan. "She gave in," he said, relieved.

"For now. And only because I backed off first," Amy said.

"You are amazing." She'd been astute enough to realize that his mother might perceive her as a threat. Roper shot her a look filled with admiration and gratitude.

She shrugged. "Years of experience at the retirement community, I guess. I just sensed she needed to feel in control of things."

"Well, it worked." Roper knew another reason why Amy had been able to get his mother to step aside for today, at least—because his mother was astute enough to sense there was more to Roper's relationship with Amy than business. She'd said as much on the phone after meeting Amy at the apartment the other day. Cassandra thought her son had a thing for Amy, which worked to Amy's benefit because his mother played nice to Roper's girlfriends.

She had spelled out her reasons to him the one and only time he'd brought a girlfriend with him to L.A. The woman hadn't had nearly Amy's intelligence and she'd grated on his mother's nerves, but Cassandra had been the gracious hostess, giving in to all the other woman's requests—to go shopping on Rodeo Drive, to tour Paramount Studios—all because, as she'd told Roper later, she knew he'd grow tired of her quickly.

And he had. He always did. The women he met and dated up until now didn't have enough substance to make him want them in his life long term.

"Time for the doctor," Amy said.

He rolled his eyes at her bossy tone. He wanted to tell her that she wasn't in charge. That he could make his own decisions. That he was the man.

Until he realized that if she hadn't been here, he would have canceled his appointment. She'd done her job, keeping him on schedule. Damn, but he liked her take-charge personality.

"Amy, do you want to join us for a late lunch this afternoon?" Sabrina called out as she and his mother walked back into the room.

Amy paused, then said, "Love to." She shot him a satisfied grin.

Knowing Amy, she figured keeping his mother

and sister busy would enable him to work uninterrupted.

She was right.

But he'd have the last laugh. Because while he
was going to his appointments, she'd be getting
grilled by his inquisitive family.

He ought to tell her, then decided against it. Amy
could handle herself.

"Can we talk before you take off?" Amy asked.

He nodded and she walked him to the door.

"Ready to rethink the lodge?" she asked.

He shook his head. "So far you've got things well
under control. When you don't, we'll talk." He threw
down the gauntlet, knowing she'd work doubly hard
to prove she could corral his family.

No escape necessary, or so he hoped.

"Promise?"

He nodded.

"Say it."

"I promise." He couldn't hold back his grin.

"I'm going to hold you to that," she said, pointing
at him for emphasis.

"I wouldn't expect anything less of you." He
grabbed her finger long enough to stop her and
glanced at her satisfied smile.

He could think of just one way to wipe the smug
grin off her face. He leaned forward, brushing a
long, lingering kiss over her lips before turning
around and walking out. Leaving them both wanting more.

ROPER WALKED OUT OF THE office of the team's orthopedist, the best in the city, and barely felt the cold winter air. He'd gone from a euphoric high, leaving Amy with a stunned expression after that kiss, to this. He'd just gotten the results of an MRI he'd had taken last week and the news wasn't good. Despite his workouts and physical therapy, his strength wasn't returning as quickly as he'd hoped. The MRI didn't show anything that would impede his progress, but the doctor also said that sometimes healing didn't occur at the pace a patient wanted. He'd have to listen to his body or risk further damage.

The doctor was warning him. Spring training might start late for him.

Or not at all.

Roper had seen many players who never bounced back after surgery, and in his case, he wasn't coming off a stellar season to start with.

Mentally he'd needed good news today. Promising news. He hadn't gotten it.

"A delay ought to go over well with the already-pissed-off fans," he muttered, kicking uselessly at an empty coffee cup littering the sidewalk. On the city streets, nobody spared him a second glance.

Someone talking to himself wasn't unusual here. He was just lucky there were no reporters around to let the world know he was losing it.

At least, since he'd seen the team doctor, he didn't have to call his coach. The doc would do it for him, which took one load off his shoulders. Roper had a couple of hours before his physical-therapy appointment, so he headed home to unwind.

As he passed the front desk with a wave to Stan, the doorman, called him back.

"What's up?" Roper asked Stan, who'd been on the day shift ever since Roper had bought the place two years ago.

"Another delivery for you." He held out a box with a familiar scrawl.

"The guy doesn't give up," Stan said, lifting his cap and scratching the top of his head.

Roper began to shrug, and the immediate soreness reminded him of his already shitty day. "He's a Renegades fanatic who doesn't think I'm earning my keep. At the moment he's got a valid point."

Stan frowned. "Maybe if he showed you some support, you'd get your groove back faster."

Roper appreciated the man's backing. "Thanks. Not much I can do but ignore it." Still, the thought of how much he'd disappointed the fans, his teammates and himself gnawed at his gut.

"I still don't like that he knows where you live."

Roper forced a laugh. He didn't like it much himself, but again, there wasn't anything he could do about it. "Half of New York City knows where I live. It's not a national secret. But I appreciate your concern."

"Yeah, well, it just doesn't sit right. I mean, the guy doesn't try to hide what he's doing. He just sends you things that don't fit in the mailboxes and have to come through me. You need to get these things screened."

He waved at an older woman passing by. "Afternoon, Mrs. Davis," he said.

"Hello, Stanley." She smiled warmly and kept walking.

"Anyway, I don't like it," he said, turning his attention back to Roper.

"It's his way of getting my attention." As if Roper could or would ignore the upset-fan letters still trickling into the stadium addressed to him.

"Why don't you open it down here? That way I can get rid of it for you afterward," Stan offered.

Roper recognized his curiosity but also his point. Who wanted more reminders of his shitty season hanging around his apartment? "Why not?"

Stan pulled a box cutter from beneath the desk. "Do you want the honors?"

Roper shook his head. "You can have them."

Stan neatly slit the box and opened the flaps, then Roper took over. He reached inside and pulled out a Ziploc bag, sealed shut.

For good reason. The contents defied description.

Roper looked, blinked and stared again. "Holy—"

"What the hell?" Stan asked, narrowing his gaze and staring at the bag in disbelief. "Is that what I think it is?"

Roper held the bag with two fingers, keeping it far

away from him. "It sure is, Stan. It's a bag of shit."
Probably dog shit.

And written on the bag in permanent marker were
the words *You Stink*.

Roper's stomach roiled in a combination of
nausea and humiliation.

"The nerve of some people. You get on upstairs
and take it easy. I'll get rid of this." Stan pulled the
bag from Roper's hand, stuffed it in the box and
stormed away, heading for the back of the lobby
where the trash was located.

Appreciating Stan's discretion, Roper nodded.
Shaken, he headed farther into the building and took
the elevator upstairs. He'd just reached the kitchen
and lowered himself into the nearest chair when his
cell phone rang.

He pulled it out of his pocket, glanced down and
groaned, answering it despite knowing better. "Hi,
Mom," he said, hearing the exhaustion in his voice.

"Hello, darling. What's wrong? You sound down.
What happened at the doctor's?"

"Just some frustrating news," he admitted. "I'm
not getting better as fast as I'd hoped." He didn't even
think of upsetting her with the news about his recent
package in the mail.

"What's up?" he asked, for the first time almost
grateful for his family to focus on.

His mother paused. "Are you sure you're okay?"

"Yes."

"I'm calling about Ben. I visited with him after

lunch and I'm horrified by where he's living. Did you know he's crashing on a friend's couch? He gave up his apartment because he couldn't pay the rent." Her voice rose in panic. "I had no idea things were so bad. He never told me."

Obviously Ben had managed to lie about where he was living until faced with his mother in the flesh.

Roper massaged the back of his suddenly stiff neck. "Mom, Ben's a big boy. There are any number of jobs he could take that would bring in a weekly salary so he could keep an apartment. He chooses not to apply for them. Just like he chooses to ignore my phone calls or discuss potential coaching jobs."

Just like his mother chose not to take acting roles she believed were beneath her. The difference was that Ben had lost enough of Roper's money that Roper no longer felt obligated to help his brother.

"You never did understand how frustrating it is for Ben to live in your shadow," she said.

Roper let out an angry groan. "I'll tell you about frustrating. I just had a doctor's appointment where I learned that despite all the work I've done in the past few months, my shoulder isn't strong enough for spring training. I've been killing myself and it just doesn't matter. So I can't summon much pity for Ben at the moment. He's brought his problems on himself."

A long pause followed, which Roper took to mean his mother finally understood how serious he was about not wanting to discuss Ben. "Is there anything I can do for *you?*" she asked, her voice softening.

"No, thanks. I'll be fine. I want to grab something to eat before my P.T. appointment, so I need to get going."

"Okay. But just one more thing? I have a situation," she said.

Roper narrowed his gaze. Did it ever end? "What kind of situation?"

"It seems that Harrison Smith followed me to New York. In fact, he's staying in the same hotel. He wants me to take that role I told you about and he's being very persistent. He sent me roses. Not real roses, mind you, but mink roses. Flowers made from fur. They are simply gorgeous. But that's not the point."

"What is?"

"He insists on having dinner tonight and I can't deal with him alone. It's getting harder and harder to resist him."

"So don't." Roper exhaled hard. "A meaty role would be good for you. Why don't you just take the part?"

"Darling, I couldn't do that. Just do me a favor and join us for dinner tonight. I'll be forever grateful."

"Ask Sabrina and Kevin."

"I did, but they have one of Kevin's business dinners. I need you, darling."

"No—"

"And bring that delightful young woman, Amy, with you."

"Delightful young woman?" Just what had happened at lunch, anyway? She hadn't said.

"Well, yes. We got to know each other earlier and she's a joy. I'd love for her to join us at dinner."

He'd love to see Amy, too, but not at a family dinner with a Hollywood director. "Mom, I've had a rough day and it's not over yet. I'm not in the mood for a long dinner."

"Good! We'll make it short. Better for me."

He glanced heavenward. She wasn't listening. If he didn't show up, he'd never hear the end of it. Maybe having dinner out would be better than eating alone in his apartment, thinking about his recent package in the mail or the doctor's report. Besides, he knew when he'd been beat.

At least there was a silver lining. His day had sucked. He deserved a break. And he needed to see Amy.

"Where and when?" he asked.

She mentioned Kelly's, a small, casual restaurant he'd been to a couple of times. "Oh, listen, that's my call-waiting," his mother said. "Your brother's on the other line. I'll see you tonight at seven."

Roper nodded, hung up, then called Amy.

After spending the day with his family already, he wouldn't have been surprised if she'd said no to dinner. But surprisingly, she agreed to join them. She even said she'd meet him at his apartment because he'd just be getting back from the physical therapist—where, after today's news, he realized he'd have to put in one hundred and fifty percent. He needed to focus on his career, not his family. And not on the beautiful woman who'd agreed to be his salvation at dinner tonight.

CHAPTER NINE

AMY WAITED IN THE KITCHEN for Roper to finish dressing. She hadn't planned on seeing him again today, but he'd sounded so down, she couldn't resist coming along to dinner tonight to make sure he was okay. And considering his mood when he'd answered the door, she was glad she'd agreed. She'd watched his mother in action this morning and again at lunch and realized how wearing the woman was on those around her. Cassandra Lee expected the world to fall at her feet. No doubt she'd become used to it in the heyday of her career. And then afterward Roper had ensured she always had everything she needed, Amy thought.

But who made sure Roper had everything he needed? she wondered.

The sound of footsteps drew her attention, and she glanced up to see Roper join her wearing a pair of black jeans and a light blue Burberry shirt. Amy wasn't into designer clothes. But the Jordan sisters were trying to change that, and thanks to them, Amy recognized the classic plaid. She had to admit, she liked that she could hold her own with Roper, a man who was always immaculately groomed, no matter what his mood.

"You look good," Amy said, the words out before she could stop them. A heated blush rushed to her cheeks.

His gaze bore into hers. "Thank you. You're looking pretty hot yourself."

She blushed deeper.

"We have a few minutes before we have to leave. Can I get you something to drink? Water? Perrier?" A smile tugged at his lips. "You see? I heard you when you said you didn't want to drink around me."

"Those weren't my exact words," she muttered. She'd only said no to a drink last time. But he'd read her mind. Which probably meant he understood her reasons. He was hard to resist when she was sober. Give her a drink and she'd succumb to his charm in an instant. "No, thank you. I'll wait until we get to the restaurant."

"Okay, then. Let me just straighten up and we'll head on over. With a little luck, Mom and Harrison Smith will be early, too, and we can get this meal over with," he said, sounding even more preoccupied than usual.

"Why do I have the feeling that you're worried about more than spending the evening with your mother?"

He shrugged, eyeing her as if deciding whether or not to talk. "I'm just sick of hearing from disgruntled fans. They're entitled to their feelings, but it would be easier if I didn't have to deal with it at home, too."

She narrowed her gaze. "So why do you? Doesn't your mail go to the stadium or directly to us at the Hot Zone?" She was pretty sure the stadium mail was automatically forwarded to the Hot Zone, protecting him from unwanted correspondence.

It was just another service the Hot Zone offered to their clients. Long ago, Micki had made sure that someone screened all clients' fan mail before being passed on to those athletes who wanted to see it. The rest was answered by someone at the PR firm with a signed photo or as directed by each client.

"Most of my mail goes the standard route. But even though I'm unlisted, it's not too hard to find out where someone in the public eye lives. This guy's been sending me stuff all season."

"At your home?" she asked.

He nodded. "You brought up a letter the other day," he admitted. "But that wasn't the worst of it." He twisted his head from side to side, obviously aggravated.

She propped her hands on her hips. "I think you need to elaborate."

He groaned. "Besides the standard letters, I've gotten a bobblehead doll with a knife in its shoulder. And then today's *package* was something else."

"A knife in its shoulder?" she asked, her voice rising. "And it was a bobblehead doll of *you?*"

"Calm down." He stepped toward her, placing a hand on her arm.

Not likely, she thought, a chill sweeping through her body. "What was in today's package?" she asked.

"Forget it. It's just some crazy fan. Fanatical. Get it? It comes with the territory of playing in the majors and getting the big bucks."

She raised an eyebrow at him in question. Did he really think he could gloss over this? "Oh, no. You aren't getting away with avoiding my question. What was in the package?"

He lowered his hand from her arm and met her gaze. "Dog shit with a note saying *You Stink*. At least I think it was from a dog," he muttered, not wanting to contemplate that thought too deeply.

She winced, both nauseated and horrified at the same time. "You have got to be kidding me! That is the most disgusting, scary thing I've ever heard. This guy is nuts!"

"It's a fan, remember? Just let it go."

"I remember Uncle Spencer telling me about the time a tennis player was stabbed during a championship match. You can't brush this off. Did you report it to the police?"

He rolled his eyes. "Now, that would be over-reacting."

She scowled at him. "Then did you mention it to someone at the Hot Zone? Did you tell Yank about the bobblehead? Of course not," she answered for him.

"Since you already know the answer, why should I bother answering the question?" he said, laughing at her.

She wasn't fooled at his attempt to change the subject. "First thing tomorrow I'm going to have all your mail forwarded to the Hot Zone. We'll make sure you get your bills and things that are safe as soon as possible."

He inclined his head. "Not a problem."

She blinked, startled by his easy agreement. "Oh."

"I'm not a glutton for punishment. I should have done that from the beginning. It's more of a mental drain than any kind of real threat. But thank you. Good idea."

"You're welcome." She exhaled hard.

"So how about we just go to dinner?" he asked.

"Sounds like a plan." Dinner wasn't the only thing on her agenda.

Now there was more than just his family eating away at him. He also had this nutty fan whose so-called gifts were just sick, and getting worse. Amy didn't want them to get dangerous. At this point, she was more sure than ever that she had to get Roper out of town.

With or without his consent.

CONSIDERING BEN HAD DEIGNED to show up, dinner had been surprisingly pleasant, Roper thought. There had been no talk of the televised pilot his mother kept turning down or Roper's career skid. Instead

Harrison Smith had led the discussion, getting to know Roper, Amy and Ben, and essentially ignoring the diva at the table. By the end of the meal, Cassandra was sulking, proving to Roper that the man had his mother wrapped around his finger. She claimed not to want the attention, but she didn't want to be ignored, either.

Roper silently applauded the man's ability to get under his mother's skin. No man had done that during Roper's lifetime.

Harrison was busy with the waiter, placing his dessert order. "The lady and I will both have crème brûlée," he said, placing his hand over Cassandra's.

Cassandra slid her hand from his. "I'd prefer the tropical sorbet. I have to watch my waistline," she said, becoming animated for the first time all evening.

Harrison snorted. "She'll have crème brûlée." He placed his hand behind her chair and leaned closer. "Are you really going to avoid your favorite dessert just to spite me?"

Cassandra sniffed but didn't reply.

"Remember when we couldn't afford more than one dessert and we shared it once a week back in film school?" the other man asked.

"You two knew each other in film school?" What rock was he living under? Roper wondered. And what else was his mother hiding?

"Mom, you're holding out on us," Ben said. "Did you and the director here have a thing going on back then?" he asked, chuckling.

"Maybe she doesn't want to share personal information at the table," Roper said to his sibling.

The waiter conspicuously cleared his throat. "Would anyone else like to order something?"

"I'll have a decaf cappuccino," Amy replied quickly, probably to kill the oncoming argument between the brothers.

"Espresso," Roper added.

"Regular coffee," Ben said.

"And two crème brûlées?" the waiter asked, double-checking with Harrison and Cassandra as he collected the small menus.

To Roper's surprise, his mother nodded. "That's fine," she said with an obviously forced sigh.

She'd caved in to the director. It didn't matter that the subject was something as insignificant as dessert. Cassandra had given in. Now that he'd witnessed her relationship with Harrison Smith firsthand, Roper knew why his mother was running scared.

The man didn't cater to Cassandra's prima donna whims and he didn't put up with her nonsense. He also knew her a lot better and perhaps more intimately than anybody had guessed. Just because Ben had asked his tacky question at the wrong time didn't mean he was wrong. Something deeper than an argument over a role was going on between these two.

With the waiter gone, Ben leaned forward, elbows on the table. "So you two have a history?"

"Your mother didn't tell you?" Harrison asked.

Cassandra visibly squirmed in her seat.

Ben shook his head. "No, Mom's been holding out."

Roper opted to add his thoughts. "Frankly, I thought you wanted her for the role in your pilot because of her past body of work," Roper said.

"That's one reason. Your mother is talented. But we also go way back to our days as struggling artists. Remember, Cassie?"

Roper nearly choked on his water.

"Cassandra," she corrected him, her haughty tone returning.

"Cassie!" Ben laughed loudly. "That's really something else." He grinned, enjoying his mother's discomfort.

Roper wasn't. He was confused by the interaction and worried about his mother's ability to handle Harrison. On the other hand, Harrison dealt with his mother extremely well. Roper was beginning to like and appreciate the man for that reason alone.

He glanced at Amy. She sat beside him and had remained quiet for most of the meal, watching the dynamics around the table much as Roper had. But that didn't mean he hadn't been intensely aware of her the entire time. She smelled delicious, her perfume a subtle but constant reminder of the always simmering attraction between them.

"It's not Cassie, Benjamin, and you know it," Cassandra finally said. "So behave."

Harrison grinned. "She's always been Cassie to me." His cell phone rang, and after checking it, he glanced up. "Would you excuse me for a minute? It's my daughter and she wouldn't call if it weren't important."

Roper nodded. He'd appreciate a minute or two with his mother without the other man's imposing presence.

"Well, well," Ben said, catching his mother's wandering gaze. "You've been keeping secrets."

"Not really. We knew each other back in the day. So what?"

"So the man remembers what your favorite dessert is. That's not something a woman takes lightly," Amy finally spoke, telling Roper his observation was on target.

Cassandra waved her hand in the air. "He has a good memory."

"Okay, *Cassie,* whatever you say." Ben finished off his drink.

Roper would never give Ben credit, but his brother had a point. Nobody had ever called his mother by such an intimate shortening of her name. Never.

His mother flushed deep.

This meal was actually turning out to be fun, as well as enlightening, Roper thought. "Okay, you two obviously had a fling and he's obviously interested again. That's not a big deal. He seems like a decent-enough guy. So the real issue is why you're fighting him so hard."

"That's obvious," Amy said when his mother remained silent. "It's because he's so intense. The man has the looks of Sean Connery, the charisma of Jack Nicholson and the persistence of a pit bull. Overwhelming." She fanned herself with her hand.

Cassandra met Amy's gaze and an unfathomable understanding flashed between the two women. Something Roper didn't for the life of him understand. "Females," he muttered.

"Just cut your mother some slack," Amy said, placing her hand on his arm. "It's obvious she needs time to adjust to Harrison's pursuit."

"Exactly," his mother said, folding her arms across her chest. "Cut me some slack, John." She turned to her other son. "You, too, Benjamin. Stop enjoying this so much. You're both encouraging Harrison. And that is something I do not need, want or appreciate."

Roper saw his opportunity and grabbed it. "If I back off, will you consider the role Harrison is offering?" He believed in a good quid pro quo and he'd just offered his mother a very fair exchange.

She opened her mouth to answer just as Harrison returned.

Taking pity on her, Roper didn't push her to decide now. But he'd definitely be discussing it with her again later.

"I'm sorry about that," Harrison said, taking his seat once more.

"Is everything okay with your daughter?" Amy asked.

He nodded. "She's in the middle of an ugly divorce and she needed my opinion on something."

"I'm sorry," Cassandra said. "That can't be easy for her." Her compassionate tone took Roper off guard.

"It isn't. She's an MBA and earns more than her husband, whom she supported while he tried to make a living screenwriting. Now he's asking for a divorce, alimony, full custody and child support. The man isn't worthy of my daughter," he said, fired up on his child's behalf. He cleared his throat. "But thank you for caring." Harrison placed his hand over Cassandra's, sending her into another frenzy of unsettled movement.

It was all Roper could do not to laugh, watching his normally composed mother fidget and fuss under a man's attention.

Half an hour later, they'd finished coffee and dessert. When Roper asked for a check, he discovered that while taking his phone call, Harrison had apparently also made arrangements to pay the entire bill. Roper thanked the man. He wasn't all that bothered, since he had the definite feeling there would be plenty of opportunities for Roper to return the favor.

Harrison didn't strike him as a man who gave up easily.

They made their way to the street. Roper held on to Amy's hand, not wanting her to hail a cab and disappear before he had a chance to talk to her alone.

But he managed to catch up to his brother when they reached the sidewalk. "Hang out for a few minutes, I want to discuss something important with you, okay?" he asked.

Ben didn't reply.

"It's good news for you, so chill," Roper muttered.

"Thank you for a lovely dinner," Amy said to the director, probably to distract everyone's attention from Roper and Ben.

"My pleasure. I've been wanting to meet the people who are close to Cassie. Perhaps next time Sabrina and Kevin can join us, as well," he said.

"Sabrina will definitely want to check things out for herself," Ben said.

Cassandra flipped her pashmina scarf around her shoulders. "I think Harrison will be back in L.A. long before we can arrange everyone's schedules," she said.

"You think wrong," Harrison said. "I've freed myself up for the foreseeable future. Nothing is more important to me than you." His voice grew deep, making Roper shift uncomfortably on the sidewalk.

Beside him, Amy squeezed his hand, seeming to understand.

"You mean, convincing me to take the role of someone's mother and *grandmother*. On TV." Cassandra straightened her shoulders in a haughty display, but beneath the pride, Roper saw the fear.

He suddenly understood. His beautiful mother was afraid that if she took the role, she'd be acknowledging her own mortality.

Harrison stepped forward and clasped her hand in

his. "I meant what I said, Cassie. Nothing is more important to me than *you*."

The two stared at each other, the silence only broken by the honking of a car horn and the screeching of tires.

"Should we leave them alone?" Amy whispered.

Ben shrugged. "Seems like it."

Roper was about to agree when his mother's voice rose higher. "Like I'm going to believe you aren't sweet-talking me in order to get me to take this godforsaken part. I'm nobody's fool," she said, before stepping into the street to hail a cab.

Before anybody could react, a yellow car pulled up and Cassandra Lee placed herself inside. And then she was gone.

Harrison turned to Roper, Amy and Ben, completely unflustered. "So happy to meet you," he said. "We'll have to do it again sometime."

Ben inserted himself between Roper and the director. "I'd be happy to. There's a script idea I've been toying with. A ballplayer who couldn't make it in the minors due to a tragic past."

Harrison nodded, listening politely. "Call me and we'll talk," he said to Ben.

"Will do." Ben then took off down the street, his wave telling Roper exactly what he could do with his request.

Harrison turned back to Roper. "It was good to meet you, too," he said, extending his hand.

Roper inclined his head and shook the other

man's hand. "She's a complicated woman," he said of his mother.

"Always was." Harrison's smile spoke of deep understanding for Cassandra's ways.

"Are you really here indefinitely?" Roper asked.

Harrison nodded. "As long as it takes," he said, then turned to Amy. "A pleasure." He lifted her hand for a kiss.

"Same here," she said, her cheeks pink.

He turned and strode down the street, hands in his leather jacket pockets, whistling as he walked.

"Hmm." Roper stared after the man, at a loss for words. "Nothing about tonight was what I expected."

"I bet not. Your brother is a character," she said.

"He was too pushy with Harrison, too crude with Mom and too eager to get away from me." He glanced at the dark sky thickened with clouds. "Frustrating," he muttered. "So what did you think of Harrison Smith?"

"A very interesting man," Amy said, her eyes sparkling with intrigue. "I know I've only recently met your mother, but I can't imagine anybody flustering her the way Harrison does." Amy rubbed her hands together briskly.

She obviously still wasn't used to the cold. "I've known her forever and I've never seen anything like it, either." He flagged an empty taxi.

The cab slowed to a stop in front of them. Roper held the door open so Amy could slide inside before joining her. She gave her address to the driver and Roper, exhausted from his day, decided not to argue.

"Does it bother you? That he's so obviously interested?" Amy asked.

Roper didn't have to think about his answer. He shook his head. "Not as long as the man's feelings are real and he isn't using her reaction to him as a means to get her to take the role."

The role, as well as the man, really had to be right for Cassandra Lee. Roper would have to do some digging into the director's past and make sure he was good enough for Roper's mother.

"Well, he seems genuine," Amy said.

"Says the woman who was ready to fall at his feet," Roper said, laughing.

She playfully smacked his shoulder. "I was not. I could see your mother's dilemma clearly, that's all. Harrison is a charming man."

"A mix of Sean Connery and Jack Nicholson and a pit bull. Is that what you like in a guy? A bulldozer?" Roper asked.

"That's an interesting question." Amy leaned her head back and glanced at him. "I haven't thought about it, really. I think it's all about chemistry and whether, like you said, the man is the real thing. The rest should come naturally." Her voice dropped lower, thicker, making him think she was referring to them.

Or maybe that's just what he wanted to believe.

Inside his pocket, his cell phone rang, interrupting the dark intimacy of the back of the cab, and Roper groaned. He pulled it out of his pocket. "What is it?" he asked.

"Now do you understand why I can't take the role or be alone with him?" His mother didn't bother to say hello first. "He wants to have lunch tomorrow to discuss the part. I need you there."

Her voice was loud enough for Amy to hear, and she groaned, too.

Roper rolled his eyes. By the time his mother let him interrupt her long enough to say he'd discuss lunch with her later tonight, the taxi had pulled up to Amy's building. While he was hanging up the phone, she'd thanked him and promised to call him from the office tomorrow to discuss mail forwarding among other things.

He'd planned to walk her in and kiss her goodnight. He'd have settled for just kissing her right there in the cab.

Instead, the opportunity to segue into any kind of a kiss was lost. He slammed his hand onto the torn leather backseat in frustration, then gave the cabbie his address.

The life of an orphan suddenly seemed appealing, he thought wryly.

AFTER LAST NIGHT, AMY realized she needed a new plan of action for Roper, and by the late afternoon, she had one in place.

Still, as she sat at her desk, she couldn't help but take one last look at the daily papers. The *Post* lay on top of the pile. Metro Jock Receives Major Shock. The article went on to discuss the frustrating news

Roper had received from his doctor and how uncon-
firmed rumors had him pushing back his start date
to weeks after the start of spring training.

She called her secretary on the intercom. "Kelly?"
"Yes?"

"Do me a favor? Please pull all the most recent
sightings and blurbs about Roper on the Internet,
TV and radio and make sure I have copies before I
leave?" She wanted to take a look at where Roper
had been when he was sighted and ask him to think
about whom he'd spoken to each time. She needed
to see if there was a connection or common denomi-
nator. Clearly someone was out to punish Roper. But
whether it was Buckley or the crazy fan or someone
in his personal circle, she had no idea.

"How the hell do they find out about these
things?" Amy asked in frustration.

"Good question. I don't got an answer, either,"
Yank Morgan said as he entered her office without
knocking, cane in hand, fluffy dog at his side.

"Hi, Yank."

"Hi, girlie. How are you doin'?"

"Fine if not for these." She ran her hand over the
stack of newspapers. "Did you see that Frank
Buckley's been picked up by satellite radio with a
corresponding TV deal? He won't just be seen and
heard in New York. The whole country will get to experience the foul man."

Yank nodded. "Lola read it to me this morning.
Don't fret about what you can't change and change

what you can. That's what I always say. In other words, forget about Buckley the Bastard."

"I would if the media would let me." She flipped over the paper that had Buckley's deal on the back and picked up the *Daily News*. It, too, had a blurb about Roper's life. "Which metro jock was spotted with his lady of the moment and his famous actress mother at an intimate family dinner at Kelly's restaurant? Could wedding bells be in the picture for either couple?"

"Argh!" She threw this edition into the trash.

"You must've just read the one about dinner. How was it anyway? I've been meaning to tell Lola I want to eat there one day soon."

Amy appreciated the subject change. "Delicious. You'll enjoy it," she promised him. "So are we all set?"

"You're ready to go. Our boy thinks you're picking him up for a business lunch with me. The limo knows to head straight up to the lodge. Dealing with the fallout is up to you." Yank let out a loud laugh that startled Noodle from where she'd plopped onto the floor.

"I can handle it," she said, repeating her new mantra, the one she'd adopted for maneuvering in the Hot Zone world. After all, she could think of many times she'd taken a hard stand with her mother, going so far as to lock her in her own home, just to keep her out of trouble.

"Of course you can. I just came by to wish you luck," Yank said. He turned, whistled and walked out, dog toddling after him.

Amy gave a silent prayer for success.

Between the stress of Roper's injury and therapy, the constant fan backlash, his mother's daily drama and the tracking of his every movement in the paper, Amy knew she was doing the right thing.

She just knew Roper would never see it the same way.

CASSANDRA DEFINITELY NEEDED a new plan of action to avoid Harrison. Running from L.A. hadn't helped. He'd followed her. She didn't know how much longer she could continue to convince John to act as a buffer and she knew better than to include Ben again. Harrison had told her Ben wanted to discuss a script with him. Her son was shameless and would use whoever crossed his path. She understood she wasn't blameless in how Ben had turned out. She'd babied him for too long. But she understood him, too, and she couldn't just cut him off, which was why she kept turning to her oldest son to help.

But who was going to help her with her director? The man was persistent in the extreme. He wanted her to return to L.A. with him as a couple and he wanted her to take that role. Television. Could she hold her head up in Hollywood after such a huge step down?

Cassandra didn't know what she feared more, the role he wanted her to play on screen or the part he wanted to play in her life.

CHAPTER TEN

ROPER GLANCED OUT THE tinted window of the car Amy had hired to pick him up and take them for lunch. He still didn't understand why he couldn't have just met her and Yank at the restaurant for this sudden meeting, but she'd insisted. Now, as he sat beside her, she remained eerily quiet.

"What restaurant are we going to, anyway?" he asked.

She shrugged. "I'm new in the city and I'm bad with names. I can't remember," she murmured. Her gaze strayed out the window and she drummed her fingertips on the hard leather armrest beneath the window.

Taking her cue, he sat in silence, watching as the scenery changed from the luxury shops on Madison Avenue to more eclectic scenery as they made their way farther north.

It wasn't until the driver turned right onto 102nd Street and merged onto FDR Drive that he spoke up. "We're leaving the city?"

"Looks that way." She didn't meet his gaze.

His gut churned with anxiety. He braced his hand on the seat in front of him and leaned forward so the driver would know he was talking to him. "Excuse me, but where are we headed?"

"Upstate," he said.

"Upstate." Roper placed his hand on Amy's jeans-clad thigh.

Faded-jeans-clad thigh, he realized now. Warm, tight yet supple. He shook off those thoughts, reminding himself he was annoyed. He looked her over, from the top of her ponytailed hair to the bottom of her Converse sneakers. Her outfit wasn't exactly business casual.

"Dammit, Amy. Don't make me guess." Because he didn't like the direction his thoughts were going.

She turned toward him, her knees nudging against him as she moved. "We're going to the lodge, and before you blow up at me, hear me out."

He stiffened in shock. "What gives you the right to kidnap me and take me somewhere I explicitly told you I did not want to go?" His anger simmered on low boil. If he'd been with anyone but Amy, he'd have lost it by now.

She straightened her shoulders and met his gaze head-on. Now that he'd been clued in, she was no longer hesitant around him, but was the determined Amy he'd grown to admire.

"Correct me if I'm wrong here, but you have a goal. You want to be ready for spring training as close to the beginning as possible, right?"

He inclined his head, unwilling to give her more than that for the moment.

"In order to get ready, you need not just to be physically ready, but mentally ready." Her eyes blazed with certainty.

When he didn't reply, she nudged his leg with hers. "Well?"

"Right," he muttered.

"Well, as far as I can see, you're far from being ready either way. If you stay in the city with your mother pulling you into her problems every five minutes, and your sister needing help planning her wedding, and your couch-potato brother hanging over your head and shit arriving at your door—and I mean that literally, as well as figuratively—you'll never have five free minutes to focus on *you*." She poked him in the chest as she spoke.

He shifted in his seat, finding it difficult to argue the point, yet unwilling to concede to her tactics. "So you took it on yourself to bring me to a place where I could get tough for the season."

"Yes."

"Care to tell me where you get off manipulating me?"

"I'm paid to make sure you're ready. Both Yank and Micki agreed we had no choice."

His cell phone rang and he grabbed it from his pants pocket.

"Who is it?" Amy asked before he could take the call.

He glanced at the screen. "My brother."

Taking him off guard, Amy reached out and swiped the phone from his hand. In an instant, she opened the window and threw the device into thin air.

"What the hell?"

Amy's heart raced a mile a minute. She truly couldn't blame him for being angry. But with the act of throwing his phone out, her heart pumped faster and more furiously in her chest. She'd scared herself while his face flushed red with anger.

"The Hot Zone will replace it," she said, repeating what Micki had told her last night when she'd called to support Amy and her plan.

They agreed that given the chance, Roper would use his phone to call and check on his family or let them know where he was. Both women were convinced, though, that once he had the opportunity to unwind and he saw how focused he could be on his career, he'd willingly go along with their plan.

"I don't believe this." He ran a hand through his hair.

"Believe it." Amy turned back toward the window, intending to ignore him.

Reverse psychology. She couldn't think of another way to work around Roper's anger. She curled her hands into fists and looked out the window, not really seeing the passing scenery.

"What's going to stop me from picking up a phone at the lodge and calling someone to come get me?" he asked.

"Nothing except your own common sense. I'm counting on the fact that you want to get healthy enough that you'll give this experiment a chance. See what relaxing without pressure does for your frame of mind."

He'd soon discover that his suite had been stripped of a telephone and the staff had been instructed not to give him access to either the house phone or anyone's personal cell phone. He could definitely find a way to leave or call home if he was downright determined, but it wouldn't be easy. And Amy hoped that by the time he found the means, he'd no longer have the desire.

She drew a deep, calming breath. "I'm betting that after a few days, you'll be thanking me for this."

"Not likely," he muttered.

"You don't need to worry about your family," she reassured him. "Micki is making herself personally available to them for any emergencies. You trust Micki to handle them, don't you?"

He didn't reply. Instead he shifted in the seat beside her and exhaled hard. Reverse psychology, Amy reminded herself, pushing aside the gnawing guilt.

Then she followed his lead and ignored him for the rest of the long car ride upstate.

A WOMAN WHO INTRODUCED herself as Lisa, the assistant manager, escorted Roper to his private suite. He wasn't surprised to see he had a dresser and closet full of his favorite brand of workout clothes, T-shirts and a note assuring him anything else he needed would be provided by the concierge—whom he had to walk downstairs to reach since he had no phone in his room.

The suite had a fully stocked kitchen, including a refrigerator and pantry, along with a set of dishes and utensils for him to use. A quick glance told him the coffeemaker was state-of-the-art and his favorite flavored beans were sitting beside the appliance along with a note.

Relax and enjoy. You need it and so does your career. Courtesy of Athletes Only and the Hot Zone.

On the nightstand, there was a list of restaurants on the premises, a room service card and a printed schedule of activities specifically put together for him. From the daily physical-therapy appointment to the orthopedist on call if there were any problems, to the gym hours and scheduled masseuse, every one of his needs had been taken care of. Despite the fact that it was already past lunchtime, even today had been booked. He had a full afternoon of rehab and relaxation waiting for him.

Obviously he could find someone with a cell phone or grab a ride to town and use a phone, but something stopped him. Maybe it was the niggling feeling in the back of his mind that Amy had a point.

Though at the moment he was loathe to give Amy credit for anything.

AMY LEFT HER SUITCASE OPEN on the bed and pulled out a swimsuit. She hadn't had a real swim since leaving Florida, not that she considered an over-chlorinated indoor pool the equivalent of what she was used to, but she'd have to make do. She had a lot of frustration and, yes, guilt, to work out and she knew no better way than a swim.

She changed and headed for the spa and gym area where the pool was located, deciding to leave her captive to his own devices for a while. And since it was winter, and most of the guests were skiing, she had the pool to herself.

She dove in and swam laps, taking the length of the pool with the crawl stroke she'd perfected as a teenager living down south. She made her way through the water, up one end and back down the other, over and over until exhaustion threatened to overwhelm her. Satisfied she'd burned calories, as well as nervous, excess energy, she drew herself up and out of the pool.

But she wasn't ready to head back to her room just yet, so she settled on a chair and relaxed, planning to wander the area and get familiar with the other amenities before going back up to shower and face Roper's anger over dinner.

As it turned out, he didn't show up for the reservation she'd booked at one of the lodge's most exclusive restaurants, nor did she see him for the next three days. She kept track of him via the staff and by checking up on him with the physical therapist and others around the resort, so she knew he hadn't escaped her so-called prison. She caught glimpses of him wandering the grounds or working out in the gym, but she left him to his own devices, grateful he hadn't attempted to borrow a phone or hitch a ride home.

She had to admit she was impressed. Even if she was growing increasingly upset and frustrated by his refusal to talk to her at all.

THREE DAYS HAD PASSED SINCE Roper arrived at the lodge. He'd relaxed for the first time in ages, though it had taken a while. He had no idea unwinding from the reality of life could take so long or be so difficult. Hell, he hadn't even realized how physically and emotionally taxed he'd been until his first massage.

At first, being out of touch from his family had been difficult. He'd worried constantly about his mother and how she was dealing with Harrison Smith. He wondered how many expenses she'd incurred without his sister's permission in planning the huge wedding. He didn't worry much about Ben, since without money, his brother was unlikely to get into too much trouble.

After a while, though, a funny thing happened. He stopped thinking about his family's problems and he started focusing on himself. Not on the negative things, like not returning in time for spring training, but on what he could do to work harder and smarter in order to get back to the game he loved. Without his time being divided, he started to get into the routine set up for him, and he began to see how distracted he'd been before. How much he'd needed this escape.

How right Amy had been.

At first he'd deliberately avoided her, missing planned meals out of spite, wanting to make a point that he might have chosen to stay here but he was still in charge. He justified his actions by telling himself that he was just doing as she'd instructed, thinking only of himself for a change. Which he was. Yet he'd catch her watching him through the gym windows or eating with some of the guests she'd obviously met during her time there. He knew she was giving him space just as he knew he was being childish by avoiding her.

He waited for her at lunch at her normal time. When she didn't show up, he asked Lisa about her. The woman told him Amy wasn't feeling well. She was laid up with a cold and said she'd be in her room if he needed anything. He didn't *need* anything, he was just starting to miss her.

Hell, he'd missed her from the minute he'd shut her out. But if she wasn't feeling well, he doubted she'd want to see him, so he had chicken soup sent to her room with a *Feel Better* note that he signed himself.

The next day, she was still out of commission. When he called, she told him that she felt awful and didn't want to give him her cold, so it was better he not stop by. He sent the doctor over instead, but respected her wishes and stayed away. Her cold lasted another three days.

In the meantime, he worked out, relaxed and fell into bed exhausted at night, earlier than he was used to. He woke each day feeling refreshed and ready to start over again. And he began to sense that his body was responding to routine, consistency and *lack of stress.*

Everything was progressing well. The only thing missing was Amy, and he figured by tomorrow, she'd either come out or he was barging in. After this past week, he'd come to the definite realization that if he was going to remain here next door to the woman he wanted more with each passing day, he was damn well going to do something about it.

His scheduled routine was finished for the day and he eased his aching body into the warm, bubbling water of the hot tub, soaking and unwinding. Every time he began to wonder how his family was doing or what their reactions were to not being able to reach him on demand, he pushed the thought out of his mind. He'd become an expert at it, and with each passing day, the guilt lessened. Amy was right—he trusted Micki to handle them. If a true emergency had cropped up, he'd have heard. He closed his eyes, tipped his head back and thought about absolutely nothing.

Much too soon, a female voice broke into his blessed silence.

"Mind if I join you?" she asked.

He forced his heavy eyelids open to see a gorgeous woman in a tiny string bikini sinking into the tub as if his answer was a foregone conclusion. Since he didn't own the rights to its usage, he supposed it was.

Her chocolate-brown hair screamed perfect dye job and her wide smile indicated perfection. Celebritylike perfection. Everything about her seemed familiar, but he couldn't place her name.

"John Roper, pleased to meet you." He extended his hand in greeting.

She grabbed it for a surprisingly strong shake. "Hannah Gregory," she said.

He snapped his fingers in the air. "'Lies Lost,'" he said, suddenly remembering her Top 40 hit. "I'm a fan."

Her smile grew wider. "Thanks. Since I have three brothers and I was born and raised in New York, I'm a die-hard Renegades fan. Nice to meet you, too," she said. Leaning back, she let herself grow more comfortable in the water.

He waited for a negative comment on his season, but it never came.

"So what are you doing here at the lodge?" he asked.

"The band wanted to get away, so here I am." She waved one arm in the air. "They went skiing. Brr," she said, her distaste for the outdoor sport obvious. "How about you? What brings you to Greenlawn?"

He contemplated how to phrase his kidnapping diplomatically. "R and R," he finally said, opting for discretion.

"That seems to be what this place is known for."

"So I hear."

She began to hum, a pleasant sound that didn't disturb him, and he shut his eyes once more.

After a few minutes, her voice once again broke the silence. "Listen, the boys and I are having a small get-together in our suite tonight. Why don't you join us?" she asked. "They'd love to meet you. Especially Mike, my drummer. He's also a fan."

Roper opened his eyes to see she wasn't even looking at him. In fact, her eyes were shut and she was enjoying the bubbling water. Clearly she wasn't flirting with him, just extending an invitation. One he appreciated, since he was ready for some human companionship here in Greenlawn.

He was surprised to realize that he was relieved the beautiful Hannah wasn't showing any interest. Though there might have been a time when her perky breasts and pretty face, all probably molded by a plastic surgeon, might have appealed to him, it was the lightly freckled Floridian who held his interest now. Despite the fact that she'd tricked him into coming up here.

Damn Amy, even out of sight she wasn't out of mind. She had obviously spoiled him for anyone else, which only served to convince him he had to act on his desire.

And what better way to break the ice after a week of not speaking than at a small party? "Sure. I'd love to come," he told Hannah. It wasn't as if he had someplace else to be tonight. He was on his own in this little slice of seclusion.

"Great." She still didn't open her eyes. "I'm catering food up to my room. That's why we love this place. We can really keep to ourselves."

He nodded. That suited his purposes just fine. He glanced up at the ceiling, then asked Hannah the question circling in his head. "Mind if I bring a friend tonight?"

She shook her head. "Not at all. The more the merrier." She rattled off her suite number, then began to chat with him about the season in a way that told him she was one of the minority—an understanding fan who knew even a million-dollar player could have a bad stretch.

By the time he climbed out of the water, he realized that despite Hannah's celebrity, she was as down-to-earth as they came. She even reminded him of Amy.

He wrapped a towel around his waist and ran his fingers through his hair. "I'll see you around eight?" he asked.

Hannah, who'd also come out of the tub and had begun to dry herself off, nodded. "Come earlier if you can't find anything to keep yourself occupied," she said.

"I might just do that."

"Do what?" a familiar female voice asked.

He jerked around to see Amy staring at them. He wondered what she'd overheard, and worse, what she thought was going on between them.

"Hey, there," he said to Amy, trying not to look or feel guilty when he had no reason.

"Hi." Amy lifted one hand in an awkward wave. The other pulled tighter on the towel that covered her one-piece bathing suit. "I didn't mean to interrupt. I just thought a sauna would be a great way to finish off this awful cold. And it's through there. The sauna, I mean." Her gaze darted from Roper to Hannah, then back again. She took a step back, and then another one, clearly intending to escape.

"Don't go." Her obvious discomfort tugged at something inside him and he wanted to reassure her. "Hannah was just inviting us to a party tonight. Hannah Gregory, meet Amy Stone. Amy, Hannah is—"

"I know who Hannah is," Amy said, extending her hand. "Nice to meet you. I love your music," she said with genuine warmth.

More warmth than she was shooting his way at the moment.

Hannah beamed at the compliment, suddenly looking even younger than she really was. Given the frosty look Amy turned his way, and considering she had walked in on the tail end of their conversation, it was obvious she thought the events at her cousin's wedding were repeating themselves. She believed she'd witnessed John Roper picking up a woman while he had another one waiting in the wings, hell, while she was upstairs sick.

Apparently Amy didn't know him as well as she

thought she did. It was time he enlightened her as to the man he really was.

He looked forward to the challenge and to ending the night exactly where he belonged. In Amy's bed.

BACK IN HER ROOM, AS AMY showered to get ready for Hannah's party, she knew there was no way she could compete with a music pop star who was gorgeous, impeccably groomed and much more worldly than Amy could ever be. Again, it wasn't that she lacked self-esteem, she just understood what it took to keep up in Roper and Hannah's world. They exuded star quality without effort, and as young as Hannah was, Amy had no doubt she'd had plastic surgery of some sort to keep that perfect body and face. So Amy wasn't even going to put herself in that league. As her mother had taught her, she should always just be herself.

Still, Amy was human and she couldn't help but wonder what Roper had thought when he'd turned from Hannah in her itsy-bitsy teenie-weenie bikini to face Amy in her Speedo one-piece racing suit.

It shouldn't matter.

But it did.

Just like she shouldn't be personally interested in Roper.

But she was.

And that truth had been driven home to her when she'd heard the sound of Roper's deep, familiar laugh coming from the whirlpool and she'd walked in on him making time with a gorgeous woman who, true to form, hung on his every word.

Amy knew she ought to have expected it, but since she hadn't talked to him in a week and their last real encounter had been an argument, she hadn't been able to laugh it off. Instead, unwanted and unbidden jealousy had swamped her and remained with her, even now.

Four days with a respiratory virus had nearly killed her, and Amy had dragged herself out of bed for the first time in days to take a sauna and visit the outside world. She hadn't expected to run into Roper, and she sure as heck thought she'd look better the first time she did. But her nose was still red, her eyes sunken and tired-looking and her choice of bathing suit wasn't exactly sexy.

She stepped out of the shower and towel-dried her hair, then used a diffuser to air-dry the curls. The one benefit to being in New York was the lack of constant humidity, but there was no getting away from the fact that she wasn't a model-thin, glossy-haired starlet. She picked clothes that suited her, but at times like these it was hard to remember that she liked herself just fine.

Drawing a deep breath, she headed over to the room number where Hannah was staying. She'd told Roper she'd meet him there, knowing she'd need time to pull herself together before seeing him again.

Voices, laughter and soft music sounded from inside. Amy knocked once and the door eased open, so she let herself inside. She took in the small group of people, immediately noticing they were dressed as casually as she was in her jeans and a loose-fitting cotton long-sleeved T-shirt. One hurdle over, she managed to relax.

Then she zeroed in on Roper sitting beside Hannah, along with a bunch of other guys who joked and talked while she strummed on her guitar. Although he was laughing and enjoying himself with the guys, Roper didn't look particularly hung up on the pretty musician. In fact, he seemed more mellow and relaxed than she'd ever seen him.

A sudden sense of peace settled over Amy as she realized she'd done the right thing by bringing him here. At that moment, he seemed to sense her presence. He turned her way, his gaze locking on hers. A welcoming smile eased the corners of his mouth upward in a grin that told her he was genuinely happy to see her.

She walked over and joined the group.

"Hi, there," Roper said, light sparkling in his eyes.

"Hi," Amy said, not wanting to interrupt the ongoing conversation.

"Join us," Hannah said.

"We're just listening to Hannah and her favorite relaxing music," one of the guys said.

The other woman rolled her eyes. "They are not. They're being guys, making crude jokes and basically ignoring me," Hannah said.

"Who's this pretty lady?" A big, dark-haired, tattooed guy asked. His easy laugh was at odds with his rougher appearance, and Amy could tell he was a teddy bear in wolf's clothing.

"I'm so bad at names." Hannah blushed. "But I remember your first name. It's Amy. Amy…?"

"Stone," Roper said, rising and stepping over to join Amy, placing a protective, possessive arm around her shoulders. "Amy Stone, meet Mike Morris, the drummer."

"Hey, don't forget about us," another of the group said.

Amy glanced over. Two identical faces, both blond-haired men, stared back at her.

"Joe and John Glover, Amy Stone." Hannah gestured between all involved. "You can see how rough it is. I'm surrounded by guys all the time. I'm glad to have another girl here." She placed her guitar beside her and jumped up. "Me and the guys, we tour together all the time, but sometimes it gets a bit much, if you know what I mean."

Amy laughed, glancing at the men she found herself suddenly surrounded by. "I can imagine."

"Don't listen to her," Mike said. "She loves us." His gaze caught Hannah's for a brief second before he quickly glanced back at the other guys.

"Like a brother, baby." She made a face at her drummer, but the stare and the connection lasted long enough to tell Amy there was something between them. Something they both fought to deny.

Hannah turned to Amy. "Come on, let's get to know each other," Hannah said, pulling her away from Roper and to the far side of the room.

She handed Amy a can of Coke and grabbed one

for herself, another thing that surprised Amy. No drugs or alcohol. Everyone here seemed high on just hanging out and enjoying life.

"So how do you know Roper?" Hannah asked Amy.

"I work for his PR firm."

"Publicist?" Hannah asked, drinking her Coke directly from the can.

Amy nodded. "But on this assignment, I'm more like his handler."

Hannah nodded. "I'm ducking my handler-manager at the moment," she said, sounding way too wise for her years.

Amy was intrigued. "Mind if I ask why?"

Hannah strode to the window and looked out. Amy joined her, struck by the beauty of the falling snow. White and full flakes dropped against the backdrop of the inky night sky. So different from Florida and yet so magnificent it took her breath away.

Hannah sighed. "My manager likes to keep me in the headlines even when I don't have a CD currently out. You know the expression, no publicity is bad publicity? Well she lives by that mantra and frankly it exhausts me."

"How so?" Amy wanted a point of comparison for Roper's life. The two sounded similar.

"I can't go out for dinner without the press finding out about it. If I call a guy friend just because I need a shoulder to cry on, the next thing I know I'm reading about how we're an item. I know this sounds selfish considering how fortunate I've been, but I need some downtime and it's been hard to get it lately." She glanced around the room at the guys in the band. "They understand and feel the same way. So we came up here without telling her where we are."

Amy placed her soda can down, unopened. "Boy, we all have a lot in common." She didn't know why she thought she could trust Hannah, but she did. Something about the sincerity she sensed in the other woman's demeanor and personality spoke to Amy. "I basically dragged Roper up here kicking and screaming for the same reasons. Nobody knows where he is and I really need to keep it that way."

Hannah turned toward Amy, her eyes full of understanding. "He's had it rough lately, hasn't he?"

"He has. Much more than he deserves. I want him to have time to regroup without personal issues pulling at him. Every day he gets here is a bonus as far as I'm concerned."

"He won't be outed by any of us, that I can promise you." Hannah crossed her heart.

Amy glanced across the room and her gaze met Roper's. He held the stare for a long moment before he winked and turned his attention back to whatever Mike was saying.

They hadn't had a real conversation since the car ride up here one week ago. Her cold had sidelined her, but watching him now, maybe it was for the best. He'd had a chance to come to grips with what she'd done and why. He'd needed to be here and he understood that now.

Amy refocused on Hannah, realizing Roper's emotional health depended on everyone's discretion, but apparently Hannah felt the same way. "I believe you'll keep his location secret."

"I will. We're in seclusion, too." Hannah leaned closer. "You care about him, don't you?"

"Of course I do. He's my client and this is my first big assignment. I can't afford to have him dissatisfied with the end result."

Hannah rolled her eyes. "I wasn't talking about liking him as a client. I saw the way you were looking at him. Not just now, which was pretty intense, but earlier at the pool. You didn't like finding him hanging out with me."

"I…" Amy opened her mouth, then shut it again. She thought about denying the other woman's words but what was the point. "Was it that obvious?" Amy asked.

Hannah nodded. "I'm afraid so."

"It wasn't personal." Amy raised her hands to her hot cheeks, embarrassed at being found out. And here she thought she'd managed to seem professional.

"I know that." Hannah waved a hand, dismissing Amy's concerns. "Want to know how I know? I mean, can I share a secret so you'll understand?"

"Absolutely," Amy said.

"I figured it out because I have the same problem

with Mike." She tipped her head toward the drummer, who still stood talking to Roper. "I'm head over heels," she said with a sigh. "We spend so much time together on the road, we know each other really well. I know he finds me attractive. I see how he looks at me, but he won't act on it."

"Why not?" Amy shot a covert look at the big man who looked as if he could handle himself with this or any woman.

"He says he doesn't want to screw with the chemistry of the band if something goes wrong. But that isn't it." Hannah shook her hair out of her face. "It's the age thing. There's ten years between us. That's an issue for him, not me. Age and Big Mama."

"Who?" Amy tried not to laugh at the name.

"My mother," Hannah said, wrinkling her nose. "And the band's manager I was telling you about earlier. I think Mike's afraid of her," Hannah whispered. "Not that he'd ever admit it."

Amy understood Hannah's situation. She wouldn't exactly say she was head over heels for Roper, at least, not yet, but the damn attraction was there and strong. But she didn't want it to interfere with her doing her job. She didn't want her private life to become public, either. Still, she couldn't deny how much she desired him or the fact that the feelings weren't going away.

Maybe she just ought to sleep with him, get it out of her system and be done with it, she thought wryly.

And then she wondered why not.

Although the idea had come to her suddenly, the

yearning between them had been building since
they'd met at the wedding and the feeling had only
grown stronger since they'd begun working together.
She swallowed hard and glanced his way. She took
in his strong presence, his sexy body, his handsome
face, and suddenly she couldn't think of anything
else.

"What do you think?" Hannah asked her, drawing
Amy's attention back to their conversation.

"About what?" She'd obviously missed everything the other woman had just said.

Hannah rolled her eyes, obviously realizing what
Amy was preoccupied with. "I said I was thinking
of just seducing Mike. Slipping into his bed and daring him to throw me out." She laughed, but Amy
could see Hannah was serious.

"Not a bad idea," Amy said, wondering if she
could pull off such a stunt herself.

"That's what I've been telling myself. We're here,
we're alone except for the twins—but they don't
care about anything except their music—and there's
no Big Mama to interrupt." Hannah's eyes flashed
with anticipation.

"I like it," Amy said, her mind already wondering
how she'd manage it herself.

"As for Big Mama, I've thought about hiring
another manager and cutting out the nepotism, but
she really means well. She's pushed and pushed and
helped us get where we are. But honestly, she needs
to back off sometimes. And if things work out be-

tween me and Mike, her interference would be a make-or-break point between us." Hannah nodded decisively.

Amy knew Hannah meant what she was saying, but as she knew from watching Roper deal with his family, it was one thing to talk a tough game, another to execute it against a well-meaning but interfering parent. "You need to be blunt and tell her to let you live your life."

Hannah sighed. "She thinks it's her job to direct my life. Tell me, is it possible to prevent a steamroller from doing its job?"

"I wish I knew," Amy said, thinking of Cassandra Lee.

Amy had spoken with Micki earlier and Cassandra had given her hell for sequestering her son and refusing to discuss his whereabouts. Micki had assured Cassandra that Roper was fine and taking care of himself for a change. She'd offered the woman anything she needed from advice to reservations. She just wouldn't give Cassandra the one thing she wanted. Her son's current address.

Amy looked into Hannah's eyes and said, "Just remember it's your life. If you don't take control of it, everyone else will."

"Sound advice," Roper said, coming up behind them.

"It is. It just isn't easy," Hannah murmured. "I should go talk to Mike. We're supposed to go over some things for this summer's upcoming concert. We'll talk later," she said to Amy.

Hannah worked her way over to her band and, with great finesse and a lot of sex appeal that included swaying hips and a full pout, managed to extricate Mike from the rest of the guys.

Impressive, Amy thought.

And when Roper strode over and cornered her, she hoped she had the nerve to act as boldly as Hannah had. What a difference a week made. Now Roper glanced at Amy with a devilish grin, all evidence of his anger at being tricked gone. So when he turned his sex appeal her way, it wasn't hard to believe in herself and her ability to act on her feelings.

Because Amy was finished fighting the attraction between them.

CHAPTER ELEVEN

ROPER STUDIED AMY, HER tight jeans and sexy loose-fitting top, and realized she fit right in here. The woman who'd been uncomfortable earlier in her one-piece bathing suit was gone. In her place was the siren who called to him day and night, in his dreams and when they were wide-awake. Like now.

She shoved her hands into her pants pockets. "So have you calmed down?" she asked.

As if he hadn't had a reason to be upset with her, he thought wryly. He wasn't fooled by her attempt to put the onus on him. But he didn't mind it, either.

He leaned against the wall, just plain enjoying her. "You mean, have I forgiven you for dragging me up here against my will?" He was teasing. He just wasn't sure whether or not she knew it yet.

She stepped closer until they were inches apart. Her scent, strawberry shampoo and pure woman, overtook his thoughts and all he could concentrate on was taking her in his arms and kissing her senseless—with no cell phone, Treo or family member interrupting them.

"I was looking out for you." She met his gaze

with those huge brown eyes that broke down his defenses.

Not that he had any left when it came to her. "I know that now." He treated her to a slow, easy, genuine smile meant to relax her and put all conflict behind them for good.

She released a puff of air, her relief that he was no longer angry evident. "So what made you come around and finally understand?"

"You did." A stray curl fell onto her forehead and he plucked it off with one hand, allowing himself the pleasure of smoothing his palm down her head in a gentle caress. "Deep in your heart, you aren't a manipulative sneaky person. Some time up here alone, no one to bother me, a workout and a whirlpool, and I relaxed enough to remember that."

"Wow. You're complimenting me." The corner of her lips turned up in a cheeky grin. "Not only have you forgiven me but you're pretty mellow."

"And you seem to be enjoying yourself, too. You must be pretty relaxed yourself."

"I wasn't, but I am now," she said.

He hoped the reason was his forgiveness, but he couldn't be sure and raised an eyebrow in question. "And what's so special about now?"

"Your calmer attitude, for one thing."

"And the other thing?" he asked.

She shrugged, her attitude playful. "Isn't a girl allowed to have secrets?" She bit down on her lower lip.

His gaze followed the movement, his gaze drawn to her sensual mouth. So she was playing coy. Miss All Business was suddenly flirting, he thought, amused. Hmm. Well, he couldn't say he minded.

She was one of the perks of being here. "I took a walk earlier and discovered an amazing place. Want to see?" he asked.

She glanced over at their hostess, who appeared pretty tied up with her drummer. "I don't think they'll miss us," she said, a mischievous glint in her eye.

"Come." He took her hand and together they walked through the lodge's main lobby where people wandered, some alone, some in small groups, while others gathered around the big-screen television at the bar.

"Do you want to stop first and have a drink?" He gestured to two empty stools in a private area.

She shook her head. "I'd rather have all my faculties tonight. Nothing to drink. But thanks, anyway."

He inclined his head and kept walking. Normally he'd think her unwillingness to indulge in alcohol was her way of reminding him they were only business associates, but something was different about her tonight. It wasn't just her light mood or her teasing. It was *her*. She hadn't removed her hand from his grasp and there was a sudden confidence emanating from her he hadn't seen since meeting her at the wedding. Whatever had brought on the change, he was thankful for it. And he had the sudden hope that her unwillingness to drink had more to do with her desire to remember each and every minute between them.

He led her past the gift and sundry shop to a point beyond the restaurants. While working off his frustration earlier, he'd come upon a solarium that was being cleaned. He let himself inside and found himself viewing a winter wonderland beyond the glass. It was a place he'd spent a quiet, contemplative hour.

The door was closed and he knocked once. When no one answered, he pushed it open and led her inside. Instead of turning on the lights, he kept the room dark, and when the door slammed shut behind them, he quietly turned the lock, giving them complete privacy.

"What is this place?" she asked.

"A sunroom," he said. "I asked Lisa and she said it's usually only open during the summer. But when I walked by, a crew was dusting and I peeked inside." He'd looked out the wall-to-wall windows at the snowy landscape beyond and immediately knew he wanted to share the sight with Amy.

She strode to the windows and stared outside. Instead of looking at the scenery, he watched her. Eyes wide, she stared at the frosty view, lit up by outdoor lights and the ski trails in the distance.

"Wow. It's beautiful," she said in awe. "I've never seen snow like this before. I mean, I've seen the dirty slush in the city this winter but nothing like this."

He hadn't realized what she'd missed growing up

in Florida. "Then I'm going to have to get you out-side to experience the snow for real while we're here."

"Ooh, I'd love that." Her voice dropped to a deeper husky sound that resonated inside him.

He stepped behind her, wrapping his arms around her waist and looking out from over her shoulder. White snow covered the bare branches and stars filled the night sky. Without even realizing it, he eased himself forward so his body pressed more fully against her back. His hands splayed across her stom-ach, and of its own volition, his penis grew hard and aching. It thrust against his jeans and pressed insis-tently against her rear end.

She sucked in a deep breath, but she didn't pro-test or try to escape his hold. Obviously much had changed and he wasn't about to question why.

He rested his chin on her shoulder. "It's beauti-ful," he said, turning his head slightly and nuzzling his lips against her neck.

"Mmm. Growing up in Florida, I always thought I had it all. Sunshine and beaches, warm weather. But now I know what I was missing. Will you really go outside with me? I want to touch the snow and feel it between my fingertips," she said, her excitement rising.

He was rising, as well.

"I want to make a snow angel like I've seen on TV," she continued.

Her enthusiasm was contagious, and he felt as if

he were experiencing the same surge of emotions as Amy—all for the first time. "I'll take you anywhere you want to go," he promised her.

She tipped her head backward. "I believe you," she whispered.

She stared out the windows some more while he continued to nuzzle her neck with his lips, which quickly turned to suckling her soft skin. He couldn't get enough of her taste, her scent, all of her.

He slipped his hands into the waistband of her jeans. She didn't object, so he let his fingertips dip lower until he passed the low band on her panties and brushed the soft hair beneath.

She sucked in a shallow breath, and at the moment, he let his waist jerk forward, seeking relief he knew he wouldn't find just yet. But that didn't mean she couldn't enjoy and he intended for her to do just that.

In the silken silence that surrounded them, he unbuttoned her jeans and lowered the zipper, never once turning her to face him.

"John?" she asked, her voice uncertain.

"We're alone," he reassured her. "I locked the door. Besides, no one comes back here. And with the thick trees out there, no one can see in. It's just us," he promised her. "Isn't that what you wanted for me? Peace and quiet? Time to focus on what's important?"

He let his words settle, let her make of them what she would. He wasn't about to think or dig too deeply into his meaning now. The words had escaped, and right now he meant them.

Before she could back away, he picked up where he'd left off, easing her jeans just low enough on her thighs to give him access, but not too low that she couldn't pull them up and get decent if she wanted.

"Trust me," he whispered in her ear.

"I do." Then, as if to prove it, she shifted and spread her legs slightly, opening for him.

He'd been waiting for this moment, more desperately than even he'd realized, and as he slid his fingers past the triangle of hair and down to her damp heat, desire the likes of which he'd never known swept over him.

A soft moan escaped her lips.

"Do you like that?" he asked, already knowing the answer. Proving his theory, he pressed his forefinger between her dewy folds. Moisture licked at his skin and a rush of heat suffused him from inside out.

If this is what nearly entering her with his finger did to him, heaven help him when they made love. And they would. Soon. But her pleasure came first. He shifted positions and slid his finger inside her.

She shook and trembled, clearly already on the verge.

"I've got you, so don't be afraid to let go." As he spoke, he pushed his fingertip into her, then slowly eased out, making sure his thumb hit on the tight nub of desire with each slide.

She clenched her hot, wet inner walls around him, which only served to increase the friction of his finger's glide. Unable to control his own body's reaction, he began to pump his hips against her back in a steady rhythm.

He had control, but barely.

And then without warning, she turned toward him, releasing his finger from between her legs, taking him off guard. With shaking hands she reached for the zipper on his jeans and pulled them down.

She glanced down and stared. "Commando," she practically stuttered.

He shrugged, then grinned.

Laughing, she wrapped her arms around his neck, but he kissed her first, reveling in the sweet welcome of her mouth. He didn't know how, but he held on to some last shred of sanity, enough to know they had to be fast. The longer they stayed, the more risk of someone wandering back here by accident, as he had this afternoon.

"We should hurry," he said.

Amy nodded. "Please tell me you have protection." She wished she'd asked before she'd acted on impulse and yanked down his pants, no matter how impressive the sight.

But her entire body was on fire, desire pulsing through her and begging for release.

"As a matter of fact, I do." He bent to extricate a condom packet from his pocket.

Though relieved, a part of her wasn't sure how to

feel about the fact that he had a condom on hand, ready to go at a moment's notice.

"Amy?" he asked as he took care of the situation.

"Hmm?"

"Wipe the frown off your pretty face and look at how old this thing is." He held up the ripped packet, obviously worn from being carried around in his wallet. "My father knocked up my mother in a day and age when it just wasn't done. I promised myself a long time ago I'd never get caught without one."

The frenzy had momentarily lapsed in favor of deeper, more important talk. She couldn't suppress a smile. How could she be upset with a man like him?

"You're one of a kind," she told him.

He grinned. "You are, too, freckles." He tapped her cheeks.

She ought to be embarrassed, but he said it in a way that made her feel cherished.

"Listen, I'd lift you and be inside of you already but I could never explain reinjuring my shoulder if I did." He grinned, but she couldn't mistake how deep his voice was, how much his need matched her own.

"Good point." She glanced around the dark room, lit only by outdoor lights creeping in. To her right was a covered bar and stools that looked just the right height for what she had in mind.

What the heck? she thought. In for a penny, as the old expression went. She was already tempting fate by letting out the bad girl she always had a hunch was inside her. She pointed to the covered stools.

Next thing she knew, Roper had pulled her over and positioned her on one of them, in the most vulnerable way she could imagine, legs spread wide, waiting, just for him. But she didn't have time to think too long.

Condom on, he pulled her toward him and tilted her back against the chair. His gaze never leaving hers, he thrust into her completely.

Amy saw stars, and not only because it had been so long since she'd had sex. He filled her body in a way that reached up, up through her throat and threatened to make her head and body explode with the perfection of the feeling.

A low groan escaped from his throat and his big body reverberated inside hers. She grabbed on to the seat of the chair and held on tight as he slid out, then thrust deep once more. He repeated the motion, and to Amy's surprise, each time she felt fuller, more intense pressure inside her.

Together they quickly found a rhythm and the pleasure built higher and faster each time his body connected completely with hers.

In.

Out.

In.

With each successive thrust, she felt more of him. Took more of him.

Gave more of herself.

He cupped her face in his hands and kissed her long and hard, branding her even more than his body was doing. His tongue swept through her mouth, taking possession as he took control—gliding out of her body slowly at first, easing back in deep, not stopping to let her catch her breath. As the passion and yearning grew, gentleness gave way to more pressure, deeper thrusts that brought her ever closer to completion. She couldn't do anything more than squeeze her body tight around his and ride out the masterful storm he created.

And just when she didn't think she could take anymore, everything inside her exploded in bright lights and the most intense pleasure she'd ever known. The sensations took her even higher, rocking her world until finally, they subsided in slow, sweet passion.

She opened her heavy eyes and found Roper staring at her, his expression intense. "Are you okay?" he asked, concern in his voice.

"Never better." The pulsing continued throughout her system as she struggled to catch her breath.

"I thought our first time would be in a bed." His gravelly voice told her he hadn't yet completely recovered, either.

"I think I'd have killed you if you stopped to go find one."

She thought about his words and their implications, which summed up the kind of man he was. For so long, she'd been consumed with avoiding anything happening between them. Meanwhile, he'd thought about their first time. He cared about where they made love.

Was it any wonder her feelings for him continued to grow?

He leaned his head back and groaned. "I locked the door, but we shouldn't continue to tempt fate."

She laughed. "Good point."

He slid out of her, his regret at leaving her obvious. After he pulled up his jeans, he gently helped her stand and fix her clothes until there were no telltale signs of dishevelment to give her away.

He then smoothed his hands over her hair and pulled her close for a long kiss before breaking apart once more. "There's a bathroom on the other side of the room. I'll be right back."

While he was gone, she stared out at the landscape, the snow and glittering lights. She was light-headed and in shock, as much from what she'd done as from the feelings attached to what she'd once considered merely a physical act.

If asked, she'd have said that she cared about the few men who'd come before Roper. Until tonight she'd have been telling the truth. But now, post-Roper, she realized she'd been so naive and ignorant.

There was sex. And there was making love. And though she'd obviously liked the men she'd been with in the past, none had ever induced such a cascading flood of emotion.

She pressed her hands against the cold window and then used her palms to cool her flushed face. But nothing eased the internal heat and nothing stopped the sudden realizations that came next.

She'd never felt this way before. So right, so un-inhibited, so free. Only with this man. And that was what she'd feared all along—that the overwhelming desire he fueled in her would overwhelm common sense. That she'd act on instinct and satisfy her desires at the expense of the consequences.

And those consequences in this case were clear. She risked losing her heart to the wrong man. A man whose life meant cameras and public scrutiny. All the things she'd been hiding from in Florida for years.

Roper released the wildness in her she'd repressed for most of her life—the part of her that was so like her mother and aunt, making public spectacles and taking risks. Tonight she and Roper had been in a secluded place with minimal to no risk of being caught bare-assed having sex in front of wall-to-wall windows, she thought.

No press around. This time.

And yet despite it all, she couldn't regret their time together here for that very reason.

It was theirs alone.

WHEN ROPER RETURNED FROM the bathroom he'd sensed Amy's withdrawal, caused no doubt by too much time alone to think about what they'd done. He'd expected regrets and recriminations. A long talk about things between them being a mistake. But she'd surprised him by linking her hand in his for the walk back to their rooms. She might be more sub-dued, but she hadn't pulled away.

Hannah's party had broken up early, a discovery they'd made when they'd found the twins, Joe and John, drinking at the lobby bar and rolling their eyes at the fact that apparently, Hannah had finally gotten her way with Mike the drummer.

Amy had seemed ridiculously pleased with the tidbit of gossip, which Roper attributed to one of those female things he'd never understand. Who cared what happened between Hannah and her band member? Since the news only served to fully restore Amy's good, playful mood, Roper decided he should not only care but be thankful.

When they reached Amy's room, she unlocked the door and pulled him inside. That was when he got to live out his fantasy of making long, slow love to her in a bed with music playing and lots of time to savor and enjoy.

Which they did, twice before she collapsed on top of him and fell fast asleep. Before he followed, he had time to watch her. She didn't snore, but she made cute little noises while she slept.

Noises, he suddenly noticed, that he didn't hear now.

He reached for her, assuming she'd rolled over to the other side of the king-size bed, but he came up empty. He forced his eyes open and discovered he was alone. A glance at the clock told him it was only 9:00 a.m., and he decided to trust that wherever Amy had gone, she hadn't run far away with morning-after regrets.

He propped one arm behind his head and stared at the ceiling. Thinking back on the night, he knew he'd seen a more adventurous side to Amy than he knew she possessed and he decided he liked it. A lot. The fact that she didn't regret hooking up in the solarium reinforced his notion that she wasn't someone he'd grow bored with too soon. She was good for him professionally and personally, he decided. And for now that was all he needed to know.

As his schedule started at ten, he headed back to his room for a quick shower. Then he stopped by the front desk to make his first request of the concierge. His plan? To fulfill a promise he'd made to Amy and show her all the ways he could make and keep her happy. Not just in bed, although he had to admit they'd gotten off to one helluva start.

AMY HAD LIKED WAKING UP next to Roper. She'd liked it too much, so she rose quietly, showered and met up with Hannah at the breakfast buffet. They walked the length of the long table together and Amy filled her plate with at least one of everything.

"I'm starving," she said, the smell of pancakes assaulting her senses.

"Sex will do that to you," Hannah said.

Amy choked. "How do you know what went on?" she asked, praying the other woman hadn't seen or heard anything from the solarium.

Hannah laughed. "Until now, it was only a guess. One based on the fact that I'm beyond ravenous and

I know what I was doing all night," she said with a grin.

"So things between you and Mike worked out?" Amy grabbed one last pastry before heading for a small table in the corner of the restaurant.

Hannah followed. "Let's say they're at least moving forward. The only way they'll be better is if he gets Big Mama's blessing. All he's ever wanted was his career and she can make or break him."

They sat at a table and immediately dug into their food. While she and Hannah ate, they exchanged life stories, Amy about growing up without a father and as the only sane one among two childlike adults. She even revealed her mother's Lady Godiva episode and what it had cost Amy in terms of not just a job, but a life among her peers, something she hadn't been able to realize or put into words until now.

And Hannah described growing up with her mother, who lived her own unfulfilled dreams through her talented daughter. Hence the reason for the other woman becoming her manager and directing Hannah's life, so that music was its only focus.

"You know you have to take control of your mother," Amy said, stabbing her fork into a piece of waffle and talking to Hannah as if she'd known her forever.

Considering they'd already confided in each other about sex and their men, Amy figured the bond was already there. She liked people and talked to them easily. So this friendship with Hannah wasn't a surprise, merely welcome.

She missed having someone to talk to. For years it had been her mother and her aunt, but with Hannah, Amy realized how badly she missed the companionship of someone her own age. A best friend.

"Not only do I know I have to take control, but I plan on doing something about it. Mike is going to kill me, but I intend to call my mother and let her know where we are." Hannah accentuated her decision with a raise of her coffee cup.

Oh, wow. That was a huge step. "What exactly do you plan to do when she gets here?" Amy asked.

"I'm going to tell my mother that she will have to make a choice. Accept my relationship with Mike without any interference or lose not just her place in my life but her position as our manager." Hannah set her cup down and met Amy's gaze, not a hint of uncertainty in her eyes.

"You love him that much," Amy said.

"I do. You don't spend that much time with someone, in the studio, on the road, and not get to know him, the good and the bad, quirks, faults and all. He's worth it to me." She nodded definitively.

"You go, girl," Amy said. She knew what Hannah was risking and yet she approved of her going after what she wanted most in life.

Hannah shook her head, her long ponytail falling over her shoulder. "Yeah, well, enough about me. Once my mother arrives it'll be pure chaos."

"When will that be?" Amy asked.

"I need another few days to savor this time with Mike. Then I'll call Mama. At which point I'm sure I'll be on your doorstep, begging for you to save me from her," Hannah said, half jokingly.

"Can I ask you a silly question?"

Hannah nodded. "Of course."

"I just realized that growing up the way I did and moving into a retirement community left me with few…okay, make that *no* real friends my age to speak of. Now I'm getting to know people at work, but I've revealed more to you than to any of them." She glanced at her water, feeling ridiculous. "But what about you? Don't you have a best friend or someone you go to when you need a shoulder? Or advice?" Why would the famous Hannah Gregory confide in Amy?

Hannah laughed. "I can see why you'd want to know, but the truth is I'm more like you than you realize. When I was young, I was tutored so I could take singing jobs, commercials, whatever Mom could line up. Now I'm in the studio or on the road. I'm with the guys all the time. The people I meet are either other performers, in which case there's jealousy or competition, or they're intimidated by me. I can't relate to them. You're the first woman I've met in ages I'd want to call my friend."

A warm, fuzzy feeling settled around Amy's heart. A friend. Silly as it seemed, she was feeling more and more complete with each passing day.

She wanted to reach across the table and hug Hannah, but the ringing of Amy's cell phone prevented her from acting on impulse. "Excuse me. Just for a second."

"Hello?" The phone number indicated it was Micki even before Amy had answered. "What's wrong?" Amy asked, because they'd agreed Micki wouldn't call and risk Roper being around and getting worked up by information from home. Amy would call her if she needed her.

"What isn't?" Micki asked.

Amy closed her eyes, realizing for the first time just how easily the real world—and Roper's problems—could intrude on her idyllic time here.

CHAPTER TWELVE

"SO WHAT'S GOING ON?" Amy asked Micki. She held the phone to her ear and mouthed an apology to Hannah.

"Cassandra Lee has camped out at my office and refuses to leave until I tell her where Roper is. I couldn't believe how attached she is to him until I found out the real reason she's parked herself at the Hot Zone." Micki sighed.

"Which has something to do with Harrison Smith?" Not a difficult guess, Amy thought.

"He followed her here and now they are both seated on my couch. Both wearing full-length furs. Cassandra has a matching hat."

"Oh, Lord." Amy held her forehead in her hand. She could just imagine the sight. "Do you have a plan? Short of divulging our whereabouts, I mean."

"As a matter of fact, I do." Micki's laugh let Amy relax a bit. "Uncle Yank is going to take them out to lunch. Or should I say Uncle Yank and his guide dog, Noodle, are going to take them out. Cassandra thinks he's going to explain why we have Roper secluded, which he will. And then I am sure she believes she'll charm him into giving out the phone number."

Micki's laughter gave away the fact that her plan wasn't as simple as Cassandra obviously believed.

"But…?" Amy asked.

"But once they order dessert, Uncle Yank plans to suggest Harrison choose someone more suited to play the role he wants for Cassandra. Someone more worthy. Someone who will come cheaper. Someone named Lola." Micki snickered.

Amy shook her head, glad she wasn't anywhere near New York City during this lunch. "Go on."

"Harrison, who is infinitely wiser and more cunning than Roper's mother, and who has a stake in the outcome of this lunch, has agreed to agree with Uncle Yank. At which point we expect Cassandra to scream, become offended that he'd give her role away to someone unknown, and then take the role back on principle," Micki said, sounding pleased with herself.

"But as soon as Cassandra comes to her senses, she'll walk away again." Amy massaged her suddenly aching temple.

"Not so fast," Micki said. "Harrison's assistant is waiting for the phone call that it's a done deal and she'll immediately 'leak' the news to the press that Cassandra Lee is back, making it impossible for the woman to dispute it or back out without looking foolish. Especially when Uncle Yank confirms Harrison's claim that she agreed."

Amy chuckled at the absurdity of it all. "You know, it's so crazy that it just might work. Anything else I need to know about?"

Micki exhaled loudly into the phone. "Well, if the role ties Cassandra up the way we hope, she'll stop booking twelve-piece bands and let her daughter and soon-to-be son-in-law plan their own small wedding."

"Twelve pieces?" Amy yelled loudly until Hannah placed her finger over her lips, reminding her she was in a quiet restaurant.

"Twelve pieces and Barry Manilow, but Cassandra claims he'll do it for free, as a favor for an old flame," Micki said.

Amy cringed. "Eew. Too much information."

"Harrison said she was full of it. And Sabrina isn't answering her phone until her mother sees reason," Micki said.

Amy raised a finger to Hannah, indicating she'd only be another minute. "Listen, you need to make sure this plan works or Roper will have a coronary," she whispered to Micki.

"I know. But I think I have it under control... except for one teensy little thing," the other woman said.

"How little?" Amy asked.

Micki grew alarmingly silent.

Amy stiffened in her seat. "What is it?"

"The stalker is at it again, except now he's turned to threats. He sent a generic baseball in a brown box to Roper's apartment. It was forwarded to the Hot Zone. Untraceable and untrackable, of course. The inscription on the ball read, 'Whack the ball or you'll be whacked instead.'"

Amy's stomach churned. "Did you—"

"Report it to the police? Yes, along with all the other incidents. At least the ones Roper told you about. They want to talk to him, but I managed to stall that for a while. And I let Vaughn know what's going on. He's hired extra security for the lodge just in case. The good news is that since the stalker sent the package to Roper's apartment as usual, we have no reason to believe he knows where Roper is."

Amy exhaled long and hard. "But the papers are quiet?"

"Just a mention by Buckley that Roper's lying low, probably hiding out in embarrassment. Roper would be pissed if he knew, but since he doesn't, all's well."

"You weren't kidding when you said everything's wrong."

"As long as you tell me everything is right there, I'll be happy," Micki said.

Amy glanced around at the dark wood decor and her peaceful surroundings. "Everything here is perfect. Roper is relaxed, baseball focused, rehabbing and he isn't worried about home. It's going exactly the way we wanted it to," Amy said.

"Excellent! I have to go, but I'll check in again soon." Micki hung up and Amy turned back to her breakfast companion. "I am so sorry about that."

"Hey, I understand when business calls. Everything okay?" Hannah asked.

Amy nodded. "Nothing my boss can't handle." Which was true. Except for the escalation in the stalker's actions, which Roper wasn't around to deal with, everything was status quo. His family was as needy and crazy as usual, but they had another audience to perform for, at least for a while.

The waiter had cleared the plates while Amy was on the phone.

Hannah leaned forward on her arms. "Then why do you look upset and worried?"

"I do?"

Hannah made a show of studying Amy. "Wrinkled brows, pursed lips, frowning…yup, you look worried."

Amy laughed. "I guess I'm just preoccupied." And concerned about how Roper would feel if he found out about the news from home. He'd want to know everything. But as long as she could shelter him, he could continue to relax, something he desperately needed to do. But she couldn't share his personal troubles with Hannah because he was her client.

So instead she decided to be up-front about her own issues—getting involved with a famous baseball player who came with a load of baggage of his own. She asked Hannah for advice.

"As someone whose life is a media mess, I'm not going to lie and tell you it's easy. I'm also not going to tell you what to do, because I've seen too many celebrity marriages break up because public life interferes." Hannah signaled for the check.

"You sound older than your years," Amy said.

"Not older, just more jaded." She glanced down. "I believe in going after what you want in life, but I also believe in weighing the odds. What's the point of getting involved with someone if it's doomed from the start? Or if you think it is?"

A shiver raced down Amy's arms. She had no answer, nor did she want to think too much about it right now. "For as long as we're up here, it isn't something I have to worry about."

Hannah inclined her head. "Good point. You might as well enjoy what you've got while you've got it."

Amy smiled. Truer words were never spoken.

She'd enjoy the here and now. Tomorrow would show up soon enough.

THERE WAS NO *AWKWARD* morning after. For the next few days, Amy and Roper fell into a routine that included sharing the same bed, then going their separate ways after breakfast while he worked out. They'd meet up again for a quickie or just to hang out and talk. She enjoyed their conversations, which ranged from politics to sports and even music. There were never silences that weren't meaningful or comfortable. There were never issues between them that couldn't be resolved with a quick discussion.

Amy could hardly believe this was a job, that she was being paid to watch over Roper. Once they returned home she was certain things wouldn't be so easy, but for now, life was good.

After a swim, Amy returned to her room, showered and changed for the day. Since Roper had an appointment with the physical therapist, she knew he'd be tied up for a while.

She lay down on the bed and memories of last night washed over her in full Technicolor detail. Every stroke, every caress replayed itself in her mind until she was as aroused now as she'd been then. By the time she realized someone had been knocking on her door for a few minutes, her entire body was on fire. She swung her legs over the side of the bed, rose and headed for the door.

On the other side was a lodge employee with fully loaded shopping bags in his hands. "These are for you, Miss Stone."

She narrowed her gaze. "Are you sure? Because I didn't order anything," she said, confused.

The young man nodded. "I'm sure. There's a note here for you. Mind if I put these inside?"

"Of course not. Come in." She pushed the door open wider and he walked in, unloading his bundles in the entry area of the room.

She tipped him, and once he was gone, she opened the note he'd left with her. *"I promised you a day in the snow. Get dressed and meet me at the lobby entrance at noon. John."*

She tore into the packages and discovered a winter wardrobe filled with items she'd never had a reason to buy for herself before. She examined the goodies one by one: a white down winter jacket with brown piping and matching snow pants, a ski hat with a pompom on top, brown gloves and thermal underwear. She checked the sizes and was shocked to discover Roper had gotten it right. Another bag revealed fur-lined snow boots and a pair of white-rimmed polarized sunglasses, especially designed for winter glare.

Excitement surged through her and she was instantly reminded of her childhood and Christmas mornings past, when she'd open all the wild and extravagant gifts beneath the tree. Thanks to her father's life insurance, her mother had been well-off enough to support them, but her uncle Spencer had always made certain she was spoiled, too. He thought of Amy as the daughter he'd never had. When Amy had found out that he was gay, but that he'd had a son, Riley, whom he'd allowed another man to raise as his own, Amy truly understood the depth of the void she could only partially fill in her uncle's life. He'd given up so much and had only begun to forge a relationship with his son now.

She turned her attention back to the gifts from Roper. She couldn't believe how he'd managed to have all these things picked and sent over so quickly, but she supposed fame and money had its perks.

And he'd chosen to bestow it on her. She marveled at his thoughtfulness and generosity, as gratitude and much more filled her heart.

A couple of hours later, she was dressed and headed for the lobby, ready for her first adventure in the snow.

ROPER'D HAD A GREAT SESSION with the physical therapist and then an appointment with the orthopedist in town. His time at the lodge had been rejuvenating. He was feeling an overall natural high. He still didn't know if he'd be ready in time for spring training, but for the first time, he could live with that because he *knew* he'd be back. He felt good about his life and career.

Amazing what some self-indulgence could do. He felt like himself again, in no small part thanks to Amy. He could think of only one way to show his gratitude, and now he waited for her by the front of the lodge, curious to see how she liked his surprise.

The shock was on him when she finally strode into the lobby, ready for a romp in the snow. Her brown curls contrasted beautifully with the white North Face down jacket he'd ordered, and her face glowed with excitement.

She caught sight of him and smiled, waving as she joined him. "I can't believe you sent me all of this!" She wrapped her arms around his neck and pulled him close, her hug of gratitude so warm and genuine, his heart beat even faster in his chest.

"My pleasure." He held out his hand and she placed hers trustingly in his.

Amy's reaction to her clothing was the same as another woman might react to diamonds or jewels. A gift from the heart, he thought. And he refused to ponder deeper.

The snow fell softly as they made their way outside. One glance at Amy in her winter gear had him on fire. It didn't matter how cold the temperature, nor did it matter that they'd made love last night. Nothing stopped the wanting. Her bright smile and genuine appreciation for the simple things was something he needed. Something he'd been unaware of until she took control.

He trusted her.

She said his family was being taken care of and he believed her. And thanks to that trust, he sensed a shift in his own outlook on the future, in his devotion to his career and his craft. All because he'd taken a time-out from his life. He no longer fought the guilt, no longer felt the desire to find a phone and check on his mother and sister. His own needs had to come first, and for once he was putting his priorities in order.

"Wow, this is way better than looking at things through the window," Amy said, bringing him back to the present.

They'd reached the back of the lodge, the place they'd viewed from the solarium where they'd also... He yanked his thoughts away from their first sexual encounter before he tackled her into the snow and had his way with her *here.* She pulled her hand from his and spun in circles, laughing and appreciating the cold winter air and the snow around their ankles. Coming to a stop, she waited while the dizziness wore off, then turned and stared off at the expanse of pure white landscape behind them.

"I can't believe I missed out on this growing up." She shook her head, staring in awe.

"Definitely something everyone should experience," he agreed.

She nodded. Without warning, she took off running—or running as best as she could run while laden down with winter wear.

"Very graceful," he called out wryly.

She paused and stuck her tongue out at him. Then, laughing, she bent down and picked up a handful of snow, packing it into a ball. "The snow is so much softer than I thought it would be," she said.

"And harder to keep together. It depends on the kind of snowfall you get, whether or not you can pack a solid snowball," he explained. "Ben and I used to build forts and have snowball fights all the time on our Colorado vacations. We'd be outdoors for hours on end."

Funny, but he hadn't thought about Ben as his fun-loving little brother in a long, long time. Age had divided them, Roper thought. Age and talent—or lack thereof.

Amy stepped closer. "Hey. What's on your mind?"

He shrugged. "I'm just thinking about how relationships change." And not for the better.

She placed her hand on his shoulder in under-standing. "They could change back if you wanted them to. Or at least you could try to reach out to Ben without any expectation and see what happens. Maybe you need to try an approach you haven't used before. One that doesn't make him feel as if he's second-best."

He met her gaze. Her cheeks were flushed red from the cold, her eyes hidden behind the sunglasses he'd chosen. She looked hot enough to melt the en-tire field they stood on.

While he was lost in thought, she had trudged through the snow until she was a decent way from him, then she wound up, took aim and threw the snowball, hitting him squarely on the shoulder.

She wiped her hands together, obviously pleased with herself. "Not bad for a rookie."

He bent down for some snow and packed a weapon of his own. "You'd better watch out because I've had a lot of practice at this," he warned her.

"Throwing or making snowballs?" she asked as she stepped backward. And back some more.

He grinned and narrowed his gaze. "Both." He pitched his ball at the same time she took off at an awkward run, so he ended up hitting her squarely in the back.

He took off after her, catching up in no time. He tackled her to the ground, bringing both of them onto the soft but thick snow. He rolled her onto her back to discover she was laughing. Having fun. Doing exactly what he'd wanted for her when he'd purchased all this winter apparel.

She gazed up at him, smiling.

His heart swelled even bigger. He cleared his throat. "Hey. Do you want to make your snow angel before you get too cold to stay out here much longer? After all, your blood is much thinner than mine, what with you being from down South and all."

"You say that like it's a bad thing. You northerners and your pasty skin, you make a pretty pathetic sight if you ask me."

He shook his head and laughed. He liked teasing her because she took it so well. "Pasty skin, huh? You say *that* like I'm unattractive and don't turn you on. Don't forget I have seen, felt and tasted some pretty distinct evidence to the contrary." With each word he spoke, he leaned closer, until his lips pressed down hard on hers.

Warmth surged through him, licking at him like flames on logs in a fireplace. She opened her mouth, letting him slip his tongue inside to delve deep and swirl around and around, devouring her because he couldn't get enough. Making him wonder if he ever would.

By the time they broke apart, panting and out of breath, he was ready to curse the confining clothing.

But she wasn't finished playing in the snow. She gave him a playful shove so he fell onto his back, carving out more room for herself. She lay down on her back and began to swipe her arms and legs in broad strokes, creating the snow angel she'd talked about earlier.

He watched her, realizing she was his angel. And despite how much time they'd spent together here, he wasn't ready to let her go just yet.

AN HOUR LATER, AMY AND Roper had showered— together—and redressed, heading down to the coffee shop for something hot to drink. Amy needed to pick up a few personal items in the shop, while Roper went ahead to get a table and put in their order.

Once seated, Roper ordered himself coffee and Amy a hot chocolate, and settled in to wait for her to return. He barely had time to take in the rustic interior when Hannah stopped by.

"Mind if I join you?" she asked, and in her usually friendly fashion, didn't wait for an answer before sliding into the booth beside him.

The waitress place their drinks down.

"Do you want something?" Roper asked Hannah.

She shook her head. "No, thanks. I just was hoping to give you a message for Amy."

"If you wait five minutes you can tell her yourself. She'll be back anytime now."

The other woman shook her head. "I need to make myself scarce." She glanced around as if looking for someone. Nervously looking for someone. "Just tell Amy that Big Mama's here and it isn't pretty. She'll understand," Hannah whispered right into Roper's ear. "Tell her to use my personal cell to reach me. I need to talk."

Roper nodded. "Who's Big Mama?" he asked, obviously too loud for Hannah's liking, because she smacked her hand right over his mouth.

"Shh. Ask Amy. She'll explain."

Women. He would have rolled his eyes but he didn't want to insult Hannah. "Whatever you say," he told Hannah.

She smiled. "You're as great as Amy thinks you are."

Amy thought he was great? Now, that was something Roper could live with, he thought wryly.

"Thanks, Roper." Hannah leaned in and placed a grateful kiss on his cheek.

At the same time a small cell-phone camera captured the moment.

Everything that came next happened in a fast-moving blur. A security guard tried to grab the phone, but the woman holding it, an Amazon by anyone's definition, ducked and ran toward the door.

Hannah yelled and took off after the woman, shrieking for her to come back. By the time security had stopped the female photographer and her phone, Roper had a hunch the photo had already been sent to the highest bidder or whoever was in place ready to receive and run with it.

He didn't plan on sticking around to find out. He had to do damage control. He groaned and swiped his hands over his eyes. Drawing a deep breath, he reached the door, coming face-to-face with Amy, who appeared stunned by the commotion around them.

"What in the world is going on?" she asked.

He explained the situation as quickly as he could, hoping she'd take it in the spirit in which he relayed the tale. He wasn't worried about himself. He was worried about Amy and her reaction to photographers. To one catching him with Hannah in what the tabloids would call a "canoodle." To their idyllic time here being over.

"Typical photographer bullshit," he said. "Hannah and the security guard went after the woman. Hannah seemed way more upset than I was." He was so used to the unwanted photographs and the way reporters twisted reality, he could ignore it with the best of them.

And the lighter he made the situation, the lighter Amy would hopefully react. Because as he'd come to realize earlier today, he wasn't ready to give her up yet. Or for his lifestyle to intrude and yank her away before he'd had a chance to cement the bond building between them.

Amy bit down on her lower lip, obviously upset. "Do you think Hannah was worried that Mike might think the two of you are more than friends? Is that why she was so upset?" Amy asked.

She was worried about Hannah and not them? Typical Amy, caring for others almost to a fault. He assumed the realities of their situation hadn't hit her yet.

"I'm not sure what had Hannah so crazy, considering she's as used to the press as I am. But she did have a message for you right before the photographer took that picture."

Amy raised her eyebrows. "What did she say?"

"She told me to tell you that Big Mama's here and it isn't pretty. Or something like that. She wants you to call her on her private cell," Roper said.

And then he remembered something else. "When Hannah ran screaming after the woman who took the picture, she called her Mama." He narrowed his gaze. "That big woman photographer was her *mother?*"

"Sounds like it. They do call her Big Mama. I guess now we know why. Was Hannah okay?" Amy asked.

"Last time I saw her she was running after her mother, so I'm really not sure."

"Do you think anyone retrieved the camera before the picture was sent?" As she spoke, Amy was pulling out her BlackBerry from her purse.

Funny how, now, she was the one in contact mode. Or maybe it wasn't so hysterical after all, Roper thought. "You do realize it doesn't matter whether or not the photo was retrieved before it was sent," he said.

Amy's eyes, which he'd grown used to seeing full of laughter and delight, now dimmed. "I know. Big Mama knows where her daughter is and that she's been with you. It won't be long before the world knows it, too."

Her voice dropped along with the light mood he'd been savoring for days. They were both keenly aware of the fact that their idyllic time together was at an end.

CHAPTER THIRTEEN

CASSANDRA PACED THE FLOOR of her hotel room in bare feet. The rooms had been renovated and hardwood floors replaced what had once been plush carpet. She appreciated the chic modern look, but the last thing she needed or wanted was for her next-door neighbor to hear her and know she was back in her room. She still didn't know who Harrison had bribed to place him in the suite next to hers, but if she ever found out, she'd make sure that person was fired.

She marched to the window and back, her silk loungewear sweeping the floors. At this rate she could save the hotel money on vacuuming and dusting. A glance at the iHome clock radio/stereo on the shelf told her that it was time for Buckley's show.

Since her son's sudden departure, she'd taken to listening to Buckley the Bastard, hoping he'd hear about Roper's whereabouts before she did. He had spies everywhere. But since Roper and Amy had been gone, all Buckley had done was call John a coward for leaving town. The man was all about name-calling. Yet he was persistent, and somehow, someway, he'd find out where her son had gone.

And she'd be listening when he revealed all. She flipped on the cable station that broadcast his radio show simultaneously.

The man droned on about hockey and she sighed.

A knock sounded at her door. She assumed it was Harrison and she sat quietly, hoping he'd go away. He knocked again.

"I died and went to heaven," she called out to the person on the other side of the door. Her stomach flipped like a schoolgirl's. Like the schoolgirl she'd once been the last time they were together, when she'd been head over heels in love with him.

She'd been in love since, but she'd never had the depth of feeling she'd had—*still* had—for Harrison. But those feelings scared her because he was as strong a personality as she was. And she'd been on her own for so long, she feared his ability to twist her to his whim would cause her to lose herself. And even if his whim suited hers, she didn't want him to know he was in control. In essence, her feelings for him and the influence he wielded over her, scared her.

"You'd be in heaven if you'd just let me in," he yelled back, his voice deep through the closed door. "We have business to discuss. I have some head shots of actors and actresses I want to screen-test for the show."

Business or not, she didn't want to be alone with him. "I'm sleeping," she called back.

"You signed the contract, Cassie. You're in this project. Working with me. So open the door." He banged harder.

She cringed and hoped the guests in the neighboring rooms didn't call and report them.

Yes, she'd signed the contract. She'd been tricked. She just wasn't sure who'd done it. One minute she'd been having lunch with Yank Morgan and Harrison, who'd insisted on coming along. She'd been certain she could charm John's whereabouts out of Yank. The next minute the subject changed from her son to the TV series and Cassandra's resistance to the project. Yank had declared he had the perfect replacement for Cassandra. An unknown. A woman who'd never acted a day in her life. He'd suggested Lola, his wife, a lovely although plain woman, who couldn't hold a candle to Cassandra, not in her heyday, and not now.

She'd looked to Harrison, expecting him to laugh. Instead he'd nodded thoughtfully and he'd *agreed.* Cassandra had lost it then. Even though she'd played into Harrison's hands, she'd stood up in the middle of the restaurant, in front of the maître d' and everyone, and announced there was nobody better to play the role than she.

Harrison had whipped out a contract and she'd *signed.* She'd signed without her agent, without her attorney, on principle and acting in anger. Next thing she knew, Harrison had called his assistant and the news had hit the press.

They'd conned her and she'd allowed herself to be conned.

Suddenly she heard Buckley's voice loud and clear again. It had turned quiet and she realized Harrison had stopped banging on the door.

"Whew." She hadn't thought he'd give in and walk away so easily.

And though it was what she'd wanted, she found herself disappointed in him, anyway. She lowered herself to the couch and five minutes later, the key card sounded in her door and housekeeping let him inside.

"Your room," the maid with a heavy accent said, smiling shyly up at him before she walked away.

The door slammed shut behind her, leaving Harrison inside Cassandra's room.

She jumped up from the couch. "Well, of all the nerve!" she said, striving for her most indignant tone.

He walked forward, toward where she stood by the couch. His masculine, sensual cologne wrapped around her, touching her inside and out.

"Cassie, Cassie. When are you going to stop fighting the inevitable?" he asked.

He was as handsome now as he'd been back then, while she'd had to endure Botox and Restylane and even a face-lift. She resented it. "I believe I stopped fighting the moment you tricked me into signing that contract." She fluttered her eyelashes and spoke too sweetly.

He laughed. "If you think you were tricked, sue me." He grinned but didn't say one gloating word.

Damn him. At least then she could have snapped right back.

He placed folders on the table by the couch. At least he hadn't lied about wanting to do business.

"Besides, I'm not talking about you giving in on the role. I'm talking about giving in on us. We're inevitable."

Her heart fluttered inside her chest. Perhaps he'd only used business as an excuse to make his way into her room. She feared her heart would be next. "No, we're not."

He shook his head in that determined way he had, his jaw clenched. "I've waited long enough for you and I'm not about to walk away now." He reached a strong, tanned hand toward her face.

She turned away before she could give in. She was afraid. Afraid of doing as he suggested and ending up as the wife of the most powerful director in Hollywood. He'd turned from movies to television and hadn't looked back. He wanted her to do the same. Then where would she be?

At his beck and call.

At his mercy.

She'd have no protective barriers left because he understood her better than any man ever had, and he got her to do things she knew weren't right for her. Or maybe they were exactly what she needed, but she feared losing control of her life—which she'd lived on her own terms for so long. She just didn't know anymore.

"Why don't we look at the head shots?" he suggested, backing off personal subjects.

Grateful, Cassandra turned back around and they settled beside each other on the couch. He opened the folder and revealed the next crop of young, beautiful perfection. They sought fame and fortune in Hollywood. She'd been like them once, wide-eyed and innocent, ready to make it big.

She was too old to consider them her competition. Rationally she understood that, but she couldn't help but be a touch envious that the hardships of life hadn't touched their youthful faces yet.

"I was thinking..." Harrison paused to flip through the photographs.

"I've had so many e-mails and phone calls asking me when I was going to touch on my favorite least-favorite subject, John Roper." Buckley's voice carried through the television, John's name capturing Cassandra's attention.

"One minute," she said to Harrison, and grabbed the remote control to raise the volume.

Buckley adjusted the microphone in front of his face. "It's been frustrating for me to have no gossip to report on Roper since he unceremoniously disappeared. Or should I say ran away?" the disgruntled man asked.

"His harassment helped drive John underground," Cassandra said bitterly. At least that was what Yank and Micki told her. That John needed time for himself or else there would be no next season for him.

He needed, they'd said, a break from the media, the fans and, yes, even his family. That remark had hurt.

Maybe because she could understand why he'd need to get away. Which didn't mean she wasn't going to scold him the next time she got her hands on him for a hug. He'd abandoned her to Harrison's clutches.

"Well, I finally have a big reveal," Buckley said proudly. "Right after this message from our sponsors."

"Are you okay?" Harrison asked, wrapping an arm around her shoulder. He understood how she felt about John abandoning her.

She wished he didn't. She wished he wouldn't be so kind or make leaning on him so easy.

Cassandra nodded and bit the inside of her cheek.

After a short break, during which neither Harrison nor Cassandra spoke, Buckley returned. "Many have been looking for our friend, John Roper, the Renegades' highest-paid coward, and *People Magazine* finally got the inside scoop."

Cassandra leaned in closer, her anticipation rising. Just where was her son?

"Inside this week's issue is a cell-phone photo taken from the Web site of pop diva Hannah Gregory in the restaurant of the exclusive lodge in Greenlawn, New York, owned by Brandon Vaughn."

A grainy but clear enough to be recognizable shot of John and the singer with her lips against his cheek showed on the television screen. Buckley continued.

"John Roper isn't away rehabilitating his shoulder and getting ready for the season. He's making time with a hot star on the Renegades' dime. Wonder what happened to Amy Stone. Our boy Roper really gets around." Buckley cleared his throat. "The phone lines have just lit up like a Christmas tree," he said, laughing. "Hey, don't shoot the messenger. I just report the truth, folks. I'll take calls next. The Buck Stops Here!"

Cassandra hit the off button on the remote. "Damn the man for being so rude to John," she said as she rose to her feet. "But thank God he was persistent and found him."

"Where are you going?" Harrison asked, jumping up to step around her and block her way.

Cassandra rolled her eyes. Men could be so dense. "I am going to see my son!" She darted around him. Now that she knew where John was, she was going to find him.

Ever since Ben and Sabrina's father had left—and good riddance—John had stepped up as man of the house. She'd come to rely on him. He was her rock. And now, when she was bound to Harrison and close to being seduced by him again, she needed her son's level head to steady her. It was what she was used to in times of crisis. And this was her own personal crisis.

Still, she wasn't surprised when Harrison hooked his arm through hers and said, "I'm going with you. I'll call my driver and he'll meet us downstairs in twenty minutes." He pulled out his cell phone. "Does that give you enough time to pack?"

She dug her heels into the floor. "Why? Why are you coming with me?" She needed to hear his reasons.

He shook his head. "I'm sorry you need to ask. Because I love you, silly woman. And you need to see your son. Where else would I be?"

Her throat filled. Fear warred with an emotion she didn't want to name. An emotion, she feared, that was close to love.

"Now, I asked if you have enough time to pack." He didn't push her to reciprocate his words, she realized.

"Yes, yes, I do," she said, grateful for him. She knew that with her behavior, she didn't deserve him. She needed to get her head on straight or she'd drive him crazy.

She grinned.

"Good," he said. "I'll go throw a few things together, too. Don't even think about leaving without me."

"I won't," she promised, meaning it.

He strode to the door.

"Harrison?" she asked, stopping him.

"Yes?" he asked, his voice gruff.

"Thank you." From the bottom of her heart, Cassandra thought.

ROPER FELT AS IF A SOAP OPERA was playing around him and he might as well watch the episode until his own reality intruded. Which he figured shouldn't be too long.

Hannah's mother had taken a room at the lodge, even though Hannah refused to deal with Big Mama until she accepted her daughter's relationship with Mike. The drummer, meanwhile, refused to speak to Hannah because she'd gone behind his back and informed her mother of their relationship before he was ready to go public.

He feared for his career, and if Roper's hunch was right, he also feared for the relationship. Roper felt sorry for all parties involved except for Big Mama, who, true to her name, was larger than life and intrusive to a fault, like some other mothers he knew too well.

Amy had already informed him that Big Mama's cell-phone photograph had appeared in *People Magazine*'s Web site the day after it had been taken. Big Mama no doubt chose the magazine on purpose, knowing she wouldn't have to wait a week to get her daughter's face splashed in the tabloids. As if Hannah's fans would forget about her in one short month. As if Roper's hate club would forget him, either. No such luck. The day after *People Magazine*'s exclusive photo was aired, Roper's nemesis Buckley picked up on the news. Between *People* and Buckley, he figured Cassandra would arrive anytime and destroy his newfound serenity.

Once again, he was the center of attention. In Hannah's circles the gossip revolved around Hannah

Gregory's top-secret new lover, baseball star John Roper. In Roper's circles, the dirt speculated that Roper's priorities were so far out of whack, he cared more about getting laid by a hot young musician than about recuperating.

Put together, Roper had been made to look like a lazy, inconsiderate, cheating pig who didn't give a rat's ass about his new girlfriend, Amy Stone, or his lucrative career. Nothing, of course, could be further from the truth.

He nursed a beer in the lobby bar, thinking about what on earth he could do to help diffuse the current situation, but nothing came to mind. Amy, meanwhile, was busy on the phone arranging an exclusive with *Sports Illustrated* to counter the bad press. Roper didn't give a damn who the media paired him with romantically as long as Amy didn't believe the hype.

She didn't.

But from the moment the picture had shown up in *People,* only to be copied on the Internet and the rest of the free world, Amy had withdrawn. She might not believe he was having an affair with Hannah, but Amy had stopped sleeping with him, anyway. And he knew why.

The world had intruded on their private time, making them fodder for public dissection. And she wasn't having any of it. It didn't matter how strong their bond was or how well they understood each other. She was going to let outside forces drive a wedge between them.

Unless he stopped her somehow.

He raised his glass to his lips at the same time his gaze settled on the front entrance, taking in the two people making their way inside.

His mother and Harrison Smith.

Both in full-length fur coats, his mother wearing a matching fur hat on her head, Harrison in a wide-brimmed cowboy hat. Both dressed in a manner guaranteed to attract attention. Lots of it.

Sure enough, the normally low-key staff grouped around the couple, bowing and scraping as if the king and queen of England themselves had arrived. Roper didn't know if the staff knew who the famous couple was. Harrison and Cassandra probably just looked important enough to warrant extra attention.

Roper finished his drink in one long sip, placed the glass on the bar and rose to greet his mother.

AMY ARRIVED IN THE LOBBY at the same time Cassandra Lee and Harrison Smith made their entrance. Her success at securing an appointment with *Sports Illustrated* to interview Roper suddenly didn't feel like such a coup. Instead all she could do was fear that he'd forget the lessons learned at the lodge about putting himself first and revert to the dutiful son who catered to his mother's every whim.

"Maybe I don't give him enough credit," she muttered.

"Give who enough credit?" Roper joined her at the bar entrance.

She hadn't meant to speak aloud. "No one," she murmured. "Have they seen you yet?" she asked, tilting her head toward his mother and the director.

He shook his head. "But it's only a matter of time."

"John!"

His mother noticed him. "That was quick," he muttered.

Amy drew in a deep breath and together they headed toward Cassandra, who was waving madly.

Harrison stepped away, having a conversation with the luggage valet.

"Darling!" Cassandra called.

Amy winced at the long-haired fur she wore, which was really noticeable in a day and age it wasn't considered politically correct.

"It's so good to see you!" Cassandra came at him with open arms, enveloping him in chinchilla.

"Isn't this a surprise," Roper said drolly, once he'd extricated himself and stepped back.

He tried to sound upset with her, but Amy couldn't help but notice the warmth and affection in his tone despite his mother's unwanted intrusion.

"You and I have so much to catch up on. I won't even scold you for dropping off the face of the earth without so much as a word to your own mother." Cassandra's pout was actress perfect.

"I think you just did," Roper said with a grin.

Ignoring the subtle rebuke, Cassandra turned to her companion. "Harrison," she called. He stepped back toward her. "Be a dear and see to our rooms. Plural, remember? That means two. Preferably on different floors or opposite ends of the hall if I have no other choice." Without waiting for an answer, she hooked her arm through her son's. "I want to hear all about your time here," she said to Roper.

Not a word to Amy, not even a greeting. Amy wasn't surprised since she was the one who had helped orchestrate the separation between the actress and her beloved son.

"Hello, Cassandra, it's nice to see you again," Amy said, unwilling to meet rudeness with rudeness.

Cassandra lifted her chin a notch. "Hello," she said stiffly.

Amy sensed the hurt behind the cool facade, but she couldn't apologize. Not without losing her edge in this situation.

"Come, darling, show me where you've been hiding out." Cassandra pivoted and tugged on Roper's arm, urging him to walk away with her.

Amy glanced at her watch before meeting Roper's gaze. "You have an appointment with the physical therapist in ten minutes," she reminded him.

Cassandra let out a frustrated, exaggerated sigh. "You've probably been seeing your therapist daily while I haven't had five minutes with you in the past two weeks. I didn't even know where to find you. Surely you can skip just one appointment so we can catch up. You can't imagine what Harrison and that horrible Yank Morgan put me through."

Amy bit the inside of her cheek to keep from telling the prima donna that she didn't deserve what Yank and Harrison had done. They'd pushed her into taking a role that would put her back in the public eye, make her a ton of money and give her back her sense of self.

No, Amy thought, watching her manipulate her son, she didn't deserve such good fortune. It was time for her to grow up. But Amy didn't expect Cassandra Lee to understand just yet. She did, however, expect Roper to make his mother see the light. Surely he'd experienced enough freedom of thought, mind and body while here to know he needed it to survive. Surely he could see his mother needed to be pushed away from him in order to make her own way in life once more.

He had to set parameters with his family and this was the ultimate test.

"John?" his mother asked.

Yes, John, what will it be? Amy wondered, but she remained silent. She folded her arms across her chest and waited for him to decide—physical therapy and his career or his mother and her whims.

Roper had never felt so torn in his entire life. There hadn't been a day when he'd ignored his mother's needs. She'd been the rock in his life after she split with his father and again when Ben and Sabrina's dad took off for good.

To his surprise now, he resented her intrusion into the progress he'd been making in his rehabilitation, his thought processes and with Amy. But as she pleaded with him now, desperation and fear in her eyes and her voice, he didn't know how to shut her out.

He'd have to explain it to her, of course, and maybe start slowly with real rules she had to follow. But he couldn't turn her away cold turkey.

Both women waited. He wanted to please them both. *Because he loved them both.*

He loved them both.

Which meant he loved Amy.

Holy shit.

His palms began to sweat and his body overheated at the sudden, but not so unexpected realization.

He needed time to process the revelation as much as he needed time to ease his mother into the way things would be between them from now on.

"I'm going to skip this one appointment and talk to my mother," he said to Amy. He met Amy's gaze, silently imploring her to understand the choice he'd made.

A flash of pure disappointment crossed her face. "I have some things to do in my room." She turned and walked away.

His stomach plummeted, but he'd just have to explain later tonight when they were alone.

When she always seemed to understand what he wanted and needed.

And he needed her.

"I AM SO DONE," AMY SAID as she pulled her suitcase out of the closet and tossed it onto the mattress.

Hannah flipped the top closed. "No, you are not. You can't walk away from Roper."

Pausing by the bed, Amy opened the suitcase again. "Watch me." She headed to the drawers and began pulling her clothes out, packing her items in the large bag. "I called the Hot Zone and Micki agreed. If Roper can't stick to his schedule within five minutes of his mother's return, then he can damn well fix his career himself."

Drawers emptied, Amy turned to the closet and laid her pants, jeans and sweaters neatly inside the suitcase, then wedged her shoes in the sides.

Hannah seated herself on the bed and curled her legs beneath her, watching Amy's manic packing. "I'm not talking about his career or your role as his publicist. I'm talking about you, Amy, the woman, walking away from John Roper, the man."

"Have *you* made any progress getting Mike to forgive you for calling your mother?" Amy asked, moving toward the bathroom for her toiletries.

"No, but he's a man and he's stubborn. But you don't see me leaving him because I don't like the decisions he's made," Hannah said, loud enough for Amy to hear as she pulled her shampoo and conditioner out of the shower.

"Here's the thing," Amy said, rejoining Hannah and continuing to pack. "I got involved with Roper while we were here at the lodge so that I could stop fighting the attraction while we were living in such close proximity. It made sense." She placed the sealed bags filled with her things into her suitcase and zipped it closed.

"Go on," Hannah said, her skepticism obvious.

Amy ignored her tone. "But now that things have blown up with the press, it's time to go home. I can't help a man who doesn't want to be helped. So I'm leaving."

"Craving satisfied, man out of your system?" Hannah asked wryly.

Amy drew a deep breath. "Exactly."

"Liar."

Maybe, Amy thought, but she wasn't about to admit it aloud. She was disappointed in Roper. Disappointed in how he handled his first crisis. And she was disappointed in herself for falling hard for a man who was the opposite of everything she wanted and needed in her life.

"I'm not going to argue with you," Amy said. "I am, however, going to insist you keep in touch. I'm new in town and I don't have many friends, remember? So when you're visiting New York, I expect to see you. And when you're home in L.A., I want you to call, okay?" Amy changed the subject. She wanted to leave one conversation on a good note.

Hannah rose from the bed and gave Amy a hug. "Okay. As long as you know I'm not finished harassing you about Roper."

Amy rolled her eyes. "Fine," she said, knowing she couldn't deter Hannah. If the woman could stare down Big Mama, Hannah had persistence and staying power.

Amy glanced at her watch. She had a car service picking her up and she needed to get going. Before she could think too long or too hard about all the reasons she didn't want to leave Roper. But she had no choice. The only way he could decide what he wanted in his life, what kind of relationship he wanted to have with his family and how he could put his career first, was for Amy to step aside. Leaving him alone to compare life before and after Amy Stone.

HE POPPED A BEER IN celebration. Roper had been found. It had been a long, dry spell. Boring. He'd had no one to blame for his troubles. Now that was over. The fun could begin again.

CHAPTER FOURTEEN

ROPER HAD BEEN HOME FOR one week and he still couldn't believe Amy had picked up and left him at the lodge.

Could. Not. Believe. It.

Worse, now that he'd shown up at the Hot Zone to get his best friend's support, Micki sat behind her desk, backing up Amy's move both professionally and personally. "So much for turning to my best friend for support," he muttered.

Micki raised her eyebrows at him, not looking at all sorry. "You turn to your best pal for the *truth.*"

He shoved his hands into his pants pockets and stared out the window at the gray sky, which matched his mood. "I had every intention of following Amy's advice after I explained things to my family. She didn't have to take it so personally."

"Well, let's see. Have you followed her advice since you've been home? Have you been as single-minded as you were at the lodge?" Micki asked.

No, he hadn't been. Because as soon as he'd returned, so had old habits. "They need me." But he planned to talk to them. Soon.

"You need you," Micki said, her voice stern. "Have you spoken with Amy since you've been back?"

He turned to face her. "She was with me at the *Sports Illustrated* interview and she set up a few more media hits to counter the Hannah thing. Just so people would know I'm coming back stronger than ever."

Micki nodded, a satisfied look on her face. "I've guided her through some of it, but she's really got a knack for this job."

"If you knew, then why did you ask?"

She grinned. "Because I am trying to get you to see the obvious. Which is that Amy is damn good at her job. She had you completely focused on your career, and the minute your family starts pulling at you, you forget all lessons learned." She leaned forward, elbows on her desk. "Amy took it personally and I can't say I blame her. That's my professional assessment. Get your head on straight again or you might as well kiss your career goodbye. You can't handle the distractions right now."

She was right.

So was Amy.

"You said that was your professional assessment. What's your personal one?" he asked, sure Micki had more to say.

"That you've fallen in love with Amy." Micki smiled with a knowing certainty.

He *had* fallen in love but he'd never admitted his feelings aloud, not even to his best friend. "And?" he asked, wanting to hear what more Micki had to say.

"She's not willing to see you on a personal level now that you're back in the city and it's driving you insane." Micki shook her head and laughed.

"And for some reason you're enjoying watching me suffer?"

"I'm enjoying the fact that you're in love for the first time in your life. That you have to work hard for something for the first time ever. That Amy isn't falling at your feet like every other woman in the universe," Micki said. "But no, I'm not enjoying watching you suffer. I just think you two have more stuff to go through. Like all couples that are meant to be."

He frowned. "You sound like a romantic."

She rose from her desk. "Just telling it like it is. Have you?" She began to collect files from her drawer, which told him she had a meeting and their time was through.

"Have I what?"

"Told Amy how you feel about her? That you're in love with her? Maybe knowing she's *the one* will help her settle things in here." Micki tapped her head. "She can't read your mind, you know."

"No, I haven't told her." He hadn't put her first, either.

He missed Amy like crazy and Micki was right. Amy was driving him insane by not falling at his feet.

"Any reason why not?" Micki asked.

He shrugged. "It's not every day I make a realization like that one. I guess I wasn't ready."

"You ought to get yourself ready," Micki suggested. "Before you lose her for good."

"Thanks for the advice," he said, coming around the desk and pulling her into a big hug, which she easily returned.

"Anytime."

He didn't bother telling Micki he wasn't holding out much hope that if he bared his heart and soul to Amy, they were guaranteed a future.

Amy wouldn't consider returning to the way things were at the lodge. She claimed it was because she was his publicist, but he didn't believe her. She had deeper reasons for avoiding him—and his bed. His life in the public eye was one heavy part of her reasoning, but he sensed there was more and he didn't know what that more was.

He wasn't even certain Amy, herself, knew why she was avoiding any emotional closeness between them. But Micki was right about one thing. Amy needed to know how he felt.

He needed to break through her defenses and hope that he was wrong.

That the three little words women loved to hear would actually make a difference.

He walked from Micki's office directly to Amy's. He was a man on a mission and not the gentleman she'd been dealing with during their time at the lodge. He was determined not only to make his point but to get her to see the error in her thinking. Either she listened or he was shit out of luck. He didn't want to think about that possibility.

He entered without knocking.

Startled, both Amy and Yank, who sat across from her desk, turned to stare.

"Roper!" they both said at the same time.

Suddenly he felt like an ass. But his reasons for barging in hadn't changed so he kept walking toward her. "Hi, Yank," he said to his agent. "Bye, Yank."

As if agreeing with Roper, Yank's fluffy dog barked.

"Of all the nerve!" Amy strode around her desk and stepped between the two men. "You can't barge in, interrupt a private meeting and expect to get your way. Yank, you aren't going anywhere," Amy said, her cheeks flushed pink with anger.

The older man leaned back in his seat. "You heard the girl. I ain't goin' nowhere," Yank said, his tone not only smug but amused.

Roper wasn't worried. He still held the trump card. "My career may suck at the moment, but I'm still worth money. If you want to be the one who gets me the deals, you'll give me and Amy some time alone." Roper stared his agent down because otherwise Yank, who loved drama and gossip as much as any female, would have kept his ass in the chair.

Yank groaned. "Man, you're taking what little fun I still get out of my life," he muttered as he rose from his seat.

"You'll survive," Roper said wryly.

"It's my office. I have the final say." Amy perched her hands on her hips.

Roper took a moment to admire her high-waisted

black slacks and fitted buttoned-down shirt, which accentuated the curves he'd learned well, both with his hands and his tongue.

He shifted positions before dealing with the task at hand. "I'm sorry to tell you this, but I'm the client. And the client is always right," Roper said to Amy. Then he turned to Yank. "Tell her I'm right."

He ran a hand through his shaggy hair and groaned. "We'll talk later, girlie," Yank said. He pulled on Noodle's leash and he and the dog strode out of the room.

They were alone. Roper might have won the battle but he didn't kid himself. He hadn't yet won the war.

Amy's heart beat fast in her chest and her head pounded so hard she thought both might explode. "How dare you!" She faced Roper and poked him hard in the chest. "This is my office. Where do you get off walking in here and calling the shots?"

Despite her words, a traitorous part of her was glad to see him. In the time since she'd been home, she'd been fighting her deepest feelings. The rational part of her understood that she and Roper were trouble waiting to happen. But looking at him now, it was difficult to remember why.

"You need to calm down and listen."

She inhaled deeply. "What?" she asked, her voice deliberately cold.

He shook his head and laughed. "You don't make things easy."

She opted for silence.

"We grew close at the lodge," he said in his most seductive voice.

She swallowed hard.

He stepped nearer. She stepped back. He stepped closer. She stepped back. The dance continued until her back hit the radiator by the window and he had her cornered.

Just as he had at the solarium. Memories and seductive heat swept through her.

"Very close," he said as he took his final step, his thighs coming into direct contact with hers. "Remember?" He stroked her cheek with his hand.

"It's over," she said in a shaky tone. Damn, she hated the effect he had on her. The longing and wanting threatened to make her forget her reasons for not being with him.

"Actually, it's just beginning." His eyes bore into hers and his fingertips stroked her face, her cheek, her throat. "I love you, Amy."

She couldn't have heard him correctly, though everything inside her turned to liquid, molten heat and a sudden yearning for so much more settled inside her chest. "You—"

He inclined his head. "I love you and I believe you love me, too."

Oh, my God. Oh, my God. How long had she dreamed of the day when the man she loved would tell her he felt the same?

And she did love Roper. She knew it in a soul-deep way and had for a while, though denying and pushing it away from her consciousness had become second nature.

"Tell me, Amy," he said, his lips inches from hers.

She was enveloped by the sensual cologne he wore that made her weak. She wanted to let herself be swept away by the dream. But she couldn't.

Because it was nothing more than a dream.

"I can't."

"No, you won't. You're scared. I understand that. I've never said those three words to any woman before in my life. But we can make it work." His tone was low and imploring.

She drew a deep breath, steadying herself. Reminding herself of the reasons she'd left the lodge and had steered clear of him since. "We can't. I gave you all the tools to fix your life. I took you away, I showed you what you needed. But the first time you were faced with a choice, you chose to cave into your family's needs."

"Let me explain."

"In a minute. I need to finish first. Until you can make that separation between yourself and your family in a way that leaves you healthy emotionally, you aren't remotely ready for the kind of relationship that love entails." Her heart and her voice cracked as she spoke.

"Are you saying you love me, too?"

When she didn't reply, the knowing smile that had teased the corners of his mouth disappeared. "I *will* handle my family. You just can't expect me to shut them down with no explanation after a lifetime of doing just the opposite."

He made sense. He did. But it wasn't enough. She merely shook her head.

"There's more bothering you than just my family," he stated with certainty.

She trembled, unwilling to admit to anything more. She couldn't put it into words herself. "The family issue's enough, considering it's not going to change."

"It will. And when it does, are you going to admit you love me? Or are you going to use the press as another excuse to stay away?" Once again, he spoke as if he knew the answer.

She wondered why he even bothered asking the question. "The press is another part of the problem," she admitted.

He narrowed his gaze. "But there's more, isn't there?"

Before she could answer, his cell phone rang.

Both Amy and Roper froze.

He glanced down at the number. "It's Ben," he said, meeting her gaze. "Ben never calls."

"Unless something's wrong. Go ahead and answer it," she said, resigned, as she raised her hand, waving him away.

She wasn't surprised at the intrusion. She supposed it was just as well. She didn't want to have this painful talk, anyway.

"I'm going to handle this. I'm going to break my

family into the way things are going to be from now on. And then I'm coming back to finish this conversation. We aren't done. Not by a long shot," he said, before answering his phone.

Oh, yes, we are, she thought as she watched him engage in the same frustrating discussion with his brother that he always had.

Then he left without another word.

They were over.

It was exactly what she told herself she wanted and needed. Yet she'd never felt so miserable in her entire life.

BEN HATED SLEEPING ON a friend's couch. He hated feeling like a loser who couldn't hold a job or make a go at any career he started. And he absolutely hated having to ask his brother for money.

"I just know I can make this gym thing work," he muttered. But Roper didn't want to talk about money. He wanted to talk to Ben about taking a demeaning coaching job. One that was beneath him.

But his big brother in the major leagues wouldn't understand that he wouldn't compromise his principles. Everything came easy for Roper. A father whose genes guaranteed talent and the magic touch with both women and baseball. So what if he was having one bad season?

It wasn't the same as having a bad life.

"Are you moping again?" his friend Dave Martin, whose couch he currently occupied, asked.

Ben shrugged. "Feeling sorry for myself, I guess."

"Well, your brother surfaced, so that ought to cheer you up. It means you can talk to him about our gym idea. My friend still hasn't found a buyer, but he is talking with some people, so you need to step up the pressure before we lose out." Dave sat down beside him and kicked his feet up on the table.

"At least you have a decent, well-paying job."

"Being a trainer at Equinnox means I work for someone else. I want to work for myself. Make my own hours, boss someone else around. I've been there more than ten years and I have the experience."

"You just don't have the money. I know." And he was counting on Ben for the cash. Or rather Ben's famous brother. "It just so happens my brother called a family meeting. I'm heading over to my mother's suite for lunch."

"Good. Just make sure you get some time alone with Roper and be your charming, persuasive self," Dave said. "Your brother shouldn't be so stingy with his money. He ought to share the wealth with his family. Besides, it's not as if he's doing anything to earn it lately," Dave said in a round of Roper-bashing Ben had become used to.

It bothered him, though. Ben didn't mind complaining about his brother, but it irked him when others did it. For all Ben's jealousy, Roper had been good to him and they *were* brothers. Which Ben was counting on to convince Roper not to give up on him just yet.

"I'm going to shower," Ben said, rising. "And for the record, it's not my charm I'm worried about. It's my brother's built-in immunity."

"Make it happen," Dave warned him. "Or else."

Or else he'd be out a couch and on the street, Ben thought, finishing his friend's sentence in his mind. There wasn't much else he could do.

AS MUCH AS ROPER WANTED a quick fix to his and Amy's problems, he also understood he had obligations to his team, and so he threw himself wholeheartedly into his rehabilitation. Not only did he hope to return as quickly as his body allowed, but he hoped to prove to Amy that he was a man who learned—from his mistakes and from good, solid advice. That he was a man who kept his word.

Through it all, he also dealt with the daily traumas from his family that never seemed to cease. Complaints from his sister that his mother was lining up people and events for the wedding she wanted no part of. Meetings with his mother and Harrison, mediating in order to keep his mother from being in breach of contract before actual work on the television project began. Ben wanting to show him the gym he wanted to invest in, all the while constantly pushing him for money.

Roper tried to tell them things had to change, but they weren't listening. Or maybe, he realized, he wasn't speaking clearly.

Just as Amy wasn't coming after him. It was time he took charge in a decisive way, then acted on it.

So he'd called a family meeting. He wasn't surprised when his mother balked at going out and insisted on hosting the family at her suite. Her new ploy to irritate Harrison was to avoid the public and the reporters questioning her about her new television series. He wanted them to be seen in public, so she adamantly refused to be seen at all.

Cassandra hadn't come to terms with her contract and she was still running from Harrison Smith's presence in her life. Ironically, Roper was beginning to accept and like the man. He appreciated the stability Harrison provided Roper's mother and how he encouraged her independence and her career even if he had to manipulate her into agreement. Harrison could aid Roper's need to free himself from his mother's neediness—Roper just had to make the break, as guilty as he felt doing it. If Cassandra chose to rely on Harrison more instead of becoming more independent, that was *her* decision.

Roper would just have to assert his priorities in a way his family couldn't misunderstand. Then he had to follow through. He hoped once his family understood, they'd support his efforts, if not now, eventually. In the meantime, he'd get his ducks in a row, so to speak, and then challenge Amy to step up as he had.

That was in a perfect world, Roper thought. He entered his mother's apartment to find his family already assembled. This was *his* world, and here, anything could happen.

"I'm glad everyone could make it," Roper said.

"I was under the impression it was a command performance," his mother said, obviously miffed.

He laughed. "Yes, it is. We're *here* at *your* command," he said. "The food looks delicious. Everyone dig in," he said, figuring they should have full stomachs before they heard what he had to say.

He chose a chicken wrap and a bottle of water and was on his way to sit beside Sabrina and Kevin when Ben grabbed his arm. "Got a minute for your brother?" he asked.

"Sure." After today Roper would control his own minutes, so he didn't mind talking to Ben now. He refrained from asking, *what can I do for you?* knowing he probably wouldn't like the answer.

They made their way to the empty kitchenette area. Ben pulled a can of Coke from the fridge, popped the top and took a long drink. Roper ate his lunch standing, waiting for his brother to talk first.

"How's the rehab?" Ben asked.

Roper wiped his mouth with a paper napkin. "Coming along," he said warily.

It pained him to realize that gone were the days when he could confide in his brother about anything—and vice versa. Sure, Roper knew Ben bounced from idea to idea and rarely held a full-time job, but he didn't understand why. Communication between the brothers had died a slow death about the same time Roper's major league career had started to soar.

"Are you still crashing on Dave's couch?"

Ben nodded. "It's not bad. He's got a fifty-inch flat screen so he can catch the Renegades away games and feel as if he's really there."

"He's a fan," Roper said.

"Season ticket holder."

Roper nodded. The small talk wasn't working for him. "What's going on?" he asked his brother.

Ben shifted from foot to foot. "Here's the thing. I need to talk to you and I don't want you to turn me down without hearing me out."

Here it comes, Roper thought. "Okay, what's your pitch?" he asked, then listened to Ben expound on the perfect gym location in SoHo and how he hoped to bring the money, while Dave would bring the experience, and together they'd set up a fantastic business.

"There's just one problem," Roper said to his brother.

"What's that?"

"You don't have the money." He had no choice but to lay it on the line for Ben in a way he'd never done before. He'd come here today to do just that with each family member, and Ben had given him the opening first.

Ben's eyes opened wide in disbelief. "But you—"

"I don't have it, either, and before you argue, call my accountant if you don't believe me. Incoming money is tied to endorsements and performance. The rest is tied up for the future. My future." He squared his shoulders and faced the brother he'd rarely refused.

This gym proposal was probably the only thing Roper had pushed aside and refused to discuss—proof he'd already been taking a stand even before Amy had entered his life.

"What about me? It's not as if I have the talent to make it the way you did." Ben's voice dropped to a whine and his expression turned to a pout.

"That's what I came here to talk about. Even if I did have the money in liquid cash, I wouldn't be giving it to you. It's time you stood on your own. You may not have what it takes to make it in the majors but you have plenty of other talents. Certainly enough to make a living and support yourself. More than support yourself, really."

Ben rolled his eyes. "Oh, here it comes again. The old 'why don't you take a high school coaching job' speech."

"Why *don't* you take a coaching job?"

"Because I'm better than that. But you wouldn't know what it's like to fall short, now would you?"

Roper had to laugh at that. "I know better than you think. I know exactly what falling short means. I know what it's like to disappoint my family and my teammates. I know what it's like to have fans boo me from the stands and throw things at me onto the field. I deal with criticism from everyday people on the street and from the media. I can't name one source

I don't get shit from, so don't tell me I don't know what it's like to lose. The difference between us is that I'm not afraid to step up to the plate. Whatever plate that may be. If I had to walk away today, I'd be damn happy to have a coaching job, Ben. No joking here." He blew out a stream of air, shocked at how direct and hard he'd been with his brother.

He glanced at Ben, who appeared stunned, too.

"I'm sure that's easier to say with money in the bank," Ben muttered.

"I put that money in the bank." He jabbed himself in the chest. "I earned it. When your father took off and mine was nowhere to be found, all I could think about was stepping up and making sure the family was taken care of. I mowed lawns while Mom worked. I did what I had to and I never asked a damn thing in return. But I'm asking now. No, I'm telling you now. Grow the fuck up. Get a job and hold your head up high for once," Roper said, his heart accelerating in his chest.

Ben looked as if Roper had slapped him.

"What's going on in here?" Cassandra asked, walking inside to join them.

Roper glanced at his younger brother. "Nothing. Give us another minute, okay, Mom?"

Cassandra nodded. "Just stop with the raised voices or I'll be thrown out of here and then—" Her eyes lit up. "Then I can find a place where Harrison will never think to look!" she said, the idea obviously just forming.

Roper shook his head and groaned. "Remember your contract, Mom. We'll talk in five minutes. Don't do anything until then," he warned her.

She laughed and walked out, probably already planning.

Roper quickly turned back to his brother. "Ben—"

"Not now. You've said enough." Arms folded over his chest, he looked like the hurt little boy Roper remembered. It took everything Roper had to steel himself against the manipulation.

"Listen, Ben, my point is this. You have more inside you than you give yourself credit for. You could do a world of good coaching kids. You could tap into their psyches—those that already believe in themselves and those that don't but should. You can steer them in the right direction from the start." He placed a hand on his brother's shoulder.

Ben shook it off.

Roper swallowed back the hurt, knowing he had to let things settle and hope someday his brother would come around. "Let's go join Mom and Sabrina," Roper said.

"Why bother? I'm finished here." Roper waited in the kitchen while his brother stormed out of the room, said his goodbyes and left, slamming the door behind him.

One down, two more to go, Roper thought.

CHAPTER FIFTEEN

ROPER GLANCED AROUND, studying the female members of his family who gazed at him with curious eyes. Ben's abrupt departure had left them stunned, Roper was sure.

"Obviously Ben's upset about something. What's going on?" Sabrina asked. She sat beside Kevin, holding his hand. At least she seemed genuinely happy.

And that, Roper thought, was what this part of his day was all about. He needed to use his sister's happiness as the springboard to give him the courage to lay down the law with his mother—and undoubtedly hurt her in the process.

Before he could speak, a noise sounded from outside the door and suddenly Harrison entered, key card in hand. Roper raised an eyebrow but didn't say a word. He already knew there was more to this relationship than his mother wanted to admit to her children *or* to herself.

"You shouldn't just barge in as if you own the place," Cassandra chided him.

He raised an eyebrow. "Considering I gave up my

own room, you can't expect me to knock first. Hello, everyone," Harrison said.

Roper shook the other man's hand.

Sabrina managed a wave. From her pale face, she hadn't known about their mother's living arrangements, either. It seemed as if Cassandra was keeping up the pretense of not wanting to be with Harrison for no one's benefit that Roper could figure, except maybe her own.

Cassandra scowled at him. "John was just about to say why he called us all together. It's a family meeting so you might want to—"

"Stay," Roper added before his mother could send the other man away. "And do not argue with me, Mom."

Harrison grinned. "Thank you," he said to Roper.

"No problem."

Cassandra needed the older man more than she wanted to admit and Roper was glad she had him, especially since he, himself, intended to take back his own life. He was grateful and relieved he wouldn't be leaving his mother alone to her own devices.

Cassandra folded her arms across her chest. "I wasn't going to argue. If Harrison wants to pretend he's part of this family, who am I to stop him?" She sniffed in her haughty way.

Harrison laughed and slung an arm around her shoulder. "Go on," he said to Roper.

"Please," Sabrina said.

Roper drew a deep breath. "Okay. Here goes. For

as long as I can remember, I've been here when you all needed me. Twenty-four/seven, at your beck and call."

"Well, I'm not sure I'd phrase it so callously," his mother said, only to be silenced by Harrison squeezing her shoulder in warning.

"You've been a wonderful son," she said, her voice sincere.

"Thank you." He wasn't fishing for compliments, just stating reality. "The thing is, that by doing everything you all wanted when you all wanted it, I've neglected my own life."

"I can see that," Sabrina said softly. "I have for a while. It's just that old habits are hard to break."

He smiled at his little sister. "Tell me about it."

"So what are you trying to say?" Sabrina asked.

"That it's time for you all to live your own lives."

"As if we haven't?" Cassandra asked.

The sad thing was that Roper knew she believed her words, which made what he had to say all the more difficult. "No, you haven't. If I was in a meeting and one of you called, I dropped everything. If I was on a date and you needed me, I cut it short. Don't get me wrong, I did it because I wanted to—"

"And you don't anymore?" his mother asked, insulted.

He wanted to say no that, of course he wanted to, he just couldn't do it anymore. But that would be a lie and he'd promised himself and Amy—even if she wasn't aware of the promise—that he'd be completely honest. For everyone's sake, including his mother.

"No, Mom, I don't want to. I want to concentrate on my career. The time I spent at the lodge showed me the difference less stress could make on both my body and my mind."

"This is all that woman's fault."

"That's not fair, Mom," Sabrina objected. "And it's not true. Besides, I thought you liked Amy. You said she's bright enough to hold her own with John, and she didn't bore you like the other bimbos he's dated." Sabrina shot him an *I'm sorry* look. "No insult intended," she said.

"None taken. And I'm glad you like Amy. Because if I have my way, she's going to be around for a long, long time."

Sabrina let out a whoop and ran to Roper, giving him a hug. "I hope you find the happiness we have," she said, nodding toward Kevin.

His mother remained silent. Sulking.

And Roper wasn't even finished yet.

"Thanks," he said to his sister. "We'll see. There's a lot to work out between us." An understatement if he ever heard one. "Still, I want to be clear on what this means to all of you."

"Do tell," Cassandra said, curled up in the corner of the couch, sulking like a petulant child.

He realized now what a complete disservice he'd done his mother by being at her beck and call. He'd never allowed her the chance to stand on her own. He hoped she did so now and didn't just transfer her needs from Roper to Harrison.

"I love you, Mom, and I will always be here for you if you need me. I want to see you. I want to have lunch or dinner with you and I want you to call me when you want to talk."

"But?" she asked.

"But you can no longer expect me to drop everything I'm doing to fix things for you. You're a grown woman with a new career and you're going to love it."

Harrison applauded.

Roper rolled his eyes. "You're also able to support yourself now, and I'm hoping you'll love the freedom it gives you. Don't close your eyes to new opportunities. Accept and embrace who you are and what you can do today, not twenty years ago," he said, hoping she heard the love and respect in his tone. "America is going to adore you on this series. It's going to open up all sorts of new doors for you. So don't be stubborn like you were with Harrison. I'm betting you're going to love what happens to you next and I want to be there to share it."

"On your terms."

Okay, so she didn't *get it* yet. He had faith that she would.

"On *our* terms, over time," he said.

"I need to lie down."

Harrison shook his head, but Roper met the other

man's gaze and silently told him he'd expected this reaction. There would be more discussion, and hopefully, understanding, in the future.

Harrison escorted Cassandra out of the room.

Roper turned to his sister and her fiancé. "As for you, Sabrina, you're marrying a good man."

Kevin cleared his throat. "Thank you," he said, clearly embarrassed.

Roper inclined his head. "Sabrina, you have the world ahead of you. If you continue to work as a paralegal, good for you. If you decide not to work, that's between you and your husband. Whatever you two decide, I stand behind you. I'll be there for you, but I won't undermine Kevin by sneaking money to you or providing things he can't. Unless he agrees," Roper said, grinning because Kevin was nodding at everything he said.

Sabrina seemed surprised but okay with his words. Relieved, even.

"One last thing. About the wedding." This was the best part of his day, Roper thought, reaching into his pocket.

And damned if he didn't deserve some fun after the nightmare he'd been through.

"Your wedding should be everything *you* both want. I want to give you the wedding of your dreams." And he already knew that Sabrina's dreams weren't his mother's. "So here," he said, walking over and handing them the check. "Plan your wedding the way you want. Or don't plan the wedding and use this toward your future. The choice is yours."

Sabrina glanced down at the paper in her hand and her eyes widened. She squealed and threw her arms around Roper's neck. "You are the best, John. The very best."

"Do it your way, baby sister," he whispered in her ear. "And be happy."

Kevin shook Roper's hand. "I can't thank you enough."

Roper shrugged. "If Mom had the money, she'd do it herself and you'd be ducking dove shit. So this is my pleasure," he said, laughing.

Kevin smiled. "She's going to have a fit when she realizes you've effectively taken away her power."

"I'm hoping that by giving it to Sabrina, she'll include Mom on the right things, shut her down when she doesn't belong, and eventually we'll all be one big happy dysfunctional family," Roper said.

"We can hope," Kevin said.

"Will that family include Amy?" Sabrina asked.

Roper groaned. "I honestly don't know."

But he couldn't wait to find out.

AMY KEPT BUSY. AT WORK SHE'D been given new clients and she'd also shadowed both Annabelle and Sophie through various events and meetings, learning by example. Her uncle Spencer was pleased with her progress at the Hot Zone and he took her to dinner to tell her so. She joined a gym and went there at night so she didn't have to spend so much time in an empty apartment. There she met other single women in a yoga class, one of whom she'd become friendly with. All and all, her life was exactly what she'd wanted when she'd planned to come to New York.

Unfortunately the life she'd imagined hadn't included John Roper. Having been with him, she was afraid she'd never be the same without him. And working at the Hot Zone, where she read the papers and blogs to keep up with damage control, guaranteed she was reminded of him daily. Buckley hadn't let up on him, but the rest of the papers had, due in the most part to the fact that he'd been at the gym every day.

But Amy was reminded of him nightly when she lay in her bed, tossing and turning. How could she not when their last encounter had included his declaration of love.

One she hadn't been able to verbally reciprocate even though she knew without a doubt, she felt it deep in her heart. How could she not love a man who was so kind and generous, thoughtful and caring? Not just to his family but to her, as well. He'd made her wish for a day in the snow come true in a way that went beyond special. He could have just taken her outside. Instead he'd planned a fantasy afternoon.

But that was the problem. No matter what they both felt in here, she thought, her hand rising to her chest, it had been a moment out of time. Real life meant obligations he couldn't extricate himself from and cameras that followed him everywhere he went.

That was a life of his choosing. Not hers.

Frustrated with her train of thought, she tossed her pen down onto her desk. Obviously she couldn't concentrate on work. A glance at her watch told her it was late in the afternoon. She'd had it for today. With nothing pressing keeping her at the office, she decided to head home.

She began packing her bag, taking select things to review with her when she heard a knock at her door. "Come in," she called, hoping nobody had an assignment that would keep her in the office later. She was more exhausted than she'd realized.

She glanced up at the same time her visitor strode inside. "Roper," she said, surprised to see him. Her stomach flipped, nerves fluttering inside her.

"Hey, there," he said casually. As if nothing important had happened the last time they'd met.

I love you. She considered that important.

He looked healthy and well. She knew from Micki and Yank that, despite his family obligations, he *had* been focusing on his recovery. Though he'd miss the beginning of spring training, the doctors were hopeful for a full recovery. But also according to Yank and Micki, his family still pulled his strings.

And he still let them.

"Let me guess. You just happened to be in the neighborhood. Visiting Yank or Micki?" She gripped the handle of her tote bag hard, yet strove for normalcy in her voice. Like in the deodorant commercial, she wouldn't let him see her sweat.

"Nope." He shut the door behind him. "I'm here to see you."

"Oh." Her mouth grew dry. "I was just leaving for the day."

"Then I can walk you out."

She shrugged. "That's fine."

He helped her on with her coat and they started for the door. "You look good," he said.

Such a simple compliment and yet she grew warm all over. "Same for you. I hear your therapy is going well," she said.

"I'm trying. The shoulder's getting stronger. It helps that I've lowered my expectations of trying to be back in time for spring training. I find I'm more focused."

They rode down the elevator and walked onto the street. "I was going to take a cab, but it's a little warmer today so I think I'll walk a bit," she said.

"Sounds good. I'll join you."

They walked in silence, but the comfortable feeling they'd found at the lodge was gone. "How's your family?" she finally asked when she couldn't stand the stiff silence between them any longer.

"Good, actually." He perked up at the question. "I'm glad you asked. It ties into the reason I wanted to talk to you. My mother has her hands full with Harrison and—"

The sudden singing noise from her cell phone

interrupted him. She dug into her jacket pocket and pulled out her phone. "Sorry," she said, glancing down and seeing a 718 phone number she didn't recognize.

"Hello?"

"Amy, it's Uncle Spencer," his warm voice said.

"Hi, Uncle Spencer," she said, more for Roper's benefit so he'd know who was on the phone. "What's up?" she asked.

Roper shoved his hands into his jacket pockets and waited patiently.

Her uncle went on to explain the reason for his call and a familiar panic settled deep in her bones. "Mom is *where?*" Amy yelled.

A young couple passing by her on the street turned and stared.

Roper immediately huddled near her side, placing a hand on her shoulder. She appreciated the support.

God, this couldn't be happening. Not when she'd just carved out a perfectly sane, normal life for herself. She shut her eyes for a brief moment before she pulled herself together.

"I'll be right there," she told her uncle, ending the call. Then she turned to Roper. "My mom and my aunt are being held by security at JFK Airport."

She stepped off the sidewalk and into the street, glancing around for a free taxi cab to take her to meet them.

Roper grasped her hand. "I have my car in the lot

downstairs. I'll drive you. It'll be cheaper and quicker. Come."

She drew a deep breath and met his gaze. "Thank you," she said, grateful for his unquestioning support.

He steered her back toward the Hot Zone offices and to the elevator leading to the underground parking garage.

"I didn't even know my mother was coming to town. Apparently they wanted to surprise me." And she hadn't seen it coming, Amy thought. "Uncle Spencer has a meeting he can't miss, so it's up to me to get them out."

"And we will," Roper assured her.

Amy was sure they would. As good as her mother and aunt were at getting into trouble, they were equally adept at talking themselves out of it. Or letting Amy do it for them. And to think, she'd been so anxious to start her new life, she'd let her mother remain in Florida unsupervised. She'd underestimated the older woman yet again.

Roper handed his ticket to the attendant and within minutes they were in his car and on their way. Amy finally started breathing again.

"I almost took the Porsche but I knew with all the stop and go traffic, there'd be no point. It was a good thing, too. At least I can fit them in the backseat."

She nodded, grateful. Even in the midst of her panic, she could see how quickly, calmly and efficiently he'd taken charge. What a guy.

"Why are they being held by security?" he asked.

"Uncle Spencer didn't give me a straight answer, which isn't surprising given my mother and aunt. I'm sure we'll find out soon enough."

There was some traffic, but it moved at a decent pace and soon they'd pulled into the airport.

"I'll drop you off, park and meet you in there," he said, easing the car to the curb in front of the terminal.

She bit down on her lip. "You can drop me off and leave. I'm sure you have somewhere more important to be and—"

He placed his hand on hers, his touch doing more to calm her than anything could. "Nothing is more important than helping you through this," he assured her.

Strong and capable. Roper had to be the perfect man.

For the first time, she could understand firsthand how and why his family had come to rely on him for everything. She couldn't allow herself to do the same, especially since she'd faulted him for responding to them on cue.

"Really, I'll be fine. I can take them home with me in a cab and—"

"I will be inside in five minutes. You'll get to them sooner if you stop arguing and go," he said, giving her a gentle yet firm push.

She inclined her head. Then, knowing she should just turn and head inside, she acted on impulse and placed a thank-you kiss on his cheek.

At least she meant for it to be on his cheek. But the scoundrel anticipated her move and with a quick shift of his head, he caused her lips to land squarely on his.

She didn't pull away. Instead she leaned in closer. Her eyes closed, and for a sweet short time, she was back at the lodge, where real life couldn't intrude. His lips parted, and his tongue swept over her lips, her teeth and then tangled with hers. Warmth eased from the pit of her stomach, shooting outward, overwhelming her senses…until a car honked, startling them and breaking the intimacy of the moment.

Flustered, she gathered her bag and darted out of the car.

ROPER MANAGED TO PARK and catch up with Amy before she was allowed in to see her relatives. A stiff man in a suit, who turned out to be the federal marshal on the plane, escorted Amy and Roper to the area where Darla and Rose were being held. The marshal explained that he worked with TSA, a component of the Department of Homeland Security and they were trying to assess whether Darla and Rose were terrorist risks.

More like attention seekers, Roper knew.

First, Amy introduced Roper to her family and they shook his hand, but they were too impatient to tell their story to spend time on pleasantries.

"So we were talking about how what happened with my luggage reminded us of the movie *Meet the Parents*," Amy's mother, Rose, said.

"And I said it wasn't *Meet the Parents,* it was the second one, *Meet the Fockers,*" Darla said.

"It was *Meet the Parents* and the stewardess—"

"They're called flight attendants now," Darla interrupted her sister.

Rose rolled her eyes. "The *flight attendant* had taken my carry-on and gave it to the handlers to put it in the cargo area. I forgot, and when the plane landed in New York, I opened the top compartment to take out my luggage and Darla reminded me that my bag wasn't there. So I said, I thought it was stupid. I could so have fit it on top."

"But the flight attendant wouldn't even let her try," Darla said. "So we were reminded of *Meet the Fockers.*"

"Meet the Parents," Rose interrupted. "And I said, in a complete and perfect impersonation of Ben Stiller, *It's not like there's a bomb in it.*"

Darla and Rose both spoke with animation, hands waving in the air. "Then some woman obviously misunderstood us and yelled, 'that old lady said she has a *bomb.*' Do I look old to you?" Rose asked Amy.

"No, Mom," Amy said through gritted teeth. "Go on with the story."

Roper held back his laughter because he could see how obviously stressed Amy was. But the women, with their bright red lipstick, overdyed hair and deep circles of rouge on their cheeks, looked more like Kewpie dolls than terrorists. And Roper thought the way they each argued their point was hilarious.

"Of course we don't look old to you," Rose said, ignoring Amy's request. "You see us all the time." Rose then took Roper off guard by walking up to him. "You're a young, handsome man. Do I look old to you?" She nudged him with her elbow and batted her thick eyelashes.

"No, ma'am," he said, holding back a chuckle. "You're beautiful."

Amy shot him a warning look that clearly said *don't humor them.* He couldn't help it, they were so cute.

"Why, thank you," Rose said. "You see, Darla?"

"What about me? Do I look old?" Darla asked him, pushing her sister out of the way.

Roper grinned. "You're absolutely breathtaking, too," he told her.

Pleased, both women relaxed and smiled. "So anyway," Rose continued, "someone yells, 'The old lady has a bomb!' And all hell broke loose. That man who brought you in here had been sitting in front of us and he turned around and practically dove over the seat. The rest of the passengers went into utter panic."

"There was nearly a stampede thanks to that crazy woman," Darla said, nodding.

Amy raised an eyebrow. "You think *she* was the crazy woman?" she asked.

Both relatives ignored her. "Next thing you know, they evacuate the plane and corral everyone into one area, except for us. They brought us in here. Apparently they had to check all the carry-on bags underneath the plane to make sure they didn't miss something in security the first time around. They thought we were planning to blow up the airport!"

"They can't be too careful these days," Roper said seriously.

Rose and Darla nodded. "We understand. If only that woman hadn't made a scene, nobody would have been detained."

"And you don't think you had anything to do with that little scene?" Amy perched her hands on her hips and confronted her family.

Roper thought they blushed, though it was hard to tell beneath the heavy rouge.

"It was a misunderstanding," Darla said. "Not that your uncle Spencer thought so. He was furious, but he promised us you'd be here to handle things."

"Of course she's here. My beautiful, smart girl always rescues us," Rose said, pulling Amy into a hug. "I've missed you."

Amy hugged her mother back. "I missed you, too." She turned to her aunt. "You, too," she said, wrapping her arms around the other woman, as well.

For all her frustration, Amy obviously genuinely adored the women in her family.

Roper watched the byplay with interest. This was the only real firsthand glimpse he'd gotten into Amy's family and background, and a few things jumped out at him immediately. Her home situation wasn't much different from his. Her mother and aunt created situations and she rescued them on command.

It didn't take a psychologist to figure out that Amy dove into handling his family so methodically not because she was used to handling her own, but because she couldn't *control* them. In managing Roper's family issues, she'd been able to take charge in a way she hadn't been able to with her own family. She saw herself in Roper, and when Roper fell back into old habits, she'd backed away.

He'd gotten some insight into Amy's emotions. But he hadn't gotten enough. With her mother here, he hoped to gain even more.

"Mom, you really should have told me you were coming for a visit," Amy said.

"And ruin the surprise? What fun would that be?"

"None at all," Amy muttered. "So how do we get you two out of here?"

Rose seated herself in a metal chair. "The grumpy air marshal said he'd be back. He had to confer with his colleagues."

"Do you think they'll do a background check like they do on the TV show *COPS?*" Aunt Darla asked, walking to the small window and glancing out.

"Oh, Lord." Amy chose the nearest chair and lowered herself into it.

Roper gave Amy's shoulder a squeeze. "Why don't I go outside and see what I can find out."

Amy glanced up. "I'd appreciate it."

"Not so fast," Rose said. "Amy introduced you

and we know you're a professional ballplayer, but she didn't say what your relationship is. What are your intentions? Because when you come to help rescue a woman's relatives from the hoosegow, then you must have some personal interest, yes?"

"Remember, my sister is like a professional lie detector," Darla said. "If you're not telling the truth, she'll sniff it out."

"Oh, for God's sake, leave him alone," Amy said. "Roper, please go find out when I can take them home," she said, pleading with him.

Because her mother and aunt were wackier than his family, he took pity on her and agreed. "Okay. When I get back, we can discuss your questions," he promised the women.

They reluctantly agreed.

So Roper headed out of the room to get Amy's mother and aunt sprung. Afterward, he thought, the real fun could begin.

CHAPTER SIXTEEN

HER FAMILY WAS FREE. Amy sensed Roper had signed a few autographs and promised tickets to Renegades games in order to hasten the release process. He hadn't said, but the people who'd eventually released her mother and aunt had been huge fans, shaking Roper's hand and thanking him. He refused to say for what.

TSA and Homeland Security actually did perform a background check on the women and discovered their penchant for getting into ridiculous trouble back in Florida. It was soon obvious terrorism wasn't an issue. Insanity was, though, Amy thought wryly. But since the incident had been more of a misunderstanding than any kind of practical joke, the women were released into the general population of New York—complete with a behavioral warning for the future.

Amy was exhausted.

"So what are we doing tonight?" Aunt Darla asked, from her seat in the back of Roper's car.

Amy closed her eyes and groaned. But at least

they hadn't started asking Roper questions about his intentions again.

"I need to make some calls and find you two a hotel. I'm afraid my apartment is too small," Amy explained. "By the time I get you settled, it'll be too late to do anything tonight." Amy turned around in time to see her mother wink at her aunt. "*What* was that wink for?" Amy asked.

"You can go home and sleep. Darla and I want to hit one of the clubs," her mother said.

"Oh, no."

"Ladies, I think I have a solution," Roper said. "Do you want to hear it?" he asked Amy.

She leaned her head back and nodded. "Yes, please." She owed him more than she could say for just being here.

"Instead of a hotel, why don't your mother and aunt share my guest room? It has two double beds and they'll have their own bathroom. And I'll be there to keep them company."

Meaning he'd make sure they didn't get into trouble by sneaking out at night.

The rest of the thought went unsaid, but it was glaringly obvious. "I couldn't impose like that," Amy said. No matter how good a solution he provided. Nobody should be subjected to dealing with her family twenty-four/seven.

"We'd love to!" Rose and Darla said at the same time, ignoring Amy as usual. "That's just so kind of you. We won't be any trouble."

"Are your fingers crossed behind your back?" Roper asked, laughing.

"You have a season to get ready for, remember? You can't afford any distractions," Amy said, her heart beating out a panicked rhythm.

Not only did Roper need to focus on his career, Amy didn't want her family getting close to the man she was trying to avoid.

"My family is a distraction for me. Your family is not," he assured her.

"You see? We're not a distraction."

Amy didn't turn around to see which one of her relatives spoke. They sounded alike and she didn't much care.

He leaned closer, never taking his eyes from the road. "It's different when nobody's pulling your emotional strings," he said softly, so only she could hear. "I can handle them and still keep all my appointments." Roper reached out and placed his hand on her thigh.

She knew he meant to reassure her but he aroused her instead. Talk about pushing emotional buttons, this man had hers down pat.

"It's still an imposition."

"Not when I offer freely. Besides, they want to stay with me."

"We do," the two chimed in from the backseat.

Amy groaned. "It looks as if I'm outnumbered."

"Wait until I call home and tell everyone we're staying with the famous John Roper. You know many of our residents are originally from New York. They still follow the Renegades and you're big news," Darla said.

"I didn't think you knew who I was when Amy introduced me," Roper said, glancing at them from the rearview mirror.

Rose laughed. "Well, we didn't want to embarrass you. We do have some sense of decorum. We know how to behave around a celebrity. Besides, who knows if the room was bugged."

"Oh, give me a break," Amy said. They'd obviously been watching too much television without her there to set up activities.

"We're almost at my apartment," Roper said.

"Good! Thank you so much for your generosity," Rose said. "We won't tell a single soul about your engagement to my daughter until you're ready to announce it publicly."

"What engagement?" Amy practically shrieked.

"The one Roper promised the guard would be happening soon, of course," her mother said, confident she had the whole situation figured out.

"Roper?" Amy asked, her head pounding hard.

He shook his head and grinned. "I promised to speak at his son's graduation."

Amy swirled around in her seat. "Did you hear that, Mom?" she asked, wanting to put an end to their inaccurate assumptions once and for all.

But both women suddenly had iPod earphones on and neither one was paying any attention.

"MAYBE IT'S TIME TO GET a job," Ben said, flipping through the Help Wanted section of the paper.

"You're giving up?" Dave, just home from work, pulled out a VitaminWater and guzzled from the bottle. "What happened with your brother?"

Ben had avoided seeing his friend for the past few days, embarrassed to admit he'd failed to get the necessary cash from his sibling. "He cut us all off," Ben admitted. "Mom, Sabrina and me. Told us it's time to stand on our own, if you can believe that." Ben could practically feel his anger and blood pressure rise at the memory. "What does he know about how rough I've got it? The guy's got the golden touch. Even with an injury, life's easy for him," Ben said.

"Damn." Dave shook his head. "I didn't want to believe he'd be so full of himself. I mean, he's a hero, even with last season's mess. But he's so damn selfish."

"You're telling me! He tried to convince me coaching is the way to go," Ben muttered. "He needs to be taken down a few pegs. Maybe then he'll stick his hand into his pocket and give something to the family that stuck by him."

Dave placed his empty bottle on the counter. "Don't you worry, I'm planning just that," his friend said.

Ben glanced up. "Planning what?"

"Remember all the times you wished someone would teach your brother a lesson?" Dave asked.

Ben didn't like Dave's tone. "Yes," Ben said warily.

"I've been doing it. It's been so easy, considering I know where he lives. A few disgruntled fan letters, a bobblehead doll with a knife in the shoulder, all meant to remind him that he's been one constant disappointment. What a waste of money on season tickets," he muttered in disgust. "I'm ordering a vegetarian pizza for dinner. Want some?"

"Make mine half plain," Ben said. "Wait a minute. You've been harassing my brother?"

Ignoring him, Dave picked up the phone and placed the food order before turning back to him. "I wouldn't call it harassing. It's more like teaching him a much-needed lesson. All that money, he should work a little harder instead of doing so much wining, dining and romancing. Pay a little respect to the fans, you know."

Ben's stomach rolled. It was one thing for him to complain about his brother, it was another to hear his friend ragging on Roper when he was down. Despite his own anger, Ben knew Roper was pissed at himself for this past year's performance. It wasn't like he'd screwed up on purpose.

"Back off," Ben warned his friend.

Dave stepped back and stared at Ben in disbelief. "You're sticking up for him now?"

"I'm just saying he works hard. When he wasn't playing well, it wasn't his fault. Just like it isn't my fault that my minor league career didn't work out,"

Ben said, hearing his words as if someone else were speaking them.

Understanding them, maybe, for the first time.

If it wasn't Roper's fault that he'd had a bad season, could it really be Roper's fault that Ben's life didn't turn out the way he'd hoped and dreamed?

Holy shit. Talk about an *aha moment*.

"This is frigging unbelievable," Dave said, pacing the kitchen. "What happened to the man who wanted his brother to suffer the way he was?"

Ben jumped up from his seat. "Those were words, man. A fantasy. We all have those. I'm not happy with my brother at the moment. But he's my brother." Hell, Ben had just come to realize he wasn't happy with himself, either.

After all, he'd leaked news of his brother's whereabouts to the press. His mother would casually mention what Roper had been up to and Ben would put an anonymous call through to Buckley, Roper's number-one nemesis. He'd tell the guy where Roper had been and with whom, usually making things seem more frivolous than they were.

Ben had gotten perverse pleasure in seeing Roper on the receiving end of bad press for once, but Ben's actions had been harmless fun, or so he'd thought at the time. Looking at Dave's twisted view, Ben was coming to see that even his phone calls had done damage to the brother he was jealous of—the brother he loved.

Dave went on to describe some of the better

packages he'd sent Roper, including the dog shit he'd paid a dog walker to hand over, and Ben thought he'd be sick.

Roper was his brother, Ben thought, repeating his own words.

The same brother who had stepped up to the plate when Ben's father took off. Who'd introduced him to coaches in the minors and who'd funded more failed businesses than Ben cared to remember. Jeez, he'd been living with his head up his ass, Ben thought.

"So do me a favor and leave Roper alone."

Dave shrugged. "Can't do that. It's too late."

Ben's skin chilled. "What do you mean?"

"The way you've been ducking me the past two days, waking up before I leave, coming home after I'm asleep, I had a feeling you struck out with big brother. So I put the ultimate revenge in motion."

Ben grabbed his friend by his shirt. "What the hell do you have planned?" he asked.

Dave laughed, but there was nothing remotely funny about the situation. "Nothing I'm going to tell you about, that's for sure. And Ben?"

"What?" he asked, releasing Dave's shirt.

"Find yourself a new couch. Mine's off-limits."

AMY SAT IN ROPER'S KITCHEN, her stomach cramping as he read, first from the *Daily News* and then the *New York Post*. He hadn't said much since she'd arrived except to warn her that her mother's adventure at the airport had made the news, thanks to an overzealous fan who'd spotted them. The guy had called the Gossip Zone, another online site. And when one rag got hold of the news, the rest followed.

Roper watched Amy warily, as if waiting for her to explode at any moment. And he was right to worry.

Amy's fuse was lit, her nerves strung tight. But she had to see the damage for herself. "Give me that."

She snatched the newspaper from Roper's hand and glanced at the article, reading aloud. "'As opening day of baseball season approaches, Renegades star John Roper is busy. Just not in the way his fans would expect.'"

As she spoke, he rose and poured his coffee into the sink, rinsing the mug and saying nothing.

She continued. "'Yesterday, the center fielder bailed his girlfriend's mother and aunt out of trouble at JFK International Airport.'" Nausea rose and remained in her throat. "Why can't my family just act like normal human beings?" Amy asked in frustration.

"Because they are who they are. Besides, that's why you love them," Roper said. His kind tone only made things worse. How was she going to fight her feelings for him?

The newspaper articles instantly reminded her of the last time her mother's antics had made the front page. How she'd lost the job she'd been so proud of, not to mention any potential career in the same field thanks to Rose's behavior. Amy knew a psychiatrist would have a field day with her inability to put the past where it belonged. But it *was* her past and she was reacting the only way she knew how.

"Give me the papers," he said. "They aren't good for anything except recycling," he said, the voice of reason. His reaction seemed strange, coming from a man used to reading about himself regularly in a none-too-flattering light.

But Amy wasn't a celebrity. She hadn't signed on for a life in front of the cameras. In fact, she'd deliberately chosen a career behind the scenes. Yet when she was with Roper, she couldn't remain there.

"I need to read the rest." She folded the newspaper in half and cleared her throat. "'Amy Stone, niece of sports agent Spencer Atkins, and newly minted publicist at the Hot Zone, has her hands full with relatives who were detained for possible terrorist activity on board an aircraft....'"

"Give me that," he muttered, grabbing the paper and tossing it into the recycling bin in disgust.

But not before she caught a glimpse of the photograph beneath the article. "There's no mistaking us," Amy said. She shook her head and groaned.

"I actually think it's a good picture," Roper said. He settled back into his chair as if nothing had occurred.

As if two elderly women with a penchant for trouble weren't in his guest room getting ready to *hit the streets of New York City* right this minute. There were probably even people with cameras waiting outside the apartment. Ones that had probably watched her come inside. Not that she'd seen anyone, but obviously, that didn't mean a thing.

"I never saw anyone with a camera at the airport." Amy said. Yet there was the picture, taken as they exited the terminal building yesterday.

Her hands grew damp at the thought of dealing with more pictures, innuendos and rumors.

"They could have had a zoom lens or a cell-phone camera. At least we know who called it in. Half the time I'm left guessing about how they found me." He eyed her with obvious concern.

She didn't respond. She was too busy worrying about avoiding more photo ops in the future.

"Everyone's looking for a way to make a buck these days," Roper finally said.

"Off of my newfound celebrity status." Since New Year's Eve, she'd somehow become a person of interest, thanks to her connection to John Roper.

She couldn't blame him for her mother's innate ability to attract trouble. Amy had been this route before. But she couldn't risk the potent combination of Roper and her mother placing her squarely in the limelight again. True, her uncle Spencer had as deep a connection to her mother and aunt as Amy herself, so she wouldn't be fired. But the idea of being the object of public ridicule after spending so many years avoiding it gave Amy more than a headache. It made her want to throw up.

She realized that Roper was staring at her, trying to figure out what was going on in her mind. "It's just insane the way the media focuses on me as your girl-friend," she said, needing to explain her reaction to him in some way he could understand.

"That's not what bothers you," Roper said.

She leaned forward in her seat. "And what does?" she asked, since he obviously thought he knew her so well.

"I'm not sure yet. But I'll let you know when I fig-ure it out," he said.

"Maybe it's that you insist on giving everyone the idea that we're a couple when you know we aren't."

He grinned, that sexy, in-control smile that drove her to distraction. "I know no such thing."

And because of his stubbornness, her mother, her aunt and even the media refused to believe that she and John were just friends. Perhaps because he made it so hard for Amy to believe it herself.

He was doing his best to charm her into his life and keep her there. Last night he'd taken them to din-ner at his friend's restaurant in Little Italy. The one where he'd brought Amy on their first date. She had a hunch he'd chosen the place on purpose, as much for the memories as the good food. He called it *their place,* which caused a stir with her relatives. After-ward they walked around and he treated them to gelato and cannoli.

Then he insisted on dropping Amy off at her apartment first, so her mother and aunt could see where she lived. Amy had allowed him to take charge because he'd had ideas to keep her mother and aunt busy for the night, tiring them out. As much as she wanted to argue with his commandeering attitude, he took the pressure off of her and she appreciated it.

He was a gentleman. A kind, sexy gentleman. And to use her mother's old-fashioned word, he was *wooing* Amy with thoughtfulness, not money. She couldn't let herself succumb, but it wasn't easy.

Last night he'd slipped his hand into hers as they walked, so she couldn't pull back without making a scene. He'd casually placed his palm on her back when they entered the restaurant and once again she'd been powerless to separate them. After a while, the gestures felt too good and she didn't want him to stop. She lay in bed last night, aroused from his touch, yearning for him to ease the ache in her heart and the one that throbbed insistently inside her body. She missed him.

Just as he obviously intended.

But that was before she'd seen the morning paper. Before the past and present collided. John Roper and her eccentric, publicity-magnet mother were a combination Amy could not handle.

"So what are we doing today?" Roper asked.

She rose from her chair. "*We* aren't doing anything. I took the day off to entertain the troops. You are going to the gym or the physical therapist or whatever else is on your schedule." If he wasn't with them, he couldn't get them on tomorrow's front page.

She could keep her mother and aunt under control for a day or two, make them happy and then send them back to Florida without argument.

"I haven't skipped a day of therapy in weeks and you know it. I have a four-o'clock appointment today and I'll be there. Meanwhile, if you have nothing specific on the agenda, I thought maybe we could all do the Statue of Liberty. Then you can take them back here to rest up for dinner while I keep my appointment."

The telephone rang before she could argue, and Roper picked it up on the first ring. "Hello?" he said, then listened.

"Hi, Mom. I can't talk right now. I have company," he said.

Amy watched with interest. He'd taken phone calls from his mother and sister last night, as well, and there was a distinct difference in how he dealt with them now, compared to the panicked acquiescence he'd used when they'd first met.

"Yes, Amy's family is still here. If you'd like you can join us for dinner tonight."

Amy winced. "No!" She waved her hands in front of her face. Between her family and the famous Cassandra Lee, there'd be more than enough drama to create ten scenes. Amy couldn't deal with it and her anxiety built higher at the mere thought.

"I'll talk to you later, Mom," Roper said. There was no hint of frustration in his voice.

If anything, things with his mother seemed

almost…normal. Such a stark contrast to the episodes Amy had witnessed in the past. It was enough to distract her from canceling tonight's dinner or arguing about today's plans. At least for now.

Roper hung up and met Amy's gaze.

"You haven't dropped everything and run to your mother, not last night and not this morning," she said, realizing exactly why things seemed so off balance to her now. "And Sabrina? Her phone call was calm. She wasn't in hysterics complaining about your mother. And Ben—"

"Isn't speaking to me at the moment, which makes things easier," Roper admitted. "But yes, something *is* different. I came to your office to talk to you about it. But then you got the phone call to rush to the airport and, well, I forgot."

Amy nodded. Subtly and not so subtly, Roper was now his own person. Not an athlete and a son pulled in a million different directions. If his family called, he spoke to them and quickly got off the phone. He met all his obligations and appointments, including those promises he'd made to Amy's mother and aunt, without running off on one emergency after another.

He was focused.

He was present in the moment.

And his career obligations—working out and meeting with the physical therapist—came first.

Wow.

"How? What happened with your family?" she asked.

"In a nutshell, I laid it on the line for them. I told them—"

Suddenly her mother's and aunt's voices sounded from the other room, growing louder as they made their way to the kitchen.

Roper shot Amy an amused glance, but she wanted to hear the rest of his story. Unfortunately her family descended on them, two small women who sounded and acted like a herd.

"We decided what we wanted to do today," Darla said. "We want to go to the Central Park Zoo."

"And then I have something special planned for tonight," Amy's mother said, her eyes sparkling.

"We're having dinner with my mother tonight," Roper said.

"Great! I can't wait to meet Cassandra Lee! And afterward she can join us. I read in the paper that the Chippendales show is in town. Can you use your pull to get us tickets?" Rose asked Roper, snuggling up to his side and batting her eyelashes.

"No, no and no!" It was time for them to go home, Amy thought.

Much as she loved them, they were already driving her crazy. And though she'd loved her job in Florida, she had to admit she'd found a peace in her short time in New York she hadn't realized existed. Her family had shattered it the moment they arrived.

And on the pragmatic side, she wasn't getting any work done. Though her uncle had given her time off, she was too new to have earned it. She needed and wanted to get back to the office. But how could she send her relatives packing after not even twenty-four hours? They'd be devastated. And hurt.

"I'll see what I can do," Roper said, chuckling. "But it's last-minute. I'm pretty sure it's too late for me to get tickets. I'm sorry."

Amy breathed a sigh of relief. Obviously he knew better than to let her mother and aunt Darla loose at a strip show in Manhattan. Short of putting them in handcuffs and chains, Amy barely knew how to contain them herself.

Whether they stayed three days or three weeks, they'd have more than enough time to wreak havoc without a trip to Chippendales on their agenda.

DAVE PUT THE FINISHING touches on his project. He'd been working on it for a while, in between shifts at the gym. It looked professional, if he did say so himself. Enough to cause trouble for John Roper. Trouble the likes of which he'd never seen before.

Ben had bailed out on him and he wouldn't be getting the money for his gym. Someone had to pay. It might as well be the high-and-mighty John Roper, Dave thought.

Laughing, he clicked Upload on his computer.

Let the fun begin.

CHAPTER SEVENTEEN

AT DINNER, ROPER BRACED himself for a clash of two women who could not be more different, but his mother and Amy's hit it off. Darla and Rose gushed over Cassandra and she ate up the attention. If his mother found Amy's family odd or eccentric, she didn't show it, for which Roper was grateful. And Harrison, ever the gentleman and ever present at Cassandra's side, kept her grounded.

The same couldn't be said for Amy's female relatives. Aunt Darla was obviously smitten with their waiter, a young man, new to his job, who didn't know what to make of the attention.

He'd taken their orders, with Rose and Darla interrupting him periodically to ask questions. Unfortunately they weren't about the daily specials.

"I have a question," Darla said for the third time. The first two times she'd interrupted the man with personal questions.

"Yes?" he asked, forcing a smile.

"It had better be about the meat," Amy said through gritted teeth.

"Oh, it is," her aunt assured her. She glanced up at the waiter. "What's your address, Hot Boy?" she asked.

Roper chuckled despite himself.

"Aunt Darla!" Amy scolded her aunt.

"I'm going to turn in the order," he said, flustered and walking away.

"Ooh, check out that rear end."

Amy slapped her hand over her forehead. "Would you cut it out?" she scolded under her breath.

"Don't be a spoilsport," her mother said. "It isn't anything personal. This is the one thing we don't miss back home—you killing our fun."

Beside him, Amy gritted her teeth. "I'd think you also miss me bailing you two out at midnight. Aunt Darla told me that my replacement makes you wait until morning."

"This is better than any movie," Cassandra said, laughing.

The waiter returned with their drinks, serving the ladies first, which was his first mistake.

Darla reached out, and before Roper realized what she intended—and definitely before Amy did— Darla pinched the waiter's behind.

The man jumped back, dropping his tray of drinks. "Sorry," he said. Red-faced, he headed back to the kitchen to get something to clean up the mess.

"That's it," Amy said, yelling at her aunt. "You need to apologize to the man."

Roper stood and placed a calming hand on her shoulder.

At the same moment, a man in a jacket and tie approached the table. "I'm sorry to disturb you, but we've had some complaints about your table being too loud," the gentleman said.

Amy's face turned red. "I apologize. We won't cause any more trouble," she promised.

"Thank you. I'll be sending a new waitress to handle your order," he said pointedly. Then he walked away quickly, leaving them all alone.

No explanations were necessary. Darla had run the other man off.

"I hope you're all happy." Amy glared at her family members.

"I didn't mean any harm," Darla said, sounding sincere and embarrassed at the same time.

Roper actually felt sorry for her.

He felt worse for Amy.

She lowered herself into her seat and the rest of the meal passed without a word from her. Her mother and aunt behaved—at least well enough not to get them kicked out of the restaurant.

His mother picked up on the tension and told stories about Hollywood, distracting Amy's family enough to pass the time.

"I heard your daughter is getting married," Rose said to Cassandra at the very end of the meal.

His mother nodded. "She's marrying a wonderful man and they're having a *small, intimate ceremony,*" she said, grudging acceptance in her tone.

Since the day Roper had laid down the law, his

mother had backed off his sister and stopped meddling in the wedding plans. Of course, the fact that Sabrina had a check in her hand meant there was nothing Cassandra could do but accept her daughter's wishes.

Just as Roper had intended.

And perhaps sensing she was at a crossroads with her son, Cassandra had changed her behavior where he was concerned, as well. Roper was sure Harrison played a strong role in his mother's turnaround and he appreciated the man more than he could say. Harrison obviously made his mother happy, in her own dysfunctional way, and that pleased Roper, too.

Roper gestured to the waitress, who picked up the credit-card slip, fully signed. They could leave whenever they were ready. And he sensed Amy had been ready a long time ago.

"Weddings are wonderful," Rose said with a sigh.

Roper nodded. "I'm going to give my sister away and we're looking forward to Kevin becoming part of the family," he said.

"Speaking of weddings," Rose said, leaning across the table and staring Roper in the eye.

"Oh, no," Amy said. "We're leaving before you can go there." She correctly guessed her mother would begin to pump Roper about his intentions regarding her daughter.

Roper knew his own intentions. Unfortunately Amy didn't share them. Instead she wanted to run from him, far and fast.

After tonight's dinner, he was starting to understand why. Now that she couldn't blame Roper's family or his choices for coming between them, she had it in for the press. But there was so much more to her feelings. When she'd first come to New York, she'd been uptight, diligently planning his life as if her career hinged on his getting it right. At the time he'd chalked it up to the fact that he was her first assignment. But their trip to the lodge proved him wrong.

Only when she'd gotten away from the pressure of her job and her family, when she'd stopped worrying about what people were going to think of her, had she been relaxed and happy. She'd enjoyed life.

There was no enjoyment in Amy now.

Her family pulled her strings the same way his family had with him.

Amy stood and he followed. Everyone at the table did the same. They left the restaurant, at which point Cassandra and Rose exchanged phone numbers. Everyone survived the embarrassment of the evening no worse for wear. Everyone except Amy.

She was barely speaking to anyone. He wished he could help her through what was going on with her family. Unfortunately, he'd learned from firsthand experience that the only person who could fix Amy's situation was Amy. After all, she'd tried desperately to change his and nothing worked until he'd stood up for his own personal space.

She needed to do the same.

AMY COULDN'T BELIEVE HER luck. Yank had arranged for an entire day's worth of activities for her family. Curly, one of his and her uncle Spencer's poker buddies, was taking some relatives into town to see the sights and they asked Amy's mother and aunt to join them. Amy showered, dressed and headed for work, determined to forget the events of last evening.

She cringed, her stomach cramping at the memory. She wondered what her father would think of last night's episode. Pushing those thoughts aside, she collected her notepad and pen and headed for the conference room for the weekly meeting. The room filled up quickly, everyone present and accounted for.

As usual, Yank called the Hot Zone meeting to order. Amy, having already learned the drill, remained standing, hands and coffee off the table until he slammed down the gavel. Then she seated herself and prepared for the list of new assignments.

Yank's first words weren't about business per se. "We're gonna have a firm party at one of the upstate country clubs," he announced without preamble. "It'll be before the start of baseball season and after the NFL draft, so nobody can make excuses. Micki's got media lined up and we're gonna make a splash just because we can," he said proudly. "Everyone needs to be there."

"This is going to be an annual event," Annabelle said. "We have corporate sponsors who want to meet our clients. It's a win-win for everyone. Date to follow soon."

"Amy and Spencer, be sure your family's back home before then. Otherwise we might have a bomb scare," Yank said, laughing.

Amy cringed.

Until her uncle added, "Similar to the fire drill you arranged New Year's Eve?"

Then Amy laughed.

"He's blamin' a blind man for trippin' over his dog! Can you believe that?" Yank asked, rising from his chair.

"I'm blaming you for being a klutz. Being blind's got nothing to do with it," Spencer said.

"Here they go again," Micki whispered to Amy, leaning close. She grabbed the gavel from her unsuspecting uncle's hands and rapped it on the rubber mat. "Move it along," she ordered.

The men sat down, obeying her without question. Another half hour passed with routine business until Frannie burst into the room without knocking. "I'm sorry to interrupt," she said, huffing and out of breath. "But I have news that can't wait."

Amy's stomach churned. She had a distinct feeling of déjà vu, taking her back to her first meeting in this room.

"Let's hear it," Yank said.

"Well, I need to see Amy privately," Frannie said, suddenly realizing all eyes were on her.

Now Amy's stomach churned again, but for good

reason. Frannie wasn't the type to get so worked up. This must really be something. Amy rose from her seat, but Micki placed a hand on her shoulder. "We're family here. Nobody is in this room except Uncle Yank, Spencer, myself, my sisters and Amy. We want to help."

Amy sat down again.

Frannie nodded. She leaned forward until she was between Amy and Micki. "There's something on the Internet Amy needs to see. Nobody else should see it," Frannie said.

That was the moment Amy realized her uncle's secretary had a laptop beneath her arm. She placed it on the table, opened it and Amy immediately recognized the banner for Buckley's blog on the top of the screen.

Everyone in the room was silent, obviously recognizing something huge was going on. Amy had never been so sick in her life.

"Ready?" Frannie asked.

"As I'll ever be," Amy muttered.

She scrolled down slowly until the headline caught Amy's eye. *Roper Bares All.* Panic rose in her throat as she tried to concentrate on the words. The effort to understand what she was seeing was futile until she saw *her* own name posted along with Roper's.

A prominent link promised to lead to "an eyeful."

She clicked.

She looked.

And she immediately wished she hadn't.

Her hands began to sweat because somehow,

there were photographs of Amy and Roper—*naked* on the Internet.

Having sex.

She ordered herself to breathe. In. Out. In. Out. Think.

She peeled open her eyelids and looked again. Thanks to the unbelievable angle of the bodies on screen, Amy tipped her head to the side to get a better glimpse.

"When did you get a tattoo?" her uncle Spencer asked from behind them.

"I didn't!" she said tightly, jumping up from her seat, nearly knocking everyone behind her over in her effort to escape the sudden stifling feeling surrounding her.

"Take it easy," Micki said, grabbing her wrist. "They're obviously doctored, so breathe. We'll figure something out."

Everyone around her spoke, but she couldn't hear anything beyond the ringing in her ears. It didn't matter that the body on the screen wasn't really hers. It was her face. And nobody who viewed this photograph would know or care that it wasn't really Amy and Roper doing the deed.

She knew her business. Perception was everything. Thanks to her relationship with Roper, she'd been violated in the most extreme and demeaning way and there was nothing she could do about it.

Tears filled her eyes, along with impotent frustration. She'd felt like this once before. Memories of her mother being photographed as Lady Godiva came back to her vividly. Guilt by association had damned her in the eyes of her employers and made her a laughingstock in the community. She'd let herself down, but worse, she felt her father's disappointment keenly. Amy had coped by withdrawing deeper into her mother's world, doing her best to help them control their behavior. Without others to judge her, she'd been able to live with the insanity.

But here in New York, she couldn't hide the same way. She hadn't signed up for the privilege of being in the public eye. Nor did she want it.

The price was too high.

She jerked away from Micki, her uncle and everyone else calling her name and headed to find the one person she could vent on. The person who'd caused this mess, intentionally or not.

To her surprise, Amy didn't have to go far to find Roper. He was waiting in her office.

ROPER HAD RECEIVED enough phone calls and e-mails about the Internet photos to know he'd better reach Amy before she had a chance to build up emotional walls against him.

She burst into the room quickly and stopped short, obviously shocked to see him. She was dressed for work, in a blazer and slacks. Professional and cute at the same time.

As usual, his heart beat faster at the sight of her. He'd accepted his feelings for her.

She hadn't.

He welcomed them.

She was still running.

"Hi." She straightened her shoulders and turned away for a second, obviously wiping tears from her eyes. He guessed she'd heard about the photos.

Anger gripped him, as it had when he'd seen the pictures the first time. This wasn't the usual paparazzi photo. Someone was going to pay.

Clearing her throat, she met his gaze. "You saved me a trip. I was just coming to find you," she said calmly. Too calmly.

Everything inside him chilled. "Well, I'm glad I saved you a trip. What's up?" he asked, trying to gauge her mood.

She walked past him, retreating behind the safety of her desk. "Let's put it out on the table, okay? I'm sure you've seen the pictures." She clasped her hands in front of her, but not before he noticed that they were shaking and her cheeks were flushed pink in embarrassment.

He wanted to wrap her in his arms and protect her from everything that had and could hurt her, but he knew better than to think it was possible. She needed to face this challenge. They needed to face it together if they ever wanted to have a future.

"I've seen them," he said, his jaw clenched tight. "And I'm going to kill the bastard who doctored them and put them up there."

"You'll have to find the person first."

He inclined his head. "I intend to. But I'm more

worried about you." This composed, sedate woman sitting in front of him wasn't the Amy he thought he'd find.

He'd figured she'd be angry and fired up. Furious at him just because he was the easiest target.

"I know how you feel about this kind of thing and I'm sorry," he said. "I can't promise you something like this won't happen again, but I swear, I'll do my best to see it doesn't."

She shook her head. "I'm afraid that's not enough. You are who you are. You're John Roper, center fielder for the best team in New York. You're a celebrity, and let's face it, you love being one. I can't ask you not to be you."

Was that a glimmer of deeper understanding he saw? A flicker of hope rose inside him that maybe, just maybe, being in this job, in this city, had taught her to come around. Could that explain the calm aura around her.

"Thank you for that. But *you're you*. We can certainly work around both," he assured her.

He stepped closer, intending to circle around the desk and take her in his arms, but her words stopped him.

"That's not possible, John, and it's naive to think it is." She drew a deep breath. "Being a couple isn't working for me. The photographers are relentless. Being friends won't work, either. Even if I were just your assistant, it wouldn't keep me out of the media spotlight. And that's just not a place I want to be. So

I've decided to ask Micki to reassign me. Permanently." Her voice cracked but her composure didn't.

The only sign that she was upset was the fact that her knuckles had turned white.

But Roper didn't have her composure. He snapped, losing his patience. In a heartbeat he strode around the desk and grasped her by the shoulders, spinning her chair around to face him.

She gasped and squirmed, but he didn't release his grip. "What is wrong with you?" she asked, emotion showing at last.

"You're wrong. This is wrong."

"Because I don't want to sleep with you anymore?" she said without meeting his gaze. "Or because I don't like your high-profile life?"

"Because you care about me as much as I care about you. You're using this 'I hate being in the public eye' thing as an excuse not to be with me," he said, his frustration at an all-time high.

She finally met his gaze. "Pardon me if it bothers me to see myself naked on the Internet!" she spat.

"We both know it isn't your body. I'll take a freaking billboard in Manhattan if that's what it takes to convince you I love you!" he yelled at her.

She stilled and stopped pulling away from him. Her eyes filled with tears. "I love you, too," she said softly.

Relief swamped him. "Then get angry at whoever is doing this to us. React, instead of being this monotone robot without feelings. Fight for us, dammit!"

She shook her head. "I can't."

He leaned closer. "Why the hell not?" he asked, seeking an answer to the one question he didn't understand. "We can ignore the press and focus on us. It isn't easy, but we can do it."

"You can. I can't."

"Because…" he prompted.

"Because when I'm with you, I'm everything I've spent a lifetime trying to avoid."

He gentled his grip on her shoulders. "In English, please. I'm just not understanding."

She swiped at a tear running down her face. "I don't want to be the crazy lady arrested by airport security for making a scene. I don't want to be caught making love to you in front of a glass window by paparazzi with cameras. No, those photos on the Internet aren't of us, *but they could have been!*"

He finally got it and let out a low groan. "You don't want to end up like your mother, and being with me increases the chances that when you finally let go and act like yourself, you'll be caught by the press."

"I lost my job once thanks to her antics. I've spent years since making sure that won't happen again."

This time he brushed her tears away with his thumb. "You can't keep running from who you are. You can't suppress your true self forever and be happy. You aren't. You won't be."

She stiffened her shoulders. "Who are you to say I'm not happy?"

"I'm the man who made love to you in front of

that window. I've seen you making snow angels for the first time. I saw you dancing and singing in the corner with Hannah when you thought no one was looking. I've seen the real you and I'm here to tell you that if you keep running away from yourself, you'll spend the rest of your life out of the spotlight like you think you want—and you'll be perfectly miserable." He lowered his hand from her face.

He looked into her eyes, and although he'd obviously hit a nerve, he hadn't changed her mind. His heart sank at the thought of walking out of here as alone as he was when he'd walked in.

"I can't do this anymore. I'll talk to Micki and she'll take care of you from now on."

"Did you hear anything I said? Or did you tune me out completely?"

"I heard you. I just don't think you're right about what I need to be happy." She folded her arms across her chest.

He was through. If Amy couldn't see she was running away, there was nothing more he could do to convince her. He had a season to prepare for and he was leaving for Florida to join the team soon. "I guess you're right. You know what you need and what you want. It sure as hell doesn't seem to be me."

She didn't argue.

"It's ironic, though. You helped me get my shit together with my family but you can't do the same for yourself." And until she was willing to try, he had nothing left to say.

Heart heavy, he turned to go.

And she didn't stop him as he walked through the door and out of her life.

AMY LEFT WORK EARLY. She wasn't in the mood to deal with people today. She couldn't look them in the eye with those photographs circulating, and to add insult to injury, she'd lost the man she loved. In fact, she'd sent him out the door without so much as a goodbye because she wasn't convinced she could handle *anything* anymore. What a mess.

She was mentally spent, and the last thing she expected to find was her mother and her aunt cooking up a storm in her kitchen. The scene was reminiscent of her childhood. Big meals, family dinners. A warm, fuzzy feeling surrounded her as she realized that maybe this was exactly what she needed. Retreating to the comfort of home and family without the outside world intruding. It had worked for her when she lived in the retirement community. It could work for her now, helping her forget about what it had cost to let Roper go.

"Hi," Amy said, announcing her presence.

"Oh, you're home," her mother said. She wiped her hands on a towel and strode across the room to give Amy a hug. "Your aunt and I were just making dinner. We thought you could use a home-cooked meal and some cheering up. Between those awful photos and you being silly enough to break up with Roper, we decided you needed your family around you."

"How do you know about my breakup with Roper?" Considering it had just officially happened earlier today.

"He called and said you might need us and suggested we come here. Of course, we pushed for an answer as to why, and when we found out, we just had to wonder what you were thinking!" her mother explained.

"I'm glad you're here." But she wasn't going to argue with them about the wisdom of the choices she made in her personal life. "A home-cooked meal sounds good. Just let me change into something comfortable and I'll be right back."

"Um… How comfortable?" her aunt asked.

Amy narrowed her gaze. "Why?"

"We're having dinner company," her mother said.

"Who?" Amy asked warily. If they'd invited Roper over, she was going to throttle them for interfering.

"While we were cooking for you, your phone rang and we answered. It was a gentleman who said he wanted to know your side of the story regarding those pictures on the Internet," her mother said.

"And so you just had to invite him over?" Amy asked, appalled, but not all that surprised.

"Well, of course!" Her aunt waved a spoon in emphasis. "You know how polite we are. Besides, the gentleman explained that you'd need someone on your side and he was the best person for the job."

Amy rubbed her burning eyes. "Does this gentleman have a name?"

"Frank Buckley from eSports," her mother said. "Amy, be a dear and get the wine that's been chilling in the refrigerator?"

Amy glanced at the ceiling and counted to ten and back again but there was no getting away from the truth. Roper had been right. She'd helped him get his life together, but she hadn't been able to do the same for herself. And as a result, she was here with her mother and her aunt, about to discuss pornographic pictures of herself with the reporter who hated Roper the most.

She had to take control and she had to do it now. Before her new life here in New York shattered beyond recognition.

"Listen, we need to talk."

Her mother nodded. "And we will. But first, you might as well change clothes. Our guest won't be here until seven and it's only three-thirty now. Why don't you get comfortable. You'll be able to change back into a nice, unwrinkled, presentable outfit later."

Amy sighed. "I'll worry about how I'm going to deal with Buckley later. First we're going to talk. The three of us, so sit. Please." She gestured to the small set of couches.

Her mother and aunt gave each other concerned glances before settling themselves on the cushions.

Amy sat down between them. "You both know how much I love you, right?"

"We love you, too," they said at the same time.

Amy swallowed hard. "What I'm going to say isn't easy, but it has to be said." She rubbed her hands against her pants, nerves setting in. These two women meant the world to her. They'd raised her, they adored her, and she felt the same way about them.

They also caused more trouble than two five-feet-one-inch women should be able to. She adored them for their quirkiness, but she needed them to keep their antics in Florida. Far from Amy—except for planned vacations.

"I'm glad you came to visit because I really missed you both."

"We're glad, too. It's been fun," her aunt Darla said.

"What's wrong? You seem sad." Her mother put her hand on Amy's shoulder.

Rose had always understood her daughter and it was no different now. Unfortunately for Amy, she was about to break her mother's heart. "Mom, in case you don't realize it, my life's a little hectic at the moment."

"Which is why it's good your aunt and I are here, right?" Her mother looked at her with her big, imploring eyes.

Amy drew a deep breath. It was now or never, she thought. She might not have been able to fight for her relationship with Roper—something she'd yet had time to analyze. But suddenly she was ready to fight for herself and her future.

She leaned forward. "It's not so good that you're here right now, Mom."

"What do you mean?" she asked, hurt in her voice.

"I came to New York to grow up," she said, looking toward the bookshelves she'd put her favorite things upon. "I thought I was doing that, but it turns out I was just running away from things," she said, more to herself than to them.

"I don't understand," her mother said. "Darla, do you understand what Amy is saying?"

Her aunt shook her head. "No, but I think she does and that's what matters."

"I left Florida to get a life. Instead, I've still been running away from one," she said, coming to the realization as she spoke.

She'd put miles between herself and her family. But it wasn't them she was running from—it was herself. It was time to stop. To deal with her past and embrace her future, one that, she hoped, included Roper.

"All I ever wanted was for you and dad to be proud of me," Amy said, taking her first step.

"I am. And he would be. Just look at you, my beautiful girl."

Amy smiled. "I love you for saying that, but don't you think that this mess with the photographers, the naked pictures…" She shook her head. "He'd be appalled."

"At the people who did it to you, yes. But not at you! He admired people with spunk. Why do you think he married me? I was the same crazy woman at eighteen that I am now. And I refuse to discuss my age, so don't ask."

Aunt Darla opened her mouth but Rose shot her a look that clearly said "Don't you dare."

Her sister shut it without speaking.

Amy laughed.

"Amy, you've got the best of both of us—my crazy side and your father's sensibility. He adored you and thought you could do no wrong, no matter what you did with your life." Then she chuckled. "Although I must say, it's a good thing those pictures aren't really of you. That I don't think he could have handled."

Amy glanced at her mother and her heart was filled with gratitude.

As she looked at the mother she'd always loved and the aunt who'd always been there for her, too, Amy came to yet another epiphany. It wasn't so bad to be like the two women sitting here.

She was glad her mother said her father would have approved of her choices. But in reality she'd already come to the conclusion, as she sat here with her mother and aunt, that it didn't matter as long as she herself approved of her choices.

In moderation, what was wrong with having fun? Unlike her relatives, Amy knew where and when to behave. So she'd made love with Roper in front of a set of windows—in a locked room facing a wintry landscape where it had been very unlikely they'd have been caught.

And if they'd been photographed? Could it be any worse than the doctored pictures on the Internet now? Amy shook her head and laughed, feeling lighter than she had in ages. She wrapped her hands around her knees, rocked back and forth and thought of all the ways she'd tried to run from Roper. All the excuses she'd made.

And that's what they were.

Excuses.

After being fired from her first job, she'd retreated home to lick her wounds—and she'd stayed there. It had been easy and fun and she never had had to worry about what people would think. Her job at the retirement community, by definition, allowed for the eccentric behavior of those around her.

Her move to New York had been more overwhelming than she'd expected, and she'd been running from her fear—fear of not being able to make it here—without knowing it. Not until Roper had pointed it out today. And even then, she'd refused to admit he was right.

"What's so funny?" her mother asked. "First you weren't happy we're here and now you're laughing."

"I think I'm just realizing what a fool I've been." About so many things.

"So is it good we're here? Or not so good we're here?" Aunt Darla asked.

Amy bit down on the inside of her cheek. "It's good you're here now…"

"But?" her mother asked.

"But next time can we schedule a visit so I can take some legitimate time off?" And give her time to plan some activities that would keep them busy and out of trouble.

"We can do that," her mother said, nodding.

"And as far as tonight's guest goes, I need you two to promise you'll stay in the background and let me do the talking. Do you understand?"

They both nodded.

"Good."

Between this afternoon and right this minute, Amy had come to some major conclusions about her behavior and her life. Both needed to change.

And Buckley was giving her a chance to do it publicly.

CHAPTER EIGHTEEN

ROPER DIDN'T THINK HIS DAY could get any worse. After leaving Amy for what seemed like the last time, he worked out, checked in with his coaches and headed home. He'd taken one look at the house-guests who'd just returned from their tour of the city and he knew he had to send them to be with Amy. She needed them—either for their moral support or to face her frustration with them and send them home. Regardless, it wasn't his problem. Unfortunately, he still cared enough to want her to have her family around her if she needed them.

An hour later, his doorbell rang and he found himself face-to-face with the last person he expected to see—his brother. As much as he wasn't in the mood for company, he hadn't seen Ben in a while.

"What's up?" Roper asked.

"Can we talk? And before you slam the door in my face, I'm not here to ask you for money, a job or anything else," his brother said, red-faced.

Curious now, Roper swung the door wide and gestured inside. "Come on in. Can I get you a beer?"

"Why not."

A few minutes later, they were settled in his living room with the TV blaring eSports Network behind them. "So what's up?" Roper asked.

Ben shifted in his seat. "A few things. First is, I called some of those contacts you gave me a while back and set up some interviews for assistant coaching jobs."

Roper couldn't believe his ears. "That's great!" He didn't want to ask what changed Ben's mind because he didn't want to ruin this step in the right direction.

"I've done some thinking and I've been an ass," Ben said. "Blaming you because my life didn't work out the way I wanted." He glanced down, not even chugging his beer the way he usually did. "A couple of the guys said if things work out and I prove myself, the head coaching position might become available. I know it's because of you but I'll take the opportunity and try."

"What's going on, Ben?" Roper had never seen his brother so subdued.

"There's something that's going to hit the news and you need to hear it from me first."

"Can't be any worse than doctored porn shots of me and Amy on the Internet," Roper muttered.

"No, but it relates to it. Turns out my friend Dave, who'd been letting me bunk there until I convinced you to fund the gym, was behind those photographs."

"What the hell? *Why?* I don't even know the guy."

Ben swallowed hard. "Yeah, well, thanks to me, he thought he knew you. My old, skewed perspective of you."

"I don't know what I want to know first. Why your view of me changed or more about Dave and the pictures," Roper muttered. "I do know I'm going over there and kill him for what he put Amy through." He flexed and unflexed his hands, anger coursing through his veins.

Ben rose and began pacing the room. "Hear me out first, then you can decide what to do. You know I was jealous of you. You know I thought fate gave me a raw deal and Dave knew it, too. Not only was he my friend, he's a Renegades season ticket holder, too, and last season's World Series disaster pissed him off big-time."

"He wouldn't be the only one," Roper said, acknowledging the truth.

"But he was more out of control than I realized. You know those packages you've been getting? The letters? The media coverage of you lately, excessive even by New York standards?"

"Yes…" Roper knew where this was going and his head felt full enough to explode. "He's been behind it all?"

"Anything I heard about you, things I griped about to him, he used against you, bro." Ben strode to him. "I had no idea. You have to believe me. I was whiny and self-centered, but you're my brother. I'd never do anything to hurt you. As soon as he told me, it was like this huge lightbulb went off in my head and I realized how messed up my own thinking has been." Ben pleaded with Roper to understand.

And he tried. Man, Roper tried. Because this was his baby brother and he wanted to believe he'd changed. "Go on."

"I moved out. Well, he kicked me out, so I moved into Mom's hotel until she goes back to L.A. But as soon as those photos surfaced, I knew it was Dave." Ben picked up his beer and took a long swig, then placed the bottle back on the table. "I hadn't given him back my key, so I let myself into his place while he was at work and checked the laptop. And bingo."

"He wasn't bright enough to delete the evidence?" Roper asked in disbelief.

"He's cocky enough to think he wouldn't get caught. But he's wrong." Ben shoved his hands into his back pockets. "Before I came here, I turned the laptop over to the police. Then I called Buckley and gave him a tip."

Roper shook his head hard. "You did that for me?"

Ben shrugged. "Maybe I also did it for me. A little redemption, you know? So maybe I could look at myself in the mirror and not hate what I see."

Roper tried not to wince. For all Ben's faults, he obviously had a good heart. And Roper knew what it was like to hate yourself at least a little bit. "Ben, it's okay. I don't hold what Dave did against you. I appreciate you stepping up to the plate for me. I do."

"Don't thank me, at least not yet. There's one

more thing you need to know," Ben said, looking down as he spoke. He drew a deep breath. "You know how Buckley's known a lot about you lately? Where you've been and who you've been with?"

"Yes," Roper said warily.

"It was me. Mom would mention things in casual conversation and I'd tip off Buckley or gawker-stalker.com," he said, self-loathing in his voice.

"I'll be damned." Amy had been right. It had been someone close to him. He shook his head in disbelief. "Why the hell would you do it? Do you hate me that much?"

His brother shook his head. "No. I thought it was funny at first. And things always seemed to go your way. I thought it would be a lark to see you twist in the wind a little. But I realize now how pathetic that is."

Roper could have bashed his brother for what he'd done, not just to him, but to Amy. Obviously, though, Ben was doing enough bashing to himself. Roper couldn't bring himself to tell his brother all was okay, but he wasn't going to add to his misery.

"What did the police say about the laptop?" he asked, bringing the subject back to Dave and what mattered at the moment.

"They need to go through the computer. Since I had a key, they aren't going to press charges against me for taking it. And I don't understand any of the legalities, you know, like whether or not they can use it as evidence. But they'll see what they find on it and go from there."

Roper drew a calming breath. He glanced at Ben and tried to see the baby brother he'd always loved. "We'll have to do the same." Roper walked over to his brother and threw an arm around his shoulder. "We go on from here," Roper said.

Ben inclined his head, meeting Roper's gaze. "I don't know what to say."

"Nothing. We're family and—"

"Hey, isn't that Amy?" Ben asked, jerking a finger toward the TV.

Roper glanced up, took one look at Amy in the pantsuit she'd worn the day they'd met at Sparks Steak House, and he grabbed the remote control to raise the volume.

He lowered himself onto the couch and watched her, interviewed in the comfort of her own living room by none other than Buckley the Bastard, himself.

"I thought it would be entertaining for my listeners to hear about a day in the life of John Roper from the woman in charge of handling his affairs for the past month," Buckley said.

"You do have a way with words," Amy said, shaking her head and laughing. Her curls fell over her shoulder in sensual disarray as she flirted with Buckley.

Roper couldn't believe his eyes.

"She's playing him," Ben said, easing himself back on the couch beside Roper.

"But I appreciate the chance to tell my story," Amy said.

"She'd better be playing him and not exposing my life for public consumption." Or his fears and insecurities to a world that already thought he was a washed-up loser. In a few weeks he'd prove them all wrong.

"Relax, man," Ben said. "I know a con when I see one. Buckley's so happy to have her talking, he doesn't realize she's the one using him."

"So the pictures that recently surfaced were doctored?" Buckley asked.

"That's right," Amy said with certainty. She didn't even flinch at the subject.

"Can you prove it?"

She shook her head. "Not yet."

"Rumor has it the police have a lead." Buckley leaned in close.

Amy shrugged delicately. "I haven't heard anything about that."

Roper glanced at his brother. "You stole that laptop. Aren't you worried?"

"No. In all likelihood, the police can't use the evidence against Dave. But at least I'll have planted doubt in the public's mind about those pictures. It's the best I can do."

Roper nodded.

He listened as Buckley questioned Amy about Roper, his habits, his dedication, his talent, trying to trip her up or get her to admit that Roper was more of a player than a dedicated athlete. He failed. Not once did Amy speak in terms other than respectful and in a way that built him up in the public eye.

She was every inch his publicist.

She was every inch the woman he loved.

"I was hoping for some juicier information when I set up this interview," Buckley said. "So far you haven't given up anything."

"I'm a publicist. My job is to be behind the camera, not in front of it."

"Yet you're here. You agreed to talk with me."

"Technically, you conned two elderly women into letting you come here to dig up dirt on John Roper. Isn't *that* the truth?" Amy asked.

Without warning, the camera panned to Rose and Darla who waved from the kitchen. Roper figured Amy must have bribed them but good to keep their mouths shut during the interview.

Buckley turned red in the face. "They invited me."

"Not to worry," Amy said, patting his hand. "I was happy to get in front of the camera."

"You were?" Roper asked aloud.

"And why is that?" Buckley asked, clearly looking for a scoop.

"Go ahead, tell them you dumped the infamous John Roper and be done with it," Roper muttered.

Beside him, Ben chuckled. "Come on, she isn't going to diss you in front of your home crowd."

"Thanks to me she's bare-assed on the Internet."

"It isn't really her."

"Like that matters?" Roper asked.

"As you can see, I come from an outgoing family." Once again the camera angle widened to include Rose and Darla, who this time hammed it up for the television audience, blowing kisses and calling out the names of friends back in Florida.

Roper winced. He could only imagine Amy's mortification. And yet she'd put this circus in motion by talking with Buckley. He leaned forward, wanting to hear more.

"But I've always shied away from being in the spotlight," Amy went on to explain.

"Which must make your relationship with Roper an uncomfortable one."

Roper didn't miss the satisfaction in the bastard's voice or the man's obvious pleasure in knowing Roper was probably watching and squirming. Which he was.

"At first, yes." Amy glanced down. "You see, I didn't realize that I was afraid of disappointing someone very special in my life. Someone who's no longer with us. My father."

"But what about today? The photos?" Buckley prodded, obviously not willing to let Amy go off on a tangent, even one Roper sensed was of the utmost importance—to him.

"Oh, he'd hate those photos," Amy said. "But he'd understand how they came into being. Just as I now understand that I idealized the man he was, the things I thought he expected of me. But I realize now my dad was just a man in love with my slightly eccentric mother."

"That's me! Darla, she's talking about me!" Rose squealed.

The camera panned back to Amy's mother, who blushed and blew kisses.

Roper grinned.

Buckley squirmed in his seat. "But those photos. Even if they aren't you, which has yet to be proved, they must have made you pretty uncomfortable," Buckley pushed.

Amy sat up straighter in her seat. "Yes, they did. Especially with my family in town, as you can imagine. But when you love someone, you can't run away from your fears."

"What did she just say?" Ben asked.

Roper wasn't sure. "I need to hear it again." He raised the volume another notch.

"So how do you like your job at the Hot Zone?" Buckley asked, changing the subject.

"I love my job, although I must admit, I wasn't as prepared for the media hype as much as I thought. But I'm ready to handle it now, both in my professional and my personal life. In other words, if you're watching, John, I was wrong. I'm sorry. And I'm ready to fight for us," she said, grinning as widely as Buckley scowled.

Roper didn't wait to hear any more. "Hold down the fort, brother. I have someplace important I need to go."

AMY PACED HER APARTMENT as time passed. Surely Roper had seen the interview or someone had called to tell him about it. So why wasn't he banging down her door? She'd be breaking down his if she wasn't afraid of them crossing in the night.

It hadn't taken long for Buckley to leave once he realized his exclusive, live interview wasn't going to bash Roper. He and his crew had wrapped up and taken off, leaving Amy alone with her applauding mother and aunt. Of course, they had gotten their own exclusive, realizing Amy had come to her senses about Roper.

Had he seen it? Did he know?

"Mom, you and Aunt Darla need to make yourselves scarce. Go to a movie or something," Amy said, rifling through her purse for money.

"Don't worry, we're leaving. And we won't be back here tonight," her mother said pointedly.

"So you and Roper can do whatever you want," Aunt Darla said. "We'll end up back at his apartment. Anyway, we have to pack. We have a flight tomorrow early in the afternoon."

"You do?" Amy turned to her family, surprised. "You didn't tell me you were going home." To her surprise, despite the chaos their surprise arrival had brought with them, Amy was sad to see them go.

"We didn't have definite plans. But after our talk tonight, we realize you need more privacy. We'll be sure to give you a heads-up before we come next time. At least we can leave knowing that you and Roper are fine," her mother said.

"You are fine, right?" Aunt Darla asked.

Amy, not wanting to worry them, merely nodded. "It's all good. Now, go out. Keep busy, *behave* and we'll have breakfast before you leave tomorrow. Will that work out timewise?"

"Yes."

They opened the door to the apartment and bumped into Roper on his way in. Another ten minutes of conversation passed, and by the time she shut the door behind her mother and aunt, nerves took over. Her stomach was in knots, her throat raw and dry.

"So." She spread her hands out beside her, then clasped them together. "Alone at last."

He glanced around the empty apartment and grinned. "Very."

"You saw the interview?"

He nodded. "I did. Shocked the hell out of me to see you in front of the camera talking about yourself."

"I bet." She bit down on the inside of her cheek. "I realize I've been driving you a little crazy with all the 'I want you but I can't be with you' stuff."

He raised an eyebrow. "Do tell."

"I tried to explain it to you through Buckley. I was living up to an idealized version of me I thought my father would have had. That's why I became a social worker, to make a difference in the world. For him. But it wasn't really right for me. Working at the retirement home was a blast. I could be myself but I had no social life. When I came to New York and started working for the Hot Zone, I found myself. I love my job. I love organizing and compartmentalizing, strategizing and finding solutions to problems like yours."

"You do it well. Just look at how you fixed me. So go on. Tell me more." He needed to hear everything she had to tell him. He wanted to understand what motivated her, her hopes and dreams, her fears and mistakes. He needed to know so they could go forward.

"Well, you know I don't want to be as out there as my mother. It's a deep-rooted fear of mine. You'd have the same one if you'd rescued Lady Godiva from jail."

He nodded. "I suppose I would."

"But I also don't want to be so repressed anymore."

"You're over it?" The wary tone in his voice told her he didn't want to live the roller coaster anymore.

Neither did she. "I'm over it. I realized that even if we'd been caught at the lodge, what's the worst thing that could have happened?"

"I don't know."

"Some sleazy photographer could have posted naked pictures of us in the papers or on the Internet. The worst has already happened and I survived," Amy said. "My family loves me no matter what."

"I'm sure it helps that it wasn't really you in those photos."

"No, but the public thinks it is. I swear to you, I've

come to terms with who you are and who I am. I know it seems like a fast turnaround, but it makes sense to me now. Almost as if I've come full circle today." She cupped his face in her hands and kissed him hard on the lips. "You need to trust me. Want to know why?"

He inclined his head. "Why?" Roper asked, going along with her.

"Because I love you, John Roper, center fielder for the New York Renegades. I can live with being plastered on the pages of the *Post* and the *News* if that's what it takes to be with you."

He shook his head, stunned. And yet, at the same time, not really all that surprised. He always knew she had the strength and spunk he'd seen in her other female family members. "Life with you isn't ever going to be boring."

She pursed her lips. "I can try for boring. I really can. I've done it fairly well at times."

He stepped close and pulled her into his arms. "I prefer you free-spirited," he said, kissing her hard on the lips. "Like at the lodge."

A low purr escaped from the back of her throat. "You know what? I can live with free-spirited," she said. "As long as I'm only that way with you." She let her hand slip between them until she cupped his hard erection in her hands.

He groaned, his body needing to escape his jeans. "I missed being able to touch you, how I want and when I want," he said, running his hands through her hair.

She moved her hand and let their bodies align. *"I love you,"* she said, meeting his gaze.

"I love you, too. Always." If this was the best life had to offer, Roper didn't need another damn thing.

EPILOGUE

New York Post—Page Six
New York Renegades center fielder, John Roper, needs extra innings to keep up with the happenings in his life. His career is back on track, as is his personal life with an impending marriage to Amy Stone, a publicist at the infamous Hot Zone PR Agency. And there's more. Somehow Roper managed to pull off a private wedding for his sister at Brandon Vaughn's mountain lodge in Greenlawn, New York, this past weekend without intrusion by the press. What makes this so surprising is that pop star Hannah Gregory and drummer Mike Morris also married this weekend at the same lodge. Roper and his fiancée joined the rest of Hannah's band as bridesmaids and groomsmen. The guests signed a confidentiality agreement, which left yours truly out in the cold. But to quote two older female guests as they exited Roper's sister's affair, it was small and too sedate for their liking. The ladies were overheard heading to the indoor pool to convince the activities director for the weekend to add naked Marco Polo to the events.

Harrison Smith's television series starring movie star Cassandra Lee as the matriarch of a family in need of guidance as they vie for a trust fund was picked up by NBC for the fall lineup.

In a related story, Dave Martin, a sports trainer, was brought in for questioning by the police in conjunction with the nude photos of Amy Stone and John Roper. Charges to be announced….

In other news, eSports columnist and reporter Frank Buckley checked himself into rehab after his wife left him for the Renegades' newest acquisition, twenty-year-old shortstop, Don Andersen. He was replaced at work by Veronica Butler, a long-time reporter at eSports. The Buck won't be stopping anywhere anytime soon, folks.

And they all lived happily ever after….

* * * * *

Watch for LUCKY CHARM,
*the first title in a new series
from Carly Phillips,
available in October 2008
wherever books are sold.*

REQUEST YOUR FREE BOOKS!

2 FREE NOVELS
FROM THE ROMANCE/SUSPENSE
COLLECTION PLUS 2 FREE GIFTS!

YES! Please send me 2 FREE novels from the Romance/Suspense Collection and my 2 FREE gifts (gifts are worth about $10). After receiving them, if I don't wish to receive any more books, I can return the shipping statement marked "cancel." If I don't cancel, I will receive 4 brand-new novels every month and be billed just $5.49 per book in the U.S. or $5.99 per book in Canada, plus 25¢ shipping and handling per book plus applicable taxes, if any*. That's a savings of at least 20% off the cover price! I understand that accepting the 2 free books and gifts places me under no obligation to buy anything. I can always return a shipment and cancel at any time. Even if I never buy another book from the Reader Service, the two free books and gifts are mine to keep forever.

185 MDN EF5Y   385 MDN EF6C

Name	(PLEASE PRINT)	
Address		Apt. #
City	State/Prov.	Zip/Postal Code

Signature (if under 18, a parent or guardian must sign)

Mail to The Reader Service:
IN U.S.A.: P.O. Box 1867, Buffalo, NY 14240-1867
IN CANADA: P.O. Box 609, Fort Erie, Ontario L2A 5X3

Not valid to current subscribers to the Romance Collection,
the Suspense Collection or the Romance/Suspense Collection.

Want to try two free books from another line?
Call 1-800-873-8635 or visit www.morefreebooks.com.

* Terms and prices subject to change without notice. N.Y. residents add applicable sales tax. Canadian residents will be charged applicable provincial taxes and GST. Offer not valid in Quebec. This offer is limited to one order per household. All orders subject to approval. Credit or debit balances in a customer's account(s) may be offset by any other outstanding balance owed by or to the customer. Please allow 4 to 6 weeks for delivery. Offer available while quantities last.

Your Privacy: Harlequin is committed to protecting your privacy. Our Privacy Policy is available online at www.eHarlequin.com or upon request from the Reader Service. From time to time we make our lists of customers available to reputable third parties who may have a product or service of interest to you. If you would prefer we not share your name and address, please check here. ☐

BOB08R

carly phillips